DAVID EBSWORTH is the pen name of writer negotiator and workers' representative fo General Workers' Union. He was born in in Wrexham, North Wales, with his wife .

Following his retirement, Dave began to write historical fiction in 2009 and has subsequently published ten novels: political thrillers set against the history of the 1745 Jacobite rebellion, the 1879 Anglo-Zulu War, the Battle of Waterloo, warlord rivalry in Sixth Century Britain, and the Spanish Civil War. His sixth book, *Until the Curtain Falls* returned to that same Spanish conflict, following the story of journalist Jack Telford, and is published in Spanish under the title *Hasta Que Caiga el Telón*. Jack Telford, as it happens, is also the main protagonist in a separate novella, *The Lisbon Labyrinth*.

Dave's *Yale Trilogy* tells the story of intrigue and mayhem around nabob, philanthropist (and slave-trader) Elihu Yale – who gave his name to Yale University – but told through the eyes of his much-maligned and largely forgotten wife, Catherine.

Each of Dave's novels has been critically acclaimed by the Historical Novel Society and been awarded the coveted B.R.A.G. Medallion for independent authors.

This tenth novel is the third of his stories about Jack Telford and takes Jack into the turmoil of the Second World War but through a series of real-life episodes, which are truly stranger than fiction.

For more information on the author and his work, visit his website at www.davidebsworth.com.

Also by David Ebsworth

The Jacobites' Apprentice
A story of the 1745 Rebellion.

The Jack Telford Series
Political thrillers set towards the end of the Spanish Civil War and
beyond.

The Assassin's Mark

Until the Curtain Falls
(published in Spanish as *Hasta Que Caiga el Telón*)

The Lisbon Labyrinth
(an ebook novella, set during the 1974 Portuguese Revolution)

The Kraals of Ulundi: A Novel of the Zulu War

The Last Campaign of Marianne Tambour: A Novel of Waterloo

The Song-Sayer's Lament
Another political thriller but this time set in the time we know as the
Dark Ages, 6th Century post-Roman Britain

The Yale Trilogy
Set in old Madras, London and northern England between 1672 and
1721

The Doubtful Diaries of Wicked Mistress Yale

Mistress Yale's Diaries, The Glorious Return

Wicked Mistress Yale, The Parting Glass

A Betrayal of Heroes

DAVID EBSWORTH

SilverWood

Published in 2021 by SilverWood Books

SilverWood Books Ltd
14 Small Street, Bristol, BS1 1DE, United Kingdom
www.silverwoodbooks.co.uk

ISBN 978-1-80042-071-7 (paperback)
ISBN 978-1-80042-072-4 (ebook)

British Library Cataloguing in Publication Data
A CIP catalogue record for this book is available from the British Library

Page design and typesetting by SilverWood Books

Dedicated to the memory of those who sacrificed themselves in the fight against fascism, in all its forms, from 1936 until 1945, as well as those who continue to confront the fresh rise of fascism's tentacles in today's world.

"In a time of universal deceit, telling the truth is a revolutionary act."

George Orwell

Author's Note

This *is* a novel. It's a work of fiction. But its background is a series of historical events, the locations in which they occurred, and the real-life characters who shaped them. They are all events taking place between 1939 and 1945, the period we generally know as the Second World War. These are, therefore, events that are relatively recent. The close families of some of those involved are still with us. But though the framework of the story is factual, the fiction has sometimes required me to composite particular episodes, timelines and personalities. And, of course, because the main protagonist, Jack Telford, is an entirely fictional figure, it must follow that all the exchanges involving him are also simple figments of my imagination.

As usual, where I have deliberately tweaked the history, I've detailed those distortions in the separate notes at the back of the book. Any other examples of the events, or the characters, being inaccurately portrayed are therefore errors on my part – or, perhaps, they are simply the way fictional Jack Telford perceived them. One way or the other, if readers come across such examples, I apologise for them, profusely, in advance.

But, overall, I hope you'll enjoy reading this as much as I enjoyed the writing!

For readers who would like to know more about the historical background, I've included my main sources in the acknowledgements at the end, but there is also a more detailed list, a bibliography, on my website, www.davidebsworth.com.

David Ebsworth
February 2021

Madrid
SPAIN
Lisbon
PORTUGAL
Alicante
Bizerta
Tunis
Gibraltar
Tangier
Oran
SP. MOR
Oujda
Fédala
Rabat
Casablanca
FRENCH MOROCCO
Bou Arfa
Agadir
CANARY ISLANDS
ALGERIA
FRENCH WEST AFRICA
Dakar
Bathurst
GAMBIA
NIGERIA
Freetown
IVORY COAST
GOLD COAST
Abidjan
Accra
Libreville
GABON
Jack Telford
May '43
0
500
1000km

October 1939

The Yemenite, Brachah Zefira

He hadn't intended to kill Fielding and he still had no idea whether he was wanted for the crime. But needs must when the devil drives.

The building invited him to enter. A polished plaque on the white wall. *British Consulate General, Rabat.* Arabic script beneath. Three storeys. A courtyard house, he thought. Archways with sweeping Islamic calligraphy, complex motifs, shaped into the stucco. *Mashrabiya* oriel windows. Intricate lattice screens of dark Moroccan cedar.

One of the studded outer gates stood open and Telford took a deep breath, carried his two cases over the raised threshold into a paved garden, past a gushing fountain, stopped before a deeply carved inner door, which opened to his exploratory touch. Inside, a wide vestibule, peaceful, cool and dark, the tinkle of more running water, ornately green-tiled floor, double staircase. To the right, a reception room. A ceiling fan whined gently while an older woman in a frock of purple printed flowers rose from behind her typewriter. Too late for him to escape again now.

'May I help?' she said.

'It's all so − quiet,' said Jack, setting down his luggage and removing his trilby. 'Considering…'

'That we're at war, you mean? Yes, all a frightful bother. It will get busier later, I suppose.'

She tried hard, he could see, not to stare at the patch covering the ruin of his left eye.

'Without doubt,' he said. 'Busier, yes. I just got off the train from Oran. A bit frantic, really. Impossible to talk of anything else. But might I speak with somebody about my papers?'

1

He had to wait a while. Nervous, half of him still wanting to run back out into the ambiguity of the city's busy streets. He was offered tea – proper tea, the woman stressed, not the mint char the locals enjoyed so much – but he politely declined, not sure he'd be able to hold the cup without spilling it, and was finally ushered up the stairs, to the consul's own office.

'Telford,' the fellow mused, as he studied the documents Jack had presented to him. He looked for all the world like Clement Attlee's twin. Same moustache. Same domed polished pate. Same paternal façade, same three-piece suit. Same pipe even. 'Telford,' he repeated, and blew a small cloud of smoke towards the ceiling. 'Are you the chap...?'

'Yes, San Sebastián. I'm afraid so.'

'You're with the *Telegraph*?'

'*Reynold's News*,' Jack corrected him, imagined there was a look of disdain. 'Though not anymore,' he added, perhaps a little too quickly. 'Freelance now, you might say.'

Freelance, yes. Like an actor between roles. It had been a long while since he'd written anything decent. A very long while. And it gnawed at him every day.

'Poor Valerie, though.'

Yes, thought Jack, and stared down at the trembling hands, which had held her under the waves. Poor Carter.

'You'll know the family, I suppose?' he said.

The consul, Mister Hurst, had been so lost in apparent reminiscence that he'd neglected the pipe, produced a box of Swan Vestas from his desk drawer and lit the thing afresh.

'Met Sir Aubrey a few times,' said Hurst. 'He's now Secretary for Overseas Trade, did you know?'

'I didn't,' Jack told him. 'For some reason word never trickled through to Oran. And not a word about it on the train.'

The sarcasm seemed to waft above the consul's head as smoothly as his tobacco smoke.

'Bad business,' said Mister Hurst.

Jack nodded, pulled a blue cigarette pack from the inside pocket of his linen jacket.

'D'you mind?' he asked, waving the pack before him. 'And

yes, bad. Twenty hours. Seemed to stop every five minutes.'

'I meant San Sebastián,' said the consul. 'Can't remember all the details, but both of you swept out to sea?'

'A year ago,' Jack lit one of the *Gauloises* to which he'd become so addicted during his months in Oran. 'Still riddled with guilt,' he lied, and set down the brass cartridge case lighter on the desk. And with guilt came the familiar feeling of ease. Hurst seemed to have no idea of the real story. So, the yarn spilled forth in its usual form, word for word, so it sometimes felt more real than the truth.

'Was that how…?' Hurst gestured with the pipe's stem towards the eye patch.

'The rocks, sir. Ripped me up pretty badly. Then there was a boat. Don't remember much, but they hauled me out, took me along the coast to a village. More than a week. Unconscious mostly. They stitched the eye though. The lid, to prevent infection. Then the *Guardia Civil* raided the place.'

'Looking for you, Mister Telford?'

'Turns out these fishermen were smugglers. But the *Civiles* hauled me off to their barracks. Seems they'd picked up a copy of an article I'd wired home. Gave me a rough time about not being authorised.'

'Just one article?' the consul smiled. 'We are talking about *Reynold's News*, after all.'

Jack laughed, settling in his part.

'Very perceptive, sir. And you're right, of course. I was suddenly on Franco's most wanted list. Ended up in prison. At San Pedro de Cardeña. Military Tribunal to hear my case, they said. Anyway, one day they sent a gang of us down to the river for a bath. And then all hell broke loose. An ambush. Some of the guards killed. A raid by *guerrilleros*. And I got caught up in the middle of it all, somehow. Took me south. To Madrid.'

'Where you got these?' He tapped his fingers on Jack's documents. 'Who was it? Milanes?'

'Mister Milanes, yes.'

The consulate in Madrid had been able to issue him an Emergency Certificate. Number 1397 (Madrid). *Not valid for more than one person. Valid only for the journey to Great Britain, leaving Madrid-Valencia/Alicante via France.*

'But you didn't go.'

'I got all the way to Alicante. The very last day of the war in Spain. And by then the only way out was a ship heading for Oran. I wasn't going to take a chance on Franco's boys catching up with me again, so here I am.'

Hurst peered at the document.

'This was signed last December,' he said. 'Christmas Day?'

'Yes, sir. But you see? No time limit.' Jack leaned forward, pointed at the relevant wording. 'And – well, there was a young woman.'

The consul leaned back in his chair, a sigh of dismay.

'She travelled with you, to Oran?' he said.

'No, she stayed in Alicante.'

That much was true, anyway. For Telford had left young Ruby Waters in Alicante, still working at the temporary consulate. She'd written to him at Oran but by then he'd decided his fondness for her was all one-sided. Still bitter about it, believed she'd deceived him.

'And now?' said Hurst. 'I assume you want to get back to Blighty. Planning to sign up?'

Jack bit his lip to stop the smile he felt forming there. For the war had brought a new dilemma. Telford was, essentially, a pacifist. He had a duty, he supposed, though this was tempered by the rage he felt against the country of his birth. He'd seen, at first hand, the dirty game played by Britain's Intelligence Services during the war in Spain and, like many others, he almost blamed Britain for causing this new and even deadlier conflict to erupt. He still had a copy of the piece he'd written for *Reynold's News*. A commentary on Britain's brokerage of the Non-Intervention Pact, and its failure to act against Italian and German bombing of innocent civilians, and especially their attacks on British merchant shipping. Other things too.

'Well,' he said, and looked Hurst intently in the eye, 'we must all do our bit, sir. Don't you think?'

*

4

He was being followed.

Telford had noted Hurst's instruction to return the following morning and accepted his recommendations, first, about a clean but modestly priced hotel, the Transatlantic – he dropped his suitcases there – and then about the main attractions this town had to offer.

He'd made a decision to leave the Chellah until tomorrow, since his onward train to Casablanca was only due to depart well past noon. Plenty of time for more sightseeing after breakfast. So, for now, he chose to start at the El Ghazel spice market just along the road, among the saffrons and cinnamons, the corianders and cumins, the fennels and fenugreeks – always such a joy to the eye and nostril, even in the most humdrum of North Africa's villages.

Then, when he headed to the muddy banks of the Bou Regreg river separating Rabat from the neighbouring town of Salé, he saw somebody slip from the shadows of the Custom House – where Jack had walked only moments before – then jump back into their anonymity as soon as Telford turned his head.

He paused for a moment, there at the outer harbour, watched a couple of Arab fishermen haul a broad-bellied boat, stripes of peeling paint, white and green, up beyond the tide line. A backward glance. Nobody there.

Yet by the time he'd followed the old fortified sea wall towards the Point and its imposing Moorish castle, there could be no mistake. It was in his bones, he supposed. All those times he was hunted in Spain. And the fear was no less forceful for its familiarity.

He didn't linger at the Almohad gates of the Kasbah, that mighty fortress, but doubled back instead through the old Muslim burial ground, plunged into the narrow alleyways of the medina. He imagined Baedeker would describe these streets as dazzling white and blue, but Jack saw them simply as sepia shades of decaying palest grey and dusty cyan. Weaving his way as inconspicuously as he was able through the *djellaba*-clad vendors and denizens, he stopped occasionally in the cover of a striped awning, a vegetable or pottery stall, each time catching a glimpse of the same Panama hat some distance behind him.

There was a marginally wider thoroughfare, the Rue Sidi Fatah according to the blue street sign, just beyond which he concealed himself behind the bole of an ancient tree, at the corner of a mosque's outer wall. And there was his pursuer. No doubt about it. The farther junction, looking this way and that. Not English, Jack was fairly certain. Linen suit in light olive. The familiar hat, the palest shade of straw. White shoes, buckskin maybe. The fellow's features sharp and tanned, clean shaven. Mediterranean. Could almost have been Spanish or Portuguese. But would he come this way? If so, Telford would have to make a run for it. He was attracting strange glances from the locals, an old man with a heavily laden donkey staring up at him from only a yard or so away.

'Min Fadhlik,' said Jack. 'S'il vous plaît.' He tried to shoo the man away, cautiously peering over his shoulder to see whether this old wretch had drawn attention to him. But there was no longer any sign of the pursuit. Still, he waited there a few more minutes before moving swiftly through another labyrinth of passages until he emerged on the Rue Souika, another mosque – enormous, this one – and another burial ground, the side wall leading him to the Boulevard Joffre, back to the river, the slipways, more blue-hulled wooden fishing boats, a couple of tramp steamers at the inner harbour, all the bustle and stink stamped on every dockside from Tilbury to Timbuktu.

Across the busy square at the end of the boulevard, rocks rising to a plateau and the Hassan Tower, just as Mister Hurst had described it. Vertiginously high, rose-red sandstone, horseshoe-shaped arches, intricate latticed patterns near its summit. But what to do? No time to play the tourist anymore, yet nor did he want to venture back towards the Transatlantic. Surely if somebody was tailing him they must know where he was staying. And he suffered a flashback, as the moviemakers might say.

His hotel in Madrid. Trapped there by bloody Fielding – Jack was still not sure exactly whose side Fielding had been on, apart from his own – and the British military attaché, Major Edwin. They planned to hand him over to the Russians in return for those documents Telford had stolen from Edwin's office. Embarrassing documents showing the extent of the blind eye Britain's high and mighty were turning to Hitler's rearmament. And it would have disposed of another problem. Jack had killed Valerie Carter-Holt.

6

Self-defence maybe, but he'd killed her all the same. An agent for the NKVD, for Stalin – though her prominent father still believed she was nothing more than a renowned and respected foreign correspondent.

'You see, Mister Telford,' Jack heard Major Edwin tell him again, 'it would cause something of a scandal back home if you were allowed to squeak about the daughter of Sir Aubrey Carter-Holt being a spy for the Comintern. Secretary to the First Lord implicated with Russian agents? It simply wouldn't do. Much better for us if we let General Kotov tidy up the mess.'

Oh yes, Kotov would certainly have done that – if he hadn't been so busy getting out of Madrid to save his own skin. And then there'd been Jack's escape at the hotel door, the running drop kick he'd managed to connect squarely under Fielding's chin, the satisfying slap as though it had been a soccer ball. Satisfying, at least, until he later discovered he'd snapped Fielding's neck. And Fielding had, at least officially, been one of His Britannic Majesty's vice-consuls. Was there a link? The retribution Jack had feared ever since?

In summary, he'd been hunted across the length and breadth of Spain, variously, by killers from the *Guardia Civil*, from the NKVD, *and* from the British intelligence services. He might now be safe from the *Civiles* and the Soviets, but his own people? He simply had no idea.

He pulled down the brim of his trilby, decision made, stepped out onto the road – and a car's horn blared at him. An old taxi, its roof piled high with mattresses and bedding, the driver screaming at him in a rare blend of French and Arabic. Telford leapt back, shouted an apology in English, then dodged between the trucks and mule carts, made it to the other side, then took the rough track skirting the modest cliff face, clambered up to all that now remained of the old red walls of the unfinished mosque. Maybe here on this flattened escarpment, in the shade of the Hassan Tower, he could try to make sense of it all. Or perhaps not.

Pursued. It entirely unnerved him. Yet the plateau was mercifully devoid of other human life, though a rising wind was beginning to blow dust devils across the broken ground. A forest of lonely columns, grandeur to challenge the most glorious of Rome's ruins, forever roofless except for the cerulean canopy above, now turning to an early evening rose pink.

He picked his way among more tumbled masonry, discovered a wide cistern, signs of an archaeological dig, a fastened tent nestling among clumps of blue aloes, a sign hanging from the flap announcing in French that all enquiries should be directed to the Mederso Museum.

Telford sat against one of the columns, sheltered from the breeze, lit a cigarette and tried to unravel the threads of his life while a hawk swooped and dived around the tower's flank, all afire now as the lowering sun blazed red upon its western wall.

His stay in Oran had been longer than planned though, in truth, there'd never really *been* a plan. He'd sailed from Alicante on the *Stanbrook* – just about the last vessel to get away with refugees on board before Franco's Italian allies swarmed into the city. And in Oran he'd worked with some of the local groups trying to provide aid to the Spanish men, women and children now herded into the French internment camp, the conditions atrocious. A concentration camp. Old warehouses surrounded by barbed wire. The men segregated from the women and kids. Senegalese guards. Worse, the vicious Algerians and Moroccans from the *Garde Mobile*. A nasty little rat for a camp commandant. And though Jack had officially resigned from *Reynold's News*, he continued to wire the occasional report to his old boss, Sydney Elliott. He had also eventually managed to speak on the telephone again with his former colleague Sheila. Yes, he'd promised, home soon. But for now, perhaps she'd be good enough to speak with his sister, arrange for money to be transferred for him, sort out his NUJ membership too, get a new union card sent out once he had a proper address.

He looked back on those six months with a mixture of nostalgia and distaste. A new purpose to his life and he'd found some form of peace, an inner calm after the terrors and turbulence of the previous half-year. But the French régime in Oran – across all Algeria it seemed – he had found brutal. His hand still troubled him too – the right hand, with which he had taken life several times. Maybe all in his head. Maybe not. But a slight paralysis all the same. And his eye – how he hated the disfigurement, the loss of his peripheral vision.

The dreams of taking his career to new heights, the elusive Pulitzer, lay in tatters. And by then the French authorities had tired of his meddling, demanded to see his papers. A problem, naturally, since Jack's documents had been lost at San Sebastián. Yet the authorities were happy that the Emergency Certificate issued in Madrid was valid for passage from Oran to Marseilles. And perhaps, they suggested, sooner rather than later, relations with Germany deteriorating by the day.

Jack agreed, begged leave to remain until his money arrived and was allowed to do so on condition he stayed away from the internment camps. By then it didn't really matter. Most of the men had been given the choice, either to join the French Foreign Legion or to serve with the forced labour squads maintaining the French railway from Oran to Bou Arfa, at the very edge of the Sahara. God help them. Their families? Some given work locally. Others with no choice but to be shipped to France, to the refugee camps – which, according to most reports, were even worse than those scattered across Algeria. To those hellholes, Barcarès, Saint-Cyprien or Argelès.

Telford's friend from the *Stanbrook*, Amado Granell, had vanished also. To where? Jack had no idea. Yet he still had no inclination to head for England. And then it was indeed war again. Poland invaded. France preparing for the conflict with Hitler. A reason for those former Republican soldiers to join the Foreign Legion after all. Their three-year fight against the fascists, against Europe's Nazis, now given new life.

He inhaled the Gauloise smoke deeply into his lungs, knowing he had no such motivation, saw the hawk dive once more.

If anything, his links to his own home country seemed ever more tenuous. There'd been a letter from his sister, still mourning the loss of their mother. Jack mourned her too, in his way. They may not have been close, but it was she who had instilled in him the principles of pacifism, especially after his father committed suicide rather than return to the horrors of the Great War. And then there'd been Ruby Waters. It had been his intention to open his heart and

9

soul to her – about how he'd so deeply believed Ruby might be his salvation. But he'd never done so. And thus, he'd lost her. Lost her to England and her duty. Bloody England. There'd been that letter shortly after he reached Oran. Her apology for abandoning him, a suggestion they might "keep in touch" – as though there'd been nothing more between them. He'd ignored it, angry and hurt and alone.

It was almost sunset and, across at the foot of the Hassan Tower, a bearded man in a blue burnoose and white turban slipped from the back of a donkey and began removing a huge padlock from the door. The *mu'azzin*, Jack guessed, though it hadn't occurred to him earlier that the structure itself must still have the status of a minaret – and therefore be actively used for the calling of the faithful to prayer. At this time of day, the *salat al-maghrib*.

Telford watched the old fellow, but his mind was set on Casablanca. He'd heard positive things about Casablanca. How Morocco in general was very different from Algeria. Opportunities. And it was as good a destination as any other. A good enough place to find out whether he was still at risk after Fielding's death and – well, after Major Edwin too. Yet he seemed to have already found the answer to this one.

Jack flicked away the stub of his cigarette and, as he did so, there was the Panama hat once more. As though the simple act of thinking about the pursuit had brought that very thing down upon his head again.

The man was scrambling up onto the plateau at its southern edge, furthest from the tower, and Telford was certain he'd not yet been observed. He eased around the side of the column, gradually backed away, a single pillar at a time, always careful to keep one of the uprights between himself and his pursuer.

He cursed himself, should have realised. For this was an obvious vantage point, the man hunting him now making his way to the rim from which he could look down on the inner harbour warehouses. But while the stalker was busy with this, Jack made his move.

The door to the tower stood open and he made a run for it. He slipped past the donkey, ducked inside, peered around the frame, breathed a sigh of relief when he saw his escape hadn't been observed. And why should anybody look for him in there?

He turned around, found himself in an entrance hall, a low wooden door to his right, a larger doorway to his left and, ahead of him, a wide opening to the ground floor chamber of the minaret. Each of their surrounds was beautifully ornate, the dim light reflecting upon gold, blue and white truncated stalactites of honeycomb vaulting and Qur'anic inscription.

All so exquisite – until the wooden door flew open and the *mu'azzin* emerged, paused in his stride, astonished to see him there, began yelling, waving his clenched fists in the air. Jack's Arabic wasn't bad now – so long as it came in short, slow doses. But this was too much, too fast, though he finally remembered the prohibition in Morocco against non-Muslims entering mosques. He tried to apologise, to pacify the old man, doffed his trilby to show respect.

'*Samehni,*' he said. Forgive me.

But as he glanced again through the outer door, he saw his pursuer staring back at him, his attention attracted by the commotion. He began to run, and Jack ran too, pressing the hat back onto his head. Running blind. Stupid. Panic. Through the second doorway, the *mu'azzin* screaming even louder.

There was a ramp of herringbone brick, perhaps ten feet wide, rising up towards the next floor, tall featureless walls on each side with shafts of light beaming down from openings high on the landing above.

He took the first ramp easily enough but the second required more effort, and now he could hear the altercation. Panama hat, inside the tower, arguing with the old Moroccan. Then somebody running up the ramps behind him. Footsteps echoing in time with his own.

'Telford!' An angry, breathless voice. Foreign accent. 'Come down. Need to talk.'

Like hell, Jack thought. Like hell. He'd been caught that way before.

But where was he going? No way out up there, surely.

Where was he? Third floor, he thought, his chest heaving as he looked into yet another chamber, though this one closed off with a wooden fence, a sign reading *Passage Interdit*. Evidence of restoration work.

'Telford, stop now!'

Jack bent double, coughing badly. But he ran again. Another ramp. And another. Panting for breath. Pain in his side. A stitch.

'God dammit,' he gasped, forced himself onwards, upwards. His time with the *guerrilleros* in Spain had toughened him, but six months of relative inactivity in Oran had done little to keep him in condition.

He came to a landing wider than the others. Windows here, traceried openings, though vertigo kept him from going too close, but almost certainly the balcony from which the *mu'azzin* would perform the *adhan*.

Telford ran on. A further barrier, this one across the next ramp itself. Another French prohibition against progressing further, but he climbed over the wooden frame and carried on regardless.

'Telford!' Rage in the voice now.

Christ! His stomach lurched, his foot crashing through crumbling bricks. Into nothing. He fell forward, his other leg almost giving way, hand scrabbling upon the broken masonry, scratching for a purchase – until he was able to haul himself up on the other side.

His heart pounded as he staggered up yet another section of ramp, his trilby lost somewhere.

With luck, he told himself, that bugger would break his bloody neck. Ahead of him there was no ramp, simply a door, bolted, and the bolt rusted tight. More rubble, and Jack picked up a lump of stone, hammered it against the rust, looking back, always back, down the slope, the pursuing footsteps getting ever closer. But it gave at last. He shouldered the ancient door open, so fast he almost fell out onto the tower's roof – or, rather, the brick dome of the upper floor. There was a low parapet, but nothing else. And so little space here he almost went over the edge. Terrified, he pushed the door closed again, leaning against it with all his weight, bracing himself, saw the sun had now set almost entirely, stars visible above. The wind stronger, whistling through the apertures of this top storey.

There was hammering on the other side of the door, his name being called again. Rock and a hard place, Jack knew. Cornered up here. How high? A hundred and fifty feet? He was petrified. Just a few yards from that terrifying drop. And the man on the other side of the door, did he have a gun? Could Jack fight him? Well, there was little choice, and he couldn't stay there forever. At least he still had the lump of stone in his hand.

'Stay back or I'll shoot,' he cried. Stupid. But anything, anything, to buy time. And maybe not so stupid after all. The hammering stopped, and the crunch of shoes on stone, on gravel, on the other side of the door telling him his pursuer was moving back. Discretion, the better part of valour.

At the same time, astonishingly close, no more than a floor or so underneath, the donkey braying. It made sense. The ramps. He doubted the old holy man could have made the climb otherwise. Then the *mu'azzin* as well, his call to prayer repeated across the city, from each of Rabat's other minarets. He could see them, their silhouettes, square fingers, against the skyline, the setting sun.

A plan. If he could climb onto the flat roof of this attic exit, built into the dome's side he could perhaps lie there, in the dark, just over the doorway, use the stone to good effect, a surprise attack from above when his pursuer finally ventured outside. He'd have to hit him hard, of course. Bloody hard.

But with his makeshift weapon in hand, he found a projecting brick in the curve of the dome, levered himself up, reached for the ornate rim above the door, managed to get a grip and crawled onto his chosen place of ambush. Yet once there it no longer seemed such a good idea. The space was smaller than it had seemed from below, the rear section sloping downwards at the same angle as the interior ramps. And the gut-wrenching dizziness, which heights afflicted upon him. The wind too. A fierce gust. And it took only one false step...

Sliding. Rolling down that treacherous incline. He cried out. No, he screamed. His belly lurched and he felt all reason desert him, arms lashing out and his fingertips ripping on every rough edge they tried to grasp.

Telford's feet smacked against the parapet and relief flooded through his tripes, until the impact shot him like a boulder from a catapult, forward again – and over the edge.

Though not entirely.

He screamed again, legs and lower torso dangling in the abyss, feet fighting in vain for a toehold upon the wall – but the whole of his left arm slung over the top and the fingers of his right hand gripping the edge.

Somewhere inside his head a small voice was telling him he could easily pull himself up from this position. But he had once foolishly been persuaded to try rock climbing, had experienced the bizarre sensation of being literally paralysed by fear, his body simply refusing to move either up or down, limbs in watery rebellion against the instructions, the desperate pleas of his brain. This was the same. Only worse. The blackness beneath him eradicated each of his senses, made him deaf to the *mu'azzin*'s calls, numb to the stone's coarse texture, unreceptive to the stink of his own acrid sweat, blind to even the possibility of salvation.

Thus, he was hardly aware of the hands stretching down to grip under his armpits and beginning to haul him back over the parapet. Nor the voice, that foreign accent again.

'Telford,' the fellow gasped, then sighed. 'Well, I suppose all the fingers of the hand are not the same. But, *ay de mi*, you are a rare one.'

The flickering candlelit ambience of the Café Mazouti could have been replicated in a hundred other joints across Algeria, or here in French Morocco – perhaps thirty round tables, each accommodating well-dressed but dimly perceived customers; ceiling fans wafting concentric circles of tobacco fug around the cellar; sounds of polite and respectful revelry; an impossibly tall waiter delivering orders from a carefully balanced silver serving tray; the chink of bottle and glass; more folk perched upon stools at the bar, and beyond the bar a piano, and a stage – little more than a shallow raised dais on which a singer stood tuning her Spanish guitar, adjusting the leather shoulder strap. She was probably Jack's own age, about thirty, tall and slim, her features either Arabic or Jewish, he couldn't tell. But attractive, green silk blouse, leaf-patterned skirts, and in her hair one of those head-dress chains decorated with small coins he had often see worn by Berber women.

'What did it mean anyway?' said Jack. He was forced to hold his liquor with two hands, for he hadn't yet stopped shaking. 'All that fingers stuff?'

'Simply a saying we have,' said the man, an air of superiority settling across his pursed lips. 'How we are not all the same. But really – stay back or I shoot?'

They'd sat trembling, each of them, on the roof of the Hassan Tower, Telford's rescuer assuring him he was friend, not foe, eventually introducing himself as Gabizon, Isaac Gabizon, and Jack hadn't hesitated to accept his suggestion they might both be well served by a shot of something strong. And it was fortunately only a short but shaky step – once they had endured an unsteady return down the ramps and the *mu'azzin*'s renewed rage – across to the old Jewish Quarter, the *mellah*, and the shabby exterior of this cabaret.

'It seemed like the best place,' said Jack, the *mahia* comforting, the warm embrace of its exotic anise tickling his throat. 'The best plan.'

'Extraordinary,' Gabizon shook his head in disbelief, closed those darkly hooded eyes as if to shut out the memory.

'I thought…' Jack stammered. 'You looked… Following me, for pity's sake. You could have just shouted to me.'

'I doubt your reaction would have been much different, *monsieur*. But I admit I had not expected it to be – *bien*, so dramatic.'

'And you're – what, again?'

'I suppose you might call me the Sultan's Jew. It's long been a tradition here. An envoy, between his royal palace and, without being immodest, the rest of the world.'

The singer earned an enthusiastic welcome with the opening chords and lines of *J'attendrai*. It had been all the rage in Oran.

'Envoy – or spy?' said Jack.

'A suspicious man.' Gabizon laughed. 'It comes from having made a few enemies, I suppose.'

'A few? That's a bit like being damned by faint praise. The only truly effective men are those who make many enemies or those who make none at all. Isn't this so?'

'There've been many? I'm impressed.'

Sarcasm, Telford knew. But he was happy to play this game a while longer.

'If you didn't know at least that much,' he said, 'why the tail? What is it you want? And Jewish – working for the sultan…'

Well, he certainly seemed to have some influence, Jack thought. The cabaret's proprietor – simply introduced to him as Corcos – had wasted no time shifting a protesting couple from this table near the stage to another at the back. Sheer deference. But now Gabizon took a swallow from his own glass, fingered the brim of the Panama hat on the table between them, next to the candlestick.

'We should try to get you cleaned up,' he said.

Jack glanced down at the linen jacket and trousers, which had earlier been so casually cream, but now stained filthy by brick dust and grime.

'I can change back at the hotel.' Jack offered his badly squashed packet of Gauloises to the man, who politely declined. 'Unless,' he said, 'you planned to offer me hospitality at the Sultan's Palace.'

'I'm afraid His Imperial Majesty has other things on his mind than entertaining guests, *Monsieur* Telford.'

'Such as?'

Gabizon shrugged.

'The war, naturally.'

'This *excuse* for a war,' Jack corrected him.

Nobody in Oran had been able to understand it either. The Germans fully engaged in Poland, only a relatively smaller army left to defend its western border along the Siegfried Line. And when a significantly larger combined French and British force had rushed to confront them it had looked certain the conflict would, indeed, be over by Christmas. Yet there they had stopped. At the French Maginot Line, despite their promises to the Poles. And ignoring, too, the Soviet seizure of eastern Poland. For two weeks, the whole world seemingly aware they were squandering this precious initiative. No more than a token advance across the Rhine, then inexplicable retreat.

'Herr Hitler understands very well,' said Gabizon, 'that neither France nor Britain has the stomach for this fight. He's still convinced

they're simply waving flags, will agree a peace as soon as they've let
him finish with the Poles.'

'And your sultan?'

The singer accepted the audience's applause with a genteel
curtsey, ran seamlessly into a pleasant rendition of *J'ai deux amours*.
Not quite Josephine Baker but good, all the same.

'Sultan Muhammad is still a young man. And a strange twist of
fate that brought him to the Sultanate.'

'I heard it was the French – thought he'd be a safer bet than the
older brothers.'

'You are a cynic, *monsieur*.' He lifted his glass, saluted the singer,
who offered him a dazzling smile in return, sang on regardless. 'It
was the sacred scholars who chose him,' said Gabizon. 'And if the
French *did* have some hope of securing a puppet, his support for
the nationalists, for the independence movement, must have been
a shock for them.'

'Nationalists,' Jack sneered, filled his glass again with the clear
eau de vie. It was going to his head. He could feel it. 'I had my
bellyful of nationalists in Spain.'

Gabizon sighed.

'Yes, Spain,' he said. '*D'accord*, we have arrived there at last.'

Jack wondered what he meant.

'The war in Spain's over,' he said. 'All done and dusted.'

He tapped the glass on the table, frowned. Memories.

'Yet you still write about them. From Oran. The refugees.
About Franco. Reports of these reprisals against anybody who
might have supported the Republic. The sultan's heard them too,
monsieur. Terrible things. Mass murders. Thousands of them.'

Franco, Jack thought. I could have killed the bastard at Burgos.
His regret at having failed to do so brought bitter bile to his throat.
Or was that just too much of the *mahia*?

'Mass murder,' he repeated. 'Like…'

'Yes, those stories too.'

Jack had been in Madrid when he'd picked up the news. Germany, the previous November. Hundreds of synagogues burned
to the ground. At least a hundred Jews murdered in their homes.
Tens of thousands rounded up and sent to prison camps. Jewish

businesses destroyed, their windows smashed. The Night of Broken Glass. And maybe comforting to think it was just Germany, but only a few years since there'd been attacks, the killing of Jews, by Frenchmen in Algeria. Then Mosley and his Blackshirts in Britain. It was everywhere. Like a cancer.

'When I arrived in Oran,' said Jack, clapping loudly, cigarette dangling from the corner of his mouth, the singer basking in the applause and skipping down from the stage, 'somebody told me there are two sorts of Jews in Morocco. The Berber Jews who've always been here. Literally always?' Gabizon nodded his head. 'And the Andalucian Jews,' Telford continued, 'who settled here after they were expelled from Spain. The Sephardim?'

'Yes,' said Gabizon. 'We are those. *Sefarad*. It is the Hebrew word for Spain. And we had hopes. The Republic. It seemed they had a willingness to attract our diaspora back to the Peninsula. After five hundred years. Imagine? But for Franco and his friends we were simply part of those responsible for all Spain's problems – the Bolsheviks, the Masons and, of course, as usual, the Jews. Always the Jews.'

'This is wonderfully educational,' said Jack, 'but like I said, the war in Spain's all over.'

A second entertainer was taking the stage, a young boy, a striped burnoose, woollen embroidered hat, deeper than a *kippah* skullcap. And a harp.

'*Bavajadas*, Telford. Spain, I think, is in your blood now.'

Jack knew he was right, but he was damned if he'd admit it.

'Beautiful tune,' he said. 'Haunting. What is it?'

'One we brought with us from the glories of Córdoba and Granada. In Ladino, we call it *Bilbilikos*. The skylarks, I think you would say.'

Jack lit another cigarette.

'And this other business,' he said. 'Me still writing about the refugees. What? Your sultan has his copy of *Reynold's News* delivered each week?'

Gabizon poured Telford one more shot of *mahia* – though Jack noted he'd not filled his own glass.

'You underestimate yourself, my friend. The sultan has eyes and ears throughout Morocco. Poor divided Morocco. But we have friends in Oran too. The Telephone and Telegraph Office, at least. Instructions for certain activities to be monitored, reported. His Imperial Majesty may never have seen *Reynold's News*, but he was intrigued by the reports you wired, *monsieur*.'

'About Spanish refugees?'

The young man was caressing the strings of his harp like an angel. Telford felt choked, emotional.

'The sultan has this strange view,' said Gabizon. 'That here we are all Moroccans. No Muslim, no Jew, no Christian. Simply Moroccans. And even those who find themselves in Morocco perhaps temporarily, through whatever circumstance or misfortune, still merit consideration. Algeria may be different but there are also labour camps here in Morocco. Spanish Republicans interned there. At Berguent and Tendrara. Maybe others by now.'

'For the railway,' Jack replied, though he was afraid he'd bumbled the word. 'I heard. But Spain? Me?'

'There are questions we cannot answer. We can be certain if Hitler continues his conquests, Europe's Jews face an unpleasant future. But how will Franco respond? What shall be the fate of Spain's Jews – more precisely those of Spanish Morocco?'

'Wait,' said Jack. 'Let me get this straight.' It was going to be difficult, his head now spinning. 'The sultan wants independence for Morocco,' he went on. '*All* of Morocco. And the Jewish communities across Morocco could go a long way towards helping him meet this ambition?'

It was no time for a lesson, but Jack knew full well that Morocco's history was long and proud – until, over the past hundred years, France and Spain, with Britain's help, had carved the country up into so-called protectorates, swamped the land with colonists, finally and at huge cost crushed any Berber insurrections – so famously in Spain's case that Franco had been able to use his Moroccan *regulares*, his Army of Africa, to pursue his defeat of the Popular Front Government. The irony. Without Hitler, without Mussolini, and particularly without those Muslim *regulares* his so-called Christian Reconquest of Spain could never have succeeded.

'An ambition, as you say,' Gabizon smiled. 'For now, it seems we are all united in one cause. To see Hitler defeated. And apart from the sultan's concerns for my people, for *all* our people, his immediate fear is that Franco will succumb to the Führer's demands for the mineral wealth of Spanish Morocco. Still more resources for Germany's arms industry. Worse, *Monsieur* Telford. Hitler may decide to help Franco yet again, this time with the expansion of his territorial dreams. All Morocco part of a reborn Spanish Empire.'

The harpist had finished his second piece, and several members of the audience offered him a standing ovation. He was, after, all, quite a performer.

'Mineral wealth?' said Jack, suddenly alert again. It was one of the things that had got him into so much trouble. Hitler rewarded by Franco, a gift of all the iron pyrites and similar materials from northern Spain he needed for Germany's rearmament – to the cost of Britain's own arms industry. And Telford had discovered the reports doctored by Major Edwin, minimising the extent of the threat, allowing a blind eye to be turned by those in the British Establishment who still favoured appeasement. Or worse, alliance with the Germans.

'Phosphates, lead, cobalt,' Gabizon explained. 'Oh, and did I mention grain? Morocco to be Germany's breadbasket. And how will your country respond, *Monsieur* Telford, when they find out all the bribes paid to Franco's generals and family may keep Spain from officially taking part in the war, but won't stop El Caudillo giving help – what is the phrase you use?'

'In kind,' Jack told him. 'And you know about the bribes.'

'Your government began paying them at the start of the year. Recognised Franco's dictatorship before the war was even finished. They say the Arabs are a devious people, *monsieur*, but *atyó*, perfidious Albion!'

'Whatever it is you want, trying to make me feel guilty about my country's responsibility for this mess isn't going to help you.'

'Then for Spain? For the Republic?' Gabizon suggested.

'I think I've heard enough.' Jack rose unsteadily from the table. 'Time to get cleaned up, as you say. Enjoyed the drink though.'

He wanted to mention the Hassan Tower, pointed vaguely towards the ceiling fans, but the words he sought somehow refused to form on his thickened tongue.

'But you'll miss the main event,' said Gabizon. 'We are hugely privileged tonight...'

Telford was about to decline but as he looked around, he saw – heard too – that the cabaret's customers had fallen into a hush of anticipation, no more than whispered conversations. There was a fellow in a suit settling himself at the piano, arranging sheet music on the instrument's rack. He turned to acknowledge a polite ripple of applause from the floor, but the ripple turned to a flood with the woman who made her entrance from a door in the wings. Beautiful. Astonishingly beautiful. Proud, the darkest, most deep-set eyes Jack thought he'd ever seen. Her hair was wild and wiry, a rope of small pearls wound through its waves. Rouged lips. Some sort of traditional dress, blue Crêpe de Chine maybe, and a black waistcoat. Jack sat again.

'Who...?'

'Don't you know?' Gabizon murmured, smiled, knowing he had scored a point or two. 'Brachah Zefira. On her way back from touring America. Landed this morning. Agreed to perform for us. Well, she's here anyway.'

There was something familiar. Even the face. But how...? And Gabizon's chatter wasn't really helping. Born in Jerusalem, he was saying. To Yemenite Jewish immigrants. Orphaned and raised by Sephardim, there in Palestine. Rose to stardom.

'I've seen her before,' said Jack, ignoring what he interpreted as a glance of some cynicism from the Sultan's Jew. 'Really.'

Yet he failed to make the connection until the pianist played a few introductory bars and she opened that profoundly captivating mouth. There was no mistaking the voice. He'd been hiding in Madrid, the house of the Republican priest, Father Lobo, and there'd been a Columbia gramophone record. This same woman. Her picture on the cover. He couldn't remember the tune, but it was like this, a Hebrew song with all the Flamenco rhythms of Andalucía. A reminder of Spain's Jewish roots, this same Sephardic tradition he'd stumbled across here. In Madrid the music had entranced him, helped him to think – at a time he'd very badly needed to do this very thing. Brachah Zefira had inspired him, given him new hope and now here she was again, in person.

21

Did he believe in fate? Some higher power shaping our lives? No, he did not. But this? Coincidence? He couldn't quite accept that either and he knew sometimes, in life, you just have to run with it.

In his room at the Transatlantic, somewhat sobered now after two *cafés noisettes* at the bar, still infatuated by Brachah Zefira's grace and elegance, he brushed his teeth, changed into his sky-blue pyjamas. But what had he promised Gabizon? Not much, he hoped. If he remembered correctly, simply to use his correspondent's credentials to visit one of the camps, ostensibly to report on France's remarkable achievement in keeping such a difficult railway route running, but then to provide private intelligence for the sultan on conditions there. No harm in this, surely. Innocent.

Telford sat on the edge of the bed, picked up the copy of *Karenina* he'd managed to buy in Oran, finished it on the train journey. But he turned to the back, read the final paragraph once again. Then he closed the volume and gazed at it for a moment, experiencing that sinking feeling with which Tolstoy always left him. What's wrong with me? he wondered. Good writing. No doubts there. Some of it philosophically profound. Yet his final reaction was the same as ever. A shrug of his shoulders. Not much of an ending. It was all – well, a bit pompous.

He set the book on the bedside table, threw open a corner of his sheets, found the light switch and wriggled down until he was comfortable, his head still fuddled but thankfully not spinning. Jack rolled onto his side – recoiled as his shin made contact with something, felt a hot needle pierce his leg. Another. The pain was immediate. Burning. He sat bolt upright, threw back the bed covers, fumbled for the switch once more, almost knocked the lamp from the table.

'Christ!' he swore. 'Jesus Christ!'

There it sat, black and ugly, three inches long. Four maybe. Its tail lifted, ready to strike again. Then it scuttled into the folds of the bedding once more, only the tip of a single claw still visible.

Jack felt sick to his stomach. He'd heard bad things about scorpion stings. Hated the little buggers. And he stumbled across to the dresser, the telephone there, managed to dial the front desk so that, five minutes later, he was being bundled into a taxi by a black-skinned bellboy. By then he was feeling drowsy, his vision blurred, his leg twitching badly and still the burning sensation, spreading now up to his thigh.

'What sort of hotel d'you call this?' he said to the manager, a dapper little fellow with white spats protruding from the bottoms of his striped trousers. 'Scorpions in your beds.'

'You will be fine, *monsieur*,' the manager assured him, flustered with embarrassment. 'The hospital is only along the road. No danger. And *mon Dieu*, you must believe this has never happened before. Never.'

'If you say so,' Jack muttered, collapsed back on the leather seats as the manager slammed the door. But as he did so, Telford saw him turn to the bellboy, heard him quite distinctly, a snort of laughter.

'No chance of scorpions in your bed,' the words played in Jack's head, over and over again, 'unless somebody puts them there on purpose.'

November 1939

Lawrence of Arabia

There'd been plenty of time to think during the twelve hours from Oudjda, and the damned song he couldn't get out of his head. From *The White Horse Inn*.

I'll join the Legion, that's what I'll do.
And in some far distant region…

Yet, all a bit old hat, really, the desert – the occasional patches of green, the wadis and trestle bridges, the goats on the line, an odd sighting of nomads and camels, brown-faced sheep and Berber tents, glimpses of the distant mountains, even the much-vaunted tunnel near Tiouli. The rest? Hard-packed desert from horizon to horizon. For most of the journey. Yes, old hat.

He wrote, of course. Habit more than anything. Yet he could not capture anything in his writing except *ennui*. And he went over those final pages of *Karenina* yet again, desperately hoping to discover some hidden message there. But nothing emerged. All as mystifying as his own conundrums.

They'd treated him with bored civility at the hospital, washed and cleaned the two purple punctures, provided analgesics. That was the extent of it. He'd rather felt as though the doctor should have made more of it. Scorpion bite, for goodness sake.

'For the very young or the very old,' the doctor had explained, 'such bites can be serious. Or those with certain allergies, prone to anaphylactic shock. Yet you, *monsieur…*'

'But in my bed?'

'I would probably prescribe a change of hotel.'

As it happened, the Transatlantic seemed rather glad to see the back of him. But yes, they had caught the creature and disposed of it. And Jack had checked every inch of his new room at the Hôtel Ville de Paris. None of that, naturally, had gone any way towards helping discover how the scorpion had found its way into his bed in the first place and though he had determined to interrogate Hurst at the consulate when he returned there for his papers, it never really went any further than a polite enquiry from Jack about whether anybody may have asked about him.

'Not so far as I'm aware, old chap,' Hurst had replied. 'Why, were you expecting somebody?'

Telford could hardly explain that he feared Major Edwin might have friends.

'Is there a military attaché here in Rabat, by any chance?' he'd said as he accepted the new Emergency Certificate, pleased to see this one also had no expiry date.

'My dear fellow, this is a French Protectorate. All those things are handled through Brigadier-General Fraser's office. Paris, you see? Occasionally one or other of the attachés might pass through on their way to Casablanca or Marrakech, but – what have you done, by the way? Saw you limping just now. Accident of some sort?'

Telford had mulled it all over as the train headed south. And when he became entirely tired of finding no answers, he thought again about Brachah Zefira. After he left Hurst, Jack had gone to meet Gabizon again, as arranged, told him about the scorpion and was rewarded with a response even more dismissive than the one he'd received from that bloody doctor.

'If somebody wanted you dead,' Gabizon had explained, as though speaking to an idiot, 'they would not have chosen scorpions.'

Telford agreed to make this trip though, as soon as the leg was better. Somewhere within him he hoped his adventure might impress the singer. An interesting talking point. And as innocently as he was able, he asked Gabizon whether she'd be performing again in Rabat.

'You'd like an introduction, I expect,' Gabizon had leered at him.

'No, I just – well...'

'Too late, my friend,' he sighed. 'Already on her way back to Tel Aviv. With her husband.'

A hammer blow.

'Husband?'

'Nardi. The piano player. You didn't know? I say husband, but they're divorced. Still performing together though. Big concerts planned back in Palestine.'

Palestine. He felt dashed, tried to hide his disappointment. Still felt disappointed as he'd gazed through the train window, imagined Lawrence and his Arab army charging across their barren terrain, those raids on the Turkish Hejaz railway between Damascus and Medina.

Lawrence. The Arabs. Jews. Palestine – the part of the Ottoman Empire mandated to Britain after the Great War, its ancient name officially restored. The Holy Land. The Arabs had been promised independence but then the Balfour Declaration allowed for an annual quota of Jewish immigrants. Later, Britain's announcement. Palestine should not as a whole be given over to a Jewish National Home, but that such a national home should exist within the boundaries of Palestine. By 1936, one-third of the population was Jewish. And, the same year, the Arabs revolted. Martial law. Britain had armed the *Haganah* Jewish militia to help them in the fight. And the British government introduced a White Paper they thought might provide a compromise. But in the best traditions of compromise, both sides saw it as a betrayal. And if they'd thought the war would help, they were only partially correct. The Jewish leader Ben Gurion had set out the thing concisely. They would fight alongside the British in this war against the Nazis as if there was no White Paper, and fight against the White Paper as if there was no war. So said *La Dépêche*.

Palestine. Thomas Edward Lawrence. Somehow it had all started with Lawrence. And somehow it had all gone so horribly wrong. What had he written in the *Seven Pillars*?

> *I loved you, so I drew these tides of*
> *Men into my hands*
> *And wrote my will across the*
> *Sky in stars*
> *To earn you freedom.*

26

Except – well, he hadn't freed them. The Arabs. Not really.

Telford found himself only marginally distracted by the other passengers who came and went at the various stations along the way – most of them seemingly in the middle of nowhere – or at the other camps, Berguent and Tendrara. What were they all doing? The French officer returning from leave to take up his prison warder duties again was easy enough to understand. But there also were European men Jack considered candidates for the social class the French would have called *bourgeoisie*, functionaries. Several Arabic or Turkish merchants. A couple of engineers or similar who spent their journey poring over technical drawings, referring to various points along the route and contracted, Telford discovered, to the Trans-Sahara Railway Company – so that, from them, he'd learned considerably more about the project.

And about the astonishing amount of labour they'd need for the task. Many, many thousands. In addition, of course, to those they needed to keep these existing lines running, to keep them from being buried by the desert's shifting sands.

He gazed out upon the desert, imagined himself, yet again, as Lawrence. There was a ridge of low mountains to the south and west but otherwise the landscape was barren and without feature, as Jack's life seemed to be also. A single tree, and the tree threw a long weak shadow as the sun went down, and the shadow brushed Telford's face as he smoked a cigarette in the doorway.

'End of the line,' he said.

'Not for me,' the Spaniard from the prison camp replied. He was using a pair of pliers within a junction box on the wall of the office. Bou Arfa's station building.

'Getting chilly.' Telford was glad he'd had the sense to pack a sweater.

'November. What d'you expect?'

More, thought Jack. He supposed he'd expected more. This cluster of ramshackle buildings, hardly even a village. A poor excuse for a hotel. A well with timber uprights and cross-piece, a bucket hanging below the pulley. The skeleton of an old truck, with the name of the now defunct manganese mining company still just visible on the side. A water tower, paint peeling from the blue rectangle with the town's name picked out in faded white. Two short dead-end sidings, a few semi-derelict wagons on the weed-grown rails. The crumbling adobe and stone detention huts surrounded by rusted barbed wire fencing. A pair of military trucks outside the camp gates, a Renault and an ancient Berliet, which could have seen service these past twenty years. A blockhouse and stabling for the garrison.

'Where in Spain?' he asked.

'Look, I've got work to do. Isn't there somebody else you could annoy, English?'

The carriages in which he'd spent all day reaching here still stood at the platform, waiting for the return journey tomorrow. And Jack wished he could be on it. But he was stuck here now, for a few days at least. The shabby diesel-electric engine stood in the head-shunt, an oil-streaked tapper in vest and braces working his way along the wheels and bogies. Beyond the locomotive – nothing. The end of the line.

'Will they build it?' said Jack, waving his cigarette towards the wilderness. 'The Trans-Sahara?'

'The commandant says next year,' the Spaniard replied, closed the junction box, his task completed, joined Jack at the door. 'Depends whether they can get the workers.'

Thirty miles away, Morocco's southern border with Algeria. Thirty more to the town of Colomb-Béchar, and the line running there from Oran, far away to the north-east. It was the great French colonial dream. To join up these two routes and then drive the railway right across the desert. All the way to sub-Saharan Africa. To Timbuktu. Fifteen hundred miles, give or take. And then on to the coast at Dakar. The same distance again.

'A friend in Rabat says they're going to start shipping out labour from the camps in France.' Jack offered the man one of his Gauloises and the Spaniard accepted, wiped his hands on the torn overalls.

'They might be better here than at Barcarès. At least they have to feed us if they want us to work. After a fashion. The food's garbage, but they feed us.'

'And this one?' said Jack. 'How long has there been a camp at Bou Arfa?'

The Spaniard snorted, spat out onto the platform.

'How long? Since the start, of course. Three shitty years. When those bastards took Córdoba and Granada, you'd have had to be crazy to stay and get shot. You know what they did in Córdoba, English?' Jack knew. 'Well, it was one way, anyhow. Get to Almería or Cartagena. Ship to Oran if you had the dough.' Actually he'd used the Spanish slang word *parné*, but Jack got the drift.

'You?' Jack asked, though he was certain this fellow had no Andalucían in his accent.

'Me?' The man laughed. '*Hombre*, no such luck. From the north, me. Only got out just before the end. From Valencia. Oran, and that shithole at Morand-Bogari. Then two weeks ago, here. And thank god somebody figured I was an engineer. Took me away from shoveling sand and breaking ballast.' He extended his hand and Jack shook it. 'Raúl Ramos,' said the Spaniard. 'What's your story?'

'Just a journalist. Telford. Jack Telford. Somebody wanted me to write about the camps. About the Spanish here. They say there's twelve thousand in Algeria and Morocco now. Most of them women and kids though, I guess. So I suppose you're right. No chance of laying fresh track unless they can fetch more men.'

Ramos flicked away the end of the cigarette. The sun had almost disappeared below the ridge to the west, and the Spaniard fiddled with a switch inside the doorway, a light coming on above their heads. As it did so, there was a crunch of boots from the farther end of the platform and a Senegalese guard plodded towards them, khaki jacket and leggings, dark blue forage cap and rifle slung at his shoulder. Ramos ducked back inside. No fraternisation with the internees, Jack had been told. Not without supervision. And the 'internees' had plainly been told the same.

'Quarter of a million of us in France,' Ramos whispered. 'Isn't that what they reckon?'

Jack heard him almost choke on the words, watched the guard begin to shine a torch through each of the carriage windows. Telford turned slowly, so he would attract no attention, saw Ramos in the shadows behind him, the dim glow from the overhead light glistening now on a tear running down the Spaniard's cheek.

'You'll get back there,' Jack murmured. 'One day.'

But Ramos shook his head.

'No, *señor*. The enemy in Spain isn't really Franco. It's the millions who don't give a damn. Half the bloody country don't care whether they live under a dictatorship or not. I was a union organiser before the war. UGT. There's nothing you can tell me about apathy, English. Nothing.'

'But the war,' said Jack. 'The war will change things.'

The Senegalese soldier had finished his check of the first two carriages, paused before starting on the third, pointed the torch at Telford.

'You, *monsieur*,' he said, in an exotic *argot* mix of French and West African. 'Hotel.'

'Straight away,' Jack shouted back, took a step away from the door, then stopped again as the guard swung his attention to the final coach. 'It will, won't it?' he said under his breath.

'Not for me it won't,' said Ramos. 'Not for lots of the others here either. If we get out of these bloody camps, personally I'd stay. Rabat maybe. Or Casablanca. Organise the union among Spanish workers in Morocco. God knows, there'll be enough of us.'

The shooting woke him. But when he put down his razor, crossed to the window and peered through the shutters, he could see nothing. On this side, only that endless desert.

He took the towel from around his neck and wiped the soap from his cheeks, lips and ears, dressed quickly, grabbed his satchel and ran downstairs. Not the best night's sleep and no, he told the shabby Frenchman who seemed to be the proprietor, no breakfast, not yet. Maybe coffee. Maybe later.

'I have tea,' the fellow shouted as Jack went out through the door.

Across the street, the station. At the platform, those same three carriages but now with a flatbed truck hooked up behind. And the engine, square and squat, its motor throbbing, filthy black exhaust smoke, the stink of burning oil, and the harsh impatience of its horn. The locomotive no longer in the head-shunt though, having been driven through the run-around loop ready to pick up the coaches for the haul back to Oudjda – the driver keen to be on his way, the horn's siren again. But, blocking his way, around the front carriage, four of the Senegalese guards and that French officer, the camp's commandant, Jack had met yesterday – the officer who'd grilled him so thoroughly on his reason for being there, scrutinised his papers.

'The sultan's staff?' the officer had said. He seemed incredibly small, parsimonious features, thick-lensed spectacles beneath a *képi* at least one size too large for his head.

'Yes, you see?' Jack had showed him the relevant section. 'His Imperial Majesty requires a report on the excellent conditions enjoyed by these refugees. To be submitted as an appendix to the Resident-General's claim for compensation from the Spanish Republican government in exile.'

'Report from the sultan?' The French lieutenant shook his head. 'I don't understand.'

'Between you and me, lieutenant, I don't understand either. Independent source, maybe – who knows? But ours not to reason why, eh?'

Jack wasn't sure he had this particular bit of French quite right, but he pointed at the Resident-General's signature again anyway. General Charles Noguès. And now he came to think of it, he also wasn't sure how Gabizon had acquired that either.

'English?'

'I have that privilege, sir,' Jack had beamed. 'And honoured to be here at this important outpost of our gallant French allies. Long live the Third Republic, *n'est-ce pas?*'

The fellow had twitched, handed back the document – and issued Jack a set of strict orders.

Towards the rear, between the last of the carriages and the flatbed truck, stood a half-dozen men in threadbare clothes, each of them leaning on a long-handled shovel. Jack sidled across to push among them, checked they couldn't be seen and passed around his packet of Gauloises.

31

He peered carefully around the mucky green side of the coach. Up front, that French lieutenant bellowed at two more of the work detail, told them to pick up the corpse Jack could now see sprawled in the sand at the feet of the Senegalese guards.

'What happened?' Jack asked in Spanish, though he was by no means certain these men were Spanish speakers. They simply didn't look like Spaniards – most of them anyhow. There was an exchange, which would have graced the Tower of Babel, the men keeping their eyes fixed always on the soldiers.

'*Señor*,' one of them replied at last, 'we have enough trouble here today. If they see us talking…'

But one of the others slapped the Spaniard on the arm, hissed at him in…

'Is he German?' said Jack. It certainly sounded like German.

'Why do you ask?'

'I was in prison. Burgos. Internationals there. Hundreds of them. Taken during the Ebro campaign. Germans among them. Austrians too. Always admired them. Men already at risk from the Nazis back home but willing to sacrifice everything by going to fight for Spain's Republic. Automatic death sentence if they were caught and sent back.'

The Spaniard translated – after a fashion. Both ways.

'Yes, he's German,' he said, then pointed to each of the others. 'That one, Yugoslavia. Him, Dutch. This comrade all the way from Cuba. Internationals as well – but stayed to fight alongside the Poles and Hungarians when the Brigades were sent home. Me and El Gordo, from Toledo.'

'What happened?'

'Since this other war started, some of us have been trying to join the Legion. Kill fascists again. But here? Seems this Lieutenant Vidal's in the pocket of the railway company. Doesn't pass on our requests. Now and then, one or two of us try to get out. But that?' He thumbed back towards the front of the train. 'Tried to hide himself under the coaches and…'

'*Tiens!*' It was one of the Senegalese guards, who'd made his way down the other side of the train and they'd not seen him. The soldier aimed his rifle at them. 'Lieutenant,' he shouted.

'Shit,' said the Spaniard, and they could hear the officer yelling instructions.

'Get that out of here,' Vidal called, then he was strutting towards them. 'And get those bastards on the truck.' He had a lanyard around his neck, a whistle attached to the lanyard. He blew it, waved to the engine driver, and the locomotive began to shunt backwards, while several of the guards hustled the labour gang onto the flat-back. Another, at the officer's instruction, grabbed Telford's arm, dragged him towards the platform. There, the lieutenant took the spectacles from his eyes, pulled a handkerchief from his uniform trousers, wiped the glasses, his face contorted with rage.

'You had instructions, didn't you?' said the officer. 'You only speak to this scum if we arrange it.'

'You're Jewish,' Jack realised. Something about the man reminded him of Gabizon. A vicious version of Gabizon. But not Sephardi, he supposed.

'And...?'

'Nothing. Nothing at all.'

The war, he thought. Reports he had no reason to disbelieve. Warsaw besieged all last month, but then? The Germans had taken the city, surrounded the main Jewish Quarter with barricades, cutting it off entirely. There'd been a quarter million Jews in Warsaw in 1939, Jack had read. Now, a hundred thousand more. Refugees. All herded into that one area. And there was a word from history for zones like this. Jews herded like animals. A *ghetto*.

'Good,' said Vidal, settled the spectacles on his nose again. 'Then you should understand, *Monsieur* Telford. Those men will be punished as soon as their work duty's finished. Until that time, consider yourself confined to your hotel. You step outside, you will be shot. You might think about this. Think very carefully. Because, personally, I don't give a shit whether you are, or are not, with the sultan.'

The punishments would be severe. The commandant, Lieutenant Vidal, had made this much clear and told Jack he had two choices. To watch or to join them. Telford's protest, that he was a British citizen, was wiped aside by the officer's scorn and the sweeping gesture of his riding crop, which so eloquently took in their surroundings, confirmed he was, here, so very far from British authority.

So, he watched. This morning's work detail, returned from four hours shovelling several small dunes from the path of the north-going train as far as Tendrara, then a tortuous return by lever-operated *draisienne* handcar – now sitting in the sidings – and its attached hopper filled with freshly crushed ballast they'd been required to drop and spread at various points, under guard all the way, back to Bou Arfa. For this.

They were all there, lined up inside the camp gates. The two Spaniards from Toledo, the Yugoslav, the Dutchman, the Cuban and the German. Two other men – Spanish as well, Jack thought, and assumed they must have been the couple who'd carried away the dead man. Behind them, all the other internees in a couple of serried ranks.

'He was part of your detail,' Vidal was screaming at the Spaniard who'd done the translation this morning. 'You are the section leader. You must have known.'

'I know…nothing,' the Spaniard replied in halting French. But he looked over at Jack. And Jack wondered whether the look was an accusation, or might it mean something else? He imagined he saw a slight nod of the head, an acknowledgement. A conspiratorial agreement.

'Liar,' shouted the lieutenant. '*Vache espagnole.* You will all spend tonight in the hole anyway.' He pointed his whip towards the pit just behind them. It looked deep, about six yards long and maybe three yards across. If these poor devils were going down there in just their work clothes, they'd freeze. 'But if you don't tell me the truth, you'll stay there.'

'Better than working for you bastards,' said the Spaniard, this time in his own language.

Jack wasn't sure whether Vidal understood or whether the insolent tone was enough in itself, but the lieutenant lashed out at the man's face with that riding crop, drew blood in a wicked line across the Spaniard's cheek. The fellow barely flinched, hardly moved – but his comrades did. All forty or fifty of them, as one. They surged forward, surrounded the work detail entirely as the

34

Senegalese guards fell back, raised their rifles, Vidal reaching for the holster flap at his hip.

The prisoners at the front of this demonstration began to tear open their shirt fronts.

'*Venga*,' one of them shouted, pushed out his chest. 'Go on, shoot. Shoot!'

Others did the same. And some of them, half-hidden at the back, seemed to have found weapons, shovels and a pick.

'Get back now,' said the lieutenant, revolver in hand, 'or we *will* fire.'

But the men didn't seem to care, moved forward another pace or two. Jack admired them for it, but it was foolish in the extreme. Maybe there were enough of them to overpower the guards – though several more Senegalese had now gathered at the other side of the barbed wire, rifles at the ready – or maybe not. Many of them would die, all the same. And the tension was only broken when one of the men, cried out, fell to the ground, convulsing, spittle at his lips. Some sort of fit. Epilepsy maybe. Enough though. His friends gathered about him and Vidal seized the moment to order his men – Jack too – back through the gates, shouting something about tomorrow, that he'd settle this tomorrow.

The building was ablaze, burning more fiercely against the still-dark sky than he could ever have imagined.

Telford considered that Vidal had made an awful mistake. He'd left him confined all the previous day in his excuse for a hotel. And once he exhausted all his obvious sources of entertainment there'd been nothing left except – well, this.

He hadn't known, of course, the punishments would run over to this morning. Simply too much time on his hands to dwell on the work detail's words yesterday. The possibility of escaping this hellhole, getting back in the fight.

It would all be a bit random, but it couldn't be helped. And, as the day dragged on, the pieces had seemed to fall into place quite nicely.

First, over bread rolls and coffee, that camp trusty Raúl Ramos, had arrived to repair a couple of ceiling fans. A piece of serendipity, which really inspired the rest of the scheme.

'Did you know him?' Jack had asked. 'The one they shot.'

'I knew him.'

'And what?'

Ramos was standing on a chair, unscrewing the cover from the fan's motor. He looked around, only one other guest at breakfast, a merchant maybe, but the man didn't seem to be following their Spanish.

'I was with him at Teruel. Andrés Villena. Met up again when we were getting out. But by then...' He grimaced, tapped the screwdriver's handle against the side of his head. '*Loco*.' Then he peered up into the motor, carefully separated a couple of the cables. 'My god,' he said. 'This wiring.'

Jack sipped at his coffee. Villena must indeed have been mad, he thought.

'Under a carriage? Where the hell did he think he was going?'

'Tendrara. The Legion uses it – like a rest camp. Place is full of whore-houses. I suppose Villena... Well, he's dead now. They wouldn't have taken him anyway. Not a madman.'

'How many more?' said Jack. 'Killed here?'

Ramos climbed down from the chair, went to the bag he'd left by the door.

'Vidal's too smart,' he said, taking out two coils of sheathed wire, one green, one brown. 'I've seen him have a man almost dragged to death behind a horse. But only almost. Understand, English? He needs us alive, not dead. Not if he can help it. He...'

The Spaniard shut his mouth quickly when that weasel of a proprietor poked his head through the door, demanded to know how long the work would take. The fellow's French was the strange *pataouète* spoken by Algerian colonists, even those spread to here in Morocco, the *pieds-noirs*, and he'd not endeared himself to Telford by a lengthy, barely intelligible diatribe about Lieutenant Vidal and others of his race. '*A bas les juifs!*' he'd said. Down with the Jews. A real Cagayous, Jack had thought, remembering the anti-Semitic comic strip character he'd come across so often in Oran.

'Excellent coffee, *monsieur*,' Jack had said, lifting the cup in salute. 'Excellent.' He waited for the wretch to disappear again.

'And the Legion,' he said. 'They're close?'

'Depends what you mean by close,' Ramos had replied. 'There's a fort, at Bou Denib. But that's – what? A hundred and fifty kilometers, I guess. Maybe a bit less. Southwest of here. There's a road, of sorts.'

He snipped off a few short lengths of wire, bared the ends, while Jack lit himself a cigarette.

'What will happen to them?' he said. 'The rest of the work detail.'

'A beating maybe. Thrown into the pit for a day or two. Vidal can't afford to be without them too long.'

Jack thought about this for a moment, finished his coffee.

'And you, Raúl, will you be here for a while? At the hotel?'

'Now? Half-hour maybe. Then back to the dump for some more gear. I'll be on this most of the day. Why?'

'No matter,' Jack had said, stubbed out the cigarette in the table's brass ashtray. 'Just a thought.'

He'd wandered to the front door, reminded himself of the camp's layout. And the station, empty now, the train already well on its way back to Oudjda with the work detail on board – to wherever *they* were bound. All day to kill, the punishments in the evening. But tomorrow? Tomorrow would bring whatever tomorrow might bring. He doubted whether he'd pull it off but it amused him, this plotting. Bloody Vidal.

Then up to his room. The window. The building cast a shadow westward in the early morning sun and there was the desert, of course. But that must be the road Ramos had mentioned. He'd not really noticed it before. He leaned further out, looked to the right, over the rest of the town. Just a few godforsaken streets, a single stubby minaret. He took the fountain pen from his inside pocket, put the end of it in his mouth, tapped the black Bakelite against his teeth, reached for his notepad and began to write. Simple Spanish. He thought about it carefully. Needed to be clear, concise.

When he was finished it was downstairs again, hoping Ramos would be back – and indeed he was, but now working in the kitchen, the proprietor there too and a Moroccan cook, stirring a cauldron of saffron-stained stew and a pot of white rice.

So, Jack waited. And waited.

'I thought you'd be all day,' he said when he finally caught Ramos on his way out.

'Now what?' said the Spaniard.

'I need you to do something.'

'*Hombre*, you think they just let me come and go?'

'Don't they?'

'They need me. For now. But you don't know what it's like, *señor*.' He glanced back towards the kitchen. 'Just to stay sane.'

'Tell me.'

'It would take too long. They'll be looking for me. What is it you want?'

Jack took two notes from his pocket.

'These,' he said. 'This one for the comrade who's with the work party. On the train. Not El Gordo, the other – I don't know his name. This one for you.'

Ramos read the second one.

'It's *you* that's mad.' He looked horrified. 'You want...' He studied the note again. 'And then...'

Jack took the pen from his inside pocket once more.

'I wrote those notes with this,' he said. 'Know where I got it?'

Ramos shook his head but not in answer to his question, Telford thought, for he was trying to push the two pieces of paper back into Jack's hand.

'Here,' he said. 'I don't want these.'

'This is Negrín's pen,' said Jack. 'You remember Negrín?'

'Don't insult me, *señor*. But his pen? I don't think so.'

Yet he still held the notes. And yes, Negrín. Jack remembered.

The airstrip at El Fondó, near Elda, Alicante. The President of the Republic waiting to fly into exile when, finally, all was lost. Jack had been with him and Negrín's last act before boarding the plane was to gift him this pen, less elaborate than the elegant Font-Pelayo Telford had previously carried, but that – well, it was best not to dwell on what had happened to the Font-Pelayo. It was enough he'd lost it in Negrín's service, and the President had recognised its sacrifice. So this simple writing tool had almost the status of a religious icon and Jack held it up before him now, fixed

Ramos with his gaze. He saw the man's head go back, incredulity in his eyes, but then they softened, the head tilting slightly.

'You're serious,' said Ramos. 'Crazy.' He stuffed the two notes in his pocket. 'But the gasoline... And the truck...'

He was gone, and Jack had no confidence he'd persuaded him to assist. So, the afternoon had been agony, not helped by the bout of diarrhea seemingly brought on by the rice and stew, and only just brought under control when he'd been summoned to witness the punishments after the work detail returned. There'd been that look too.

'I know...nothing,' the Spaniard had told Vidal, then glanced over at Jack. An acknowledgement? Or a conspiratorial agreement?

But there'd been no sign of Ramos during the punishment parade and its minor rebellion, and he was still pondering matters when he returned to his hotel room. There at the foot of the bed, was a *Phénix* beer bottle – and yes, half-filled with gasoline. Not much and by now Jack had convinced himself the plan was stupid anyway. It had assumed the status of a schoolboy prank. He was angry with Vidal. Of course he was, though all the same how would this play out? He'd only come here in the first place to – why *had* he come?

It kept him awake most of the night, fully dressed. And the few snatches of sleep were filled with the wildest fearful fantasies. But by five he'd been wide awake.

What the hell have I done? he thought. By then he was convinced. The section leader's nod had given him the go-ahead. And with Ramos he'd invoked Negrín. A double-edged blade. It might have helped persuade the Spaniard but it had served also to commit Telford. Almost a sacred solicitation. But to what end? Help a handful of men to reach the Legion? How had they put it – to get back in the fight? Well, that was *their* choice maybe, but it wasn't his.

It all seemed so bloody pompous somehow. He'd believed himself qualified to interfere. Yet now? This whole camp would be expecting – something. Of course, he could feign illness, more stomach troubles – because this wasn't so far from the truth. Then he could simply wait it out, take tomorrow's train back, tell Gabizon it had all been something of a waste of time. After all, he'd never see any of these men again. Would he?

'Oh, Christ,' he said, and picked up the bottle, his handkerchief, his cartridge case lighter. And he crept down the stairs with his heart beating so fast he was convinced it must wake the whole hotel.

The building was so beautifully ablaze. It had all happened so fast. He'd learned how to make petrol bombs well enough while he was with the *guerrilleros*, and this one worked just fine. Soaked handkerchief for the fuse, lit while he stood in the dim hallway outside the kitchen, then the bottle tossed inside the room and the door shut again, Jack up the stairs once more as fast as he was able. How long? And which of his possessions would he save? He only had the smaller of his cases with him and nothing in there he especially valued. His satchel, of course. He'd have to save the satchel. But how would he explain being dressed? He couldn't. So, he'd stripped off his shirt, trousers and socks, put on the pyjamas, shoes on his bare feet, shrugged himself back into the jacket. And again he waited, sitting on the bed.

It seemed he waited forever, convinced himself the bottle bomb had malfunctioned. He'd seen that happen before. Yet after a while the faintest of wood smoke smells had reached him. And a noise. Was it a noise? Almost a trembling in the fabric of the building. Jack decided to take a look, set a hand against the grotesquely papered wall. It was warm and yes, throbbing.

He opened the bedroom door and recoiled in horror. Heat. And the whole landing filled with black smoke, a dense cloud roiling around the ceiling.

Telford slammed the door shut again, saw the insidious fingers of the monster groping, writhing under its lower edge.

The window. He could get out through the window. Yet by the time he reached the shutters he knew there was something else very badly wrong.

Where was everybody else? There weren't *many* other guests in the hotel but...

He grabbed his discarded trousers from the floor, the water pitcher from the bowl on the nightstand, soaked and balled the garment and clamped the dripping linen to his face as he charged back out into the horror.

'Fire!' he yelled, taking the bundle from his mouth and the smoke stinging his eyes. '*Fuego!*' He thought he'd choke. '*Au secours! Au feu!*'

He stumbled out into the corridor, set his hand against the baking wall he could no longer see, felt his way along to the next door, hammered upon it. Nothing. But then coughing ahead of him, a dim light in the darkness and a shape, somebody pushing past him. Jack tried to ask for help, but the smog was filling his own lungs. He needed to get out, knew he was becoming confused, no longer thinking straight. And he found himself at the end of the landing, the shuttered window there, but the shutters firmly closed.

What happened next? He had no idea. He'd tried to ask himself which way to turn. But it was hot. So bloody hot. The more he tried to think, the worse it all became. Thumping his fist against two more closed doors, a third door left open, and his struggle to stop himself going inside, the deadly lure illusion of sanctuary. Yet he managed to shout once more. No reply. Staggering further, feeling the banisters just too late – found himself pitching forward, reached for the handrail, cracked his head, tumbled down the rest of the stairs.

End of the line, he'd thought. The heat. An inferno. Then somebody had spoken to him, took hold of his wrist and dragged him along the hallway.

He remembered nothing else until his head cleared a little, out on the dirt road, and somebody slapped his face. The hotel owner. Of all people. The bloody proprietor.

'*Maré de Déo, monsieur,*' he gasped in that weird *patois*. Mother of God. 'If you hadn't raised the alarm…'

Jack couldn't have answered even if he'd possessed the words. Breathing fresh air again only made the coughing worse. Barely conscious. The noise deafening. A roaring beast, the flames of hell, his face afire. A tocsin bell tolling inside his skull. Shouts and running feet. A final flood of emotion. Relief. He knew just how close he'd come.

The hotel was a lost cause, but Jack now saw there was a real risk to the whole neighbourhood. What had he expected – a fire brigade? But Bou Arfa responded with the next best thing. Citizens everywhere, the spout of the water tower swung into action, the precious liquid gushing down to supply a hastily arranged bucket chain, and some ancient wheeled pump deployed at the well, a leaking hose spluttering, splashing the only two roofs its impotence could reach.

Among the locals Jack could see prisoners, Lieutenant Vidal in his shirt and uniform trousers, screaming orders, lashing any perceived reluctance with his riding crop. Good god, he'd emptied the camp.

But what for? Telford asked himself. What the hell did I do it for? He thought of those painful sections of the *Seven Pillars*, Lawrence's remorse. His guilt. The duplicity. The cruelty. The sacrifice. The betrayal.

Yet in the midst of it all he saw a Senegalese guard running, frantic, towards his commandant, pointing, yelling.

Just outside the camp gates, one of the trucks roared into life, its headlight beams dazzling. Men were clambering on board. Many men. Even as it ground into gear, sped towards the road, they were still trying to grab for its sides, several of them falling in the dust.

Shouting. Shots. Vidal and a few soldiers running for the second lorry, the Renault. A short sharp protest as its engine turned over. And over. And over. The lieutenant's bellow of rage when it finally became clear it was never going to start.

The cheer that went up from the antiquated Berliet as it rattled past, silhouetted against the blaze – and disappeared down the track to Bou Denib. And the line from the same song ran through Jack's head.

You won't see my heels for the dust.

December 1939

Paquita Gorroño

A few burns or other injuries sustained by those who'd helped fight the fire. The doctor at Bou Arfa had been kept busy most of the day with the hotel's smoke-damaged guests.

Lieutenant Vidal had eventually found a mechanic who could get the Renault running again and it was after dark when he returned from a belated and fruitless pursuit of his fugitives.

Jack was offered alternative lodging for his one remaining night in town – a grubby yet welcome little room above Bou Arfa's only other bar. From there he was summoned, still dressed in his pyjamas and jacket, to the commandant's office in the blockhouse – where he sat without invitation on the only available chair while Vidal stood at a wall map, thumped his fist against the defiant expanse of the Sahara.

'Well, *monsieur*,' he'd said, 'what can you tell me? It was sabotage, of course.'

'Sabotage, how?'

'It must be obvious, no? The fire. You think those scum decided on the spur of the moment? One of the trucks tampered with?'

'Really?'

'The injector pipes all cut.' Jack coughed, remembered his proposition to Ramos, closed his tired eye and pressed his knuckle against it. 'Smoke?' said Vidal.

'Yes,' Telford replied, 'it was...' But when he opened his eye again, he saw the lieutenant was offering a silver case and, inside, black-papered cigarettes with gold filters. Sobranie. The last time he'd seen one of those was during his interrogation at Burgos.

43

'Thanks,' he said, and took one. 'Lost mine in the fire and the bar only sells those bloody Egyptian things. Bit strong for me.'

He dug in the pocket of his soot-stained jacket for his lighter.

'Didn't lose your lighter, I see,' said the lieutenant. 'Fortunate. Personally, my cigarettes and lighter are never more than inches away from each other. But I suppose we're all different.'

'As you say.'

Jack recalled how Gabizon had said something similar. All the fingers of the hand are not the same.

'And your bag.' Vidal pointed at Jack's satchel. 'You saved it.'

'Instinct, I guess. Being a journalist all these years. Always keep the writing close, eh? Grabbed it and ran.'

As it happened, his first concern had been for Negrín's pen and after his fall down the stairs, the rough manner of his rescue, he'd been astonished to find it still intact, still in his pocket. But then he'd always attached some mystical quality to it.

'I'd like to see,' said Vidal. 'Writers. I've always been curious. May I? Your notebook – whatever you use?'

'There's nothing to interest you.'

Jack's defiance was perhaps bolstered by whatever small success he may have thought accomplished by the escape.

'*Monsieur* Telford, let me explain something.' He slammed a hand against the telephone on his desk. 'I am waiting for the officer in command at Bou Denib to return my call. I will have those Reds back here before the train leaves tomorrow morning. Understand? And when I get them again they *will* tell me what I need to know. You may think somebody has been very clever here but I can assure you there will be a price to pay. And I am not especially particular about who should settle the account. Now, your notebook.'

He held out his palm and Jack carefully handed him the book. Vidal skimmed the pages.

'I'm afraid most of it's in English,' he said.

'That's not a problem, *monsieur*. Let me…'

The lieutenant hitched his spectacles further up his nose, ran a finger, line by line, along the most recent scribbles.

'As you see, I've not had time to write very much about the camp,' said Jack. 'Just those few general observations about how efficient everything seems to be.' He waited for Vidal's reaction, saw the lieutenant tap the last couple of paragraphs, nod his head in acknowledgement, in appreciation. They were, in truth, the paragraphs in which Jack had made notes about Villena's shooting, about the punishment pit.

'*Bien*,' said Vidal and passed the notebook back, 'this afternoon I will arrange for some of the Reds to return early from the quarry. Only a few. But you may interview them. Record the names of those you speak with. Eye-witness statements, you see? Bring the statements here tonight. In French, of course. I shall have them typed, signed and stamped. In the morning, before you board the train, I will need to see the papers again.'

'Of course, lieutenant. I would have it no other way.'

Vidal studied him briefly, seemed fascinated by the eye patch, and Jack knew the Frenchman needed this, a positive report, to hide the inefficiency of the escape.

'Strange though,' said the commandant. 'The fire. You really have no idea?'

'I just assumed – well, faulty wiring perhaps?'

Vidal beamed at him, as though a veil was lifted from his vision.

'Of course.' He nodded his head vigorously. 'I should have realised. Yes, the wiring.'

They were all rehearsed statements, naturally. Entirely predictable. Vidal's chosen stool pigeons. But they looked pretty enough, those official documents.

And Jack was then pleased to note, as the train had slowly pulled out of the station next day, that Vidal had been wrong. The escaped prisoners had not been returned to the camp.

He'd allowed himself a priggish smile, and his only regret that he'd not been able to find Raúl Ramos anywhere. Well, if the man's got any sense, he thought, he'll have been on the Berliet as well. And now he had a whole twelve hours back to Oudjda to write his real report.

Yes, the throwaway line about the wiring? It had meant nothing to him. Not then. Indeed, he'd been deluded enough to think he might have put Vidal off the scent.

'They shot him?' Jack murmured.

There was newsreel. Grainy images of the Soviets at war in Finland. A short homage to Douglas Fairbanks, dead just days earlier. British bombers in action – against a German naval base somewhere. French *poilus* – Jack struggled to think of them as anything else, soldiers of a bygone era – along the Maginot Line in joyous preparation for the Christmas everybody still hoped would see it all over.

'Tortured him first, I imagine,' murmured Gabizon. 'The report wasn't very clear. Eight men escaped. One executed.'

There weren't many audience members scattered across the plush red seats at the Théâtre La Renaissance, and those who'd paid for this matinee showing were a rowdy bunch. A fine cinema, though, standing right next to Telford's Hôtel Ville de Paris, on Avenue Dar-el Maghzen and entered through those white arched cloisters at street level.

'But they shot him,' Jack repeated, numb with the news, almost sick with self-reproach, the last echoes of the victory cheer from the escaping Berliet finally silenced.

'A man called Ramos, yes. Same fellow?'

'The camp's handyman. A trusty. Maybe not as trusted as I thought.'

The upper half of the cinema screen was only visible through a tobacco haze. It reminded Jack of the awful smoke-filled corridors of Bou Arfa. But then the newsreel ended and the lights came up.

'Seems he confessed. Setting fire to the hotel. You had a lucky escape.'

Apart from all the previous guilt, now this. The delusion that he'd set Vidal on a false trail when, in truth, he now seemed to have set the commandant on Ramos's trail. Guilt. Like the grief following the death of Lawrence's young Arab companion, Farraj. Yet at least when Lawrence had been forced to put his bullet through the boy's brain, Farraj had begged God to give him peace. He doubted Raúl Ramos would have been so generous in his final moments.

'Lucky, yes,' said Jack.

'Lose anything valuable?'

Oh indeed, Jack thought. He'd felt it ever since he got back to

Rabat. Something missing, though he wasn't quite certain what it might be. Had he known? Deep inside?

'Nothing much. Couple of shirts. Socks. My best sweater. Suit. Travel bag.'

And *Karenina*, of course. But Tolstoy he could always replace. No, it wasn't the book. In any case, he'd paid a visit to the library on the Rue Marchand, managed to find a copy of Gogol's *Dead Souls* in the English translation section.

'I'm certain the sultan would be happy to meet any reasonable costs you might have incurred, *Monsieur* Telford. He was more than pleased with the report.'

Thank god for that, thought Jack. His money was running a bit thin now and he doubted he'd be able to get any more wired over.

'Really?' he said. 'I've still got some receipts I think.'

'You seem a little distant, my friend. Is there something…?'

'It wasn't a good experience.' He looked around to see whether they might be overheard but most of the neighbouring seats were still empty. For a moment he considered the possibility of telling him. Telling it all. But only for a moment. 'And the report,' he said. 'What next?'

'The one you wrote for Vidal? Filed away for posterity. The other? It will form part of a dossier the sultan plans to send to the Red Cross.' The lights dimmed again, and the screen showed the opening credits for tonight's main feature. Duvivier's *Pépé le Moko*. He wasn't sure why they were showing it again, but maybe a response to Hollywood's recent release of their own version – *Algiers*, starring Charles Boyer and some new starlet, Hedy Lamarr. 'Oh,' whispered Gabizon, as Jean Gabin's name flashed up among the credits, 'and to some friends among the Popular Movement.'

'Is there one?'

They kept their voices low, nobody really close enough to hear, but those hushed side-of-the-mouth tones reserved especially for cinemas. Almost inaudible against the amplified soundtrack of the film.

'More or less. New groups sprung up. After the nationalists' Action Committee was outlawed. Two years ago already – can you believe it? The National Party. And the Popular Movement.

The religious and the secular. A simplistic distinction, but puts it in perspective.'

'And the sultan favours the secular?'

'Not entirely. Republicans, for the most part. May call themselves the Popular Movement but...'

'No popular support?'

'Precisely.'

Jack settled in his seat, lit a Gauloise, partly troubling about Ramos, partly focused on Gabin's eponymous hero. A powerful gangster, worshipped in the warren of the old town, the *casbah*, but safe there from the police, wanting to take him down for the trail of bank robberies and murdered officers of the law left in his wake. Typical Duvivier. Somewhat tongue in cheek, the characters amusing stereotypes. But it was also the setting that fascinated Jack. Algiers, of course.

'Is it the same? In Algiers?' Jack whispered.

His only experience of Algeria had been Oran. And he knew how the first Resident-General of Morocco, Lyautey, had insisted that here, rather than be annexed entirely to France as Algeria had been, there should only be one government, the sultan's *Makhzan*, protected by France.

'The *casbah*? A lawless place. Algiers, you see?' The screen portrayed a rabbit warren of twisting alleyways, secret passages, impenetrable to the police. 'But is it really any different here? The labyrinth may outwardly appear more elegant, but still French bureaucrats doing their best to manipulate the sultan. The *Imazighen*, the Berbers, defrauded of their lands by greedy colonists. French planners designing model cities like Casablanca and driving the locals into tin-shack *bidonville* slums on the outskirts. There is much here that is wrong, *Monsieur* Telford.'

'Is this why we're watching *Pépé le Moko*?'

'It's my favourite film,' said Gabizon. 'All these contradictions. You see? He's a complex figure, isn't he? The clothes. The style. The management skills. The paternal care of his gang. If he'd been on the right side of the law – well, who knows what he might have been. But his nostalgia. For Paris. Perhaps for his lost innocence. And you, *monsieur*? Nostalgic too?'

'To walk the streets of London again? I can't say that I do.'

No, he thought. Not nostalgia. But a certain sense of self-pity in his exile. A lack of purpose, a lack of connection to his present. He was certain the French must have an expression for it – the French had pithy expressions for just about everything – though he couldn't recall just now. But poor Pépé, he might be a big man in the *casbah* but he was trapped there, whereas in Montmartre, where he longed to be…

'Of course,' said Gabizon, 'we know Pépé is doomed, do we not? Inevitable. A symbol. The futility of any struggle for positive change.'

'Struggle? The National Party's? Or your Popular Movement?'

Gabizon laughed quietly.

'I've seen it all before, my friend. All the nationalist fervour of the past ten years. The strikes. Demonstrations over water rights. They only went so far. Simply wanted our French masters to be better colonisers. But they were put down anyway. So now we begin to demand independence. Can you imagine how they'll react to that?'

On the screen, the French police inspector had a plan. Needing to lure Pépé out of the *casbah*. A woman, of course. The gangster infatuated with Gaby – and despite Gaby already having a rich lover, the inspector knew she had plans to run off to Pépé's hideaway.

'Like those in power always react,' said Jack. 'Set traps. Give them just enough rope. Encourage protest. Then pretend it's revolution. Put it down, before the real revolution can even get off the ground.'

The police inspector had tricked Gaby into believing Pépé was dead. If so, why remain in Algiers. No, she'd sail away with her rich lover instead. And now all that remained was to let poor stupid Pépé know which dock she'd be leaving from.

'You see, *Monsieur* Telford? It's why I love Duvivier. Pépé could simply accept his lot. Enjoy this lifestyle he leads. But no, the *casbah*'s not good enough for him. Good enough for the Arabs, for the Jews, for the exiles, for the world's outcasts. But for a white Frenchman?' He tutted with his tongue. 'No, as a white Frenchman, the world owes him something more. Not the gypsy girl he tosses aside so easily. Something more.'

Pépé le Moko was racing for the wharves of Algiers, but the scene suddenly faded to atmospheric camera tricks, images, memories of Paris. In his mind, Pépé would always have Paris.

'I can't help thinking you're trying to make a point. You think Pépé's me?'

'I believe, *monsieur*, that like Gabin's hero, you need your Paris too. Not a place perhaps, but certainly a purpose. And perhaps there is a convergence of interests here: the sultan; the Sephardim; the Popular Movement; Spain's exiles; and a certain Jack Telford. Perhaps *HaShem* has brought us all together in this place for a purpose.'

'You'd need to explain that to me,' said Jack, as he watched Pépé reach the dockside, buy his ticket for Gaby's boat and then be arrested as soon as he boarded.

'It's this way,' Gabizon told him. 'Here the French won't naturalise Muslims or Jews. We remain subjects of the sultan only. But what does this make us? Muslims and Jews suffer at the hands of colonists. Insults. Attacks. Not really French. If not really French then we should be fully Moroccan, no?'

'I thought you told me the sultan has set all this aside. The war.'

'We don't know what's going to happen with this war – except that it won't be over by Christmas.'

'If it's anything like Spain,' said Jack, 'I know this much. If we summon up the worst possible images of what might happen – the very worst – we still won't even come close to the reality.'

'Then we should all do our best to work towards what might come after, don't you think? For Morocco. For us Jews. For Spain. There's somebody I'd like you to meet.'

'A woman?'

'How did you know?'

'Who is she?'

'Spanish. Says she's heard of you, *monsieur*.'

On the screen, Pépé watched Gaby's ship sail away from the other side of the closed dockyard gates. He screamed her name, but the sound was drowned away to nothing by the ship's foghorn. Then the gangster took the concealed knife from inside his suit, killed himself.

'Heard of me?' said Jack, but he was somewhere else entirely. Two places, really. The station at Bou Arfa. And another dockside.

'Are you sure there's nothing wrong?' Gabizon asked him.

'I was surprised to learn you were still in Rabat, Mister Telford,' said the vice-consul.

'I was surprised to get your note, sir.'

There'd been a hand-written letter, delivered to the hotel.

'You still have plans to head for Blighty, I assume?'

'That might depend on what you have to tell us,' said Jack, glancing around the small gathering of English folk clustered in an upstairs salon of the consulate. He tipped his new trilby to them, removed the hat and spun it round in his hands. In the centre of the room, a table, beneath the grumbling ceiling fan, and on the table a Bush wireless.

'Not me, old boy. The Beeb. And superb news.'

Jack needed some of this. He'd become something of a recluse since his visit to the cinema with Gabizon.

'Well,' he said, 'I plan to leave for Casablanca in a few days, and from there…'

'Good man,' said Hurst. 'Good man. But now let's get this show on the road. Ladies and gentlemen,' he cried, 'apologies for the cloak and dagger but you may not know the BBC has been broadcasting this announcement regularly through the day. Some news from yesterday. The South Atlantic.' He glanced at his watch. 'Just about now, I think.'

The wireless was already warmed up and the vice-consul stepped over to turn up the volume. There were a couple of minor items and then the news reader's voice took on a more studied tone, almost a hint of excitement. Almost.

One of Germany's famous pocket battleships, designed as the most powerful ten-thousand-ton vessel afloat, is now lying in Montevideo harbour with gaping holes in her hull after the engagement with three smaller British ships. The vessel is either the Admiral Scheer *or the* Graf Spee *– these are sister ships.*

There was a murmur of appreciation from those gathered in the room.

Now, thought Jack, who was this? The voice. Not Alvar Lidell, certainly. So Frank Phillips then?

'Oh,' said Mister Hurst, 'she's the *Graf Spee* right enough. We had confirmation an hour ago. Langsdorff the skipper.'

A small cheer went up, the men slapping each other on the back, the ladies touching excited gloved fingers to their own necks, their lips, their stylish *chapeaux*, their coiffured hair.

'At last,' said one of the gentlemen, 'an end to this *drôle de guerre*. Now we can get at them.'

'Quiet, quiet,' snapped a woman Jack took to be the fellow's wife. 'We shall miss it.'

It appears that the German ship attacked HMS Ajax when the small British cruiser was convoying a French liner. The cruisers Exeter and Achilles responded to a call for help and they came up at full speed. They opened fire on the German vessel and the Exeter took fire repeatedly.

'Still can't believe it,' said Mister Hurst. '*Ajax* and *Achilles* are only bantamweights compared to the *Graf Spee*. They'd have been so badly clobbered. Brave fellows. Hearts of oak, yes?'

Jack decided he should take some notes, reached into his satchel for the notepad, and he noticed a fellow a few feet away, just apart from the others, arms folded, leaning with nonchalance against the wall. He was perhaps Jack's own age, hair slicked down with brilliantine. A pencil moustache, camel-coloured jacket and trousers.

Under cover of darkness, says the New York Times, the German battleship again changed course and finally reached Montevideo. Here she claimed sanctuary.

'Nice suit,' Jack said to the man. 'Does it come with the job?'

'You must be Telford.'

The British losses are not yet known.

'And you, one of our gallant military attachés?'

'Dear me, so obvious? Fox,' the fellow said. 'Phillip Fox.'

Telford laughed.

'You couldn't make it up, could you?' he said. 'Fox – really?'

'Sorry?' said Fox.

'Oh, nothing. I was thinking about something else. But will they, d'you think? Let the *Graf Spee* stay there – in Montevideo?'

And then, other news, the vice-consul turning down the volume, clapping his hands together.

'That's all there is for now, I'm afraid,' he said. 'But wonderful, I'm sure you'll all agree. Britannia rules the waves, what? And we'll keep you in touch, if we're able.'

'Montevideo?' said Fox. 'The Uruguayans are a funny old bunch. Neutral but friendly to us. And there's Article Seventeen. Hague Convention. They'll only give Langsdorff seventy-two hours for repairs. After? Well, she'll likely be interned for the duration.'

'Sounds like a lot of damage to fix in three days.'

'Doesn't it? Langsdorff's old school though. Expect he'll try to fight his way out, regardless.'

'May I quote you?'

'Surprised you troubled to ask, old boy. Here, have one of these?'

'Capstan?' said Jack, his voice full of wonder. 'Full Strength? Sweet Jesus.' If he had his time over again, he would have brought a suitcase full when he'd headed off from London. Fifteen months ago. It was supposed to be a week. A week on Franco's War Route across northern Spain. But he still remembered where he'd enjoyed the last of them. Galdakao. Before it all went so horribly wrong. Fox lit the cigarette for him and Jack inhaled deeply, made himself a little light-headed. 'But surprised?' he said. 'Why surprised?'

People were leaving, thanking the vice-consul, repeating snatches from the broadcast.

'Played a bit fast and loose, didn't you?' said Fox. 'Couple of the pieces you wrote for *Reynold's News*. Stuff that would have been better kept under wraps. Papers you stole, without wishing to put too fine a point on the thing.'

Jack felt a frisson of fear run down his back, the old sensation of being hunted again.

'You a friend of his? Of Edwin's?'

'We are – acquainted. Or were, at least.'

'Where is he?'

'Now? Oh, I've no idea. They eventually shipped him home. Can you imagine what it's like, Telford – losing both legs?'

Jack's stomach lurched. Before he'd sailed on the *Stanbrook*, Major Edwin had been taken to the hospital and there'd been too many other things going on for news to come through about his condition. But he'd known it must be bad. Edwin had been trying to kill him, silence him. The entrance to the air raid shelter in Alicante. Direct hit by an Italian bomber, Jack thrown clear and Edwin buried by the concrete. But Jack had stopped him from being crushed entirely – though the thought had occurred to him then, as it did now, that he might have saved Major Edwin more out of malice than mercy for, at the very least, the fellow was surely going to be crippled for life.

'Of course not,' Jack snarled. 'But then I remember also thinking at the time – if there *should* be another war, another carnage like the last one, it would all be down to pro-Hitler traitors like Major bloody Edwin.'

He threw down the remaining half of the Capstan with a sharp flick of his fingers and hurried for the stairs, offering thanks to Mister Hurst as he left.

'Did you hear the other news?' said the vice-consul, and Telford jerked to an abrupt halt.

'No,' he said. 'I'm sorry. That was rude. I was in a hurry...'

'Not at all,' said Hurst. 'Not at all. And nowhere near as important. But I thought you'd like to know. Atlanta. Georgia.'

'I'm sorry, I don't follow...'

'Great heavens, man. Film of the decade. *Gone with the Wind*. Premiere today. And they say we'll get to see it here early in the New Year.'

Jack laughed, despite himself.

'Yes,' he said, 'this *is* good news.'

As it happened, he had a real soft spot for Leslie Howard. He'd seen him in *Intermezzo* with Bergman not long before he left for Spain. And as Blakeney in *The Scarlet Pimpernel*. Superb.

'But I expect you'll beat us to it,' said Hurst. 'If you're back in Blighty.'

'Yes,' said Jack, 'I expect so.'

He nodded a final farewell and went down past the reception room where the same secretary gave him a jaunty wave.

'Glad tidings, Mister Telford,' she cried. 'About the *Graf Spee*.'

He waved back, walked through the vestibule, out past that fountain in the courtyard, set the trilby back upon his head. On the street a troop of *spahis* in ceremonial uniform trotted past, sky-blue baggy trousers, scarlet tunics, voluminous white turbans and flowing blue burnoose over a cloak of white. He waited for them to pass.

'Impressive fellows.'

Fox had come up behind him. Silent.

'You want something?' said Jack.

'You really believe Major Edwin was a traitor, Mister Telford?'

'Let me see. Providing false reports, masking the way Hitler's been able to build so many tanks and planes – at the cost of Britain's own defences. Then his links to Franco's fascist killers, to those who financed the coup – like Juan March. A traitor? Oh yes, like all those back home, who'd rather see Europe under Hitler's boot heel than disturb their own vested interests.'

'Our intelligence services sometimes need to take action for the greater good. Move in mysterious ways. You know this, I think.'

'I know the bastard tried to kill me.'

And Fielding too, he thought. No mention of Fielding. So maybe Ruby Waters had been right. When he'd finally told her the full story she'd been certain nobody in the Establishment would want too much fuss about Fielding. A vice-consul? Yes, but one with more than a passive involvement with Carter-Holt, and with that Soviet general in Madrid. In Spain he often felt like he'd fallen down some Lewis Carroll rabbit hole, and here it was again.

'Yet here you are,' said Fox, 'still with us. And over there…' he pointed vaguely towards the coast, '…we still have Gibraltar. Might not have done if fellows like Edwin hadn't kept Franco onside. But you must appreciate, Mister Telford, things are somewhat different now. At war, after all. Must all be more careful, don't you think?'

'Oh, I seem to have a charmed life, Mister – what is your rank, by the way?'

'Captain,' Fox smiled.

'Captain,' Jack repeated. 'Well, Captain Fox, not too long ago somebody reminded me how my enemies have a habit of meeting unfortunate accidents.'

That had been Ruby Waters too. He touched the brim of his trilby as a farewell salute and, as the last of the *spahis* went by, he stepped out into the street.

'By the way,' Fox shouted after him, 'Mister Hurst tells me you had a nasty brush with a scorpion. All better now, I hope? And just shows how prone we can *all* be to accidents, Telford.'

The concierge at the hotel's reception desk wore an anxious frown. His mouth gaped open, and as Jack crossed the lobby towards him, a word of greeting still forming on his lips, his arm was seized. A uniform cuff braided with silver chevrons, a black sleeve and above the *gendarmerie* officer's tunic collar, a hardened soldier's face, scarred, shadowed by the peak of his *képi*. He held a leather briefcase under his arm.

'*Monsieur* Telford, you will come with us.'

There were two more of these military policemen and, with Jack protesting all the way, they hauled him outside and into a waiting Renault Juvaquatre *camionette*, an army green shooting brake. But they refused to answer any of his questions until they'd arrived at their headquarters, out to the west of the city, near the stadium and the sultan's *Garde Noire* barracks.

'You intend to hold me here?' said Jack.

It was a small cell. Basement. Metal table – with the briefcase upon it – and two chairs. Precious little else. The walls painted bottle green below, cream above.

'Have you committed a crime?'

'These days I'm never sure.'

The officer snapped his fingers, pointed at Jack's satchel.

'It is a problem for your kind, I suppose,' he said, and gave the bag's contents a cursory inspection.

'My...?'

'We received a report from Lieutenant Vidal at Bou Arfa. Concerned you might have had some involvement in a recent escape from the labour camp there. A bunch of Reds. That you might be involved in disseminating propaganda materials unfavourable to the Third Republic. This would be serious enough in itself, of course, but...'

He passed back the satchel.

'This is a matter for the *gendarmerie*?' said Jack. 'Not the police?'

'An army matter, *monsieur*. Possibly state security also.'

'Then I can assure you, the only thing I've disseminated is the report Lieutenant Vidal himself signed. I delivered it to the sultan.' This was true enough, he supposed. The more private report still sat in draft form on Gabizon's desk, so far as he knew, waiting to be compiled into some dossier or other. But disseminated? No, you could hardly say that. 'If you don't believe me,' said Jack, 'I'd be happy for you to search my room.'

'We already did so.'

Telford found himself clutching the cold steel edges of the chair seat. This was all too familiar, and when the officer reached into the briefcase, took out a cigar tube, he thought he might faint. A similar room in Burgos, where the *Guardia Civil* lieutenant, Turbides, had burned out Jack's left eye.

'You searched my room?' he managed to say, his thighs pressed tight together against the very real possibility he might soil himself. His bladder threatened to betray him.

'You thought I needed – what do you call them? A warrant? No, this seems a case of flagrant offence. Perhaps sedition.'

Jack would have protested, but he clamped his lips tight, knew he must not anger this man any further, and he watched compliantly as the officer unscrewed the lid of the tube, slid out the cigar, bit the end, then fished in the briefcase again.

'Want to use mine?' said Jack, desperately hoping this Frenchman might be different from Turbides, to be civilised, to be humane. Any minor infringement of his rights instantly forgiven. After all, what was there to find? And so he took the cartridge case lighter from his pocket, offered it across the table.

'I was looking for this.' The officer produced a battered sketch book, brandished it in front of Jack's face. 'Yours, I assume?'

'Yes, mine. But you've no bloody right...'

'Such rage, *Monsieur* Telford. Guilt, perhaps?'

'Guilt? Why in god's name should I feel guilty? It belonged to a friend.'

'I guessed that much, *monsieur*. A good friend?'

Sergio Sifre's sketch book. Jack had brought it from Alicante, had promised himself he would do something with those beautiful drawings. Sifre's illustrations of Lorca's poetry. *La señorita del abanico...*

'Yes. A good friend.'

'And you, *monsieur*, you have a wife?'

'No, why?'

'Fiancée?'

'No.'

'A mistress then? At least a mistress? A lover, perhaps.'

'Nobody.'

The officer thumbed through towards the back of the book. 'Him?'

Jack had forgotten. Life drawings of Fidel Constantino Sánchez. The Spanish captain. Jack had saved his life, carried him through the Republican lines north of Madrid, carried him on his back. One of Telford's finer moments. Each of the sketches a wonderful likeness. And yes, erotic. Intimate, in only the way Fidel's lover could have captured him. Jack still missed him. Both of them. Good friends. And the memories choked him.

'The last time I looked,' he said, 'there was no law in France against homosexuality. Not since the Revolution, god bless it.'

'But there are laws to protect public morality, *monsieur*. Or is this the right title for you? I'm never sure. An *homme-femme?*'

It would be so easy, he thought. The denial. But he was damned if he was going to give this bastard the satisfaction. And anyway, there was still a bond, between himself and Fidel.

'I read something Gide wrote,' said Jack, 'about him preferring to be hated for what he is than loved for what he is not.'

'Hate? I'll tell you about hate. I imagine what such dogs get up to and it makes me want to vomit. All my time in Paris. A sewer of creatures like you. Degenerates. Invading everything – the arts, philosophy, politics.'

'Are we finished here?' Jack stood, spent a moment lighting a Gauloise. 'And I assume you won't be wanting to keep that?'

He held out his hand for the sketch book.

'Filth,' said the officer, tossed the book onto the table. 'But we will be watching you.'

'And all this nonsense about helping the escape?'

'We found no evidence to support Lieutenant Vidal's suspicions. Only this.' He waved a finger at the sketch book as Jack pushed the thing into his satchel. 'But there is no doubt that sexual inversion leads to political subversion. As I say, we shall be watching.'

Jack thought about his Gogol. *Dead Souls*. A piece he'd read only the previous night. *"However stupid a fool's words may be, they are sometimes enough to confound an intelligent man."*

A demonstration, a protest. Not many, perhaps a hundred but no more. Mostly women but a fair number of men too. A couple of Spanish Republican flags and another, which Gabizon told him belonged to the Popular Movement. And across the front of this modest column, a long banner, reading *Worldwide Committee of Women Against War and Fascism*. In French, Spanish and Arabic, in that order, one below the other. Behind the banner, a dozen women, two men, all well dressed, carrying the painted canvas at waist height.

'Communist Party?' said Jack as he stood with Gabizon on the corner of the Boulevard Galliéni, near the Municipal Market, watching them march past. He remembered a couple of articles about Sylvia Pankhurst's involvement. And the French woman, Gabrielle Duchêne. He'd done an interview as well with the Labour MP, Ellen Wilkinson about her own support for this organisation.

'Oh yes,' said Gabizon. '*Señora* Gorroño. About as Red as they come. Does it bother you?'

'That her?' Something about the young woman at the very centre of the leading group. Who did she resemble? Constance Bennett maybe. Small, neat. Square-ish, honest face, fire in her eyes, a smile on the lips, dark hair piled high at one side of the head. 'And no, some of my best friends are Communists. Or at least they were.'

'You've changed *Monsieur* Telford. Somehow – sharper. Your brush with the law?'

It had been a few days and at least he now knew the name of his interrogator. Captain Edouard, Commander, Rabat's *Brigade de Gendarmerie*. An eventful enough few days, a broadcast by the First Lord himself, Churchill, confirming the *Graf Spee* had been sunk – scuttled in fact by her skipper, Langsdorff. And Langsdorff, according to the French papers, now dead. Suicide in his Montevideo hotel room.

'I'm still heading for Casablanca,' said Jack, as they followed the red, yellow and purple flags of the small procession across to the piece of waste ground opposite. There were speeches – even hecklers – and a barnstorming performance from the same young woman, but an hour later they were all sitting together in the Bar Tahona de Carmen, enjoying a cold beer and an old guitar player in the corner. There'd been introductions. Francesca Gorroño, though everybody called her Paquita, it seemed.

'Well?' she said. 'What did you think?'

'I've not heard anything so stirring since I saw Dolores at the Plaza Mayor in Madrid.'

Paquita accepted a Gauloise from him. And yes, he thought, she has that same intensity as *La Pasionaria*. Dolores Ibárruri. The Spanish Republic's Passion Flower.

'I was with her in Paris,' said Paquita. 'During the summer. She told me a strange story. About Elda, the Yuste Position. Franco's agents. She said they'd all have been dead, Negrín included, except for this Englishman. And an army captain, Fidel...'

'Fidel Constantino,' Jack reminded her. 'But I barely met her – Dolores, I mean.'

The beer was good. French. Bière de Garde. Ice-cold. And the old man was strumming some percussive flamenco rhythm, his friends hand-clapping, *las palmas*, almost a separate accompaniment rather than in time to the beat.

'So, it *was* you,' she said. 'Small world, is it not? When Isaac told me about you...' Gabizon offered him a slight smile at this shared intimacy, '...I thought you must be the same. Dolores said there was something about you, *Señor* Telford. You sailed on the *Stanbrook*?'

'I did. And you?'

She explained her life story in that peculiarly Spanish way, no detail omitted, no stone left unturned. But basically she'd studied in Paris, returned to Madrid only to be evacuated to Valencia when her home city was besieged. In Valencia she'd worked as a secretary within the Ministry of Public Information. Later a refugee across the French border, and an internment camp. Her husband too. But she'd an uncle in Rabat and, with somewhere to go, the necessary papers completed, they'd been given leave to travel and then remain, the husband now a truck driver, she a nanny.

'That is,' she said, 'when I'm not organising. I don't suppose we'll ever hold another congress. Not now. Women against fascism. We've all been overtaken by events, don't you think? But the fight will go on. *No pasarán.*'

Two women who'd been sitting at a neighbouring table got up to leave, came over to kiss her on both cheeks, said their goodbyes.

'Following in the Passion Flower's footsteps,' said Gabizon, and sipped at his golden beer.

'Perhaps,' said Paquita. 'I'd like to think so. But you know the strange thing? Those of us who are part of the Committee – in France, in England, every one of the allied countries – we could each provide a list of all the Fifth Columnists, every likely traitor. Because they'll be the very same animals who've been writing terrible things to us for years now. Letters to the papers. Sign their names because they know nobody will take notice of us. We're only women. Reds too. And worse for me, Spanish. Who the hell ever listens to Spanish women?'

'They listened to Dolores,' said Jack, stubbing out his cigarette. 'In Madrid. Everywhere else she spoke.'

'There, maybe,' she said. 'But it was always the problem. That it came more easily for women in Spain to follow Franco. Centuries of being indoctrinated by the Church to know their place.'

Jack was sure she was right. It was the thing which made Ibárruri so exceptional. He'd admired Dolores. Inspired him as she had inspired so many to stand firm in the fight against Franco's fascists. But there had always been those stories too. Her part in the destruction of the Marxist Workers' Party, the POUM. Her role in the suppression of Trotskyites. And her reported view that, when the life of a people is threatened, it's better to convict a hundred innocents than to acquit a single guilty person. But none of this was for here, for now.

'To be honest,' he said, 'I'd not realised there were so many Spaniards in these parts. One of the men at Bou Arfa…' he paused,

61

painfully remembered it had been Raúl Ramos, '...told me how many had fled here from Córdoba and Granada'

'There's not a city in Morocco without a Spanish enclave,' Paquita told him. 'All we have to do is mobilise them.'

'Mobilise them, for...?'

'The war, of course,' she said. 'Did you imagine it's over? Apart from anything else, we have to raise funds. Help the men in the camps. Food and clothes. Leaflets too, when we can get them inside. Encourage them to sign up for the Legion. Isaac told me you were there, when the boys escaped from Bou Arfa.'

'Yes, it was quite a sight.' He signalled to the white-aproned *camarero*, ordered three more bottles.

'And then,' said Gabizon, 'there's always Franco. I told you our hopes for independence have all been set aside for the duration of the war. But Franco has no such rein on his ambitions. There've been broadcasts every day calling for nationalists here in Morocco and Algeria urging insurrection. And tracts like this...' he pulled a crumpled flyer from his pocket, '...calling for a rising against the French. And there'll be hotheads here who'll listen to them. Exactly what Hitler wants naturally.'

'So much for neutrality,' said Jack. 'And the bribes.'

'I told you,' said Gabizon, 'payment in kind. And this is just the beginning. All the intelligence we've received is that Franco has eyes on the whole of Morocco. He hopes Hitler will help him get it.'

In the corner, one of the guitar player's companions was singing now, a tune Jack knew well. *Santa Bárbara Bendita*.

'This war,' said Paquita. 'It's about so much more than defeating Germany. About the world order, about how our lives will be governed for the future.'

Jack laughed. 'My old editor had this view that the sovereign states of Europe have been struggling since the French Revolution to reconcile our various political systems. How this war, if it came, would be a European civil war, though fought on a global stage.'

'It began at the gates of Madrid,' she said. 'Three years ago. Not with the invasion of Poland.'

''You'd like Sydney Elliott,' said Jack, raising his voice to be heard over the singing, which had now been taken up by most of those in the bar. 'And this is pleasant. But I'm guessing you didn't want to meet me simply because I was with Dolores at Elda. I was there when she flew out, by the way. But I don't think she noticed me that day.'

There was the repeated refrain of the song, with much foot stamping, fists thumping out the beat on tabletops.

'It must have been – difficult,' said Paquita. 'But you played your part, *señor*. All your work helping to expose the capitalists who were betraying your country. You think that's finished?'

'Do I seriously think corporation America and big business Britain won't simply want to get on with their greed? To get on with their comfortable lives and their luxury holidays? Of course they will. But we're at war now. Whatever they might want…'

Paquita shook her head. 'Comrade,' she said, 'as we speak, British investments in Germany have never been higher. You have the Bank of England to thank for this. Sir Montagu Norman and his Anglo-German Transfer Agreement. You know, of course, as late as January this year the Governor was proposing that poor Herr Hitler should be compensated by British taxpayers for the costs he'd incurred by helping Franco in Spain.'

'No, I didn't.'

'Well you should, *Señor* Telford. You know why? Because it was your own paper, *Reynold's News*, carried the story. Seriously, compensation for blowing Guernica to hell. And your bloody government was thinking of accepting the Bank of England's suggestion. A minor miracle they didn't go through with it. You know what we think? That the only reason they didn't was down to *Reynold's News*, the backlash from the article.'

The rabbit hole, yet again. And outside a black police van raced past, its klaxon blaring.

'You didn't think Hitler was only financed in Germany?' said Gabizon. 'That would be laughable.'

'The conservative élites,' said Paquita, 'the privileged of all the great powers, including England, share every single aim of the Nazis – disdain for any real democracy, hatred and a language of fear against Republics, Jews, trade unions, Socialists, the decadence of modern art.'

'They think,' said Gabizon, 'they have Hitler on a leash but perhaps, just perhaps, they're now beginning to realise they have a tiger by the tail. They won't care though. They'll be happy and rich, regardless of what happens. And when it's all over they'll wring their hands and say they were duped, or they didn't know. But they'll still be privileged. They'll still be the élite. And when you go back to pretending your world's governed by politicians, *Monsieur* Telford, they'll still be there, above those puppets, pulling their strings.'

The waiter again, and Paquita called for the bill. She had to get back to work.

'No, let me,' said Jack, and fumbled in his pocket for his wallet. 'But you expect me to expose all this? Think anybody would believe me?'

'Perhaps just those the Allies think are friends,' said Gorroño. 'Of course there are purely German investors among the Nazis. Creatures like Helene Bechstein. Another Jew hater. Isn't this the worst irony, that the manufacturer of such beautiful pianos should be Hitler's personal etiquette tutor?'

'Yes, I know about Bechstein,' said Jack. 'And the steel barons, the war mongers, like Thyssen and Krupp. Old news, isn't it?'

'But it's the others,' she said. 'IBM conducting the last German census but, really, gathering information about Germany's Jews. Woolworth's. Singer sewing machines. Coca Cola. That most anti-semitic of all Americans, Henry Ford – his Cologne factory churning out Nazi army vehicles. General Motors with an eighty percent share in Opel. J.P. Morgan upto his neck with Germany's General Electric. And Rockefeller? Standard Oil has a twenty-five percent share in I.G. Farben's gasoline business. Just imagine the profits they'll all make from this war, regardless of which side wins. Imagine the strings they're pulling at this very moment.'

Jack left a ten *franc* note.

'Oh, I can imagine right enough,' he said, as they came out onto the street. 'And Sydney Elliott may be happy to publish a pithy piece about Rockefeller or Henry Ford. But it's hardly going to make headlines.'

'Then write this, *Señor* Telford,' Paquita insisted, glancing at her watch. 'Write about Spain. About our war still going on.'

'And maybe a trip to Tangier or Ceuta,' said Gabizon. 'See if you can use your cover as a journalist to make links with our friends there.'

'I told you. I'm heading for Casablanca. You want me to leave there, go into Spanish Morocco?'

'*Monsieur* Telford, Casablanca is hardly the *casbah* in Algiers and, with respect, you are no Pépé le Moko. You'd be safe enough.'

Paquita laughed.

'I really must go,' she said. 'But who would suspect an Englishman in Spanish Morocco? And you can at least write about our boys still fighting fascism. You're all we've got, I think.'

They exchanged cheek kisses. Who would suspect an Englishman, indeed! Jack thought, and conjured up images of the *Guardia Civil* lieutenant, Turbides. But she'd moved him. That fire in her dark eyes.

'I think I owe Fidel Constantino this much, at least.'

She nodded, turned to leave, but then stopped.

'And where is the gallant *capitán* now. Escaped with you on the *Stanbrook*?'

'Fidel?' he said. 'No, he's dead.' He could barely force the words out of his throat. 'And his lover, Sergio Sifre. Shot each other on the quayside at Alicante along with so many others. They couldn't bear to leave Spain. Knew what would happen if they were taken by Franco. Only one solution.'

Yes, I owe them, he thought. Fidel and Sergio. And now Raúl Ramos too.

The Bar Tahona de Carmen fell silent. New Year's Eve and Franco was broadcasting to the Spanish nation. Not a live broadcast since it required onward re-transmission from the private stations in Spanish Morocco. But it was chilling.

'*It is necessary to call out insidiousness and libel,*' the dictator was saying, '*and to shut the mouths of slanderers.*'

There were gasps and sobs, merely muted cries of defiance. For almost everybody in the bar still had relatives in Spain. And there were already stories, awful stories, about precisely what Franco might mean when he spoke of closing mouths.

'Where there is a murmurer, a harvester of alarm, there is always a traitor.'

It was an open invitation to a witch hunt. To point fingers at annoying neighbours. At political rivals.

And I could have killed the bastard, thought Jack yet again. At Burgos.

Tomorrow he would leave for Casablanca, as planned. But as he watched Paquita Gorroño get to her feet, make another impassioned plea for resistance to this infamy, Telford knew he'd reached another crossroads in his life. He had no illusions about this young woman's politics. He knew the gulf which existed between the sincere passion for freedom, peace and equality exhibited by communist supporters like Paquita – and Fidel Constantino, of course – and that of Stalin and the Soviet leadership. But he knew, like Fidel, he would have followed her to hell and back. That his life would never be the same.

January – July 1940

Archibald Dickson

Casablanca. He'd arrived late in a foggy morning on the first day of January. The Hôtel du Touring on the Rue de l'Horloge. A single room for fifteen *francs* per night and the neighbouring Restaurant Languedoc where he could eat decently but cheaply. Then the search for gainful employment. He offered his services to Casablanca's English language newspaper. He provided translation services to an engineering firm doing business with the company Independent Pneumatics in Chicago, Illinois. He even succeeded in almost befriending that head of the local *gendarmerie*, Commandant Réchard. And he wrote to London. To the BBC. He had a contact there – through the Republican priest Father Lobo he'd met in Madrid – a fellow called Barea, now working for the European Service, Spanish Section, but previously one of the Spanish Republic's main censors. He wrote to Barea, though there was no reply – not then anyway. And nothing either from the Associated Press cooperative.

But it bothered Jack only a little. He'd begun to settle in Casablanca. It struck him as being surprisingly modern, clean, European, the streets busy with traffic, elegant gardens. The Arab medina he found disappointing, smaller, less romantic than he'd imagined. But the dockside bars and cafés delighted him.

Through Gabizon he'd made contact with the *Alliance Israélite Universelle*, the Worldwide Jewish Alliance. The organisation had opened its first school in Rabat at the turn of the century and now there were AIU schools all over Morocco. And they were pleased to offer Jack, on Gabizon's recommendation – he knew he'd never otherwise, as a Gentile, have been accepted – some sessional work teaching English at the Jewish college on Boulevard Moulay Youssef, just along from the Place de la Fraternité and the British consulate on Boulevard d'Anfa.

He'd found a place to live. A small house at a rent he could afford on the north side of the medina, a few minutes walk from the old Portuguese bastion, La Sqala, close to the wall, a small but pleasant square with a couple of trees, just off the Sidi Belyout and an easy walk to the *souk* in one direction – where he'd managed to haggle reasonably well for most of the things he needed to make it feel like home – and the *hammam* bath house in the other. There was a stench, of course, from the local tannery pits, like a palette of giant paint pots, but the prevailing winds seemed generally in his favour. Among the treasures he'd won, a Victor portable gramophone and a few decent records. Including Brachah Zefira. *La Voix de Son Maître.*

At the same time, through Paquita Gorroño's links, he started to find his way around the Spanish community. Rather, the *two* Spanish communities. It took Jack only days to realise that the second largest chunk of Casablanca's population – though a long way after the French, naturally – were Spaniards. It was Spanish traders, after all, who'd given the place its present name when it was little more than a fishing village. But in the twenties, waves of immigrants began to arrive in what was, by then, a new and gleaming white Moroccan metropolis. The first waves came seeking relief from starvation in Spain itself. But the next influx? During and after the civil war.

Many of the original settlers were devout Catholics, worshipping at the Iglesia San Buenaventura – the oldest Christian church in the city – and supporters of Franco. But not all. There were plenty, as well, who'd welcomed Spain's Republic. And among those who arrived in the past two years, not all were fleeing the fascists. Some just wanted an end to the fighting, had arrived here long before the final exodus. But regardless of their politics all those early incomers had, like Paquita Gorroño's uncle in Rabat, provided legitimate destinations for the refugees who came after – destinations other than the internment camps.

So, two Spanish communities. Dyed in the wool monarchists, traditional Catholics and friends of Franco on the one hand. The broad church of the Republic on the other – and these latter divided, naturally, into all their usual factions. The Anarchists blamed the Communists for the Republic's defeat. The Communists blamed the Trotskyists. And the Socialists blamed everybody but themselves.

Yet Telford moved easily enough between the various threads of this Republican warp and weft. And by Easter, they seemed to have found common cause. A general strike. The day before it was scheduled to take place, Paquita herself turned up, invited him to meet some of her comrades – including Julián Netto, who'd also been on the *Stanbrook*.

'You see?' said Netto. 'Two Spains. Always two Spains.'

They ordered a jug of *tinto* in the cigar smoke-filled bar at the junction of several claustrophobic streets deep in the old medina. Like every other bar in North Africa, it seemed, many of the customers preferred to take their tobacco through *shisha* pipes. The crumbling ochre walls in the alleyway leading north were daubed with the slogans *Arriba España* and *Viva Franco*, those of the lane running west adorned with *Muera Franco* and *No Pasarán*.

'How long's that one been there?' Jack shook his head. 'They did though, didn't they? Get past, I mean.'

'*Hombre*, they did?' shouted Paquita, as she scattered strike notices among the other customers. 'As I recall, they never got into Madrid until the war was over and there was nobody there to stop them. But as long as Madrid was defended, they could not pass. Never would have done if Casado and those bloody Socialists hadn't betrayed Negrín.'

A ragged cheer from the older men, all in matching black berets it seemed, fists thumping on tables. There it is again, thought Jack. The blame. In this case she might be right. He'd been closer than most, after all. But it didn't really take them anywhere. Not now.

'Still,' he said, sniffing at his wine glass, 'it really is still going on here. The civil war.'

'No, *señor*,' Paquita came over, waved a finger in his face. 'That's shit, Jack.' She'd taken to calling him Jack, almost in the French style, *Jacques*. 'Not right. It's more like – like time's stood still. Frozen, like it's still February '36. Franco's consulate here watches our every move and sometimes there's a broken head, even a shooting or two, but otherwise we glower at each other across the divide. As though it's not yet happened and, in this other universe, our side can still win. We have our own newspaper, they have *ABC* – always a couple of days old, but...'

'And the strike?' said Jack. 'It'll be supported?'

Paquita sat on the bench next to him, shook her head in exasperation.

'Members seem solid,' Julián shrugged, and Telford already knew him for a militant member of the *Unión General de Trabajadores de Casablanca*, the General Union of Workers, UGT, aligned to the Spanish Socialist Workers Party, PSOE, but also with a strong presence from the Spanish Communist Party, the PCE. They might be banned in mainland Spain now, but here they still functioned. Strange.

'What does this mean, Jack?' Paquita scowled at him. 'That you'll only cover the story if there's a big turnout?'

'Your husband on strike?' said Jack.

'Of course not. Weren't you listening? This is just Casablanca.'

He felt himself chastened, though he did wonder about the principle of solidarity, one town's workers with another's. He liked her, all the same. But only just. So damned strident.

'I'll wire it to Elliott whatever happens,' Jack told her. He was a regular now at the *Grande Poste*. All telegrams and other communications only in French. 'But there *is* a war on. Likely to be other things.'

'Is there?' she said. 'You'd hardly know it. The bloody French still think it'll soon be over.'

He could understand. It was still this joke war, as the French themselves called it. German bombers had attacked the fleet at Scapa Flow. The Winter War between Russia and Finland had come to an end. Paul Reynaud had become France's new Prime Minister. That was about it. Except...

'Out there,' said Jack, pointing away to where he supposed the ocean must be, pointing past the donkey and four-wheeled cart trying to negotiate its way through the impossibly narrow street. 'Out there. It's why the cruise ships have stopped coming, isn't it? The reason your taxi drivers, your dockyard workers, your waiters...'

'The waiters are all Anarchists,' said Julián. 'Not ours.'

Jack laughed, topped up their glasses again. Not a bad bit of red, as it happened.

'Spanish waiters are *always* bloody Anarchists,' he said, remembering Madrid. 'But whether they're in CNT, the FAI or any other damned thing, they've all had their wages slashed.'

The cruise ships had indeed stopped arriving. Natural enough. At least, for those that had to risk the Atlantic or the Bay of Biscay. They were still coming in from other parts of the Med though. From the ports of southern France – French holidaymakers, as though there really was no war. From Italy too. And there was the big question of the day – whether Mussolini would continue to sit on the fence. Perhaps, the French said, he'd had enough in Spain. The fifty thousand Italian troops he sent to help Franco hadn't exactly had an easy time.

'Not just the tourists either,' said Paquita.

'Tell me about it,' Jack replied, for this portion of his own income had dried up, the engineering firm no longer needing translation services since they'd been forced to give up shipping to Independent Pneumatics. Lots of companies in similar dire straits and the *franc* tumbling day by day. 'But, my god, is it always this cold in March?'

Beastly cold, he thought to himself.

'Well,' said Paquita, 'tomorrow we'll see what happens. But for now, how much of the city have you seen? Only Bousbir, I bet.'

He smiled, passed around the Gauloises – to half the old men too, as it turned out. Beyond the window, on a low-slung telephone wire, a trio of finches twittered and wheezed, flew and settled again, flashes of yellow and green.

'Bousbir?' he said. 'No, I wouldn't dare. Passed it though. Went to wander round the new medina. When I got here I couldn't work out why there weren't so many Moors on the streets as in Rabat. Why the medina was so dull.'

'The *bidonvilles*,' said Julián.

The *bidonvilles* indeed. It wasn't as though Oran and Rabat didn't have their own slums. But here, as the city had grown so quickly, he now knew it had become a magnet for poor Arabs from out in the sticks, but they'd been confined to the tin shack shanties around the edges of town.

'If things go right,' said Paquita, 'some of them will join us. The CGT's been helping to organise the Moroccan Workers' Unions. Phosphate miners. Others. Goes without saying that even with our wages cut, we're still getting a damned sight more than the *moros*.'

'Pretty obvious,' said Jack. 'And if things don't go right?'

She bit her top lip.

'Then things might get a bit rough.' She waved her hands in the air, as though to set this unfortunate idea free.

In the Place de France there were flags. The unions, various youth organisations, the Women's World Committee. Perhaps three hundred demonstrators. A few of the bars closed, maybe a bit less traffic than normal, but otherwise it hardly seemed like a general strike. A Galician piper though, to lead the march. And plenty of French policemen.

Jack was alone, towards the rear of the gathering, both Paquita and Julián up front, holding another street-wide banner.

'How far?' he said to a young man at his side and holding up a placard with a CNT poster pasted upon its plywood board. 'The march.'

'From here,' said the lad, 'along d'Anfa, past the consulates, then the *plaza de toros*, back around the Petit Lycée, here again for the speeches. If we make it this far.'

'Make it this far, did you say?'

'Falange.' The young man's look was insulting. But understandable. You could almost smell trouble cooking amid the more normal odours of woodsmoke and sweet spice. Overhead, seagulls screeched.

'Storm coming,' said Jack.

'Probably when we pass the consulate.'

But the lad was wrong. No sign of life at Franco's consulate there in Casa – as Jack had eventually grown to call the city, along with everybody else. A couple of soldiers, from Spain's own Foreign Legion just inside the gates. Otherwise, nothing. Except the marchers stopping to sing the *Himno de Riego*. No, nothing –

until they reached the bullring, which the French called *Les Arènes*. It had stood here a long while but rebuilt, apparently, within the past ten years, the walls around its entrance towers plastered with gaudy posters, recent and forthcoming *corridas*.

'You go?' Jack had asked the young man when it came in sight, the marchers now singing the *Internationale*.

'*El toreo*? No way. That's a pastime for tourists and *facciosos*.'

Telford had the boy's story now. Manolo, his uncle, aunt, mother and two sisters had escaped from Cartagena in the family fishing smack just days before their home city fell to the Nationalists. Sailed south to Oran. Fuel and provisions. Then three solid days and nights due west to Tangier, the neutral International Zone. More fuel and food. Two more days and nights at sea in a raging Atlantic storm to reach Casablanca, where yet another uncle was part of the local fishing fleet. Manolo's family had joined the fleet, been fishing ever since. But now the market for their catches was drying up.

And Telford had heard this about the *corrida* before, though never seen Hemingway make the point. Just the glorification of the spectacle, the tradition, the heroic skills of those taking part. *Death in the Afternoon*. Even more pompous than Tolstoy. But it was one of the main things in Spain marking the political divide, *aficionados* of the bullfight, *la faena*, on one side, those who decried its brutality and outmoded ritual on the other. He was still mulling this over when the fighting began.

The war finally came to Casablanca that same weekend. The explosion.

Jack had gone to the lido, the *art décoratif* swimming pool, a precisely rectangular sea lake, blinding white on the headland, just beyond the old military hospital. The water was cold, the salt stung some of the cuts and grazes he'd sustained during Wednesday's brawl, and the diving boards gave him vertigo, just looking at them. But he needed its vitality. And it was pleasant to sit in the sun with his writing. It reminded him of halcyon days at Grimley-on-Severn, or a couple of romantic episodes he'd enjoyed in more recent years at Droitwich and Sandford Parks. Nostalgia, he thought, the gloss we put on our neglect.

But yes, pleasant in the sun. At least, it had been pleasant until he was dragged into the company of Brigade Commandant Réchard, his brother and their wives. All *Marie Claire* maillot-style beige swimsuits, green palm tree designs, slender shoulder straps, the men with bare chests, both of them muscular, tanned. Glasses of ice-cold Lillet Blanc. Deckchairs.

'I had to rescue him,' Réchard said to the others. 'From my own cells. Can you imagine?'

'It was those thugs of Franco's who should have been arrested, Louis. Not me.'

'Arrested? Never. Protective custody, my friend.' He reached over, stroked the arm of his wife, Monique. 'For your own good. You're mixing with the wrong sort, I fear.'

They'd come from nowhere, a swarm of them with cudgels – knives too, he thought. Maybe from the main gates of the bull-ring. Jack had no idea. All so fast. But there'd been blood, many people injured, Telford himself knocked down, kicked, spat upon. And the police? Réchard's *gendarmes*? Showed no sign of either surprise or action. Not until later – and then only to move in for the arrest of the strikers. Nobody but the strikers. Well, he'd seen this before.

'Yes, mixing with the wrong crowd indeed,' said Jack, and gave them a wistful smile. 'This isn't good for my reputation.'

Réchard laughed, knocked back the last of his cocktail.

'Of course not,' he said. 'Telford the revolutionary. Telford the Red. Did you know, my dears? Our friend escaped from Alicante on the last boat out. I bet *El Caudillo* would have paid a pretty penny for your scalp, no?'

He was being sarcastic. Of course he was. But not too far from the mark. Yes, the mark, he thought. Jack Telford, everybody's dupe. Carter-Holt had certainly seen him that way. Carter-Holt the assassin and he, the assassin's mark, her fall guy, her patsy. Bitch.

'I was just writing about this very thing,' he said. 'Before I was so rudely interrupted.' The four of them laughed again. 'About the *Stanbrook*.'

'May we see?' said Réchard, though he'd already reached over and snatched Jack's notepad.

'No, Louis,' Monique scolded him. 'Let *Monsieur* Telford tell us his story.'

'My god, no.' Réchard threw up his hands in horror. 'Once he starts, you can never shut him up again.'

Over in the dockyard, the sound of a ship's foghorn, a single long blast, but immediately taken up by others, a series of foghorn salutes. From the sundeck, Jack could see the smoke from her stack. Late afternoon, and one of the French destroyers going out on patrol.

'Well,' he said, 'this one's only short. My old editor's still keen on new articles about the war in Spain, so I've been working on this. The Spanish Civil War, the conflict that began and ended with a Welshman. His paper has a big following in the *Pays de Galles*.'

'And did it?' said Monique. 'Begin and end this way?'

'More or less,' said Jack. She was an attractive woman, a few years older than him, but with skin the texture of milk, a thick mop of blond curls, rouged lips. And she seemed interested. 'It all began with a pilot called Bebb. Welshman. Because Franco had a problem. He knew their military coup could never work without his Army of Africa. Their Moroccan troops. And Franco was their commander – they'd never act without him. But Franco was stuck in the Canary Isles. So, weeks before the insurrection was due to begin, they hired Bebb to fly from London, to collect Franco, deliver him to Spanish Morocco. *Et voilà*.'

'And your British authorities knew nothing of this, I suppose?' said Réchard, in disbelief.

'Quite the reverse,' Jack smiled. 'Bebb carried with him a certain Major Hugh Pollard, an agent of the British intelligence services.' Well, this was the story Carter-Holt had told him and he'd never doubted that on this, at least, she was telling the truth. 'It seems they knew about the planned coup weeks in advance but didn't bother to tell the Spanish government.'

'Perfidious Albion,' said Réchard's brother, Jean-François, an officer at the local army camp in Mediouna.

'You're not the first person to remind me,' Jack replied.

'But who can blame them?' The brother scowled. 'Good old Franco. There's the real enemy, *Monsieur* Telford. The Reds.

They'll eat us all alive if they get the chance. Louis was joking, I hope. You're not part of those filth?'

Jack had heard this so many times. The common view, among French army officers in particular. And the *Petit Marocain* hardly let a day go by without some article praising Franco's new Spain. He was about to deliver his usual riposte about the Republican Government having been democratically elected, the Communist Party only one element within the Popular Front. The will of the people. But he never quite got there.

'*Monsieur* Telford,' Réchard stopped him, 'is simply an honest foreign correspondent. Following his stories wherever they might take him. And fallen in love with our fair city, so graced us by his decision to stay a while. Isn't it so, Telford?'

Jack pulled a face, a neutral face. But the brother announced he was going for a swim, took his wife with him, gave Jack a look of disdain as he passed, while Monique muttered something sounding like an apology.

'Please,' she said, when they'd gone, Jean-François diving athletically into the water, '*this* story – this fellow Pollard, you know what happened to him?'

Réchard summoned the waiter with a click of his fingers, ordered more drinks.

'As it happens,' Jack told her, 'he was mentioned in *The Times* recently – when I finally got to see a copy. Some reference to our new military attaché in Madrid. Pollard there as a senior advisor. His reward, I suppose. And there was mention of his early career. Coincidence, I suppose. Seems he'd spent time here in Morocco. The revolt by the old sultan's brother. Thirty years ago? Didn't say which side he was on though.'

'And the Welshman who, you say, ended the war?' said Réchard.

'Not actually ended it, Louis. The war just ended *with* him. The Welsh skipper of the *Stanbrook*. Dickson.'

He briefly told them the tale, by which time Jean-François was back, his dark-haired wife in tow, and both of them furious.

'That was quick,' said Réchard. 'Something wrong?'

'Those,' raged his brother, and pointed back towards the pool. 'Who the hell let them in?'

A couple of girls, young women, in the water but their arms resting, folded, on the poolside tiles – and those arms covered in tattoos, pink flowers, images of green interwoven vine stems. And what? Birds maybe. The girls laughed together, European features, handsome enough but hard, a toughness about them.

'*Putains*,' murmured Monique, while Jean-François and his wife rubbed themselves on their towels, frantic rubbing, as though to wipe away some contamination.

'Can't you have them thrown out?' said the brother. 'My god, they'll pollute the water.'

'On what charge?' Réchard shrugged. 'If, as I suspect, they're Bousbir women...' One of the girls waggled her fingers at him, flashed a coquettish and, Jack thought, familiar smile, which Réchard tried hard to ignore. 'Well, this is probably their day off – and they don't look like Jews, do they? If not, there's no law against them using the pool. It's municipal, after all.'

Jack stood, lit himself a Gauloise, moved away a few feet, left them to this family quarrel, studied the girls out the corner of his good eye. The cruise ships may have stopped coming but he'd seen the way a trickle of different traffic was beginning to replace it. Poles, for example. Hungarians, Lithuanians, Latvians and others. Getting out of their own countries – to escape the Germans on one side, Russians on the other. It didn't really matter. Circuitous routes bringing them to this crossroads in Casablanca. The hope of freedom in America. But always, always those unfortunates who, for a thousand reasons, would fall into the hands of pimps. Or those, maybe, who'd never known any other life than prostitution anyway.

'You're commander of the *gendarmerie*, aren't you?' said the brother. 'What more reason do you need, dammit?'

He stormed off towards the changing rooms, dragging his wife behind him, but then...

Jack would later remember the blast of blistering air, so sudden, so severe, it drove the breath from his lungs, drove the cigarette from his fingers, made him stagger back towards the water.

Then a flash, the already bright afternoon illuminated with the purest white light. Painful. And the flash ripped apart by a sound like the end of worlds. He would never adequately describe it.

A savage roar, but so loud it literally deafened him, the screams all around muted to the merest echoes.

A mantle of smoke rising in the shape of a black mushroom, out there in the channel beyond the breakwater. Within the cloud, gouts of flame, each jet tossing black specks towards the heavens.

More explosions, folk here in the lido clutching each other, shielding their eyes, their shouts of alarm now beginning to drill through his ear drums. Some people running, others throwing themselves down on the tiles.

There'd been sirens, arrests. Those German nationals still with leave to remain in Casa now rounded up under suspicion of sabotage. But within days it had become apparent that the destroyer *La Railleuse* had been cut in half by the accidental explosion of one or more of her torpedoes, the scale of the blast magnified by the compressed air in the torpedo compartment. Or something of the kind. Jack was never good on technical detail. But twenty-eight of her crew dead. Dozens more seriously wounded. The huts of the old military hospital were pressed back into service for their care. And every low tide, the broken remains of her hull and superstructure appeared afresh, sitting in the shallows, the sandbanks onto which the explosion had tossed her. A regular reminder to them all.

Yes, war had come to Casablanca and, after that Easter weekend, there'd been no stopping it.

Jack recalled the fellow at the BBC broadcast, the consulate in Rabat, about the *Graf Spee* – the fellow who'd called for an end to the *drôle de guerre*, the joke war, the phoney war. Well, he thought, I hope he's happy now. They must have each awoken to the same news, he supposed. Six weeks ago. Mid-May. Was that all? Six bloody weeks.

The French and British had planned such a foolproof strategy. The Maginot line, stretching all the way up France's eastern border. Then the protection of the Ardennes Forest, an entirely impenetrable barrier immediately north of the line. Finally, the might of the combined British Expeditionary Force, the French First Army and Belgian Divisions protecting territory between the

Ardennes and the coast. The Allies with more tanks and planes than the *Boches*.

And it had all seemed to be playing out according to the predicted scenarios. Shame about the Netherlands, of course. The invasion. The surrender four days later. Within those four days, the Germans pushing into Belgium.

'There,' somebody had said, 'same old Germans. No imagination.'

The bars of Casablanca swilling with champagne. News of the French victory – tactical victory anyhow – at Hannut. French Morocco's own infantry regiments in action at Gembloux, the Hun decisively repulsed.

Within those same four days, however – four days, for pity's sake – the unimaginative Germans had pushed through those "impenetrable" Ardennes forests, the British and French commanders unable to comprehend the speed with which this was all happening. Good god, nobody had imagined...

On the same day as the Dutch surrendered, that fourth day after the German offensive began, the enemy were on the Meuse and taken Sedan, then ran straight to the Channel, near Abbeville, neatly splitting the British and French to the north from Paris, the Maginot Line and the rest of the French army to the south.

Well, this was how Jack remembered it all. Afterwards? The disbelief. The acrimony. But the conviction that the Germans had overstretched themselves. Made a fatal error. Maybe it would all work out fine in the end. And, for a while, it looked like they were right.

The *Petit Marocain* suddenly forgot its obsession with Franco. They'd found a new hero to turn back the tide. A French colonel, Charles de Gaulle. Three days of fighting in a counter-attack. A village called Stonne, not far from Sedan, the village changing hands seventeen times, the French eventually having to withdraw for lack of air support – though for every Frenchman who'd sacrificed his life, they'd left three Germans dead.

And the withdrawal? Only so far as the town of Montcornet, where de Gaulle had, for a while at least, driven off the *Wehrmacht* in total confusion.

Whole articles were devoted to this latterday paladin, comparing him to Charlemagne's faithful champion Roland – though Jack wasn't sure whether it was helpful to invoke images of Roland's legendary but suicidal last stand at Roncevaux – reminding readers that the colonel had fought with distinction, been wounded many times during the Great War, decorated with the *Croix de Guerre*, endured thirty-two months in a German prisoner-of-war camp.

Stories about how, at six feet five inches, de Gaulle had bestridden the battlefields, always upright, ramrod straight, bullets and shell bursts all around, inspiring his men in their own tenacity. In the end, it had been the French high command who'd ordered his division to pull back – though when he did so he took a mass of German prisoners with him and, as at Stonne, he'd made the enemy pay a catastrophic price for their tactical victory.

Perhaps there was hope after all. And though he did not pick this up immediately, it seemed on the same day it had all kicked off, the second week in May, after the awful news of Britain's disastrous Norway campaign, the House of Commons finally lost faith in that old fool Chamberlain, and the First Sea Lord, Winston Churchill, was invited by the king to form a new government, to become Prime Minister – even though the whole world seemed to know how the disastrous Norway campaign had been Churchill's initiative in the first place.

The folk from Gibraltar began to arrive about this same time, the last week in May. A thousand of them, more or less, ferried to Casablanca every two or three days on board an Egyptian freighter hired by the British Governor on the Rock. Each group the same. Families, uprooted with their sad suitcases, most of them reasonably dressed, some poorer than others, but not a man, woman or child among them without that haunted fear in their eyes, the lot of refugees everywhere.

They'd arrived without visas and nobody seemed sure why this should be, but Jack knew here was a story Sydney Elliott would definitely want. So, a few days after the second group had landed he made his way to find them in one of the dance halls, Le Temple on Rue Colbert, the *ville nouvelle*, set aside for their temporary accommodation.

It was a bright day, and he lingered a while in the *souk*, pushed his way through hanging *djellabas*, burnooses and women's caftans; bathed himself in the fresh bakery smells of flatbreads in shoulder-high stacks and the tangy aromas from crates of citrus; ran his fingers through dried coriander, cumin and cardamoms in their overflowing burlap bags; revelled in the glorious reds and silvers, blues and golds of slippers, tassels and rugs; gazed at his distorted image, the curse of the eye patch, in the burnished copperware; and pressed himself into the crowd, against the whitewashed walls, each time a merchant's mule train wound its way through the labyrinth, the drivers screaming *'Balek, balek!'* Make way, indeed.

He did so, reached the dance hall and persuaded the *gendarmes* guarding the doors that he had legitimate business there.

'You can check with Commandant Réchard,' he said, the name itself enough to grant him entrance.

Inside it already had the smell of a hospital, those layers of stale food, excrement and disinfectant, one on top of the other. Curtains hung from wires, forming tiny cubicles, the barest level of privacy for the mattresses or piles of straw filling every available inch of floor space. Like an oven, the ceiling fans not working. And most shunned his approaches, until he found a couple, sitting against the wall, propped against their luggage, reading to a child of perhaps five or six. The girl sat on her mother's lap. Just a vest and a tartan skirt, the woman wearing a cotton print frock, copra blue with tiny white daisies, both of them drenched in sweat.

'Hello,' he said to the girl and produced from his satchel a leaf-wrapped bundle of dates he'd bought in the *souk*. 'Would you like one? Is she allowed?' he asked the couple, really as an afterthought.

'Why not?' said the man, and gratefully accepted one of Jack's Gauloises. His flannel trousers were stained with oil and rust, his open-necked shirt no longer white.

'I'm Telford. Jack Telford. I write for an English newspaper. Well, sometimes. *Reynold's News.'*

They knew it well. The man's brother ran a newsagent's shop on Tuckey's Lane, the Callejón del Jarro, he said. It was usually a week behind but that was OK. Sunday was Sunday, after all.

'And what would *domingo* be without *Reynold's News*?' he said, told Jack his name was José. José Linares. 'This, *mi esposa*, Lydia.' Then he ruffled the child's hair. 'And *nuestra hija*, Morena.'

Jack was trying hard to follow this mix of Spanish and English, the Gibraltarian *llanito*, but José's accent was pleasant, softly sibilant, like the Andalucians he'd known.

'Your family Spanish originally?' he said.

'No way!' José protested. 'British. Always British.' But he understood the question well enough. Jack had never visited the Rock but he knew its inhabitants had roots, yes of course deep into Spain and Portugal, but also into Genoa, Sicily and Malta. British blood too? Without doubt.

'And how do you feel about all this?' said Jack. 'Angry?'

José looked around, sniffed at the rancid air.

'It's not good here, *hombre*. Our *familia*, all separated. *Mi hermano* in some other place. And *mi madre* – we don't know. But why angry? There's a war. We play our part, no? And Gibraltar, she needs more *soldados*, more planes, more ships. Not shopkeepers.'

'Is that what you did?'

Jack couldn't quite see José behind the counter at Liptons or Marks and Spencer.

'Shipping clerk,' said José. 'The Anchor Line on Main Street. *La ironía*, no? We always dreamed of sailing away somewhere. And now...'

His wife Lydia put a hand on José's shoulder, while little Morena pulled at the waistband of his trousers.

'Read, *Papa*,' she insisted.

'And what are you reading?' Jack turned the front of the book in José's hand so he could see. *Alice's Adventures in Wonderland*. He should have guessed.

'I'll read it,' Lydia told her, took the book from her husband.

'I heard,' said Jack, once the girl was settled again, 'they're moving out all non-essential residents. How many is that exactly, José, do you know?'

'Thirteen thousand. Fourteen, *quizás*. They need the *espacio*, for more military.'

There were plans for more dance halls to be pressed into service, A camp out at Aïn Chok too.

'I guess the government thought Gib was fairly safe,' said Jack. 'Franco neutral. But now the Italians, nobody knowing which way Mussolini would jump – you're probably safer away from the place.'

'We had a nice house,' said Lydia, and a tear rolled down her cheek. José put his arm round her shoulders.

'You always said you hated it, woman,' he said. 'But we'll get back there. Soon, I think. Beat the *alemanes*, then...'

'Then we all go home again,' said Jack. 'But did you have trouble getting in?'

That problem about visas. But also the *Sûreté* had been checking for Spanish Republicans – those who'd managed to take refuge on the Rock – bizarrely believing they might be Fifth Columnists. Jack made a mental note to ask Paquita. But José simply shook his head, spoke only of a few formalities.

'*Mama*, I have to *pipí*,' said the girl, and Lydia took her off to the queue waiting to use the buckets hidden behind another set of curtain screens.

'Tell me, *señor*,' said José. 'It is right, *verdad*? Soon?'

'I hope so,' Jack replied, but he knew he could have been more convincing. Because the rest of the news was pretty grim.

They continued to arrive all through early June, along with the rest of Europe's outcasts – and the foul miasma of defeat.

'There's an old Berber proverb,' said Commandant Réchard, running a finger around the rim of his glass. 'An army of sheep led by a lion may defeat an army of lions led by a sheep. Our forces in France, *Monsieur* Telford. Lions led by sheep.'

The headlines. *Le Petit Marocain*. The paper lay on the table between them outside the café of the Hôtel Excelsior. The green awning sheltered them from the sun, just turned noon according to the clock high in the Moorish-style tower opposite, against the medina wall. The Place de France again. But at least it was more peaceful there on the terrace, and the other customers were careful to keep a respectful distance between themselves and the Commandant. The *brasserie* inside was, as usual, packed – all those with business to conduct. And with the influx of new refugees, there was a lot of new business. A new *accordéoniste* too, it seemed.

'Again,' said Jack. 'It just happens over and over again.'

He thought about his father. The horror of the trenches, the cannon fodder – *kanonenfutter*, as the Germans had called it. The insane attacks. For a while it looked like, this time, they'd learned. The British Expeditionary Force and the French First Army opening a mobile offensive, to drive through the German lines, join with the French armies in the south. Yet after the reported initial French and British success at Arras it all went quiet, the offensive abandoned and, before anybody knew it was happening, at the end of May, the BEF – and much of the French First Army – was being evacuated from the beaches of Dunkirk. Réchard stabbed his finger at the photograph on the front page.

'I never thought this could happen again either,' he said. 'Look at this. Millions of refugees on the roads. Always refugees. An Exodus.'

'And Dunkirk,' said Jack. He'd tried to imagine it so many times. Like Alicante. But a hundred times worse. Two hundred times. With bullets and bombs.

'Your government betrayed us, you know? Perfidious bloody Albion. You *goddams*. Made the decision to evacuate without speaking to us first. Rather than follow Weygand's plan and attack. Attack.'

He thumped his fist on the table, the glasses bouncing, slopping some of their wine onto the white cloth, two dark stains.

'How do you know that?' said Jack.

'Oh, believe me. I know.'

A local beggar with a badly deformed leg hobbled towards them, a monkey sitting on his shoulder and turning acrobatic tricks whenever its chain was pulled. Réchard threw a couple of *sous* into the man's cup.

'And then,' said the Commandant, 'your precious Royal Navy gave priority to the English. Left decent Frenchmen to rot. In the beginning anyway.'

'I don't think…' Jack began, but Réchard was in full flow.

'What will your papers say, Telford? A great victory, I suppose. But I wager there won't be a mention of the thirty-five thousand Frenchmen who sacrificed themselves to cover the evacuation.'

'British too,' said Jack. 'Second Division, remember? And without them a hundred thousand other Frenchmen wouldn't have got away either.'

By the fourth of June it had all been over at Dunkirk, and the *Marocain*'s new hero, de Gaulle, promoted to Brigadier-General. Prime Minister Paul Reynaud had appointed him as a government minister as well. Then a second German offensive.

'They should have been thrown into the fight,' said Réchard. Weygand's army, supported by the British 51st Highland Division had done well, but they were facing impossible odds. 'If we'd had those other divisions, Paris wouldn't be surrounded now. Left to its fate.'

He accepted one of Jack's cigarettes.

'And now,' said Telford, 'we're supposed to accept that the Reich can't be beaten. Further resistance futile.'

'Even if the *Boches* do win, what other way is there to preserve the honour of France – other than resistance?'

Jack smiled, flicked away some of the ash, which had fallen on his grey flannels.

'My god, Louis, I spoke to a friend in Rabat yesterday. She said exactly the same.'

He'd been at the *Grande Poste*, wired his story about the Gibraltarians and telephoned Paquita Gorroño at the same time.

'One of your Red friends?' Louis smiled.

'Make a difference? Does it matter which side of the political divide they follow, so long as they're *résistants*?'

'I just pray for Paris,' said Réchard. 'Open city – what does that even mean? We save the buildings, if we're lucky. But abandon the heart of France to German jackboots?'

Out in the square, buses ran past at regular intervals, horns blasting at the laden donkeys. Against the medina wall opposite, white-robed Berbers displayed their terracotta pots behind the long line of fancy horse-drawn carriages waiting for the tourists. And in the middle of the road a camel rider swayed past, his beast pulling a string of four mules, each mule carrying a black-swathed woman and huge cargo baskets. There were flies buzzing about, the smells of dust, manure, cigar smoke – and the heady scent of garlic from the *brasserie*.

'Louis,' said Jack, 'I invited you to ask a favour.'

'I didn't expect it could be anything else. What is it you want?'

'When I came over on the *Stanbrook*, there was a man. Granell. He went into one of the camps. Might it be possible – to find him?'

'You think I've nothing better to do? And if he's another Red, he's probably where he belongs.'

'If you're looking for resistance, Louis, Amado Granell and his comrades will be in the front line – as they've been for the past three years.'

'Needle in a haystack, I think. Besides, I have family matters to deal with. Jean-François shipped out this morning. Marseille.'

'The Italians?'

Mussolini finally off the fence, declared war on France and Britain.

'Bloody cowards,' said Réchard. 'Useless *macaronis*. Vultures. Think they smell us already dead. Give them a few days and they'll be coming for us too. But they'll get a warmer welcome than they expect.'

'Looks like it was the right move though, getting all those civilians out of Gibraltar. The Rock will be their first target.'

Jack had been back to visit José and his family several times. Still in the dance hall, conditions there appalling.

'They need moving,' said Réchard.

'Then house them. Or build a decent camp. My god, you can build an entire walled town for your whores, Louis.'

'Bousbir? You'll go there once too often, my friend.' Réchard wagged a finger at him. 'The girls there are clean – for the most part. But...' Jack was struggling to find the correct protest. That he'd only been back there to research. Yet somehow – 'Anyway,' the Commandant pressed on, 'there's Aïn Chok.'

'The old typhus camp? I don't think so. Anyway, it's already full. But *Madame* Bénatar's got plans.'

'The lawyer. The Jew?'

Hélène Bénatar was another Casa legend, made her name as the first woman lawyer in town. Widowed just six months earlier. Jack had met her through the *Alliance Israélite Universelle* and she was now determined to set up a refugee committee.

'Are there two?' said Jack. 'And what about Granell?'

'What plans? The Bénatar woman?'

Jack picked up his glass, swirled the green-tinted wine around inside.

'A committee,' he said. 'Pull people together. People with influence who can make sure new refugees are treated decently.'

'Jews, you mean?'

'No, Louis. Not just Jews. Bloody hell, don't you know how many more there'll be – if France falls?'

Even with the distance between them and the nearest customers, Jack saw heads turn, faces twisted in contempt, enraged whispering. Réchard tossed the stub of his cigarette out into the street, where a bunch of Arab urchins descended upon it, fought each other for this prize.

'I'll try to find your Spaniard,' he barked. 'But no more of this nonsense. France won't fall. Not ever.'

Telford had rarely felt such grief. He wept. He wept openly. As did everybody else in the audience at the Cinéma Théatre Rialto. Jack was there alone, wished it were otherwise, for those others, who clung to each other in the darkness, shared at least some crumb of comfort.

Another newsreel, the projectionist's flickering searchlight piercing the fog of war. British Pathé, emotional French commentary over the original English. Tragedy in two tongues. Paris. Friday 14th June. A week ago. Rank upon rank of German soldiers marching down the Champs-Élysées. Tanks. Nazi salutes. A *Wehrmacht* band. Motorbikes and sidecars. Motorised infanty. Swastikas being hung from public buildings, the Arc de Triomphe. Tearful bystanders. And the barricades of sandbags stacked for the defence that never happened.

There'd been fresh footage flown in almost every day. It caused a pain he couldn't erase. Indeed, it got worse. For, like everybody else, he was addicted to this daily dosage of disaster. Yesterday he'd been here twice, convinced there must be happier news. And when it wasn't newsreel it was the papers, scanning each of them for some small sign of salvation.

Yet it never came, and now a short clip showing fighting along the Maginot Line, bitter, strong but futile French resistance. The German breakthrough here as well.

Then Pathé again, British tanks crossing the border from Egypt into Libya, dust clouds, the Italian Fort Capuzzo captured. But this so pathetically short of levelling the scales. Somehow the pit of despair seemed even deeper.

Finally, coverage of a second Dunkirk, this time the start of evacuations – British and French troops – from Brest.

Somebody shouted *'Vive la France!'* in a choking sob, while another poor soul began to sing *La Marseillaise*, but only got to the second line and, with nobody else joining in, the woman's voice broke entirely after *'Le jour de gloire...'*

There, he thought, nothing left. And it all seemed so inadequate. His contribution to this war? A few articles. His teaching at the school. So bloody inadequate.

How could it be that those same words, just days later, and now in the midst of even greater despair, could provide so much hope, such solace? *'Vive la France!'*

'Long live Free France in honour and independence!'

Same words, same sentiment, but spoken by one man in a BBC studio such a distance away. De Gaulle once more. There was a map on the wall. Europe and North Africa. Pastel pinks, greens, blues and yellows, and Jack calculated the distance between Casablanca and London.

'Radio will never be the same again,' he said, almost to himself, though he still had to make an effort to control his emotions. He knew only a couple of the others who'd been invited. The widowed lawyer, Hélène Bénatar. The same Captain Phillip Fox with the David Niven moustache he'd met in Rabat. A civil engineer called Williamson, working on the new developments out on the Anfa Hill, and a mining consultant, Bromley, from the phosphate mines near Boujniba – both of whom he knew from the Excelsior, and neither of whom he very much liked. The rest, the usual mix of British expatriates, men and women, with family or business interests in this part of the world.

'Will they listen to him though?' said Bond, the consul there in Casablanca. Jack hadn't heard him approach but gratefully accepted the tumbler of whisky he was offering. And then one of Bond's Chesterfields.

'Something about the whole concept,' Telford told him. 'This isn't Goebbels using the airwaves for propaganda. Or *Band Waggon* to soothe our nerves. Has it ever been used to start a revolution before? Here's a man forced to leave his own country and rallying his people to the cause, rallying resistance. For freedom. Liberty. How could they not listen to him?'

He'd passed the consulate many times. Number Sixty, Boulevard d'Anfa. Reasonably new. A modest green street door, up four broad steps, gave onto a garden with eucalyptus trees, around three sides of which nestled the white single storey building, the public office and meeting room straight ahead, just next to the waiting area. And Mister Bond had, like Hurst in Rabat, been happy to offer his facilities, for a chosen audience to hear the broadcast. And after the broadcast, a modest supper, drinks and sandwiches. Honey-soaked Moroccan pastries.

'You know he made a similar speech four days ago? Though I don't think anybody heard it,' said Fox. 'And anyway, it was somewhat overshadowed by dear Winston.'

They'd all heard the broadcast too, the same speech he'd earlier delivered to the Commons. Almost Shakespearean. Something about the Battle of France now over, the Battle of Britain about to begin. And, even if the British Empire lasted a thousand years, men would still reckon this was their finest hour. Telford thought he'd never been so deeply moved by anything in his life.

'Well, that was before this damned armistice,' he said. 'Nothing like the prospect of being hanged to concentrate the mind. Isn't this what they say?'

Word had hit the streets earlier. The shock and horror of it all. But de Gaulle had provided more of the details.

'As long as the allies continue the war,' he'd said, *'the government of France has no right to surrender to the enemy.'*

No other vanquished country had done so. The Poles, the Norwegians, the Belgians, the Dutch – each of their legitimate governments had gone into exile, not accepted defeat.

'And Pétain?' said the mining consultant. Had he slept in that lightweight linen suit? 'What do we make of Pétain?'

'Pétain may have been a hero of the Great War,' said *Madame* Bénatar. Her amiable face was flushed with anger, her oddly ill-shaped teeth gritted. Jack loved her accented English, French naturally, but with a light hint of Hebrew. Yiddish, perhaps? He was never quite certain. 'But now – they say he's always been close to Hitler. Shared views, of course.'

Prime Minister Réynaud had resigned a few days earlier and Pétain had replaced him, the French Cabinet bitterly divided over how they should respond.

'And willingly went off,' said Jack, 'as the first French ambassador to Francoist Spain.'

He looked over at *Madame* Bénatar. She was biting her lip, fear in her eyes, and he could almost read her mind. Given what they'd heard about Germany's treatment of the Jews everywhere else, what would be the fate of her people in occupied France? Or under Vichy for that matter.

'It'll never work, will it?' said the civil engineer. A dapper fellow, blue blazer and beige slacks. 'This idea of the Germans occupying Paris, carving up the rest of France. And Algeria? Protectorates like poor Morocco – now all part of this so-called *zone libre.* Free? What a poor jest. They say the Germans now have almost two million Frenchmen as prisoners. Two million. Can you imagine? Two million hostages. Pétain's puppet government now at Vichy.'

Jack ran his finger over the wall map. There it was. Vichy. Almost slap in the middle of France. Except, this was a France which no longer existed, and Bond – or one of his staff – had drawn a neat line, black ink. From Burgundy, west almost as far at Tours on the Loire, then south to the Pyrenees but leaving the whole of the western and northern coasts in German hands.

'Spa town, isn't it?' he said, though he knew the answer.

'I heard from Keeling,' called Mister Bond from the other side of the room. 'At Tangier. Bloody Franco's taken over the place. The international zone all gone to hell in a handcart.'

'Franco? His army there?' said Jack.

'Tangier annexed into Spanish Morocco. His *regulares*. Martial law.'

'Dammit,' said Jack. 'Muslim *regulares* to win his so-called Christian crusade in Spain but wasted no time at all shipping them back here when it was all over.'

'We protested, naturally. What price Franco's neutrality now? What if he allows the Germans to launch yet another offensive? This time against Egypt, through Tangier.'

'But Tangier,' said *Madame* Bénatar. 'It's been a safe haven for so many. For so long.'

'There are Republican refugees there,' Jack replied. 'Good god in heaven, they'll be dead men now.'

'Others too,' said Bénatar. 'There'll be still more refugees from there. Millions more from the occupied zone too. And they speak of atrocities. Terrible atrocities. A hundred thousand colonial troops captured by the *Boches*. Men from all over Africa, the West Indies, Indochina. Many of them being butchered as we speak. By the master race.'

'Who the hell cares about a few Reds in Tangier?' said Bromley the miner. 'Or whatever wogs the Frenchies may have been stupid enough to rely on. And refugees? I, for one, am sick of having the word pushed down my throat every five minutes.'

There were appreciative nods among several others in the room. Jack's blood boiled. He decided to thump the fool. But Hélène Bénatar set a hand on his arm.

'You'd better get used to the idea, Mister Bromley,' she said. 'Soon you won't be able to move in Casa for refugees. A good time to go back to England, perhaps.'

'I would too,' Bromley growled, 'except it's full of Johnny Foreigners already. Jew kids from Austria and god knows where else arriving by the shipload...'

He stopped. He looked about him. This time simply embarrassed glances exchanged among the others, or folk turning away. Jack knew half of them probably wanted to applaud but something in *Madame* Bénatar's demeanour would have halted even the most rabid of anti-Semites.

'Please, sir,' said Burton, 'I must ask you to desist.'

Throw the swine out, thought Jack. Why don't you? But Bromley simply pushed himself into the gathering, went straight for the whisky bottle at the refreshments table.

'Well, France has made its bed,' said Williamson the engineer. 'But Bromley's right. What about England? We're alone now.'

'Alone?' said Captain Fox. He offered his cigarette case to those around him. 'Hardly alone, old boy. The Empire. Canada as our bread basket. All the meat we'll ever need from Australia and New Zealand. Literally millions of men available from India and all those aforementioned places. Great heavens, we couldn't be *less* alone. De Gaulle may have been playing to the gallery a bit. But he's right on this, Mister Williamson. This war's not over by a long chalk. Not for France. Not for anybody.'

'I call upon all Frenchmen who want to remain free to listen to my voice and follow me,' de Gaulle had said. But Jack was cynical about the numbers who might heed his call. Yet, maybe. Just maybe it would be enough.

'All this about weapons,' said Williamson. 'He said they still have weapons. But Vichy has all the weapons, doesn't it? Help from America? What planet is the fellow on? America would be mad to get involved in another European war. Anyway, Vichy's now recognised across the globe. And Free France – what *is* that, precisely?'

'It's all bluff, surely,' Jack told him. 'But sometimes – look, I'm no poker player…'

'If the powers of freedom ultimately triumph over those of servitude…' De Gaulle's words had been strong, confident, *'…what will be the fate of a France which has submitted to the enemy?'*

Triumph? Had he really spoken of triumph? Bloody hell, thought Jack, this was utopian. An impossible dream. Who *was* this man? De Gaulle was the head of nothing but a mere concept. Nothing to back him up. Nothing but Free France. Yet Free France didn't exist. Not yet, anyway. And could it ever?

He thanked Bond for his hospitality, promised Hélène Bénatar that yes, he'd be happy to help in some modest way with her Committee for the Assistance of Foreign Refugees, said a curt goodbye to Williamson and thought seriously about blacking Bromley's eye before he left. But he didn't, simply made his way back out into the garden where he found Captain Fox enjoying a smoke.

'Nice night,' said Fox, and gazed up at the overcast sky. Just growing dark, except for the glow of his cigarette and the last creases of crimson in the west. The longest day. Felt like it too.

They'd exchanged the briefest of greetings when Jack arrived. He'd been surprised to see Fox there – but not *too* surprised.

'How d'you do, Mister Telford?' Fox had asked, while Jack was being relieved of his trilby by Bond's secretary. 'Well, I hope?'

'As Oedipus might have said, Captain,' Jack had replied, 'that's a little complex.'

He'd been pleased with himself, thought of his old friend Max Weston. The Cornish comedian had left the battlefield tour bus after Covadonga, with his wife and manager Marguerite. A tearful parting – from Max, at least. But Marguerite? Well, there'd been the rather embarrassing incident in the woman's bedroom. And where might they be now? Had she succeeded in sealing the contract with Ealing for *Mexican Max*? Jack had written to the studios, just once, from Madrid, asking them to pass on a letter he'd enclosed, though he'd never received a reply. Or perhaps it was waiting for him there. And now, the war. Max had almost been excited by the prospect, the chance to entertain the troops and Jack had advised him to maybe add some music to his act. The ukulele, perhaps. The jokes were appalling, of course – almost as bad as the Oedipus thing.

'Very good, old boy,' Fox had smiled. 'Not heard that one in a long time. But no more scorpion trouble, I trust?'

Jack had looked around the gathering, noticed Bromley among them.

'I'd take a scorpion in place of one or two in this room any time,' he'd said.

'Pleasant, yes,' said Jack now as he walked past. Then he stopped, there in the garden. 'But no warning tonight? No cautionary tales about possible accidents?'

'You think I put it there,' Fox laughed. 'Your bloody scorpion. You do, don't you? How absolutely priceless.'

'Is it so unlikely?'

'What d'you think this is, Telford – an Agatha Christie? Come on, be a sport. Walk with me. Clear the air, what?'

'I'm going home,' said Jack, set the trilby on his head and pushed open the street door, skipped down the steps and turned left onto Boulevard d'Anfa, Fox's footfall following behind.

'Then let me join you. Never entirely safe to be out alone at night.'

'I've always felt safe enough here,' Telford lied. A brushful of bravado. 'Present company excluded.'

Even at this hour of the evening, the Boulevard d'Anfa – Jack always thought calling this particular section a boulevard was wonderful hyperbole – was its normal chaos of trucks, motor cars, camels and carts, and he picked his way through the roadside rubble, glad of the occasional headlight to illuminate their path or the blazing galvanised bucket braziers that passed for streetlamps. Across the city, the *mu'azzins* were calling the first *adhan*. Ten o'clock then, and the street vendors beginning to rise from their places, ready themselves for the night prayer, the *Isha*.

'I found out what happened to your Major Edwin, by the way,' said Fox. 'Desk job. Couldn't be anything else, of course. London.'

'I'm a wanted man then?' Telford said it flippantly, though he dreaded the answer, was certain this was the reason for the captain's pursuit of him. He stopped, turned to confront Fox. 'If so, why don't you do whatever it is you're supposed to?'

Fox shrugged.

'There's a file, I'm told. But no action pending. All just too messy for us, I imagine. As you said, something of a cloud around the major's methods. Though still something of a hero among the young bucks – losing his legs like that in the line of duty. Casualty of war. But it seems you knew another of our old colleagues – Fielding? Vice-consul at San Sebastián, wasn't he? Never had the pleasure. Died in Madrid. Killed in some brawl. But even darker clouds there. You wouldn't know anything about this, would you? Nobody wants to talk about Fielding.'

He spoke the name as though it were noxious.

'No, nothing,' Jack told him and continued to walk.

'Now, why don't I believe you, Telford? What was it you said – enemies and unfortunate accidents?'

Jack heard again that slap as his foot had connected with Fielding's chin.

'I was just trying to impress. Nasty habit of mine, I'm afraid.'

Was Fox telling him the truth? If so, it sounded like he had nothing to fear. A weight lifted from him. Though it left the question of Carter-Holt's father, Sir Aubrey. Now Secretary for Overseas Trade, Hurst had told him in Rabat. But had he accepted the version of his daughter's death, which Jack had disseminated? It simply seemed odd he'd heard nothing from him. No attempt to verify the story, speak with the only person who witnessed the family tragedy. Perhaps, of course, Sir Aubrey Carter-Holt simply didn't care. But odd.

'Ah, back in civilisation,' said Fox.

They'd reached the Place de Verdun. Electric streetlamps. Palm trees. Lights beckoning from several of the bars and bistros.

'I first met Fielding on one of Franco's battlefield tours,' Jack told him. 'War Routes of the North. Long story.'

He'd thought about them a lot, as it happened. Were they still running? He supposed they might be. Even now. More difficult, of course, with the war. But there were still three scheduled flights each week from Bristol Whitchurch to Lisbon – and back again. From there, easy enough to reach Madrid. He didn't suppose the powerful and wealthy would let a small thing like a war spoil their holidays abroad. And since so many of the powerful and wealthy also seemed to be admirers of Franco – well, a match made in heaven. He made a mental note to ask Paquita, next time he chased her for news of Granell.

'Then let me buy you a drink, and you can tell me,' said Fox. He pointed to the Café de Verdun and they dodged a few cars and bicycles to reach that side of the square, while the *mu'azzins* called the *iqamah*, the final call to prayer.

'No,' said Jack. 'When I said a long story, I meant it. And not one I especially want to share. Anyway, I'm more intrigued by whatever it is you're after, *old boy*.'

They sat outside, ordered coffee and cognacs, lit cigarettes. They were just around the corner from Franco's consulate.

'Still, I'd like to hear it one day – about Fielding. But you, Telford – honestly? For now I'm just interested in what you thought of the broadcast. As a journalist. There was cynicism painted all over your face at times. I was watching.'

'It was clever stuff. Not quite the same way with words as Winston. Two of a kind though. But the difference? Clever, what you said. About all the resources the old man has at his disposal. Empire. But de Gaulle? Playing with an empty hand.'

Inside there was a party in progress. Music, dancing and gaiety. It seemed to make the point.

'Is he?' said Fox. 'And you shouldn't set too much store by that infernal racket. There'll be plenty more like them – having a good time simply because it's over. For France anyway. Or so they think.'

'You know something the rest of us…'

'Off the record?'

'Of course.'

The captain picked a piece of tobacco from his lip, squinted at Jack through half-closed eyelids, then turned his attention to the shapely calves of two young women, arm in arm, laughing together as they joined the celebration.

'You saw the ships today?' Fox said at last.

'Arrived on one tide, sailed again on the next.'

It had been a busy day on the waterfront. A convoy of four French troopships, though seemingly without any troops, anchored in the approaches. An escort of two destroyers went out to meet them, herded them out to sea again. An American destroyer, the USS *Herbert*, as well, docking on some diplomatic mission of neutrality. And then, finally, at five o'clock, the French battleship *Jean Bert* had limped into port. She'd only been launched the previous month and had escaped from Saint-Nazaire a few days ago, still incomplete and damaged as she'd left there in a German bombing raid – but what would happen with her now was anybody's guess. Fox leaned across the table, lowered his voice.

'Those troopships? Strictly confidential. Though they're away safely enough now. But still, the less that know, the better, yes?

Bound for Dakar. And then the security of Fort Kayès. Deep in the Sahara.'

'Carrying?'

The captain mouthed the words, almost without a sound.

'The last of France's gold reserves. More than a thousand tonnes. Belgian and Polish gold ingots on board too. Those three countries have been sending their reserves abroad for a while – France for the past two years. America. Canada. More recently Martinique.'

'But it's Vichy gold. Isn't it?'

'At least it's not already in Germany's hands. And in the end? It all depends how things play out. If de Gaulle's gamble pays off, if he can make Free France a reality, if he can persuade enough people that triumph is, after all, a possibility – then the gold becomes valid surety, collateral, for him as much as for Pétain.'

'Is this a state secret?' said Jack. 'Or am I the only fool in Casa who's in the dark on this?'

A shoeshine boy in a striped *djellaba* carried his box towards them and Jack haggled with him until they reached a price.

'You're one of the privileged few, Mister Telford,' said Fox as the lad started work on Jack's dusty leather loafers.

'Why?'

'Truth? I may need your help. Unless I miss my guess, we'll be forced to close our consulates in Morocco before very long. And I...'

'But Vichy's neutral. We're in the *zone libre*, for pity's sake. Why would...?'

They shared fresh cigarettes, Jack's *Gauloises* this time.

'It doesn't matter,' said Fox. 'Let's just call it a hunch. Why are you looking at me like that? Oh, very well.' He lowered his voice again. 'It's the French navy, of course. We have no idea what will happen with it. But if there's the slightest chance of it falling into German hands... Anyway, the consulates – if I'm right then my own movements will be restricted. Quite seriously restricted. I need eyes and ears, Telford. Ah, apologies – one eye, at least. And you're a resourceful fellow when you set your mind to it.'

He was smiling, and though Jack had determined to ignore the jibe about his eye, he found himself lifting his left hand from the table, resting his head against the raised fingertips in a way which hid the patch. It had become something of a habit. One he must break.

'Eyes and ears on what, precisely?' he said.

'Anything that catches your attention, I suppose. Your friend Réchard, for example – it would be good to know where he stands. On Vichy, if you get my drift. But just generally, see which way the wind blows.'

'And where will you be – on the off-chance I decide to help?'

'Oh, here and there,' said Fox. 'Here and there.'

It was menacing. Outside the consulate, an angry crowd of French naval ratings, all white short-sleeved tops, or striped vests, sun helmets or caps with red pompoms. Even a few officers' uniforms among them. Local civilians too. But all baying for blood. And Réchard's *gendarmes* forming a cordon to hold them back.

'Assassins!' they yelled. English murderers.

Jack had been delivering more food and water to the Linares family – he'd finally found them in a pitiable condition among the thousands of others forced to spend those same two days out on the open quaysides – he'd set off in hot pursuit. The consulate would have been his next stop anyway. But he hadn't expected this, and he thought twice before slipping around the back of the police line and up the steps.

Inside, the consulate itself was in turmoil, the staff working like Trojans, shifting paperwork to the back of a black sedan, a taxi, waiting at the side door on the Boulevard Moulay Youssef.

'Why don't they do something?' a young woman shouted. 'Mutiny, isn't it? It would never happen with our boys.'

Jack wanted to remind her about the strike at Invergordon. A thousand matelots of His Majesty's Royal Navy. When? Nine years ago, it would have been. Though by then the girl had disappeared and Jack had other things on his mind. Fox's prediction, of course. The French navy, he'd said. And he'd been right. But before that, there'd been the *Massilia*. Just after the armistice and she'd come sailing into Casa, carrying two dozen members of the French government – at least, those who'd been in favour of keeping their government free, in exile, even though France itself may have fallen. Decent men, like Georges Mandel, who'd sailed here from Bordeaux with this very intention. Heroes, but they'd been betrayed, of course, the armistice signed while they were at sea. Behind their backs, so to speak. On their arrival in port, confined aboard the *Massilia* on the orders of the *Sûreté*.

'What the hell's going to happen?' Jack had asked Réchard over another glass of wine, this time at the Café du Commerce. 'It's like – I'm scared to breathe. Everything on hold while we wait to see. Which way will Morocco jump?'

'We're part of Vichy now,' Réchard had replied. 'All this with Mandel – a resistance government? Pie in the sky, I think. Though between you and me, my friend...'

'Yes?'

Réchard shrugged his shoulders.

'Nothing,' he said. 'Nothing. It seems certain Noguès will confirm Morocco's loyalty to the deal and then – that will be the end of our *Monsieur* Mandel.'

'Arrest him? You can't, surely?'

'You think I'd have a choice? And anyway, he's a Jew.'

Jack had been chilled by the casual nature of the comment. But Réchard had been right. There'd been another broadcast. This time Charles Noguès, French Morocco's Resident-General, his personal support for the armistice, the support of all loyal Frenchman in the protectorate, the integrity of all French North Africa. Two days more and Mandel indeed arrested, along with fellow-passenger Édouard Daladier, until May the Prime Minister – Daladier, who'd been with Chamberlain at Munich. Where would they end up now? Jack wondered. In some German concentration camp, he supposed. A few days later and news about that other supporter of a resistance government, the man who'd taken over from Daladier, Paul Reynaud, had also been arrested as a traitor. All of them gone. All those who could perhaps have made Free France a reality. And the news hadn't got any better. Reports in the papers. Claims Hitler now wanted Vichy's cooperation in the building of airfields for the *Luftwaffe* around Casablanca. And British attempts at negotiations with Pétain to make sure the French navy couldn't fall into Hitler's hands as well.

After all, it was still the second most powerful in Europe after Britain's own fleet.

In the middle of all this, Telford had been back to visit José Linares at the Temple dance hall again, took them food, a doll and more books for Morena.

'Any word of your family?' Jack had asked. 'Your mother?'

'She's with *mi hermano* now. He found out where she was, arranged for her to join him. I don't know how. They were talking about putting us all together. A new *sitio*. At Roches–Noires. You know it?' Jack knew it. Mostly an industrial area, east edge of the city, but he'd been out that way a couple of times. Once to the bowling club with Réchard, on the Rue de Dinant, a *pétanque* championship.

'José, it's not going to happen. Not now. You've heard the news?'

Jack had looked around the hall. More space, at least. Some of the Gibraltar folk had managed to bring out decent amounts of money and, whether through bribery or not, had apparently rented property. But most, like José, had no such means. And now...

'The guards here,' whispered Lydia. 'They don't treat us the same. Not since – is it true?'

'Yesterday,' said Jack. 'Our navy launched an attack on the French fleet at Mers-el-Kébir. Oran.' He wanted to call it a sneak attack, because this was the way it had been reported in *Le Petit Marocain* and others. Protests that the Vichy government was acting honourably, had given assurance after assurance to Britain about the measures put in place to make sure their ships could never fall into German hands. But the attack had happened anyway. No warning. None. French ships seized in Plymouth and Portsmouth. And at Mers-el-Kébir the French battleships, destroyers and gunboats shot to bits in a naval and aerial bombardment. More than a thousand French dead.

'We're at war then? With the French?' said José. '*Dios mío.*'

Jack watched Morena running around with the doll, blissfully unaware.

'I've no idea what will happen,' he'd said. 'But my friend in the *Gendarmerie*'s let me know the Resident-General wants you all gone again. Says that when you arrived, Britain and France were on the same side. But now…'

'They'll send us back?' said Lydia.

'To our home?' José shouted. 'How can they? Now we have no home. Nothing.'

Telford couldn't bring himself to tell them the whole story. Since the armistice more ships had been arriving. Upwards of a dozen every day. So many, there weren't enough berths for them. Forced to anchor offshore in the merciless heat and with their provisions exhausted. From Bordeaux. From Marseille. Other places. Each ship bringing hundreds more refugees. French, of course. Mostly French. But among them just about every other nationality in Europe. Many Jews. More dance halls taken over, sections of the old army camps pressed into service, holding pens within the waterfront warehouses. Hélène and her teams of volunteers working themselves to death, round the clock, trying to provide whatever help they could.

And getting rid of the fourteen thousand Gibraltarians, the *llanitos*, would go a long way towards helping the authorities with their dilemma. In any case, Réchard had warned him, the British had been told in the most brutal language. If the Gibraltarians didn't leave Casablanca immediately, the Resident-General could no longer guarantee their safety.

It was into this cauldron that Commodore Creighton had sailed, just as Archibald Dickson had, the previous year, sailed into Alicante.

Jack had been there, on Casablanca's quayside, to cover the story the arrival of this new convoy. Except Creighton had sailed in, of course, with all those evacuated French soldiers. And when Jack had tried to get a comment from him, it hadn't been a good first meeting.

'You're a reporter?' snapped this particular skipper, not Dickson. At least, Jack assumed he was a skipper, though something about his manner spoke of even higher authority. As did the amount of braid on the sleeves of the dark naval uniform jacket he wore about his shoulders, over the tropical whites beneath, for there was a sharp cold wind blowing in from the Atlantic, despite the

North African sunshine and clear summer skies. But another hero, Jack thought. He must be, for he was weathered and gnarled as an ancient oak, the wrinkles deeply etched around his eyes from a lifetime peering into the teeth of a gale, the lines sliced there by sea salt spray. His escort, a much younger officer and a rating carrying a slung rifle.

'I am, sir, yes,' said Jack, holding up the notebook the old fellow had so plainly spotted. Telford spoke with an amount of trepidation, for the way the officer spat out the word *reporter* didn't bode well for the rest of the conversation. 'I was supposed to be covering the story of the Gibraltarians, but then this...'

Behind them, a remarkable sight. The thousands of Gibraltarians the new régime now wanted out of Morocco, even though they'd only arrived over the past month or so. Impossible for Jack to spot any of the families among them he already knew, even though he'd searched frantically for more than an hour. They were being herded in a huge column of thirteen or fourteen thousand souls stretching from here to the Customs House, then all around the inner harbour with its fishing fleet, past the fish market, past the grain silos of the Quai Delande towards the British ships now berthed around Casablanca's *Môle du Commerce*, at the mouth of the Outer Basin – but those ships busily hauling up gangways, having discharged their cargoes. Cargoes? Fifteen thousand Frenchmen being funnelled in the opposite direction, away from the ships. The twin columns side by side, but the Gibraltarians goaded along by the rifle butts and bayonets of the *gendarmerie*, while the two groups were separated by a line of Senegalese soldiers, directing all manner of abuse, catcalls, at the miserable and dejected recent arrivals. Yes, Jack had seen this before as well, the defeated remains of the Republican army trudging into Alicante.

'Exempt then?' said the officer.

Telford was still trying to assimilate the scene, the shouting, the total chaos, to which this fellow seemed entirely oblivious.

'Exempt?' he said.

'Journalists, dammit. From conscription. You look fit enough.'

Jack knew that somewhere, back in England, call-up papers would be waiting for him. And he supposed, one fine day, especially now, they'd catch up with him here. He hadn't set out to be a dodger especially but – well, all in good time.

'I think there may be a problem with the eye,' said Jack, and he flicked his fingers towards the patch. But then he thought of Nelson and felt a fool.

'For a Board to decide, isn't it?' Jack agreed that yes, it was. 'And who's the consul here?' said the officer. 'Bloody hell-hole. D'you know where the Port Admiral's office might be?'

But the question was answered without Jack's help by a French naval lieutenant, who'd come scurrying towards them.

'We have instructions, Captain,' he said in breathless but passable English.

'I have already explained to one of your officers.'

'God's teeth,' the Englishman thundered at him. '*Captain*, did you say? I'll have you know, sir, I am *Commodore* Creighton. Commodore of Ocean Convoys. And I have instruction to simply clean and restock my vessels. Nothing more, you understand? My god, can you not smell the state of my ships. All this time at sea with fifteen thousand men in our holds. Fifteen thousand of *your* men. Frenchmen. Not ours. So, instructions, lieutenant. No refugees. None. *Pas de…*'

The lieutenant turned to Jack, reverted to French, introduced himself as Lieutenant Vaisseau. Telford returned the compliment.

'*Monsieur* Telford, might you translate? I would hate to be misunderstood.'

Jack was surprised there was no sign of Brigade Commandant Réchard. He'd come to know Réchard passably well in the six months he'd been in Casablanca. When he'd first got there, Réchard had signed his *permit de séjour*, his temporary leave to remain. Twelve months. But they were hardly close friends. And certainly not since the French surrender. More accurately, since Mers-el-Kébir. In any case, he agreed, explained as much to Creighton.

'What is there to misunderstand?' the commodore growled. 'What? Vichy's supposed to be neutral, isn't it? Therefore, we're entitled to our seventy-two hours, are we not? Well, tell the wretch.' Jack couldn't help thinking of the *Graf Spee*, but he explained anyway. Not quite verbatim, but near enough. 'And remind him, will you?'

said Creighton. 'Their bloody destroyers threatened to sink us.'

A flock of seagulls screeched overhead, supplemented the other ubiquitous quayside cries of cranes, dock railway diesels and bustling tugboats.

'I think the commodore needs to understand,' said Vaisseau, 'that neutrality is hardly a word we'd expect to hear on British lips after your Royal Navy – the cowards' attack. Our fleet, sir. Twelve hundred French sailors murdered. And our orders are clear, *Monsieur* Telford. I might not like them personally but the Gibraltarians, they are British citizens. When they arrived here, they arrived as allies. Not our responsibility, but citizens of our allies. Now, though…'

Telford translated and, while Commodore Creighton cursed and fulminated, demanded again to see the French Port Admiral, he turned to Vaisseau.

'Now they're an embarrassment to Vichy because of your new German masters,' said Jack.

'Our German *friends*,' Vaisseau replied. 'And you must tell Commodore Creighton that the Admiral has already insisted there is no room for negotiation here. None. If he does not agree to take them, his ship – all these ships – shall be arrested, interned.'

On the day after Creighton's arrival Jack had sent a telegram to Paquita Gorroño, suggesting a time when he could call her at the Bar Tahona de Carmen, where he knew they had a telephone, then waited during much of the afternoon at the *Grande Poste* for a booth, the queue running around the block – and most of those waiting recently arrived refugees it seemed. You could tell. The clothes, the babble of languages, the suitcases, the fractious children, the desperate faces of the lost and lonely.

'Paquita,' he'd said, when an operator finally connected them, 'you know fifteen thousand men from the French army landed here yesterday?'

'We heard, comrade. You know where they're being processed?'

'They've been shipped to a camp just outside town. A couple of camps anyway.'

It was like an oven inside the grey-painted telephone booth, the box offering little insulation also from the general hubbub in the post office, or from the raised voices of those in the neighbouring booths.

'Our people among them?' she asked, and Telford knew she meant former soldiers of the Republic.

'Paquita, it's hard to hear you,' he shouted. 'But yes, must be. I'll try to get there. I'd like to collect some stories. Spanish Republicans still fighting fascism, but now in the French Foreign Legion – that angle.'

'We've had some rough figures for those who died in France. Hundreds. Mainly from the Legion's three infantry regiments of foreign volunteers, one of them almost entirely Spanish. Our boys, Jack.'

'But what now?' he said. 'Find themselves with no war to fight again. Trapped in an army which presently counts Hitler and Mussolini among its friends. And Granell, did you find him?'

He looked out through the window in his door, at the folk waiting impatiently in line, craning their necks to see whether any of those in the booths might be nearing the end of their calls.

'Not yet,' she told him, 'but we're still searching.'

They'd agreed to speak again later in the week. But it plagued Jack. He could almost feel the anguish of those Spaniards who wished to continue the fight – but were presently part of an army that was, at best, now neutral and, at worst, sympathetic to Germany and Italy. It still plagued him when he caught up with Creighton at the consulate, in the bustle of Mister Bond's office. Creighton himself in the consul's chair, using the telephone. He raised a hand in recognition when he saw Jack.

'Ah, Telford,' said the consul. 'You heard the news? It's de Gaulle. He's going to lead a Free French military parade through London. To the Cenotaph. Bastille Day.'

Churchill had recognised the Brigadier-General as the official leader of Free France at the end of June. By the time of Mers-el-Kébir this didn't seem to mean very much, almost an empty gesture. But this?

'How many?' said Jack.

105

'On the day? Only a few hundred. But he claims to now have seven thousand men. Strange as it may seem, the attack on their fleet appears to have done the trick. Convinced his people we're deadly serious. It's a good start, Mister Telford.'

Jack was pretty certain it must have had the opposite effect as well, but he bit his tongue.

'He'd do well with that mob outside,' he said, 'to boost his numbers. Where the hell is their shore patrol?'

'We meet again, Mister Telford,' said Commodore Creighton, replacing the handset. 'And I think we need to understand how high feelings must be running among those fellows. No excuse for indiscipline, naturally. But still.'

Jack nodded. Yes, there'd be sailors out there with brothers, friends, among the dead at Mers-el-Kébir.

'And this?' Jack said to the consul as another junior clerk carried away more files. 'You're closing?'

'No choice. Resident-General Noguès has made it clear we're not welcome any more. The American Consul General, Mister Goold, will seal the place for us. And they'll look after matters on our behalf until we're able to open again. Rabat's closing too.'

'Back to Blighty?'

'Gibraltar first. Commodore Creighton has kindly agreed to take us.'

'With the *llanitos*, I hope? My god, Commodore, they can't survive another day on the quayside.'

'You think I like it any better than you, sir?' said Creighton. 'We just 'phoned the Port Admiral. Tried to persuade him one last time. A few more days. Give them some decent shelter while we finish cleaning the ships. He refused. Filthy mess. But I've no choice. We have to get those people out of here today.'

Jack breathed a sigh of relief, lit a Gauloise.

'To Gibraltar?' he said.

'We can be there in twelve hours. After that – I can't say.'

'They're British citizens,' said Jack. 'They'll go back to England, surely.'

'Mister Telford,' Creighton stood from behind the desk, 'they're not even wanted in Gibraltar. I shouldn't say this, but it was put to me in no uncertain terms not to take them back. They had a hard enough time getting rid of them in the first place, or so they told me. My orders are clear. To leave them here. But unthinkable. Can't do it. So, I'll deliver them to the Rock, regardless. Beyond that? Yes, some to England. Though not many. The last I heard, Jamaica has agreed to take two thousand. The rest, Mauritius and Portugal. South Africa as well – though they won't take anybody of Spanish extraction.'

'My god, are you serious?' Jack began, then stopped himself again. 'I'm sorry, Commodore. Not your fault. And I greatly admire your decision.' He was thinking about another skipper, of course, who'd faced a similar dilemma – Dickson and his orders from the ship owners that he must leave all those people on the quayside at Alicante. And Telford had his own duty, reached inside his pocket and took out an envelope, removed the folded paper it contained. 'Then Mister Bond,' he said, 'would you look at this? Perhaps see your way clear to signing it?'

Bond picked up his spectacles from the clutter on his desk, read the words Jack had typed. Then he took off the glasses again, chewed on the temple tips while he thought about the content.

'You know this won't carry any weight, don't you?' he said. 'But it might help, I suppose. Now where did I put...?'

He began searching among his papers, and Jack reached into his own inside pocket again, took out Negrín's pen.

'Here, sir, use mine.' Bond thanked him, admired the pen for a moment, then signed, found the official stamp and applied that also, while Jack turned to Creighton. 'Excuse me, Commodore, but how are you getting back?'

The taxi outside, Bond told him. Need to avoid those fellows at the front. And yes, said Creighton, he'd be happy to give Jack a lift.

All so horribly familiar. A quayside, but this time Casablanca. And thousands of displaced refugees, men, women and children, with nowhere to turn except, perhaps, to the humanity of just one man. Jack watched them from the *Bureau du Port*, the dock offices. Parrots screeched overhead and the place stank, as it always did, of hemp, oil and fish, though not as badly as the nauseating stench from the fifteen British merchant vessels so recently berthed.

The last occasion? Alicante. Fifteen months earlier. Hordes of people fleeing from Franco's fascists, his Italian allies. Most of them knowing the best they could expect, if they couldn't get away, was the concentration camp, their children stolen from them to be re-educated. The worst? A firing squad. To be buried in unmarked mass graves. They'd been promised ships to carry them abroad. Maybe they'd been promised by the very Ministry for Public Information in Valencia at which Paquita Gorroño had worked, Telford didn't know. But one way or the other there'd been no ships. Just one. A British tramp steamer, the *Stanbrook*, and her skipper, Archibald Dickson, with the strictest of instructions that he must get out of the port safely, with his cargo of tobacco, saffron and oranges – and under no circumstances, none, must he consider taking refugees on board.

Jack had been there. Seen the man's turmoil, his eventual orders to the crew, a crew of just twenty men – and Telford knew a few of them – to dump their cargoes back on the quayside and allow just a few dozen of those desperate thousands on board. The *Stanbrook* wasn't a big vessel, two hundred feet maybe, but Dickson had then allowed another few dozen up the gangway. Then a further bunch. And another. Until her decks were packed with almost two thousand souls. Jack among them. For he was on the *Guardia Civil's* death lists too.

And at midnight, with every light doused, Dickson had navigated his way out of Alicante harbour, out through the iron ring of Italian U-boats blockading the port and landed them all safely at Oran two days later. There the French had treated the refugees barbarically, but this was old hat, and now nothing surprised him. For here it was, repeating itself once more.

'How is she?' said Jack, and ran his hand gently through Morena's hair. The girl stirred, moaned quietly.

José and his family – his entire family now, the brother and sister-in-law, their three children, his black-garbed ancient mother and an equally elderly cousin – were exactly where he'd left them, at the side of the harbour's fish market and fishermen's association, the *confrérie de pêcheurs*. They'd rigged up a filthy tarpaulin to keep them from the worst of the heat. But even so, two days out there in the baking sun. The stink of fish. The constant screaming of seagulls.

'She has a fever,' said Lydia Linares. 'But at least she's asleep.'

The old mother muttered something through rotting teeth, something Jack didn't quite catch. But he looked around to see the Senegalese soldiers – that human barbed wire fence – wilting in the heat. They'd been there as long as the Gibraltarians, naturally, but there was no empathy of shared discomfort there. Quite the reverse.

'Look,' he said, 'I've just come back from the consulate. They'll be putting you on the ships soon. And yes, back to Gibraltar.'

He'd expected to see hope, excitement perhaps, in José's eyes, yet he found there only lethargy.

'Home,' said Linares, though without enthusiasm.

'No,' Jack told him. 'Only a day or two. Then it will be other boats. To other places.'

'England?' said José's brother.

'Perhaps. Though I'm not sure it's the safest place to be right now. Hitler's going to turn his attention there next, that's for sure.'

He knew what was coming, perhaps better than many. He'd seen at first hand the handiwork of Germany's bombers. At Durango and Guernica. In Madrid and Alicante.

'But *hombre*,' said José, 'we're British. If England has to fight, we should be there.'

'I thought you might say so,' said Jack, thinking how little his country deserved such loyalty. But he handed over the straw basket he'd brought. Goat's milk. Honey-soaked *ktefa*. Almond *briouats* and *m'hanncha* snake cake. Flatbread and cheese. All for the journey. 'Oh, and this.' He reached into his satchel and took out the letter Bond had signed. 'Look, it's not much. But in Gibraltar there'll be detention camps, everybody sorted into groups – depending on where they decide to send you all. Then there'll be a wait for ships. You must try to stay together. And show them this...'

José read the letter carefully, shared it with his brother.

To whom it may concern. This is to confirm that the family of José Linares is known to me, and that he has facility for accommodation, as well as sponsorship and self-sufficiency in London, through the good offices of Mr

109

Sydney Elliott, editor, Reynold's News. Then Elliott's address and Bond's official details, his signature, his stamp.

Jack still found it difficult to believe how easy it had been, wished he'd done the same for others. But he'd wired Elliott from the *Grande Poste.* Sydney would know people who could help, the same way he'd helped those Basque refugee kids in '37.

'Señor...' Linares began. 'Why us?'

Why? Jack thought. Chance he supposed. And something Archibald Dickson had said to him on the voyage to Oran. They'd been talking about fate, about the random nature of life, about the lottery that led two thousand to safety on the *Stanbrook* and left those countless others to their problematic futures, almost certain death, back in Alicante.

'You simply can't save them all,' Dickson had said. 'In life you must simply save who you can.'

'Like I said, José,' Jack told Linares, 'it probably won't help. In the end it's just a piece of paper. It's nothing. But look, I've written my friend's number on the bottom. Fingers crossed you'll end up in England and, if so, call him.'

But there were trucks now, rumbling along the wharves, *gendarmes* spilling from the vehicles, orders shouted to the Senegalese guards. To his left, Jack could see some of the local fishermen, passing down the lines of those about to be evacuated, handing out cups of water, portions of fried fish, and there was Manolo among them – the young man who'd been with him on the strike demonstration. They waved to each other, just at the precise moment when Telford felt a hand on his shoulder. Réchard.

'If you don't get out of here,' said the Frenchman, 'you're likely to find yourself in Gibraltar by tomorrow morning.'

'This,' Jack snapped and pointed to those huddled masses. 'It's barbaric, Louis. Just bloody barbaric.'

'It's necessity, *Monsieur* Telford,' Réchard shouted, before giving orders to the soldiers, told them to get everybody on their feet, to get them moving. Then he stopped looked back over his shoulder. 'It's war, my friend.'

The Senegalese were galvanised into action.

'*Levez-vous!*' they yelled. '*Allez, allez.*' Up, get up.

They began dragging people to their feet, prodding the slowest with their bayonets. And when one of them noticed Lydia struggling to lift Morena in her arms, the devil raised his boot, kicked her backside. José grabbed at the man and was smacked in the face by the soldier's rifle butt.

'You!' Jack yelled as he ran back to them, but another of the guards stuck out his foot, sent Telford sprawling across the sleepers of the dock's railway track. 'Bastard,' he spat, wiped blood from a split lip. But the soldier was staring at him down the barrel of his own gun, the point of his bayonet perilously close to Jack's throat.

And there he stayed as the sad procession trudged on towards the waiting wharves. It was the last he saw of them, lost them in the crowds. But later he at least found Creighton once more. He was standing at the foot of the *Balfe*'s gangway, checking his inventories.

'Well, Telford, we'll be under way before long. But good god, man, your lip.'

'Nothing serious,' he lied. It was beginning to swell badly, to slur his speech. And it felt like one of his teeth was loose.

'Did you find your friends?'

'I did, sir. Though lost them again now, I'm afraid.'

'Too bad. But we'll look after them all. As well as we're able. Keep them all on the decks anyhow. The holds still not fit for pigs, I'm afraid. And anyway, all these children. They'd have to go down the ladders. Dangerous. Too damned dangerous. But you'll write all this up, I suppose.'

'It feels a bit too much like *déjà vu* for me, sir. Alicante. A skipper there with the same problem. Managed to cram nearly two thousand on decks much smaller than these. It's been a privilege, Commodore. Really.'

'We do what we can, Mister Telford. No more and no less.'

They shook hands, the last of the *Balfe*'s allocated thousand about to board. And for just a minute, he was tempted to join them. Head back to England. But then he almost imagined he saw Fidel Constantino, Sergio Sifre and now Raúl Ramos too, waiting for him on the quayside. No, his unfinished business, by whatever fate had brought him, was here in North Africa. For now.

'Yes, he said something similar. Captain Dickson. Have you come across him by any chance?'

'Dickson? Can't say I have.'

'Well, *bon voyage* anyway. Think I'll just have one last look for my friends.'

He lifted his fist in a last salute, walked away. Actually, Jack knew he'd stay in the harbour and watch them all leave. It seemed the least he could do.

'Wait, Telford.' Jack had gone no more than a dozen paces, turned to see Creighton puzzling over something. 'Dickson, you say? Master of the *Stanbrook*?'

'The same, sir.' Jack conjured up his memory of Captain Dickson, his battered cap. And the First Engineer, Henry Lillystone. Seventy and still at sea. Brilliant mechanic and taken Jack under his wing.

'I'm sorry, old man. Yes, I do remember now. But you didn't know? Must have been – November, if I'm not mistaken. U-boat attack in the North Sea. The *Stanbrook* went down with all hands I'm afraid. No survivors.'

October – December 1940

Hélène Bénatar

Where had it all begun? At the Excelsior, naturally. But the Excelsior of their new world, the world of Vichy and the thousand-year Reich. He recalled his arrival in Burgos, two years back, to find the place full of strutting Germans and Italians. Here, today, the same. No longer a respectful distance either, between Réchard and the other customers. Now the Commandant was lucky to have a table on the terrace at all, little choice but to rub shoulders, literally, with the *Boches*. And on this day, towards the end of October, they'd been out in force. Loud, as only Germans could be loud, one of them, beige civilian suit and a Nazi armband, stood at their table – in truth, five or six tables pulled together – amusing his audience with some anecdote or other but pausing now and then, the gap-toothed grin falling from his thick, damp lips, eyes rolling theatrically in his head, one hand caressing his heavily pomaded hair, the other gesturing towards the brasserie where, as usual, there was music playing on the gramophone. Good music, Telford thought, even though the sound was metallic, tinny. Josephine Baker singing *Sous le ciel d'Afrique*. He'd not long bought the same record to add to his collection, and *Princesse Tam-Tam* might not be his favourite film, but it had its attractions.

'Who is he, Louis, d'you know?'

'You've not met?' murmured Réchard. 'Auer. The Führer's top official here. Diplomat. With the Armistice Committee. But he's Gestapo. Tells me it's his mission to persuade Berlin to take more interest in North Africa. And I don't think he means just making sure the terms of the armistice are met.'

'You!' Auer shouted at one of the waiters. Jack knew the man.

Fernando. And yes, another Anarchist. 'You! Turn off that *neger* racket, can't you?'

Telford spoke little of their language but it took no imagination to know what the German word meant, planted there within Auer's French.

'Of course,' said Fernando. Jack had never known him be so polite. 'Right away, *mein herr.*' He finished serving the drinks, disappeared into the brasserie, while Auer made some aside to his *Wehrmacht* and black-uniformed SS friends, fists now resting on his hips. The music stopped, the smile returning to his face.

'Shit,' Jack whispered, brought the cognac glass to his own lips, though he didn't drink.

Auer continued his story.

'Be careful, my friend,' Réchard told him. 'These are dangerous times. And the look on your face would sour cream. It rather gives you away.'

True enough, Jack supposed. He felt as though his honeymoon with Casablanca had been over for a while. He'd been wedded to the place yet presently found that the almost physical passion, which once so endeared him to his new love, had become tedious, monotonous. For the French to treat the town as an amusement park, a playground, before the surrender had been endearing. Now it seemed the epitome of betrayal. And that the Germans, the Italians, should defile the old girl in the same way? Almost unbearable. Something else had changed as well, for it no longer seemed possible to conduct any form of business unless it took place in one of the town's more disreputable bars, or the casino, or the bordellos of Bousbir. As though Casablanca had become a whore herself.

'How can you stand it, Louis? Bad enough for me. But you...'

'Me? Just glad I'm not in Algiers.'

The news from Algiers seemed worse every week. A month back, the windows of Jewish-owned stores there were smashed by thugs from Doriot's French Popular Party. People attacked, heads broken. Two weeks ago, the citizenship of more than one hundred thousand Algerian Jews simply rescinded. By Pétain. By Vichy. Made them stateless, refugees in their own land. Their property confiscated, stripped of jobs in government, as teachers, as journalists, in finance, and limiting the numbers who could work as doctors, nurses, lawyers. There was talk as well of internment camps, of being required to wear patches, the yellow star, stitched to their clothing.

But now, music again in the *brasserie*. Fernando smirked in the doorway, caught Auer's attention, cocked his head and cupped his ear with his hand.

'Better, *mein herr?*'

Rina Ketty's version of *J'Attendrai*. I will wait. The song had become an informal anthem. For those no longer waiting for love but, rather, for liberation. Auer looked furious, caught the smiles on one or two of the customers' faces, extended an imperious arm, fingers stretched wide towards Réchard as though demanding some action and Jack noticed the almost imperceptible nod the commandant offered him in return.

'Excuse me a moment,' said Réchard, and stood from the table. Jack grabbed his wrist.

'Louis...'

Réchard glared down at Telford's hand.

'Stay out of this, *monsieur*,' he growled, dragged his sleeve from Jack's wrist. Jack felt abashed. He'd taken a liberty. His association with Réchard could not be classed as a beautiful friendship but they'd certainly grown closer. Last Sunday, for example, the commandant's invitation to join himself and Monique at the races.

Quite an excursion. Out to the Anfa track, the hippodrome, but first Réchard's guided tour of the area, the villas of the locally rich and famous perched around the hillsides overlooking the sea, and a drive past the Hôtel Anfa, now almost entirely taken over by the German Armistice Committee, all six floors, and the red banners of the Reich with their swastikas hanging down each side of the building's bullnose façade. Two hundred staff, Réchard told him. God only knew how many German soldiers besides. They could hear their machine gun practice down on the beach. At least, Telford *hoped* it was practice. There'd been rumours.

But all seemed normal enough – normal, at least, for this rabbit hole world in which he now found himself – by the time they'd parked outside the racetrack's functionally modern white grandstand building. All the usual suspects, Jack had laughed later as they picked up their programmes. The entrance lobby was packed with race-goers, guttural German everywhere, though hardly a uniform in sight – their pretense at maintaining a low profile. He'd half-expected to find Captain Fox, though he hadn't seen him since their last encounter at the Café de Verdun, but just ahead of them were the civil engineer Williamson and that despicable wretch Bromley, the mining consultant. Jack thought he must feel in good company here with these Nazis. 'And the fellow who has Bromley's ear?' he said.

'New boy in town,' Réchard replied. 'Let's say hello.'

He linked arms with Monique, still studying her race card. They made a handsome couple, he in his immaculate dress whites, she in scarlet satin.

'This one,' said Monique. 'For the three o'clock. My hairdresser says...'

The rest was lost in a babble of introductions – frigidly curt where Bromley was concerned. But the stranger? Older, though athletic. Hatchet-faced, eyes the palest blue Jack had ever seen. Welch, he'd said. Kingsley Welch. A trade delegation from London.

'But working with the Americans I'm told,' said Réchard.

'A helping hand,' Welch smiled. There was something resentful about it, haughty, as though he was bored having to answer the same question, time and time again. 'Nothing more. Greasing the wheels. But we expect the Yanks to conclude their deal with Vichy in a matter of months. A US-Morocco trade deal. Won't that be something?'

'Will it help with the rationing, *Monsieur* Welch?' said Monique.

Tea, sugar, petrol already in limited supply, prices going through the roof, complaints about taxes – and shortages.

'Probably not, my dear,' Welch told her, then ran his tongue along his lower lip, gazed down at her cleavage. Monique blushed. 'But it might just steal a march on the Germans, don't you think?'

Réchard, however, was more concerned about missing the start, invited them all to his private glass fronted box and balcony on the first floor. The opening spectacle, a *t'bourida*, the *fantasia*, as the French called it. Fifteen scarlet-robed riders, blue capes, turbans, facing them along the rail, saluting the audience with a display of their long Kabyle muskets, then regrouping across the width of the racetrack in a dressed line until, with a shout, they started the *talqa*, the charge on their tasselled Arabian mounts – the line perfectly maintained as they thundered down the track for the finish, two hundred yards, where their muzzle-loaders fired in a volley, more accurately a single deafening report. That was the skill of the thing.

'Magnificent,' said Welch. 'Bloody magnificent. And you, Mister Telford, how long are you in Casablanca? Business here?'

Really, he didn't seem very interested. Almost as though he already knew the answer.

'In a manner of speaking. I'm a correspondent.' No reaction. There was usually a reaction. 'But I'll be away in Rabat next week. It seems I'm wanted there for some reason.'

Welch put an arm around Jack's shoulder, led him away to the bar.

'Rabat, yes. Miss the place. And what do you make of all this?' Welch asked him. 'Can't quite get one's head accustomed to seeing the French as the enemy, don't you think?'

'A problem for all of us.'

The loudspeaker system announced the impending start of the first race, the *Derby des Trois Ans*, for three-year-old colts and fillies, nineteen hundred metres.

'Coming down to the paddock?' Monique shouted to him as she and her husband headed for the staircase.

'Think I'll stay here,' he said. 'Enjoy a gin and tonic. But please, Mister Welch, join them. I should catch up with a few people while I'm here.'

In truth he'd seen somebody who troubled him. He knew the man, Chabat, a weasel renowned throughout the medina as an informant. And now here he was with a bunch of these Germans in their Sunday best, and the only man in uniform, General von Wulisch. Jack had seen him often enough, monocled, parading around town in his open-topped Mercedes 770. Jack ordered his drink, settled himself behind one of the pillars, lit a cigarette, watched Chabat a while, wondered what was going on and finally took himself down to the paddock. The smells of straw and manure from the stables, caftan-robed boys grooming their charges, photographers, local journalists, laughter and cheering, the race commentator over the sound system announcing runners and riders, the soft thud of hooves on the sands of the parade ground, that slight oily scent of horse, and the sweet fragrance of the pink flowers from the daphne bushes surrounding the paddock itself. He found Réchard peering through his binoculars as the horses gathered at the starting line.

'Louis, do you have a moment?' he'd said.

'We have money riding on this race,' said Réchard. 'Won't it wait?'

'It's Chabat,' Jack told him, as quietly as he was able. 'What's he up to, d'you know?'

'My god, Telford, not here.' He looked around, checked they couldn't be heard.

'They're off,' shouted Monique. The starter's flag went down and the ground shook as the horses went straight to the gallop.

'Why are you asking?' said Réchard, taking Jack's arm and leading him away from the crowd.

'I just saw him with the Germans. And is it true, Louis? Word on the street says he told them about hidden weapons at Roches-Noires.'

Hitler had given instructions to Vichy about heavily limiting the size of the French army – and it was an open secret that some of the local army officers had been acting on their own initiative, hiding guns and ammunition, despite the severe penalties they faced.

'Why the hell do you always have to put me in this position? But strictly off the record yes, it's true. And my unfortunate duty to arrest those responsible. But these days *Monsieur* Chabat seems to have an entirely different scheme.'

'Which is?'

'Not here,' he murmured. 'Let's go up on the terrace.' He turned back to his wife. 'Monique,' he shouted, 'I'm going to show Telford the view from the top deck.'

She smiled and waved.

'Don't worry, Commandant,' said Welch, 'we'll keep an eye on her.'

Réchard touched fingertips to the peak of his *képi*, led the way back to the stairs, while the commentator worked himself into a frenzy. Jack wanted to ask about Welch, but the commandant was already busy acknowledging the greetings of those still inside, and between those greetings he began to answer Telford's question. In short, staccato bursts.

'The soldiers who landed here in July – remember?' Of course, he remembered. The Gibraltarians going out, the dejected soldiers of defeated France coming in.

'They all signed up again, didn't they?'

'Not all of them, no. Some deserters. Most of them heading south. Brazzaville. Or Fort Lamy. But others? Seems they'll only settle for London. And London means they have to get to Gibraltar first. It would take a swine like Chabat to come up with this one. A team of his bastards doing the round of the bars, making it known they can arrange passage. If the deserters are desperate enough, they'll hand over two hundred *francs*. Then it's by truck to Fédala. Boat. But find the *Sûreté* waiting for them. Or the Germans maybe. After that? Anybody's guess.'

'And if he doesn't find deserters, presumably there are plenty of other marks out there for scum like him to fleece.'

They paused briefly at the top of the first staircase. The bar again. Chabat still there with the Germans. He looked up, caught Jack staring at him, turned to glance at Réchard.

'Come on,' said the commandant, making some show of ac-knowledgement, a raised hand, almost a Nazi salute, to von Wulisch.

Yes, plenty of marks in Casablanca, Jack thought as they head-ed up to the second floor. He'd seen the queues at the American consulate. All those refugees, more every day, heading for the USA, needed visas. Pending visa decisions they'd be given a temporary *permit de séjour* – if they were lucky. Before they could get one they'd have to provide the documentation for their visas. About sponsors in the USA. About proof of their finances. About their onward travel tickets, usually by ship from Lisbon, which they must already have purchased. If they couldn't provide them, there was no choice. The internment camps. But some of them who'd escaped might have managed to bring portable wealth with them, hidden diamonds, rubies, emeralds, gold jewellery. And those folk were the constant prey of phoney boat skippers, bogus shipping agents, forgers, pickpockets. No, Casa wasn't pretty any more. Yet there, in the sun, the green parasols of the grandstand's terrace, the sea in the distance, it was still hard not to love the place just a little.

'I'm sorry, Louis,' he said, when they found a quiet corner of the spectators' wall. 'Bad luck.'

Réchard was tearing up his betting slip, the race over, the horses cantering back towards the paddock, Monique's filly come in a poor fifth.

'You win some and then… But why this interest in Chabat? No story there for you, not if you don't want your throat cut.'

'Curiosity, really. It's working with Bénatar and the refugees, I suppose.'

'I always preferred Voltaire on curiosity, rather than this nonsense about cats,' said Réchard. 'Judge a man by his questions, no? But that reminds me. Your Spanish friend, Granell. Managed to track him down. Camp Morand. Not there now though. Tried to escape. Twice. Transferred to Bossuet.'

'Where the hell's that?'

'In this case, *Monsieur* Telford, even Voltaire would say the same. You don't want to know. Old fortress at Dheya. He'll not come out of there alive.'

Jack remembered the first time he'd seen Amado on the deck of the *Stanbrook*. Cool as a cucumber among all the misery of defeat. His only possession? A Browning automatic rifle.

'I'd not bet on that one either, Louis. He'll end up fighting the Nazis again, one way or the other. For de Gaulle as well, I'm guessing.'

They lit cigarettes, sauntered across to the rooftop bar for a beer, fifty minutes until the next race.

'De Gaulle? Finished now, I think. Men here who might have – well, not any more.'

Jack laughed.

'You, Louis?'

A cooling breeze had come up from the northwest, from the Atlantic, wafting the palm fronds on the farther side of the track.

'That would be treason. And you know what happens to traitors.'

Early August, and a Vichy court had sentenced de Gaulle to death *in absentia*, stripped him of his rank, his property. And then, at the end of the previous month, the last week in September, they'd received news of the general's failed attempt to take Dakar for the Free French. True, Britain's navy had their own part in the failure but Free France now consisted of no more than a few thousand men in England plus the French Congo and Chad – more or less. There'd been repercussions.

He'd been teaching one of his English classes when the whole city was shaken to its roots by the Amiot bombers roaring overhead with their Bloch fighter escorts from the Médiouna airfield. On their way to bomb Gibraltar it later transpired. Two days of bombing, *Le Petit Marocain* with proudly displayed photographs of the damage they'd done. And Jack had hoped to god the Linares family wasn't still there. But would they have been any safer in England? Hell, the Blitz. It didn't bear thinking about.

'These days,' said Jack, 'one man's treason is another's patriotism. One fellow's resistance, the other side's terrorism.'

'That's the bloody pacifist in you. A habit you'll have to break, *monsieur*. Perhaps you'd be less philosophical if you'd been in England these past few months.'

Pacifist? Jack thought. He would once have said so. Yet the blood of at least three people on his hands. And he'd followed the news from home like a man possessed. Bought every paper he was able to understand. Even picked up a copy of the Germans' own propaganda sheets, just to balance things up. A different perspective. The Battle of Britain, Churchill had called it. Heroic. Hurricanes and Spitfires against the German bombers trying to destroy the country's airfields. Hundreds of pilots from all corners of the world – Poles, New Zealanders, Canadians and the rest – flying alongside Britain's own boys. Hitler's invasion fleets waiting on the Vichy French coast until Britain's air defences were destroyed. How long could it last? Not long, he'd been certain. But then, at the end of August, a change in the strategy, British bombers in large-scale attacks on Berlin. The Germans in retaliation switching their focus for more intensive bombing of London and other civilian targets. Jack had wrestled with the ethics, remembered Guernica – but he didn't wrestle with it long. The Blitz. And Britain's cities at the mercy of Hitler's Heinkels and Dorniers, though the RAF's airfields largely left alone. The new fighters now in production able to turn the tide until, finally, around the time the Free French and Royal Navy were taking a pounding at Dakar, Hitler was forced to abandon his plans for the invasion – for now, at least. The Blitz still raging but…

'You're right,' said Jack. 'I've never felt so useless in my life. Managed to telephone my sister – did I say?'

'She's in London?'

'No, Worcester. And she's safe. They've only had one attack. A lone bomber. A few people killed. Lots injured. But that's all there's been. Fingers crossed.'

'Worcester – it's near London?'

'No. What we call the West Midlands. South of Birmingham. He raised his hand, pointed with the other forefinger. London,' he said. 'Here, Birmingham. On the River Severn. Pretty. I was at school there. My father ran the Old Worcester Bank in town. Before the war – the last one.'

Dammit, what was this? Nostalgia again. He slapped his hand on the top of the wall, caught a glimpse of Monique's scarlet frock over in the paddock, posing in the line for a souvenir photograph.

'Let's hope it will all be over soon,' said Réchard.

'It'll get far worse before it gets better, Louis. And it's payback time for both our countries, don't you think? We turned a blind eye to Ethiopia, to Spain, to Czechoslovakia – and for all the help we gave Poland we might as well have not bothered declaring war. Makes you wonder. But Chabat – why do I ask about Chabat? Because he may be on the wrong side. He may be a bastard. Still, for all that, he's doing something. Wicked as it might be, and even if it's only for the money, Louis. But me…'

Yes, it had been quite an excursion. But this had been the previous Sunday and now, at the Excelsior, he'd still been thinking about Chabat, about his own inertia, when Réchard returned from inside the *brasserie*, saluted the Germans as he passed. And the music had changed again. One of Wilfried Sommer's jolly little numbers.

Auf Dem Dach Der Welt. Jack hadn't a clue about the lyrics but he always thought of it as Blitzkreig jazz. Nazi swing. Oh, the *Boches* knew how to have a good time alright.

'Well, Louis?' said Jack. 'Just doing your job? Fernando sacked now?'

Réchard counted out change from his pocket, threw it on the table.

'Perhaps you've outlived your welcome here, *Monsieur* Telford. And don't ever lay your hands on me like that again. Understand?'

Jack stubbed out his cigarette, picked up his trilby and stood as well.

'Oh, I'll be out of your hair soon enough, Louis. For now. Rabat. I told you, I've had an invitation. But I'll be back.'

His Sherifian Majesty, *Sidi* Muhammad ben Youssef, Lord Muhammad, settled himself on his cushion. The sixteenth day of *Ramadan*, and the *Maghrib* sunset prayers bringing the day's fasting to an end. The sultan picked up his eating bowl from the enormous silver tray between them and fingered a good helping of goat *tajine* into his mouth. The attendant at his side leaned over at once to clean a dribble of juice from the imperial chin – or rather from the dark stubble framing the sultan's mellow features. Or perhaps, thought Jack, it was to save the pure white *djellaba* from serious stain. Saffron, he knew to his own cost, could be the very devil.

'You see?' said the sultan. 'I like to lead a simple life.'

'Yes, I see that, Highness,' Jack replied, trying his best not to stare – either at the jet and gold damascene screen gleaming in the lamplight just behind *Sidi* Muhammad, or at the two members of his Black Guard who flanked him. The biggest men he'd ever seen in his life.

'I like to drive, of course. You could write this?'

'Should I? Which car, sir – your favourite?'

Jack imagined there must be many.

'I have one, Mister Telford. One only. I am a modern man. The readers of this magazine should know that, I think.'

Telford liked the fellow. He was twenty-nine. Two young sons sitting on their own cushions around the colossal tray also, there in the sultan's private apartments. Modern, yes, he thought. The stories were legend. How he'd inherited a harem of a thousand women yet, in one supremely progressive sweep of the royal prerogative had reduced the number down to a mere one hundred. Jack bit his lip to prevent a smile, wondered what happened to redundant royal concubines.

'And you enjoy tennis, I think?' he asked instead.

'Walking too. In my garden. I am a keen gardener.'

The garden. Telford had been taken to see. You could have fitted Hyde Park inside the grounds easily. Gabizon had met him at the station, driven him to the hotel – the Ville de Paris, of course, not the Transatlantic with its venomous arachnids – then collected him again as it grew dark, back to the Place Lyautey and south into that district of the city Jack still considered to be the Sultanate Quarter. The Imperial education offices and college, the grand library, the seemingly endless barracks of the Black Guard, open parkland stretching down to the parade grounds and the sprawling green and white Dar al-Makhzan Palace itself.

'You're certain, Highness, that the editors actually want me to write this article?' There was a collective gasp from the white-robed ministers, a dozen of them, also seated within this circle. 'I apologise, sir, I meant no discourtesy but I have no contract with Henry Luce. And I assume his editorial team would have expected this photographer they've sent to write the captions. It's the normal way for *Life*, I imagine.'

He looked around for help but neither Gabizon, nor the two boys, nor the twelve wise men returned his baleful stare. And he thought about a passage he liked in the *Seven Pillars*, the one in which Lawrence describes his first meeting with Feisal. The breach of etiquette when he told the prince that yes, he liked Wadi Safra well enough – though it was far from Damascus. As if to say: what are you doing here, so far from the place you *should* be? But then – well, Lawrence was about to help launch the Arab Revolt. And Jack? Fine, it was only an article for *Life* magazine, not quite the same league, yet he hoped *Sidi* Muhammad might show something of the same good grace Sherif Feisal had extended to young Captain Lawrence.

124

'But how could I trust them, Mister Telford? They are Americans. I admire them, yet I do not quite trust them. But our friend Gabizon spoke to Mister Luce's young lady. He told them you are my press officer. They have assured us they will print that which may be written.' He seemed pleased with himself, while Jack fought hard against his own rising fit of pique. One of those moments of outrage. Against the presumption. About how nice to have at least been asked. Yet – well, perhaps he should speak to Gabizon later. 'But admire them,' *Sidi* Muhammad went on, 'yes. When our guests have gone and the photographs are taken, you must come to my villa. Across the garden. We have electric cookers there. Westinghouse, Mister Telford.'

'Guests, sir?'

Telford was not entirely comfortable. Partly it was sitting for so long on the marble floor, cushion or no cushion. Partly, the simple truth. He had never taken too well to eating with his fingers – easier to scoop up the rices and meats on chunks of flatbread. Partly the lack of preparation. Gabizon had told him that *Sidi* Muhammad, having been so immensely impressed with the Bou Arfa report, now wished to be interviewed, open himself more to the outside world. In preparation for – what, exactly? And now this. He felt he was being played for a fool.

'You did not tell him?' the sultan asked Gabizon in the most benign of rebukes.

'Highness…' Some of Gabizon's food shot from his mouth.

'Never mind. You see, Mister Telford, General Weygand comes to visit tomorrow afternoon. He is Delegate General for all French Africa now, did you know?'

'I did, sir, yes. But I can't be certain whether he thinks his jurisdiction also covers the territories held by Free France.'

'Then you shall ask him, my friend. What do you say, Gabizon? *Le loup dans la bergerie, non?*'

The wolf in the sheepfold. Jack almost gagged on his goat.

'Highness…' he began, but the sultan smiled, held up his hand.

'Merely my childish jest, Mister Telford. Yet you shall observe. The throne room is well equipped for that purpose. But not for

125

photographers. So it shall be you, and nobody else, who may then tell the readers of *Life* magazine how skilful are we Moors in the arts of diplomacy.'

And so it came to pass, late the following afternoon, Jack enjoying another grandstand view, this time from the parapet above the main gate. But still annoyed.

'Why the hell didn't you tell me?'

Gabizon had made himself scarce as soon as yesterday evening's meal was done and he'd been conveyed back and forth by one of the sultan's drivers alone.

'Because you might not have come,' said Gabizon, and Jack had no immediate answer.

The small convoy of black limousines rolled down past the cluster of buildings on the far side of the dusty parade ground and the sultan's mounted military band struck up *La Marseillaise*. They then moved swiftly into *Maréchal, Nous Voilà!* New order. *La Marseillaise* no longer permitted performance unless followed immediately by this Vichy anthem to Pétain. Black Guard infantrymen lining the approach road – the same scarlet tunics, white and red turbans – presented arms, and the same tall sub-Saharan black warriors from the tribes far to the south. A troop of cavalry lowered their lances. It was all so precisely timed, the cars halting outside the gate, their passengers dripping with army and navy braid, a few diplomats in black suits, stiff winged shirt collars. The American photographer at his work.

'Weygand?' said Jack, almost a rhetorical question, for the man's face had been a regular feature of the front pages ever since Telford arrived on the *Stanbrook*. The sparse moustache, pinched cheeks, the trademark jodhpurs and riding boots. A khaki chestful of medals and the sun gleaming on the mass of gold oak leaves adorning his *képi*. At his side, almost, another face from the papers, the more slender but equally decorated figure of Noguès, no longer Morocco's Resident-General, now Inspector-General instead for the French Army in North Africa. Noguès had been quoted as saying this was a great honour – though even the urchins on the street knew it for a demotion.

'Weygand,' Gabizon whispered as, below them, *Sidi* Muhammad stepped from the crowd of his own matching ministers, that

126

gathering of pure white robes, to accept the formal salute of the French officers. At his side, one of his attendants waving a white banner. Peace and harmony.

'I read Harris,' said Jack. '*France, Spain and the Rif.* Not changed, has it? Not a single European in the *Makhzan*. Not even you.'

'I am the closest creature he has to a European,' Gabizon replied. 'But no, not part of his court. Merely the Sultan's Jew – I told you this. But come, we need to take our place.'

Gabizon led him down through a series of alleyways, between the houses, which the sultan rented to trusted workers in the city, skirting the inner courtyard until they reached that part of the complex with its reception chambers leading one by one to the throne room. And the throne room was magnificent. The rugs, he thought. Rich reds and blues all over the entire marble floor. A colossal chandelier and a colonnade of Moorish arched columns running the length of each side. Within the archways, *mashrabiya* screens, and behind the screens a passage in which Jack and Gabizon sequestered themselves, nostrils relishing the pine resin aromas of the lattice. But it was hot in there, airless. Yet the meeting was mercifully short. The formalities. The sultan's apology that *Ramadan* prevented them from sharing food but if the generals should care to eat – but no, they did not. Perhaps some water only. *Sidi* Muhammad edged towards his throne, the low double-seated chair, gilded arms and legs, the cushion and backrest red velvet, and he waved a hand toward the two matching seats provided specifically for the generals, the rest of their entourage standing behind.

'Gentlemen,' he said, 'you are both most welcome. But you especially, General Weygand, to this most loyal Protectorate. And General Noguès, you have been our shield. We wish you well with your new duties, yet these are dark days and my people are troubled by whatever might come next.'

'Only a year, Highness,' Noguès replied, 'since we broadcast together from this very throne room. So full of hope. Confidence. And now, all those sons of Morocco who fell in the battle for France, or made prisoners-of-war...'

'Fell in battle, General – or murdered by Germany's army after they were told to lay down their arms? So many thousands of

127

them. My staff, my ministers,' he gestured towards the members of his *Makhzan,* 'overwhelmed daily by the numbers of mothers and wives begging us to know the fate of sons and husbands and fathers.'

'We have heard the stories, Highness,' said Weygand. 'But I am here to assure you that the sacrifice of your people shall not be forgotten, nor the devotion shown to Morocco by General Noguès diminished.'

'*Our* people,' Gabizon whispered in Jack's ear. 'We die on the battlefields of France but still not *their* people.'

'Truly?' said the sultan. 'You shall have your Residency at Algiers, I understand. While the Germans have their own in the heart of Morocco, at Casablanca, the Hôtel Anfa. How long, General, before our instructions come directly from Berlin, before my people are treated like the Jews of Warsaw?'

'The Jewish question,' Weygand replied, 'is one also troubling our own government, sir. We cannot afford to have fifth columnists undermining our efforts – whether they may be Freemasons, or Reds or, yes, Jews.' Jack could sense Gabizon bristling at his side. 'You must understand this, surely?' the general went on. 'I am certain we shall all receive instruction from Vichy in due course, and we hope we have your assurance that the necessary edict, your *dahir,* will follow immediately after.'

'General,' said *Sidi* Muhammad, 'I confess I have never understood these obsessions with the Jews. Did they not fight and die for you at Sedan, at Arras and everywhere else? But here the Jews are among the seven million under my direct rule, are they not? After all, the Israelites were here long before the Prophet – peace be upon Him – brought us to Islam. Long before we Arabians settled here from the east. Perhaps even before the *Imazighen,* the free men you call Berbers – though that is before history even began. We have a saying. Scratch a Berber and you will find a Jew. But here there is no Jew, no Berber, no Arab, no black Haratin from the south, only Moroccans. We are a *shlada,* a salad, different elements chopped into a single dish.'

'Still, you will comply, I trust,' said Weygand.

'These days, General, I suppose we must all comply – at least to the level the times require.'

Well, thought Jack, the sultan knows this much at least. It would take only a word from Vichy to the German Armistice Committee, from the Armistice Committee to Berlin, and Morocco would be crawling with Hitler's tanks.

'As you say, Highness,' said Noguès, 'not entirely the world any of us would choose. But I hope you will always remember my devotion, my loyalty, to Morocco.'

The tone of the man's voice, the hint of bitterness behind the words, told Jack just how much Noguès must resent his demotion. Telford could almost taste it.

'And there shall be no direct orders from Berlin, sir,' Weygand insisted. But he glanced around at his officers – hoping for reassurance? Jack wondered. Or was it simply that he might be overstepping his mark, not certain whether one of his subordinates might report his words back to Vichy? 'Marshal Pétain will not allow such a disgrace, you may be certain.'

Not the world any of them would have chosen indeed, thought Jack. Weygand might be loyal to Pétain but Vichy had hardly reciprocated, the general out of favour now, and dispatched here almost to exile.

'But these negotiations with the Americans, Highness,' said Noguès, taking a handkerchief from his pocket and wiping the sweat from his neck. 'Perhaps it might be wise to put those on hold? I'm sure Marshal Pétain would be keen to have our involvement.'

'The Americans?' said the sultan. 'Oh, the negotiations make slow progress, my friends. And you may rest assured we shall keep you informed.' He paused for a moment, to gauge the response. But there wasn't one. Testing them, Jack thought, for weakness. And there, he'd found one. 'Yet I was hoping,' *Sidi* Muhammad pressed ahead, 'that you might have spoken to me of Franco.'

'Franco?' Noguès repeated, earned himself a scowl of reproach from Weygand.

'You do not know, General?' *Sidi* Muhammad smiled, as though he had found a second weakness. 'There are problems with Spain. Franco wants our phosphates, it seems. He needs Morocco. All of Morocco. The start of a new Spanish empire, perhaps. To rebuild their ruined economy.'

'These are merely rumours,' said Weygand. 'Naturally, but...'

'If France cannot protect Morocco from Spain, sir, then Morocco must protect itself.'

'Highness, I was briefed about these sentiments you possess. Towards the nationalist faction among your people. Understandable, perhaps. But you must not view the armistice as anything but a temporary imperative. Not a defeat, merely a transition from one state to another. The end of failed republicanism. Our new French State.'

'And the occupied zone?'

'Unacceptable, of course. But it shall not last forever. A temporary expediency only.'

'Expediency, General. But I can see it in your eyes. You are a Frenchman. And the horror of Paris, of France, occupied by the Germans. I cannot imagine how my heart should break if I were in your position. Oh, but perhaps – for you see, gentlemen, never a tear shed for my own country's occupation by France. An irony, no?' But Jack could see no shred of discomfort from the generals and their staff while, from outside, somewhere in the distance, a *mu'azzin*'s cry. 'Ah,' said the sultan, 'the hour of *Asr*. Time for our prayers, gentlemen. I hope you will forgive us if we bring this audience to an end.'

'Naturally, Highness,' said Noguès. 'But the Jews, sir?'

'The Jews are People of the Scriptures, General. They deserve as much protection as falls within my power to afford them. Yet let us see what Marshal Pétain demands of us.'

The sultan stood from his throne, formal farewells and obeisances, the Frenchmen waiting while *Sidi* Muhammad was escorted from the chamber. In their hidden passageway, Jack was glad to escape his dark and dusty confinement, but Gabizon held him back, for the sultan had stopped, turned to face Weygand once more.

'You know, General,' he said, 'there are many things this war must sweep aside.'

Later, as they sat together in the limousine, returning Telford to the Hôtel Ville de Paris, Jack asked what he'd meant.

'His Imperial Highness,' Gabizon replied, 'claims ascendancy from the daughter of the Prophet – peace be upon Him. He says

Fatima the Resplendent One came to him in a vision, told him the Americans cannot be trusted but that it shall be the Americans who will help set his people free.'

'But for the war to sweep things aside,' said Jack, 'mustn't we first win? Free France must win. Feels like a long shot though. Just now, I mean.'

'If this is written, then yes, Allah – God – will show us the way.'

'I think I may already have found a small way to point Allah in the right direction.' And he explained about Chabat, the way that filthy piece of scum was betraying those wanting to fight for de Gaulle – Jack's own modest scheme for thwarting Chabat's snitches. 'What do you think?' said Jack.

'I think you have found a way to fight your own corner of this war, *Monsieur* Telford. You must do it. But if you want names of those who might help more directly you should speak with *Madame* Bénatar again.'

By the time they were back in the town centre another of Rabat's fogs had settled.

'I'll do that,' said Jack. 'I should be back there tomorrow night.'

'And got enough for the article?'

'You should still have warned me.' He'd spent the morning following the photographer around the palace complex and grounds, a rare privilege. Pictures of the crimson and gold royal carriage. The sultan's mosque. The two boys at their studies in the Imperial College. And several posed images of *Sidi* Muhammad's ministers and wise men bowing to the ground and chanting *How great is the sultan!* as though he were truly there in their midst. Wonderful stuff. But yes, he said, enough.

The robed chauffeur came around to open Jack's door outside the hotel, and Telford gave them a cheery wave as he crossed towards the entrance steps.

'Wait!' shouted Gabizon. Jack turned to see him leaning out of the Ford Mercury convertible sedan – a gift, naturally, from the American trade delegation – with Jack's satchel in his hand. Dammit, he'd left it on the back seat, walked towards the car, smiling, hand stretched out, wondering what Henry Ford might make of his gift being so freely used by the Sultan's Jew.

'I'd forget my own head,' he began, 'if it weren't…'

Gabizon had jumped out of the car, stood quickly in front of him, smiling and, in that instant, there was a single *crack*, Gabizon thrown forward, the smile still fixed on his lips, into Jack's arms. Telford's hand cradled the back of the man's head, and it came away matted with blood, hair and brains.

They buried him the following day in Rabat's Jewish cemetery, the sultan himself in attendance.

'And so it begins,' said *Sidi* Muhammad as he passed Telford when it was all over. 'Such a hatred for the Jews. But why him? The most gentle of men. I shall miss him so very much.'

'Me too, Highness.' It was about as much as Jack could manage. Beyond words, though his brain played tricks once more. Outside the Café de Salesas, Madrid. The waiter shot by the *Paco* Fifth Columnist sniper. Only Jack now knew the target hadn't, after all, been any of the politicians there with him in the doorway that night.

And back at the hotel he collapsed on the bed, at first not noticing the business card – a calling card, perhaps more accurately, for when he sat up again, there it was. No text on either side. Simply a motif. A plainly printed image of a black scorpion.

'Dead,' said Paquita Gorroño. 'I heard. I only met him a few times, but he seemed a good man.'

'Sometimes people just creep into your life,' Jack told her, 'without you even noticing they're there. It was only after I left the cemetery, I think. Realised I counted him as a friend.'

Her husband brought them coffee he'd been brewing on the stove. She was running her classes from their rooms now – Vichy's requirement that a woman's place was in the home. And Manuel laid off from his work on the trucks.

'They gave you a hard time?' Paquita asked him.

It had been the same Captain Edouard who'd interrogated him earlier – all that nonsense about Sergio's sketchbook. And whether Jack himself was…

'Honestly?' he said. 'I don't think he gave a damn. Muttered something about the usual suspects but who the hell would these be?'

'They certainly won't touch those pigs in the PP,' said Manuel. He sat at their kitchen table in his vest and braces, reading the paper by the light streaming through the balcony shutters.

'That's where I'd look,' said Paquita. 'Our very own Nazis. But a shooting? There've been plenty of Jews beaten up but this…'

'I'm not sure,' said Jack. He was thinking about Madrid again, told them the story.

'Scorpion?' Paquita looked at him as though he was mad. 'And this sniper in Madrid – turned out to be one of Franco's agents. But after you? Why the hell should they still be chasing you? Here?'

She was right. Of course, she was right. Why indeed?

'I don't know. But Franco's name keeps cropping up. Doesn't feel like coincidence.'

He saw her exchange a glance with her husband.

'Where exactly?' she said, suddenly wary. 'What have you heard, comrade?'

Her tone angered him.

'Look, I've had enough interrogation for one day. And Gabizon…'

'He told you something.'

'Nothing. For god's sake, this is ridiculous. We saw a meeting between the sultan and Weygand. That's all. The sultan worried about Franco's designs on French Morocco. But not news.'

'The *Makhzan*? Well, weren't *you* privileged? And the Americans? Did they talk about the Americans?'

'Got a mention, yes. Trade deal. Weygand seems bothered by it.'

'So?'

'Nothing. That was all.'

'Oil embargo?'

Jack hunched his shoulders, lifted his hands in the air, showed her his empty palms.

'What oil embargo?'

There was a rustle of Manuel's *Petit Marocain*, her husband now entirely hidden behind its spread pages.

'It seems,' she said, 'your Mister Churchill has been busy. Word from our people in London. Doesn't trust Franco to stay neutral.

But can't be seen to do anything himself. Gibraltar. So persuaded Roosevelt to impose an oil embargo against Spain. Some pretext or other. But maybe make Franco think twice about joining forces with Hitler. That's the idea.'

Jack smiled. How did she know all this?

'Something the sultan shared with Gabizon,' Jack told her. 'A vision. Somehow it could be the Americans who'd help set Morocco free. And Spain as well maybe?'

'The dream,' she said. 'Defeat for Germany and Italy. Defeat for Franco. Independence for Morocco. Spain a Republic once more.'

There was a gleam in her eye – something she wasn't telling him.

'We know where Granell is, by the way,' he said. 'He'd been at Camp Morand. But not there now. Some fortress or other. Bossuet?'

She grimaced, and Manuel set down his paper.

'Shit!' he said. 'Show him the report.'

'Later,' Paquita replied. 'Red Cross report – about Morand. Pitiful. Disease and starvation. Wicked punishments. Bloody French. They're the enemy now, comrade. The Republic's enemy. But Morand, bad as it is, is a playground compared to Bossuet. Pity. We could have used some of the boys.'

'Used them? Won't they have been through enough?'

'Something else we picked up from London. An intercept. Letter from Franco's brother-in-law in Berlin. It seems the Germans will only help Spain take Morocco if Franco agrees to then let them have bases at Agadir and Mogador Island. Franco's due to meet Hitler in person at Hendaye – and we have a small part to play in mixing things up a bit.'

'What the hell does that mean?'

He saw Manuel shake his head at Paquita.

'No details,' she said. 'Not the details. But there are plenty of nationalists in Spanish Morocco. Strange bedfellows but if we stir up enough trouble there, convince Franco he's more likely to lose Ceuta and Melilla to the independence movement than gain Rabat and Casablanca – well…'

'And if we all play enough small parts…' said Jack. Wasn't that what Isaac Gabizon had suggested, more or less? 'There's a debt

I have to pay,' he said, and explained his own modest plan. He'd thought they would laugh, but they didn't.

'You'll need a boat,' she'd said. 'Reliable skipper. At Casa. You remember Manolo?' Of course, he did. The brawl during the strike march. 'But the men you need? Better speak with *Madame* Bénatar about that one.'

'We all have a part to play for our passions,' said Jack. '*Countless as the sands of the sea are human emotions.* Isn't this right?'

'Gogol?' said Manuel. 'You read Gogol?'

Jack nodded.

'You are a strange man, *Señor* Telford.' Paquita had smiled. 'But I don't understand. If Franco is still trying to have you killed...'

After his visit to the sultan's palace, after Gabizon's death, the train journey back to Casablanca had been a nightmare. He'd not been able to get Isaac out of his head, a sense of abject sadness. He'd written some lines, almost a eulogy, yet had no idea where to send it. But it helped – a little – just to put pen to paper. Negrín's pen. And by then he'd been certain. How in god's name could Gabizon have been the target? No, this was something to do with Spain again, though it hurt his brain, trying to fathom the reason.

Spain. He remembered one of their first conversations, Jack trying to tell him the war in Spain was all over. 'But I think it is in your blood now,' Gabizon had replied. Well, he'd been right then, and it was still right now.

There were crazy thoughts. Franco due to meet Hitler at Hendaye. *I could have killed the bastard in Burgos,* he thought, yet again. Would it be as easy in Hendaye? He remembered the station there, on his way to the War Routes tour, just the other side of the Spanish border at Irún. He thought about the station layout, but he knew it was all pie in the sky, focused instead on this less ambitious plan, to strike a more modest blow.

So he'd headed home, locked himself away like a hermit for days on end, chain smoking, drinking too much, ignoring every ring of the bell outside the courtyard gate, playing Brachah Zefira over and over, torturing himself with memories of Gabizon, of doomed Pépé le Moko. Yes, a symbol. Doomed Isaac Gabizon.

Doomed Archibald Dickson. Raúl Ramos at Bou Arfa. Fidel and Sergio.

But finally he'd stirred himself, tidied his notes, wandered off to the *Grande Poste*, wired his *Life* article to Luce's assistant with word that Gabizon was dead and any further correspondence or transactions – payment, he hoped – should be sent to him direct at his address on the Place d'Oléandre, off the Sidi Belyout.

He picked up the papers, bought some food in the *souk*, then back to the house, skimmed through *Le Petit Marocain* and spotted there a mention of Hélène Bénatar. She was holding a fundraiser on behalf of the refugees, at the Art School in the Place Bel Air, an exhibition of Denise Bellon's photographs, those she'd taken on her last visit to Casa and especially at Bousbir. *Reflections on Bousbir*, that was the name of the exhibition. He'd taken a leave of absence from the classes, told Hélène he'd be away a week. But it had been two. And she needed every volunteer for the refugee work. Telford knew he'd let her down, but he found her at the Art School itself, getting ready for the opening.

'Isn't this breaking the new bloody rules?' he said.

'You were with him?'

There were crates everywhere, arrived from Lyon, Hélène in a flowered pinafore, busy with a crowbar to prise open one of the boxes before parting the packing straw and lifting out a framed picture.

'When he was shot. Then at the hospital. They couldn't do anything for him.'

'I still can't believe it. Jack what's happening here?'

'I wish I could tell you.'

'Well, you finally turned up,' she replied, without any real rancour, scolding him only with her benign, gap-toothed smile and those kindly eyes. The Vichy statute had come into force just after Jack's return from Rabat and then, two days ago, the sultan's own *dahir* – the statute watered down, though not by much. What had he said? We must all comply – at least to the level the times require.

'Fortunately this place qualifies as a Jewish school,' said Hélène. 'It seems, thanks to the sultan, we're only prohibited from teaching gentiles. Teaching our own? That's apparently still allowed. I can't help thinking – if Isaac had still been here…'

Jews now barred in Morocco also from work as civil servants, armed service officers, teachers, journalists.

'Nice reward. All those Jewish boys you helped recruit for the French army.'

'Two thousand,' she said. 'Just from Morocco. And now – dead, or prisoners-of-war. Or treated like vermin as refugees back here.'

Telford looked around the room. In the centre of the wall next to them stood an enormous and ornate seven-branch *menorah*, from one of the old Córdoba synagogues according to the plaque. Around it a display of timeworn *ketubot*, those Jewish marriage contracts, themselves precious works of art, images of intertwined vines and branches, flowers and fruits in sweet pastel pinks, blues and lilacs, exotic birdlife, arcane symbols in circles of rich ochre hues, and the careful calligraphy of the Hebrew texts.

'Those are quite something.' Jack admired them very much.

'Some of them are ancient,' she told him. 'And rare. We're lucky to have them. The families now gone. Or gifted to the school. Many of the refugees come to visit them, to remember all they've been forced to leave behind.'

'How many on the books? The refugees.'

'Just now? Nearly nine hundred.' She held up the photograph. A young woman's face, staring out through the open door of a cane birdcage, her mouth gagged by a black silk scarf with a rose design where her lips should be. 'All those we can help,' she went on, 'with housing, food, a bit of cash here and there. What do you think? Does it look right there?'

'Yes, perfect. And the rest?'

'There's an internment camp at Sidi-el-Ayachi. Nearly two hundred more there.' She set down the frame, picked up a hammer and nail from the top of another crate. 'But Jack, it's inhuman. The Red Cross reports – at first I didn't believe them.' She hammered in the nail. 'Oh, and some Spaniards there. Republican soldiers who'd reached Gibraltar, but then shipped out here with all the others.'

Réchard had mentioned something, a few months back. The Gibraltarians had all been vetted, of course. Not easy, given that nobody had proper visas, but they'd managed somehow, to identify the "Reds" among the real *llanitos*.

'You've been?' He lit a cigarette, rummaged in the packing case, pulled out a second photograph, wrapped in wadding paper.

'To Sidi-el-Ayachi?' said Hélène. 'Not yet. But I went to Aïn Chok. You don't want to know.'

'Oh, I do, Nella.' He'd taken to using this diminutive a while back, picked it up from her other familiars. 'Covering some of these stories isn't much, but great and small alike, we each have a place in the fight against the Nazis. I know this now. Isaac Gabizon taught me this. Hell,' he waved his arm around the room, 'even a show of photos from the Bousbir bordellos.'

'Then get your jacket off, *Monsieur* Telford. Sleeves rolled up. There's plenty to do.'

They spent the afternoon displaying the pictures, all of them indeed images of the Bousbir women, but especially the Jewish girls.

'Why the Jewish girls?' Telford asked.

'Denise is Jewish. One of the Hulmanns, before she married. Sees herself as a surrealist. And when she was here in Morocco, told me she'd never seen anything that so summed up what surrealism stood for as decent Jewish girls sunk into prostitution. I kept in touch after she went back to France, saw some of her pictures in *Match*. Decided she might be willing to help us.'

'I've never made sense of it,' he said when they finally paused for mint tea. 'This hatred. I was at university in Manchester. England. Big Jewish community there. But no problems. Then along comes Mosley, the Blackshirts. A few loud-mouthed speeches, and suddenly every problem in the world is the fault of the Jews. Orthodox Jews attacked on the streets. It was like – a cancer. As though, as soon as it was exposed to the air, it just spread like wildfire.'

'Always this way.' She stared down into the tea leaves. 'As it has always been. More than two thousand years.'

'I've read *Mein Kampf*, Nella.'

'Makes you feel filthy just turning the pages, no?'

'And I thought I understood,' said Jack, pinching the bridge of his nose. 'How decent people could be beguiled by the nonsense.

At least Hitler's logic – if that's the word for it. This obsession – the world's races in a deadly contest. Survival of the fittest. Semites the greatest threat to Aryans.'

'I know their putrid arguments, Jack. Because we take up space the Aryan race needs for its own expansion. Because we use our so-called weapons – democracy, communism, capitalism – to debilitate the other races of humanity.'

'You're supposed to have used those same weapons to cause Germany's defeat and humiliation in the Great War, then to undermine Weimar.'

'And Hitler believes we can and did mobilise the other so-called inferior peoples – gypsies, Slavs, Asiatics, homosexuals, blacks – to aid them in their humiliation.'

'All nonsense,' said Jack. 'But I heard the same nonsense from Mosley, yet…'

'It still isn't enough,' she said. 'Is it? To explain two thousand years and more of segregation, of seeing us as something less than human, as the scapegoats for every problem under the sun.'

'For the bitter, naked need to sweep you away.'

'Josephus tells us, Jack, that at about the time Jesus the Nazarene was crucified in Jerusalem, fifty thousand Jews were massacred in Alexandria. The truth, Jack? This terror of the Jew has been instilled into generation after generation, driven deep into the minds of so many, as deeply entrenched as fear of the dark.'

'Or deadly disease, Nella.'

'Primeval. Hitler may have convinced himself he has rational reasons for his hatred, but the simple fact? It is bred into his very bones.'

'Like it was bred into those who persecuted Dreyfus in France.'

'Oh, we killed the Christ, didn't you know? Or we caused the Black Death. Every generation, something different to lay at our door, the fear and superstition reinforced.' She picked up one of the nails, turned it over in her fingers. 'Driven deeper into their being, pressed yet deeper into their emotions. *Your* emotions, Jack.'

'Mine? No, Nella.' The denial began to form on his lips but the reproach in those usually sympathetic eyes was unbearable. 'Countless as the sands of the sea,' he said.

'The first step,' she told him, 'is simply to see it exists. After that...'

He looked over at his haversack, half hidden in the folds of his jacket on a chair in the corner. And he remembered how he'd struggled with his own prejudice when he was first awakened to the relationship between Fidel and Sergio. It was Ruby Waters who'd opened his eyes, and he had travelled a road, from an initial sense of stupidity, to something approaching revulsion, to a final understanding that his moral outrage at homosexuality was, again, no more than something he'd inherited. Nobody was born with this outrage, this bias, it had to be taught – in the home, in the family, at school, at the university. So he had rationalised the thing. Unlearned the prejudice, so far as he was able. Conscious it was still there, somewhere. But confined now, imprisoned.

'I know,' he said. 'After that, we can at least civilise the beast. D'you mind if I show you something?' Of course not, she'd said, and went to tidy away the tea tray.

'Jack,' she smiled, when he'd handed her Sergio's sketchbook and she turned some of the pages. 'These are wonderful.'

'I brought it just in case. Promised myself I'd do something with it but never had any decent ideas. But now? Well, I thought...'

'You'd like me to display this? I'd be more than happy. And I know somebody in town who can produce lithographic prints. These would sell, I know they would. But the artist...'

'He's dead, Nella. Alicante.'

'I'm sorry,' she told him, reached the back of the book and, as she turned the last page, a photograph fluttered out. She bent to pick it up.

'Oh, is that where it went?' Jack began, reached for it, but she half turned.

'It's you, Jack. And – now who is this exquisite creature at your side, my friend?'

'Nobody. Nobody at all.'

'Really? Something about your posture, *Monsieur* Telford. And the girl...'

It was nonsense, of course. Christmas Day, two years before. The consulate in Madrid. He'd only just met her. And if he'd been foolish enough to believe there *was* anything between them – well, that had come much later. Or not, he thought.

'A secretary at the consulate. Madrid. Ruby.'

Although she'd finally admitted that Ruby wasn't even her name, and he'd never found out what it might really be. Just, Ruby.

'And this sour-looking devil?'

'Military Attaché.' Now minus his legs, Jack thought. 'British Intelligence Service. Nasty little creature called Major Edwin.'

Somehow the rest of the story tumbled out. A brief account anyway. Her reaction? Pretty much the same as Paquita's had been. A calling card with a scorpion insignia – really?

'You're serious?' she said. 'You think this sniper was trying to kill *you*? Not Gabizon?'

'Sounds absurd, doesn't it?'

'No more absurd than somebody trying to kill Isaac, I suppose.'

'And the girl, Nella – Ruby, or whatever her name is – she told me I should find a place where I could get to grips with all this. The stuff I'd seen in Spain. Maybe this – I don't know what's going on, that's the truth. I thought it might be here. Sanctuary in Casablanca, you know? But now...'

'Now you're stuck here, holding your breath. Waiting. That's what we do in Casa. Wait. And hope Mister Goold at the American consulate will carry on helping us at least get a few to Lisbon. But will they herd the rest of us into the *mellah*? Like a ghetto? I've no idea.'

'Thank god for the Americans,' said Jack. 'Funding still coming through then?'

'And a new man in town. Murphy. Robert Murphy. Wining and dining Vichy, so they say.'

'Trade agreement,' said Jack. 'They're pushing through a trade agreement for Morocco.'

'Well, he's doubled up their capacity for dealing with all our people who want papers for the States. Though still such a backlog – lots of those poor devils being preyed on by...'

'Chabat and his gangs.'

'Somebody needs to shoot that creature,' she said, 'but...'

There was a ruckus from outside. Chanting. *La Mort aux Juifs.*

'Stay here,' Jack told her, suddenly more angry than he would have believed possible.

'Jack, leave them.' But he couldn't. Of course he couldn't. Not after their conversation.

'Nella, stay inside,' he yelled as they reached the lobby, the outside door. Yet she didn't. Of course she didn't.

There were ten of them, nine men, one woman. Respectable-looking. *Bourgeoisie*, Jack thought. One of the men with a can of yellow paint. A Star of David now daubed on the wall. The rest still shouting. *La Mort aux Juifs*. But louder now, as they saw him.

'*Hey, les fascistes, allez chier!*' Piss off, he yelled at them, went to grab the paint brush, found himself being pushed hard in the chest, another of the brutes aiming a blow at him. And then there was Hélène. She'd picked up a broom from just inside the vestibule, swung it now so it caught Jack's attacker full in the face. Jack kicked out at the wretch with the paint, caught him in the crotch, made him squeal, the contents of his can now splashed all over the floor. Bénatar still swinging the broom, the scum from the Popular Party falling back but cursing her to hell, the woman screeching like a banshee, every foul anti-Jewish insult she could conjure up. A policeman's whistle, one of the local constables from the *Préfecture*, emerging from the *pissoir* on the opposite side of the square.

Later, when they'd narrowly managed, themselves, to avoid being arrested – always easier to arrest a Jew than members of the PP, Hélène told him – though forced to clean up the paint as part of the process, he tried to explain his rage to her. Something to do with the attempt on his life. His need for revenge. And he realised he'd never in his life felt vengeful before. Not even with Carter-Holt. That was survival.

'Before,' he said. 'You talked about those poor buggers being preyed upon by Chabat and his thugs.' And he told her his plan, as he'd told Paquita Gorroño.

'Jack,' she'd said. 'There are things – look, at Rabat, a few other places, groups forming.'

'*Résistants?*'

'If you like, yes.'

'And here?'

'There are men who might help you. But, Jack, there's always a price to pay. You must know that. For every action, a reaction. The Torah teaches us this, as if we didn't already know. And some of these men, my friend – are you certain about this?'

Drowning. Telford never imagined he would die from drowning, though his nightmares often whipped him with the weighted lead lashes of Carter-Holt's own death. He was certain she'd intended to kill him, of course, there in the gentle swell of San Sebastián's bay, a bit more than two years earlier. The ornamental hairpin. Poisoned, he'd realised; grabbed her wrists until she'd been forced to drop it. Her screams of protest as he took hold of those dark wet curls, pushed her down, felt her nails clawing at his belly, struggled as she broke free of the surface just once, her eyes wide with terror. The coughing. The gagging. Her final shriek before he forced her under again, almost going down himself as he fought to tread water. Then the stillness before her mouth burst open and the sea filled her lungs, claimed her, jerked her backwards, dragged her from his grip. And now – his turn?

His stomach lurched again as the fishing boat bucked and tossed, Jack wedging himself, arms and legs braced, in the wheelhouse doorway. Somehow it was all made worse by a thorough blackness broken only by the whitecaps coming up behind them like rows of ravenous, roaring fangs. The pitching navigation lights might pinpoint their position for other vessels, but on board they were invisible.

'I was a bloody fool to let you talk me into this,' he yelled over the storm.

Manolo swung the wheel, rode the next wave as it lifted the stern high. He laughed and glanced back over his shoulder, face like a Rembrandt portrait, only the features on one side illuminated by the instrument panel's intermittent glow.

'Tío,' he shouted back to his uncle, still working at the transom despite this filthy weather. 'He thinks this is rough.'

Ancient Uncle Emilio, brown and wrinkled as a walnut, was tidying the hooks, the *ganchos*, hundreds of them, with the help of a dark lantern, around the rim of the cut-down oil drum in which their long-line was now neatly coiled again, the floats back in the stern locker, the flagged end-marker buoys hanging in their rack, and the modest catch spread over the tarpaulin hiding the contraband they'd secured in the shallow hatch beneath the foredeck. Emilio shook his head, his whole body moving in perfect synchronicity with the squeezebox regularity of the *Nuestra Señora's* own peaks and troughs.

'This?' he yelled. '*Hostia*, nothing more than a few ripples.'

'And if I remember right,' said Manolo, 'it was you insisted on coming along. Sea legs – wasn't that what you reckoned?'

To be fair, the journey out had been easier than he'd imagined. The four Frenchmen smuggled safely to Gibraltar in just twenty-eight hours. Manolo knew the channels and state of the tide around Casa like the back of his hand, but they'd sailed out at four in the morning in a thin, cold fog with a dozen more of the *palangriers*, the boat's dark red mizzen raised and her engine throbbing enthusiastically. The watch of a token Vichy gunboat at the harbour mouth had turned a searchlight on them, given a cheerful wave while the Frenchmen lay hidden behind the bulwarks, and a British corvette from the blockade squadron must have been so used to the fishing boats that they didn't spare them even a cursory glance.

Yes, easier than he'd thought. And besides, by then it was in for a penny, in for a pound. His part in the mission to pick up the Frenchmen. His part, along with the two nameless Jewish fellows – they couldn't have been anything else, he was certain – in stopping the old Renault van on the road to Fédala just after midnight, pushing the driver around, then convincing the passengers – it hadn't been easy – they were being tricked, that the only thing waiting for them in Fédala was an arrest for treason. At least, convincing four of them; two more refusing to believe their story and eventually left behind. Then back to Casa's *Port de Pêche*, where the *Nuestra Señora* was waiting for them and the two Jewish *résistants* had wished them well on their voyage.

'*Haberes buenos*,' one of them had said. A Ladino phrase, Jack was sure. And it made perfect sense. Hélène had made the contact after all, hadn't she?

By the time they raised Rabat hours later, away to starboard, Manolo had them all practising their fishermen's skills – at least a dumb-show, since they couldn't afford to waste bait, he'd insisted. But if push came to shove, they might have to do it for real. Still, they'd simply followed the rest of the *palangriers*, all through the day, sleeping by turns the following night, attracting little attention in the shipping lanes between Tangier and Ceuta, keeping as far as they could from the Spanish Moroccan sardine boats heading out at daybreak – their second daybreak, of course – along the coast. And, with Ceuta itself no more than ten miles to the southeast, Manolo broke away from the fleet, leaving them to their fishing grounds between there and the tiny island of Alborán, their hunt for whiting, mackerel, scabbardfish, pomfret, bonito, sardines and hake.

Due north and into the Algeciras bay, spluttering towards the small harbour of La Línea de la Concepción, the pretext of engine trouble. Past the superstructure of the Italian tanker *Olterra*, sabotaged by British commandos back in June and scuttled here by her crew. And in La Línea, the smuggler who would get the Frenchmen over the border to Gibraltar, hopefully for their onward journey to London and de Gaulle's enlistment offices – the same smuggler who'd already brought their return cargo of tea and sugar from the Rock itself.

'Well,' Jack had pressed Manolo as they manhandled the small crates into the fish hold, covered them with the canvas, took on board more buckets of ice, 'did he find out anything?'

'Nothing,' Manolo replied. 'They could have gone anywhere.'

Jack had heard back from Sydney Elliott, as late as last month, and no sign of the Linares family. Wherever they were, it certainly wasn't London. He was bitterly disappointed. Hardly knew them, for pity's sake. But at least he'd felt, for a short while, as though he might have made a difference. Yet the disappointment had somehow brought him there, as well. To this other *refus absurd*, this illogical resistance against Vichy, against the Nazis, against – well, he was no longer sure he could count them all. But Elliott had at least sent him a few back copies of *Reynold's News* and, more importantly, his updated NUJ card. A sheaf of his favourite cartoons penned by Carl Giles. There was also a letter from Sydney. Giles still with them for, though he'd been called up, he was ironically too short-sighted to serve. A few humorous anecdotes about the clashes between Carl and Elliott's recently appointed news editor, Arnold Russell. Carl still the good Socialist, Sydney had quipped, and Russell quite the opposite. But the cartoons – quite a change from Giles's *Young Ernie* stuff. More sophisticated. Making light of the German invasion threat, Nazi parachutists landing among the lions at Whipsnade. Or the lone drinker at a pub table, under the notice repeating Churchill's Cabinet War Room dictum: *Please understand there is no depression in this house and we are not interested in the possibilities of defeat – they do not exist.* Jack had that one pinned on the wall in his house. Illogical resistance, but resistance all the same.

They'd spent much of the day avoiding the *Guardia Civil* and taking turns with the engine hatches lifted, feigning repairs. Cheese and bread, rough red wine and then, mid-afternoon, out to sea, Jack initially helping Emilio pay out the long-line, each hook baited with silver sprats on the hanging threads, the *barandillos*; after every fifty hooks a makeshift weight, and every hundred hooks an orange float with its own uphaul.

'*Joder*,' Emilio swore every few minutes, 'you may look the part, but we'll be here for a week.' Jack had been quite proud of himself, his striped fisherman's top, his eye patch, his unkempt black hair, his tanned features. But now they were so exasperated by his clumsiness that Manolo reluctantly assigned him to the helm, strict instructions about how to keep them on course. Then with the floats snaking away behind them, the marker buoys' fluttering rags just visible in the distance, nothing to do but wait, while away a few hours cleaning the boat, more bread and cheese, a few three-handers of *Ronda* in the tiny cabin below, or snatching some sleep, all the time wallowing in the swells and crazy currents of the Straits.

The catch was brought in as the weather worsened and Manolo's skills now needed at the wheel to stop them floundering, Jack working like the devil to follow Emilio's bellowed instruction, much of it carried away on the wind, the rest lost in translation. Telford's Spanish was good but, as now, he often realised how many massive gaps there were in his vocabulary – words with which the kids of these fishermen would be familiar from the age of three.

But he managed – just. Sliding about on the small afterdeck, barely able to hold on with the worst of the swells, yet the fish in all their rainbow colours prised off the hooks and tossed, thrashing, into the waiting creels, the process repeated so many times that Jack lost track. Exhausting though. And the storm, when it broke fully, simply drained him even beyond the point of exhaustion.

'Gut them later,' yelled Emilio. 'Rest now.'

Jack woke, the sea now settled again, hunched in a corner of the wheelhouse, literally under Manolo's feet.

'Trouble,' said the Spaniard. Another fog. Another dawn. Yet seagulls, there must have been a hundred of them, screeching, piercing the mist like dive bombers for the fish innards trailing in the *Nuestra Señora*'s wake.

'Quick,' said Emilio, 'help me get this one in the hold.'

The last of the baskets. He'd gutted the rest while Jack slept. Hundreds of the damned things. But Telford helped him drag the small creel forrard, both of them keeping low, dumped the contents into the evil-smelling hold then threw in their final bucket of ice, yet all the time nervous glances over the top of the gunwale. Away to starboard, another of the *palangriers*, heading into port. Good timing on Manolo's part. But ahead of them, blocking the channel, that same Vichy gunboat and a seaman with a loudhailer ordering them to come alongside.

Manolo had switched off the engine, played the mizzen sail to bring them neatly alongside the gunboat.

'Just act normal, my friend,' he hissed at Jack. 'You look like a frightened bloody rabbit.'

At the gunboat's rail a French naval officer and two ratings with rifles by a boarding ladder.

'Whose vessel is this?' the officer demanded as his men made them fast.

'Need some fresh fish, Lieutenant?' Manolo shouted back. 'Decent catch. Plenty to spare.'

The officer didn't reply, sent his men down to jump onto the *Nuestra Señora*'s deck.

'Spanish?' he said with some distaste when he'd followed them down. His fingers played with the lanyard attached to the butt of his holstered revolver.

'No, sir. Moroccan.'

'And these?'

The swell rocked them gently against the gunboat's grey hull.

'My uncle Emilio. And his son Julio. My cousin.'

'Reds?'

Jack tried to look simple, fixed a stupid grin on his face as he watched Manolo bristle for the first time.

'That a problem, Lieutenant?'

The officer glowered at him, contemptuous. Not worth a response.

'Check below,' he said to one of the ratings. 'And Fronsac,' he told the other, 'the fish hold.'

'I told you,' said Manolo, 'if it's fish you want...'

The lieutenant made his way towards the foredeck, where his man was already loosening the straps, lifting the hatch.

'Get in there,' he said.

'Sir?'

'I want some of those fish shifted.'

Christ, thought Jack. And he couldn't keep up the masquerade anymore. He was shaking like the proverbial leaf. Uncle Emilio was beside him at the transom, slowly twisting the bitter end of a mooring rope between his hands, Manolo scambling forward.

'But Lieutenant...' he said.

'But sir...' the rating complained.

Paquita had warned him, of course. Manolo's a good comrade, she'd said. He'll do it. But he's fighting his own *guerrilla* just now. You'll laugh but he's been doing a bit more than fishing. Thinks it's his patriotic duty to make sure we Moroccans aren't starved of our mint tea. So, tea and sugar coming in – only our green gunpowder tea, of course. Proceeds either going to union funds or the Free French. At the same time, Vichy losing their tax revenue. And the blockade? Jack had asked. She'd laughed at him. Though now...

'That was an order, dammit,' the lieutenant shouted. 'I need to see if there's anything else down there.'

*

148

The sea erupted a hundred yards from the *Nuestra Señora*, a gout of water following quickly upon a bark of thunder away beyond the gunboat.

'Back on board – now!' yelled the lieutenant, half-dragging the rating, Fronsac, from the hold. 'Lively,' he shouted, nodded frantically in response to a lookout's cry, signalled with one arm to the helmsman and pushed the second seaman up the boarding ladder with the other. The gunboat's engines roared into life and sailors rushed to toss the warps down onto the fishing boat's deck. 'Follow us into port – quick as you like,' the lieutenant called to Manolo, even as they were swinging away into the channel, another shell bursting in the waves only feet from their bow.

'God bless them,' Jack muttered as they caught their first glimpse of the British corvette again. 'But where the hell are you going?' he cried as Manolo opened the throttle and swung the *Señora* in the opposite direction from Casa.

'Are you in your right mind?' Uncle Emilio replied. 'Follow them into port carrying this lot?'

'Then dump it overboard.'

'Maniac. You know what those crates are worth?'

'Then…'

'Fédala, of course,' shouted Manolo. 'Not the best place but we've friends there. And it's not far.'

The *Nuestra Señora* was docked, and unloaded by Manolo's circle of smuggler friends there at Fédala.

'You'll have to go back to Casa sooner or later,' Jack said to him. 'And that gunboat's going to be waiting.'

'I'll tell them there was no way I was going to risk running past those English bastards when I could put into Fédala instead. The *lonja* here will let us sell the catch. Sorted. We head home tomorrow night.'

'They'll wonder where your best deckhand's gone.'

The truth was, he was glad to be getting off the boat. But Uncle Emilio snorted with derision.

'We'll tell them we tossed you overboard with all the other shit,' he laughed.

'Take no notice,' said Manolo. 'But listen, comrade, you did good. Useless as a fisherman, but apart from that – maybe another time, no?'

Jack took the bus back to Casablanca. He was filthy, unshaven, stunk of fish and diesel. Cold. So he walked quickly back to his house, stopped when he arrived at the outside gate. It stood open. He pushed it cautiously, caught a glimpse of a uniform, the pale khaki of the *Sûreté Nationale*, the national police force. There was a young officer, toothbrush moustache, cape draped around his shoulders.

'Seize him,' he shouted, and two of the policemen grabbed his arms, dragged him back into the alley, along to the street where he was bundled into a black Citroën. To the *Sûreté* offices, two blocks away from the *Gendarmerie*. The cells, where he waited an hour until Colonel Maurice Herviot came to interview him. Jack knew him by sight and by reputation. Tough, a scar on his left cheek. Looked like a knife wound. But impeccable uniform. Rumours that he had no great love for Pétain.

'What's this all about?' Jack stood from the bare bed frame, trying hard to display outrage rather than the trepidation sluicing through his veins. It was another recollection of the past, this time Burgos, the *Guardia Civil* lieutenant there, the cigar with which he'd taken Telford's eye. There were still times when…

'I don't have time to waste on theatricals, Telford,' said Herviot. 'That's you, isn't it? You may be well connected but this won't help you. All I need is the names of your accomplices. Now, sit down.'

Well connected? Jack thought. Who does he mean – Réchard? The sultan? The former wouldn't care and the latter wouldn't know. Not now. But he did as he was told, tried to expunge Manolo and Uncle Emilio from his brain, determined not to think about how persuasive these policemen could be.

'No accomplices,' Jack told him, his guts cramping violently when the colonel took a leather cigar case from his uniform pocket, a cutter and lighter.

'Are you a simpleton? We have the witnesses.'

'Witnesses to what?' Telford began, then realised he was

150

barking up the wrong tree. This wasn't about the boat. Not directly. The truck driver, the one they'd stopped on the way to Fédala. Maybe, as well, the two idiots who'd refused to go with Jack and his companions.

'Listen, Colonel,' he said, his reasonable voice, 'I've been out with the fishing boats these past few days. We all need to eat. No crime, is it?'

'Sweet Lady, Mother of God,' said Herviot. 'Smells like it. But it was you, Telford. The description.' He touched a finger to his left eye.

'I'm the only man in Casa with an eye patch?'

'Simple enough to get you identified. But now, the others. When did you sail and who with?'

He'd snipped the end off the cigar, flicked the lighter into action.

'It would have been – hell, you lose track of time at sea. But I tell you, Colonel, you've got this wrong. Fetch your witnesses, by all means.'

'When? And who?'

'When?' Jack assumed a look of painful memory loss. 'What's this – the fourteenth? Five days ago, so we would have sailed – early hours of Tuesday morning.'

'Doesn't give you an alibi for the Monday night. But you know that already, don't you? What's your game, Telford?'

'No game, and why should I need an alibi?'

'Your shipmates?'

'The Monday night?' Jack laughed. 'There was the big festival for Saint Denis. There must have been a hundred people will confirm my shipmates, as you call them, were in the Fishermen's Hall that evening. The whole evening. They were still drunk when we cast off.'

'But you, Telford?'

'I love France, Colonel. But I didn't feel qualified to celebrate her patron saint. That's not a crime either, I don't think. Not yet. I was at home.'

'You mean *Free* France, I suppose?' he sneered.

'How could anybody not love a free France?'

'Two other friends then? The truck driver saw two men. Besides you. Not fishermen though, perhaps.'

Jack wondered if he should call the colonel's bluff, say to him: So what? We stopped a truck, offered the occupants an alternative lift. Back into town. After that – well, who knew?

'And suppose I *was* there?' he said. 'What *is* the crime, exactly?'

He saw Herviot's face relax into a grin, cigar smoke blowing through his teeth.

'I'll take this as a confession, I think. And the crime? Well, there was the hijacking of a truck. It's a start. A truck belonging to Luc Chabat. But after that? *Monsieur* Chabat himself turning up dead, murdered, just two hours later.'

'Chabat? But…'

'Nice act, Telford. But it'll be the *guillotine* for you, my friend.'

His night in the cell seemed endless. No mattress, no sleep, no window to help him calculate the hour. Too much time to think. He had no idea what would happen to him in the morning, but he'd have to cross that bridge when he reached it. For now there were simply confusions.

He'd met the men Hélène knew, and they'd begun the process of hanging about the bars, listening to the conversations until they finally overheard the one they sought. A man offered the chance of a boat from Fédala to Gibraltar. Two hundred *francs*. The confusion? *'Somebody needs to shoot that creature,'* she'd said. And now, apparently, Chabat was indeed dead. But surely…

It all became confused somehow, with his own fate. And yes, he'd have to deal with this in due course. Yet, there in the darkness, it was impossible not to think about how he might now never get to see the fruition of those dreams – any of them – he'd come to cherish. Freedom for Morocco and Morocco's Jews. The destruction of fascism. Spain taken back for the Republic. Victory for Free France. For the Free World.

Well, that part, at least, seemed to be gaining ground. After the disaster of Dakar back in September, by the middle of November news had arrived of success in Gabon, the last area of French Equatorial

Africa – with Chad, Cameroon and the French Congo – to be taken from Vichy. The fighting had been vicious, but the Gabonese capital Libreville finally falling to de Gaulle's army. Although perhaps more accurate to say the armies of a new name for the headlines, a man called Leclerc. The name played on Jack's mind, there in his cell, waiting for the morning he dreaded while, at the same time, wishing this night of uncertainties would stop tormenting him.

And as sometimes happens during such waking nights, there was a song going round and round in his head. Brachah Zefira, naturally. He'd loaned his gramophone and some records to Hélène for the opening of the exhibition. It was appropriate, since Zefira had sent her a message of support. She'd been on the circuit, all across Palestine, cultural crossroads of the Arab world. Everywhere. Safed and Haifa. Tiberias and Nablus. Tel Aviv and Jaffa. Jerusalem, Bethlehem and Hebron. Performing for the many Jewish refugees from Nazi-occupied Europe arriving in Palestine itself. Yet on the day of the opening, towards the end of November – as it happened, the very day Jack had met with Hélène's contacts among the Casablanca *résistants* – there'd been fresh and more tragic news. Almost two thousand refugees on a French liner, the *Patria*, in the harbour at Haifa, being deported by the British from their Palestinian Mandate because the Jews in question had no valid entry permits. An explosion, the hull ripped apart and the *Patria* sinking in mere minutes, hundreds trapped below decks. Hundreds killed, men, women and children. Accusations. Rumours. And among them, the story that seemed to stick. A bomb. Planted by the Jewish underground armed resistance group, the *Haganah*, in an effort simply to disable the vessel, prevent the deportations – a plan which, if true, had gone horribly wrong. The story had run through the visitors to the opening like wildfire, the joy of the event washed away in the tears, the reproach, the pain. One fellow's resistance, the other side's terrorism, he thought, yet again, there in the darkness, Brachah Zefira's guttural contralto playing on the turntable of his brain, her exotic features mingling with images of Ruby Waters – but all of it finally swept aside by the sound of a key in the cell door. Jack stood, afraid but ready for defiance, his fists balled at his sides.

'You,' said Jack, his mouth gaping open.

'Get out of there, now,' Réchard snapped. 'There's not much time.'

'But Colonel Herviot...' protested the policeman who'd unlocked the door.

'If Colonel Herviot wants to complain,' Réchard told him, 'he knows where to find me. Come on, Telford, shift yourself. This falls within the jurisdiction of the *Gendarmerie* now,' he called back over his shoulder, as one of his men hustled Jack along the corridor and up the stairs.

'Where are we going?' he said.

'Lucky for you, *monsieur*, that we caught Luc Chabat's real killer late last night. And that you've got friends with some influence.'

'You, Louis?'

'Me, Telford? No, not me.' They paused on the ground floor while Réchard argued with another of the *Sûreté*'s young officers, a junior inspector. 'My only part in this is to get you out of here and then deal with your *permit de séjour*. And even then, a simple matter of not renewing it. Revoked. That's the deal. For their part, you're free, for mine, you're out of my hair. For good.'

They were on the street. Not even dawn yet, though it was hard to tell. Another Casablanca fog. There was a black sedan, its engine running, the boot open.

'You said for *their* part. Who?'

'It was quite a network. Your Anarchist waiter friend at the Excelsior – Fernando? And yes, he's still working there. That night, at the *brasserie*, I only told him to keep his head down for a couple of weeks.' Telford began working on an apology but Réchard was in a hurry. 'Anyway, he overheard Herviot reporting to the Germans there last night. Linked you to the resistance. The waiter phoned *Madame* Bénatar, who put through a call to the sultan himself. Let's just say he called in a favour or two.'

'Louis, listen...'

'Shut your mouth and get in the car.'

Jack turned to the vehicle, noticed the driver for the first time, standing on the running board.

'Christ, it's...'

'Vidal, yes. Your friend from Bou Arfa. Only he's not Lieutenant

Vidal anymore. Cashiered from the army, like all the other Jews. Not that I mind this personally, but you'll have a lot of catching up to do, I guess. You've got a long road ahead of you both.'

'Herviot's not just going to give up on this, is he? Where the hell am I supposed to go. And with *him*?'

He saw Vidal toss away the stub of a cigarette, then give Jack a glance of pure contempt before swinging down into the driver's seat. It looked as though he was talking to somebody in the back.

'He's no happier about this than you are. But he's heading south all the same.'

Jack crossed to the car, bent down to peer through the rear window. A hand waved behind the glass, the window winding down a fraction.

'Good morning, Telford. Fancy a cruise?'

Jack recoiled. Captain Phillip Fox, smoothing his pencil moustache.

'You see, Telford?' said Réchard. 'You won't be going alone. I wouldn't trust you. Captain Fox is heading down to liaise with the Free French garrisons. Vidal as his guide. Golden opportunity to send you as well. And no, Colonel Herviot won't give up on this. He'll still want to pursue you for the hijacking at least. But I'll find somebody to carry the can if you've escaped. And he'll look for you here, or Rabat maybe. Whereas you, *Monsieur* Telford, will by then have disappeared in the opposite direction.'

'The garrisons,' Jack stammered. 'You mean...?'

'Libreville to be precise. Tramp steamer. But you'll pick her up at Agadir. They'll not be looking for you that way. And more chance of avoiding the blockade. She's due to dock at Dakar but the skipper will keep you all under wraps. Her final port of call? Abidjan, Ivory Coast.'

'Hell of a long way,' said Jack.

'But from there,' said Fox through the gap at the top of the glass, 'we should be able to get across into Nigeria. Our very own Nigeria, old boy. Maybe a boat from Lagos to Libreville – the new Free French garrison there.'

'My things, Louis. I can't go like this.'

But Réchard dragged him to the back of the car, showed him the contents of the boot.

'Captain Fox took care of everything for you. From your house – oh, it's confiscated, by the way. Property of the *Gendarmerie* now. But all the essentials are here. Now, get going. They'll have to put up with your stink until you reach the ship, but...'

'Wait,' said Jack. 'There was a pen.'

'Got it here, old man.' Fox held it through the window. 'Was rather hoping you wouldn't notice. Oh, and this. Present from *Madame* Bénatar.' Jack took Negrín's pen, then accepted the gift. It was the photo. Him and Ruby Waters in Madrid. 'Sent a message. Couple of messages really. Says she'll take good care of your book and your records, if that makes any sense? And she wishes you *mazel tov*. Orders you to keep writing.'

'And one last thing,' said Réchard. 'In the boot. A few home comforts for the voyage. Courtesy of our old friend Kingsley Welch. Still working with the Americans but asks if you'll make sure to keep in touch with him. Anything which might be useful.'

By now he'd pushed Jack around to the other rear passenger door, opened it wide.

'Louis, if you caught Chabat's killer, and Herviot's only after me for the truck...'

'You're going, Telford, and that's the end of it.' He pressed Jack's head down, forced him inside. 'I'll say goodbye to Monique for you, but I don't expect we'll see you back in Casablanca any time soon.'

January – March 1941

Leclerc

A strange new world awaited him. Jack knew it.

'You're serious, Telford?' Fox had said to him on the fifth evening after they'd sailed from Agadir on board the tramp steamer, *Gautier*. 'Black scorpion?'

'Thank god the sea's settled.' Telford flicked the stub of his cigarette over the stern rail. It was going to be a beautiful sunset and the coast of Africa, away to the east, had already been swallowed by the twilight, while the ship itself had lapsed into a more benign throbbing roll after the pitch and toss of the past few days.

'I read about it in Egypt,' said Fox. 'Gabizon. Nonsense about an accidental shooting. But the sultan...'

'Convinced it was some maniac, some Jew hater, in the Popular Party but the *Sûreté* not willing to confront them.' Jack shrugged his shoulders. 'And who knows?' he said. 'Maybe he's right after all.'

He shivered. A chill wind, though it did nothing to dispel the stink of diesel oil permeating every inch of this old vessel, even the food.

'But this thing with the scorpion – you've been reading too much John Buchan, old boy.'

'The card was real enough.'

The skipper came down the ladder behind them.

'Five minutes,' he shouted, then made his way forrard along the side deck.

Five minutes until the change of watch, and they'd be confined once more to their small cabin. There were only a few of the twenty-man motley crew Captain Nilsson seemed to trust and, for the most part, he'd decided it would be best to keep them under wraps – as the Yanks might say – at least, as much as possible.

'And our friend below?' said Fox. 'What is it with you two?'

'Vidal? Just can't make him out – can you? I told you, at Bou Arfa he treated those men like scum. Worse. Stories – well, never mind. But did everything to stop them signing up for the Legion. Christ, these weren't criminals. Men who'd been fighting the Nazis for three years. The sort of men France needed.'

'Reds, Mister Telford. Spanish Reds. France might have needed them. But not the French army. And maybe he did them a favour. They'd probably have died in France anyway. Or ended up in Sachsenhausen.'

'A favour? Not the Vidal I saw in operation at Bou Arfa. And now here he is, cashiered from the army because he's a Jew, but doing his patriotic duty by going off to join the Free French. Not that he'll be fit for anything by the time we get there – *if* we get there.'

Vidal had barely moved from his bunk through the whole voyage. *Mal de mer.* Though mere seasickness hardly seemed to do it justice. Telford had never seen anybody so ill, and though both he and Fox had done their best to keep some water down him, to stop him dying from dehydration, it had been a struggle.

'We'll get there,' said Fox. 'Never fear. I just haven't a clue what we'll do with you when we arrive, my friend. And Vidal? Whatever it is between you – not just some conundrum about his hypocrisy, I don't think.'

There'd been one brief respite in Vidal's condition. Two nights before. And Fox had gone off to fetch food. Big mistake, as it turned out. But it had given Jack the chance to get a few things off his chest.

'Listen, you bastard. It was me who lit your bloody fire. Not Ramos.'

Vidal had managed the ghost of a smile, his already parsimonious features now almost like parchment, translucent.

'Guilt, *Monsieur* Telford?' he murmured. 'It was you who mentioned the wiring, no? And it wasn't you supplied the gasoline. Obviously not. Or cut the injector pipes on the other truck. Besides, he confessed.'

'Confessed – what, after you tortured the poor bugger?'

'Just doing my job.'

'And they just wanted to join your own rotten bloody army. For Christ's sake…'

'My job.'

Jack couldn't now even remember what he'd said by way of reply, looked out at the phosphorescent whiteness of the wake churning away into the black oblivion beyond.

'Something between me and Vidal?' He turned to Fox, rubbed at the weary ache behind the eye patch. 'Come on,' he said. 'Time to go below. And I may have been reading too much Buchan, Captain, but you – too much Margery Allingham.'

Tomorrow they would arrive in Dakar, and the skipper's plan required them to stay in the cabin for the whole two days he expected to be there while they unloaded their cargo of submarine cable, wheat and pulses before their next stop at Conakry to offload the bales of wool and cotton which seemed to fill much of the hold. But Jack was determined to at least take a look at the damage left in Dakar after the British bombardment of the previous year.

And if there were any awkward questions about the passenger manifest, Vidal might at least be useful. Captain Nilsson had listed him, and him alone, as the cabin's occupant. Vidal still had his uniform and it was unlikely the port customs officials would bother greatly about a Vichy officer heading for Abidjan. Jack and Fox would simply have to keep out of sight.

Telford had been tempted on more than one occasion to tell Fox the whole story about Bou Arfa. But he understood Fox as little as he understood Vidal.

They'd arrived in Abidjan two days before Christmas, remained hidden on the *Gautier* while still more bales of cotton and wool, casks of Moroccan wine, were hauled ashore by Ivory Coast dockworkers, and the first enormous sacks of cacao and groundnuts were swung into the steamer's belly for the return journey.

Fourteen days of virtual confinement in their cabin with Vidal's stinking vomit and bile, yet the worst hours were those final few, while they fretted for nightfall. But the Swedish skipper hadn't wasted any time. One of his deckhands was a Kru seaman from Freetown but with family in Abidjan and a cousin who regularly drove freight from here into the British Gold Coast, hostilities having had barely any impact on trade between the neighbouring regions. Thus they bade a grateful farewell to Captain Nilsson, slung their belongings – Jack's two cases and his satchel, Fox's fine leather travelling bags, as well as Vidal's canvas military valise and grip – into the back of Cousin Dido's truck, and climbed aboard, settling themselves among the sacks of coffee beans he was delivering to Cape Coast Castle almost three hundred miles away. It wasn't going to be a comfortable journey.

They shared more stories of their backgrounds – though Vidal remained as sullen as ever – or they sank into long silences, hammered on the sides of the cab whenever they needed to relieve themselves, drank from their water bottles. And they smoked.

'No Sobranies anymore?' said Jack, as he offered Vidal one of the Sana filter-tips from the tin the skipper had supplied them as a parting gift. They weren't bad. Swedish, but not bad.

'Filthy bloody things,' Vidal shouted back. 'Keep them.'

He was sitting on the cab's roof, facing backwards, peering out between the fraké trees and tropical undergrowth to catch a last glimpse of the Aby lagoons below them and to their right.

'Please yourself,' said Jack. 'But watch out,' he yelled.

'And why…'

Vidal's infuriated face spat the words, as the low-hanging branch cracked the back of the Frenchman's head and sent him sprawling among the sacks. Fox barely managed to catch the thick-lensed spectacles before they flew off the lorry.

'We've still got a long way to go on this damned thing,' he said, offering a helping hand – and the glasses – to Vidal, but holding tight to the truck's side with the other while they bounced and swayed along the jungle road.

'Leave me alone,' said Vidal, snatching the spectacles. He hooked the wire frames back around his ears as the rain began.

'Just our luck.' Jack shook his head, tried to cover his cases under a couple of loose sacks. Cousin Dido brought the truck to a halt, opened the driver's door and handed them up a waterproof poncho.

'The only one I've got,' he said. 'Have to share.'

Fat chance, thought Jack, but then he saw his companions were better prepared than himself, Vidal's valise revealing a military rain cape, and Fox's travelling bag a lightweight trenchcoat.

'Looks like it's yours, Telford,' Fox laughed. 'And thank god this is the dry season, eh?'

'Been here before?'

'Only Accra. On my way to Cape Town a few years back.'

They passed through yet another village of huts, people bustling about, oblivious to the downpour. A marketplace, splashes of reds and yellows, greens and brown ochres. And somehow Telford managed to sleep, startled back to consciousness as the truck bumped off the road itself and came to a halt among the trees. The rain had stopped, at least, replaced by a permeating mist.

'Only a half-mile to the border point,' said Dido. He looked worried, clambered up into the back of the wagon, shifting the heavy sacks to hide their coats, the cape, their belongings.

'Careful with those,' said Jack.

But Cousin Dido ignored him.

'You walk now. That way.' He pointed to a track leading off into the jungle. 'Follow until you reach the river. Then turn.' He waved his right hand. 'To the bridge. I will be on the other side. Do not let them see you.'

The path was easy enough to follow, but the green canopy above them dripped so much it was like being back in the rain. Steamy, prickling heat. It sapped Telford's strength, made him feel sick.

'After the border,' Jack gasped, pushing his way through some hanging lianas, almost tripping on a root. 'How much further – d'you remember?'

'Good question,' Fox replied. 'About fifty miles from Elubo to Axim. Dido says we'll stop there. If all goes well, of course. On the coast.'

'Christ, how I'd love a swim. Some decent food.'

He could almost hear the waves rasping back and forth at the shingle on a beach, smell the scallops, shrimps and fresh fish cooking over an open brushwood fire, picture the orange and purple of an African sunset. But here there were just these menacing green

161

mansions, a fandango of bullfrogs, the occasional flash of crimson wings, sweat running into his eye. What had he expected? This was a world of which he knew little except some half-remembered childhood lessons about the Dark Continent. Livingstone and Stanley. Pygmies. Mud huts. Never dreamed he might be here – how, somehow, Isaac Gabizon, Paquita Gorroño, Hélène Bénatar, Louis Réchard, had all conspired to guide his steps.

'You'll be lucky, old boy. Another eighty miles, I think, from Axim to Cape Coast Castle.'

'And is there – a castle?'

Vidal was just ahead of them and Jack was surprised at the ease with which he trod the track.

'Oh, indeed. I had the pleasure while I was at Accra. Relic of our glorious past. One of our slaver forts. Grim, Telford. Grim. But you might get a chance to explore. We'll probably be stuck there over Christmas. Though Dido says there are plenty of ships these days. Leclerc's set up a proper little trade route, it seems. Between our boys on the Gold Coast and Gabon. If we're lucky we may be able to sail straight to Libreville.'

'Ever met Leclerc?'

Telford stumbled again, cursed himself as Fox caught his elbow.

'Never had the pleasure. Must have something about him though. To make such a name for himself. They say he walks with a limp. Always carries a walking stick.'

'Fell from his horse,' said Vidal, over his shoulder. 'Riding accident at Saumur.'

Jack exchanged a glance with Fox. It had come as something of a surprise, this sudden unsolicited gift of information.

'You know him?' said Fox.

'I was at St. Cyr.'

'Cavalryman?' Jack asked.

'Administrator, *monsieur*,' Vidal replied. 'Just the job for a Jew, no?'

If they expected more, they were doomed to disappointment.

'And when we get to Libreville,' said Jack, 'what then, Captain?'

'Simply an assessment. Strengths and weaknesses, that sort of thing. Report to Cairo. There's an outfit there. Long Range Desert Group, as they now seem to be calling themselves. Heard of them?'

'Like Lawrence,' Jack smiled, brushed some sort of sticky web from his face. But yes, strangely he'd seen a copy of the *Evening Standard* in the Café du Commerce before the Gibraltar trip, left there by one of the British expatriates, he'd assumed. A couple of weeks old. But a headline. *We are now in Libya!* They'd called them the Long Range Patrol Unit, though. Desert fighters. Volunteers – New Zealanders, Southern Rhodesians, British Guardsmen.

'With luck,' said Fox, 'they'll agree to work with Leclerc. But what about you, Lieutenant? You've never told us your own plans.'

'I'm not a lieutenant anymore,' Vidal replied. They broke through the last of the vegetation, emerged onto the muddy bank of a wide, fast-flowing river.

'Maybe there'll be a cosy little prison camp for you to look after,' Jack growled, though in English, almost to himself. But as he did so, his legs went from under him. He slithered down the slope, grabbing ineffectually at the few sparse roots and plunged, feet first, down the final short drop and was immediately dragged down, swept by the current. He'd taken a breath, almost instinct, before he hit the water. Now, panic. Expected to come up again. Yet...

Telford pulled for the surface, felt something tighten round his ankle. Fingers. A hand. It held him. Panic. And as much as he tried to scream some logic to himself, that it could not be a hand, still the certainty persisted. He tried to double over. To reach down. Towards whatever sprite anchored him there. The effort of doing so merely drove precious air from his lungs. Aching. Water forcing its way up his nostrils, urging him to suck it inside.

His free leg tried to run, cycled uselessly in the depths. Burning in his chest now and throat constricted. He gripped beneath his chin, choking himself in some absurd attempt to avoid inhaling. The sun, he thought. Where is the sun? Nowhere. Yet there was light all around. Some strange sepia light. Jack let go of his throat, flailed his arms at the light. The light spoke to him, somehow. About the weight pressing down upon him, against his head, his chest. A thin trickle of bubbles danced up past his eyes. An apology formed inside his brain. To Carter-Holt? To God? His lips parted and a final, feeble vomit of breath spewed from his mouth. Then, nothing.

*

'Somebody told me once,' said Fox, 'how nobody ever remembers the drowning itself. Only the time immediately before.'

'Comforting.' But it wasn't, of course. Jack was trembling, couldn't stop. Abject terror filling him as, in truth, it hadn't done when he was in the water. Shock, he told himself. Shock. And terrible nausea. He felt cold. How was it possible to feel cold, here of all places? But he sat in a puddle of water, trying to peel off the sodden jacket. Fox was the same, dripping wet.

'Well, you said you fancied a swim, Telford.'

'I couldn't get free.'

'Weed of some sort. Look.'

Still traces of it wrapped about his sock. His shoe had gone. A flock of emerald parrots screeched past and, in the jungle, the chatter of monkeys.

'Vidal?'

'Gone to find the truck. Bring back one of the coats, something to get you dry.'

'Can't stop shaking,' said Jack.

'Natural enough, my friend. Need to get you to a doctor though, and pretty damned quick. God alone knows what you must have swallowed. Good job I was on hand to apply the old artificial respiration, though.'

'And to get me out.'

'Good god, no,' Fox laughed. 'That was Vidal.'

Telford swam. In the sea. Or, at least, in the wide, wide estuary, to the eastern margin of which clung Libreville.

He swam in the rain, for it had rained ever since their arrival, two days earlier. New Year's Day.

He swam because he feared it might be his last chance for a long time. Tomorrow they would hopefully begin the journey northwards again, more than two thousand miles through French Equatorial Africa to reach Chad, and this opposite side of the vast Sahara. Could they simply have crossed its wastes in the first place? Perhaps. But nobody except a madman would have thought of it. And besides, they'd then had no idea precisely where de Gaulle and Leclerc might be. And their ability to catch up with the Free French forces depended on the papers Fox hoped they'd be able to collect from the Acting Governor Delegate for Gabon at the Government Palace. The captain, however, seemed reasonably certain there'd be no problem – though Jack's precise status still seemed uncertain.

He swam, also, because he must. His near drowning in the Tano River had left him, for the first time in his life, with a fear of the water. Like falling off a horse, he supposed. And he thought about Leclerc – while he showered and dressed in the changing rooms of the Nombakélé beach's Club Bretonnet, a favourite destination for the French residents, though the waiters and attendants, of course, all ebon-faced Myene, Fang or Kande, perhaps immigrant Yoruba. Outside it still rained – though here in Libreville this didn't seem to matter much, and he set off along the Route de Glass, the coastal dirt road with its fringe of palms, back into town. He almost choked in a carrot-coloured cloud of dust as a logging truck, felled Okoumé trees, passed him outside the shipping offices of the *Chargeurs Réunis* – responsible, it turned out, for their passage from Cape Coast Castle on the French freighter, which had made stops *en route* at Accra and Douala. He paused at the beachside market, among African women with babies swaddled to their backs, admired a troupe of tam-tam drummers and dancers, all emerald green and saffron yellow *boubou* robes, wound turbans in every complimentary shade. There was food here as well, goat-stuffed purple eggplant and spiced cassava he ate from a banana leaf while he shopped for different footwear, something more appropriate than the rattan loafers bought to replace the shoe lost in the Tano. Something more appropriate for the afternoon's meeting with Lieutenant Colonel Parant.

But, first, back to the Hôtel Central, then his appointment at the hospital for his yellow fever jabs and, afterwards, the commemorative service he'd decided to attend at Saint-Pierre.

A memorial service. Telford was still shocked. It should have been a solemn affair, respectful. A local Mpongwè man, a veteran of the Great War, had come out of retirement to fight in France. Commanded a mixed force of Senegalese and Gabonese. Fought so fiercely there were only fifteen left alive from the entire company when they were forced to surrender. And the Germans had refused to recognise his rank. How could a *neger* be a captain? Shot him like a dog.

'There was hardly anybody there,' Telford explained, as they drank coffee in the Acting Governor Delegate's spacious office, its window shutters thrown wide to permit the cooling ocean breeze, a pleasantly suffused light and a fair amount of tropical rain. He shifted uncomfortably on his chair, his backside throbbing from the bloody needle, the humiliation of fainting as the damned thing went in still eating at him.

'The locals mostly decided to boycott,' said the white-suited African on the divan opposite. He was – well, round. His head, his corpulent body, his fingers. *Monsieur* Éboué, Governor General of French Equatorial Africa, had come all the way from Brazzaville, it seemed, for the meeting. 'And all but the closest family prefer a more private ceremony.'

'Without Bishop Tardy, that is,' growled Lieutenant Colonel Parant – stocky, wire-rimmed glasses, cropped hair cut high above his ears.

'Strange service,' Jack replied. 'And I gather I'm not telling tales out of school if I say he wasn't exactly glowing about the Gaullists.'

'Let me guess,' said Parant. 'The Free French not true French at all? Vichy the only legitimate government of France?'

'I've heard plenty of open grumbling since we got here, sir,' said Fox, 'about the food shortages. About Brazzaville.'

'About me, you mean.' Félix Éboué grimaced. 'Yes, this would be Bishop Tardy as well. Stirring up the people.'

'All the same,' said Jack, 'to use an occasion like this...'

The Governor General and the Acting Governor Delegate each shrugged their shoulders at the same time. What else could you expect?

'But tell me, Mister Telford,' said Éboué, now in perfect English, 'we are so starved of news here. How is this terrible war affecting your Football League?'

It wasn't precisely the question Jack was expecting but he carefully explained how the league divisions had been split – Football League North and Football League South. It was considered safer.

Sensible, said the Governor General, and waxed lyrical for several minutes about the respective merits of Preston North End and Crystal Palace.

'I'm afraid I've not really been keeping up,' Jack told him, and Fox made some apology about being more a rugby and cricket man.

The Governor pushed himself out of his easy chair, took himself to one of the windows, gazed out at the sea.

'Disappointing,' he said, without looking at them. 'I have such hopes that English football might be one of the things which could pull us together in these difficult times.'

'I fear it may take more than this, Excellency,' said Lieutenant Colonel Parant, opening the drawer of his desk. 'But here are your papers, gentlemen. Captain Fox, your permit to travel. And Mister Telford, I spoke with General de Gaulle this morning. He was satisfied with your credentials, happy to allow you accreditation as a correspondent on behalf of Free France – though you may not submit any articles until they've been approved. Is it understood?'

It was all a bit sudden. Official accreditation? He'd rather hoped he might go along for the ride, pick and choose the stories he wanted to write – as he'd always done.

'Do I get a uniform?' said Telford. It fell on stony ground.

'The normal arrangement. We transport you into the war zone, we feed you, provide shelter. Clothing? Yes, I suppose so. You certainly won't be much use in the desert dressed like that. In return, you follow military discipline and the censorship rules. Colonel Leclerc will appoint the necessary liaison once you reach his headquarters. But a word of warning, Telford, the Colonel has no time for journalists.'

Censorship? And no time for journalists? Jack was still trying to frame a suitable response, but Fox cut in.

'I'm sure Mister Telford understands the contract, sir,' he said. 'And we leave when, exactly? Tomorrow?'

'The convoy leaves at dawn. We assume you'll liaise with Cairo once you reach Fort Lamy.'

'Indeed, sir. If not before. And might I ask – about Lieutenant Vidal?'

'Lieutenant? Cashiered, wasn't he? Not sure he'll be any use

167

to us, but he can join the other volunteers, I suppose. Chad's responsibility to make a decision, not mine. He can ride with the Reds.'

'Reds?' said Jack.

'Spaniards, *Monsieur* Telford. Deserters from the Legion, mostly. Already enough of the buggers in the garrison here. But they keep arriving. Two here, three there. This bunch we're sending up to the Colonel.'

'Censorship?' Jack fulminated as they headed back to the hotel – though they took the scenic route, down from the Plateau with its gleaming white colonial elegance, to the Port Môle.

'For pity's sake, Telford. What did you expect?'

Fox opened the umbrella which Governor Éboué had kindly lent them.

'Maybe a rank or something. But the stuff about English football – pulling them all together?'

Through the trees below them, along both sides of Rue Gambetta, were the red or green wooden shacks, corrugated roofs, which seemed to provide most of Libreville's housing. It all looked peaceful enough.

'Most of the old Vichy officials,' said Fox, 'are still in prison here. Masson, the previous governor, hanged himself rather than surrender to Parant and Leclerc when they took the town.'

'But still plenty of Vichy's cronies on the loose and making mischief.' Jack was thinking about the bishop again, Tardy. Out beyond the breakwater, a dozen dugout canoes, fishermen casting their nets like fluttering birds' wings upon the waters.

'Not the worst place to fetch up, what?' Fox offered him a cigarette as they sheltered under the umbrella. Jack had been thinking the same, wished they could have had more time here. 'But add to that?' Fox went on. 'All the usual frictions between civil and military administrators, between the towns and the rural outposts. They've got their hands full. Football, though? Just an obsession of Éboué's, I think. Not a bad fellow, I reckon.'

They turned inland along Cours Pasteur. An army truck stopped just ahead of them, its bow frames brushing through overhanging palm leaves, Free French sailors – from Port-Gentil maybe – in white vests and sun helmets, jumping down from the back and heading across to a brothel on the other side of the street. Laughter from the girls who ran out to greet them, naked breasts with tribal scars, which looked like they'd been raked by a leopard's claws.

'Reminds you of Bousbir, no?'

'Fair enough,' said Fox. 'Those girls will be far from home as well. Yoruba, maybe. Nigeria? The local women here are a different kettle of fish. Did you know? The Gabonese. Hardly any ethnic boundaries between the tribes. Bantu, apparently. Like the Zulu. My god, they're impressive devils. Clan systems. Like the Scots, I suppose. The clan chieftains send their young men off to the army. See it as their feudal duty. But many of the women have these secret societies. Njembe. Put the fear of god into the men around here, apparently. Pride themselves on not being scarred. No wounds – anywhere, old boy, if you get my drift?' Jack was rather afraid that, yes, he might, and decided to change the subject.

'What about Éboué, though?' he said. 'Made me wonder. Did anybody ask the Africans whether they wanted to be Vichy or Free French? I suppose not. Maybe they didn't want either. Paquita and the comrades would have put it all down to colonialism – outdated imperialism, I guess. Not even spared a thought. Only as cannon fodder. Éboué made me think perhaps I'd got some of it wrong.'

Outside the Hôtel Central, the rain had stopped. Fox flapped the brolly open and closed a few times, startled the cattle being driven past by a small boy with a stick, their hides almost the same shade as the red clay of the road.

'He was already Governor of Chad,' Fox told him. 'And he didn't need any asking, Telford. Brought Chad over to de Gaulle almost as soon as the general made his broadcast. And the people of Chad praised him from the rooftops in the process.'

They waited while some young French officers in tropical khaki argued vehemently in the doorway.

'But here?' said Jack. 'Civil war.'

'Among the white man, maybe. And only a few dozen killed.' They'd finally managed to get inside, collected their keys, Fox handing over the umbrella and asking the desk clerk to make sure it found its way back to the Palais du Gouvernement. 'Time for a drink before we eat?'

'I'll need to pack. And one of us should let Vidal know, I suppose. Besides, I should go to the Post Office, try and get a wire through. It seems I'm now a war correspondent without anybody to write for. Better try the syndicates again. Get some money sent out. But yes, why not? A quick one, perhaps, while you finish your story.'

'Not much to tell, really,' said Fox as they made their way to the bar. 'Locals voted with their feet. When Leclerc and Parant came out of the jungle, the Gabonese units could have stayed with Vichy. It was a Vichy stronghold, after all.'

'I should be more familiar with all this.' Jack ordered a gin and tonic. 'You know your stuff.'

'Same for me,' Fox told the waiter. 'And you'll not impress de Gaulle as a war correspondent, Mister Telford, unless you do the same. He's a stickler for detail. But his boys could never have won. Not without the locals. And they didn't stay with Vichy. Don't underestimate them, old man. The people of Africa – for the most part, anyway – know damned well what they're fighting against.'

'And *for*, I suppose,' said Jack. 'I thought the same during the memorial service. Go and ask the man's family whether they'd rather have Vichy and Hitler than de Gaulle.'

'For now, at least. They joined up with Leclerc all the way. Free France no longer just an empty idea – a few thousand émigrés in London. Now Free France is a piece of real estate. French Equatorial Africa, bigger than France itself. And Churchill's managed to get some agreement with Vichy. Whatever they or Free France respectively now hold should stand for the next year at least. No more hostilities.'

'It's a miracle,' said Jack, took his glass from the waiter, sipped at the gin through crushed ice.

'A miracle which means de Gaulle can now get on with fighting the real enemy without having to watch his back all the time. And you, sir, are going to be on hand to tell the world how he gets on.'

'You expect us to ride with this piece of shit?'

A face Jack remembered. The last time he'd seen the man was at Bou Arfa. El Gordo – wasn't that what he'd called himself? But now he had Vidal by the throat, pinned against the back of the lorry and surrounded by a small but angry crowd. It was raining again.

'Comrade,' said Jack, setting down his kitbag and touching El Gordo's shoulder, but cautiously. 'Remember me?'

The man's impatient scowl as he turned to face Telford faded to a crooked smile.

'English,' he said. 'All the saints, how…?'

'Believe it or not,' said Jack, 'because of him.'

He nodded towards Vidal, looked around the others, saw a couple more faces he thought he recognised. The second Toledan – the fellow who'd done the translating? He still carried the scar left by Vidal's riding crop, a very personal score to settle. One of the others as well? There was a flicker of acknowledgement from them both.

'This turd?' El Gordo snarled.

'What's going on?' yelled the French lieutenant, splashing through the ochre puddles, marching down the line of trucks, the convoy which was now his responsibility. Just behind the lieutenant, rifle at the ready, a sergeant and up ahead, at the side of the lieutenant's open-topped scout car, Fox smoked a cigarette. 'Bloody Reds again,' said the lieutenant. 'And you…'

He pointed an accusing finger in Jack's direction. Telford raised his hands in mock surrender.

'Just trying to pour some oil on the waters, Lieutenant.'

'Shit,' said the officer, 'another one who can't understand a simple bloody order. Get moving. On the lorries, now.'

'Not with this son of a whore,' El Gordo shouted, but at least he'd let go Vidal's throat.

'Told you, sir,' said the sergeant. '*Rosbifs*, Jews and Reds. More trouble than they're worth. The bunch of them.'

'Get them on the trucks anyway, Sergeant. Or shoot the bastards. I don't care which.'

El Gordo spat at Vidal's feet.

'It's a long way from here to Fort Lamy,' said the Spaniard. 'We finish this later.'

'I'll look forward to it,' Vidal replied, setting the spectacles more squarely on his nose.

'Maybe you'd better take my place,' Jack told him, jerking his thumb towards the lorry behind them. 'I'll ride here.' And Telford didn't wait for an answer, grabbed his bag and pushed El Gordo past the Frenchman, up onto the Bedford's back. But, amid the handshakes and greetings, he kept his eye on Vidal as he joined those filling the final truck.

'What did you mean?' said El Gordo, as the convoy lurched into motion. 'Here because of that pig.'

It had struck Jack at Bou Arfa how the man's nickname must have been intended as a joke for, like most of the inmates under Vidal's supervision there, he'd been all skin and bones. But now he'd begun to fill out again towards what, Telford assumed, must have been his regular build. Like a brick shithouse, as Sydney Elliott might have said. Solid. Dependable.

'The Legion must have agreed with you,' he said. 'I take it you made it – to Bou Denib.'

'We made it, English. Thanks to you.'

The other Spaniard shouted to him from the open rear of the truck.

'But some of the others weren't so lucky, comrade. Remember the Cuban boy, César Fuentes? And the Dutchman, Meijers? The Legion broke them, both of them.'

Jack saw nods of agreement from four, maybe five, of the soldiers, realised they understood.

'All from Spain?' he said.

And the rest of their first morning, thirty miles, along the new Kango road eastwards, to Nkan – where they would turn north towards Cameroon – was filled with a bewildering array of back-stories. The other *toledano*, the translator, the man with the scarred cheek, introduced himself as Alonso Vorje – though he seemed to prefer the soubriquet Alemán. The German from the work party was also there, Reiter, and the Yugoslav, Markovich. Two Spaniards

172

who'd also escaped with them from Bou Arfa. They'd been posted to Dakar but when de Gaulle's attack there had been imminent, they'd be damned if they would kill the very Frenchmen who wanted to keep fighting the Nazis. They deserted, a whole bunch of them, made their way here. Garrison duty ever since. But now Leclerc was looking for volunteers – so here they were.

Telford, for his part, told him about his own reason for being there, about his work with Paquita Gorroño, and about his brush with death on the Tano.

'And the evil little swine saved your life?' said El Gordo.

The rest of the men thought it was hilarious.

'He's here, isn't he?' said Jack. It seemed like mitigation, at least. Whatever Vidal had done before, however Vichy had rewarded him by cashiering him from the army, like them he still wanted to fight the Nazis. But he knew this was unlikely to wash with these men.

'You saw the camp,' said Alemán. 'You were there, when those pigs killed Villena.'

'You don't know…' Jack began. 'After you got away. Ramos – they shot Ramos.'

The hilarity faded away.

'You should have let me kill him, English,' said El Gordo. 'But there'll be another day.'

'No,' said Jack. 'You don't understand. Ramos. It was my fault.'

'Well,' said Fox, 'looks like you may see some action, Mister Telford.'

It had taken them eight days, the six hundred miles from Libreville to Bertoua, where the dense jungles further south gave way to the savannah of north-eastern Cameroon. Still another two weeks to reach Fort Lamy. And no real certainty Leclerc would be there, even then. At Yaoundé, Fox had picked up an encrypted wire from his superiors in Cairo. Two patrols from the Long Range Desert Group dispatched to link up with Leclerc's men. Joint operations. Two commanders.

'You know either of them?' Jack asked him.

'Met Clayton once. Kiwi, of course. The Frenchman – Massu, did they say? Don't know him.'

By the time they reached Bertoua it was all over, but they'd gathered at the District Administrator's office to hear the BBC broadcast, also from Cairo, to confirm the success of raids against Italian bases, and especially a place called Murzuk. Praise for the two British units, New Zealanders and Scots Guards. Fulsome praise for the Free French forces. There'd been a great deal of poring over maps.

'Christ,' said Jack as they shared a cigarette outside, 'the middle of nowhere.'

By a rough measurement, Murzuk was fifteen hundred miles across the desert west of Cairo, and about the same distance, also across the desert, north from Leclerc's base at Fort Lamy in Chad. It made Lawrence's attack on Aqaba look modest by comparison – though Lawrence, of course, never had the advantage of Maitland and Laffly trucks. But even so, fifteen hundred miles…

Across the dirt road, outside the reed-thatched huts of the locals, there were mounds of green bananas for sale, pineapples, cauldrons of rice ready to feed the convoy – the soldiers' tents pitched around the artesian well in the sparse gardens of the administration buildings. Women in bright *kabbas* carried impossible loads upon their heads, and the men sat impassively in the shade, watching them pass.

'The middle of nowhere, old boy,' Fox smiled, running a finger along his pencil moustache, 'is precisely where we're headed.'

The six-foot Sara with tribal scars down each cheek shouldered Telford aside like a raging bull, sent him sprawling in the dust, rolled him over and over. Jack spat dirt, tried to sit, yelled in pain as bootstuds ground into his ankle.

'Christ, watch out,' he screamed in redundant English, got to his knees in time to see Alemán – the bloody fool who'd trodden on him – bring down the big Sara in a dirty tackle, well inside the penalty area.

For pity's sake, Jack thought, as bearded *Père* Bronner's whistle screeched. Not now. Five minutes left? Can't be much longer.

The mule was still on the pitch, as it had been since the start of this furious second half. Nobody even seemed to notice the damned thing anymore. It ambled back and forth nibbling at the few sparse tufts of vegetation along the sideline with its fringe of trees providing the spectators' only shade from the harsh Sunday afternoon glare. Jack limped over to join his team-mates where they jostled with the Chadians, both for a slice of precious shade and also to keep as close to the penalty spot as they could manage. He was dripping with stinking sweat, his singlet soaked and stained, the red stripes, which had originally graced the sides of his knickerbocker shorts – presented by the local women to this hastily assembled International XI after church parade this morning at the Jesuit mission – now hanging in tatters against his bruised shins.

'Back, back,' yelled *Père* Bronner, blowing his whistle again in their faces. '*Dix mètres, dix mètres.*'

It was the Spaniards, of course, determined as always that, if there was a rule, it must surely have been meant to be broken.

'Come on, boys,' Jack shouted. 'Play the game.'

And, as the same Sara centre forward prepared to take the kick – El Gordo bouncing on his goal line ready to save the day – Telford watched the mule trotting towards them, like a linesman coming over to offer their reverend referee some much-needed advice. Across the road he could see the arched walls of Fort Lamy's marketplace, and beyond the walls, the pointed minaret of the Grand Mosque at the town's southern extremity. Almost eight hundred miles from Bertoua, three weeks since they left Libreville – only to discover Leclerc was no longer here, headed north, to Ounianga-Kebir, seven hundred and fifty miles further still. And on Tuesday they'd be on the road again. But, now…

'Shit,' said the Yugoslav, Markovich, as the ball sailed into the back of the net – or so Jack thought of it, since there was, factually, no net, simply the posts.

'We've still got five minutes,' shouted another of the Spaniards, the one who called himself Beto. 'We can do this.'

'Sounds familiar?' laughed Alemán, and slapped Telford on the back. 'Come on, English. This time we win, no?'

But they didn't. Not this time either. Though, by god, Jack thought, they don't give up easily. It had run right to the final whistle, the whole team, even Telford and the other two fullbacks, El Gordo the keeper as well, up there in the Chadian team's half, fighting like fury. And then came the excuses, the good-humoured recriminations, while they collapsed among the trees and swallowed down pots of *billi-billi* red millet beer. There was food as well, *biya* balls and smoked fish dipped in spicy saffron sauce. All courtesy of the Sara women and the crowd from the sidelines but attracting a fresh cloud of whining insects.

'It was the bloody mule,' said El Gordo. 'Winked at me, I swear it did.'

'Fine game, my friends,' smiled the Chadian skipper, their centre forward, of course – Eze Tolabye, as he'd introduced himself. He settled himself among them, sucking some of the bright yellow *banda* between his lips from a banana leaf. Good French, better than Jack's own. They all did. Or seemed to. Was this strange? He wasn't sure. The French had been in Chad – how long? Forty years? Another land grab to help them expand French Equatorial Africa.

'What was here?' Jack asked him. 'Before the French?'

'The river only,' said Eze. 'More or less. A village. Small. A slavers' village. They called it Am Djamena. When the French soldiers drove out the slavers, they built the fort. Yes?'

'Reminds me of Bou Arfa,' Markovich snarled.

'It's growing on me,' Jack replied. 'And big.' It must be a mile, at least, he'd calculated, from there to the oasis where they were camped, north, along Rue du Colonel Moll, the streets of mixed shacks and colonial bungalows, up beyond the Place de l'Étoile and the administrative centre towards the airfield.

'Big? Of course,' Eze told them. 'My people grew cotton, raised cattle. But now they all come to the town. Work in the cotton mills.'

'Working for the French,' said Alemán.

'My father, my grandfather, my uncles, they still remember the slavers. But we fight for France now – and who can say? This time they might see us.'

This bloody war, thought Jack, swatting aside another of those damned *tick-tick* flies. Everybody expects so much from it. Morocco's Jews. Spain's Republicans. And these boys. A whole battalion of them up at the camp. They'd be leaving on Tuesday, to join Leclerc.

'As you say, Eze – who knows? And fighting for Leclerc. Have you met him yet?'

'Leclerc,' said Reiter, the German, and spat on the ground. 'They say he's fascist as well. Rich bastard. Just hates Hitler a bit more than he hates decent Socialists.'

The Spaniards laughed, nodded their agreement.

'Hey, Abia,' Eze shouted, still in French, to another of the forwards, 'this Englishman wants to know about Leclerc. Come, tell him the story.' He turned to Jack. 'He is Bassa,' he said. 'Of the Yaoundé men.'

They'd picked up a further truckload of troops in Cameroon, and Jack was still struggling with the bewildering number of tribes, clans and dialects. But the Bassa, he thought, were much like the Gabonese back in Libreville. Another Bantu people? Well, according to Fox this was the case, anyway.

'What can I tell you, my friend?' said Abia, squatting with his millet beer next to Jack. 'In my village they tell this story. About how this man Leclerc was a chief among the tribes of the French. But he died fighting many enemies and fell from his horse.' Jack was about to correct him, but he knew better than to spoil a good yarn. 'Dead ten years,' Abia gazed up at the sky, 'though he still watched over his people. He brought them great prosperity. Strong magic. But then, one day, when he slept deep within his grave, the fork-tailed drongo brought him word. Word that his great city had been taken by a German corporal. Leclerc did not even know this corporal's name but in a great rage he rose from his grave, flew across the seas, for his legs were broken, and said: "See, now I am a colonel. I shall make myself invisible, bring war to this German, to his Italian friends, and warriors will ride upon my wings." You understand, English? We are the warriors who ride on his wings.'

Later, Telford swam. In the very place he would never have expected. He wasn't sure how he'd imagined the colonial outpost. But not this. And after three weeks on the road the slow green waters of the River Chari, the private beach below the Hôtel de Fort Lamy, presented a minor miracle. There were just the hippos to worry about. And the story Abia the Bassa had told them.

Leclerc. Jack didn't know what to make of the man – or, at least, the man's reputation. Fox had filled in a few of the gaps. The name, Leclerc, as much a *nom de guerre* as El Gordo, or Alemán, those of most of the other Spaniards among the volunteers. Leclerc, a name as common, and with the same origins, as Clark back home. Nobby Leclerc, Telford smiled to himself, as he breast-stroked cautiously close to the shoreline, watching out for hostile wildlife. And he pictured the man, the cavalryman Philippe François Marie de Hautecloque, privileged son of Picardy's Comte and Comtesse de Hautecloque, showing his forged papers as the lowly wine merchant Leclerc, to help him get out of the German occupied zone, and then keeping the identity, to protect his family, when he'd escaped to London and joined de Gaulle. Leclerc. The stuff the Spaniards had picked up about him. How, at the start of Franco's insurrection, Leclerc – like most of the French military, all the devout Catholics anyway – had been sympathetic to Spain's rebel generals, supported their so-called crusade against the atheist Reds. Was it right? Had his sympathies changed now? And would having a common foe allow these soldiers of Spain to fight for a man who'd despised their beliefs? The enemies of my enemy, thought Jack, as a flock of black and white cranes swept above him, across the river and towards the African sunset.

Christ, he wondered, are there crocodiles? I never thought to ask about crocodiles. He'd never seen one. But what a wealth of nature he'd enjoyed on the long days of his journey. The savanna. Buffalo and rhino. Elephant and giraffe. Antelope and zebra. Even a cheetah. Monkeys everywhere. But no crocodiles. And, thankfully, no more scorpions.

Heaven be praised for some good news, he thought, as he read the first of the messages waiting for him the following morning at Fort Lamy's post office.

This one from Sydney Elliott in London, the authorisation Jack had wired from Libreville for the transfer of funds, all sorted, and the confirmation details from Lloyds for the cash to be collected, upon provision of the required identifications, from the temporary branch for the Bank of British West Africa established only a few months earlier. All part of the deal between de Gaulle and his new friends in London. The RAF in British Nigeria able to use Fort Lamy's airfield, Chad's production purchased in sterling through Nigeria's banking system, and Chad's supply of oil guaranteed. Neat. Jack's only problem? He still had no passport, just those temporary travel documents from Rabat and his accreditation letter as a foreign correspondent signed by de Gaulle himself. Well, if this wasn't good enough...

He leaned against one of the white columns at the front of the *Grande Poste*, lit himself a cigarette and gazed out across the wide, wasteland roundabout, boasting the name Place de l'Étoile, this hub of Fort Lamy's road network. He ran his fingers inside the collar of his uniform shirt, flicked away some of the sweat. Too ferociously hot to be Paris, and no Arc de Triomphe. Would there ever be one? A monument to the glorious fallen of French Equatorial Africa? He didn't think so. No, these would be their only memorials: the rich aromas of rotting fruit; petrol fumes; horns blaring from trucks trundling around the Étoile's outer rim, the circular Boulevard de Strasbourg. But along the Avenue de la République were most of the main administrative buildings and around the corner, he knew, he'd find the provisional branch of the bank, attached to the offices serving the British government's agents here in Chad – now including Captain Fox.

'Waiting for a booth?' Vidal, now in his own light khaki shirt and shorts. Jack hadn't noticed him earlier but he'd plainly also just come out of the post office. The Frenchman took off his sun helmet, used his handkerchief to wipe inside the headband.

'Me? No. Just picked these up.' Telford waved the telegrams at him. 'You?'

Relationships were still pretty frigid, but Jack owed him. For his life. And, while he knew the Frenchman deserved just about every-thing the Spaniards frequently threw at him, it had now all become a bit much. Vidal had been beaten twice and there were almost daily incidents – excrement in his food seemed to be a favourite.

'Trying to get through to my mother. My father. Still in Paris.'
'They stayed?'
'Thought they'd be safe – after the armistice. But now? Last

time we spoke, my father had been forced to hand over his business to some non-Jewish neighbour. No compensation. Nothing.'

Vidal lit a cigarette himself, glanced back inside to see whether his number had come up yet.

'The paper,' said Jack. 'They've been bombing synagogues. In Paris.'

It had been all over the front page of *L'Éveil de Cameroun*, the copy he'd picked up in Yaoundé. It had cut him perhaps even more than news of the German occupation itself. He had fond memories of Paris.

'That too,' said Vidal.

'Germans?'

'Our very own French Nazis.'

'I'm sorry,' Jack told him, and he meant it. The world was mad, suffering from some weird virus, which affected only the collective mind.

'Why sorry?' Vidal seemed genuinely surprised.

'Collaborators. All those friends of Pétain, of Vichy…'

'Pétain? The Lion of Verdun. He is a hero, *Monsieur* Telford. But surrounded by rogues for advisors? Of course. Though his actions against the damned republicans, the Reds, the Freemasons…'

'The Jews?' said Jack. 'You can't be serious. Pétain's upto his neck in anti-Jewish laws. You, for pity's sake. The way they threw you out of the army.'

'The work of others,' Vidal snapped. 'Not Pétain.'

'Then why the hell are you here? And is this why you wouldn't pass on the Spaniards' requests for transfer to the Legion?'

Vidal turned the sun helmet in his hands, stared at the blue, white and red *tricolore* emblem on its side, ran his fingers over the scarlet Cross of Lorraine at its heart.

'More Reds inside our army?' he muttered, tossing away his half-smoked cigarette. 'Just what France needs, eh? You've seen them. Can't take orders. No respect for authority. And why am I here? Because I'd hoped, *monsieur*, there'd be a chance to join your *British* Army. Perhaps I'll still get the chance.'

'Is this because of the rank thing?'

Jack gestured towards the double chevrons on Vidal's epaulettes.

'A sergeant,' Vidal spat. 'They make me a sergeant. And why? Because they will trust rank only to so very few of the blacks. I may be a Jew, but a white Jew is still worth marginally more than a black. Didn't Gabizon teach you that much, at least?' He turned to look back inside once more. 'Ah, my number, Telford.' And without another word he headed for the doors.

'Hey, Vidal.' The Frenchman stopped, swung around, holding the door open. 'I've got to go get some funds,' Jack shouted. 'What's best? French *francs*, French West Africans or *Neptunes*?'

'West Africans, of course.'

'Thanks, and good luck – getting through, I mean.'

This time there was no backward glance, only the door swinging shut, and Jack was left with the image of Isaac Gabizon again, falling into his arms. It was hard to shift. But what the hell would he make of all this? Men like Vidal still loyal to Pétain despite the way he'd been personally treated. Nor was he alone. Telford knew it. There'd been tales of deserters, men already abandoning these Free French territories and heading back west, for the Vichy-controlled Ivory Coast, Dahomey, French Sudan or Mauretania. It was all so very fragile.

And Gabizon? Jack still lived in the shadow of his death, always looking over his shoulder, certain that, if it had indeed been an attempt on his own life, it was likely the threat would remain whenever he returned to civilisation – or perhaps sooner. But why? He still had no idea.

He walked down the steps, turned left along the avenue, reading again the second of his messages. This one forwarded from Libreville. The London bureau chief of Associated Press, Robert Bunnelle. Jack had met him once, along with Bunnelle's wife. Elliott had spoken with him and, if he was still with Leclerc's forces, Bunnelle was prepared to offer one of AP's third-party packages – infinitely inferior to the contracts for their own bureau correspondents but not to be sniffed at, all the same. Telford, in return, to build up a beat around the military capabilities of Leclerc and the Fighting French. His reports would be wired direct and exclusively to Bunnelle, though nothing in the offer prevented him sending unrelated articles to *Reynold's*

News. Payment by results. He'd wired back to Bunnelle. Accepted the offer.

'A beat?' said Fox, looking up from his paperwork through a haze of tobacco smoke. Jack had drawn his French West Africans and wandered through the collection of zinc-roofed huts now serving as some ramshackle consulate for the British attachés. He hadn't even been challenged. But the place was very much a work in progress, local Chadians still decorating the timber walls, or working on the fixtures. The nostalgic odours of fresh paint. The rasp of a saw, a carpenter cutting the bottom from an oversized door.

'Like bobbies on a beat. Instead of reporting news in general, you build up an expertise on a particular patch. Just concentrate on that area. Get to know it inside out. Build up sources. More insight and analysis maybe.'

'You think there's a Pulitzer in this, Jack? Becoming the world's expert on Leclerc. This is just a sideshow, old boy. And you'll never get close to Leclerc. You know he hates journalists.'

Fox scowled over at the carpenter. The fellow had taken now to singing at the top of his voice to the beat of his crosscut saw.

'I was thinking of a slightly different beat, Captain. Leclerc and the Fighting French, certainly. But the stories of all these men who aren't French at all – the Spanish, the Africans, and the rest – but making Free France a reality. Without them – well, it just wouldn't exist, would it?'

Fox pursed his lips, head swaying cobra-like as he tried to fathom whether Jack's plan might have legs. Behind him a wireless set crackled a broadcast relayed from Radio Colonial Paris. Ray Ventura's dance music, *Aux Îles Vent-Debut*. Memories of seaside resorts. Swimming at Deauville after his last assignment in Paris in '37.

'Maybe,' said Fox. 'But here's good news. Wire from Faya-Largeau. French contingent just got back from the raid on Murzuk. The captain – Massu. Even more of a success than we thought. Airfield destroyed.'

'Casualties?'

'One of the New Zealanders.' Fox glanced at the message. 'Hewson. And their Kiwi C.O. – Clayton, taken prisoner in an ambush on the way back. Another French officer killed. A few wounded. And this Massu, sounds like quite a fellow. Shot in the leg but cauterised the wound with his own cigarette.' Jack winced. 'Get to meet him, I expect,' said Fox, then shot an irate glance at the joiner, slammed his hand on the desk. 'For pity's sake,' he yelled, 'can't you stop your caterwauling.'

The African simply offered Fox the most disarming of smiles.

'Fellow's just happy in his work, Captain,' said Telford. 'And can't wait,' he went on, wondering – not for the first time – how he'd manage to keep himself safe from the horrors of war. 'To meet Massu. But I wanted to ask you about this.'

Jack showed him the third of his messages, another of those forwarded to Fort Lamy. At least it turned the captain's attention away from the joiner.

'Decent of him, what?' said Fox, as he read the sparse text. From Kingsley Welch. Jack had a rough recollection of his hatchet-face, those ice-blue eyes, and the few luxuries he'd sent for them to consume on their voyage south from Agadir.

HOPE THIS FINDS YOU STOP, said the wire. *MAY HAVE STORY STOP KEEP IN TOUCH STOP.*

Telford flapped away a fly buzzing around his ears, tugged at the shirt sticking to his back.

'He still with the trade delegation – working with the Yanks?'

'How would I know, old boy? As much in the dark as you. But suppose so, yes. Why d'you ask?'

'No reason, not really. Might be a scoop to be had, though – the trade deal with Morocco.' Yes, Jack told himself. But he barely knew the man, hadn't really taken to him, truth be told. And Welch must have known plenty of other correspondents. Greeks bearing gifts, he thought. The sultan, maybe? Perhaps this was the link. Still, he'd think about it.

'Probably won't mean much to folk back home, though. Caught up on the news yet?'

At Libreville the papers had given plenty of coverage to the Blitz, not just the continuing raids on London but the concentrated attacks there'd been, day after day, on cities like Southampton, Sheffield, Liverpool and Manchester, each of them punished in their turn. But better moments, like the British victory at Sidi Barrani. At Yaoundé, Fox had picked up word of the beatings taken by Cardiff and Bristol, Wavell's action around Tobruk, Roosevelt inaugurated for a third term.

'Not much,' said Jack. 'But one of the local boys from the football team's a huge boxing fan – tells me Joe Louis knocked out Red Burman.'

A red-headed lieutenant at the adjoining desk looked up.

'Fifth round at Madison Square,' he said. 'Quite a show. And, by the by, anyone fancy a cup of Rosie? Still some in the pot, I think.'

Jack shook his head, then changed his mind.

'Actually...' Telford smiled, and the lieutenant jumped up from his chair.

'Well,' said Fox, 'apart from all that, we seem to be doing OK in Libya. In the east, as well. Here's the big one, though. Seems like Jerry's sending out an expeditionary force to help the Italians. Hitler not very impressed by their performance. So he's sending one of his favourite generals out with them. Rommel. Made quite a name for himself in France.'

'Christ, they were unstoppable in France.'

He thought about the victories Britain and its allies had secured in North Africa, or in Italian Eritrea, and he knew they were important. But important maybe like Luton Town beating Plymouth Argyle in the Second Division. It felt like treason, but he couldn't help it. And the gains made by the Free French here? He kept seeing those reports of the German panzers sweeping across France itself. Unstoppable indeed. He balanced those images against the tatterdemalion outfit with which he was travelling.

'That was then, and this is now, as they say,' said Fox. 'And all packed for tomorrow? Great heavens, Telford, you even *look* like a war correspondent now.' Jack fingered his armband, white, with the single word *Presse* in bold black letters. 'Want me to arrange for you to travel up front?'

The captain's optimism did little to lift Jack's gloom, but he'd have to make the best of it. And besides, the young lieutenant had just come back with an enamel mug.

'Take sugar, sir?' he asked. Jack declined, but he held the warm cup between his hands. Counter-intuitive perhaps but at this moment, tropical heat or no tropical heat, he knew a refreshing cup of tea would hit just the right spot.

'Travel with the officers?' Telford forced a laugh. 'Bad for my image, I'm afraid. No, I'll be travelling with the *tirailleurs*. Get to know them better.'

'Good god,' said Fox. 'Taking things a bit far, don't you think?'

'It's never what I'd expected.' Jack steadied himself, hanging from one of the truck's bow frames, the canvas rolled up against the cab. The barren, stony desert – yes, this much was predictable after a whole week of it. And the sprawl of nomadic huts, mud-brick buildings on the outskirts. But the trees? The verdant oasis, palms so abundant you almost couldn't see the town itself? The evening rose-rimmed rock formations rising from its northern shores, fingers stretching out like a giant's hand reaching into the Sahara? He'd forseen none of it.

'After all this time?' laughed Eze Tolabye. 'We can still surprise you?'

It was a fair point. After a whole week travelling with these *tirailleurs* – these black riflemen from every part of French Equatorial Africa – Jack knew he'd learned a lot. Yet everything he learned simply helped to highlight how much more he had yet to understand, and how complex was their involvement in a war which wasn't their own. In other ways, though, they were little different from soldiers everywhere – grumbles about their food, shared bawdy jokes, constant banter about the whores of this place or that, their respective sexual exploits.

'There's not a day goes by, Eze,' said Jack, 'without you surprising me.'

The language, apart from anything else. These men could switch at the drop of a hat from tongue to tongue: Arabic and Sara; Bassa and Ewondo; Fang and Myene. Jack had picked up the odd few words of each. But whenever he was among them it was always French, literally their *lingua franca*. A kaleidoscope of French, this was true – for each of them spoke it in their own fashion, warped

185

by their respective accents – but French, all the same, once he'd tuned his ear to it.

'Shall we also surprise the Flying Lion Leclerc, English, do you think?' said Abia the Bassa. 'The last time he saw us, we were just recruits. In rags, with broomsticks and machetes for weapons.'

They'd told Jack the story over and over. About Leclerc's arrival in Cameroon when Yaoundé had still been controlled by Vichy, when Free France was no more than an outline on a Frenchman's map. Well, this lot were more than just a mirage, and no mistake. A whole mobile batallion of them, trained in the camps at Brazzaville and Libreville, their uniforms a rare mixture of odds and sods, in every shade of khaki, many still without decent boots – and here, on the trucks, mostly bare feet anyhow. Or simple rope sandals, like those Jack now favoured, in imitation of Leclerc himself. On their heads, a few sun helmets, the occasional beret or forage cap, or those *chechia* brimless red hats he'd seen so often in Morocco. Even the occasional turban, favoured by the Hadjerai Muslims among the men from this northern-most part of Chad.

'You still think the Germans would have given you better?' said Jack.

'Have you never seen their *Askaris*, English?' Abia replied. 'I still remember them, marching through Yaoundé.'

He'd told this story many times. How, as a boy, when Cameroon was still a German colony, before it was carved up by France and Britain at the end of their world war – the previous one – German had been his second language. About how he'd hated having to learn French. And he regaled them now with one of the songs he'd sung as a kid, *Der Luftballon*.

'Lovely people, the Germans,' said Diguéal, another of the Gabonese, a Sara, like Eze Tolabye. A sense of humour as wild as Max Weston's. 'Just a shame they want to kill anybody who's not got white skin and hair like dried straw.'

They all laughed, slapped Abia the German-lover on the back as the truck ground to a halt outside a mud-brick blockhouse with an open slope running down towards a small green pool. The tailgate dropped and the company lieutenant shouted up at them.

'Down,' he yelled. 'Tents there.'

He pointed at the slope. The *tirailleurs* smiled at each other, a few giggles, and Jack found it hard to keep his face straight as well. He'd seen it a few times now – mainly during their halt at Faya-Largeau – this habit of so many officers and NCOs to talk with the Africans in this bizarre pidgin French. Of course, there must be plenty among the volunteers who had no French, but Jack hadn't yet come across any. It was the simple assumption of the officers that these men must all somehow be illiterate. The same lazy ignorance causing them to label this entire rainbow alliance of black Africans, regardless of their actual place of origin, as Senegalese.

But at Faya-Largeau they'd also come across Massu – still limping after his eye-watering piece of self-inflicted first aid – and the men who'd returned with him from Murzuk. Men hardened by their experiences, like the Spanish Republicans. Drinking men. Pirates, Jack had thought. It's what they remind me of.

'And where will you sleep, English?' Eze asked him, jumping to the ground. 'With the officers?'

'Why?' said Jack. 'Don't you want me?'

'You,' called the officer. 'Correspondent?'

Jack shrugged, gestured towards his armband and received instruction he must see *le patron* immediately, the boss. Eze offered to look after his kitbag, and Jack pushed his way through the travel-worn men disembarking from the other lorries, saw Vidal at one point and, at another, received a friendly wave from El Gordo and the other Spaniards.

Telford was dog-tired. Like the rest, he'd simply now been on the road too long and this final stretch by far the worst. A week, north from Fort Lamy to Lake Chad and then north-east into the desert, barely a track to follow. The meagre settlements at Tourba and Massakory, Moussoro and Salal, Koro Toro and Faya-Largeau, then finally here, Ounianga-Kebir.

The last thing he needed now was any sort of confrontation. To be honest, Leclerc's reputation, his contempt for Jack's profession, made him almost believe he'd be put back on the first south-bound truck, but he found the colonel, finally, in the enclosure of rusted barbed wire – an enclosure full of black or flaking green oil drums, *tirailleurs* running around with heavy, grey fuel cans. And there were camels here, many camels, most of their riders dark-skinned nomads from the desert, but a few Europeans among them – all of them, however, barely identifiable as soldiers, for their ragged outer robes, the turbans, the veils covering so many faces. The French Camel Corps, a *Compagnie Méhariste*.

Ah, thought Jack, this is more like it. Lawrence!

But what were they doing? The officers in Leclerc's entourage shouted their orders and the riders began bringing the camels to their knees, while the *tirailleurs* helped them strap can after can to the beasts' saddle hooks.

Leclerc gave some final instruction, turned and noticed Jack, limped towards him.

'*Monsieur* Telford, I presume.'

A couple of inches taller than Jack, his short-sleeved bushjacket seemed a size too large for his slender arms. The toothbrush moustache looked wild, untrimmed and the badge on the front of his pith helmet was in imminent danger of coming away entirely from its stitching – the Cross of Lorraine sitting upon an anchor, Jack noted, the emblem of France's colonial forces.

'It's a great honour, Colonel,' said Jack, and wished he'd thought of something more original, but he was thinking of Abia the Bassa's legend, Leclerc's self-promotion to the rank. *See, now I am a Colonel.*

'Honour? Honour is precisely the reason you're here. Nothing more and nothing less. The honour of France.'

The colonel headed off towards a collection of vehicles parked alongside the blockhouse – dozens of trucks, a couple of armoured cars, two pieces of heavy artillery – and Telford wasn't entirely sure whether he'd been dismissed or was required to follow. He chose the latter.

'Yes, sir. Precisely the brief I've received from AP. In-depth reports on how Fighting France achieves its victories. Like Murzuk, Colonel. I was told you'd appoint a liaison for me.'

'No, Telford. You'll liaise with me. Nobody else. Understand?' The *tirailleurs* guarding the vehicle compound snapped to attention smartly enough, but one of them also offered Leclerc a friendly smile. 'These fellows,' muttered the colonel as he returned the salute.

'I've been travelling with them,' said Jack, feeling the need to defend his new friends. 'A good bunch.'

Leclerc stopped, rounded on him, tapped his walking cane on the ground, again and again.

'And think you know them, I suppose? Typical bloody journalist. Spend five minutes somewhere and think you've the right to share your personal warped views with the world. A good bunch. Is this what passes for in-depth analysis in your book, *monsieur*?'

'Look, Colonel…' Jack began, but Leclerc had already moved on to another of his officers, inspecting a truck with its bonnet open, a mechanic working on the engine. Words exchanged, the officer's assurance that, yes, they'd be ready.

'Tomorrow, Lafitte. Final inspection tomorrow.'

Leclerc slapped the fellow on the back, turned to Telford once more.

'Captain Fox with you?'

'Delayed at Faya-Largeau, sir. But should be here this evening.'

'He's a good man.' The colonel shifted his weight onto his good leg, lifted the malacca stick. It was very fine. 'By repute, anyway. His chief gave me this. General Spears – know him?'

Jack shook his head.

'But, Colonel…'

Leclerc was on the move again, glancing up at the cloudless skies, back towards the blockhouse.

'You know the history of my country, *monsieur*? Of course, you do. The Gallic tribes, each happier to be at war with its neighbours than to unite against the Romans. It is the curse of France and always has been, to this day. Perhaps forever. The reason we must present a different face, convince our few allies that, despite everything, Fighting France is a united force, worthy of support. And if you cannot help us in this goal, Telford, you might as well return to England now.'

The colonel returned more salutes, this time from soldiers with familiar white *képis*. More deserters from the Legion, Jack supposed.

'My contract with Associated Press requires me to find the spirit at the heart of Free France, sir. To find it and sell its story to the world, warts and all.'

'Oh, there shall be no warts, *monsieur*. Our secret, how we have just as many Vichy supporters deserting us for French West Africa as we have friends of Free France coming in. These rifts within our own ranks, they are precisely the reason why the Americans dismiss us as an irrelevance. Only the British take us seriously. And you shall write nothing which does not meet my approval.'

'Lieutenant Colonel Parant explained the censorship rules to me very carefully. I might not like them, but I'm no fool, Colonel. And when I said your *tirailleurs* are a good bunch, it was simply my shorthand. I'd like to tell their story in more detail. Without the gloss. If I simply said they'd all volunteered from some patriotic duty to the glory of France, nobody would believe me anyway. But their individual stories, the simple soldiers' stories – enlisting for the pay, for the adventure, for following friends into service, for the escape from nagging wives, for their obligation to their headmen – that's what will grip folk. And then how they've found their loyalty to France – to you, Colonel, or to General de Gaulle – through their individual and collective journeys.'

It had been interesting. Most of them didn't have a political bone in their bodies, yet there were those like Eze Tolabye, who would all have expressed the thing differently, though dreamed of a day when their towns, their rivers, their forest, their grasslands, even the treacherous *fesh-fesh* sinking sands of their deserts, were once more their own. And they seemed to understand – most, anyway – how the least menacing scenario in which this dream might become a reality was the one in which France willingly granted them their freedom. Simply released them. But to reach this distant place in the sun? First, France herself must be defended.

'Sounds like hogwash to me,' said Leclerc. 'But in a few days, we'll see. Have you ever fired a weapon, Telford?'

'Once or twice, sir.' It was twice. And neither occasion one which Jack would have wished to remember. 'But I won't need a gun now.'

At the studded gateway to the blockhouse, a uniformed clerk – another Sara, Jack thought – was waiting with papers to be signed. But nothing with which to sign them. Telford noted the twitch, the tic, which erupted in Leclerc's cheek. Jack reached into his top pocket, took out Negrín's pen. Leclerc admired it but Jack chose not to explain its provenance.

'No gun?' said the colonel, snatching the documents, casually perusing them. 'Then you're a fool. That armband won't protect you from Italian or German bullets. They've no more respect for the press than I have.'

He began to sign the papers, one by one.

'Another raid, Colonel?'

'Two days. We march on Kufra.'

'Kufra...'

'The Kufra Oasis, *Monsieur* Telford. Across the desert, and the desert here as enormous as northern Europe. You have been in Paris?'

Leclerc handed back the documents and pen, while the clerk disappeared into the shadows of the gateway.

'I have.'

'Bordeaux?'

'Yes. By train.'

Jack wondered whether he'd be invited inside but the colonel seemed intent on surveying his domain, squinting first at one area, then another. Instinctive, the way any good sailor constantly checks each section of his standing and running rigging, without even thinking about the process, yet finding every potential fault. Finally, his eyes rested on the camels, now plodding out in a long train onto the track leading north.

'Then you know the distance we must travel to reach Kufra,' said Leclerc. 'A little less than Berlin to Warsaw. Except – we must make the journey by truck. Across some of the most inhospitable terrain in the world.'

'The camels, sir?'

'We can't make the journey without refuelling, and we don't have enough trucks to carry the men and all the fuel we'll need. But the camels will establish fuel and supply dumps for us along the way.'

'How long d'you think you'll be away, Colonel?'

'I assumed you'd be coming with me, Telford. No? You and those rogues you've been travelling with. I suspect most of them have no taste for modern warfare, but we'll see.'

As he spoke, a platoon of *tirailleurs* marched past, at their drill, their feet stamping up and down theatrically. *Left, right, left, right,* they yelled. Jack felt as though he'd been rebuked, but the truth? He very much wanted to be part of the raid, but thought it protocol to wait until he was invited or instructed. He'd wanted to impress Leclerc but seemed only to have irritated the man.

'The Saras in particular seem to have quite a reputation as ferocious warriors, don't they?' he said.

'Handsome devils, to be sure. And some of them served me well in Cameroon and Gabon. But these new recruits? So many of them. And can they fight?'

'Well the Spaniards certainly can.'

Leclerc looked at him in disbelief, scornful.

'More Reds? Dear Lord, did those imbeciles send me more Reds? Don't they understand? We're fighting Italians here. Professional Italian soldiers. The same fellows that chased you – you and your communist friends, Telford – out of Alicante.'

Jack took it as a personal affront, though it was only what El Gordo and his comrades had warned him would be Leclerc's attitude.

'I think, Colonel, perhaps you've not been fully briefed...'

'You think you're in a better position than me, *monsieur*, to analyse the military situation in Spain. Generalísimo Franco, his German and Italians allies, his *Moros* – my god, how I wish I had a few companies of *goumiers* under my command again – but they outmanouevred your Republican Bolsheviks at almost every turn.'

'You admire them, sir?'

'I respect them, Telford. Yet they are the enemy now. The enemies of France.'

In the distance, the throb of an aircraft's engines, and coming their way. Jack flinched, a habit he'd picked up during the bombing raids on Alicante. A flurry of activity at the sandbagged gun emplacement just along from the blockhouse, Leclerc impassive but shielding his eyes, peering at the rapidly growing black dot. A French officer standing atop the wall of sandbags focused his binoculars.

'Our own, sir,' shouted the officer. 'One of the Blenheims.'

Jack gripped his own right hand, to still the shaking.

'And me, Colonel,' he said. 'I'd hardly classify myself as a Red, as you put it, But are my sympathies with the Republic? Oh hell, yes, certainly. You know it. So why agree to me being here?'

'Because I once had the pleasure of reading a piece you wrote. About the Saar Plebiscite. It was perceptive. Honest, as well. You may have misguided politics, but I think you have integrity. You predicted all this – most of it anyway. That if such huge numbers of ordinary people could vote in favour of their territory willingly becoming part of Nazi Germany, then would this not feed Hitler's hunger for Austria, for Czechoslovakia? For the rest of the world? If more people had read it, heeded the warning signs...'

Telford was astonished. But he remembered the article. Of course, he did. He'd covered the plebiscite, along with Sheila Grant Duff. Close colleague and friend, too professional to allow herself ever to be anything more. Jack wondered how she was. Or *where* she was.

'I'm amazed you read it, sir.'

Leclerc stabbed the tip of his cane against the stones again.

'I have to be honest. A cousin of mine sent it to me, Telford. Xavier. He was an admirer of your work, seemed to share your misguided opinions. But he visited Dachau, reported on conditions there, the killings. Charted the rise of the Nazis, like yourself. And I asked our friends in London to check you out.'

'You said he *was* an admirer. Did I upset him?' Telford laughed.

'Poisoned during his last investigation in Germany.' Jack winced. Guilt. Stupid, stupid – though Leclerc didn't seem particularly troubled. 'The Nazis, of course,' the colonel went on. 'He suffered three months in agony before he died. We had our differences, but my cousin, all the same.'

But does this make it easier to understand the man? Jack wondered. Some of the contradictions.

'I'm sorry for your loss, Colonel. It must make this fight against the Nazis very personal.'

Leclerc chewed his lower lip, looked at Telford as though he was calculating whether this was an impertinence bordering on insubordination.

'Is this war not personal for us all, *monsieur?*'

'It's this way, *Monsieur* Telford,' said Leclerc, four days later, 'the patrols are back – and all the signs show that the Italians know we're coming.'

It had taken them two days to reach the oasis at El-Zurgh, just five miles south of Kufra itself. An ancient wind from deep in the Sahara's soul rattled the canvas of the headquarters tent flaps, and Jack had been astonished to receive the colonel's invitation to a personal briefing.

'You'll have to call it off, Colonel?'

'Call it off? On the contrary, here's the story you'll have to tell. How, first, we reconnoitred in force. Then how we destroyed their gun trucks. And, finally, how we took the oasis itself.'

Isn't there something about not counting our chickens? Jack mused. He watched Leclerc take a yellow tin of Manila cheroots from the breast pocket of his khaki shirt, fitted one into a mother of pearl holder, rummaged in the loose-fitting *sirwal* breeches.

'Of course, sir.' Jack produced his own cartridge case lighter, flicked it into action, and the colonel nodded his appreciation, blew a thin stream of smoke towards the tent's roof.

'Your Captain Fox seems to think a direct attack will be suicidal, the enemy certain to have been reinforced. Kept reminding me how well the Italians know the desert. But what they don't know, Telford, is that it's now our desert – *my* desert.'

Jack studied the map spread across Leclerc's table. The vast empty ochre shading this section of the Fezzan, and the clearly marked grey ridge of rock running from left to right. Hanging from the escarpment's lower edge, a U-shape basin, maybe two miles across, of separated green clumps, a necklace of small villages and their surrounding palm groves. At the heart of the horseshoe, two small blue-coloured lakes – the palm trees depicted more densely around their shores – and a larger village, El-Giof. Immediately to the right of the horseshoe, an airfield, its runways plainly marked. And at the upper left-hand tip of the horseshoe, another settlement with its adjoining fortress, El-Taj. This was the Kufra Oasis. Impossibly remote. It must once have been a storybook place.

'Your destiny, Colonel – are you happy if I write it this way?'

'This time last year I was leading pointless patrols to nowhere. The joke war. The wasted chance to destroy Hitler while they were still focused on Poland. But now? Yes, my place in history.'

'Action again, at last.'

Jack hadn't intended any criticism, but he saw Leclerc bristle. His tic again.

'What do you mean, *monsieur* – finally?' he growled. 'Have you been listening to this nonsense about Murzuk?'

Common currency among the *tirailleurs* – how France was happy to send them out to die while their commander amused himself flying back and forth in his aeroplanes, still living the high life of the French *milord*. Unjust, but there, regardless.

'Some of the new boys don't understand the need for reconnaissance. But those who've already seen you in action, sir...'

'Well, you may write it as you please, Telford, so long as it sticks to the theme – Free France, united, fighting, victorious.'

Jack smiled, remembered the words he'd heard Leclerc exchange earlier with his adjutant, dealing with his correspondence, his governance of the provinces under his control. Something to the effect that he would rather govern three hundred Chadians than three dozen French civilians. Damned divisions everywhere, he'd said. The thing which actually defined Free France, the divisions – the administrator, the settler, the merchant, the mine operator, each accusing the other of every kind of crime, of conspiracy, of forming all manner of factions.

'I'll write it, Colonel – if you can promise to get me back here in one piece.'

'Get you back, Telford? When I said you were coming with us, I didn't mean into the fighting itself. And tonight, *monsieur*, there will be fighting.'

Still no gun. Jack had refused Leclerc's final attempt to persuade him. And the colonel's repeated efforts to dissuade him from joining the expedition.

Telford wondered whether he might have made a mistake. He trudged along towards the rear of this central patrol, a mixed party of hand-picked former Legionnaires, a couple of the Spaniards, three other Frenchmen, a dozen battle-hardened *tirailleurs* and a few Toubou nomads as guides, Leclerc himself up front. Above them, the night sky was filled with more stars than Jack would have believed possible. He was awed, emotional, and had stumbled several times, paying more attention to the Milky Way than to where he walked. He'd promised Leclerc his damaged eyesight would present no impediment, but now, scrabbling about on this rock-strewn track, he wasn't so sure. And it was cold. The tail-end of the desert winter, somebody had said. Bloody cold, despite his borrowed greatcoat. He'd managed to fasten his *Presse* armband around the left sleeve, almost like a talisman – fretted now that the white canvas might make him a target. Yet all these things helped him, perhaps. Took his mind off the turmoil in his guts. In his satchel was a flask of cognac, though he resisted the temptation.

Somewhere behind them, in the darkness, were the vehicles. A fallback position in a wadi, roughly halfway between El-Zurgh and the village of El-Giof. As far as Leclerc dared convey them in the fifteen Bedford trucks. Jack knew now he should have stayed there – with their small force of reserves; with Medical Captain, Mauric; with the chaplain and sometimes football referee, *Père* Bronner; with the emergency supplies; and with the comforting LRDG Chevrolet command car, now gifted to Leclerc along with its decent radio kit and fancy navigational gadgets. From the wadi, another small patrol had set out as well, with the tall, fair-haired lieutenant, Jacques de Guillebon, heading off to the right, northeastwards, to check out the airfield.

'All good, English,' whispered Alemán.

'Silence,' somebody hissed from further up the line, and Jack patted the scar-faced Spaniard on the shoulder by way of reassurance which, in truth, he didn't feel. But it was comforting. Somebody cared.

They came down a slope, palm fronds silhouetted above them and rustling waving in the wind. One of the *tirailleurs* swore in his own tongue and, again, the angry admonition. Keep quiet. For there were buildings here, ghostly shapes in the blackness.

The crunch of their boots on the gravel seemed at once absurdly loud, the whole place otherwise eerily silent. Deserted, perhaps. Or maybe simply a trap waiting to be sprung. Jack thought he saw a movement, away to their right, felt himself freeze like a frightened rabbit until the goat skittered away, as far as its tether would allow. They stopped in an open square, not very big, palm trees all around, but a few empty market stalls, a modest adobe mosque on the far side with a stubby, pointed minaret. Another small building in front of them, a radio mast rising from its roof. There was a voice – Leclerc, Jack thought, or maybe it was the lieutenant in the party, Arnaud – and then the crash and clatter of metal on metal. One of the Legionnaires, smashing at the padlock. Other men detailed to take up position at the corners of the square.

Oh, good god, Jack thought. What about keeping quiet? This was going to bring holy hell down on their heads. Yet, as the door swung open, silence still reigned supreme in the village. Where the hell were the Italians? All asleep in the fort? A dog barked. And then another. From inside the building, the sounds of destruction. The radio, Jack imagined.

In the square itself, Leclerc taking Lieutenant Arnaud by the shoulder.

'As we agreed, Lieutenant,' he said. 'A section. Keep an eye on the fort. Let me know how the land lies. We rendezvous at...' He clapped a hand around the dial of his watch. 'Zero two hundred if there's no problem. If there is – send up a flare. Got it?'

Arnaud picked his men, including Alemán, and they trotted off down the narrow lane to the left between more houses and huts, while Leclerc consulted with one of the Toubous, shining a torch on a roughly sketched map of the oasis. He still had his stick, Jack noticed. No gun either. But he also saw the colonel raise himself on the tips of his toes, look over the heads of his men until he spotted Telford. A curt nod of his head, nothing more. Yet Jack felt as a puppy must do when it's scratched and fondled between the ears by its master. Foolish, yet somehow comforting that his presence was at least acknowledged.

They were on the move again, past the mosque and down to a house – larger than most of the others, though still very simple – where Leclerc rapped on the door with his cane. Gentle at first, then more insistent when there was no answer. His men were spread out along the alleyway, weapons at the ready.

'*Aftah!*' shouted the colonel. Open up. There was a reply from within, a brief exchange in Arabic between Leclerc and whoever was inside. Polite enough, an explanation. This was now French territory, the colonel here to take command of the village, needed to speak to the headman. Pretty audacious, Jack decided. Yet the door opened, as bidden. A few more courteous words, Leclerc shining his torch in the face of the gnarled old fellow, yet invited across the threshold. '*Monsieur* Telford,' said the colonel, 'with me, if you please.'

Telford was stunned, but obeyed, joined Leclerc and the same Toubou scout. Not exactly what he'd expected, took out his notepad and jotted down all he could as the headman wiped sleep from his eyes, instructed his puzzled wife – or perhaps she was a daughter – to bring them mint tea – then dutifully answered the colonel's questions, all put in perfect Arabic, about the Italian dispositions, about the fortress and a dozen other details. Though, just as the tea arrived – and, hell, how much Jack would have loved a sip or two – this incongruous scene was shattered. An explosion.

He took a step towards the door, thrust the notepad back into his satchel.

'Colonel?'

'No need to panic, Telford. Sounds like Guillebon's found the airfield, wouldn't you say?'

Outside, the men all looked skyward, a red flare blotting out the stars and, at a signal from Leclerc, a wave of the malacca walking stick, they ran towards it. There were shots somewhere ahead of them. Scattered shots as they reached the end of El-Giof's houses.

Jack could see nothing out there but a blaze, lighting up the outline of a fence. A wire fence. Hard to know how far. Two hundred yards, maybe? A flash away to the left, and then another gunshot. A burst of automatic fire in response as the falling scarlet flare gave one final flourish and died. And what was the smell? Burning gasoline, of course. Acrid smoke wafting towards them. Telford's own sweat. He almost fell, tripped on a boulder, swore as helping hands steadied him. One of the *tirailleurs* dragging Jack towards the gulley into which Leclerc had led them, more men – Guillebon's patrol, surely – coming towards them, crouching low, from the opposite direction. Away to the left, another flare, this time green.

All hell let loose. Tracer fire, arcing towards them. The rattle of machine guns, the whine of bullets overhead, and the *splat, splat, splat* as stone and sand were ripped from the desert's flesh.

'Seems like they're awake at last,' shouted Leclerc. 'Well, let's give them some back.'

The Chadian next to Telford eased his carbine over the gulley's parapet, slipped off the safety catch and aimed in the general direction from which the firefly tracers seemed to originate. The soldier pulled the trigger and worked the bolt. Eight times in quick succession until Jack's ears rang and his nostrils filled with the stink of cordite. Then another clip of ammunition pressed down into the Berthier's magazine.

A shout from back towards the houses.

'*Étoile! Étoile!*'

The password. Arnaud's boys scampering across to them, bent low. One of them hit and spinning to the ground, then dragged into this makeshift trench, Jack helping to pull the fellow, another of the *tirailleurs*, further into safety, Telford's hands slicked and slippery with blood from a wound he couldn't see.

Searchlights slicing through the dark. Lots of them, dancing up and down. But then the roar of engines, the grinding of gears. Not searchlights after all, but the headlamp beams of fifteen Bedford trucks. The cavalry, thought Jack. Thank god for the cavalry.

There was a ragged cheer from the trench. But then the unmistakable sound of the nearest truck stuck in the *fesh-fesh*, the straining engine, the tyres churning up sand. Men jumping from the back of the Bedford, yelling and heaving. Another one stuck, away to the right, near the airfield's perimeter fence – now clearly visible in the flashes of gunfire.

To the left, that beautiful Chevrolet, thundering up to join the line, another of the lieutenants at the Vickers machine gun, though now hurled backwards as enemy fire ripped across its bonnet, tore through the driver. Its wheel smashed against a rock, and Telford watched, horrified, as it spun crazily into the air, rolled over, burst into flames, screeched across the stony ground. There were screams, one of the occupants staggering towards them, a living torch.

'Down,' shouted Arnaud. 'Get down.'

They all obeyed as the Chevrolet exploded, showering them with blazing debris, the *tirailleur* alongside Jack taking a piece of steel plate which sliced through his neck. Telford tasted the man's blood, brought up bile, buried his head beneath his arms to shut out the nightmare.

It went on until first light. What time? Jack looked at his own watch. He'd bought this one at Libreville, his old one ruined in the Tano River. Six fifteen. They'd been there over three hours, but the firing had died down some time back. Still sporadic shooting but relatively quiet now.

More green flares. But whose?

'Who fired the last one?' Leclerc shouted. His own orders, last night, had been that they'd put up a green Very flare when it was time to withdraw. But where had this one come from? From Guillebon, now over on the far right, inside the airfield itself? He'd apparently managed to destroy a second Italian plane during the night. Yet whoever had sent up the flare, the men over there had plainly taken it to be the instruction to pull out.

Three of the Bedfords had been destroyed, as well as the Chevrolet, but at least the remaining trucks had been dug out of the sand and in the dawning gloom it was possible to make out the tracks again, despite the chilly mist rising all around them.

'Time to go, *mon ami*,' Arnaud murmured in Jack's ear, his hand on Telford's shoulder. They'd shrouded the dead *tirailleur* in a cape, and the lieutenant now detailed a couple of other Chadians to get the body over to the lorries, where another of the dead and several wounded men were being pushed aboard.

A thin skirmish line formed a rearguad in the gulley, while Jack found himself thrust up into a cab, alongside one of the former Legionnaires, weaponless, shot in the shoulder and almost unconscious from lack of blood.

'He'll be fine,' said the driver, crunching the truck into gear and steering them around one of the burning Bedfords. Yet it took

Jack a moment to realise the man had spoken to him in English. No, not English. A bloody Yank.

'The accent...' Telford mumbled. His lips were parched and his eye hurt like hell, stinging from lack of sleep, from hours of acrid smoke, from drifting ash.

'You like it, mister? Born in Montréal, raised in the Bronx. How d'you reckon them beans?'

It turned out he — his family — were French Canadians. Originally, at least. Considered it his duty to work his passage across the Atlantic, join the fight for France, though by the time he reached Europe, France had already fallen. An early volunteer for de Gaulle.

'Will we get through?' said Jack, settling the Legionnaire's head against his satchel for a pillow. He fished in the greatcoat pocket, found his smokes, lit one, another for the driver. Max, he called himself.

'Shit, friend, I drove a taxi for a living. In New York City. Drove a Checker. And *nothing* ever stops a Checker driver. Helluva night though. Hey, watch out!'

A plane. Italian bomber. Machine gun bullets kicking up the road alongside them. Max swerved to the left as a bomb took the lorry in front of them. Jack braced himself against the dashboard, while the Yankee driver spun the steering wheel, pressed his foot on the accelerator, gave the blazing Bedford a wide berth, swung them past and onwards, rattling down the track.

'I thought we'd destroyed the airfield,' said Jack, then realised this one must have come from one of the many other Italian bases.

'Sweet Mary be praised there's only one of them,' said Max, and ducked his head, watching the Caproni angle away, circling around for another pass.

'And thank god for this fog,' Jack murmured.

The sky was much lighter now, but the mist thicker. It rolled over the rim of the depression down which they were driving, made the track hard to see, but must also be making it difficult for the plane.

'Not far now,' Max told him and, sure enough, minutes later they were swinging into the red, rock-walled wadi of their fallback position. There they waited, while the medical officer, Captain Mauric, with the help of the bearded chaplain, patched up the wounded – including Lieutenant Arnaud. Jack hadn't even realised he'd been hit. But a bullet in his arm, removed without anaesthetic though with the help of Jack's cognac.

The Italian bomber flew over a few more times, but only made one more attempt at strafing them, hit nothing, and headed back from wherever he'd come.

'Well, sir,' said Jack, when he found Leclerc again, 'success?'

'You don't sound certain, *Monsieur* Telford.'

Fair comment, thought Jack. In truth? It all seemed like a monstrous waste. Two planes destroyed. Worth the lives lost?

'Personally,' he said, 'I consider it a major victory just to have survived.'

He was still shaking but fell in alongside Leclerc as the colonel made his rounds, a supportive word here, check on a vehicle there.

'Our losses were light. And we've now walked the terrain. Invaluable. The photographs we've taken of Kufra only tell us part of the story. Some of the reconnaissance has been contradictory. A garrison of six hundred? Or twice that strength. Or the garrison abandoned the place entirely. Well, we know it's not the latter. And their headman seems to confirm it's nearer the six hundred mark. The thing we didn't know? The heavy machine gun fire we took – the old man says a company of Auto-Saharianas arrived a few days ago.'

The Italian equivalent of the Long Range Desert Group, fast vehicles armed with heavy machine guns. And the LRDG was very much on everybody's mind later in the day, when they were on the move once more and came across remains of Clayton's ambush. Three abandoned and broken trucks, half-buried in the sand – and the bodies of those who'd once served in them. Desiccated bodies, part-mummified by the desert, even the flies no longer interested in them. But Leclerc, devout Catholic, decided they should receive a decent Christian burial, alongside the dead from the raid – so that there, at the wells of Sarra, on Saturday afternoon, 8th February, under the cruel sun, *Père* Bronner conducted a full Mass for the Dead.

*

Jack looked out of his window at the Hôtel Général Largeau. Across from him, beyond a clump of palms and a dusty square, was the mosque, men performing their ablutions around the troughs at the outer wall in time for the *Dhuhr* morning prayers. To his right, the market, quiet at last after the chaos since dawn. And beyond the market, the house where he'd spent the night with Dina.

The name, she'd told him, meant Life, and she belonged to the Daza clan.

Telford didn't pretend to understand a fraction of what she'd told him in the intervals between their lovemaking, but if he had the thing even vaguely right then she had some standing among the Toubou as an *oga*, a single woman of independent means. Her French was excellent, as it happened, yet she'd only seemed able to explain the complexities of her people's culture, at best in Arabic, often in her native Tebu. Not easy.

For his part, Jack had shared his anxieties about going back into the fighting. Yes, he'd said, very soon. A day or two. And yes, Kufra again, he was certain.

He'd been invited to a *soirée* at Dina's place by a couple of the French officers. An evening of entertainment. Music, drumming by white-veiled Toubou men in saffron robes, and dancing from a line of ululating girls draped in indigo, lime and scarlet. Singing, some amusing Trenet tunes by handsome Lieutenant de Guillebon. Gramophone records – Josephine Baker among the favourites. And did Telford know she was now in Casablanca? Conversation, about almost anything except the war, and he'd found himself, at one point, engaged in a furious debate about Gogol's *Taras Bulba*. Yes, Guillebon had said, the Cossacks understood a thing or two about the Jews, knew how to sort those devils out alright.

And then there'd been the women. The French officers' women. Massu was there, still limping from his injury at Murzuk. At his side, an astonishingly beautiful companion, also Toubou, whom he introduced as Moido.

Did I not notice this in Libreville? Jack asked himself. Or did I just have my eye shut, as usual? In Casa, there'd been Bousbir. But that was different. These women, on the arms of the Frenchmen of Faya-Largeau – the captains, Geoffroy, Massu of course, and the major who was no older than the captains, *Commandant* Dio – seemed more like wives than casual liaisons. Not Leclerc though, nor Rennepont, both with a reputation for almost monastic moral rectitude. Telford had enjoyed one or two short-lived relationships himself over the past year or more. Of course, he had. Yet nothing had stuck. Something about his senseless anger, his confusion, towards Ruby Waters.

'A stunner, is she not, old man?' Fox had said to him as they sipped ice-cold beers.

Telford tried to appraise their hostess, as he knew was expected of him. Reclining on a low divan, laughing with two of the unattached younger officers. Proud as a princess. Wide, ebony eyes. Almost as dark-skinned as the Sara. Her hair, with its silver braid-chains, a rare shade of blue-black. Gem-studded earring through the right corner of her nostril, and a robe of stark yellow, embroidered with gold thread, a turban cut from the same cloth.

'A stunner,' Jack agreed, prompting Fox to give him one of those garbled lessons in racial identities of which he was so fond. The Toubou – or *Gorane*, as they were in Arabic – and their caste system. The serving women here, all women of the lowest class, the *kamaja*, descendants of slaves and still little more than slaves themselves. But could it be true – the thing Fox had told him when they'd arrived? Nomadic warlords here, dealing in slaves even now, and this *oga*, this woman of independent means, the daughter of just such a warlord? And now their hostess was on her feet, weaving her way towards him.

'And how's the writing?' the captain asked, when he saw Jack had tired of the lecture. Yet, by then, she was smiling up at him.

'*Monsieur* Telford,' she said. 'I am sorry we have not had the chance to speak.'

'I had no idea I was so well known.'

'We do not have so many famous journalists in Faya.' Jack was always a sucker for flattery, and now it made him laugh. 'But do you like to see blood, *monsieur*? Blood – and sweat. Exquisite agony.'

Was it perfume she wore? Some exotic oil? But this wasn't precisely the conversation he'd expected. Her French, though, was equally exotic.

'Is this a professional question, *al-a'anesah*?' Jack used the Arabic greeting, since *mademoiselle* did not quite seem to fit the occasion.

She laughed as well.

'No, *monsieur.*' She clapped her hands, the bracelets around her wrists tinkling like a dancer's *sajat* finger cymbals, and she called to her guests. 'Gentlemen, we have entertainment for you all.'

They followed her, and a tail of attendants, into the garden. Two evil-looking fellows, naked from the waist up, except for their turbans, exercising their sword arms. Long, double-edged, wicked blades, the guards almost non-existent, a thong from the brass pommel securing the hilt to each warrior's wrist. The mens' shoulders and chests patterned with tribal markings, those same raised blisters, scarified with ash, Telford had first seen on the Yoruba of the south and common among so many of the *tirailleurs*.

'The writing?' Jack reminded Fox, while they waited for the performance to start. 'It's good. I finally sent my first piece to London. Wired it this morning.'

To Bunnelle, as instructed.

In a raid to rival Lawrence of Arabia's attack on Aqaba, Free French Colonel Philippe Leclerc has led his forces across five hundred miles of the most inhospitable desert in the world to strike at the heart of the Italian Empire.

There were a few sparse details, the Kufra Oasis named, the airfield destroyed, heavy casualties inflicted on the enemy. It was hardly the deep analysis Bunnelle had demanded, but it was a good introductory piece.

'Seriously?' said the captain. 'Are those fellows making wagers?'

Telford followed his gaze, saw those same young officers handing money to an ancient Toubou retainer.

'Just a display, surely.' Though Jack wasn't entirely certain.

'Leclerc happy with it?' Fox asked him. 'The article?'

'Hated it. Only liked the part where I mentioned how the *tirailleurs* tell stories about him. Christ!'

The first clash of steel startled him, as though a firecracker had exploded behind him. Still nervous, he supposed, after Kufra. He managed to watch the first few blows, heard the officers yelling their encouragement to one or other of the fighters, saw the perspiration begin to slick their black torsos – and caught their hostess watching his every move.

He nodded in her direction, could have sworn something passed between them. Something he could almost taste.

'The *tirailleurs*?' said Fox.

'They seem to have no more doubts about him.'

No, indeed. A hundred variations on the story Abia the Bassa had told them. Leclerc back from the Land of the Spirits to free them, to free France.

The soldiers, he'd written, *from Chad, Cameroon, Gabon and the Congo call him the Flying Lion, already a legend among these African men who fight every day for the freedom of France.*

'And you, Telford – what d'you think of *le patron* now?'

One of the Toubou warriors had taken a cut across the biceps, the blood dripping down his arm impossibly red.

'Hell,' said Jack, the idea dawning on him that this was an exhibition of a more serious kind. Blood sport. 'I can't watch this.' Yet he felt like a hypocrite. What else was a war correspondent than a spectator of humanity's blood sports? Had he not written down, over the days since they'd got back, every damned detail of what he'd seen at Kufra, stored away for his future use? Wasn't this the beat he'd accepted? To understand all this, in depth. He swallowed hard. 'But Leclerc?' he said. 'You heard about the plane?'

'You believe the story?'

'I wasn't there. Massu and the others are just laughing it off, but…'

One of the Blenheims hadn't come back from a reconnaissance mission, but there'd been no search for them. The word was that the colonel had refused to allow one, had no need for incompetents.

'What was it the Bard said?' Fox flinched as one of the swordsmen came close to decapitating the other. '*Thou cold-blooded slave?*' It's what happens to commanders, Telford. They become slaves to impossible decisions, bury their own confusion under harsh words.'

Jack had come pretty much to the same conclusion, and he knew better than to accept the soldiers' stories at face value. Still, he also knew there was rarely smoke without some evidence of fire.

'Well, he certainly has *sang-froid*,' he said, and had prayed the same quality might rub off on him, also. 'Isn't this what you'd say? Steady as a rock under fire. Calm. Listen, why don't we go back inside? Get another beer?'

Sang-froid, thought Jack, as they pushed their way into the house again, to drive away those bloody nightmares. But Leclerc had, at least, reluctantly approved the article, with one small proviso. A few additional lines, to keep the enemy guessing, claiming that the Flying Lion's troops now looked forward to a well-deserved rest. The colonel doubted whether Associated Press would syndicate the article in time to trick the Italians, but the Post Office system here leaked like a colander, he'd said. It might add to the other ruses they'd put in place to cover Leclerc's real intentions.

'He told you what he's planning, I suppose?' said Fox, offering Telford a cigarette.

'You think he'd trust a bloody journalist so much? No – and those boys are being pretty tight-lipped. Look at them, playing the same game.' The officers, crowding the doorway. 'Pretending they've got all the time in the world, like they've no intention of ever going back in action. All waiting for word from de Gaulle, I suppose. See what comes next.'

Inside, there was food laid out. Deep-fried cheese balls. And some sort of *daraba*, like they'd eaten at Fort Lamy. Meat – goat presumably – baked in rice and what smelled like a peanut sauce. Stuffed flatbreads. Better than the corn *boule* porridge, the manioc cakes, the watermelons, the staple diet among the enlisted men – and from which Jack had determined to escape for a few days, spending some of his French West Africans on his hotel room.

Outside, the chime of steel on steel, grunts of the fighters louder now, shouts from the spectators.

'And you, Telford, how was your first taste of action?'

'I've seen action before, Captain.'

'Like this?'

'Not quite. Oh, and by the way, I wired Welch. You think we should try some?'

Jack stirred the meat and rice with one of the spoons. One of the serving girls ran over to help, but Fox waved her aside. Telford

207

had felt guilty. Welch had sent the message, asked him to keep in touch when they were leaving Casa, and then his wire, telling Jack he might have a story. Well, better late than never.

'Probably wants to blow his own trumpet about this trade deal he's helped the Yanks cook up with *Sidi* Mohammed.' Fox picked up a terracotta pot. 'Looks good,' said the captain. 'Would you mind, old boy?'

Telford served up a portion, thought about spooning a second helping into a bowl of his own, then changed his mind. He'd lost his appetite, it seemed. And, anyway, it was less than polite to eat when he'd not been invited to do so.

'Paquita mentioned this fellow Murphy,' Jack mumbled. 'Last time I was with her. You know him?'

'Murphy, yes,' said Fox, biting on a chunk of flatbread, and plainly not sharing Jack's inhibitions. 'Seems to think North Africa's now just an extension of their back yard in South America. Part of Washington's fiefdom. Not going to join me?'

A final flurry of the blades out in the garden, a scream, and a yell of triumph from the French officers.

'Good god,' said Jack, spinning around. 'They haven't...'

Jack caught her scent long before their hostess spoke.

'You were hungry, *messieurs*,' she said. 'But perhaps what we have here might be too rich for your tastes.' Then she turned towards the door also, when she saw the relief on Jack's face. Both fighters brought inside, the one still bleeding from his arm, the other with a gore-soaked cloth pressed to his chest yet still very much alive. 'The skill,' she smiled, 'lies in delivering a wound to your opponent's body which is not fatal – but could so easily have been so. Badges of honour for the warriors. Captain Massu tells me German and Austrian swordsmen also call them bragging scars. Is this correct?'

'Still hundreds of such dueling societies in Germany, my dear,' said Fox. 'Or were, until recently. They call them *mensur* scars. Normally delivered to the face, though. The chap who founded their Gestapo has a whole bunch of them. Ugly brute.'

'The face?' she said. 'How barbaric.'

'That's the Germans for you,' Jack quipped.

'I should like to talk more with you, *Monsieur* Telford. About the Germans. About your writing. Perhaps later.'

And they did so. Later. Among so many other things. Long into the night. Long after the other guests had gone. Long after Fox had left him with those words of caution.

'Look, Telford,' he'd whispered, pulling him from the company of Guillebon, Arnaud and Dio, 'you don't have to do this.'

'Now, listen…' Jack began, angry at the impertinence. He looked around to locate their hostess again. He didn't want to lose sight of her, still wasn't sure he'd read the signs correctly – though her latest invitation had been explicit enough.

'No, you fool,' Fox snapped. 'I mean, you don't have to go back. Into the fighting. You can write your damned reports from here.'

Oh, thought Jack, I've certainly considered the possibility, but…

'Hardly a way to win the Pulitzer,' he said. 'But nice to know somebody cares, I suppose.'

'And this?' The captain flicked a surreptitious glance towards the woman, smirked at him, a schoolboy's wink. 'Good luck, old boy. But remember, careless talk costs lives. Keep mum, yes?'

Yet, in the dark, many sweet hours later, he did indeed find himself wrapped in the repeated pleasures gifted him by Dina, the Draza warlord's daughter. By then he had long since forgotten to ask the true source of her independent means. By then, also, the captain's reminder was the last thing on his mind as he shared those anxieties about returning to the fray. And yes, he'd said, very soon. A day or two. And yes, Kufra again, he was certain.

Diguéal's final jest died on his lips at the moment their truck reached the top of the dune. Blazing midday sun. Exhaust smoke and acrid hot motor oil. It was a joke at Vidal's expense.

'These Frenchmen are stupid,' he'd shouted, in French, for the benefit of the collective, over the protests of their labouring engine. 'Last night I asked our sergeant what he thought about all the millions of stars we could see. But I was sorry I asked the question. Truly, he talked for an hour. An hour! God this and God that. Then, my brothers, he asked me what I thought. And I told him – I thought somebody had stolen our tent.'

There were groans, weary curses, from the other *tirailleurs*. From Abia the Bassa. From Eze Tolabye and Diguéal's poet friend, N'Donon. From Mahamet the Hadjerai corporal. From Dillah and Rimdaga, the Cameroonian veterans who'd been with Leclerc from the very first. From Mogaye Doumra. And simply quizzical looks from the four other Africans Jack still couldn't name, despite these three days they'd spent together since leaving Faya-Largeau – more accurately, names he still couldn't pronounce, despite their efforts to teach him.

'Tobacco?' One of them had nudged Jack's leg while Diguéal was telling his joke.

Those four had little French between them either, and no common language, it seemed. Men from deep within the forests of Gabon and the Congo, yet with a certain reputation as fighters. Chosen men, like the rest of the three hundred *tirailleurs* Leclerc's officers had organised for this expedition – though most of those three hundred still behind them, back at the wells of Sarra. Chosen men, carrying the best of the ancient rifles with which their battalion had been equipped. And, on this vehicle, only one modern automatic weapon, the Browning nestled betwee N'Donon's knees.

'Cigarettes.' Jack had told the Gabonese, passed around his packet of Melachrinos.

Vidal himself was in the dust-shrouded truck just ahead of them and to the right, clinging to the spade grips of the heavy machine gun mounted behind the cab. Alongside him, El Gordo. It looked like they were arguing. But it was progress, at least. The Spaniard had told Jack he still planned to kill the bastard. Just not yet. And Leclerc's cousin, Captain Rennepont – another de Hauteclocque serving here under a *nom de guerre* – commanding this six-vehicle section of the advance party, had insisted, at the point of his pistol, they should travel in the same Bedford, take charge of the ten Africans on board.

'They cannot be so stupid, these Frenchmen,' Eze Tolabye had slapped Diguéal on the back, 'if they have all of us fighting for them. Even our Sergeant Vidal, who they hated so much for being a Jew that he is no longer an officer. Just a sergeant. It is the next thing to dog shit.'

Beyond Vidal's truck, just disappearing behind a lower dune, a real League of Nations in one of the Maitlands, driven by Max, the New York taxi driver, with Rennepont himself alongside him, cleaning the muck from his spectacles. In the back, Alemán and three more of the Spaniards –– the corporals José García and Nebot, Sergeant Torres – and the former *brigadistas*, Markovich the Yugoslav, Reiter the German. The rest – so far as Jack could see – all Frenchmen.

'How much further?' yelled Dillah, one of the Yaoundé men.

Jack looked through the cloud of sand churning behind them. The Laffly scout car, also with a mounted machine gun, and Leclerc's pith helmet, the colonel himself half-standing, shouting instructions to his driver.

'Just over this rise, maybe,' said Jack.

Somewhere, away to their right, the second six-vehicle section, with Geoffroy in command, should be heading for the airfield. There maybe, where the tops of palm trees were being swallowed by yet another dust cloud.

'Then why does the Flying Lion not bring us all together?' said Eze. 'All at once.'

Leclerc's plan, this fast-moving, two-pronged cavalry action. Take the Italians by surprise. Establish a bridgehead – was that what he'd called it? Then bring up the rest of the column, the other forty-odd trucks, their heavier equipment, the remaining three hundred troops, the majority of them more of Free France's enlisted black Africans.

'Our sergeant...' Diguéal began, the telltale smile of another quip forming as they crested the dune, and a bullet ripped the life from him, tossed him forward into Eze's arms. And *prang, prang, prang* – more shots hitting the truck's cab and chassis, the Bedford slewing down the farther slope.

Jack grabbed for one of the bow frames, almost went over the side, caught a glimpse of the fortress rising from a shimmering mirage, Italian trucks just below them, roiling dirt devils behind them, their heavy machine guns spitting fire, which Telford felt rather than heard, kicking up spout after spout of desert sand and stone.

The *tirailleurs* fell over each other among the backpacks and blanket rolls sliding across the floor, fumbling at their rifles, though the poet N'Donon had already braced himself against the Bedford's cab, the automatic rifle's return fire deafening.

Jack sat on the truck's floor, his left arm wrapped stupidly around his head, covering his eye-patch, as though somehow the flesh and bone of his own limb might shield him.

Leclerc's scout car roared past, the colonel standing, mouthing something, waving his arm. Take cover, perhaps.

And they did, the Bedford sweeping around, heading back up the slope, N'Donon with his foot braced against the tail gate, firing the automatic weapon. Vidal's truck followed them, the Italian Auto-Saharianas as well – Christ, where had they all come from? Twelve of them? Fifteen?

Jack saw El Gordo, swaying as Vidal's vehicle rocked from side to side on the broken ground, trying to level his carbine. He saw the skimming stone trail of bullet strikes, closing the gap, relentless, between the the pursuing gun truck and their target. Vidal swung the Vickers round, but he didn't fire. Instead, he jumped forward, knocked the Spaniard sideways, then jerked back, hit again and again.

Telford heard himself scream something, though he had no idea what it might have been. And he yelled again when N'Donon was hit, sat on the floor of the Bedford, gazing down at his stomach, fingers interlaced across the wound, blood oozing between them, running down onto his crotch.

They bounced back over the rim of the rise, where the remaining three trucks in Rennepont's section had already stopped, his men scrambling to form a firing line along the sandy crest. Jack's truck swung to a halt beside them, Abia the Bassa now picking up the fallen Browning, squeezing off shots while Eze cradled N'Donon in his arms.

'Help!' he yelled. 'Medic!'

A few scattered shots from the firing line, but not many.

'For god's sake, shoot,' Jack shouted, throwing himself down among the men on the ridge. 'Why don't you shoot?'

But the reason, he knew, was obvious. All the time it had taken to get there. The blown tyres. The overheated engines. The terrible heat. The broken springs. And the sandstorms. At least one every day – and now their weapons so full of grit and filth they would have posed more danger to their own soldiers than to the enemy.

Yet here came Leclerc in the scout car, and Rennepont's Maitland. The cousins, the additional troops, ran to join the line – Leclerc's malacca cane more a hindrance than a help on the shifting sands – Italian bullets still pinning them down, ripping through the palm trees all around.

'We use the bayonet, Colonel?' Rennepont offered Leclerc a gap-toothed smile, pushed the spectacles further up the bridge of his nose.

'We're cavalrymen, Pierre,' Leclerc growled. 'Sabre, perhaps. But the bayonet – that's for the bloody infantry.' He pushed himself up, shouted along the line. 'Get these damned weapons cleaned. What are you waiting for? And you, Pierre, get me three of the gun trucks up here.'

Vidal's body was being pulled from the lorry – by El Gordo. The Spaniard searched among the firing line, caught Jack's eye.

'What the hell was he doing, English? Bloody fool of a Jew.'

A few yards away, the dead body of Diguéal as well. And N'Donon, writhing in agony, Eze Tolabye still at his side, still shouting for the medic.

Jack was more worried about the Italians, though – expected them to come up the hill any moment. Yet, when he risked a glance down at them, they were still circling, in their billowing thunderheads, but coming no closer.

And now Leclerc had his three trucks, each with a mounted machine gun. The colonel climbed back into his scout car, signalled for the three lorries to follow, and they drove off westwards, staying below the line of the dunes.

'Pierre,' he shouted back to Rennepont, 'be ready to pursue.'

Jack thought he must be mad. Outnumbered three to one. At least three to one. And pursue? How the hell...?

Two more trucks arrived. The chaplain, *Père* Bronner with his stupid bloody waist-length beard, and Medical Captain Mauric. Another machine gun. And a mortar crew.

At Jack's side, the Spaniard Alemán, working the action on his rifle and shooting down at the Saharianas, the incoming fire now slackening a bit.

'Walked into this one, didn't we?' snarled the Spaniard, rolling onto his side to push home fresh ammunition, the stripper clip spinning into the air as he pushed home the bolt. 'Bloody officers. As pretty an ambush as I ever saw. Bastards knew we were coming, right enough.'

Behind them, Captain Rennepont was shouting instructions, readying his remaining lorries for the pursuit, which he, at least, seemed convinced would come.

Ambush? thought Jack while, below them, in the rolling stretch of desert between here and the Kufra fortress of El-Taj, he watched Leclerc's four vehicles appear, as if from nowhere, throwing up more clouds of dust in their wake. Like smokescreens, weaving this way and that, mingling with the haze already hanging from the Saharianas. Now and then, the glimpse of a truck, rattle of a machine gun, the dead desert earth trembling beneath him, cordite stinging his nose, almost blinded by the light, flames and screams. An explosion, filthy black smoke billowing through the veil of war. And the firing line now fully in action – whenever, that is, they had a chance to identify a target in all the confusion and smog.

But it began to ease, at last, the action, the dust clouds, moving away from them. The Italians in retreat?

'Now, boys!' shouted Rennepont, running for his truck, the New York taxi driver already revving its engine, his machine gunner ratcheting back the cocking lever on the Vickers.

The men left on the firing crest shielded their eyes from the dirt they threw up, the sand showering them, as Rennepont led the charge, chased the Italians back towards the fortress while, miraculously, as the dust literally settled, Leclerc's scout car, his lorries, headed back – seemingly unscathed, intact – towards his own lines. Out there on the sand, the burning wreckage, the scattered corpses, of three enemy vehicles.

A ragged cheer went up along the dune's ridge.

Miracle, thought Jack. But he also thought about something else. About poor dead Vidal, of course. About the dead Africans,

Diguéal and N'Donon – for *Père* Bronner had long since given him the last rites, whether he wanted them or not, and Medical Captain Mauric had long since given up the fight to save him. And about the thing Alemán the Spaniard had said. Ambush. So yes, he couldn't help it – thinking about Dina, beautifully exquisite Dina. About how he'd told her. Back in action very soon, he'd said. A day or two. And, of course, Kufra again, he was certain. So very certain.

It plagued him all through the night.

They'd fallen back just a little way to a line of wadis, easily defensible rock gulleys, like a natural trench line, which eventually ran into that same El-Giof village, where Captain Geoffroy's section anchored their right flank.

Telford should have slept. But how can any man sleep after all this? And there was the nagging guilt. She couldn't have, could she? Not Dina. He could almost still taste her on his lips. Yet there was the recollection of Fox as well. Careless talk costs lives. And if it was right, how long now, Jack – the list of dead at your door?

He ate by himself, alone except for his ghosts. Corn *boule*, naturally, woodsmoke on the air from the cook fires. Alone under another majestic, star-filled sky, cut just occasionally by a burst of tracer fire. But otherwise, it was quiet. Strangely quiet. Respect for the dead, side by side under their blankets, waiting to be buried tomorrow. Vidal. One of the Legionnaires. And the four Africans – Diguéal, N'Donon and two more. Quiet, and cold.

Jack set down the mess tin, fished in his satchel for the trusty flashlight, jotted some notes. A quick sketch map showing the fort now under observation on three sides by Leclerc's thinly spread sections. The airfield, also taken now.

When he'd finished, scoured the mess tin with sand, secured it to his backpack, relieved himself at the latrines – it was a thing of no small wonder to him, this speed with which, at every stop, Leclerc's army could dig latrines – he wandered down the line looking for his friends, his brothers-in-arms now, he supposed.

Here, as well, it was unusually silent, whispered conversations in the dark, in place of the normal bawdy banter.

'In the fort,' murmured Abia the Bassa when he finally found them, 'there are men like us?'

'Men?' said Jack. 'What – African men, do you mean?'

'*Askaris*. Yes.'

'I suppose so.'

'But not in their battle trucks,' said Eze Tolabye.

'I didn't see any,' said Jack. 'Today, I mean. But it was hard to tell.'

Fair point, all the same, Jack thought to himself. He'd picked up this much, at least. That those Auto-Sahariana Companies were pretty much like the Long Range Desert Group – fast lorries, hand-picked crews. And he'd heard the officers say more than once how much they'd like to get their hands on the Breda heavy machine guns they carried.

Eze spat on the ground.

'There,' he told Abia. 'I told you. It's why the French are different from your Germans and Italians. Here we get to fight on the battle trucks, the same as the white men.'

Jack wanted to ask whether Eze had ever seen a white man digging latrines though, or running behind the convoys, sweeping away the tyre tracks left in the sand, as he'd observed a few times when Leclerc was bothered about leaving a trail for enemy planes to follow. The officers even designated men for this specific task, the *tirailleurs balayeuses*. But he bit his tongue, admired instead the diligence with which Eze was cleaning the Browning automatic rifle he'd inherited from N'Donon.

'Fine weapon,' Telford told him.

What's the protocol, he wondered, for the officers to decide which of these men get to have the decent stuff, and which get the guns already old when the last war started?

'A fine weapon,' Eze agreed, and Jack saw the envy in the eyes of the men around him.

'I know another man who carried the same.' Telford saw Amado Granell again in his mind's eye. On board the *Stanbrook* with not a single possession except his beloved Browning. Where was he now? Still in that hellhole? What had Réchard and Paquita called it – Bossuet?

'Is he dead now, this man?' said Abia.

Jack passed around his cigarettes.

'I hope not. He was a good man. Spanish. I'd like to meet him again someday.'

'They are a strange tribe, the Spanish, are they not?' Eze smiled at him.

An explosion, away to the right. But loud enough to break the stillness. Sudden enough to almost send Telford back to the latrines. Flames, some distance away.

'My god,' he said. 'I wish they'd tell us when they're going to do that.'

The airfield, he was almost certain. The boys having fun blowing up the Italian planes.

'And the fort,' said Eze, 'will our big gun destroy this also?'

'If it gets here,' Jack replied.

One of artillery lieutenant Ceccaldi's trucks had broken down, several miles back. The truck on which Leclerc's 75 millimeter field gun was mounted. Leclerc had been furious but eventually told Ceccaldi they'd have to abandon it, almost impossible to shift it, there anyway. But Ceccaldi had rolled up his sleeves, opened the bonnet of the lorry.

'We'll fix it, sir,' Ceccaldi had told the colonel.

'Then join us when you can, Roger,' Leclerc had replied.

But, so far, there'd been no sign of either Ceccaldi or the Seventy-Five.

'Well,' said Abia the Bassa, 'I hope it gets here soon. Before we all end up sleeping with Diguéal.'

Jack left them to it, moved on to find El Gordo and the Spaniards as a second explosion, less severe than the first, started another blaze. Definitely the airfield.

He found them by the singing. A low voice, though still gravel-throated, like the rest of them. The song Jack knew so well. *Si me quieres escribir...* Sometimes he'd heard it sung as a raucous marching song, but tonight it was a melancholy lullaby.

If you want to write me, you know where I'm posted – the Third Mixed Brigade, up on the front line.

It was Beto, this singer. Jack still didn't know much about him. From somewhere around the outskirts of Madrid, he thought.

Never spoke much though. And tonight Beto was in good company. Telford had never heard the Spaniards so quiet.

He found El Gordo whittling at a piece of plank, slicing away with his knife.

'He saved my life, English,' he said. 'The bastard saved my life.'

Jack stupidly found himself biting back a tear. For himself? For Vidal? For his bone-aching weariness? And he saw how, on one side of the board, El Gordo had carved a Star of David, and the simple words, *Vidal, Teniente, Ejército Francés* underneath. Would Leclerc allow the marker to stand? Spanish? Vidal's former rank?

'He saved mine as well,' Telford replied. And he heard Beto start on another verse, the one about Gandesa, the reference to the Muslim *regulares* they'd fought there. *Hay un moro Mohamed.*

But Beto had changed the words. *Un facista italiano.*

Italian fascists now the enemy here. As they'd been so many times in Spain also.

That was war for you.

Dawn, and Jack's first proper daytime view of the Kufra Oasis – in reality, not a single oasis at all, but a cluster of them, each with its own village. Beyond the Kufra bowl, running the full lenth of the horizon, the rising sun splashed rose-pink across the shadows of the rock escarpment he remembered from Leclerc's map.

From his vantage point on the highest of the surrounding dunes, he could see the mud brick El-Taj fortress, away to the left, perhaps a mile distant. There was a bastion at each corner. Fox had told him the Italians had built it on the site of an old monastery, a *zawiya*, of the Senussi fanatics who'd put up such stubborn resistance to the invaders.

Next to the fort, the village of El-Taj itself, buildings and a minaret thrusting through its surrounding cluster of palms.

Closer, down at the heart of the basin, the two salt lakes, sapphire blue, just visible through more palm groves, and the village of El-Giof. It looked different in daylight, larger than Jack remembered from the night-time raid, artesian wells among its wigwam-thatched huts and its square adobe dwellings. There, the radio mast. And the village mosque.

To the right, a couple of additional palm groves and settlements, just beyond the airfield. And here, at the southern extremity of the broad depression, the wadis, flanked by yet more waving palm fronds and still more villages. From the nearest, the pastoral peacefulness of bleating goats, the clank of their bells, and the scent of baking bread.

Thousands upon thousands of date palms, thinly scattered on the higher ground around the basin's edge but thickest about the clusters of dwellings, a sure sign of sweet water there in abundance. But where the hell does it come from? Jack wondered. And he was still pondering the geology of this place when he heard the incoming bombers.

The throbbing grew closer, Telford running down the slope in panic, his rope sandals sinking into the sand until he tripped, rolled, came upright again, desperate for the relative safety of the wadi – and the wadi alive now with shouting men also heading for cover, or manning the truck-mounted machine guns. He scrambled down among boulders and sharp rocks, while the first of the planes reached them. Twin-engined, like the ones he'd seen and heard over Madrid and Alicante. He recognised the silhouette, the same discordant note of the engines. *Give-in. Give-in. Give-in.* Capronis. The same warning whistle of their falling bombs as Jack pressed himself beneath an overhanging ledge of sandstone, which trembled and shook with the first explosion, showering him with gravel.

Machine gun fire now. From the wadi itself. Close. A second explosion, a third, a fourth; the whole earth heaving beneath him. Bile in his throat. A further shower of dust and dirt. He pulled his knees even tighter towards his belly, forced himself against the rock until it became an agony of pain, his hands clamped over his ears.

Give-in. Give-in. Give-in.

More bomb bursts, but not so close. He risked a cautious peek from his womb-like shelter. Somebody running past. Then a cheer. The shadow of another Caproni passed over the gulley away to Jack's left, but its strident demands had changed now to a stammering protest. He saw the plane itself, one of its engines spluttering, black smoke trailing behind, while the pilot banked sharply. Further away, the bombing went on, but the *crump, crump, crump* more intermittent.

Jack followed a couple of *tirailleurs* up the side of the wadi, hand over hand on the rocks, until they could see the damaged Caproni heading north again. They watched it as the smoking engine burst fully into flame, as it lost altitude, as it disappeared over the cliffs ridges beyond the oasis, as the fireball of its crash rose into the air, as the remaining bombers headed back to base.

There was damage, one of the Lafflys ablaze, but as Telford wandered through the wadi's meandering path – greetings here and there from those he'd come to know – all the way to El-Giof and a little beyond – he was astonished to see no evidence of injury. Not a single casualty, not here, anyway, apart from yesterday's dead, still wrapped in their blanket shrouds.

He looked at his watch, seven-thirty, then held it close to his ear, checked it was still working.

And in the village, he found Leclerc and his scout car, with Captain Geoffroy, checking a strongpoint they'd established at the now deserted *carabinieri* post. Through the trees, he could see – and smell – the closest of the two salt lakes, and beyond, half a mile away, the village and fort of El-Taj, hazy, quivering on their higher ground.

'Still with us then, *Monsieur* Telford,' said the colonel, setting his hand on Geoffroy's shoulder. 'It's a good position, André. Just need to hold until Dio gets here.'

Geoffroy scratched his stubbled chin. He was a thin-faced man, no moustache, but otherwise this whole bunch of fellows around Leclerc were much of a muchness. All broadly the same age – about Jack's own age, as it happened – and mostly knew each other already from the military academy at St. Cyr. More binding them together than just their ranks, or their passion for Free France. Something to interest Bunnelle, Telford imagined. The personal stories, the ties that bind.

'Italians?' Geoffroy laughed. 'Hold them 'til Christmas, if we need to, sir.'

'Those Capronis will be back, I suppose?' said Jack, and he ducked, despite himself, with the burst of fire, the tracers from the fortress. The soldiers around him didn't even flinch.

'Not for a while,' said Leclerc. 'Now, André, I'm going to see what's happening with Pierre. The airfield seems secure enough but it's the Saharianas we need to worry about. If they turn our flank...'

'Spotters are out, Colonel. We'll see the buggers long before they see us.'

Guetteurs, thought Jack. Not scouts. Spotters, then. Sounded about right. Must add this one to the vocab. There were still a dozen new words each day he had to pick up. Lists at the back of his precious notebook. Always something. Separate lists for the French, the Arabic, the Sara Ngambay – and, more recently, the Tebu words Dina had spoken to him in their lovemaking. And there, the guilt again.

'I'm sure we will, Captain,' said Leclerc. 'Now, Telford, you'll come with me.'

Jack looked back towards the wadis.

'I thought, sir – the burial detail...'

'Time for the dead later. For now, you have somewhere else to be?'

'No, I...' He found himself squeezing into the back of the scout car, next to the machine gunner.

They came, as if from nowhere, only moments after Leclerc had finished inspecting Rennepont's position up beyond the fortress. At least a dozen of the Italian gun trucks, though it was hard to tell for the clouds of sand and dust shrouding their precise numbers. And if they'd intended to turn the French flank, they'd underestimated the colonel's cousin very badly, for he'd extended their line neatly enough, his men dug in along a series of dunes and rock ridges west of El-Taj and a mobile reserve, his command post, at the northernmost point, to anchor the line.

'I'll take three of them,' Leclerc shouted, and pointed at each of the lorries he wanted, signalled for the drivers to start their engines. 'You know what to do, Pierre.'

He leapt back into the scout car while Jack was still trying to climb out.

'Colonel...' Telford began but then he was thrown back into the narrow dickie seat, all the passenger space left after the modification now providing the V15R with the bow frame mount for its Reibel machine gun and small armoured shield.

Jack doubted Leclerc even remembered he was there, as they roared and bounced through a desert valley between Rennepont's command post and the next of his ridge-top positions. And when he wrote up his notes, later that night, it had all become a familiar jumble of post-action impressions. Snatches of memory. How they'd taken the first of the Auto-Saharianas from the side, the Reibel riddling the thing with bullets, exploding the fuel cans strapped to its body.

How he'd been showered with cartridge cases, hundreds of them, from the Reibel, deafened by the noise, choked by the smoke and smell, as the scout car's legionnaire gunner blasted away without even a pause, except to take a new magazine from Telford's trembling hands – literally, one every minute.

How Jack had sweated with relief as they headed back towards their own line of dunes, thinking that, thank god, Leclerc must have seen sense – then saw one of the Italians right on their tail, the *clang, clang, clang* of shots ricocheting off the Laffly's metal.

How this pursuing gun truck had careered into a gulley after it hit the crossfire trap into which Leclerc had lured his enemy.

How the colonel had done it a second time, and a third.

How they'd almost collided with one of their own Bedfords as the Italians finally turned tail.

How Captain Rennepont had come out to meet them, ready for the pursuit, with four more trucks.

'Keep them away, Pierre,' Leclerc had shouted as their vehicles ran alongside each other. 'This time for good. Chase them to the ends of the earth, if you need to. Dio will be up soon, and then we'll finish this.'

Rennepont offered his commander and cousin a half salute, and they were away, his truck drivers needing no instruction to put themselves between the Auto-Saharianas and the fortress, despite the fire now coming from its nearest bastion.

'If you don't mind me saying, Colonel...' Jack began as they headed back along the wadi. He was still shaking.

Leclerc spun in his seat.

'My god, Telford,' he said, 'I'd forgotten...'

He stopped himself, straightened in his seat, told the driver to go a little faster.

'No apology needed, sir,' said Jack, and smiled, despite himself, seeing the grimace, the warning shake of the head offered him by the legionnaire.

'Apology? Damn you, Telford. If you're not up to all this...'

'I was simply going to say, Colonel, there seems to be a horse loose.'

He'd glimpsed it a few times, through gaps in the rock walls. Out there, where they'd been fighting only half an hour earlier. A white horse, Arab stallion unless he was mistaken. And saddled. It made him think of that crazy football match at Libreville. They watched it – Jack, and Eze Tolabye, Abia the Bassa and a couple of the Spaniards – while they feasted on bread and goat's cheese, watched it through the commotion of Commandant Louis Dio's arrival with the bulk of the column. All those extra trucks, men, machine guns and mortars. But still no sign of Ceccaldi and his 75-millimeter field gun.

The El-Giof village – now hopefully safe from attack by the Auto-Saharianas, and just about out of range from the fort – became witness to more activity than it had done for the past fifty years, lorries coming and going with supplies, extra provisions brought in by patrols dispatched to the neighbouring settlements from which they'd been instructed to pay good money for livestock, corn – and dates. Of course, dates. So, when Jack went to find Leclerc again, he found him, setting up his headquarters at the same abandoned *carabinieri* building, the whole place surrounded by the freshly purchased goats, and a few camels. The noise, the smell...

'The gun, Louis,' Leclerc was saying, leaning against the doorpost and smoking a cheroot. 'Where is Ceccaldi and the bloody gun?'

They told how, when Leclerc had first arrived in London, Dio was the first to follow him, rallying to his side. He had the handsome features of Charles Boyer, but with a deeply cleft chin and a pencil moustache. Today, he sported a white *képi* and a plain *shesh* head scarf wrapped around his neck.

'Still behind us, sir,' said Dio.

'It will take forever to break down those walls without it.'

Dio was peering out through the palm trees, towards and beyond the salt lakes.

'Then I'll go and hurry him along, shall I?'

'Do it,' said Leclerc. 'Take the scout car.'

Jack followed Dio's gaze.

'Great heavens,' said the commandant, 'that horse. What's it doing out there?'

'Seems to have escaped from El-Taj when Pierre chased the Autos through earlier.'

'Then I've no need of the scout car, sir.'

Dio saluted, strolled off through the palm grove, and Leclerc watched him go, a thin smile on his lips. But others followed, African *tirailleurs* and Europeans soldiers alike, gathered just inside the tree line while Dio himself moved out into the desert, towards the fortress, towards the white stallion, still trotting aimlessly around the open ground.

Crack. A shot from the fort kicked up dust only a few yards from the commandant, who responded by fishing out a cigarette and lighting it. More shots, yet Dio wandered on, scornful of the danger. The horse stopped, turned its head to observe his approach. Something about the cavalry, maybe, Jack thought. Smell, perhaps. He'd always been somewhat nervous around horses, himself, rather envied those who shared the obvious bond between beast and horseman. And now Dio had thrown away his cigarette stump, held the stallion's chin in his hands, soothed its skittering when another bullet whined away from a nearby rock.

Telford imagined him whispering into the creature's nostrils, saw him gently gather the reins, swing himself into the saddle, lean into the white mane to pat the stallion's shoulder. For a moment they stood there, Dio looking about, as though to get his bearings. Another bullet threw up dirt no more than a foot or so away from them, the horse half-rearing, then steadied under its rider's hands. Jack realised how long he – each of those alongside him, perhaps – had been holding his breath. He turned to seek out Leclerc, though the colonel was nowhere to be seen. Didn't he care what would happen? Could he so easily afford to lose a major? Or was he really so confident of *Commandant* Dio that concern was entirely irrelevant?

A cheer, the second of the morning, and Telford saw Dio now trotting the stallion sedately in a wide circle – not heading south towards Ceccaldi and his field gun, but instead offering the Italians a display of his equestrian skills.

The Italians, in turn, showed their own appreciation with a machine gun salute from the corner bastion, setting Dio and his mount to the canter, just ahead of the bullets' tattoo.

The whole French camp was out now, roaring their approval as Dio swept the *képi* from his head, waved it around, once, twice, three times, and set off southwards at the gallop.

Oh, the French, thought Jack, almost choked by a sense of pride and joy he knew was excessive. But truly, he didn't care. *Éclat*, or *élan*. Whatever the word, it was bloody marvellous.

Dio was back an hour later, and Lieutenant Ceccaldi came with him, the Seventy-Five's long barrel and breech wrapped carefully so that, an hour later again, at noon precisely, the artillery officer punched his first neat, round hole through the fortress wall. An equally neat explosion inside the fort, causing the Italian mortars to kick off again in response.

Over the next sixty minutes, Ceccaldi fired two more of his precious and carefully rationed shells with wonderful accuracy and, at one o'clock, all fell silent.

It seemed to Jack the Italians must somehow have known about the burial detail. Former Lieutenant Jules Vidal had died valiantly enough, Jack supposed. They laid him to rest in the wadi where they'd camped, buried along with their four other dead – one more white Frenchman and three black Chadians, including the joker, Diguéal – Vidal's marker carved with a Star of David and a few special words from the chaplain, *Père* Bronner. Something about them all being one in the eyes of God. Something about God's good grace in sparing them a higher deathcount.

The silence endured all through *Père* Bronner's words, and if Colonel Philippe Leclerc had any objections to the words El Gordo had carved on Vidal's marker, the fictional restoration of his former rank, he certainly kept them to himself.

Jack never saw the ghost himself. He was too busy trying to master the art of floating in the larger of the salt lakes. Well, this wasn't quite right. What he'd been trying to do was to swim breaststroke, but no, he'd decided after almost ten days, it was impossible, the buoyancy in the water flipped him over onto his back every time.

But at least his desert sores had healed. They'd stung like hell at first, but finally those ugly open ulcers disappeared, as they'd done for the rest of the sufferers, perhaps half of the column. And for the bleeding feet of the *tirailleurs*, whose inadequate footwear had finally failed them.

Jack was wondering what his gran would have said about this. She'd had a mantra, whenever they'd made those excursions to Grimley lido.

'Swimming, John,' she would say, every time, 'is the best form of exercise for both body and mind. Swimming in the sea is better than swimming in a pool. Swimming in a pool is better than no swimming at all.'

The slightly oily waters of the Sahara's sapphire salt lakes had, for some reason, never appeared on her list. And he still pictured her in his mind's eye while he doused himself with water from the nearest of the wells and Eze Tolabye brought him the news.

'They sent out a white angel, a spirit of some kind, to tell the Flying Lion he must stop shooting and talk to them. To make peace, in the name of God.'

According to Alemán, though, it had been an *Askari* boy soldier – Leclerc flying into a rage that the Italians had sent a child. A personal affront, and the boy chased back to the fortress with some forthright words for their commander. Later, an officer with a white flag. But a lieutenant only. Insult added to Leclerc's injury – the lieutenant not only sent packing, but orders given to Ceccaldi for him to step up the fire from his Seventy-Five.

'Quite a shot,' said El Gordo, over the collective cry of delight, the whistles of admiration, as the fort's flagpole toppled to one side and the Italian flag fell.

Ten days, each much the same as the one before. You could almost set your watch by the daytime mortar and artillery shells, as regular as a church clock chiming the hour and half-hour. Ten days, during which they had turned into a bunch of brigands. Occasional high spots, when he was called to accompany Leclerc on his trips around the other villages, his diplomatic missions to win over the headmen. Or the afternoon when two twin-engined Martins and the old Blenheim had flown in to drop a few bombs around the fortress. Or the day Rennepont had come back, having chased the Auto-Saharianas for two days, a hundred and fifty miles, until he was sure they were never going to return.

'And the lessons, Gordo,' said Jack, 'how are they going?'

They smoked together and watched a 75 millimeter shell punch yet another hole in the fort's wall.

'The boys are natural-born Marxists,' the Spaniard replied. 'No illusions about colonialism and empire-building. Just biding their time, I reckon. Cheeky buggers. One of them chirped up last night and asked Alemán how it came about that, if we hated this capitalism so much, we're here fighting for the French.'

Jack laughed.

'And you told him what, exactly? You're here fighting the Nazis – the enemy of us all, Capitalists and Socialists alike?'

'No way. We told them the truth. Here fighting for Paris. It might not mean anything to you, English, but for us – we were brought up on stories of the Paris Commune. By the time I was twelve, I'd read Vallès. *L'Insurgé*. So yes, for Paris. Not for the bloody Eiffel Tower or Notre-Dame, but for the Paris of the barricades.'

And the nights? They'd been mostly quiet – in a perverse, wartime sort of way. Again, regular tracer fire, back and forth. The raid Dio had led against one of the bastions. Grenades, and Dio himself badly wounded in the process, sent back to Faya-Largeau. But little sleep and lots of time to think. Or to read. Jack had calmed his fears by borrowing books and burrowing inside the pages by the light from his torch.

Gide's *Les Faux-monnayeurs*, the Counterfeiters. Not what he would have expected from Guillebon, with its themes of adolescent sexuality and erotic relationships between some of the male characters. But it had made him think about Fidel and Sergio, caused him to write to Paquita, persuade Leclerc to allow his letter

– duly censored, of course – to go off with the dispatches. Sent her a copy of his will, for what it was worth. He'd enquired about the sketchbook, hoped it would remain in safe hands. And thinking of Sergio's pictures had inspired him to scribble some sketches of his own. Simple line drawings of the landscape, his companions' faces.

And apart from the Gide, a detective story, a *Disque Rouge* copy of Charles Foleÿ's *Le Chasseur Nocturne*. Trashy, but entertaining enough to help quell at least some of his terrors.

Yet that night, the night after the white angel, the *Askari* spirit, had visited his message of peace upon them, there was little time for reading. The Italians, it seemed, were enraged also by Leclerc's rejection, mortar shells screaming down upon the colonel's positions, Jack pressed against the rock wall of the wadi among the Spaniards.

'Just trying to soften us up,' said Beto. 'In the hope we give them better terms. It was like this at Guadalajara. Roatta's Italians. We thought we had them licked. Then one night they threw up this bombardment like you've never seen. Next day we counterattacked and they surrendered by the thousand. Pissing Italians.'

It was more words than he'd spoken since joining them. He was from Cuenca, and this seemed to be just about as much as anybody knew.

'Let's hope you get back there soon,' said Jack. 'To Spain.'

'What for?' said Beto. 'A bad joke now, English. Concentration camps. Killings. But does anybody talk about this? No. If Franco gets a mention at all anymore, it's about how much he loves the bloody movies. Good old Franco. Musical comedies again. Spain on the mend.'

'And your family – still in Cuenca?'

Beto turned his head away.

'The last I heard, my wife had been shot. And my two boys? My little girl? She was two, last time I saw her. Taken away to have their minds turned. To be taught that yes, their mother was executed. But taught, as well, how this was because she was a traitor to Spain. Their *papi* as well. God knows where they are. You know what they call those places, *señor*? Social Aid homes. Bloody Social Aid. No, English, if I go back to Spain now it would be to kill every last bastard one of them.'

Jack had seen for himself. Where? A village, west of Pamplona, when he was heading for Burgos. To kill Franco – only he'd failed, of course. But no point telling this to Beto, so he rolled on his back, scratched at the beard he, like so many of the others, had sprouted.

But no sleep, not really. And just after dawn – that Saturday, the first day of March, Telford calculated – with the bombardment long since ended, they heard an unfamiliar sound. A car engine. An ordinary car, a compact little Fiat with an open top, an officer standing inside with a white flag. It drove down towards El-Giof, and Jack missed the beginning of the lecture Leclerc delivered to its occupants, but he was there in time to hear the colonel tell the officer he had no intention of parleying. An unconditional surrender required no discussion. In time to hear Leclerc order them back to the fort.

Yet, as the Fiat's engine growled back into life, as the driver drove the vehicle in a wide arc in front of the *carabinieri* post, the officer plainly trying to take in as much detail of their positions as he was able, Jack thought Leclerc must have had a change of heart, saw him limp towards the car once more. The colonel looked around, spotted Telford.

'You, *monsieur*. With me, if you please. I need a record of this.'

And without another word, to the protests of the Italian, he stepped smartly onto the Fiat's running board.

'Oh, my god,' said Jack. He had to run like blazes, but he made it, just about, as the car picked up speed. Telford clung to the other side. His Italian was minimal but it wasn't hard to understand the gist of the officer's objections. But Jack's only thought, as they raced towards the open gates of the El-Taj fortress, was that both he and the Flying Lion were likely, at best, to see out the rest of this damned conflict in a prisoner-of-war camp.

The Italian colonel, Colonna, was far older than Jack had imagined. A mop of white hair, his face lined with seventy years of hardship. Jack had become accustomed, he supposed, to the comparatively youthful nature of the Free French officers. And nothing about Colonna was what he'd expected.

'You have no right to be here,' he shouted in accented French, as though Leclerc was some policeman who'd barged into his house without a warrant. 'No right. I only wanted to parley.'

'That's the *Croix de Guerre* you're wearing,' said Leclerc.

'I won it fighting for your damned side in the last one. An irony, yes?'

Jack felt as though he were the uninvited intruder at a wedding, but he took notes. Colonna's claustrophic office inside the fort. A ceiling fan wafting welcome cool air upon them. Two more Italian officers whispering angrily at each other in the corner behind him. Smart uniforms. Clean. And Colonna sporting his medals. Hell, what must we look like? Telford thought to himself. Beggars at the gate.

Jack's own bearded face, his head, his eye-patch, were wrapped in a filthy long scarf, only his eye and his blistered nose visible. His uniform shirt and shorts were now in tatters, the *Presse* arm-band tied on with string, his sandals falling apart. And Leclerc was little better. His rope sandals might be intact, but those baggy *sirwal* breeches, the double-breasted safari jacket, both repaired in a dozen places, like patchwork quilts. The puggaree band around his pith helmet had lost some of its stitching, hung down over his left ear. But he tapped the end of his cane in the familiar, impatient gesture, against the flagstones of the office floor. The twitch in his cheek.

'An irony?' he said, 'I suppose so. But your cause is lost, Colonel, and I'm running out of patience. Let me tell you how this ends, sir. With my own men in control of your fortress.'

'Blacks?'

For the first time, Leclerc's impressive self-assurance faltered.

'You command *Askaris*, do you not?' he said, at last. 'My *tirailleurs* are no different.'

'Precisely,' said Colonna. 'You cannot mean...'

'Colonel Colonna, you will gather your officers, if you please. At once.'

To Jack's astonishment, Colonna gave the order to his adjutant, and Leclerc was led outside onto the parade ground. The gates still stood open, and there was the Laffly scout car, Rennepont and

Guillebon arguing with the confused sentries, palpable relief when they saw Leclerc.

'Pierre,' he murmured to his cousin, 'do it quietly but go and bring up as many of the trucks as we can spare. And get somebody to radio the British. Tell them, we've taken Kufra and have rather a lot of prisoners we need shipping off to Cairo. Sharpish.'

And so, it came to pass. The following day's parade when the astonished Italians stacked their weapons in front of this small and ragged band of their conquerors, the polyglot, multi-national soldiers of Free France.

Père Bronner offered up thanks to this same god for their deliverance, the warm desert wind blowing the absurdly long beard against the pages of his bible. Like the rest of the hundred or so tramps gathered within the walls, Jack was choked by both the dust and the moment as the French *Tricolore*, with its Free French Cross of Lorraine, snapped up the parade ground's restored flagpole.

The Italians' own flag had come down yesterday, of course. It was now in the custody of the *toledano*, El Gordo, entrusted to him by Leclerc in recognition that he, like the rest of the small Spanish squad, had been fighting the Italians for almost five years. But if El Gordo had indeed begun to put back some of his natural bulk, it was no longer so. Now, like Jack, his sun-faded khaki shirt hung from his shoulders and none of them had shaved for days. A few pith helmets in evidence but mostly their heads wrapped in any form of turban they'd been able to fashion from the materials available.

It was all a very long way indeed from the steaming jungle wet season of Gabon, eighteen hundred miles to the south. Some journey, which had brought him here, like Lawrence crossing the pitiless desert for the attack on Aqaba.

Around them, the equipment they'd captured, waiting to be carried off. Heavy machine guns, crates of other weapons, masses of supplies. Food – hell, they'd be living on macaroni for the next month, but did anybody care? Beyond the supplies, the fourteen Fiat, Lancia and Ceirano trucks, complete with spares, which would take this precious booty back to base.

The priest's prayers concluded, Leclerc stepping out from the ranks to join him. The colonel's limp seemed less pronounced today. He leaned more easily upon his cane, and the brim of his sun helmet shaded most of his lean face, the square moustache even more unruly now within Leclerc's own stubble. But the speech was short, his throat as parched as the rest of them, the blown sand making some of the words hard to hear. Words for those they'd lost, though. Another blow struck to restore the glory, the pride, of France – Free France. Then he glanced up at their flag, crackling in the wind.

'Swear,' Leclerc shouted, and Jack thought the catch in his voice was more emotion than raw throat, 'that you will never lay down your arms until our colours, our beautiful colours, are flying afresh on Strasbourg Cathedral.'

It was something to this effect, anyway, though Jack was never certain, afterwards, when he tried to record the moment. But he was absolutely positive about the response. Tears carved narrow gulleys down grime-smeared cheeks of even the toughest and regardless of their race. Telford knew the oath might mean something slightly different for all those on parade. The colours they imagined would vary – for those natives of France itself; for the French who'd made Morocco or Algeria their home; for the Muslims from those same colonies; for the black fighters of Equatorial Africa; and for the exiles from Republican Spain. Different colours, their true colours, but one meaning. Until the Nazis were beaten.

'We swear,' said the men.

Later, Jack had an opportunity to speak with Colonel Colonna himself.

'Excuse me, sir,' he'd said in his poor Italian. 'A question? Were you in Spain? Alicante, perhaps?'

'With Gambara?' Colonna replied. 'The *Truppe Volontarie*?' The old man spat on the ground. 'What do you take me for, *signore* – a fascist?'

December 1941 – July 1942

Dudley Anne Harmon

'It was your piece about Kufra,' said the girl, looking up from her typewriter. 'Inspired me, Mister Telford. To come and see for myself.'

The *Danse Macabre* played from the wireless set in the corner, the reception terrible considering it was being relayed through the equipment just downstairs, and the transmitter up on the roof. The bare bulb flickered, attracted its customary cloud of insects and Jack slapped at one that had strayed to his neck.

'Your missionary zeal?' he replied. 'And all the way from Washington. I suppose I should be impressed.'

She was tall, blond. Lanky, he reckoned the Yanks would say. Angular in a Katharine Hepburn sort of way.

'You have something against missionaries? Or is it women journalists? Besides, it wasn't just me – who caught the Kufra bug.'

This was true, at least. Since word of Kufra had reached the outside world, men had come flocking to Leclerc's side. More Frenchmen, naturally, but other volunteers – young Poles, Spaniards, even some Germans.

'If I'd known it was going to get this crowded, Miss Harmon, I might have worded the piece differently. And no, I've nothing against women journalists. Only those working for our rivals.'

He picked up his cigarettes from his own desk – Lucky Strikes from the shipment recently arrived from Pointe Noire. She frowned at him.

'I don't think we Unipressers see any real competition from AP – not where radio news is concerned, at least. The future, Mister Telford, not the past. And a filthy habit, by the way. Would you mind doing it outside? But missionaries. You never answered me. An atheist, I suspect, like your Spanish friends.'

'I think the technical term is agnostic. It's not just that I don't *know* about creation and the function of our universe, it's that I know I *can't* know.' He slapped at his neck again. 'Any more than these damned mosquitos could comprehend Paris.'

'If you opened your heart to Jesus, He would speak to you. And then you *would* know.'

Jack shook out one of the Luckies, collected his cartridge case lighter, picked up his new trilby.

'I think you're right, Miss Harmon. Filthy habit. I'll take it outside with me.'

He headed down the creaking staircase, fulminating over her mention of radio news and taking it easy, his ribs still giving him gyp after – well, he preferred not to remember.

He'd learned to look down his nose at the United Press, still viewed in the industry as a cheap and amateurish – aggressive – alternative to AP. But Scripps's correspondents *did* seem to beat the hell out of everybody else when it came to radio news.

Two days after the Kufra surrender, Jack had been back at Faya-Largeau, wired his story to Bunnelle and to the Information Service here in Brazzaville itself, along with a short statement from Leclerc. *'I am happy to inform you…'* and so on.

Jack would later be congratulated that, the same night, early in March, the statement had been picked up by Reuters, and his own piece made headlines in the following day's edition of the New York Times.

Today, the whole world must see Free France – Fighting France – as an equal partner in the struggle against the Axis powers. For, this morning, the French Tricolore, with its Cross of Lorraine, flies above the fortress of Kufra, in the Libyan desert – a fortress Mussolini once thought impregnable. And here are the warriors responsible for its capture. Frenchmen, of course, like their commander, Colonel Philippe Leclerc, and the gallant major, Louis Dio. But their colonial warriors as well, men from Fort Lamy, from Yaoundé, from Bagui and Douala.

He'd also mentioned the Spaniards – though Leclerc had struck his pencil through this sentence, despite Jack's protests.

Not the Reds, he'd said. The colonel had done the same with the paragraph explaining how, under the condition that the *Tricolore* should continue to fly above the fortress, Kufra had been left in the hands of another unit of New Zealanders from the British Long Range Desert Group.

It was good work, all the same. But something missing. The immediacy of the human voice. And he recalled the broadcast about the *Graf Spee*, the excitement of the delivery, despite not even being an eye-witness account. He'd many times imagined Alvar Lidell reading out Jack's copy – even though this wasn't the way the Beeb operated. But radio news. If only! He'd made the suggestion to Leclerc many times. Their own radio station, that's what they needed. Something better than the service provided by the local Club Radio. Or the relayed broadcasts from the Beeb's Radio Londres. Certainly better than the Vichy propaganda they picked up from Radio Dakar. But so far…

The tickertape machine in the downstairs office was working overtime as he pushed his way out onto the street, rubbing at his aching chest. It was a busy night on Avenue Savorgnan, a truck caught in the traffic, wailing from the few men and women in the back, all of them with zinc identification cards around their necks and guarded by a *tirailleur*, a headscarf wrapped tightly round his face. Bound for the quarantine camp beyond the stadium. More outbreaks of sleeping sickness at Poto-Poto and the workers' camp out past M'Pila.

He headed for the river, hoped there might be some relief from the steaming heat there – some relief from Harmon as well. It had all turned sour so fast. And yes, he'd been peeved about having to share the windowless cell in the Information Service building, but she'd initially been pleasant enough. Admirable, in her way. A heck of a journey. And a long way from her gossip column for the *Washington Post*.

'You've met the Roosevelts?' he'd asked, after she'd managed to drop the name into one of their early chats.

'Oh, the White House receptions, Mister Telford. And the foreign envoys – all perfect little gentlemen on the face of it. Though, my goodness, I could have predicted how all this would turn out as far back as '37. The frigid nods from the Germans. The false smiles of the Italians. The suave *bonhomie* of the French. The pretense at chivalry and self-effacement of you Brits. The bowing and scraping of the Japanese. But behind their eyes? You could see that every one of them despised each of the others in just about equal measure.'

Yes, he'd thought, sharp enough. Maybe it's what came of having journalism in your blood. Her father, Dudley Harmon Senior. And her mother – though tragically dead now, she'd told him.

He stood near the brickyard gates, watched the lights of the ferry shimmering on the water, maybe a mile upstream, as it made the crossing from Léopoldville to this Brazza side of the Congo. He'd made the trip himself a few times already, liked it over there, liked the Belgians he'd met. It was a bit confused, King Leopold and the monarchists still favouring pro-Vichy neutrality, but the Belgian government in exile supporting the Allies – even to the extent of a trade deal with Britain.

There were lights, as well, from the windows across the river, all along the waterfront of Léo's Kinshasa district.

'But gossip columnist to war correspondent,' he'd said to her. 'A bit of a stretch?'

'Like I told you,' she'd snapped back, 'those White House receptions. If you ever want to see a real war zone…'

A real war zone, he thought, flicked the stub of the Lucky into the river. The gall of the bloody woman.

Not for the first time, he wondered whether he'd made the right decision. It hadn't been entirely in his own hands, naturally. A confluence of tidal forces. First, Leclerc's preparations to shift his base from Faya-Largeau to Zouar, in preparation for the colonel's planned new expedition, the conquest of the entire Fezzan – and Jack's uncertainty about whether he could cope with the violent hardship of it all. Second, Bunnelle's insistence that they needed stories from the very heart of Free France, Brazzaville itself – and he'd picked up word United Press were sending out their own correspondent, for the same reasons. Third, he was still not entirely fit after – after what had happened. The plane.

Fourth? The fourth factor was Dina. He'd returned to Faya intent on confrontation but, at their first reunion – well, his superstitions had evaporated with the heady aroma of her scent. And it had taken his discovery of her other liaisons – he wasn't hypocritical enough to call them infidelities, for their lovemaking had never been conditional on any pretense of mutual commitment – to affect a parting of their ways. No real acrimony. She'd tired of him, he knew, though he still harboured some unease about the simultaneous nature of her promiscuities, rather than the promiscuities themselves.

The fifth factor was somewhat linked to the fourth. Promiscuity, yes, that was the thing. It had begun as euphoria, of course. Free France's first major victory. And, as with all such things, some of the victors developing an overstated sense of their own significance – viewing Kufra rather through the wrong end of the telescope. Conquering heroes with a lifestyle to match. Rampant behaviour viewed by Leclerc himself – and more so by his cousin, Pierre Rennepont – as scandalous, immoral and unbecoming. But Leclerc still reliant on the loyalty of those against whom Rennepont railed, unable to act, while Pierre himself had insisted on a transfer to another command. Promiscuity, the *enfant terrible* of inaction – Leclerc's original intention of linking up with the British in Cyrenaica, all of eastern coastal Libya, dashed when Rommel's Afrika Korps had driven the British all the way back to Tobruk and the borders of Egypt. And, thus thwarted, eight months of frustration and *ennui* among the Free French forces. Worst among the officers.

It had all come to a wickedly barbaric head, an otherwise valiant lieutenant, Petit, returning from a patrol earlier than expected, finding his Toubou wife in bed with another man – his African batman. Petit had taken his knife to the poor bastard's genitals, bled him to death. There should have been a court martial, of course. But the impact, Leclerc had decided, might have damaged morale even more than the crime itself, and Petit had been sent from the colonel's side, like a whipped dog, disgraced to a desk job in Douala. But the discord left behind by the incident? It had weighed as heavily on Jack, as with many of his comrades-in-arms.

'If any of *us* had committed such a crime...' Eze Tolabye had pressed him.

And he had no answer – only, for Telford, there was an option to escape from its gravity.

A sixth thing. Maybe it was the consequence of that pressure, a fixation inside his obsession, but he'd become convinced, once again, he was being followed. He'd thought, initially, perhaps one of Dina's many paramours, for it had begun on the last occasion he'd left her house. Another shadow within the shadows. Perhaps something to do with what he'd seen and heard in Cairo. But it kept happening, and he'd taken to making sure he was subsequently never alone.

Finally, Captain Fox recalled to Brazzaville as well. It had seemed like too good an opportunity to miss, company for the long and tedious journey south again. Chance to recuperate. And Brazza had another pull, since both Alemán and El Gordo had already been transferred there, each promoted to sergeant and sent to the new training facility for officers and NCOs.

The journey took all of November, just about – by the end of which he was missing his comrades, missing the desert, even missing the beard. Yet here he was, for the time being, at least, three hundred miles up the Congo river, blistering as the rainy season extended into the end of this first week in December.

It had begun again before he got back to the Information Service building but as he ran through the door, he knew something was very, very wrong. The tickertape machine once more. But otherwise, silence apart from the snatches of broadcast. From Radio Londres? It must be.

...air attacks on United States naval base...
...Pacific...
...messages from Tokyo...
...formal declaration of war...
...Hawaiian Islands and the Philippines...
...press secretary Stephen Early...
...four US Navy battleships sunk...
...three cruisers...
...significant loss of life...

Jack ran for the stairs, found Dudley Anne Harmon weeping at the wireless set, her hands clasped together in prayer.

Before Jack's arrival in Brazzaville, before Lieutenant Petit castrated his paramour's lover, before Captain Rennepont went off to join Colonel Koenig's 13th Demi-Brigade of the Foreign Legion – Free French units of the Legion, naturally, and replete with still more Spanish Republicans – there was the incident in Cairo.

'Fly?' Jack had said. 'I've never flown in my life and have no intention of starting now. Christ, how many planes have we lost already?'

It was true. Flying across the Sahara was notoriously problematic. Sandstorms choking engines. The difficulties of navigation. The impossibility of enduring in the desert even if the crash itself could be survived. Jack was a great admirer of the aviator and writer, Antoine de Saint-Exupéry, something of a hero in Casablanca for his part in establishing regular flights between Casa and Dakar, ten years earlier. But Telford loved his writing, recalled the piece he'd written about his crash in the desert, back in '35. It was a miracle he'd lived to tell the tale, and the story was now a full-length novel, though Jack still hadn't had a chance to read it – wasn't sure he wanted to, now. The stuff of nightmares.

'Don't you want to see the pyramids, old boy?' Fox had suggested. 'The wonders of the Nile?'

'Not if it means flying.'

'Get out of Faya for a while?'

'Not fair,' Jack frowned. 'Get thee behind me, satan. For god's sake, it's – what, a thousand miles?'

'The Blenheim's got a range of fifteen hundred. More or less, anyway.'

It was cold comfort, but Telford was finally left with little choice, Fox having convinced Leclerc how useful Jack's presence might be. If the captain was to succeed in his mission, to convince the top brass in Cairo that Leclerc's demands for extra equipment were more than just token posturing, then the potential threat of negative press coverage could be a powerful ally.

'In this?' he said, bent like a chimpanzee under the constraint of the parachute strapped to his backside, clinging tightly to the brace of paper sick bags and the intercom cable, shambling towards the Blenheim – the plane's Cross of Lorraine proud on its fuselage – in company with Fox and the three-man crew.

'Safe in our hands, *Monsieur* Telford,' said their skipper, Popeye Pezon, and pushed his navigator onto the wing, from whence the wireless operator had already scrambled up the bomber's sides, to an opening above the cockpit. 'Ah, no,' Pezon laughed, as Jack prepared to follow them, 'our honoured passengers get to use the guest entrance.' He indicated the open hatch just behind the wing's trailing edge, and by the time Jack was helped by a groundcrew sergeant to haul himself inside, the French airmen had lowered themselves down from the upper opening, Pezon and the navigator climbing over into the cockpit, the wireless operator settled at his station next to a circular contraption – the turret, Jack could see, for the glazed dome and machine gun on top of the fuselage itself.

They followed the instructions from their briefing, settled themselves in the seat well, a narrow cargo space, with the heads of Pezon and Coli the navigator pretty much blocking out their view forward and, towards the rear, just a few feet separating them from that turret. Telford nervously fastened his shoulder straps, plugged in the twin cables from his headset. He pulled across the face mask attached to his canvas flying helmet, wondered whether he should try the microphone button, but the mask stunk of rubber and something like vomit. He gagged, simply let the thing hang loose. A thumbs-up from the groundcrew sergeant and the hatch was slammed shut on Jack's panic. But no going back, and there he was, trapped inside a cigar tube of thin olive-green metal, flimsy airframes. And rivets – lots of rivets.

'All good now?' shouted Fox over the skipper's pre-flight checks and crackling exchanges from the seat well's loud-speaker grille, with the caravan serving as a control tower. But Jack couldn't hear even his own reply as the engines rumbled into life, first one, then the other, the entire hull juddering, thrashing about, fit to shake itself apart when Pezon pushed open the throttles and, through the small window in the hatch, the world of Faya-Largeau began to slip past. Bumping along the ground, Telford's knuckles white where he gripped the edges of his fold-down seat.

They stopped again. Jack felt them swing around. He relaxed, but only for the moment before the engines were pressed to full throttle, the noise impossible, the smell of oil and smoke, the vibrations in the hull, in Telford's lungs. Faster, faster until the Blenheim's tail came up – and, with it, Jack's breakfast.

'What d'you think of it now, old boy?' Fox leaned over the tool chest in the seat well, lifted the flap of Jack's helmet and yelled in his ear.

The navigator had surrendered his own fold-down seat, and Jack perched alongside Popeye Pezon, the trials of the six-hour journey largely forgotten as they banked over the Giza pyramids, over the Sphinx, the Nile and the sprawl of Cairo itself, its islands and its gardens, away to the right as they made their approach to RAF Cairo West, rather than the main aerodrome on the opposite side of the city.

'I suppose I could get used to it,' Jack shouted back. He'd recovered from his initial discomfort, slept a while, enjoyed wireless operator Nemo's demonstration of the turret, even controlled the thing himself for a few minutes, the hydraulics raising the dome and affording Jack one of the most memorable occasions of his life. There he was, the sensation of being entirely outside the aircraft, at once terrifying and awesome, looking out through the plexiglass over the curve of the fuselage, the blur of the propellors only feet from him, sun glinting on the rivets, the desert's expanse stretching away, impossibly far in all directions, then curving up to meet the sky. It was beautiful. More beautiful than anything he could have imagined.

And though some of his trepidation returned when they came in for the landing, the ground rushing up to meet them, he surprised himself by enjoying the bounce and skip of their first touchdown, the gentle thump as the Blenheim's wheels brought them safely to earth.

'Smoothest flight I ever made,' Fox told the orderly after they'd completed all the formalities and were being driven along the Mena Road. 'Not even a wrinkle.'

Jack thought this might be tempting fate for the return trip, but he'd forgotten his superstitions by the evening. They sat on the terrace bar of the Mena Hotel, sipping gin and tonic, looking out through green latticed archways, the palm trees of the hotel gardens, at the pyramid of Cheops. So near and yet…

'Well, it's all arranged,' said Fox. 'Tomorrow morning. Meeting with the Old Man. See what he says. Afterwards – all in the hands of the top brass.'

'Just a shame,' Jack murmured, thumbing through the extensive *Services Guide to Cairo* he'd found waiting for him in his room. 'Risk life and limb, come all this way, and don't get to do the sights.'

'No time, I'm afraid. You're on duty, Telford. Remember?'

'Just not sure how much use I'll be.'

If he'd been honest, he might have admitted that the prospect of a meeting with General Spears was almost as daunting as his earlier fear of flying. Leclerc's reputation had been formidable enough. But Spears?

Yet the following morning, Sunday – after the long tram ride from Giza into the centre of Cairo itself – found Jack being offered a deckchair at the extensive El-Gezira Sporting Club, just south of the island's Legation District.

'Thought you might like to see the match,' said the general. 'Easier to chat here than at the Officers' Club.'

'I'd not expected…' Jack began. 'The war, sir.' Both teams in their whites, the first of the New Zealanders heading out onto the pitch, going in to bat against the Australians. 'Hard to imagine Rommel's only two hundred miles away.'

'I think what Mister Telford means…' Fox stammered.

The general waved for the Egyptian waiter, serving tea to other spectators, an assortment of uniforms, men and women, civilians.

'Journalist, ain't he?' barked Spears. 'Seems to pick his words carefully enough, from what I've read. Not bad. De Gaulle liked your piece about Kufra, by the way. Did you know?'

He must be sixty, Jack thought, but he had fire and intelligence in his eyes, perhaps a little overweight, but his height carried it well enough. The general sat, gestured for Telford and Fox to do likewise.

'Kind of you, sir,' said Jack, accepting a cup and saucer from the waiter.

'Kind be damned. It's what you get paid for, ain't it? You'd not be here if we didn't think you'd be useful.'

'Or perhaps beggars can't be choosers, sir? There's hardly a queue of fools like me lining up to tell de Gaulle's story, is there?'

Jack wondered whether he'd just made sure this would be a very short interview indeed, while Spears turned his attention to the game.

'Pie-can!' the general murmured, as an Australian at third slip fumbled an easy catch off only the bowler's second delivery. 'And I'm sure you're not in the least taken in by all this, Mister Telford. Just two weeks ago, those Kiwi boys out there were fighting in Syria against Vichy. Shot to hell, for the most part. The Aussies? They're the first we managed to get out of Tobruk. And if it wasn't for Tobruk, it would be the Afrika Korps sitting here now, not us. But it's the waiting. To get back on the offensive, back into action. All this? We call it morale-raising, don't you know?'

There was a ripple of applause from the crowd as the Kiwi batsman belted the ball to the boundary through deep square leg.

'Precisely the problem at Faya,' said Fox. 'Only they've not been under siege for three months like the poor devils at Tobruk.'

'And how are you coping with the weather, Mister Telford?' The general brushed a finger knuckle against his carefully clipped moustache. 'Not quite Blighty, what?'

No, not quite, thought Jack, and he looked past the white scoreboard, through the palms on the riverbank, saw the funnel of a Nile steamer as it passed through a raised drawbridge. The boat's whistle blew, a curl of black smoke against the palest of blue skies. And beyond, more of Cairo's sprawl, housing blocks, domes and minarets. The mixed aroma of sewer and spice.

'Not so severe as the desert, General,' he said. 'And it's been so long since I was in Blighty...'

'All strangers in strange lands now. Isn't that the way of it, Fox?'

What did Jack know about Spears? Close confidant of Churchill, many years in the Commons, and when Winston became Prime Minister, he'd been appointed as personal liaison to the French government, later escaped with de Gaulle back to London. He'd been the head of the British Mission to Free France ever since. Ever since? Telford thought. My god, it's only been a year.

'Hard to imagine ever being back there again,' said Fox. 'But this helps.'

He nodded towards the cricket pitch. There was some altercation, an argument with the umpire. And Fox was right, this could have been the local village green, back home, except for the scorched grass.

'If it's not impertinent, General,' said Jack, 'Your good lady wife – she's safe, I trust?'

'Mary?' Spears replied. 'You know her?'

'Only through her writing, sir. I had the privilege of reading *Sarah Gay*. But she's nursing again, I understand.'

'Her ambulance unit was in Syria. She's in Beirut just now. Bloody business, all of it. I doubt the poor devils in Baghdad and Basra, Damascus or Beirut will ever want to see a European face again.'

Where had it all started? The Germans inciting an Arab revolt in Britain's Kingdom of Iraq mandate – to divert yet more British forces from Libya and Rommel's offensive. It had worked as well, left the way open for the Afrika Korps to slice across Cyrenaica like a knife through butter. In Iraq, the battles had been fought all through May and though the rebels were defeated, the cost especially to the civilian population had been horrendous.

And then, in Vichy-controlled Syria, Pétain's puppet, General Dantz – who had infamously surrendered Paris to the Germans – had given the Luftwaffe access to French airfields, enabling Hitler's planes to support the Iraqi insurgents but also to strike deep into British territory in the Middle East. Of course, on the world stage, it had all been eclipsed by the news – Hitler's invasion of Russia – but at Faya…

'She was in the thick of it, sir?' said Fox.

The general clapped his hands as the New Zealanders hit a beautifully placed six.

'Syria, yes. I just thank the Lord it was over quickly. A month. But how did it play out, gentlemen, among Leclerc's men?'

A month, which had only ended a few days ago, mid-July. It had hit the forces at Faya-Largeau very badly indeed. A combined British and French force invading Syria. And while there'd been fighting already, of course, between Vichy France and Free France – at Dakar, for example – this was something else. Relentless fighting between each side's Foreign Legion units, the Vichy ranks predominantly filled by German and White Russian *émigré* legionnaires, and those of de Gaulle's battalions, large numbers of Spaniards. As though Spain's own civil war, El Gordo had said, with sad longing in his eyes, was still being fought out, by proxy, in Syria and Lebanon.

'Not well, sir,' Fox replied. 'They were already suffering from boredom and inactivity. And suddenly it seemed as if everyone at Faya knew somebody who was fighting in Syria. Or wanted to be there. Or was horrified that here was France fighting France – again. It just made things worse. All the more reason, General, to get them the supplies they need – help Leclerc launch his offensive in the Fezzan.'

'It might help unruffle de Gaulle's feathers,' said Spears. 'Furious, you know? Dantz beaten into surrender – but the damned fellow refusing to hand over his sword to anybody but us.'

The Egyptian waiter again. More tea, and sponge cake.

'And you think, General,' said Fox, 'the War Office will meet Leclerc's demands?'

'It's a hell of a list. But tomorrow? Well, tomorrow we'll know. For now...'

The satisfying smack of leather on willow, the Kiwi batsmen making two more runs.

'For now, sir,' said Jack, 'is there anything I can do to help?'

'There's a bit of a shindig at Shepheard's tonight, as it happens. Helpful if you can put yourself about a bit. We'll point you in the right direction. Just so the War Office whallahs know you're here. They can censor you, of course, but not so easy if you're sending stuff to our American friends. God bless America, eh?'

'Indeed,' said Jack, and imagined Spears was thinking about far more than just Roosevelt. His wife, Mary Borden, American herself, had privately funded and operated a nursing unit and ambulance service on the Western Front. A whole raft of books to her credit. And now, with this new war, nursing again, just about anywhere there'd been fighting. First in France, then across the Middle East. She must be sixty as well, Jack supposed. 'And good news, sir. About Mrs Spears. Let's hope she gets here safely.'

He'd been waiting at the bar for ten minutes already, the queue hardly moving. But it was better, Jack supposed, than the boredom of the reception upstairs. He'd done his duty, of course, introduced by Fox, or by General Spears himself, to an array of civil servants, high-ranking officers and a few diplomats, asked the correctly pointed questions, dropped a few names, scattered some hints – then escaped the oriental opulence, the stained glass, the dimmed lights, and the pharaonic columns of the ballroom, for what he'd supposed might be a quiet drink.

'Is it always like this?' he said to the trio of young women just ahead of him. Pale khaki skirts and belted tunics of the ATS. They'd been laughing together, but one of them, he was certain, had turned to smile at him a couple of times. Hard to tell in the candlelight.

'You should see the Long Bar on a *busy* night,' said another of the threesome, a brunette with high cheekbones and the widest mouth Jack had ever seen.

'The long bar?' he laughed and looked around. 'What's long about it – except the time it takes to get a drink.'

'Well, that's rather the point,' said the girl who'd maybe smiled at him. Short dark hair, pursed lips, small scar at the side of her chin. 'Just a silly nickname. But you know what we say around here...' The other two joined her in the rehearsed chorus. 'If nothing else stops Rommel, the Long Bar certainly will!'

'Now, ladies,' yelled the barman, over the heads of customers who'd already been served and were hogging the barstools. New York accent, white tuxedo, black bowtie. He ran a hand through centre-parted wavy hair, shouted instructions to a couple of African lads in white *djellabas* and each with a red *tarboosh* on his head. They seemed to have at least a dozen customers apiece.

'Set them up, Joe,' cried the girl with the scarred chin.

'Buzzards, Miss Valerie?' said the barman, and winked at her.

'You bet,' she replied, and returned the wink. 'Oh, and Joe, make it four, would you?' She turned to Jack. 'You will join us, Mister...?'

'Telford,' he said. 'Jack Telford. And, really, it's very kind but...'

'The least we can do, Mister Telford. Isn't it, girls? Succour for the stranger in our midst, and all that.'

Her two friends agreed, even the quiet one. A little more rounded than the others, auburn curls spilling out from under her cap.

'And all this winking with the barman?' said Jack, and watched as the fellow poured both gin and bourbon into a silver shaker.

'Private joke,' said the girl apparently called Valerie. 'They're not really called Buzzards, not precisely. Joe invented them. Suffering Bs – you get the gist.'

The drinks were passed over. A bit of fizz, ice, sprigs of mint.

'Yes, I get it,' said Jack. 'But please, Valerie, you must let me...'

'We wouldn't hear of it, Mister Telford.' She handed Joe the barman a twenty-five *piastre* note. 'And my friends call me Val, by the way.'

Jack took a sip, barely able to get it to his lips for the press of the crowd. Ginger ale, a hint of lime. Angostura, he thought.

'Well, that's got some bite to it,' he said, and lifted his glass. 'And I knew another Valerie once. Your health, ladies.'

'Oh, Mister Telford, the way you spoke her name – somebody special, perhaps?'

'Not in the way you might think,' Jack replied, thought for a moment he saw Carter-Holt's face there, among the crowd. 'But would you mind? Perhaps the terrace?'

Valerie led the way, and to Jack's surprise, it was the third girl, the auburn-haired quiet one, who linked his arm.

'I'm Pamela,' she said. They were all drivers, Pamela told him. Chauffeuses, when they were feeling posh.

In the darkened palm garden below the terrace bar, a military band was playing. The streetlights remained unlit in deference to the blackout, but the large open windows of shops across the street gleamed with defiance to the threat of attack. A dimout, thought Jack.

From those same shops, where Sinclair's Pharmacy was still doing a roaring trade, beyond the railings and the standing line of hopeful horse-drawn carriages with their piles of dung, came another smell, of roasting meat. Here on the shadow-filled terrace itself, waiters scurried about, each sporting a short, red Ottoman jacket and matching *tarboosh*. Valerie managed to grab the only available table, just being abandoned by a pasty-faced French officer with only one leg, helped up onto his crutches by drunken companions, and by the time Jack and the three young women settled in the wicker chairs, Pamela had shared with the others that Mister Telford was a famous war correspondent. They all swapped stories, tidbits about where they hailed from, back in Blighty – Pamela the most exotic of them, as it turned out. Alderney. And yes, they'd all been evacuated, all the residents of the island, just over a year ago. Last June.

'And have you seen the pyramids yet, Jack?' said Brenda the brunette.

'This afternoon,' he told them. 'But just Cheops and then the Sphinx.'

'Disappointing, aren't they?' said Valerie. 'And the stink.'

'You can't *not* see them, I suppose. And I did get to ride a camel. Two longstanding ambitions in one afternoon. But I know what you mean. When I got back to the hotel – I'm staying at the Mena – there I was, sipping beer almost in the shadow of the Great Pyramid of Giza, dwarfed by five thousand years of human history. Climbing and crawling about inside the thing may have been a bit of a let-down, but seeing it like that? I don't think I've ever felt so emotional about simply being somewhere.'

'But surely,' she laughed, 'being here with us...'

Jack was about to respond with a fast and flirty quip when he experienced the somewhat supernatural sensation of being watched. He turned his head towards the double doors from the bar.

'You're a dark horse, Telford.' The hatchet face of Kingsley Welch beaming at him, and though Welch made some pretense at surprise, as though he'd just noticed him as he came onto the terrace, Jack had the distinct impression he'd been under observation for some little while. 'Here you are, in Cairo as well. Small world. And not with one young beauty in tow, but three. How splendid.'

Without waiting for an invitation, Welch pulled over another chair, set his martini glass down on their table. But the girls didn't

248

seem to mind, especially when he insisted on ordering another round of drinks, and Jack made the introductions.

'Old acquaintances from Casablanca,' he explained. 'Mister Welch...'

'Kingsley,' Welch interrupted, leered at the young ATS drivers. 'You must call me Kingsley.'

'Well,' said Jack. 'Involved with the Yanks in trade negotiations, anyway. In Cairo for the same reason, I'm guessing?'

Welch nodded, offered cigarettes from his gold-plated case.

'Shared the news with Telford here, so he could make even more of a name for himself. Not that he needed my help in this regard, of course. My goodness, the Kufra story, old boy. He was in the thick of the fighting, did you know?'

They didn't, but Welch soon told them, to Jack's embarrassment. Yet while the fellow blathered, Jack recalled how grateful he'd been for the wire about the trade deal – not to mention, much earlier, those few luxuries Welch had sent for their voyage, the day he, Fox and Vidal had left Casablanca. And the trade deal itself? Telford had replied to the wire and Welch sent details to Faya-Largeau. The US deal finally secured, in December, with Vichy's representatives and with *Sidi* Muhammad, to supply tin, sugar, gasoline to Morocco, in exchange for wheat, hides, cork, silicon and zinc ores.

'A rather fanciful account, I'm afraid,' said Jack, as Welch embellished the story of Kufra's actual surrender. Yet he couldn't help being flattered himself by the glances of admiration he was now receiving from the chauffeuses, while the waiter set out their drinks and received a more than generous gratuity.

'Is that where you were wounded, Jack?' Pamela lifted a tentative finger towards her own left eye.

'The patch?' said Welch before Jack could reply. 'Heavens, no. A much older battle scar, I think. Man of mystery, our Mister Telford. Spain, wasn't it? Gun-running for the Reds, or something.'

Flippant, jocose, yet Jack was suddenly sure Welch knew precisely how he'd lost his eye. Why the certainty? Because Welch was that sort of man, who would have made it his business to find out.

'It *was* Spain,' Jack told them. 'But just a stupid swimming accident. San Sebastián. The woman I mentioned, the other Valerie, drowned there, I'm afraid.'

Gasps and condolences from the girls.

'Tragic,' said Welch. 'I had no idea.' Liar, thought Jack, but Welch had quickly moved on. 'But you see, girls? What did I tell you? Drink with Mister Telford at your own peril. Uncommon occurrence of mishaps wherever he travels. What was the name of the old Jew in Casa, Telford – Gabizon?'

Jack chewed on his lip, hearing the contempt in Welch's voice, trying to decide whether the fellow was provoking him or was simply as crass as he appeared to be.

'Another friend, Jack?' said Val.

'No, wait,' said Welch. 'Now I feel like a ghost at the wedding. Too much tragedy. Why not tell them about the headline you wrote, Telford? This was for an article he penned, my dears, about those trade negotiations he mentioned. *Champion Deal for one of America's First Champions*, wasn't that it, Telford?'

It had been the point of Welch's news – how even the war could not break the bond between the United States and one of its oldest allies, one of the first foreign powers to recognise America's independence, as far back as 1777.

'Makes me wince every time I think about it now,' said Jack. 'Hackneyed.'

'Not at all, old boy. You see, ladies, part of the deal included agricultural spare parts. Champion spark plugs. Champion, yes?'

Banal, indeed. Still, Jack had sent the piece off to Bunnelle, though had no idea whether it was ever picked up.

'Well, I think it's clever,' Pamela told him, set her hand on his arm. 'And how long have we got you for, Jack?'

'If everything goes according to plan, I fly back to Brazzaville tomorrow afternoon.'

She was staring up into his eyes.

'Then we should make the most of every moment,' she said, though Telford was somewhat distracted by two things. First, the knowing wink from Welch he could see from the corner of his eye. And, second, that Welch had never even bothered to enquire what Jack was doing there.

He rode the Number Fifteen tram, early next morning, from the Mena, seven miles to downtown Cairo. They'd been held up once already at the El-Gala English Bridge, waiting for a whole fleet of *feluccas* to sail through, and when they were stopped again in a jam on the boulevard leading to the next swingbridge, the traffic backed up to Opera Square, he jumped off at the Grand Continental, tugged his forelock in salute to the equestrian statue of Ibrahim Pasha, deciding to walk. He was too early for the museum to open anyway, so he strolled the rest of the way, admired the bronze lions at the end of the El-Gezira bridge and, when the steamers had gone on their way, up and down the Nile, the bridge closed once more, the tram rattling past, he crossed towards the east bank with the mixed throng.

He stopped halfway, watched the boats, soaked up the atmosphere, but mainly thought about the finale to last night. Christ, mortification. The three women had invited Telford and Welch back to their lodging for a nightcap – a tired old euphemism. He should have simply said no, but a combination of the cocktails, his curiosity about Welch, and his juvenile desire to preserve his dignity in the face of the women's goading, all led him to that shameful denouement.

They were lodging at an attractive houseboat, the *Lotus*, moored across from the Sporting Club, but during their attempt to sneak aboard in the darkness, a door swung open on the upper deck and they were caught in the beam of a flashlight.

'Dammit,' Pamela had murmured. 'Miss Perry.'

A shrill, matron's voice.

'Who's with you, girls? Men? You know the rules, don't you?'

'Yes, Miss Perry,' Val called back. 'Just saying goodnight.'

'The rules, Miss Beck. You will see me in the morning.'

There'd been a general retreat back across the gangway, Miss Perry yelling at them about lights out, Welch trying to persuade them they should all go with him to the Continental. And there'd been general accord until Jack finally demurred. All a bit seedy, somehow. He remembered how disgusted he'd been by the sordid way Welch had eyeballed Monique Réchard at the Anfa racetrack.

251

God, it seemed so long ago. He'd meant to ask after Réchard, missed the man, he found. But now...

The argument had broken the spell: Pamela insisting that if Jack wasn't going, then neither was she; the attempts by Valerie and Brenda the brunette to cajole her; their teasing of Telford; Welch's sneering aspersions, his snide comments; and the two young womens' eventual disappearance into the night with the man literally old enough to be their grandfather.

'See?' Pamela had said. 'That old witch – Miss Perry – she's gone now. With just two of us, and we make no noise...'

It had taken him an age to disentangle himself, apologies if he'd led her up the garden path, her insistence, a few desperate kisses somehow tasting of sour milk, a sullen separation, and Jack's promise he'd write.

Yes, mortification, he thought, and rejoined the morning crowd crossing the bridge. Here was a place where the entire world came together, where Kipling should have come to see how wrong he was. About never the twain shall meet. Khaki uniforms, linen suits, European skirts, veil, *tarboosh* and trilby. Trucks and motor cars and camels. He'd been woken, of course, by the sunrise summons of the *mu'azzins* but now the city was all honking horns, the babble of chatter, the occasional throb of an aircraft overhead and all eyes turned skywards in case it might, this time, be the *Boches*.

At the farther end of the bridge, to the right, was Shepheard's Hotel again, but Jack swung north to the wide expanse of the Tahrîr Square and its Egyptian Museum of Antiquities. There wasn't much time. He had to meet Fox back at the Mena by noon. But he knew he might never pass this way again.

Solid and somehow Italianate. He passed through the entrance gates, largely ignored the gardens, skipped the ground floor collection of papyrus and coins, feeling like a Philistine for doing so and almost apologising to the uniformed attendants. Indeed, he paused only briefly in the double-height hall at the museum's heart, with its colossal twin statues. Just long enough to take the notepad from his satchel and begin a quick pencil sketch – only to receive a severe reprimand.

'Can you not read?' the guard yelled at him in Arabic.

All photography, sketching or drawing strictly forbidden.

Yes, it was prominent enough. An apology.

'And the Mummy Hall, is it open today?' he asked in English, not a clue what the Arabic word for *mummy* might be.

'Before say want,' the Egyptian replied. Well, it was fair enough. Pretty much what the concierge at the Mena had told him. Book in advance.

Jack spent a few respectful minutes among the other visitors, mostly service personnel, admiring the statues, taller than the columns of the ground floor, framed against the archways above. He poked his head into many of the forty-two rooms, spent more time in those that drew him, tried to decipher the typewritten descriptions in Arabic, French or English, on faded, yellowing cards, though many of the artefacts without any explanation whatsoever. Mummy masks, the wonders of Thebes, the palettes of hieroglyphics, more glorious statues, busts, coffins, figurines of gleaming gold, perfectly preserved sandals, sarcophagi and steles.

Then the first floor, a glance at the relics of the later dynasties, and his ultimate goal. Tutankhamun's treasure rooms. The stuff of legend. He wandered through the jewel hall, peered over the shoulders of those pressed around the case containing the gold burial mask, glanced inside one of the nested coffins. Yes, they were impressive, but he was drawn back to the almost deserted rooms with the French archaeologist Montent's most recent discoveries from Tanis, and these he found irresistible. Bracelets of blue and gold bearing the eyes of Horus. A face mask to at least rival that of King Tut.

He glanced at his watch. Almost time to go, but he decided to see the gardens before he left, emerged into the furnace blast of late-morning, turned right out of the main entrance, wandered past the miniature sphinxes and smaller obelisks, the floating lily-pads, heading for the semi-circular white marble mausoleum for the great Egyptologist, Auguste Mariette, Mariette Pasha, without whose dedication, Jack knew, this museum might never have come to fruition. But he stopped dead before he reached the monument, saw two men partly hidden in the shadow of a date palm.

Kingsley Welch again. In some sort of heated discussion with his companion, a large and ugly brute, almost Slavic features.

Jack had no desire to speak to Welch, but his curiosity got the better of him. A guide, with a trio of French officers came by, one of them on crutches, a missing leg. The same fellow from last night? Jack wasn't sure, but he tagged along behind them, all the same, trying to conceal himself. A small world, indeed.

At their approach, Welch and the other man fell silent, turned their backs, lowered their heads.

Telford walked more quickly, overtook the French officers on the steps to the tomb, Mariette's statue with its folded arms above him, but keeping the Frenchmen and their guide between himself and the palm tree. He edged around the curve of the monument, with its added busts of all those other notables – more egyptologists, he supposed – and ambled with as much nonchalance as he could muster to a great sandstone stele set in the parched lawn just alongside. He squatted down behind, glad of its shade, as well as its vantage point.

The Frenchmen moved on and, as they did so, he heard Welch's voice again. The same insistent confrontation. The other man barking back at him. Yet the whole exchange muted, clandestine. Why? Telford wondered. And he cursed again his own lack of German – for this, indeed, was the language of their disagreement.

An explosion of glass. Telford instinctively closed his eye, lifted his arms to protect his face. Too late to stop whatever slammed into his cheek. Blood running down his chin and onto his neck. He put his fingers there, stared at the wet, crimson smear as he pulled them away again, then up at the hole where the plane's temperature gauges had been.

He'd felt its passing, the bullet. Bullet? Didn't seem to do it justice, Jack thought, his guts heaving. He took in the size of the hole, turned to see the corresponding exit wound in the Blenheim's port side, just above Fox's head.

The captain was reaching for him, mouthing something. The plane slewed to one side again, and Jack grabbed for the rim of the seat well to steady himself, despite his shoulder straps.

'Just a sliver of glass,' Fox yelled. 'Here…'

He turned his head, searching this way and that, as though their enemy might be there inside the plane, then reached into the pocket of his uniform shorts, through the parachute harness, pulled out a handkerchief. A swift movement and he was showing Telford the piece of glass he'd pulled from his cheek with one hand, pressing the hankie against the cut with his other.

There'd been no warning. One minute, drowsy in the now familiar throb of the Blenheim's engines, the usual soporific bathos of a return journey. Cairo far behind them. The subterfuge of sleep to help him ignore Fox's earlier annoyance. He'd ruined the captain's otherwise splendid good humour. Word from the War Office. Leclerc to receive – grudgingly – four hundred additional trucks, ten armoured cars, six American Seventy-Fives and four Bofors guns. Less than the colonel had demanded. More than he'd expected.

But Jack had almost brushed the news aside.

'I tell you,' he'd insisted, 'it was Welch. Speaking German. Clearly a secret meeting.'

'German,' Fox had replied. 'You're sure it was German? Not Dutch, perhaps?'

'Well – no, dammit, it was German. I'm certain.'

'For pity's sake, Telford,' the captain had barked at him. 'Where the hell do you get all this nonsense from? Did he hand this fellow a card with a black scorpion on it, by any chance?'

The argument had continued all the way to the plane and, since then, they'd fallen into a sullen silence, this pretense at dozing on Jack's part. Yet he'd kept his eye half open, watching Nemo working at his wireless set, a few feet away, in the cramped confines of the depressed gun turret, fiddling with the valves. It had been giving him trouble since takeoff.

Jack had seen the man suddenly become alert, cracking his head against the turret's frame as he tried to sit upright. Some instinct immediately before…

Three juddering hammer blows in quick succession, each louder than the one before, each shaking the Blenheim harder than the last. The third shattered those gauges. The cloud of glittering shards had seemed to almost hang in the air, until that whistle above his head, the stinging slap against his cheek. The wind brushed through his hair. Popeye Pezon had banked sharply to starboard. The previously peaceful thrum of the engines now turned to a scream of rage when the pilot threw open the throttle. Over this again, a louder, deafening roar. All so fast. The light from the hatch window blotted out for an instant only. Then, also, stolen from the cockpit, returning as the attacking banshee's pandemonium vanished into the distance. In its place, yelling inside the Blenheim. The whirr and clang of hydraulics as Nemo elevated himself and the turret. The turret rotating. The machine gun's cocking handle ratcheted back.

'Four o'clock,' Nemo's voice crackled through Jack's headset. 'High.'

The raging plane shuddered into another turn. Fox pressed the handkerchief harder against Jack's cheek, tossing away the glass splinter.

Fast, Jack thought. Isn't this what they'd said at the briefing? Might be called a bomber, Pezon had boasted, but we can outrun most things. Most…

The Vickers machine gun drowned out almost everything else. Short burst, empty shells raining down out of the turret, bouncing off the fuselage floor, a tinkling cascade of brass casings.

'Need to get up,' Jack shouted, fumbling with the snap buckle at his waist. 'Should help.'

'Nothing to do,' Fox gripped his arm. 'Be in the way.'

'Another on our tail, skipper.' Nemo, the intercom. The turret's hydraulics again, but the thing turning so slowly, Jack couldn't believe it might keep track of the incoming fighers. 'Coming in low. Corkscrew. Corkscrew.'

The Blenheim jinked left, then right. Left again. The cabin pungent with cordite.

'Hang on to something.' Popeye Pezon's voice on the intercom, then yelling, urgent. 'Now!'

Jack grabbed for one of the webbing straps holding some sort of valise to the fuselage side. Fox did likewise, just as the Blenheim tilted on its side. Telford was left momentarily hanging in his shoulder straps, head lolling downwards, the empty cartridge cases showering around them.

The straps cut into his shoulders as the plane, Jack's brain, rolled over completely, upside down. The rush of vertigo when it briefly levelled once more.

'And again,' he heard Nemo shout. The machine gun. Another burst. More shell cases.

'Hang on,' called the pilot, and the manoeuvre repeated, this time the opposite way, anti-clockwise. This time, as well, Jack lost any semblance of self-control. Terror, like nothing ever before.

The Blenheim flattened out, banked.

Jack had trouble breathing. Agony in his chest. Fox had braced himself against the side of the seat well, and Jack braced himself against Fox. He looked to the turret, where Nemo's legs and feet, crabbed sideways, tried to work the control pedals. Almost impossible at that angle. Jack could just see the machine guns grips, depressed almost to the wireless operator's knees, the Vickers blazing away and now spewing casings in a continuous burst, until the magazine was empty.

'Got the bastard!' Nemo shouted, chucked down the empty magazine, must have begun to fit another, the plane flying straight and level again. A small cheer from the crew, from Fox as well, while Jack tried to look through the hatch window, to spot the enemy Nemo had taken down. But nothing. Not at first. But then – yes, there. Above them. Nothing more than a speck in the beginning but growing by the second. Flashes of light. Pretty, he thought. A stupid thought. He remembered Nemo, pulled the stinking face mask across, pressed the button in its nose.

'Nine o'clock,' he screamed. 'High.'

He felt his heart thumping as the fighter dropped out of the sky towards them.

'I see him,' the wireless operator shouted back.

The turret began to swing slowly. Too slowly. Jack heard the screech of the fighter's engine over their own, the *thump, thump, thump* of the enemy plane's cannon, the ripping of the Blenheim's metal skin, the dome shattering, a storm of plexiglass fragments. The fighter roared overhead, and the Blenheim banked again. Nemo's legs jerked, then the feet swung loose in the sardine can turret. There was blood, trickling down his shoe.

'Get him out of there,' shouted Fox.

'Émile…' The intercom. Fox used his mask microphone, while Jack unfastened his straps, tore off his helmet and climbed out of the seat well. He fell heavily against one of the alloy airframes when the plane banked yet again, felt something crack in his chest. But he hauled himself upright, ducked his head into the turret, winced with the pain. Impossible to reach the handlebar controls from there, but he could just about get to Nemo's waist strap, turned the Quick Release to unlock it, pressed the plate to free him. The man was moaning, and Jack gripped his legs, pulled him down. Couldn't shift him though, until Fox joined him, helped get him to the floor.

'Eyes,' Nemo cried. There was a wound in the side of his head. Still bleeding. And badly. But his drained, milky face was like a pin cushion. Slivers of plexiglass. His eyes closed, the lids sprinkled with glass dust.

'Need water,' said Jack. 'And medical kit.'

Telford stopped the wireless operator from lifting his hand to his face.

'Blind?' Nemo murmured. Surprise in his voice. A lost look. No, not lost. Abandoned.

'Don't touch,' Jack yelled. 'Dust in your eyes. We'll rinse them out.'

The Blenheim slipped to port, the roar of the fighter again. No hits this time, thank god. Fox had the flask, tried to ease one of Nemo's eyes open, pour water onto the badly bloodshot mess. Jack picked up the first aid package, ripped open a linen corner, took out one of the morphia ampoules, the sterilised gauze, the wound dressing. He took the water flask, washed the head wound, rolled up the fellow's sleeve and used the ampoule's syringe. There was a pencil in the package. Jack looked at his watch, filled in the card. The time, the date, his initials, tied the string through one of the buttonholes in Nemo's shirt.

'Christ,' he heard Fox say. He turned. The captain was standing, hanging on to the turret's frame, staring forward. 'Again.'

Telford saw the fighter, coming straight for them. Head-on. Popeye Pezon peering through the bead sight, firing the wing machine gun. Tracers curving outwards. More tracers coming in. Collision course.

'Pull out,' Jack yelled, his guts frozen. 'For god's sake, pull out.'

But Pezon didn't. And the windscreen exploded. All hell let loose. A howling gale filled the Blenheim. The ricochet *prang* as a bullet bounced off the turret frame. The plane lurched. Jack fell backwards, banged his head, another stab of misery in his chest.

'Oh, my god,' Fox shouted, still clinging to the frame, his voice barely audible for the screeching wind, but reaching out a hand to help Telford.

The Blenheim had gone into a shallow dive, the engines' pitch growing higher. And higher.

'Why...?' Jack began. But then he saw why. Just about, through his stinging, tear-filled eye.

The navigator was leaning across the cockpit, struggling like a maniac to pull Pezon's slumped, lifeless body from the pilot's seat with one hand, wrestling the control column with the other, his foot braced against the instrument panel yoke. He turned his head towards them, frantic, goggles pulled down. His mouth opened and his bellow of fear and anguish carried back to them on the wind.

'Jesus!'

After that – well, after that...

The full horror of those sneak Japanese air attacks emerged over the few days after he'd found Harmon weeping at the wireless set. The worst damage at a place called Pearl Harbor in the Hawaiian Islands. Four American battleships sunk. Cruisers and destroyers. Over two thousand neutral Americans killed. And not just Hawaii, but other raids against the Philippines, Guam, Wake Island – and British bases at Singapore and Hong Kong.

The following day, the United States declaration of war against Japan and, three days later, Germany and Italy's declaration of war against the Yanks.

'I've two cousins,' Harmon told Telford, a week after the first news reached them. They'd gone to watch the Kyébé-Kyébé puppet dancers, just up the road from the office, the public gardens in the Place Savorgnan. 'Brothers. Both at Hickam Field.'

The name meant nothing to him, but it felt like a breakthrough, the first time she'd made any attempt to talk with him. Plenty of praying, though. And maybe that wasn't so bad. If it gave her comfort.

'If there's anything I can do…' he said.

'They are in God's hands, Mister Telford,' she replied. The shortest, most eloquent dismissal he'd ever heard.

Almost Christmas, and hot as hell. No relief from it, just the shade here from the palm fronds above. The dancers were shrouded from head to foot with sacking, only *this* sacking had been painted in pale khaki, a Cross of Lorraine, and the wooden puppet heads above could have been mistaken for nobody except de Gaulle. The nose, the *képi*.

'According to Leclerc, Miss Harmon, so are we all. In God's hands. Seems fairly convinced the Almighty must have driven the Japs to this atrocity, just as He drove the *Boches* to invade Russia. Suicide, now it's stirred up your great grizzly bear of a nation.'

'These guys seem to think it's de Gaulle who makes all the miracles,' she said.

'The Chief of Battles,' Jack murmured, as the dancers cavorted. This was the way in which the locals styled the general now. They told great stories. How Hitler had sent his planes to bomb Brazzaville, but de Gaulle had created a magic mist, made the town invisible. 'They think he performs witchcraft.'

'And does it work?'

'We've not been bombed, have we? That's how magic operates, no? It works for the folk who believe it works.'

Like religion, he thought, but didn't dare say so.

'And you, Mister Telford? Our Lord seems to have taken a hand in your own affairs. Unless you think it was magic as well.'

'What d'you mean?' said Jack, and lit himself a cigarette, careful to blow the smoke away from her.

'They say you crashed. In the desert.'

'They do? Then I suppose it must be right.'

He tried not to think about it. Five months. His ribs still not fully healed. Shortness of breath. More nightmares.

'The pilot died,' she said. 'True?'

'In the crash, yes.'

A lie. The burst of fire, which shattered the cockpit's plexiglass, had almost cut Popeye Pezon in two. If it hadn't, Telford doubted they'd have been able to haul him out of his seat, wrestle him over into the well, allow the navigator to get at the column, to slow their doomed descent.

'Going for a Burton,' Fox had shouted. Only there was no drink for them to go down into – just the desert. It was the first time Jack had seen any sign of fear from the captain.

'You can fly?' Jack had screamed in the navigator's ear.

A shake of the man's head.

'I watched Popeye, though,' he'd called back, the controls vibrating under his hands, the ground racing towards them. 'But the train...'

He frantically worked a spade-grip handle back and forth, and it took a few seconds.

'The bloody undercarriage?' Jack yelled. *Le train d'atterrissage.*

No time to use the hand pump instead, and they'd hit moments later, though Jack remembered none of the actual crash. Only coming-to – bleeding, battered, badly bruised – in the twisted, tilting wreckage. Fox had survived, helped drag him out of the Blenheim. Then poor blind Nemo.

'A miracle, I guess,' said Dudley Anne Harmon now, while the *tam-tam* drums beat and the puppet dancers spun in wild frenzy. 'The pilot living long enough to land you safely.'

'A miracle,' Jack agreed. 'No argument there.'

'The fighters – Italian or German?'

'I didn't see them. Not properly. But Captain Fox said afterwards they were Messerschmitts. German, you know?'

'Yes, I managed to work that out.'

'Well, another miracle. Wherever they'd come from, they must have been at the very limit of their range. Otherwise, the last one – it would have finished us off.'

A miracle they'd survived at all. More of a miracle the Blenheim came down, not in the desert itself, but at the Ma'tan as-Sarra oasis, where the plane had ploughed into a fortunately abandoned building and the local Toubous had taken word to a nearby Long Range Desert Group patrol. Southern Rhodesians. A miracle, yet he'd never even known the navigator's name.

Christmas again. Jack's fourth away from England. Last year, in Abidjan, on his way to Libreville. The year before, Rabat. And Christmas '38, at the consulate in Madrid – with Ruby. He shook the thought back into its box, closed the lid, pushed his way out of the Sacré-Coeur's incense fug, long past midnight, temperature in its upper-seventies, even now, and the angelic voices of the Bakongo choir, the final notes of *Bel Astre Que J'Adore*, still in his ears.

'Pretty sight,' said Harmon. They stood on the open ground outside the church and there, from the *butte*, from the Plateau de L'Aiglon, Brazzaville was spread out below them, the blackout observed even more carelessly here than it had been in Cairo. But then, he supposed, there *was* that story about de Gaulle spreading a cloak of invisibility over the place.

'And only we can see it, Miss Harmon,' he replied, not really caring very much whether she shared the joke. Yet it was the first time he'd seen her in skirts, rather than slacks. A white linen dress with green print flowers. It somehow made her seem less lanky.

Beyond La Corniche, the inky blackness of the river and, a mile away, the lights of Léopoldville's Kinshasa district.

'It's sad,' she said. 'Being away from home at Christmas, don't you think? Only it's not been the same, not since Mom died. Your mother still alive, Mister Telford?'

There was a note of hope in her voice, as though there might be some chance of surrogacy here.

'Afraid not,' he told her, as they fell in with the crowd heading down Avenue Foch. Army officers, civilians and their wives, all the mingled races of Brazzaville. Those of a certain class, anyway. 'And where would you have been now, if you were still in Washington? Not at Catholic Midnight Mass, I'm guessing.'

'Oh, at St. Paul's. Family tradition. The Carol Candlelight Service. Not midnight though. A little earlier. Ten, and *after* dinner, not before it.'

She'd raised more than an eyebrow when he explained tonight's traditions, exactly as Massu had explained it to *him*.

'Lutheran?'

'How did you know, Mister Telford? Never mind, you don't need to answer. I'm just glad you talked me into coming along. I hadn't taken you for a Catholic, lapsed or otherwise.'

She'd wanted, of course, to attend the service at the Moravian chapel, but he'd persuaded her that the Sacré-Coeur choir was allegedly something special. Not to be missed. And when they'd sung *Les Anges Dans Nos Campagnes*...

'I'm not,' he said, lit a cigarette, spun her the usual line. How everybody always *took* him for a Catholic, ever since he was a kid. Something to do with his perpetual feeling of guilt about one thing or another. How it must, over the years, have etched some sense of Catholicism into his features.

'And agnostic.' She looked up into the night sky, the stars still bright, despite the street lamps. 'How can you doubt,' she said, 'when you simply have to see God's glory all around you? When you must have heard His voice so plainly through the choir back there.'

'You'd think,' he told her, 'if God had intended me to be spiritual, He would have wired me that way, no? It's not as though I wasn't open to the idea – not when I was younger, at least. But now...'

They'd reached the town hall, the *mairie*. Despite its single storey, the colonial elegance of the building and its courtyard gardens dominated the farther side of the palm-fringed square – a half-circle, in truth – where Avenue Foch ended.

'Are you sure I'm invited?' she said.

'Just an oversight on the colonel's part, I'm sure.'

'He despises me. Why would there have been an invitation?'

'If you've never sat through *Le Réveillon*,' he said, 'you might be sorry I brought you along. And he doesn't despise you – well...'

In the foyer, he gave his name to an adjutant, explained there must be some mistake – his invitation from *le patron*, and definitely an invitation for two.

'*Monsieur* Telford.' It was Massu, just behind him, an elegant young woman on his arm, another officer at his side, a fellow with a distinctive red beard. 'Is there a problem?'

'They don't seem to have Miss Harmon on the list. Just an error, I think.'

'Error?' said Massu. He looked, as usual, as though there was something evil-smelling on his moustache, his nostrils pinched. 'Come on, man,' he snapped at the adjutant, 'this is Telford. Famous journalist. And I need to eat.' The adjutant attempted a protest, but Massu pushed them past, towards the doors, leading into the council chamber, now set with long tables and chairs, many of them already occupied. '*Et voilà*,' the captain laughed. 'This is Dronne, by the way. Telford was at Kufra, Raymond. Nerves of steel, haven't you, Telford? Look, there is your friend, Fox. Come, sit with us.'

Fox didn't exactly look excited to see him, and Jack wasn't certain whether Massu was poking fun. Nerves of steel? But Jack was happy to let it pass. A jazz combo played in the corner, a quintet. A competent enough medley of *Hot Club de France* numbers.

'You weren't on the list either, were you?' Harmon whispered as extra seats were found, exchanged greetings with Fox, with Guillebon, with Geoffroy, with another new lieutenant, Girard, with their respective companions. Introductions between those who'd not met before, while Leclerc's chaplain, *Père* Bronner, said a simple blessing for the meal they were about to receive.

'We're in, aren't we?' Jack murmured, accepted a glass of wine from Fox, glanced at the still empty top table. 'Wine? I didn't know we still had any.'

'The last of it,' said Geoffroy. 'The rest was so bad, we had to turn it over to the distillery. Medical grade disinfectant, now. You see, the sacrifices we make?'

Irony, of course. For they *had* all made sacrifices. Out there, in the desert. Here, with the shortages and the rationing. So unlike the affluence of the *Réveillon* he'd enjoyed two years before, in Rabat. But tonight? Tonight, there'd be only relative frugality. For here came the first offering. Caviar. Not much of it, but caviar, all the same.

'No, not for me,' Harmon was saying to the waiter working their end of the table. 'Great heavens, sacrifices? Have you seen what the people in Poto-Poto and M'pila are eating?'

Her French was good. He knew this already. But, strangely, he'd noticed, it was more heavily American accented than her English.

'The bush monkeys?' said one of the new young officers, further along. 'If they'd enlist, or join the labour gangs, they'd eat just fine.'

The woman at Massu's side exchanged a frown with Guillebon's companion. An athletic woman – Bakongo, Jack thought.

'Can you blame them?' Telford said. 'I think I'd hide in the forest as well if I was going to end up treated like a dog. Pounding wild rubber vines? Scratching in the dirt for gold? Chained to the road gangs? And then what? Not even the luxury of a ration card. Just – nothing.'

'We have a war to win, *monsieur*,' said the young man, and Jack could have slapped the silly devil. 'Those are the resources we need. The patriotic duty of these people to play their part.'

'They must often wonder,' Telford told him, 'for whose benefit it's being fought, wouldn't you say, *mademoiselle…*?'

He turned to Jacques de Guillebon's friend, the Bakongo woman – a nurse, Jack had gathered from the introductions. Massu's companion was also a nurse, but white, from Bordeaux.

'Christelle,' the African nurse reminded him in English, lowered her eyes, settled to her caviar. 'My name is Christelle.'

'You speak English,' said Harmon. 'What a relief. Tires me so, speaking in French for so long.'

Jack was caught now, politeness and the temptation of an easy conversation in English dragging him one way, his wish to see the young officer put in his place pulling him the other.

'Play their part, Hiver?' Massu had rounded on the man. 'You should have been at Kufra, you fool.'

Christelle was explaining how she'd learned her English – her friend too, Véronique, Massu's replacement for Moido, it seemed – learning to be a nurse under Madame Eugénie Éboué and the Englishwoman, Susan Travers. Did Harmon know her? Serving with the Legion. With Koenig, she said. A knowing look.

'Drink,' said Geoffroy, and topped up Jack's glass. 'After this, we'll be on the rum, I'm afraid.'

It had been the news this week. Lend-Lease extended to the Free French. A shipment of Thompson sub-machine guns. From the British, supplies of tin helmets, bully beef – and rum. Copious quantities of rum.

'And when does the great man arrive?' asked Telford, nodding at the top table.

As if on cue, all eyes turned to the doors, the rising ripple of guests getting to their feet, the musicians striking up La Marseillaise.

Allons enfants de la Patrie, Le jour de gloire est arrivé!

Jack had never heard the anthem sung without Gallic emotion but, since the fall of Paris, my god, it was hard for anybody to keep a dry eye. Anybody, even these battle-stained brothers-in-arms. And no chance, here, that anybody was going to observe the Vichy requirement for the Marseillaise to always be followed by their paean to Pétain. But Telford could never quite get past those strange lines at the end of the chorus, exhorting citizens to water their fields with the blood – the impure blood – of their enemies. He often wondered why nobody had ever bothered to apply an editor's pen. Yet, on this occasion, he simply joined in, as awed as everybody else by de Gaulle's presence, his ramrod solemnity as the Marseillaise filled the room, Governor General Félix Éboué at his side. And Madame Eugénie, the nurse, almost as well-built as her husband, all white taffeta and lace. Then the High Commissioner, Adolphe Sicé with his wife also, and four smaller children. Finally, Leclerc himself.

'Dammit, we missed the caviar,' he joked, loudly, as they finally took their seats. At least, Jack assumed it was a joke. You could never quite tell with Leclerc. He wondered whether the lieutenant, Hiver, also classed Éboué as a bush monkey, but Massu was still berating the fellow.

'I don't think you understand, sir,' said Hiver. 'They head for the trees every time they see us coming.'

Oysters being served now, one of the few things Jack couldn't stomach. But Harmon seemed to have set aside her disdain at this decadence, swallowed down his helping, as well as her own, and keeping up a steady stream of inquisitive dialogue with Christelle and Véronique.

266

'How was Cairo, Jacques?' Telford said to Guillebon. 'You met Auchinleck.'

'Your sepoy general? He doesn't think we can go forward...' he glanced around to see who might be listening. 'Go forward, by ourselves. I told him, with more equipment...'

Jack remembered the Mark Twain story, the detectives trying to find an elephant that was there, under their noses, all the time. And here's our elephant, he thought. The Fezzan. Nobody mentioned it in public, but most of Brazza knew this was where they were heading next. He recalled, also, the map he'd once seen, spread across Leclerc's table. The vast Fezzan desert, the size of France, the vicious heart of the harsh Sahara, the entire southwestern region of Libya. Italian strongholds at every one of the few habitable zones.

Guillebon had turned to Fox.

'No point looking at me, old boy,' said the captain, and glowered at Jack.

They barely spoke now, not since Jack had raised those questions about Welch. Telford hadn't been able to let it go, of course. Like a dog with a bone. Until Fox had tired of him entirely. Afterwards, Jack had pursued his inquiries elsewhere. A wire to Sydney Elliott. A sparse message back. Welch's address in Surrey. Connection to Standard Oil. A few other minor details, but only for the past ten years. Before that, nothing.

Speeches. Governor Éboué in his pristine white suit, on his feet to welcome them. To this *Réveillon*, this awakening, this Christmas Eve vigil. For none knew what may come next, he was saying. *Père Noël* or *Père Fouettard*.

'*Fouettard?*' Harmon whispered.

'Bogeyman,' Jack murmured. 'Father Christmas gives presents to good children. *Père Fouettard* gives the naughty ones lumps of coal, or beats the living daylights out of them.'

'Charming,' she giggled, as terrine of *foie gras* was served, the scarlet-uniformed waiters in a pantomime of exaggerated effort to make as little noise as possible. But Jack saw the expression on Lieutenant Hiver's face, the distaste as he looked from his plate, up at the tribal scars of his own wide-eyed waiter, back again. It was nothing unusual, of course. There'd been times when he'd seen legionnaires, parched with thirst in the desert, but still refusing to drink from the proffered water bottle of a *tirailleur*. Yet it seemed worse now, this new intake of recruits and officer cadets bringing with them prejudices far darker than those of the colonial old hands.

'We must be cautious, my friends,' Éboué was saying. 'But cautious in the knowledge that Our Lord is with us and shall deliver us victory in His name. For tonight, though, we may eat our fill and enjoy this communion, secure in the knowledge our holy father has given us his blessing.'

They'd all heard the broadcast from the Vatican, the previous evening. The pope's permission for the faithful to dispense with fasting and abstinence for so long as this war should last. Except, of course, on Ash Wednesdays and Good Fridays. Surely the war could never sink to such a level that it would obviate the need for fasting and abstinence on Ash Wednesday or Good Friday. Surely not.

Jack could see the look of annoyance on Leclerc's face. Not about fasting and abstinence, plainly. No, another open secret here. Leclerc desperate to attack the Fezzan, but the Governor-General, de Gaulle as well, both having their doubts about the timing.

There was a muted round of applause as Éboué took his seat again, accepted an admiring pat on the arm from Madame Eugénie. At the top table, also, some dispute apparently about who should speak next.

'And what do you think, *Monsieur* Telford?' said ginger-bearded Captain Dronne. 'Caution?'

Jack was somewhat surprised by the question. He'd become a familiar figure, here at Brazzaville. Among Leclerc's men, too. His work familiar also. But he couldn't recall anybody asking his opinion about military strategy before.

'I think Auchinleck would love us to create a diversion,' he said, noticed for the first time how piercingly blue were this young officer's eyes. 'And the British are doing well enough just now. Tobruk relieved, and so on. But if we're checked again, as we were in March…'

'Why in heaven's name should you think so, Telford?' Fox barked at him.

'Why?' said Jack. 'Our best Australian divisions withdrawn to go and fight the Japanese. Rommel supplied with new and better tanks – isn't this what we've been told? And what is it *le patron* always says? It's logistics that win or lose wars. It probably all depends on who's got the best oil supplies.'

He'd heard Leclerc lecture his officers often enough, his bitter memories of the campaigns in France, their tanks abandoned for lack of fuel. How, if only they'd had oil…

It made him think of Welch again. Standard Oil. And Paquita Gorroño's own lecture. About the American companies, which would make money from the war, regardless of which side might win. Thomas Watson's IBM used to conduct the 1937 German census but, particularly, to tabulate information about Germany's Jews. Woolworth's. Singer sewing machines. Coca Cola. Henry Ford's German subsidiary, building V8 engines for Hitler's forces, and his factory at Cologne churning out army vehicles. The General Motors eighty percent share in Opel, and Opel building the German army's favourite trucks. J.P. Morgan's interests in Germany's General Electric. Rockefeller and Standard Oil's twenty-five percent share in I.G. Farben's gasoline business. Welch connected to Standard Oil. But a German link? It all seemed a bit thin.

'Oil supplies?' said Geoffroy. 'Don't make me laugh. We haven't even got spares. You know how Jacques here has been repairing his radiators?' He slapped Massu on the back. 'With gazelle skins, Véronique.' He laughed in the nurse's face, a little the worse for his wine. 'Gazelles.'

'At Uigh-el-Kebir,' said Massu, 'the locals use them for just about everything. We're bloody good at it now, living off the land.'

Uigh-el-Kebir. Nobody was supposed to mention the location. Not really. But Massu had been turning the place into a forward base for months now. Far beyond Faya-Largeau. Beyond Zouar. Across the Libyan border, at the very edge of the Fezzan. And the new recruits being sent up from Brazza no longer had to suffer the entire journey on the jungle roads. Now, the paddle steamer *Fondère* carried them all the way to Bangui, towing barges loaded with the trucks to take them the rest of the way to Fort Lamy and beyond.

Luxury, thought Jack, as they were served *escargots* and High

Commissioner Sicé delivered his own few words. Telford had never met him, but his photo was always in the local paper and he was a familiar figure, often seen with the family in his open-topped limousine, driving on the Corniche. A medical man, he'd been director of the Pasteur Institute here. And now, also as head of the Free French medical services, he'd made some great improvements to the welfare of their troops. But Jack admired him mostly because they shared something in common. Sicé had also survived an air crash, in the jungle, the previous February.

'What about you, Captain Dronne?' said Harmon, as Sicé sat down again. 'The cautious approach – or go straight at them?'

'You promise not to quote me?'

'Strictly off the record?'

'Don't trust her, Captain,' said Jack. 'She's with United Press. American, into the bargain. Entirely without scruples.'

She rolled her eyes, was about to offer some waspish response, but the room had fallen silent. De Gaulle finally on his feet, Jack taking Negrín's pen, his small notebook, from inside his jacket.

'The traveller,' de Gaulle began, with a distant, philosophical air, 'who climbs a mountain, stops at times to measure the distance he's already come, and to check he's still on the right path towards the summit.'

It was a similar line to the one taken by the general back in November. London. The Albert Hall. And widely reported.

'And so we gather, this Christmas, here in this new heart of France, a brief moment of peace, by God's grace, this short respite from the trials of war, to fortify ourselves afresh, to confirm our progress along the hard road towards the liberation of our country, our beautiful France – Joan of Arc's France, which we all serve.'

Everybody in the room on their feet. But de Gaulle settled them quickly.

'But no lengthy orations tonight,' he said. 'For, in this company, none are needed. You are the men, the women, who have answered our nation's call in the first hour of her fresh awakening, her own *Réveillon*. Each of you with a role to play, each of you important. Regardless of origin or opinion, all we need to know about this new France, the flame of which shall outshine the old.'

Jack took notes, watched the Adam's apple bobbing up and down at the general's throat. His delivery was eloquent, measured. Cold passion. The sweeping hand, the pointing finger, as articulate as the words. And there was promise here. A distinct move away from the *Action Française* politics with which de Gaulle had been more generally associated. Bunnelle would be interested in this.

'And yes, I know you all want to hasten the end of our conflict. But we must each understand the nature of this war. It will require endurance, patience. Not just *élan*. The mountain path along which our duty takes us is long and hard. But perhaps we are near to a turning point. Perhaps, at this Christmas time, Berlin has chosen the route onto an icy slope that shall plunge our enemies into the abyss. Perhaps Rome, as the Englishman, Lord Byron once said, shall again become "the lone mother of dead empires." Yet, whatever may be the length and cost of our inevitable victory, there remains no other path for ourselves than to remain, until the very end, Frenchmen – Frenchmen born, or Frenchmen by choice – worthy of France herself.'

The chamber upon its feet again. Another rendition of *La Marseillaise*. And, while the message was clear – patience, no prospect of the major campaign they'd all expected – Leclerc's features remained frigid, impassive through the rest of the *Réveillon*; the *Coquilles Sant Jacques*; the roast duck, with its orange sauce; the fried wildfowl – peacock, francolin and quail; the cheeses; the thirteen desserts representing Jesus and the Twelve Apostles; the *Bûche de Noël*; and all the champagne they'd been able to muster with which to wash it all down.

The following week's *Réveillon*, of course, was a very different affair. Because it brought not simply a New Year in its wake, but also sudden death.

A *Réveillon* for Saint-Sylvestre. For the *jour de l'an*. A sultry night, storm brewing, somewhere. Everybody dressed to the nines, despite the heat, there on Poto-Poto's Grande Place, only a short step from Jack's room at the Hôtel de La Poste. He'd been tempted to stay there, never a great enthusiast of New Year's Eve and its forced geniality, its sour and melancholy aftertaste.

'I don't believe you ever answered Miss Harmon's question,' he said to Captain Dronne, as they shared a cold beer at the bar of *Le Dancing Chez-Nous*. 'The cautious approach – or go straight at them?'

Dronne scratched at his red beard, looked over the heads of the crowd in the yard of this tropical *guinguette*, out through the gates, towards the square itself.

'I'd forgotten,' he said. 'She's quite a girl. And me? Straight at them, of course. We won't get the chance, though. Not yet. So, all a bit academic.'

Jack liked him. A shared passion for journalism – in which Dronne had graduated, on top of his law degree. They were about the same age, Dronne having worked as a colonial administrator in Cameroon – and one of de Gaulle's "first hour" volunteers who'd helped rally Yaoundé for Free France. Now, attached to their tribal militia flying columns, their *Groupes Nomades*, in northern Chad, but presently serving a spell, teaching, at Brazza's school for new officers.

'At least until we see whether Rommel's as much in disarray as we'd like to think,' said Jack.

'Your own people, Fox and others, seem pretty convinced.'

Fox? It had been a mere irritant before, the fellow's angry dismissal of his questions about Welch, but now he'd begun to wonder whether there might be something deeper here. A sense of the rabbit hole again, tonight illuminated by the sharp white blade of a sickle-shaped moon.

'We'll see, Captain,' he said. 'But how are you coping with the Spaniards?'

Telford nodded towards Alemán and El Gordo, also enjoying a beer, and posted down here to help with weapons training.

'You know them?'

'Long story. Your lot had them in a prison camp in Morocco. In a roundabout way, I helped them escape. They joined the Legion, ended up here.'

Jack looked around at some of the other fresh-faced young men, most of them already drunk. Men basking in the purchased pleasures, the bartered affections of bare female shoulders and lingerie straps. Men from England and South America, from Canada and Sweden, from India and the Far East. Men with French names and French connections through a mother, a father, a grandparent. But a bit wet behind the ears. No military experience for the most part. And he wondered whether it had been like this when the International Brigade volunteers first began to arrive in Spain. Fire in their bellies. But soldiers?

'Hey, English,' shouted Alemán. 'Where's your girl tonight?'

'Not my girl. And she's out there somewhere.' He waved his beer glass out towards the Grande Place, the music, the dancing, the Latin rhythms of the rumba – all the rage just now, thanks to Radio Congo Belge. It seemed to be the only thing they played these days.

She was with Fox. They'd been seeing a lot of each other. Had this added to his irritation? He admired Harmon's writing, though he'd never have said so to her face. But she'd written some neat pieces, coined the phrase about Brazzaville being the little Paris of Free France, as much at the heart of the war as Moscow or London. He'd told her he hated hyperbole, of course, but it had just been pique. Yet, underneath, he knew she wasn't entirely comfortable here. Leclerc despised her, for one thing. Or so she claimed.

'The American woman again,' said Dronne. 'She asked me what I thought about Vichy. I told her they don't represent true France. They're part of the old Europe, wanting to sit on the sidelines and watch the others tear themselves to pieces so Vichy can emerge as top dog when it's all over. I despise them. Cowards, and worse. So many of them openly admirers of Hitler.'

'We had enough of those in Britain,' Jack replied. He'd had this conversation before. 'It could so easily have gone the same way for us, I suppose. An armistice. Mosley given power as puppet Chancellor. Lord bloody Tavistock or somebody as Prime Minister. Edward brought back from the Bahamas to sit on the throne again. A batch of Nazi-loving ministers to make it all look respectable. Rothermere and the *Daily Mail* spreading their Goebbels propaganda. Churchill and our own *résistant* government in exile – Toronto, maybe. Or Cairo. Planning how to get our own country back.'

'And instead?' said Dronne. 'What is Churchill's plan now? If this goes badly, if the Allies defeat Germany without Free France sitting at the table as an equal, what then? France treated as a vanquished foe? Britain able to snatch up our colonies, add them to their empire?'

'Is that what de Gaulle thinks?'

'It's what we *all* think. Vichy's not the only one trapped in the old Europe, *Monsieur* Telford. The Europe of winners and losers.'

'Then you'd better make damned sure Free France *is* sitting at the table, Captain Dronne. Don't you think?'

Telford took his leave. Yes, he liked Dronne.

Almost midnight. And on the stage in the Grande Place, they'd set up a radio and a loudspeaker although, for now, the band was still in full swing. He'd stay just long enough to see in the New Year, he decided, then back to his room.

The crowd of dancing revellers, as mixed as Poto-Poto itself. Originally built as a district reserved for white residents only – this still elegant and privileged European quarter. But, as waves of migrants had poured into town from the north, new blocks had been added, carefully segregated, one from the other, along tribal and ethnic lines. For the Sara, the Bateke, the Zande, the M'bochi, and so on. Yet the Grande Place formed a melting pot, where Telford had taken to bringing himself each Sunday, to see the dancers and their *tam-tam* drums. Or, during the week, to visit the phonograph shops that seemed to fill every street. He'd even found a place willing to rent him an old machine, to hire precious records – though the deposit was a bit steep. And, of course, nostalgia had forced him to take copies of those favourites he'd left in Hélène Bénatar's safekeeping.

Would he ever get back there? Another wave of New Year's Eve dark melancholia.

'All alone, *Monsieur* Telford?'

It was Leclerc. Jack had been too deep in his own thoughts to notice his approach. And, unusually, here was the man so recently appointed by de Gaulle to the rank of general, but with only a couple of adjutants about him, rather than his usual entourage.

'You as well, General?'

'I was working in my office. Only the lizards on the wall for company. But this drew me. Made me think of Thérèse and the children.'

Six of them, Jack knew. He offered Leclerc a cigarette, but the general shook his head, tapped the malacca cane on the ground.

'Still in Amiens?' Telford asked.

'Tailly,' said Leclerc. 'But close to Amiens, yes. You have family, in England?'

'A sister only. No wife.'

'Mine won't even be sure if I'm still alive. And I've no idea whether she's free anymore. The *Boches* know who I am now, after your damned article, Telford.'

'The photographs? At Kufra? They weren't my photographs, General.' No, they'd been *Père* Bronner's. An Agfa Box Forty-Four, of all things. 'You think she'll be in danger?'

Leclerc took off the plain forage cap he'd been wearing, wiped his brow.

'This heat,' he said. 'But the reports from France? The coldest winter anybody can remember. And the food shortages. People starving. Even if Thérèse is free...'

He didn't finish the sentence. There was no need. His wife will now know, at least, as would the *Boches*, that Philippe de Hautecloque was none other than Leclerc of Kufra. Vichy had already stripped the absent de Hautecloque of his nationality, of course. But would there be other reprisals against his family during this bitter second winter of the German occupation?

Around them, excitement had begun to mount, a countdown from somebody on the stage, a microphone in his hand. *Ten, nine...*

'I'm sure she'll be safe, sir,' said Jack.

Eight, seven...

'Well, happy end of year celebrations to you, *Monsieur* Telford,' said Leclerc and shook Jack's hand.

Six, five...

The general moved on, and Jack looked around again for Harmon. No sign of her.

Four, three...

He caught a movement from the corner of his eye. Something not quite right, a man moving towards him. Close. Too close.

Two, one…

Cries all around of *Bonne Année*. A smell of garlic as somebody threw an arm around his shoulder, a man's bristles scraping his face as he was kissed on the cheeks, not twice but four times. *La Bise.*

He tried to pull away. But couldn't. And the bastard whispered in his ear, then punched him. Hard. In the stomach.

An explosion. His hearing dulled. The night lit by a million extra stars. Fireworks overhead and, for some reason, deep within his being. Singing. The tune of *Auld Lang's Syne.*

Faut-il nous quitter sans espoir,
Sans espoir de retour?

Must we be leaving without hope,
Without hope of a return?

The man who'd thumped him was backing through the crowd, but Jack saw only his face. Like – well, like a close-up shot in a movie, the features artistically just out of focus.

That pressure inside his guts turned to a tingling sensation, like the blood surging back into a limb previously gone to sleep. Pain now. Some of the revellers protesting at being so rudely pushed aside.

The singing had shifted to some other distant place. The chorus.

Ce n'est qu'un au revoir, mes frères,
Ce n'est qu'un au revoir…

It's only a farewell, my friends,
It's only a farewell…

Somebody screamed, and people moved away from him, their joy turned to fear, revulsion.

He was hot. Not just the weather. But a fire burning inside. And his legs were beginning to fail him, felt weak.

He finally looked down, his white shirt stained crimson, something trickling along his thigh.

'Oh, god…' he said.

Oui, nous nous reverrons, mes frères,
Ce n'est qu'un au revoir.

Yes, we will meet again, my friends,
It's only a farewell.

The words echoed inside his brain. The heat turned to an icy chill. And he fell.

'Hanged himself?' Telford shifted uncomfortably in the wicker recliner, fished for his cigarettes in the pocket of his dressing gown. It brought back the pain, the memory.

'How many times?' said Harmon, pushed herself from the veranda's railing, snatched the packet from him. Her hair was tied back today with a bright red headscarf. Very Hepburn.

'For god's sake...'

'You will not blaspheme under my roof, Mister Telford. And you opened the wound twice, remember? Coughing?'

'Two months ago, Miss Harmon. It was two months ago.'

He found it hard to believe they'd never moved past that level of formality, though he still recalled Harmon's look of horror when he'd suggested, since she'd been good enough to take him in, help his convalescence, perhaps they might consider shifting to first names.

'And yes,' she said, sniffed at the pack of Luckies. 'They found him last night apparently. In his cell.'

The door from the house opened and Harmon's Congolese cook, Junelle, brought them tinkling glasses of iced orange and ginger.

'So, there goes any chance,' said Jack, thanked Junelle and sipped at his drink.

Harmon had been at his bedside in the hospital when he'd woken from the fever – for though the knife wound had been serious enough it was the subsequent infection which nearly killed him. She'd been reading to him. The bible. But it was, he knew, the thought which counted.

'This is your white whale, then?' she said. 'This obsession with a plot against your life?'

'I refuse to discuss it further with non-believers.'

'It's not that I don't believe you, Mister Telford. Just more – well, I'm agnostic on the matter. Isn't that what you'd say? It's not just that I don't *know* whether somebody's trying to murder you, it's that I know I *can't* know.'

'Amusing,' said Jack, and picked up a sheaf of hand-written papers from the table next to him. 'But can I trust you with this, at least?'

She took the document from him.

'I have both professional *and* religious ethics. It shall be taken to the office this very afternoon, typed up on the mill and then sent on its way. The photos as well.'

He lifted the manilla envelope of photographs from the table. They were superb. Leclerc's trucks emerging from clouds of sand across the Fezzan. The general himself in forage cap and sheepskin coat, directing an attack with his cane. Italian prisoners. And the other heroes of their raids. Dio – now Colonel Dio. Guillebon, Massu, Dronne, Geoffroy and Girard, three of the Spaniards, among those he recognised, despite their ragged dress, their unruly beards, their arab headgear.

For, though they'd been denied the full-blown campaign for which Leclerc had longed, de Gaulle had given them authority for a hit-and-run raid against the Italians – and it had been Dronne's responsibility, under Leclerc's direct orders, to keep a journalistic account of the action specifically for Telford's use. Jack, in turn, had arranged for a wire to be sent to Bunnelle, and Bunnelle had responded. *Time* magazine, he'd said, were looking for a feature about the Free French. It had to be the *right* feature, but if Telford had something in the pipeline…

This was the fight for which they had waited, Jack wrote. *Last year they launched a daring attack, deep into the desert, against an Italian fortress at Kufra. It was a feat to rival Lawrence of Arabia's assault on the Turks at Aqaba. But if Kufra was the Free French equivalent of Aqaba, this latest series of raids must surely rival Lawrence's later campaign against the Hejaz railway during the Arab Revolt. 1,200 miles across Libya's Fezzan Desert. A force of five hundred. A wasteland as large as France itself, and a motorised assault, with only compass and the stars to help them find their way. The sun burning the flesh from their faces. The treacherous sands. And, at the end of their journey, the Italians waiting for them in their fortified strongholds.*

It had been stirring stuff. Jack was pleased with it. Just the right amount of detail. Four Italian garrisons taken by surprise and overpowered, at Tedjéré, Gatroun, T'Messa and Ouaou-el-Kebir. Eight others seriously damaged. Huge amounts of enemy equipment, destroyed or captured. A phased withdrawal, southwards, early in March. Eight dead and fifteen wounded. Fifty Italian prisoners taken and three of their regimental colours surrendered.

'These really *are* very good,' said Harmon, shuffling the images.

'You'll need to get somebody to help,' Jack told her, but he was admiring the green-tiled dome of St. Anne's Basilica, just a block away along the boulevard, lined with mango trees and bright with deep lilac bougainvilleas.

Jack's connection to the Associated Press, exploited by the Information Services after Kufra, to have a portable Wirephoto machine installed.

'No, Mister Telford. I won't – need help, I mean.'

He'd been patronising again. He knew it. But the photos made him think about that fellow's face. Thin. Hollow cheeks, unshaven. It had taken several weeks for the local gendarmerie to track him down and, in the end, an informant. Anton Le Breux, the name of the would-be assassin. Father French, Mother Czech. Here among the volunteers and, when finally arrested, insisting it had been a case of mistaken identity. A feud gone wrong. Interrogation – and Telford dreaded to think how this must have been conducted. But they'd not managed to shake his story. And now? Just the warped memory of whatever Le Breux had said, those whispered words.

Cher mistère. That's what he remembered. Beloved mystery – whatever the hell it meant.

'Your own piece,' he said, in lieu of an apology, 'I wish I'd stolen some of it now. You gave the Spaniards a mention. They'll be delighted. And the general. Great heavens, he's certainly keen to bring the Americans on board, isn't he?'

General Leclerc is a remarkable soldier, she'd written. *He and his men, French, Spanish and Africans, are the Allies' defence here in central Africa.*

It was a generous comment, about Leclerc. For he'd never have returned the compliment. She'd gone on to explain how the new American liaison officer, Colonel Cunningham, had tried to persuade Leclerc that the Fezzan raids could bring nothing but suicide, how Leclerc had responded by saying, 'Nothing ventured, nothing gained.'

Harmon thanked him, then seemed to think better of it.

'Mister Telford,' she said, 'I've never known you to offer me a compliment without an ulterior motive. What is it? An American angle?'

He laughed, then cried out, clutched at his stomach.

'Oh, it hurts,' he said.

'You know what the doctors said. Laughing is an excellent therapy. Keeps the muscles in the area exercised.'

They'd cleaned it and dressed it twice each day. From what he could remember. Stuffing the puncture wound with some sort of cotton-like fabric soaked in – well, he had no idea. But the strangest sensation.

'It only hurts when I laugh,' he said. Not strictly true, but he was remembering something the comedian, Max Weston, had once told him. 'But an American angle? As it happens, over Christmas. Something reminded me – about the companies who'll profit from this war through business with both sides.'

'Don't make *me* laugh either,' she said. 'One of our reporters at the Post tried to put together an exposé – what, must have been the middle of thirty-nine. On the back of all those other pals of Hitler trying to make us think the Nazis were just good ol' boys. Lindbergh. America First. The Bund. The Silver Legion. Irish Catholics in their so-called Christian Front. Great heavens, Mister Telford, have you any idea how many Nazi supporters turned up for their rally at Madison Square that February? Twenty thousand. Twenty.'

'Yes, I remember. And your reporter?'

'He was reminded – very politely – of his patriotic duty to self-censor anything which might not be in the national interests. He was reminded, also, that he might very well be stepping on the toes of the Feds.'

'Didn't it infringe his rights under the First Amendment?'

'Don't be ridiculous, Mister Telford.'

He almost laughed again, stopped himself.

'But do you think it will change, now? After Pearl Harbor, I mean. Henry Ford, J.P. Morgan, Rockefeller and the rest. They'll not be allowed to carry on profiteering, surely? Fine, no need to look at me like that. I was being ridiculous again.'

'It's a story somebody should tell, all the same. Say, why not write it for your friend in London. Your *Reynold's News*?'

'Not a bad idea,' he said. 'Not bad at all. I'll think about it. But, for now, d'you think I might have just *one* cigarette?'

'The doctors tell me I was lucky,' he told Leclerc, when he was honoured by a visit from the man himself the very next day. 'No permanent damage to the internal organs.'

'Still painful?' said the general. He shifted himself on the straight-backed chair Harmon had set out next to Telford's recliner, then took off the pith helmet, set it down on the veranda floor beside him. It was overcast, sticky, a storm on the way.

'Only when I laugh,' Jack lied again. It was permanently sore. Well, sore hardly did the thing justice. He'd had a frozen shoulder, a while back, in England. Muscle pain. Hurt like the very devil for weeks. But this? You could have multiplied that pain a hundred times and poured it all here into this one knot inside his abdomen. Yet when he touched his fingers near the wound, there was no sensation in the flesh. Nerve damage, they'd said. Needs time. But the scar tissue? It would always remain. Something to which he'd have to become accustomed. He would feel it whenever he stretched, for example. Something foreign within his body.

'We're trying to look after him, General,' said Harmon.

Leclerc glanced in her direction, sniffed, then turned back to Telford.

'A pity you couldn't be with us, *monsieur*. In the Fezzan. And now this fellow has hanged himself. Hard to believe. But a fact of life, I suppose. Some of these men who come to us, a few only, who come to join the Legion, or just as volunteers – criminal types, hoping to hide their pasts or their heinous villainy inside our ranks. Well, we shall root those out. And, meanwhile, this article you wrote, with Dronne's help – a great service to France if your agency manages to get it published.'

'There's already interest, sir. From *Time* magazine, they tell me. Possibly this month.'

'Might I offer you some refreshment, General?' Harmon asked.

'No,' said Leclerc, without even bothering to look at her. Then he seemed to reconsider. 'Yes. Some water.'

It was imperious. But Dudley Anne Harmon took the hint, left them alone.

'It was kind of Miss Harmon,' said Jack, feeling the unfamiliar need to defend her. 'To take me in. I'd never have managed at the hotel.'

'Not my place to trouble over your morals, *Monsieur* Telford. Difficult enough to control the officers under my direct control. And you are a civilian, after all. Besides, I know what they say about me. The men.'

Leclerc's rigid morality. They put him on a pedestal. Of course, they did. Yet there were jokes. Affectionate, but jokes, all the same.

'Perhaps they'd be less critical if you weren't so quick to judge us all, General.'

Jack blamed his medication. It was sometimes as though he were drunk. Normally, he would never have let his mouth run away with him like this. Not to Leclerc, anyway. He began to mutter an apology.

'Never mind…' said Leclerc, though whatever followed was lost in the roar of aircraft engines. One of the giant Pan American clippers taking off from the river. They'd been flying in and out since last August. The Congo route, from Miami. A connection to the flights from Accra to Karachi.

'There is no morality question here, General. Miss Harmon is simply a good Samaritan. And even if my spirit was willing – which it most certainly isn't – you can rest assured the flesh is very definitely too weak.'

'Americans,' said Leclerc. He stood, straightened his sweat-stained uniform shorts, went to the veranda railing, followed the clipper's flight, as it was silhouetted against a vomit-yellow sky, already rumbling with distant thunder.

'Like Miss Harmon, sir. They suddenly seem to be everywhere, don't they? But you wouldn't catch me up in that thing on a day like this.' Sheet lightning from horizon to horizon. 'My flying days are over. And I should have offered you congratulations, I think. Or should I?'

Leclerc had been promoted. Now de Gaulle's senior commander, for all of French Equatorial Africa.

'A desk job, here at Brazzaville? It's an honour, *Monsieur* Telford. I know it is. But this is no time for us to be sitting around here. There's a war to be won. Do you know the *Boches* bombed Lamy? Not the Italians, but the *Boches*.'

Telford knew. The Germans on the offensive again everywhere. The Eighth Army pushed back to what was now being called the Gazala Line. Rommel in Derna. And in the Far East? Singapore fallen to the Japanese after a series of disastrous British defeats on land and sea. Stories of atrocities in the weeks which followed. The British unprepared, too certain of their own invincibility.

'Yes, General. Plenty of time to keep up with the news.'

The rain began. Drops the size of golf balls, hammering on the veranda roof.

'You've no radio here?'

'Doesn't work. But Miss Harmon…'

Leclerc cut across him, stepped back from the railing.

'Roosevelt,' he said, and positioned his chair afresh, away from the veranda's edge. 'His fireside chat. Hitler's U-boats.' Jack knew all about that, the Battle of the Atlantic still raging, hundreds of convoy ships sunk, a long way from the glory days, a year ago, when the *Bismarck* had been sent to the bottom. 'And all this in the Pacific,' Leclerc shook his head in dismay. 'But can we trust him, *Monsieur* Telford? This is the question. When Roosevelt tells us, despite the setbacks, we'll soon have the offensive again, should we believe him? And when he talks about the united nations of the Allies, where does he see France?'

'I'm beginning to get the feeling, General,' said Jack, 'this wasn't entirely a social visit.'

'You have a part to play,' Leclerc told him. 'These articles you're writing, they put Free France back before the eyes of the world. Without those, without the occasional headline, France is nothing but Vichy, and Vichy nothing but Hitler's lackey. Look at the way they've allowed us to be humiliated in Indochina. And those traitors – Pétain, Darlan now Vice-President. Prime Minister of France.' He snorted with derision.

'I still don't understand...'

'Something in the air, *monsieur*. Rumours of the Allies – the Americans – undertaking something important. Something which may be vital for France. *Our* France.'

'Invasion?'

'Not that. Not yet. But something. *Le patron* says we need eyes and ears in Oran. And I agree.'

Telford remembered the stink of those wicked warehouses the French authorities had used for the refugees before they built the more permanent internment camps. He remembered the Spanish women, the children, who'd died there.

'Yes, but not mine, General? I've seen and heard enough of Oran already.'

The veranda door was pushed open, Harmon backing through the netted screen with a tray, a jug of water, glasses.

'You have no servant, *mademoiselle*?' Leclerc snapped at her, plainly unhappy with the interruption.

'Indeed, I do, General.' She set down the tray on a small mahogany table. 'Several. Only now, it seems, they're to be forced to have work cards. And they don't like it. I'm expecting a picket line any day now. Water?'

She offered him the glass she'd poured.

'The work cards are the responsibility of the Chamber of Commerce, my dear. And designed to apply some control. You don't want your servants simply leaving you because the house next door is offering a few extra *sous*? This way, they can't start with a new employer until they've been signed off by their old one.'

'And yesterday, General, one of my boys was detained because he wasn't carrying his card. As a result, no breakfast. No, sir.'

Telford knew she was teasing, but she'd certainly ruffled Leclerc's feathers.

'Well, I have to go,' he said, and snatched up his helmet.

'Oh, such a pity,' she muttered. 'I heard you mention President Roosevelt. The walls are a bit thin, I'm afraid. And I thought – well, me being American and all, and accredited as a correspondent here…the Information Services, you know. I just thought perhaps it might be *me* you'd speak to, General, rather than Mister Telford. And won't you finish your drink?'

It was as though she did not exist. Leclerc limped to the veranda steps, used the cane to help himself down onto the street, now awash with water. He waved to the staff car, waiting for him just down the road.

'Remember what I said, *Monsieur* Telford,' he called back. 'Eyes and ears. No rush. But when you're fit for duty again…'

They watched him drive away.

'He's impossible,' said Harmon, her mouth set in a petulant pout. 'But you can't not love the man, can you?'

'That's charitable. I suppose it comes from writing for the *Christian Science Monitor*. But don't you ever get angry, Miss Harmon? Just a *bit* frustrated?'

'Me? I'm a Washington Senators fan, Mister Telford. You learn to take anger and frustration in your stride. We've got Anderson, though. Great pitcher. Really socked it to DiMaggio last June.'

'Seriously,' said Jack. 'You come all the way here. And it's not just Leclerc, is it? Like you say, the general could be forgiven. But the whole outfit. The Information Service hardly plays you to your strengths. I've seen how many times your opinions get ignored.'

'You think I have some, then – strengths? And this place? Well, I'll certainly never complain about Washington again. But it's been good for me, helped me cut my teeth. It would have killed me to write gossip column for the rest of my life. No, Mister Telford. Like you, I'm in the war now. And in the war, I'll stay. Scripps has been happy with my pieces. I just need to wait for a new assignment.'

'You're a hero,' said Jack. And he meant it.

'I heard,' she said. 'I know I shouldn't. But Oran – you'll go?'

'Not if I can help it. And I'm not likely to win the Pulitzer there, am I?'

*

They are no longer simply the Free French, Harmon had written. *They are now the Fighting French. And, just as Texans always urge us to "Remember the Alamo!" those who have stood beside General Charles de Gaulle and his valiant commanders shall now and always proudly say, "Remember Bir Hakeim."*

It was a wonderful piece and even Leclerc, four months after he'd so rudely dismissed her on the veranda of her house, was forced to acknowledge the part she'd played in making Bir Hakeim such a household name. Telford, of course, was certain her prediction that all manner of streets, buildings and much more besides would be named in Bir Hakeim's honour – well, this this was simply shameless hyperbole, surely.

Yet now she was leaving. Family summons, and she wasn't very happy about it. She'd picked up the first suggestion she should return home, back at the end of April, just before the excursion she'd planned for Jack's birthday. His thirty-fourth. Scary. He was up and about again by then, naturally, though still feeling fragile. But she'd persuaded Fox to borrow one of those scout cars the Americans called Jeeps.

'I thought it was high time you boys made friends again,' she shouted, as they hit the dirt river road just beyond the Bacongo village and caught their first glimpse – in truth, they heard it long before it came into view – of the Kintambo Rapids.

'The Congo's a different beast this side of town,' said Fox, ignoring her comment, just as Jack had chosen to do.

Fox was right, of course. Upstream, beyond Brazza on the north bank and Léo on the south, the brown Deep Mighty opened out into a virtual lake, a dozen miles wide, with its mass of smaller islets and the huge M'Bamou Island at its heart. The Stanley Pool. The Malebo, as the locals named it. Papyrus swamps around its edges, carpets of evil-looking vegetation floating on the river lake's tranquil course. He'd taken a couple of trips there, by dugout pirogue, when he first arrived. To see the wildlife. He'd been disappointed.

'Like dropping off the edge of the world,' he yelled, stood with the help of the windshield to get a better view. There was another wide bay, where the Île des Singes split the Congo's flow, but on the farther side, the river narrowed – relatively, at least – forced into half its previous great width, and the tranquil waters upstream now transformed into breakers to match anything Jack had ever seen at sea, before they plunged out of sight over the first of those cataracts which ran for the next two hundred miles towards the ocean. 'Welcome to the Livingstone Falls, Miss Harmon.' Fox brought the Jeep to a standstill. 'You two should feel at home here, what? Named by the great journalist himself.'

There was a spit of sand, dried mud, at the river's edge, a group of local boys, entirely naked, playing in the waves, a flock of long-legged cranes overhead, the roar of the rapids, and the sickly-sweet scent of the jungle at their back.

'Stanley?' she said, and jumped from the vehicle, lifted down the picnic basket Junelle had filled for them.

There was a copy of *Through the Dark Continent* in her house, and Jack had read it – twice. They'd spent more than just a few evenings debating Stanley's contribution to exploration and to the *New York Herald*. Harmon was intrigued by his almost accidental legacy to missionary Christianity, his rescue of Livingstone.

'He was at Shiloh,' Fox offered, handing down a green metal ice chest with their water and wine. 'Did you know? For the Confederates. Then fought for the other side. Strange character.'

'Under two flags,' said Jack, and spread out the blanket they'd brought. 'Now, who does this remind me of?'

'That guy, Welch, you mentioned?' Harmon laughed. 'You're serious, Mister Telford? You still think he's some sort of German spy?'

Jack looked to Fox, expecting the normal rebuke, yet there was none, simply the captain staring out at the raging rapids. His reticence was far more disturbing.

'Well, Captain?' Telford said. He opened the wicker basket, explored the banana leaf parcels. Moambe chicken.

'Really, Telford. You've no idea...'

'I know somebody else tried to kill me on New Year's Eve. Coincidence, I suppose you'd say?' He handed one of the parcels to Harmon, who settled on her knees beside him.

'Mister Telford said the man was a Czech, Captain. You were in Prague, weren't you?'

Fox opened the ice chest, fished out a bottle of white wine and the opener.

'Great heavens, Miss Marple, am I a suspect now?'

Jack had never quite fathomed the relationship between them. More intimacy than was shared between Harmon and himself. Far more. It was obvious. But always, in public, this same formality.

'*Cher mystère*,' Jack muttered, held out a glass for Fox to fill.

'What's that, old man?'

'Nothing much,' said Jack. He meant it, as well. Anton Le Breux may indeed have come close to killing him. But, really? A link with what had happened before? Occam's razor. The solution with the fewest assumptions. The simplest answer, that Le Breux was telling the truth. Drunk. Mistaken identity. Suicide by guilt, driven by the brutality of his interrogation. 'But, by the way, I had a letter from an old acquaintance today. Asked to be reminded. Hélène Bénatar.'

'Do tell,' said Harmon, sipped at her own wine. 'I sense romance in the air. Mister Telford scurried away to read it in private. Another *mystère*, methinks.'

'Not that.' Jack shook his head. 'And didn't want to spoil the mood. Grim news. The Jews in Casablanca not being treated well. And you know all Jews in Holland, other occupied countries, forced to wear the yellow badge? Star of David. But this wasn't the worst of it. Rumours of Jews being massacred. Belarus.'

The month had been thin on better news. Japanese victory in Bataan. The siege of Malta now intensified, the island presently under constant attack by the Luftwaffe. And, should it fall, supply lines to Cairo, to the Eighth Army – that would put an end to North Africa. The strange story, how the king had awarded the George Cross to the island itself. Would it be enough to stiffen morale?

'Bloody Vichy. The *Boches* might be one thing. But Vichy. And that swine Laval now second to Pétain again.'

'But General Giraud escaped,' said Harmon. 'Good news, isn't it?'

'Rather depends on whether he's able to stay free,' Fox replied.

'Do we know whether he's a Vichy man?' said Jack.

Giraud had been captured during the fighting in the Ardennes, imprisoned in some German castle. And now? In hiding. Somewhere.

'Certainly no admirer of de Gaulle,' said Fox, 'and loyal to Pétain, I'm told. But whether he'd support these collaborators with the Germans – well, the jury's out, as they say.'

They'd spent the rest of the afternoon peacefully enough, Telford sharing with Harmon more stories of his time in Casablanca but, privately, mulling over Fox's reticence to talk about Welch. Far more intriguing than the stabbing. And what did he mean? *You've no idea...*

'A little bird tells me Leclerc wants you back there,' said the captain. 'Up north. That right, old man?'

'Oran, to be precise,' Harmon jumped in. 'Though nobody's supposed to know this, naturally.'

'Well, I won't be going,' said Jack.

'And nor shall I, boys,' Harmon laughed. 'Be going, I mean. I had this letter from my father. Wants me back in Massachusetts. Selene, my youngest sister. Getting married – well, it's a long story. But I've written back, told Dad I can't make it.'

'But I suppose,' Telford said, 'I'd better be looking for new digs. Now I'm fit and well again.'

'Don't you dare,' she told him. 'Our stuffy old house wouldn't be the same without you, Mister Telford. And look what Junelle's packed. A birthday cake! Well, coconut pie, but it'll have to do.'

'Look,' he said to her. 'New union card.'

It had arrived with a letter from Sydney Elliott.

'Goodness,' Harmon laughed, as they helped themselves to glasses of punch. 'How old is that photograph?'

It was turning into quite a party. A strange one. The town hall again, the *mairie*. To celebrate a defeat, of all things. A defeat which, already by the start of July, had assumed the status of heroic legend. Yes, as Harmon had said, like the Alamo.

'You can still tell it's me, patch or no patch. Can't you?'

She grimaced, and he slipped the booklet back into his wallet.

'It's not really the patch. More...'

He had no need to be told. He'd looked in the mirror that morning, held up the NUJ card, complete now with its Associated Press accreditation, presented it alongside the face even *he* didn't recognise. No, not the patch. It was the weather-worn wrinkles, the beginnings of grey at his temples, the ears even more pronounced than when he'd been younger.

'Never mind,' he said. 'And you're going, after all?'

'As we Yanks say, these days, I'll be back.'

It would have been amusing, except for the news from the Pacific. Corregidor – at least offset by the Americans' victory at Midway. While, here, there was little to raise the spirits except this glorious setback. Was there such a thing as a Pyrrhic defeat?

'Dance?' said Jack.

They set down their glasses, squeezed their way out onto the floor. The band was playing a jitterbug number, *When The Saints Go Marching In*. Not really Telford's thing, but with this many other dancers, it didn't matter much. Even Jack's clumsy feet couldn't go too far wrong.

'You never asked me to dance before,' she said.

'You never asked me either,' he laughed. 'You're flying? The clipper?'

'Chance would be a fine thing, Mister Telford. No, a freighter, out of Pointe-Noire. Norwegian. Booked into the Hôtel Ottino first. By the railroad station. Journey will take forever but beggars can't be choosers.'

'What? World-famous correspondent? Couldn't see Hemingway slumming it on a tramp steamer.'

'No, but Martha Gelhorn would have done. The difference perhaps, between us all. Correspondents. You men, us women.'

Oh Lord, I want to be in that number...

The band slipped straight into another one. *Peckin'*.

'Mind if we sit this one out, Miss Harmon?'

She agreed, and they returned to their drinks. He'd miss her. Good company. Those other sightseeing trips. A couple of evenings across the river to Léopoldville. A jazz club or two. The cinema to see *L'Homme du Niger*.

Some investigative journalism together, as well, despite the rivalry. A visit to the new factory, literally a sweatshop, churning out uniforms for the thousands of new recruits, volunteers and pressed men alike. And then to the prison yard, where women from Poto-Poto and Bacongo pounded vines, extracted the sap, then boiled it. It stank. It was pitiful. But this wild rubber campaign, repeated in a thousand places all over French Equatorial Africa, was the only way to replace the supplies of rubber now cut off from the Far East. Yet both stories, the factory and the prison yard, only fit for publication in the press if heavily camouflaged as positive fables of patriotic war effort.

They'd decided not to bother. Yes, good company.

'I shall miss you as well, Mister Telford,' she said, as though she'd read his mind. 'Fresh air?'

'Why not? And you can give me the inside story. How you managed to snatch the Bir Hakeim scoop from under my nose.'

Jack spent time, when the first reports of the fighting came in, poring over the campaign maps with Fox. The Gazala Line. It had stretched from the Libyan coast, west of Tobruk, southwards into the desert. Not really a single line at all but a series of positions – squares of defensive terrain, minefields and the rest – each of which must be held if they were to stop Rommel reaching Cairo and the Suez Canal.

At the southern end of the line, the fortress of Bir Hakeim. It was there that General Marie-Pierre Koenig's First Free French Brigade was dispatched, to hold the Allied extreme left flank. A big area. Many square miles. Not just the fort itself, but a maze of barbed wire and gun emplacements, a rabbit warren of underground bunkers. Minefields, naturally. It had all looked solid enough.

But by the middle of June, word reached Brazza of the way it had played out. The defenders living underground, only coming out at night, or to counterattack, once they were surrounded by the Germans and Italians. How they learned that, one by one, the positions to the north of them, each of the other Allied positions, had fallen. Until Bir Hakeim itself *was* the line.

Two battalions of the Free French Foreign Legion, their 13th Demi-Brigade. Six hundred men with the Pacific Batallion, from French Polynesia. Eight hundred mainly Congolese Africans of the Oubangui-Chari March Batallion.

They'd held out for a fortnight. Yes, a bit like the Alamo.

And they'd not had a Travis. Merely a Travers. Susan Travers, of course. The Englishwoman who'd been a nurse, there in Brazza,

291

then gone off to join the Foreign Legion. The woman the other legionnaires called *La Miss*. Ended up as Koenig's driver. More besides. And when Koenig had been flown to Brazza, a debriefing with de Gaulle, Travers came with him.

'It was quite a reunion,' said Harmon, as they wandered into the open courtyard gardens behind the *mairie*. The night sky full of cloud, the palm fronds rustling together, angry in the gathering wind. 'You remember the two nurses we met on Christmas Eve? Véronique and Christelle. Véronique managed to wangle the invitation for me. Madame Éboué was there, also. So, while you were trying to piece together the official line from headquarters, I was able to make my home run. Funny though. They'd all worked as nurses together, but now – well, like *this* Travers was a different person. It all seemed friendly enough on the outside. I guess being in the actual fighting, like that...'

'It changes you,' said Jack. He lit a cigarette, for she'd long since given up trying to stop him – at least, outside the house.

'You, Mister Telford? Kufra, did it change *you*?'

'Heavens, Jack Telford? No, I fear nothing ever changes old Jack. But you got to speak with her, in the end. Must have been difficult, knowing what to leave out of the article.'

'Not difficult at all. She's quite the chatterbox. Apart from anything else, I wasn't going to include all the smut about how she'd started her affair with Koenig. And the things she had to say about Koenig's wife! Good gracious, no. But when he was sent off to the Gazala Line, given the job of defending Bir Hakeim, she went with him. And *that* was the story. Hey, you guys...'

A courting couple – the polite term for them – came staggering through the French windows, groping at each other's clothes, and crashed straight into Harmon, too drunk even to notice.

'You told it well,' said Jack, when the lovers had stumbled off towards the black shadows of the shrubbery. 'My own stuff read like one of de Gaulle's communiqués. But you captured the real sense of it all. Those quotes you got from her about baking hot during the day and almost freezing to death at night, hardly any food or water. Fifteen days, surrounded by Rommel's finest, hammered non-stop by their guns, by Stuka attacks. No, Kufra wasn't like that, Miss Harmon.'

'I managed to get those stories about the Spaniards in there, as well. Did you like those? I thought you might.'

Indeed, he had. She'd neatly tied up the fact that those almost four thousand Free French defenders of Bir Hakeim had included Africans from Chad, Cameroon and Senegal, Tahitians, Madagascans, even some Americans and Canadians. But five hundred of them – five hundred – were Spanish Republicans.

'Was it true?' said Jack, crushing out the stub of his Lucky Strike. 'The bit about how the *Boches* turned up with a white flag, tried to persuade them they could avoid further bloodshed with a surrender?'

She laughed.

'Maybe apocryphal. But Susan Travers swore it was true. That she heard one of the Spaniards asking what the hell they wanted. And another of the Spaniards said, I think they want to surrender.'

He laughed with her.

'Sounds like them.'

'Travers said they annoyed quite a few of the others, though. Kept saying this was nothing compared to Madrid. Is it true, Mister Telford? Was Madrid that bad?'

'I only got there towards the end. But at the beginning? The fighting in the university?' He remembered the stories he'd been told by the priest, Father Lobo. What had he said? On a battlefield there are no atheists. He thought of telling Harmon, decided not to bother. 'Yes, it was bad.'

The courting couple in the bushes were going at it hammer and tongs.

'What drives them?' said Harmon and, for a moment, Jack thought she meant... 'D'you mind if we go back inside, Mister Telford? I'm no prude, but...'

They went back through the double doors. The music seemed louder somehow, more frantic, distinctly more inebriated.

'Another drink?' he said, but she shook her head.

'The Spaniards,' she shouted. 'That's what I don't understand. They fought for how long in Spain? Three years. Then join the Legion and fight in France. Syria and Iraq. Now here. How do they do it? Why?'

'Really? I have no idea. The dream, maybe, one day, they'll get Spain back again. Maybe. Hell, I always thought the Brits, the Yanks, the French and Germans all had their share of stubborn national pride. But those Spaniards, they're something else, Miss Harmon.'

They exchanged waves, across the dancefloor, with Massu, and the nurse, Véronique. It was lively. Gay abandon. Swirling skirts, green and beige, red and cream. Khaki uniforms. Some sailors here from Pointe-Noire. Civilians in white open-necked shirts.

'The same during the breakout, it seems,' Harmon was saying, led him around the side of the room. Greetings here and there with people they knew. 'Some of the stories Miss Travers told me. She was a bit free and easy, mind, with her complaints about how she and Koenig hadn't been able – well, you know. Not there in the desert, anyway.'

'Too damned cold, I expect,' Jack laughed. 'And your face, Miss Harmon. Skip the sex, then. But that was some image. Koenig sitting on the roof of the car with his feet on her shoulders, helping her steer in the dark. Through the minefields.'

'Then realised she had no brakes. A dozen bullet holes in the car and the brake fluid pipes shot through. Had to crash into the back of a truck to slow them down.'

She slammed her hands together, for emphasis.

'But they made it,' said Jack. 'Koenig got almost the whole brigade out. Miracle.'

'The work of the Almighty, Mister Telford.'

'You think so?'

'Of course.'

They'd made their way around to the doors at the far side of the hall, slipped out into the foyer. There were clusters of folk gathered out there, chatting, smoking.

'You do know, Miss Harmon, the one true enemy of reason is certainty?'

She would have responded, but Fox arrived just then. In uniform. He stood in the entrance lobby for a moment, looked around, then spotted them, made his way across. But no smiles, no greeting.

'What is it?' she said, for the captain's face was a rigid mask.

'I had to meet General Leclerc,' he replied. 'The news – all bad, I'm afraid.'

This celebration of Bir Hakeim itself seemed misplaced, for only days after the Gazala Line collapsed, Tobruk also fell, and the British had fallen back to a line only a hundred and fifty miles or so from Cairo. A line stretching inland from a place Jack had never heard of. El Alamein. And everybody knew that, if Rommel punctured the line, it was all over. So far, it held, but for how long?

'Rommel?' said Jack.

'In a way,' Fox murmured. 'But not here, eh?' He nodded toward the outer doors and they followed him into the courtyard.

'What's the word?' Jack offered him a cigarette. It looked like he needed one, and Fox accepted the offer.

'Hitler's threatening to execute all French prisoners-of-war taken at Bir Hakeim. And anybody who'd been fighting for the Free French. Reminding us Vichy is neutral, of course. So, any French units fighting them must be renegades.'

Harmon gasped.

'Will they carry through the threat?' she said. 'And how many?'

'We don't know. Somebody reckons they took eight hundred prisoners. But de Gaulle's making an announcement on the BBC tomorrow, promising we'll have no option but to respond in the same fashion.'

A convoy of army trucks roared down the road towards them, turned into the crescent, which formed this extremity of the Avenue Foch.

'No prisoners?' said Jack. 'Surely…'

'Rommel will ignore Hitler's order, we're sure of that. But there's more. From Prague. Hitler's revenge for Heydrich's assassination.'

Reinhard Heydrich, one of Hitler's highest-ranking henchmen, the Führer's iron fist in Bohemia and Moravia, dead in the aftermath of an ambush.

'Revenge?'

'An entire village. Lidice. Wiped from the face of the earth. Hundreds of men and women murdered. Children.'

Harmon looked at him in disbelief, horror on her face.

'Children?' she said. 'Deliberately?'

Jack realised how hardened they'd all become to the death of innocents. Bombing of civilians. Children as well? Yes, of course. But somehow, it seemed the world had managed – for the most part, anyway – to cast a shroud over the war's collateral children's deaths. As though they might have been struck down by any of those other three Horsemen of the Apocalypse.

'I think they called them executions,' said Fox. 'Reprisals. As though this makes it right for them. Excusable, therefore, I suppose they think.'

'How many?' said Jack. 'The children.'

'Eighty. Ninety, maybe. We don't know. But some of them no more than babes in arms. Executed.'

'The savages,' Harmon said. She turned away, set both hands against the wall. 'How is this possible?'

'If we were able to understand that, Miss Harmon,' said Fox, 'we'd have to be as depraved as the Nazis themselves. All you can do is tell the story, isn't it? Make people understand what we're fighting for. When do you leave?'

'For pity's sake, I think I'm going to be sick.'

'Why don't I take you back to the house?' said Jack.

'No,' she snapped. 'Think I need to be on my own. But you're sure about this, Captain Fox? Not the children...'

'We're sure. And certain you don't want company, old girl?' She shook her head. 'I'll see you before you sail?' said Fox.

She offered him a thin smile and was gone.

'My god, unbelievable,' said Jack. 'And how did Leclerc take it?'

'Stricken. Children of his own. But *they* seem safe. He's heard from his wife. Good news there, at least. Seems her husband is famous, receiving gifts of food parcels from all over France. *Pour le Général.* Other than that, he's chomping at the bit, waiting to get back in the fight. But it all depends on what happens next. Whether we can hold Rommel. And that's where I'm bound, old boy. Back to Cairo. He's asked me to work on you again. Oran?'

'A bit hard to think about it, just now.'

'Shall we walk – find a bar?' said Fox.

Jack glanced back inside the town hall.

'The place on the Corniche?' Fox set his officer's cap back on his head, nodded his agreement. 'Think we'll ever see her again?' said Jack, as they wandered around towards the river.

'No question, old man. None at all. But god alone knows where we'll all be by then?'

'You?' said Jack.

'Cairo, for now, at least. So, a parting of the ways for all of us.' There was heavy traffic on the Corniche. And beyond, on the river, the lights of boats. Over there, Léopoldville. 'And you, Telford? Whatever the Yanks are planning in Oran – as though it's not obvious – they're not sharing it with de Gaulle. Not cricket, old boy, not by a long shot. You *will* go, I think. How could you not?'

How indeed? All those ghosts, the dead, whispering in his ear about duty, about destiny. Yes, he'd go to Oran, or wherever Leclerc sent him. But first…

'Listen,' he said, 'last time I asked you about Kingsley Welch, you said I had no idea. What did you mean?'

They stopped outside the Bar Benin.

'I meant it. You should leave that one alone, Telford. About Welch, at least. Just stay out of it. But Lidice and the rest. I was in Prague itself for a while, remember? Something struck me. You've got your notebook?' Jack handed over his pad, and Fox wrote on a blank page. This…

Černý štír. It's what he scribbled.

'What's this?' said Jack.

'It's Czech. I was thinking about what you'd said.'

'I still don't understand.'

'Depending on where you are in Czechoslovakia, they pronounce it like – well, like share-knee-stair.'

'Share… Wait, *cher mystère?*'

'Precisely.'

'And it means?'

'Haven't you guessed? Look, I set no store whatsoever in your conspiracy theories. But it means – *black scorpion.*'

October–December 1942

Colonel Bill Eddy

'If they catch you,' Leclerc had said, 'of course, you will be shot.'

And now, here he was, back where his misadventures in the Dark Continent had all begun. Oran. And in danger of that very thing. Being caught.

He waited in line for the Vichy officials to check his papers, hoping to god they'd pass muster.

'But why me?' he'd said to the general.

'Because you have an eye for detail, *Monsieur* Telford. Because your friend, Captain Fox believes your cover as a journalist – an Irish journalist – may give you access to useful people and places. To the Americans. And because this may just present you with stories that will make you famous. Whatever happens up there, we rely on you to make sure Free France is part of those stories. Isn't this enough?'

He handed over the documents.

'*Monsieur…*' The official squinted at the name. 'O'Hare?'

'That's right,' Jack replied. He'd been practising French with an Irish accent all the way here from Lisbon, but it still didn't work very well. 'Edward O'Hare. But my friends call me Butch.'

'*Putsch?*' said the official.

'No,' said Jack. But he thought, well, not just yet anyway. He might have found a better alias, but he'd been inspired by one of the pieces in a copy of *Life* magazine which had turned up in Brazza when all the Yanks began to arrive. Their first air ace, who'd single-handedly saved the carrier *Lexington* from being bombed by the Japs. February. It was a hell of a story, and Jack had added O'Hare to his growing pantheon of heroes.

'Correspondent,' said the official, and studied the forged union card. His phoney accreditation to the *Irish Press*. De Valera's paper, naturally. 'And where will you be staying?'

'At the Hôtel d'Angleterre.' Jack had been a bit surprised to find there *was* such a place. After all, the British weren't exactly popular, not after that sneak attack by the Royal Navy on the French fleet at Mers-el-Kébir, just across the bay. He'd been able to still see the damage from the deck of the Portuguese freighter which brought him here, just as the *Stanbrook* had done, three years earlier.

At least this part of his odyssey had been painless enough, and two days in Lisbon had helped him recover from the trip. Hell, he'd sworn he'd never fly again. Yet he'd ended up making not one flight, but two. First, the PanAm clipper from Léopoldville, its stop at Freetown. And, from there, the BOAC Boeing – another flying boat, of course – inbound from Lagos to London but stopping at Lisbon.

He could have sailed, naturally, from Pointe-Noire, as Harmon had done. But a combination of Leclerc's insistence there should be no further delay, added to the news that her freighter had been torpedoed, sunk in the Atlantic, all conspired to force him back into the air. Besides, it suited him to get away. Ever since Fox's revelation, all his old nightmares had returned. It wasn't that he'd feel any safer in Oran, but just the change of scene, this false identity, might make him more elusive for a while.

'The length of your visit, *monsieur*?'

'A month. No more.'

He hoped not, anyway.

'Approved.' The official fiddled with the date mechanism of his stamp, turned to a blank page in Butch O'Hare's passport, marked it accordingly.

Telford picked up his case, moved along to the customs desk, showed the contents. Then the same with his satchel. A cursory search, no more.

A taxi to his hotel. Not to the Angleterre, though. That had been a lie. No, the Métropole was more his style, and closer to his pocket. Nice. He paid the driver, took a quick look around the Place Kléber. Small roundabout at its heart, three ancient palm

299

trees and a fountain, a flock of green parakeets screeching above the tramlines. A decent cluster of shops – a pharmacy, a gentlemen's outfitter, a barber, a shipping office, a small brasserie – and the cries of *mu'azzins* from the local mosques. Over the rooftops and storks' nests, westwards, soaring over the city, the thousand-foot Murjajo heights he remembered from his earlier time here, with the old fortress of Santa Cruz at the summit.

The reception desk at the Métropole was helpful. Yes, they had two telephone cabins and their own switchboard, and he had to wait no more than twenty minutes for his call to be put through to the American consulate in Algiers, the number Fox had given him. He asked for Colonel Eddy, waited another five minutes.

'Hello. Bill Eddy speaking.'

Powerful voice. American, of course. Precise, clipped but without any obvious regional accent.

'*Colonel* Eddy?'

'That's me. Who's this?'

'My name's O'Hare, Colonel.' Jack wasn't sure whether to try the Irish accent here also, decided against. 'Correspondent. Fox suggested I should give you a ring?'

Silence for a moment.

'Oh, Foxy. Sure. He sent me a wire. Said you might call. How is he?'

Jack explained that he was fine, wondered whether the colonel would be willing to do the interview. About growing up in Lebanon, his parents both missionaries. His own paper, the *Irish Press* was interested in the story, but so was the *Christian Science Monitor*. His colleague, Miss Harmon. Yes, a lucky escape. Good to have this mutual connection. As it happened, Colonel Eddy was planning to be in Oran in a couple of days – perhaps Wednesday evening? Six? And how about the Brasserie Le Cintra?

Jack spent much of the following day familiarising himself afresh with Oran's busy streets. It all seemed so very different. As though, three years ago, he'd only seen the place through the suffering eyes of the *Stanbrook*'s passengers and all those other internees already here.

He'd strolled off towards the Château-Neuf ramparts, realised he'd never properly noticed how much Oran's architecture owed to those other Spaniards, who'd taken this area from the Moors long before the French, in turn, took it from the Ottoman Turks. There was something, the smells of baking bread, of cigars, even the sewerage, that reminded him of Alicante. It had its own aroma – like a distillery, since most of the cars and trucks here were running on alcohol. He still despised Oran, for the way it had treated those Republican refugees, but it was plainly a hive of history, another melting pot of cultures.

From the west bastion of the fortifications, he looked down the rocky slopes onto those very warehouses into which the refugees had been herded. Spread out before him were the seedy dockyards, the railway sidings, the filthy factories, the grain elevators, the circular storage tanks of the oil terminal. All smoke and steam, industrial clamour, swinging cranes and soulful seagulls. Just beyond, the jetties and quaysides themselves, jutting out into the harbour, crammed today with vessels – fishing fleet, freighters, colliers and tankers, as well as Vichy's destroyers and smaller ships lined along the breakwater running all the way from Fort Lamoune to his left, to the outer harbour, a mile and a half to his right. And all that lower area contained by the cliffs upon the top of which Oran itself sprawled.

There was this difference. When he'd been here before, he never troubled to so constantly look over his shoulder. The shadow of the black scorpion. The sense of menace, only heightened when he followed a different route back into town, wanting to check out the Brasserie Le Cintra, make sure he knew how to find it before his meeting with Colonel Eddy. But that's when he saw the first of the closed offices, boarded-up shops, the slogans daubed on walls and shuttered windows. *Down with the Jews. Death to the Jews.* The occasional swastika. How many thousands of Jews in Oran alone, now stripped by Vichy of their French citizenship, their jobs, their places at university?

The Great Synagogue, on Boulevard Magenta, was still open, but men busy scrubbing yet more painted insults from its walls, and Jack was almost ploughed down by a tram as he stopped to watch them, on the brink of volunteering to help, his fists clenched in futile fury. The world at war with fascism, yet here, in a place which should have been a beacon for this fight, here was the beast itself.

It was his own sense of guilt, inadequacy – and yes, his selfish hunger – that made him turn away, follow Boulevard Joffre back towards the hotel. And at the corner of the Place Ben Daoud, his eye caught sight of a bookshop, *La Grande Librairie de Vienne*. Perfect. He needed something new, crossed the tramlines, spotted the notice in the window.

Aujourd'hui.

L'Étranger.

Dédicace du livre deMonsieur Albert Camus par son auteur.

Today. The Outsider. Signing of the book by Mister Albert Camus, by its author.

Camus? Jack didn't think he'd ever heard of him. And then he noticed how those final words, *by its author*, had been crossed out and, underneath, in much smaller text, replaced with, *by the author's wife.*

Really? Unknown author, can't even take the trouble to turn up for his own signing. He decided not to bother, crossed to the fountain in the middle of the square, shaded by the walls of Saint André, sat himself on the fountain's marble surround. But he still needed a book. And not the shop's fault, he supposed, that this fellow wasn't going to honour them with his presence. Typical bloody author. He smoked a cigarette, back on the Gauloises now, then sauntered down the slope again.

There were copies in the window. Plain cream cover, of course. Just the author's name, the title, and the word *roman*. Novel. But a decent one? Jack thought he wouldn't bother, would look for something better. Maybe a Balzac he'd not read yet. Or something Russian in French translation.

He walked into the dark interior, saw the half-dozen chairs set out in faint expectation, received a curt welcome from the plump old lady with *pince-nez* glasses behind the counter, and an immeasurably more effusive hello from the slender creature half-hidden by one of the iron columns supporting the store's balcony shelves. Her face pale as the covers of those books on a table by her side. Pretty but fragile, porcelain, framed by waves of long black hair.

'I thought for a while nobody would come,' she said, her voice trembling a little. 'So good of you.'

'Actually...' he began, then decided simply to sit. It was cool in there. The smell of paper and print, mingled with – what the hell *was* that perfume?

She supposed she should wait, she murmured, see if anybody else arrived. But, on the other hand, she didn't have a great deal to say.

'I could just do it all again,' she laughed.

'And I could pretend to be a crowd,' said Jack. 'Applaud loudly at the end of every sentence. Maybe attract a few more passers-by for you.'

'Then I shall begin.' She coughed, picked up a slip of paper, launched into the prepared speech. An apology. She and her husband were booked to head home from Paris to Algeria two weeks ago. For this important signing, his first novel. But already very well received. Another presentation in Algiers itself. Two, in fact. But then Albert taken ill. Nothing too serious. Simply a recurrent condition, and insisted she should make the journey alone, fulfil the appointments on her husband's behalf. An introduction. Francine Faure, she said. Now *Madame* Camus. And she would personally ensure that, if anybody wished to purchase the book, cared to leave an address, Albert would make sure he wrote a personally signed letter of thanks, arrange to sign the novel in retrospect as well. She thanked her audience for taking the trouble to be there.

'Bravo!' shouted Jack, clapped his hands together.

The proprietor glowered at him.

'Can I tempt you with a copy, *monsieur*?' said Francine. 'I'll make sure Albert signs it for you when he's back.'

'I think I'd be happier if *you'd* sign it,' Jack replied, then cursed himself, didn't want to buy the damned thing at all. 'What's it about, anyway?'

'An ordinary man. Caught up in mayhem.'

'There's no such thing. An ordinary man, I mean. Not now.'

'You? You're extraordinary, *monsieur...*?

Jack thought long and hard.

'O'Hare, *Madame* Camus. Francine? My friends call me Butch.'

'*Putsch?*'

Not again. Telford decided he'd have to drop the nickname.

'Others call me Jack. And this ordinary man, what happens to him?' He flicked open a copy from her table, turned to the first page. 'Not bad. Economical with his words, your husband. Reminds me of Hemingway. Or John Dos Passos, maybe.'

'I don't think anybody else is going to turn up, do you, Jack?'

'Then maybe you'd allow me to buy you dinner.'

'Not unless you buy the book.'

They shared grilled fish in the brasserie of the Hôtel Saint-Marc. She was easy company. This idyll of first assignations. Always plenty to fill the conversation, the first time. Jack's stories of his life amended to fit his new *alter ego*. And Francine? Married two years. Albert's second wife. His illness? Tuberculosis. It had driven them to France back in August. But – well, they'd had problems. She was too coy to explain. But she had her teaching post here in Oran. And Albert, he would join her in due course. A busy time for him.

It was a pleasant evening, good wine. Shared politics. Her grandmother a Berber Jew. All this, Vichy's treatment of Algeria's Jewish community. *Action Française*, allowed to run riot. And one thing simply led to another.

'So, who's the woman?' It wasn't really the greeting he'd expected, but Colonel Eddy wasn't exactly what he'd expected either.

Jack wriggled on the red velvet upholstery of the sofa. Their booth in the Brasserie Le Cintra. It was doubly uncomfortable, simply because Francine had made such a point about this being Albert's favourite eating place.

'You mean Francine Camus.'

'If you'd said, *which woman*, mister, I'd have been straight out the door. You make a habit of this sort of thing?'

'Look, Colonel, I have to assume that if you know about Francine, you must have had somebody follow me. So, forgive me, but shouldn't it be *me* who plays Mister Outraged in this scenario?

And if you had me followed, you already know who she is. Wife of the *Paris-Soir* editor.'

Colonel Eddy called one of the Algerian waiters, ordered a tomato juice for himself. Perfect Arabic. And for Jack? A beer. There was silence between them while, in the background, loud chatter from the other booths, easy music on the gramophone. The colonel had the physique of a rugby player, his features almost Slavic, the uniform immaculate.

'I don't suffer fools gladly,' said Eddy, at last. 'No, sir. And just now I can't decide what makes you the bigger fool. The woman you don't know from Adam. Or that you couldn't even figure out you were being followed. What did you tell her?'

So much for looking over my shoulder, thought Jack. Or was this bloke simply lying through his teeth?

The waiter came back with their drinks, wiped the table with a corner of his scarlet apron.

'Menus, gentlemen?' he said.

'Not yet,' Jack growled. 'I may not be staying.'

'Nobody's keeping you here,' said the colonel, as the waiter backed away. 'You wanted to meet – remember? On your head, one way or the other. But I'm guessing your friend, *Charles*, won't be best pleased if he's sent you all the way here for nothing.'

He pronounced the word *Charles* in the French fashion.

'I won't be the only iron in his fire,' Telford replied.

'No, you're certainly not. But I already had the chance to figure out the rest of them. And *you* may not be hungry, mister, but I could eat a horse.' He called back the waiter. 'Well?' he said to Jack. 'You staying, or not?'

'I didn't tell her anything,' said Jack, while the colonel ordered the duck, with chicory and *dauphinoises*. 'We're just good friends, as they say. And I'll have the same,' Telford told the waiter. 'Nothing about...' he began when the fellow had disappeared back to the kitchens.

'Don't waste your breath. She already spilled the beans.'

'She's...'

'I think it's called serendipity. Of all the bookshops in Oran, eh? But at least I was able to put together some of the pieces about you, *Monsieur* O'Hare. Interesting Spanish connections. You know the president wishes now that we'd taken a different line with Spain? Franco's coup. No place in the community of nations, he says, for governments founded on the principles of fascism. Helped by Hitler and Mussolini. How did we not see this coming?'

'But will he do anything about it? You know how many Spaniards are fighting for Free France, Colonel. You must do.'

Colonel Eddy glanced around the room, made sure they weren't overheard. Apart from the ceiling fans, the décor was pure Paris.

'Whole network of them in Tangier,' the colonel murmured. 'Melilla and Ceuta as well. Ready to give *Señor* Franco a bloody nose if he doesn't play ball. They've been training for a year now.'

'A friend of mine from Rabat's been mixing things up there. Paquita Gorroño.'

Eddy leaned back into the seat, looked at Jack as though seeing him for the first time.

'You certainly get yourself around, don't you?'

'Seen her?'

'Not for a while. But she's well enough. Plenty of grit, that girl. Plenty. And yes, the president's promised we'll put Spain back on the right track again before too long.'

Jack was a bit overcome. Emotion. Bloody stupid, he knew. But it was like coming home after a long journey. Hard to put into words. He looked away, drank some of his beer.

'You believe him?' he said.

The colonel wiped tomato juice from his upper lip.

'He's the president, isn't he?'

Jack had a pithy answer to this one, but he held his tongue.

'The Spanish boys will be glad to know,' he said. 'But isn't this dangerous intelligence to share with a fool, sir?'

'Only the wisest of men knows *himself* for a fool, mister. Isn't that what your Shakespeare reckons? Besides, I read what you wrote about Kufra. Our friend *Charles* hoping you'll do the same here?'

'If somebody will tell him what's going on, yes.'

Their food arrived. Jack ordered another beer, fished in his jacket for the Gauloises.

'Not while I'm eating.' Eddy waved a fork at him. 'No, sir.' Jack slipped the cigarettes back into his pocket. 'And you know the score here. All under orders not to involve your friends. Better they don't know.'

Jack set down his own knife and fork, his turn to glance around at the brasserie's other customers. He almost expected to see German or Italian uniforms here, representatives of the Armistice Commission. Theoretically, at least, Algeria was still neutral territory. But the diners were simply a predictable bunch of Vichy officers and their women, or the town's more affluent civilians.

'You think they're stupid?' Jack hissed. 'His place in London's got its own network, Colonel. GIs landing in England by the thousand. For months now. Enough for an invasion. The only question is, *where*? Not France, that's obvious.'

'Orders are orders, mister. I just serve the president.'

'And does the president have no idea what they've been through? You read about Kufra. And the Fezzan. Well, just the tip of the iceberg, sir. The fighting in France itself. Libya. Syria. Iraq. Indochina. And now you want them cut out of the picture?'

'Your friend *Charles* doesn't help himself, you know? But that's not it. Not really. There's always the long game to be played. A wise man would know this. The assets still loyal to old Uncle Philippe, they could bring us quite a windfall.'

Jack chewed on a piece of duck. Uncle Philippe? Pétain, of course. Leclerc had said something similar. De Gaulle was simply all rage about being kept out of the plans being hatched between Churchill and Roosevelt, whatever they were. But Leclerc had tapped his fingers on the maps.

'The papers say France is divided in three,' Leclerc had said. 'Occupied France. Vichy. And Free France, here. That's nonsense. Vichy in the Southern Zone isn't the same as Vichy in Africa. How could it be? And what would happen if, God willing, the British pushed Rommel out of the desert, into the sea? What if the British marched into Algeria? Or Morocco? Vichy's supporters there, how would they jump then? How much would that depend on whether we could live with them again, or they with us?'

It suddenly didn't feel like such a fantasy. The forty-mile line between El Alamein and the Qattara Depression still held, Rommel's attacks wavering.

'You must be able to give them something,' said Jack. The colonel wiped his mouth with a napkin.

'Not bad,' he said. 'The food here. But I told you, I have my orders. And much as those in high places might not trust your friend *Charles*, there are many of them who don't entirely have faith in the services *we* provide here, either. Maybe don't like the company we keep – your Spanish Commie friends, among others.'

What had Fox told him? Eddy was, officially, an Assistant Naval Attaché. Marine Corps. More than that, he wouldn't say. But America's intelligence services, without doubt.

'*My* Spanish Commie friends? I don't think so. But can't you even give me a date?'

Colonel Eddy laughed.

'You think *anybody* knows? Just put these few things together in your mind, mister,' he whispered. 'Fourteen hundred ships. The Atlantic. U-boats. You know about U-boats. Look what happened to Annie Harmon. Chance in a million she was picked up with the survivors.'

'Small world,' said Jack. 'How do you know her?'

'Family connection. And she interviewed me. About my folks. Missionaries, you know?'

Jack knew.

'She didn't want to go back to the States,' he said. 'Miss Harmon.'

'Well, that's duty for you. But what was I saying? Oh sure, U-boats. And the Big Double-U. Weather. Weather at sea, this time of year. Any one of three or four possible destinations. And just now...'

'Then how...?'

'Listen, you want to play in this game, or not? If you do, then here's the deal. You scratch my back, maybe. Things we need. A friend of mine, Frank. He needs certain information. Casablanca. It's what he calls hydrographic information, you follow?'

'Tides?'

'Oh, a lot more than that, my friend. Somebody who knows those waters – on them, in them, under them – like the backs of their hands. Foxy said…'

'So,' Jack whispered, 'landing at Casa, then. This what you're saying?'

Eddy leaned over the table, affected a stage whisper in return.

'My friend Frank's department is gathering hydrographic information about Casablanca, yes. Along with Primorsk on the Russian Baltic, Stavanger in Norway and a dozen other places. Can you help us with Casablanca or not?'

Manolo, thought Jack. Uncle Emilio. Hopefully they were still around. But what was Eddy telling him? Fourteen hundred ships. One hell of an armada. And when he thought about it, bringing that lot here? How far? Much more than a thousand sea miles at the very least, through enemy patrolled waters. No, that was madness. Invasion of Norway or Russia made more sense. Or was this just what Colonel Eddy was supposed to make everybody think? He had no choice but to play along, report back to Leclerc.

'I know just the boy,' he said. 'Anything else?'

'Yes. This paper you're supposed to be working for – the *Irish Press*? Can you make it happen, for real?'

'I guess so. What d'you need?'

'Some of our units are in Ireland. It would be helpful if there were interviews. You know the sort of thing. Interviews that would get past the censors. For real. Chit-chat stuff. Human interest. But the names of the GIs carefully chosen. Scandanavian names. Mainly Norwegian.'

Jack imagined Colonel Eddy's world, just for a moment. The million pieces of misinformation scattered across the globe for their enemies to gather, the impossible puzzle set for them to solve. Where were they *actually* headed, those thousands of American troops?

'You've got it. Anything else?'

'More difficult. There's another paper in Beirut, *Le Jour*. I can make the connections. But we need stories. Subtle. But good news. On good authority, isn't that what you hacks say? Word about how some of their shortages will soon be at an end.'

'I'm not sure I understand.'

'You don't need to. Just write. It's your job.'

'I think that's the Marine Corps you're talking about, Colonel. No need to make sense of the orders – just follow them? Well, good luck trying to get your Spaniards on board.'

'All the same, you only get what you need to know. Want coffee?'

'Good idea,' said Jack, as Eddy waved for the waiter. 'And in return for me delivering the goods?'

'Maybe I give you an inside track. So, if anything *does* happen, you can work your usual magic for our friend *Charles*, heap praise on the part played by the Free French *résistants* in – well, whatever it might be. And *wherever* it might be.'

Jack remembered Hélène's mention of her *résistant* contacts in Casablanca.

'Not many of them in Norway or Russia, I don't think,' he said. 'But here? *Résistants?*'

'Oh, yes. *Pieds-noirs.* Spanish as well. Play your cards right and I might let you meet an old friend.'

Jack could rarely recall such absolute joy.

'My god,' he said. 'Amado.'

He threw his arms around Granell's half-starved frame, felt the Spaniard wince, then kissed him on both cheeks.

'Telford,' Amado laughed. 'I never thought to see you again.' He fell into Valenciano, his first language. Jack had forgotten most of what he'd learned in Alicante, yet he could follow the gist well enough, managed to explain that, now, he also had a *nom de guerre*. O'Hare. Amado was impressed. 'But hell,' he said, 'who am I kidding? I never expected to see anything beyond barbed wire and prison walls.'

Colonel Eddy had given him the address, the Cité Berr gymnasium, just beyond the Périphique. But it had taken Jack some time to recognise his old acquaintance from the *Stanbrook*. He'd always thought of Granell as a thin man: thin features; thin, sharp nose; thin smile – though always a ready one. Yet now – he'd seen healthier skeletons, his skin like tanned leather.

'And here?' Jack used his ordinary Spanish, his Castellano,

glanced around the hall. 'You need the exercise?'

There were other men. In the boxing ring. At the parallel bars. Leaning against the vaulting horse. With the dumbbells and barbells. But they'd all stopped whatever they'd been doing, stared back at Telford. Cold, unfriendly stares. All except one, a face that seemed vaguely familiar.

'He's a comrade,' Granell shouted in French, over his shoulder, as he picked up a jacket from a hook behind the door, slipped it on over his vest, and the red neckerchief knotted at his throat. 'And exercise?' he said to Jack. 'Colonel Bill insists we should all keep fit. Just in case.' He winked. 'But now I have to work, my friend. Want to help me?'

'Depends whether it involves any lifting.' Jack laughed. 'Not very good at lifting any more.'

'There might be *some* lifting involved. But nothing we can't manage between us. Come on.'

'I still can't believe this,' said Jack. 'I want to know everything, Major. *Everything.*'

'It's a long time since I was a major, *camarada*. But time for that later. We've got a tram to catch. You've been here in Oran all this time?'

Jack gave him a potted account of his travels as they dodged the trucks, the donkey carts, the camels and the occasional stray dog on the Périphique, made their way to the stop at the Pont Luc, the end of the Cemetery Line, waited for the tram.

'We never forgot what you tried to do for us,' said Granell. 'Never.'

'It was precious little, all the same.' Telford offered him a cigarette. The green tramcar rattled towards them, screeched to a halt and began to disgorge its passengers. 'And I managed to follow your own movements for a while. A friend in the *gendarmerie* at Casablanca. Tracked you to Morand. And then to Bossuet. Some fortress – at Dheya? Said you'd never come out of there alive. I saw some of the Red Cross reports. My god. Oh, there was a young woman in Rabat. Paquita. Gorroño. Know her?'

Granell shook his head. The driver changed his destination boards, yelled reprimands in Arabic at those in the queue trying to board his vehicle prematurely, while the conductor swung his trolley pole around.

'No,' said Granell. 'And, as you see, I *did* get out alive. Twice, as it happens. The first time, another escape. After that, so they could send me to Djelfa. Hell, Telford, if your friends thought Bossuet was bad...'

They jostled their way onto the tram, packed into this wooden crate on wheels and smelling, strangely, of sardines. Standing room only, hanging from the ceiling straps.

'You escaped from there?'

The tramcar lurched into action.

'Me and Campos. You saw him at the gym?'

'He was on the *Stanbrook* as well?'

'No, interned in Tenerife. Labour camp. Escaped somehow and landed up in Oran. Straight into the camps again. And finally to Djelfa. We were there a year. From not long after they opened the place. A thousand of us. Half of them Spanish. The others – I don't know. Jews mainly. Some criminals. I'd not been there long when... Typhoid. The food, of course, if that's what you can call the muck they gave us. Killed – what? A hundred, I guess. Bloody French.'

'How did you get out?'

'Work detail. The guards had this thing. We could escape any time we wanted. The desert would kill us anyway. Well, after a year in Djelfa, dying in the desert seemed like a good option. Two hundred miles of it. To Algiers. Then here. To Oran.' He ducked his head, read the name on the next tram stop. 'Sebastopol,' he said.

The conductor managed to squeeze his way to them and Jack paid both their fares.

'My friend in the *gendarmerie*,' said Jack. 'I told him once, if he was looking for resistance, you'd be his man, Major. Is this what you're doing here? For the *bloody* French?'

'I told you. Not a major. Not anymore. Another lifetime. Another man. And no, not for the French.'

For the Americans then, thought Jack. For Colonel Bill Eddy. A motorised machine gun regiment, he remembered. Wasn't this what Granell had told him on the *Stanbrook*? And what else? Born somewhere near Valencia but moved to a place... Orihuela. That was it. The name had rung a bell. A convoy arriving in Madrid when things had been bad there. A convoy of food, fruit and vegetables from Orihuela. It had been painted all over the sides of the trucks.

'But your family,' he said, 'your wife – does she know?'

'It's the worst thing about the camps. They let you write letters. But you never know whether they really send them. And, occasionally, some new prisoners arrive. They always bring rumours. Stories. Killings in this town or that. Impossible to know what's true. Still, when I got to Algiers, I sent Aurora a postcard. No details. Just to let her know. Hoping she's still there.'

'You fixed motorbikes,' Jack remembered, and Granell swung away from him. There was single sob, like a gasp for breath.

Telford's turn to peer out the window, saw they were passing the same bookshop, thought about Francine.

'It's how I survived,' Granell said, at last. 'Fixing things.'

'I was at the camp at Bou Arfa. There was another man there who fixed things. From Valencia, as it happens. Engineer. Raúl Ramos?'

Granell shook his head.

'Don't know him. What happened?'

'He died. My fault.'

They got off at the terminus, Place Foch, walked a couple of streets, passed the crumbling flight of stairs climbing up to the Rue de Wagram, found their way to the Rue de l'Aqueduc.

'Give me the address,' Jack said. 'Your workshop. I'll get in touch with our consulate in Alicante – if it's still open. See whether somebody can get a letter sent over from your wife.'

'The colonel's done the same. Nothing back yet.'

'Might not do any harm, all the same,' said Jack. He tried to remember the Spanish for *belt and braces*, decided not to bother.

They'd stopped outside an abandoned pawnbroker's. This was mostly the Jewish Quarter, *Action Française* slogans again, some window shutters smashed. But the building across the street, at number eighteen, had a prominent red light above its door. And a sign, *Le Sélect*. Granell surveyed its upper floors, then the street, first one way, then the other. There were a few people about, but not many. And no traffic.

'You have a handkerchief or something?' he said.

Jack pulled the hankie form his pocket, offered it to Granell, glanced over at the brothel.

'But why…?'

'Don't be a fool,' said Amado. 'It's for…' He looked Telford full in the face, settled his gaze on the eye patch. 'Well, maybe not. A mask wouldn't help much, I suppose. But you can keep watch, can't you?'

He was gone before Jack could answer, pulled his own *bandana* up around his nose and, as he reached the bordello's front entrance, dragged a small revolver from his pocket.

'Christ,' Jack murmured, shrank back into the pawnbroker's doorway.

He heard a scream from inside the brothel, a single shot. Shouting, a man's enraged voice. A silence that went on and on, Jack looking frantically up and down the road, expecting the police at any moment. Another scream. Granell back on the street, the neckerchief still around his face. A small canvas bag in his hand.

'Don't just stand there,' he cried. 'Run!'

They ran. Dodged through an alley, through the traffic on the Rue des Jardins, into the warren of alleyways beyond. A police whistle, and Granell stopped, ducked around a corner, both of them out of breath.

'Walk,' he said and stuffed the sack inside his jacket, stripped off the *bandana*. 'Casual. This way.'

'That's the Prefect's Office,' said Jack, recognising the side of the building.

'Exactly.'

And so they strolled, straight past the police headquarters.

'Where are we going?' Jack asked him. 'And is this what you do, now?'

'Robbing brothels? Why not? And we only rob the ones used by those Vichy bastards. Where are we going? Your hotel, of course. Hell, Jack, you should have seen the face on that pig behind the first door I kicked open – well, his arse, anyway.'

'You shot him?'

'*Jesús*, no. Just a bullet into the ceiling.'

'But…'

'How else d'you think we manage to buy guns?'

'The Americans…'

'All talk and few nuts. They promised us plenty. A submarine, the colonel said. Decent weapons, he told us. Nothing. Don't get me wrong. Not his fault, I guess. So, the Lord helps those who help themselves.'

'You're an atheist.'

'You know what I mean.'

They'd reached the hotel, took the lift to Jack's floor.

'But if there were no weapons,' said Jack, operating the controls, 'no submarine, doesn't that mean the Americans aren't coming this way, after all.'

'Or maybe they just trust us to use our own initiative.'

'Not big on trust though, the Americans. Certainly don't trust de Gaulle.'

Amado spat on the lift floor as it came to a halt and Jack slid open the grille.

'Bloody French,' Granell said again.

They reached Jack's room.

'They're not all the same, Amado. I've been with Leclerc. Nearly two years. Kufra, all the rest. Here, inside. Want a drink?'

He poured Granell a cognac from the bottle on his bedside cabinet.

'Kufra? We heard about Kufra, even in Bossuet. And I'm no fool, Telford. I *know* they're not all the same. My god, some of the Frenchies who fought for us in Spain. Did you ever come across Putz? My god, there was a man. Might be a Communist but…'

'Some of Leclerc's men at Kufra were Spanish comrades, as well. Men who'd escaped from the camps, like you. Or deserted from Vichy's Legion. Good Republican boys.'

He told him about El Gordo, Alemán and the others, while they counted the money.

'I suppose de Gaulle promised them he'll sort out Franco?'

He emptied the bag on Jack's bed, began to sort out the banknotes and the coins.

'Like Roosevelt, you mean. And these – *centimes*, tens and twenties. What the hell can you buy in a bordello with small change?'

'Tea? And yes, like Roosevelt. But what else do we have, Jack? And whatever happens, the fight's not done yet. Not until Hitler and Mussolini are smashed into the dust. So, for now? De Gaulle, your Leclerc, Colonel Eddy – the enemies of our enemy.'

That seems to come up a lot these days, Jack thought to himself. As philosophies go. He began to straighten some of the bigger notes. Hundreds and fifties. But even a hundred? Jack did a quick calculation. Three quid.

'So this? Rob a few brothels? And wait – for what?'

'For the message. *Hello Robert, Franklin's Coming.*'

'Seriously?'

'Your BBC, *inglés*. Dammit, now I've lost count.' He started again.

'Robert?'

'Murphy.'

'Of course,' said Jack. Robert Murphy, Roosevelt's personal representative in North Africa. He'd negotiated that trade deal between the USA and Morocco. 'Well, how much?'

'Just short of fifteen thousand *francs*.'

Jack tried to calculate how many brothel services this might be.

'Sounds impressive, doesn't it?' he said. 'But what would that buy you – get your Browning back?'

Jack remembered him on board the *Stanbrook*. Not a single possession but his automatic rifle.

'Best weapon I ever handled. Sure, the gun runners would want about fifteen thousand for a BAR. Three hundred dollars. And apart from the brothels? There's always a bit of sabotage to be done, maps to be drawn, timetables and work schedules to be checked. But I tell you, Jack, it's a lot better than Djelfa.'

'Big network, the *résistants*?'

'Who knows? Colonel Eddy runs a tight ship. Through a local man. Calls himself Leduc, but never met him. Five of us in our cell. Three of us, Spaniards. Two local Jewish boys. We all know each other. But that's it. We hear stuff. Mostly Jews, they say. A few hundred in Algiers. The same here in Oran. Enough to make a difference. If they come.'

They came. Or, at least, the BBC broadcast, the message in French.

'Allo, Robert. Franklin arrive!'

That first Saturday evening in November, late evening, a few hours after Jack's second meeting with Colonel Eddy, after a frustrating afternoon at the *Grande Poste*, trying to get a wire through to Leclerc in Brazzaville. An update. Coded, after a fashion. After an even more frustrating tryst with Francine. Almost a different woman. A nervous wreck. Tears she couldn't explain.

'This is it!' shouted Granell.

They'd been at the gym again, Jack lounging under the palm trees in the yard, watching the night sky, the wireless set just inside the door.

'We heard,' said Jack. 'What now?' He jumped up from the deckchair, poked his head through the open doorway. 'It's happening?'

'We go to the meeting point,' Granell told him. Inside, it was all bustle, the other members of Amado's cell grabbing coats and caps. Jack had never worked out how they managed to keep the place to themselves – and Amado wasn't about to share the secrets. 'But you don't have to come, Jack.'

'Are you joking? I may be Leclerc's only representative in this little adventure,' said Jack. But, in all honesty? His guts trembled. It took him all his time to control the shaking hands. Since the stabbing, he knew he'd lost his nerve. What little he'd had in the first place.

'Listen,' Amado cried. 'We split up. You know where we're heading. Telford, with me, if you're sure.'

He wasn't. Sure. Far from it. But he picked up his jacket, his satchel, and followed Granell anyhow. Lost his bearings somewhat, this eastern part of town he didn't know very well. But hurrying, silent – through Arbes-Ville, he guessed. Montplaisant, maybe. Darkened streets, dogs barking, past the occasional dimly lit bar. Until they came out on what he was pretty sure must be the Avenue

317

de Tunis, industrial buildings across the tram line running down its centre.

'There,' said Granell, and pointed to a darkened yard, open gates, the occasional deeper shadow flitting inside. 'Wait!'

He pushed Jack back against the wall, waited until a tram – empty, as it happened – had trundled past, then led them over the road, into the yard. The night air was heavy with the stinging scent of chemicals but, here, overlaid with the smells of raw timber, resin, iron and burned wood. In the darkness, Jack could just make out stacks of barrels to his right. Cobblestones beneath his feet. Movement of others he could sense rather than actually see. Then, a building, the bulk of a warehouse. A doorway. Granell mumbled something, a password perhaps. They were ushered through.

Inside, still no lights. But Jack's vision was adjusting now. A workshop. A passageway. Finally, an area more open than the others. Lanterns, but dim, casting strange shapes up onto the walls. People. Mostly men. Handful of women. Echoes of a dozen whispered anxious conversations.

'Amado, here.' That other Spaniard from the gym, Campos. All present and correct, his whole group.

'Is this all?' Granell peered around. A loading bay, Jack guessed. 'And where's Leduc?' No response, a few shrugs. 'Typical,' he murmured in Jack's ear, then turned to the gathered *résistants*. 'Fine, listen, he'll be here. But, for now, let's get busy. Miguel,' he said to the other Spaniard, 'find the weapons crates. They should be over there, behind that stack of barrels. You two,' he pointed at his young Jewish cell members, 'on the gate. Everybody else, hold tight until we get things sorted. And who's got the armbands?' Somebody raised a hand. 'A couple of you help spread them around.'

'Not a major anymore,' Jack said to him. 'Is that what you said?'

'Old habits,' Granell smiled. 'And needs must. But keep an eye on things.' Then he whispered. 'Especially the bunch edging towards the door.'

Jack saw them. Six of them. Waverers. You could tell a mile away, muttering to each other, lowered eyes. He walked over to them. One in a uniform Jack didn't recognise, the others fingering the white armbands they'd been given.

'Here,' said Jack, 'want help with the armbands? And what *does* the VP stand for?'

'English?' said one of the men.

'The accent still that bad? Irish, really.' It seemed better to keep up the pretense. 'War correspondent. Here to make you all famous. *Time* magazine? For the Americans.'

'They're really coming?'

'You think I'd be here if they weren't? But VP?'

'*Volontaires de Place*, of course,' said another of the waverers, the lad with the uniform. Jack was none the wiser. Local volunteers? Probably near enough. He nodded his head in any case. 'They were made for Vichy collaborators to use. But we've commandeered them. Might confuse them, no?'

'Of course,' said Jack. 'Should have worked that out. But here come the guns. Good luck – maybe interview you later?'

The weapon crates were cracked open. Rifles. Campos the Canary Islander and Granell's team handing them out, boxes of ammunition.

'Hell,' Amado said to him, 'look at the state of these. Lebels. These damned things haven't seen service for forty years. Can you handle one, Telford?'

'Me? No, I'm a journalist. From the Americans?'

'No. Some Vichy colonel – supposed to be friendly to the cause. Better than nothing, I suppose.'

'And the proceeds of your brothel raids? The gun runners?'

'There.' He pointed to a smaller crate. 'Two sten guns and six grenades. The brothels haven't been doing too good. Oh, thank god.'

He'd turned towards the door. A newcomer. A neat man, carefully parted wavy hair, thin moustache, trilby, an attaché case. Telford's own age, or thereabouts, waving his free hand, all apologies. But he looked weary, bent under the many troubles piled on his shoulders.

'The buses,' he was saying. 'Still no buses. Come, everybody. Gather round.'

'Leduc?' said Jack.

'Of course,' Amado replied. 'Let's see what he's got to tell us.'

There was a table. Leduc opened his case, spread a large map.

'Look, the buses will be here. And you're all armed? Yes, good. The Americans on their way, of course. Had to wait for the weather. But I'm assured... Well, our assignments.'

He began to name each cell, their codenames anyway. Allocated them variously, either by individual group, or two or three groups together. To the electric power station above the outer harbour. To the local police station on the Rue Darzew — imperative the radio there must be taken intact. The cutting by which the main road, the train line, ran down to the port. The telephone exchange. The *Grande Poste*.

'Us?' said Amado. 'Saved the best until last?'

Leduc lifted a hand to his tired face, rubbed at his chin.

'You, Spanish? And the rest of you. Not easy. But the two batteries this side of town. Gambetta. Ravin Blanc. We're supposed to take them. Put them out of action. If we can.'

'Gun emplacements,' said Amado. 'Concrete bunkers. Nine-inch guns. And we've got... What?' He picked up a rifle in one hand, a grenade in the other. 'These?'

'Colonel Tostain,' said Leduc, 'assured me this afternoon there won't be any opposition. You just need to turn up – when the buses arrive. And, well...'

'You believe him? A Vichy officer?'

'He's on our side,' Leduc insisted. 'He'll be here soon. To help.'

'And the buses?' said Granell.

'They'll be here.'

But Jack could see the doubt on some of the volunteers' faces. Muttering again.

They settled down to wait, Amado and some of the more experienced men doing the rounds, instruction for those unsure about the weapons. Jack made some notes, went to chat with two men in army tunics. It turned out they'd been in the army – until the army decided it didn't want Jews anymore.

'Do we know what's happening anywhere else?' one of them asked.

Granell had already told him there were likely to be landings all along the coast. But where? And what was happening? He had no idea. Only the message.

Allo, Robert. Franklin arrive!

He certainly bloody hoped so.

Time dragged. There was open grumbling. They said they're coming, some complained. But not when. What if it's tomorrow, not tonight? It'll be Sunday, and would they attack on Sunday? And at night? Surely not at night.

It took Leduc all of his persuasive skills to stop some of them drifting away, promising they'd come back in the morning.

'No, no,' shouted Leduc. 'It *will* be tonight.'

'This isn't good,' Amado said to Telford. 'He's doing his best, but...'

He shook his head.

'What's his background?' said Jack. 'D'you know?'

'He had a factory, I think. Maybe this one, I don't know. But he joined up when the war started. Lieutenant. Served locally. But got into trouble for putting out de Gaulle leaflets after the surrender. And then just demobbed with the rest of the Jews. Since then – he's been working for this, I guess. A cousin in Algiers. Organised these groups, helped to train them. And Leduc's just another *nom de guerre*. Of course, it is.'

'Free French then? Sounds like I might have found my story.'

Leduc – or whatever his real name might be – wandered over to them.

'Listen,' he said to Amado, 'can you keep on top of things here? I'm going up to the office, phone José. Find out what's happening in Algiers. Then chase up the buses.'

'If you want my advice, skipper,' Granell gripped his shoulder, 'I'd be sharp about it. We'll not hold them much longer.'

But Granell agreed he would, indeed, keep on top of things. And he was good at it. Made the various groups go over the plans twice more. Inspected the weapons. He had an easy sense of humour, made them laugh, lifted them. It had been the *Shabbat* for most of them, of course, and he joked about that as well.

Leduc came back. No news from Algiers. It seemed pretty much the same there as here in Oran. But at least the buses had arrived. Some local garage owner, according to Granell. And the fuel? Well this, at least, was apparently courtesy of the Americans. Jack looked at his watch. Almost midnight.

'Let's go,' shouted Amado. 'My groups – here.'

A moment of truth. He glanced at Jack, raised an eyebrow. Everything within Telford screamed at him to stay precisely where he was. But, of course, he didn't.

Shots. In the dark. Somewhere over towards the centre of town. But only a few. And otherwise, just another night in Oran.

The buses, the various assault groups driven away to their respective objectives.

'It's good news, isn't it?' Jack asked Granell, as they climbed out of their own vehicle. Four cells, twenty men. 'This quiet? There can't have been any resistance from Vichy after all.'

'Maybe,' said Granell. 'But sometimes…'

They'd stopped on the edge of scrubland. Ahead of them, the outline of a large building, silhouetted against the moonlit Mediterranean.

'Barracks?' said Jack. 'But where are the guns?'

'Down the cliff face.' Amado issued quick instructions to his men, scattered them by sections, in cover, shallow ravines across the otherwise open ground. 'You're right though. Too bloody quiet.' There weren't even sentries at the barrack gates.

Granell whistled to Miguel Campos, gestured for him to swing around to the right. But they'd not gone a dozen paces before, on the road from town, there were headlights, the crunch of tyres on gravel, a car screeching to a halt near the bus. Leduc, leaping from the passenger seat.

'No,' he yelled, 'it's a trap. Get back.'

All hell broke loose. Tracer fire threading towards them from the barracks.

The volunteers in full retreat, bullets kicking up dirt all around. A man went down, and Granell ran back, grabbed him under the arms, dragged him towards the bus, bundled him on board.

'Let's get out of here,' he shouted, but the young Berber driver stared back at him, wide-eyed with terror.

Leduc jumped onto the bus behind him.

'Be brave, boy,' he said, gripped the lad's shoulder. 'Come on, or we'll all be killed.'

'Where?' said the driver, grinding the gears, ducking his head as a bullet shattered one of the side windows. Everybody hit the floor.

'Police station,' yelled Leduc. 'Rue Darzew.' He lifted his head cautiously, checked his car was following.

'What happened?' Granell asked him. 'What the *hell* happened?'

'The colonel,' Leduc replied, 'Tostain. Decided he'd better come clean with General Boisseau.'

'So, we have nothing?' said Jack.

'No, we took every objective. Almost no resistance. It seems Boisseau decided to throw all his forces into opposing the landings – here, at least. Boisseau has no idea of our strength, but he's obviously decided he can deal with us after he's stopped the Americans. And since they still have the shore batteries, he might be right.'

The bus swayed and screeched through the Gambetta district.

'What about Algiers?' Granell demanded. 'Everywhere else – have they landed?'

'Heard nothing.' Leduc lowered himself onto an empty seat. 'How is he?' he asked those tending the wounded man.

'He'll live,' somebody told him.

Jack looked out the shattered window. They were crossing a railway bridge, lights below. This is bad, he thought. Very bad.

The telephone rang and Granell answered. His men at the police station windows watched him, hope or fear making them grip their rifles more tightly. And Telford, squatting near the door to the cells where they'd imprisoned the sergeant and his two constables, watched him.

'Yes,' said Amado. 'Yes.' A long pause, the crackle of a voice on the other end of the line. 'Yes, sure.'

'Well?' said Jack, after Granell had put down the handset.

'In Algiers. They've arrested Darlan.'

There was a muted cheer from the men, though some confusion. Admiral Darlan, head of the Vichy government until Laval had replaced him, but still effectively commander of Vichy's armed forces? Jack supposed so.

'What the hell's he doing in Algiers?' he said. 'And you mean – arrested by *us*?'

Granell laughed.

'Flew in yesterday. A visit to his son, according to Leduc. Bad timing. But, otherwise, everything still the same.'

Leduc had set up his headquarters at the Préfecture, kept one of the telephone lines open, called regularly to say, yes, the Americans were still on their way, that all the major nerve centres in Algiers remained in the hands of the *résistants*. Here in Oran, of course. All they needed to do was keep their own nerve. Until morning, he thought. Until morning.

Jack hauled himself to his feet, crossed the office and offered Amado one of his Gauloises.

'Listen,' he said, 'you mind if I go outside? It seems quiet enough and I'd like to see for myself.'

'De Gaulle might not like it if you get shot.'

'I doubt he'd be *too* bothered. And there's not been any shooting for hours.'

They let him out through the yard and gate on Rue Darzew. It was remarkably silent. It might be two in the morning, but this Miramar district would still normally not have yet entirely settled for the night. Yet there was nothing, except an occasional dog barking in the distance. And Miramar? Of course, just a couple of blocks north to the Boulevard Front de Mer, the view from the cliffs, down onto the oil depot, the port, and the sea. There were a few white lamps showing in the docks themselves, but mainly the harbour lights, blinking their individual sequences, dancing in the darkness, a score of them, red or green, spreading from his left, on each jetty and section of the sea wall, as far as the harbour entrance away to his right. Beyond the entance, more lights. Channel markers. It was – peaceful. Somehow not quite real. Something haunting, fey, about a harbour at night.

Until the *whoosh* of a red flare broke the spell.

A siren. Then a second.

The dockside alive. Headlights, trucks on the move. And, one by one, the channel markers stopped flashing, the red and green lights.

Thunder, though not thunder. The big guns of the batteries above Mers-el-Kébir lit up the night, a couple of miles away to the northwest, and he could feel the ground shake, even where he stood. Then another battery, closer. At Roseville, he thought.

My god, this is it, he said to himself, wondered whether he should head back to Granell, decided Amado would be able to work it out for himself. And, anyway, maybe it was just a false alarm. Everything gone quiet. No more firing. Just darkness again, down below.

It was bizarre.

He waited. Until a second flare.

This one lit up the shape of two ships in the approaches. Sirens again, this time more strident. They didn't stop. More flares. And, now, every battery opened fire. Deafening, shells screaming through the night sky. Great fountains of water shot up all around the leading vessel. But no hits. Yet she didn't fire back. Why the hell not?

And the second salvo from one of the batteries certainly found its mark. Explosions on the vessel's superstructure, flames, as she swung around through the gap in the boom at the harbour's entrance.

A destroyer – though Jack thought she might be too small for a destroyer – running a gauntlet now, firing not just from shore batteries but also from the Vichy warships in the port. Their heavy guns, but anti-aircraft weapons as well. *Pom, pom, pom, pom.*

Still no return fire. Instead, they ran up a huge Stars and Stripes. It was torn to shreds in seconds. Insane. Yet, now, one of the Vichy ships had swung out to meet her. They almost collided. They *did* collide, each of their port sides scraping against the other, the terrible shriek of steel on steel.

There was another flare and searchlights from the Vichy vessel illuminating the entire deck of the incoming destroyer. And there, crammed onto her decks, soldiers sent to take the town. The Vichy ship poured fire into them from no more than a few yards, and Jack had to turn away.

'What the hell's happening?'

It was Granell. The others from the police station. Civilians, pouring from the streets just behind the Boulevard Front de Mer. A few cars and, from one of them, Leduc. Jack noticed people gathering in small clusters, pointing to the armbands, the weapons. Many pulled back, kept their distance. But others started shouting.

'What's going on?' they yelled. 'What have you done?'

There were insults.

'Americans,' shouted Leduc. 'Americans sent to save us.'

'From what? Save us from what?'

Down below, an even greater explosion. A cloud of flame and black smoke billowed skywards.

'My god,' said Granell. 'Must have hit one of her magazines.'

Jack saw her smash into the sea wall, slew sideways and drift further towards the western end of the port, still taking fire while, back at the harbour entrance, a second Allied ship had braved the shore batteries – but missed the gap in the defensive boom, swinging to starboard, finally finding the opening. Yet her guns remained silent.

'Why don't they fight back?' said Jack.

'They've been told the Vichy forces will surrender,' said Leduc. 'Told there'll only be token resistance. They must have no orders to return fire.'

'Not even now?' Granell buried his head in both hands, as that second ship began to lower boats, soldiers swarming over her sides down nets, but dropping like flies as machine guns cut them to pieces.

Shells ripped through her gun turrets, her decks. Part of her foredeck heaved upwards, torn apart by an explosion. Fire. The stink of burning timber and oil carried to them, along with the stench of burning flesh.

The ship's bows slammed into the end of the nearest jetty. She was hit again when her engines went into full astern, dragged her backwards past some sort of floating dry dock. More shells pounded into her.

'What the hell do we do?' said Jack.

Away to their left, the first Allied ship had reached the farther, inner end of the harbour. She was listing badly, the shore batteries not bothering with her anymore, but small arms fire killing every living soul who ventured onto her ravaged decks. The slaughter went on, as the vessel began to sink, her crew trying to abandon her, but most dying in the water – though a couple of her lifeboats managed to pull away from her side, each flying a white flag, even if it didn't save them.

'I'm going to get through to Algiers,' Leduc shouted, gripping Granell's arm. 'Let Eddy know what's happening here. And then – we pull back to the Prefect's Office. Hold there as long as we can.'

He ran for his car. Amado gathered his men.

But Jack stayed, prayed in vain that something would happen to save the second ship, now limping foward again. Yet she steamed, already ablaze almost from stem to stern, alongside another Vichy destroyer. He saw the destroyer's guns swing, slowly, deliberately, towards her. The broadside, pointblank, cut through her. One explosion below decks. Another. And another. One final explosion, bigger than the rest, amidships. She slewed around, no longer under any form of control, simply her own momentum carrying her into the dock basin almost directly below, just two small launches in the water, carrying her pitifully few survivors away.

They had counted the passing of the morning most strangely. For even the regular firing, the occasional echoing rattle of machine guns, sporadic explosions, weren't enough to stop the *mu'azzins* calling the faithful to worship. The first prayers, the *Fajr*, had come and gone while it was still dark, around six. A couple of hours later, sunrise, the same. And now, almost one in the afternoon, the *Dhuhr*.

'Just another day in old Oran,' said Granell.

They crouched behind the barricades thrown up along the railings of the police headquarters.

'Funny,' Jack replied. 'You can see my hotel room from here.' He pointed across to the Place Kléber. But the buildings in the square, including his own hotel, were now occupied by the soldiers of Vichy France.

Much had happened in the past nine hours. They now knew that the two Allied ships sunk in the harbour weren't American at all. British. Not destroyers but sloops, escort vessels. The *Walney* and the *Hartland*. Survivors – those that there were – still being fished out of the water, taken as prisoners. The local Vichy commander, General Boisseau, on the strength of his victory, finally felt secure enough to turn his attention to the *résistants*. Some of their objectives were quickly taken back – the electric power station, the cutting to the port – but others still held. And one of the outlying groups kept possession of the bridge away to the southwest, at Pont Albin, which Vichy troops had tried to destroy.

'Maybe we should go over and ask them whether they'd mind us having a quick shave,' said Amado, rubbing at the stubble on his chin. 'Or a bath.'

'How far d'you think they'll have got?'

Jack flinched as a sniper's bullet ricocheted off the iron railing, whined away into the distance.

'The Americans? Not much further than when you asked me half an hour ago, I guess. I took you for a more patient man than this, *Señor* Telford.'

'Leduc said soon,' Telford replied.

'At least he made contact. And at least they've landed. After last night…'

Leduc had briefed them. His cousin in Algiers. Fighting there as well. Many of the *résistants* dead. But Americans on the beaches. Close to Algiers itself. Here, not far from Oran. In Morocco, heavy fighting around Casablanca.

They'd gathered around the wireless set to hear those broadcasts to the world. One from de Gaulle, praising the part played by Free French fighters in support of the landings, calling on the Allies to now hasten the relief of these same heroes of the Liberation, effectively under siege in their own towns. They'd listened, and they'd been cheered by de Gaulle's words. The general was there with them in spirit, even if he'd been excluded from the plans.

'It would have been different,' said Jack. 'If Leclerc had been here. Or de Gaulle himself.'

'Put no faith in saviours, English,' Amado growled. 'They always let you down.'

'Remind me to tell you the stories, some time. The ones the *tirailleurs* tell about him. The Juju General. Do you know he once threw a magic cloak over the whole of Brazzaville, saved the town from German bombers?'

They both laughed.

'And Giraud?' said Granell. 'Do they also tell stories about Giraud?'

There'd been a second broadcast. This one from General Giraud. No longer in hiding, it seemed, after his escape from the Germans. With the American commanders, he'd said.

'A different sort of story,' Jack told him. He remembered what Fox had said. Giraud no admirer of de Gaulle. Loyal to Pétain. But loyal to Vichy as well? That remained to be seen.

'Well,' Amado smiled, 'it looks like Giraud's going to be here long before our Cyrano. *Hola Oran, viene Giraud.* For me, I don't give a damn about either of them. Bloody French.'

The third broadcast? From Vichy General Boisseau. *Loyal French citizens of Oran, our forces last night defeated an attempted invasion of our sovereign territory...*

Four hundred American soldiers, more than half of them dead, the rest wounded and most now prisoners of war. Two hundred seamen of the Royal Navy killed or wounded on the *Walney* and the *Hartland*. Elsewhere, Boisseau claimed, failed landings, the Americans being driven back into the sea. Most of the *résistants* had refused to believe it. But during the morning some had slipped away.

For the rest? They remained, as de Gaulle had said, under siege.

The second night. And how many attacks beaten back during the day? Six? Seven? Harmon would have been proud of them. Just like the bloody Alamo.

They'd had word from Leduc's cousin in Algiers. The Americans had finally taken the town, relieved the defenders, late in the evening – by which time Vichy's Admiral Darlan had been released.

At Casablanca, the fighting had been tough, and, like Oran, some of the town was in the hands of resistance fighters, besieged by Vichy loyalists, and the Vichy loyalists themselves under siege by the Americans. Jack wondered whether the hydrographic wisdom of Manolo and Uncle Emilio had, after all, been useful to Colonel Eddy's intelligence services.

In Oran itself? Drunk on their success against the *Walney* and the *Hartland*, the Vichy destroyers had put to sea, determined to wreak havoc on the rest of the Allied invasion fleet. Reports said they had failed miserably, every one of their vessels either sunk or scuttled in the shallows. There'd also been word of American paratroopers, landing just to the south, around La Sénia aerodrome. But no sign of them any closer.

'Think they'll come tomorrow?' said Jack. He was working at a typewriter, the top floor of the Préfecture, working up the outline for a piece about the siege. The desk lamp flickered. Bloody nuisance.

Across from him, the man who called himself Leduc had just put down the phone.

'They'd better,' he replied. 'At the last count we were down to five rounds each. After that...'

'No dynamite?'

'Dynamite?'

Jack smiled.

'When I was in Spain, in the north, I heard this story about Asturian miners who'd held off a whole division of Italians with nothing but a few sticks of dynamite and rocks. They held out on this mountain somewhere for a week.'

'And then?'

'I think the Italians wiped them out – though this isn't the point of the story. But listen, this piece I'm writing. Assuming the Americans get here, your *nom de guerre*. I think readers will want to know your real name. And if they don't get here, it's not going to make a whole lot of difference.'

'It might make a difference to my family. If there are reprisals.'

'You think anonymity will help them?'

'No, I don't. And my name, *monsieur*? It's Carcassonne. Roger Carcassonne. My cousin, in Algiers, is José Aboulker. And you?'

Jack smiled, reached over to shake hands.

'Telford,' he said. 'My real name's Jack Telford. And when did you start organising your groups. Do they have a name, by the way?'

They'd been organising, it turned out, for two years. Almost four hundred *résistants* in Algiers alone. Yes, mainly Jewish, enraged by Vichy's anti-Semitic laws, the seizure of their property, the theft of their nationality as Frenchmen. Some army officers among them, men who despised Vichy and all it stood for. They'd called themselves the Géo Gras Group – because they'd trained at the gymnasium of former boxing champion Gras, though their true purpose kept from him.

'But I can't claim the credit for this,' said Leduc – Carcassonne. 'There were many before me. Atlan, Libine, Bouchara. Here, I'll list them for you.' He began writing names on a sheet of paper. 'At least all of them in Algiers will be safe now. Me, I was a bit of a latecomer.'

He handed over the list, moved over to the wireless. The local station was still off the air but Radio-Maroc was broadcasting from Rabat and Carcassonne played the dial, gasped with delight when he'd eradicated the worst of the whistling and wheezing. Brachah Zefira.

'Here they come again,' shouted Campos.

'Only shoot when you've got a clear target,' said Granell, from his own post at the windows. 'Clear targets only.'

Jack saw Carcassonne pick up his rifle, take his place at a sandbagged window.

'Christ,' said Miguel, 'they've got artillery.'

Telford heard the gun's report at the same time its shell smashed the outside wall. The sound of its impact battered his ear drums. Dust filled his nostrils, his eye. The wall buckled but held, the plaster cracking from floor to ceiling, white paint flakes showering down like a snowstorm. The lights flashed once or twice, then went out, plunged them into darkness.

Granell wiped a hand across his face, aimed through the window, dropped back into cover as machine gun bullets ripped apart the outside shutters.

Below, there was an explosion, shouts. And there were shots. From the defenders.

'They're coming through,' somebody called from downstairs.

'Pin those bloody gunners,' cried Granell, and ran for the staircase. Campos followed him. So did Jack.

The double doors to the courtyard were blown apart, Vichy soldiers in helmets trying to force their way inside, one of them already dead in the doorway, the *résistants*, also in the shadows, sheltering behind desks and filing cabinets.

Granell crouched at the foot of the stairs, Miguel Campos just behind him, and Telford sprawled flat on the landing, wondering what the hell he thought he was doing there. Amado worked the bolt action on the Lebel, five times, five shots, three of the attackers going down, caught in the crossfire. The rest fell back.

'Get that doorway blocked up again,' Granell shouted. He jumped down the final few steps, crouched with his back to the wall, picked up one of the fallen *poilus*' helmets, set it on his own head. Then he reached cautiously to the khaki canvas pouch on another of the dead soldiers. He grinned, held up a grenade.

'See?' he said. '*Limoncitos*.' He pulled out two more. 'Now...' Bullets cracked into the brickwork. 'Miguel,' he called to the Canary Islander, 'back upstairs, make sure they keep those bastards pinned.'

He slipped through the doorway before anybody could stop him. More shots, then it all fell silent again.

A couple of the defenders edged over, dragged the bodies clear, began building a furniture barricade. Jack crept downstairs, peered around the side of the rolltop they'd manhandled into position. Good solid walnut. But he could see nothing out there. Pitch black. He helped carry chairs, another cabinet, stacked them as solidly as they were able.

'No,' he yelled, 'leave a gap. For Granell...'

Somewhere outside, the *crump* of an explosion. Two more. *Crump, crump.*

Shots.

Jack held his breath. But there was something about Granell. Nine lives, he thought, as Amado slipped back through the barricade. He sat on the floor, short of breath, but grinning.

'No more mountain gun,' he said. 'Need a drink, though.'

Almost dawn. And there'd been no shooting for three hours. Everybody else asleep.

'At least it's not as bad as Madrid,' said Granell.

'You were there – the start of the siege?'

'Bloody university. Hell, Jack, I'd never want to be anywhere like that again.'

'I knew somebody else who was there. A priest. Father Lobo.'

Granell laughed, lifted a water bottle to his lips, shook it when not a single drop came out.

'What I'd give for a coffee,' he said. 'But, my god, small world hardly does it justice, no?'

They swapped stories, their voices low, easy Spanish: about the priest; about how Granell had ended up in Madrid; about their childhoods – Amado's in Burriana, Jack's in Worcester; about the respective tragedies of their fathers' deaths.

'Mind if I take some notes?' said Jack, lifting the notepad from his satchel, and the pen.

'Nice, Jack – the pen.'

Telford held it up, shared his cigarettes.

'Did I ever tell you the story?'

He hadn't, but now he did.

'Hell,' said Amado. 'Negrín? Never got to meet him. And that's how you came to be in Alicante? But doesn't quite explain you being on the *Stanbrook*. Could have gone home – back to England.'

He stood, stretched his arms, checked out the window. There was fog, but tinged with first light's sulphurous yellow.

'Don't think you'd believe me if I told you.'

'Try me,' murmured Granell.

Telford thought about it. To how many people had he ever told the truth? The whole truth. To Ruby Waters, that was about it. So why should he trust Granell with it? The Spaniard was ten years older than Jack but seemed more. Only the eyes spoke of a younger man.

'Well, I suppose…'

He kept it as concise as possible. The tour bus. Santiago de Compostela and Carter-Holt's failed scheme to assassinate Franco. Her attempt to kill Jack when he'd finally worked it all out. Burgos. The complicated web of those who'd wanted to see him dead – and maybe *still* sought that end. Black scorpion. Gabizon. The stabbing.

'Think I'm mad?' he said, when he'd finished.

'You've made enemies in high places, Jack. You sure it's only *one* of them trying to murder you?'

'Christ,' said Telford, sarcastically, 'I never thought of that.'

'Just drove through their lines,' said Colonel Eddy. 'Put up a white flag on the Jeep and – well, heck, here I am.'

Jack saw how Eddy walked with a limp. He'd not noticed before. At their earlier meetings, the colonel had only stood to shake Telford's hand but now, as he inspected the damage, the falter in his step was pronounced.

'And you need guides, Colonel?' Carcassonne was confused.

They still held the Préfecture. A couple of half-hearted attacks during the morning but sounds of more determined fighting away to the east, then to the south, the heavy artillery in the forts above Oran firing all through the forenoon at more distant targets. Overhead, twice – no, three times – dogfights as Vichy's fighters tried to take down Allied planes. And, every hour, terrible eruptions, naval guns hurling high explosive shells against Vichy strongpoints.

'We took the airfield at Tafaraoui a while back. But the other airfield – La Sénia? Trying to get a foothold since early morning, but the fire from that fort up on the heights...'

'Santa Cruz?' said Granell.

'Sure, Santa Cruz,' Colonel Eddy smiled. 'Keeping the boys pinned down. You know the best way to get up there? We have some Rangers who'd be glad of a few pointers.'

'What's it worth, Colonel?' Amado laughed. 'We get to invade Cartagena next?'

'Next, you help Ward's First Armoured Division get past the Saint-Philippe fort. But before we talk about Franco, we can at least get the rest of your Commie comrades out of the labour camps here in Algeria, over in Morocco.'

'Yes, sure we will,' Granell sneered. 'Like the submarine we were promised. The guns.'

He held out his rifle, worked the bolt a few times. Empty, of course. It struck Jack that Colonel Bill Eddy wasn't entirely accustomed to having broken promises thrown back in his face.

'It's war, mister. Sometimes we don't get quite what we want. None of us. But I guess the Rangers will do just fine without you.'

'Just one problem,' said Granell, 'how do we get out of *this* place?'

'Same way I got in. White flag. Touch and go. This talk of a ceasefire… But with ammo boxes? We'd never have gotten through.'

The colonel leaned against a bullet-pocked pillar, rubbed at his thigh.

'Can I come along for the ride?' said Jack.

He hoped to hell they'd say no, and he wasn't disappointed.

'Mister Telford,' said the colonel, 'you already played your part. All those little deceptions. Rumour here, newspaper article there. They add up. Seems we managed to convince them we were heading for Malta. A hundred ships, but no U-boat attacks. Luftwaffe's attention diverted elsewhere. Minimal damage. We did good. All of you,' he offered a half-salute to the assembled *résistants*, 'did good.' Yet he took Jack by the arm, led him towards the cells, switched to English. 'But perhaps one thing you *could* do.'

The policemen still held behind bars got to their feet, demanded to know when they'd be released, but Colonel Eddy told them to be patient. Maybe a ceasefire, maybe not.

'You mean it, Colonel,' said Jack, 'about getting the Spaniards out of the camps?' Eddy shrugged his shoulders, rubbed at his leg again. 'You wounded, sir.'

'War wound, sure. But an old one. And your Spanish friends. Why not? They may be Commies, but if they're anything like Granell, we need them on our side. The French as well. But, see, there's the problem. This work we do, Mister Telford – intelligence work – well, sometimes I think those of us responsible for it should all go to hell.'

'Dirty work, sir, but somebody has to do it.'

'Don't get me wrong, the sabotage, the interrogations, that's one thing. I even had a few ideas about how we could dispose of our German friends in Casablanca and Algiers – though the big boys wouldn't wear it. No, it's the lies we tell our friends. Probably just me. The problem of being raised by missionaries, maybe.'

'Perhaps you need a priest, Colonel. This is shaping up towards a confession.'

'Nobody likes a smart aleck, mister. And what I need is somebody to get word through to de Gaulle. He may already know, but the fellows at the top – my superiors, Telford, you get my drift? They're already talking to Darlan. An armistice. For all French Africa. After everything the Free French have done – de Gaulle, Leclerc, Carcassonne's men here, the others in Algiers – they at least deserve somebody to be honest with them.'

'The deal?' said Jack. 'They're not part of it?'

Colonel Eddy shook his head.

'Darlan will be High Commissioner, at least for French North Africa. Maybe more than that. And Giraud will be in command of French forces in Africa. All of them.'

The betrayals had become much worse. It might be the first night of Hanukkah, but the celebration was muted.

'A toast anyway,' said Carcassonne, once all his guests had gathered. 'To Monsieur Telford and his brave article.'

Roger had swapped his suit and his rifle for a green sleeveless jumper, an elegantly patterned *kippah*.

There'd been nothing valiant about it. A simple record of the action in the harbour, the siege, the arrival of American tanks in the city, the continuing naval bombardment which finally led to the surrender of the Vichy forces. Hundreds dead on both sides, and the hospitals filled with wounded. It had been Jack's interviews with the Allied wounded that had maybe marked out the piece. Interviews with the injured *résistants* who'd made it clear they were fighting for Free France. Interviews with American casualties happy to spit on Vichy's name. He'd even picked up news of Harmon from one of them, a United Press correspondent, Disher. Poor devil had been on the *Walney*. Shot to hell. Twenty-five wounds. But survived and, predictably, not feeling exactly friendly towards the Vichy French. Bunnelle had loved it.

'It wasn't me made all the sacrifices,' said Jack. 'Not bad wine, though.' He lifted the glass, accepted the toast anyway.

'And not a drop of Christian children's blood spilled in its production,' said Carcassonne's younger brother, Pierre. 'Well, not much, anyhow.'

'That's not funny, Pierre,' murmured his fiancée, Ingrid. Short black hair, flowered frock. Polish, Jack imagined. Czech, maybe. He'd have to ask later.

'No, it's not,' Roger Carcassonne snapped. 'Not funny at all. After all we've been through. And here we are, back where we started.' He snatched a lurid leaflet from the hall table, shook it in the air.

'I don't get it,' said the American soldier at Jack's side.

'Seriously?' Jack had said when he'd met him in the hospital. 'Benjamin Franklin?'

The boy's arm was still in a sling. Jewish, of course. From New York, and invited by the Carcassonnes – as had become the custom among Oran's Jewish families – to enjoy a simple home-cooked meal or, in this case, the Hanukkah celebrations. Jewish boys far from home and temporarily adopted by Jewish folk in this strange and distant land.

'What's the problem?' Franklin urged him now, no more French than the few schoolboy essentials from his US Army phrase book.

'French Nazis,' said Jack. 'Back on the streets again. *Action Française*. Latest leaflet. Back to claiming that Jews kill Christian kids, use their blood to make *matzos*. Or to fortify their wine.'

The Yank laughed.

'That old chestnut again?' he said. 'These guys don't take this stuff seriously, do they?'

When had Jack first come across it? His old journalism course. A session on this very thing. A phrase which had come from the States itself. Newspaper reports after some incident there. The blood libel, a journalist had called it. A legend almost a thousand years old. Deep-rooted accusation that Jews regularly murdered Christian boys and used their blood in rituals. And now *Action Française* was propagating the nonsense yet again, just as Hitler's fanatics had done, over and over.

'Hard not to take it seriously,' said Jack, 'with everything else going on.'

'Enough gloom,' shouted Roger's wife, another Hélène. A handsome woman, pale pink cardigan. She snatched the leaflet from her husband's hand, balled it, tossed it to the floor. 'I'll have you know this wine comes from my uncle's own vines at Médéa.

'Merlot,' said Francine Camus. 'It's excellent.'

She was still teaching. There'd been a painful parting of the ways. Albert was coming back, she'd said. All just too difficult. Too costly. But then, with Vichy's surrender of Algeria and Morocco, Hitler had lost patience with Pétain, invaded the whole of previously unoccupied France, worried that the main Vichy naval fleet at Toulon would fall into Allied hands. Well, Pétain wasn't about to let this happen, but neither was he prepared to hand it to the Germans either. And now the fleet lay scuttled in Toulon's harbour.

The plans of Francine's husband, Albert, had also been scuttled. Trapped in a France occupied in its entirety by German and Italian forces. So, an equally painful reunion with Jack. Could he forgive her? she'd said. Of course, he'd said, far too readily – if she could forgive *him*. His real name. Telford, he'd said. Not O'Hare. Trapped, within a trap, within another trap. But in this strange world they presently all inhabited, it hadn't even raised an eyebrow when Jack turned up at the Carcassonnes with her on his arm.

'Glad you like it *Madame* Camus,' said Roger. 'And pleased you could join us. I understand our grandmothers were friends.'

'Mama?' said Carcassonne's mother. She pulled her dressing gown more tightly around her. 'You mean mama?'

'Yes, mother. Clara Albert, you remember?' She didn't.

The Carcassonnes' house stood just beyond the Etz Haim school. A small courtyard and then the house itself, all garish wallpaper, Hebrew hangings everywhere.

'Getting dark,' said Hélène.

Carcassonne hugged her.

'Then we shall light the first candle, my love.'

They carried their drinks back to the hallway, past an old piano, at the front door. The *menorah* was elaborate, its central plaque brass, inlaid with silver and copper damascene threads. It hung alongside the family's *mezuzah* scroll. Around the outside of the plaque, hollowed receptacles and, in the middle of the plaque, a cup apart, into which Roger poured oil, but left it unlit.

'The *shamash*,' whispered Francine. 'Saved until the final night. In this family, at least. My grandmother followed a different way entirely. That, from the *shamash,* each of the other Hanukkah lights must be kindled. As many different beliefs about the *shamash* as there are tribes of Israel, Jack. More besides.'

Carcassonne had filled the first of the *menorah*'s outer receptacles, the one on the right, lit it with a spill Hélène handed to him. A curl of black smoke, the scent of burning oil, a short Hebrew blessing Jack didn't understand.

'Thanks for God's commandment,' Francine murmured, 'that Hanukkah should bring light to the world.'

Well, it was needed, thought Jack. There'd been weeks of mixed blessings. Casablanca taken, a day or so after Oran, but only with the loss of hundreds more on each side. After a great naval battle, one Vichy battleship, a cruiser, six destroyers, sunk or put out of action by the Americans. Then word that Rommel had been smashed. El Alamein, the Germans falling back across Libya, but still a serious threat, reinforced through Tunisia.

An armistice signed by Admiral Darlan and the American General Eisenhower. But no involvement in the process by the Free French or Jewish *résistants*. The only concession? A few Jewish doctors and lawyers allowed to reopen their practices. The rest of Vichy's anti-Jewish laws still firmly in place.

Jack had met Bill Eddy just once since then, and the colonel hadn't seemed particularly happy to see him.

'Well, Colonel,' Jack had said, 'is this the outcome you promised everybody? Darlan?'

'The top brass consider him the least bad option, mister. Maybe not my choice but who am I to argue?'

'You?' Jack had said. 'You're the man who made all this happen, aren't you? Support for the *résistants*. All those little deceptions to keep Hitler and Mussolini guessing. But now, what have we got? Some of the Géo Gras boys in Algiers arrested for putting up de Gaulle posters. And all those promises there'd be justice for Algeria's Jews?'

'Things you've got to accept, Jack. You not woken up yet? To how much some of these Frenchies despise the Jews? Hell, some of them believe Jews aren't even human. No, don't laugh, my friend. You know I'm right. So just imagine how much it stung them to get thrown in prison by those same Jews. If they hated them before...'

At the Carcassonnes' house, there was a second blessing of the light, this time, Francine told him, for the King of the Universe, who had performed miracles for the Jewish people, in that same season.

'Miracles?' said Pierre. 'And now forsaken us.'

Roger scolded him. Impiety. But Jack still remembered that meeting with Bill Eddy.

'Accept?' Jack had said. 'No, I don't think so. I know *this*, Colonel. How we have to understand the world before we can change it. But that's a damned long way from accepting it.'

'I'm trying to get Bob Murphy to meet the community leaders,' Eddy had replied, 'but everybody needs to be patient, Telford. There's a lot at stake here. All those Spanish boys to be released from the camps, for one thing. You think it's easy? You think anybody up there wants me releasing Commies all over the place. Hell, d'you even know how many of them there are?'

Jack had a fair idea. From Granell and the others.

'I know you're doing your best, Colonel,' he'd said. 'But Murphy?'

Telford recalled Captain Fox's bitter summary of Robert Murphy, the man who saw North Africa as just a potential extension of America's fiefdom.

'Bob Murphy is the president's personal voice here. Did you forget?'

'No, I didn't forget. Is that what this is about? Just another trade deal?'

That was about as far as their conversation had gone. Almost. And, to the background incantation of a third blessing, a longer prayer, he heard old *Madame* Carcassonne.

'Clara Albert, did you say?' She tugged at the sleeve of Francine's royal blue blouse. 'One of the Benichous?'

'Nothing so grand, I'm afraid,' Francine replied.

Roger opened a prayer book, began to recite a psalm, in French.

'I will exalt you, O Lord, for you lifted me out of the depths and did not let my enemies rejoice over me.'

'Rejoice over us?' said Pierre. 'What do you call it when they've arrested so many of our friends. For what reason? No charges, nothing.'

It had been the last day of November, five days earlier, and Giraud had issued arrest warrants. For the cousin, young José Aboulker. For José's father. For most of the Géo Gras Group's leadership in Algiers. Arrested, it seemed, for no other apparent reason than that they were, indeed, members of the group.

'Pierre,' said Hélène, 'for pity's sake. Tonight?'

'And Colonel Eddy has promised,' said Roger. 'He will make sure they get justice.'

Jack wasn't so sure, but he kept it to himself. Yet Eddy had certainly fulfilled that other commitment. The local Morand internment camp was being emptied – though there seemed to be no progress emptying the camps elsewhere – the Spaniards recruited into a new unit, the African Free Corps. Granell, Campos from the Canary Islands, *el canario*, and others had gone off to join them, reunited with old comrades. Under the command of another Vichy general, but still – back in uniform. Training, they said, for a campaign against the Germans in Tunisia. But Amado had embraced him like a brother, tears in his eyes, for he'd received a letter from his wife, Aurora – thanks, it seemed, to Jack's message to the consulate in Alicante. Telford had made a tentative inquiry at the same time. Did they have a forwarding address for Ruby Waters? Yet there'd been no response, and he was glad. Yes, glad.

There was food, served by a young girl. Potato and leek pancakes. Spinach pastries. Fried fish in spicy tomato sauce. Rice-stuffed peppers. And *bimuelos*, fried dumplings, drizzled with orange and honey.

'You think we can trust them, the Americans?' said Pierre.

'Please,' said Hélène, trying to avoid looking at young Benjamin Franklin who, himself, seemed much taken with the girl. 'Our guest…'

Jack wondered whether he should tell them, decided instead to lighten the mood, to involve the GI in a more acceptable form of social intercourse.

'Benny,' he said, 'tell them the story about the landing, about using your French.'

The lad obliged. They'd hit the beach. There were Vichy

soldiers in the dunes. But neither side seemed to know whether they should fire on the other.

'So, I start yelling. *Nous sommes Américains. Nous sommes Américains.*' His accent was execrable, of course, but Jack did his best to translate. 'Hell, I was so nervous I squeezed the trigger. And I couldn't stop. Like my finger froze. Emptied the whole magazine. But those other guys, the Frenchies, they just stuck up their hands. I took twelve of them prisoner, all on my lonesome.'

Jack spared him the indignity of telling them how, later, young Benny had tried to shoot down a Spitfire, thinking it was German.

Besides, the Yank had brought Hanukkah presents. Canned peaches, cigarettes and soap. In exchange, they presented him with a *dreidel* spinning top.

'I ain't seen one of these since I was a kid,' said wide-eyed Benjamin. 'But this one's a beauty.'

And it was. Ivory. Old.

'Been in our family a long time,' said Hélène. 'But there'll be no more children now. And perhaps you, the other boys in your regiment...'

There were tears in her eyes and Jack, still the diplomat, remembered the piano.

'Did you know that Francine teaches music?' he said.

'No, Jack...' she demurred. But the family insisted. And those fingers. She began with Bach. *Jesu, Joy of Man's Desiring.* Ingrid hummed along, while Pierre hit the wine some more. He was stony-faced, itching to hit back at anyone and everyone. Telford understood very well. The injustice meted out to the Géo Gras Group was intolerable.

Francine switched to a brighter melody. The whole family sang. A Hanukkah song. Something familiar about the tune. But Jack was thinking about his final exchange with Colonel Bill Eddy.

'Listen,' Eddy had said to him, 'you want to help? Then do what you're good at, mister. You got the connections. Get a piece in the *Washington Post. New York Times.* The *Los Angeles Times.* Maybe, for good measure, the *Wall Street Journal.* Pile it on thick. How the good ol' U.S. of A. has promised the Jews of Algeria and Morocco they'd have their rights as French citizens restored. How, instead, we're helping to send those same Jews to concentration camps – no different than the Nazis. You write that, Mister Telford, and I'll personally make sure the headlines get put under the president's nose.' The colonel chewed on his lip for a moment, a look of pure concentration crumbling his features. 'Maybe I can push things along from my end,' he said.

January – April 1943

Josephine Baker

'Darlan dead?' Jack repeated.

He was sitting at the Gorroños' kitchen table again, drinking their coffee, nibbling at a piece of stale spongecake. Boxing Day, on his way back to Casablanca, but breaking his journey here in Rabat. News of the assassination had been everywhere when he got off the train.

'And his killer already arrested – and executed,' Paquita told him.

They'd both lost weight since he saw them last. The green paint was flaking from their walls. Jack offered Manuel a Gauloise and Paquita took one, as well. Not much on their shelves, so far as he could see, except a couple of baguettes and cans of condensed milk.

'Christ, that was quick,' said Jack. 'Already executed? Who was he?'

'A young royalist,' said Paquita. 'Ferdinand Bonnier. Twenty. Darlan had been meeting the American, Murphy. Bonnier killed Darlan just afterwards. Revolver. Shot him in the face.'

Manuel turned his copy of the *Petit Marocain*, so Jack could see the latest news for himself.

'Don't know the name,' said Jack. 'One of the *résistants*?'

'It's the strange thing,' said Manuel Gorroño. 'No, he wasn't.'

'More to it than meets the eye, then,' Telford replied. And he remembered what Bill Eddy had said. Darlan the least bad option. But maybe this was no longer the case. He must have become an embarrassment, surely.

'And you played no small part in this yourself, comrade – no?' Paquita smiled. 'Newspaper articles in the United States?

All those questions about why the Allies have been supporting a collaborationist?'

'Didn't seem to have done much good. Plenty of good men still in concentration camps. And here?' He glanced through into their living room, paperwork scattered across the floor, exercise books and handbills piled on one of the chairs. 'Still working from home? Teaching?'

She gave him a summary. Languages mainly. But some geography and basic arithmetic.

'We thought it would be different,' she said, 'when the Americans got here, but it seems, in Morocco, a woman's place is still at the kitchen sink – whether it's Pétain's Morocco or Roosevelt's Morocco. Darlan dead, though, at least. There's a rumour that when Bonnier killed the swine, he shouted about how he'd freed France. But Darlan already replaced by Giraud. How will this change anything?'

'Well, I suppose at least Giraud hates the Germans,' said Jack. 'More than you could say about Darlan.'

Convenient, he thought. Just happened to be meeting Murphy before he was killed. And Colonel Eddy? Telford remembered another of his schemes, according to Carcassonne. To kill all the most senior German officers in Algiers and Oran. He'd never gone forward with the plan, but would he seriously have balked at doing away with Darlan? He didn't think so. And what exactly had he meant? Jack didn't want to consider what Bill Eddy might consider as falling within the remit of "pushing things along."

'You know Manolo and his uncle helped the American landings?' said Paquita. 'Corrected their navigation charts?'

From the street below, the scream of steel on steel, the enraged rumble of a passing American tank, gasoline fumes curling up through their window shutters.

'I put in a word for them. An American colonel, Bill Eddy. As a matter of fact...' He was about to speak his mind, about Darlan's assassination. But now it all just seemed too deranged. 'As a matter of fact, he's a great admirer of our mutual friend.' She looked puzzled. 'Amado Granell,' he explained. 'He was there. With the *résistants*. I'll tell you the whole story one day.'

'A small world,' she said and he told her more about the other Spaniards he'd encountered. Reminiscence about her dream that all those Republicans interned by Vichy might be mobilised for the war, this continuation of *their* war. The war which had come to them in Rabat as well, though the fighting not as severe as elsewhere.

'And, when you wrote,' she said, 'this stabbing. Nothing to do with the other thing, with Gabizon? The shooting?'

'I'm not sure you're going to believe this...'

'Not another mysterious message?'

'I told you. I'm not sure I even believe it myself. But when the bastard knifed me, he said something. I thought it was French, but turns out – well, it may have been Czech. Czech for...black scorpion. Lunacy, don't you think?'

'It's the world that's mad, comrade,' said Manuel. 'And this American colonel. Contacts at Tangier? Melilla and Ceuta?'

'Very definitely,' said Jack. 'Your own people come across him?'

'Tangier still under Franco's boot. So-called neutral territory, of course. But we've got a whole network there, backed by the Americans. If Madrid puts a foot wrong...' He made a cutting gesture across his throat. 'There's an American liaison officer there. Promised, when Hitler's been crushed, Tangier will be the springboard for our reconquest of Spain.'

'It's never going to happen,' Paquita snapped at him. There was a stream of invective in Spanish so fast that Jack couldn't follow all of it. 'I've told you before,' she finally said, more slowly. 'We can't trust any of them. Need to keep building the grassroots.'

She spent a few moments telling Jack about her most recent work with the Spanish unions across Morocco.

'And, meanwhile?' he said. 'Algiers – apart from this boy's execution. Other reprisals?'

'It's given Giraud an excuse to arrest even more of the *résistants*. Dozens of them.'

'God damn him.'

'How long will you stay?'

'A couple of days. I need to pay a visit to Gabizon's grave. And I want to try and interview *Sidi* Muhammad again. Before I carry on to Casablanca.'

'Why Casa? Nothing for you in Oran anymore?'

It was a good question. He'd promised Francine he'd be back, of course. But she'd not believed him. He could tell. One last painful dinner together and...

'You love Casa so much?' said Manuel.

'Old friends there,' said Jack. 'And, besides, Bill Eddy gave me a hot tip. Said I should head that way. No idea why – but I guess I'll find out before too long.'

'Never thought I'd hear myself say this,' said Louis Réchard, 'but it's good to have you back.'

Cognac outside the Excelsior. The Place de France. Only...

'I'd hardly have recognised the place. What happened to Auer?'

It wasn't just the absence of Nazi uniforms. The whole place had been redecorated. Very modern, very – American. Geometric patterns which hurt his eye, and American flags everywhere. The music was different. Brash. And in the square itself, across to the clock tower, through a light mist, the occasional camel, bike or donkey cart almost lost among the American trucks and Jeeps. Casablanca filled with unfamiliar faces, GIs guarding every palm tree or manning roadblocks, the streets throbbing to the sight and sound of armoured vehicles by the score.

'I had the honour,' Louis smiled, 'of making sure the Americans knew where he was hiding. Him and the rest of his Gestapo friends. They rounded them up, along with all the other members of the Armistice Committee. But you? Where are you staying?'

'Back at the Touring – and lucky to find a room even there. This town's suddenly a bit overcrowded.'

'Papers?'

'I was hoping you wouldn't ask.'

He reluctantly explained about the travel documents. O'Hare. Louis promised that Jack's secret was safe with him.

'Really, Louis. I think, with you, another man's secrets are just collateral to be saved against a rainy day.'

Louis smiled – pleased, Jack thought, with this back-handed quip.

He'd done all he'd promised in Rabat and, yes, he'd managed to arrange a brief interview with *Sidi* Muhammad, an exchange of anecdotes about Gabizon – and Jack had taken the trouble to mention his friend, a Spanish woman, a skilled teacher, if the Imperial College might happen to have a vacancy. The sultan promised to let him know.

'Your old house?' said Réchard.

'You'd know better than me. New tenant, I imagine.' Réchard promised to find out. 'I'd appreciate it,' Jack went on. 'I've been keeping a low profile. Look, I need to know. Are they still looking for me?'

Fernando breezed over, greeted Jack like a long-lost friend, replenished their glasses.

'Herviot?' said Réchard. 'He's just been relieved of his duties. Ironic. Getting rid of him because, as it turned out, he'd also been helping the *résistants*. But they'd already pinned Chabat's murder on somebody else. You're in the clear, *Monsieur* Telford. At least, so far as the *Sûreté*'s concerned. And your consulate's opened again in Rabat. I suggest you get some updated papers. For whatever other enemies you may have, however...'

A Gallic shrug of the shoulders.

They chatted a while. Snippets of their news. About Monique. About Réchard's family. About Brazzaville. About Kufra. But mainly about the fighting in Casa itself. Worse even than Oran, that was clear. The bitter defence against the Americans mounted by Resident-General Noguès – who Jack had last seen in person from behind the secret screen in the the sultan's throne room.

'You kept your head down, I hope?' said Jack.

'You think we had a choice? Noguès put our streets under the control of those fascist bastards in the SOL.' Darnand's *Service d'Ordre Légionnaire*, the military wing of *Action Française*. 'And then the rumours the Americans were going to bomb us.' He waved a hand around the bar. 'I was here, as it happens. When we got word of the ceasefire. The war with America over. You remember the old *accordéoniste*? He was here as well, somebody trying to teach him the tune for *The Star-Spangled Banner*. But, in the end, we just all sang *La Marseillaise*. Happier things, though,' Louis smiled, at last.

'Did you know we're going to be famous?'

'The film?' said Jack. 'Why d'you think I came back?'

He needed to find the right moment. If anybody in Casablanca knew what was likely to be happening here, whatever it was about which Eddy had tipped him the wink, it would be Louis. Yet it was the other big news. The release of Bogart's long-awaited latest movie. It had premiered in New York back in November. Supposed to be a masterpiece.

'Then you'll be disappointed,' Réchard replied. 'It's not going to be shown here. Vichy's arm still has a long reach. Through Darlan. Until – well, through Giraud now. And the Americans don't want to upset them. Enough problems with these riots. Muslims one minute, Jews the next. But listen, tonight. The Americans are opening a new club. And you'll never guess who's performing...'

There'd been rumours she was dead. Only a month or so back. He'd read the reports in Oran. In *France Dimanche*. Yet, there she was, her name on the billboard outside the entrance.

The American Red Cross Liberty Club stood just along from the Vox Cinema. The corner where the Avenue du Général Moinier met the Rue Chevandier-de-Valdrôme. A pretty little park across the street and a busy tram stop just outside.

'So, what happened to her, d'you know?' said Jack, as he followed Réchard and Monique up the few red-carpeted steps into the former hotel.

'Arrived here not long after you left,' Louis told him, showed their invitations to a couple of GIs acting as doormen. 'Toured Spain. A spell in Marrakech. Next thing I heard, she'd been brought here. The Comte Clinic. Abscess in her abdomen. But then, complications. Have I got that right, my dear?' he said to his wife.

Telford tried to remember how he'd first found out she was in Casablanca. The *soirée*, of course, at Dina's house. Faya-Largeau. One of her records had been playing. It was Guillebon who'd mentioned it.

'A little more complicated, I think,' said Monique. Another white-gloved soldier showed them to a table, reasonably close to the stage. 'Women's problems. Then peritonitis. Other things. But stayed in the hospital – oh, how long? A year. No, it will have been eighteen months.'

'My god,' said Jack. 'She must really have been at death's door.' He glanced around the room. 'And is this really going to work?'

It was one of those things. The only place in town where white GIs and coloured GIs were allowed to mix, socially. Great initiative. But strange to think that a country as civilised as America should still have a segregated army at all. How did this stack against what he'd seen and heard in Brazzaville, for example? Racism a-plenty, of course, among so many of the French officers. All those references to bush monkeys and the rest. But had he ever come across places where black and white soldiers weren't allowed to share a bar? He couldn't recall any. And he wondered what Eze Tolabye, or Abia the Bassa, would make of it all – wondered where they were, these days.

'I suppose,' said Réchard, 'you can lead the horse to water, but...'

He didn't need to say any more. Whether by accident or design, the soldiers seemed to have gravitated, by colour, to the tables on either one side of the room, or the other. Far more white faces than black. But everybody in their best uniforms. Women at their tables. Local women, Jack supposed, scattered pretty evenly across both sides. But a dazzling and rowdy array of pale khaki, or frocks in every raibow shade, a haze of cigarette smoke and candle flames flickering. And the atmosphere was good, the floor filling up nicely, smells of strong coffee and cheap perfume.

'The women...' he began.

'Don't ask,' Réchard stopped him. 'But if you ever get some free time, you should have a look at the instruction booklet they've all been given about the hazards of intercourse in all its lurid forms. It's very entertaining.'

Monique slapped his arm.

'Louis!' she scolded him.

The room was buzzing, at least. Waiter service, just for this opening night, it seemed. They ordered wine, red.

'Bousbir?'

'Guided tours only,' Réchard laughed.

From the side of the stage, another entrance, a procession of tuxedos, glittering ball gowns, rows of medal ribbons on uniformed chests, a smattering of applause from among the rest of the audience, as these guests of honour were shown to the vacant front row tables. Jack recognised Noguès, still slim, silver-haired, dark olive uniform jacket, boots and jodphurs.

'Those two?' said Jack, flicked a clandestine finger towards two of the suited civilians.

'Russell and Reid,' Louis murmured. 'From the American consulate. Dragged off to god knows where when the landings began. Never thought we'd see them again. But, thank heaven, eventually returned unharmed. Came back to a cheering crowd, as it happens.'

'Ah,' Jack smiled. 'Now, there's a face you'd not forget in a hurry.'

Picture in all the papers, of course. Patton.

Behind Patton, two more civilians, the first of them a tall man with a chiselled face, though chiselled by a somewhat inept sculptor. He'd been in the papers. Murphy, Roosevelt's personal envoy to North Africa. But, at Murphy's side, a face Telford didn't recognise. And nor, it seemed, did Louis. Tall, aristocratic, walrus moustache.

As they took their seats, a more informal uniform, shirt sleeves, skipped up onto the stage, grabbed the microphone.

'*Lieutenant* Williams,' Monique whispered.

A black lieutenant, Jack thought. Well, that's progress.

'Ladies and gentlemen,' Williams began, 'distinguished guests, it gives me the greatest pleasure, on behalf of the American Red Cross, to welcome you here tonight. Our very first Liberty Club – the first of many, here in North Africa, we hope.' He paused, glanced towards Patton for some encouragement, though the general was already deep in conversation with Noguès. Williams pressed on, told the audience how privileged he was to be able to welcome back to the stage, for the first time in far too long, one of the most celebrated artistes of all time, their very own Black Pearl – Miss Josephine Baker.

Enthusiastic applause. The curtain behind him opened. And there she was. A six-piece army combo on the stage as well. Four white boys. Two coloureds.

She wore a simple print frock, blue, with *broderie anglaise* at the throat and sleeves. A far cry from the banana skirt some of the GIs might have been hoping for. And a yellow bourgainvillea flower in her hair. All skin and bones though.

'Hi, everybody.' Only two words but Jack felt the electric current run through the room. A thousand volts. 'Well, say hi back. Make me feel at home. No, wait,' she waved her arms, silenced their shouts. 'This *is* my home now. And for you boys, I guess – for a while, at least.'

They yelled back, clapped and whistled and cheered. She nodded to the band, the opening notes for the introduction to *Si j'étais blanche*.

'Nice choice,' Jack whispered, but she'd sung no more than the first few words when she stopped, the combo left quietly playing the background refrain.

'Hey,' she said, 'why are you black boys all sitting over there? And you white boys...' She waved a hand towards the other side of the hall. 'Say, this won't do.' She pouted at Patton. Those lips, thought Jack. Coy Clara Bow one minute, screwball Carole Lombard the next. 'Heck, General, ain't these men supposed to be mingling? You gonna send them to fight the Germans that way?' She switched to her best gruff general's voice. 'OK, you black guys, you can only shoot those Nazis over there. The rest, they're just...' She switched back to her own sweet voice, all smiles. 'Think you can shake them about a bit, General?'

Patton stared at her, expressionless, for what seemed like a long time, the musicians still playing the intro, over and over. But, in the end, he stood, glowered around the room.

'Well?' he growled. 'You heard the lady. Mingle!'

And while the GIs slowly began to obey the order, Josephine Baker sang that first number.

Anybody expecting the crazy antics of *Princesse Tam-Tam* or her *Danse Sauvage* would have been disappointed. But the voice? Jack felt the strength of her words reverberate through his soul.

At its end, stamping, more whistles, wild applause, while Baker ran straight into a livelier version of *Bye Bye Blackbird*.

To finish, an apology.

'I can't tell you how happy this makes me,' she said. 'To be back on the stage like this. I guess you all know I've not been well lately – hey, no need for all that. I'm fine now. But three songs, about my limit for tonight.' A few catcalls, and she laughed, the bubbling wide-eyed laughter for which she was famous. 'It won't be the last, though. I promised Lieutenant Williams – well, I promised him, wherever you boys are in North Africa, I'll be there as well. And if anybody's listening out there,' she cupped both hands around her mouth and yelled, 'I'll be doing the same for the soldiers of Fighting France.'

A roar of approval from the crowd.

'Certainly knows how to play a room,' said Jack. But, by then, she was mothering them, explaining her third song.

'You know,' she said, 'it's true I have not one love, but two. My own country. But Paris as well. I was just a kid when I got there. All the way from St. Louis. Nineteen – just nineteen. And staying in a hotel. Not a hotel for coloured folks either. Just a hotel, you know. This white waiter calling me *mademoiselle*. Paris opened its heart to me, so this is my song for all of you.'

J'ai deux amours. Two loves have I, my country and Paris.

Jack saw Réchard's eyes – and Monique's – brim with tears.

Louis made the introduction. He'd had some official business with her when she'd been in hospital. The introductions made, Réchard took Monique to the dancefloor.

'Oh my,' said Josephine, 'another Jack for my collection.' She clutched her companion's arm, squeezed it, smiled up at him. A bit like an older version of Leslie Howard, same wavy hair, and a neat Ronald Colman moustache, laughter lines at the corner of his eyes. Telford was puzzled. 'And you want to interview me?'

'Do you mind?' said Jack. 'Not an interview, not really.'

Up close, he could see the dark rings beneath the makeup around her eyes. And the eyes? Something almost oriental about them.

'Sure,' she said. 'Why not? About time we started telling the world I'm not dead after all. And I don't know many Englishmen.'

She spoke those last few words with seemingly genuine awe, as though he might be some exotic creature. Of course, he fell in love with her at once, mumbled some pathetic response.

'This is my secretary, Jacques Hébert,' she said, and Jack shook hands across the table with her companion. But her secretary? Bodyguard he might have believed.

'So, Miss Baker,' said Jack, 'more...'

'Hey, you just wait a minute, mister,' she stopped him. 'You can call me Josephine. Josie, if you like. But *Miss Baker*? You kidding me?'

Telford laughed, apologised.

'Fine. Josie, then. I was going to say, more recuperation – after tonight?'

'Hell, no,' she laughed. 'We're going straight from here to the Hôtel Anfa. Another show. Just a short one again. But it'll be quite an entrance. Why not come along?'

He was tempted, but by the time he was ready to say yes, Robert Murphy had wandered across to the table, the fellow with the hefty moustache at his side.

'Miss Baker,' said Murphy, and Jack was pleased she didn't correct him, extend the same informality that he, Jack Telford, now enjoyed with one of the most famous women in the world. 'We have to leave now but I just wanted to say how much we enjoyed the show – and the offer to entertain the boys? Swell.'

He wasn't at all what Jack had expected. Soft-spoken. Mild-mannered. And Baker waved aside his thanks.

'It's nothing. Nothing. But, say, do you know my friend?' As it happened, Jack had felt the fellow studying him carefully. 'His name's Jack. Jack Telford. He's a journalist.'

It had felt quite normal when Louis had introduced him to her this way. But he'd still not quite shaken off the security of travelling as the Irishman, O'Hare. He felt suddenly exposed, naked to the world.

'Oh yes,' said Murphy. 'We know Mister Telford. Though never had the pleasure.' He held out his hand. Jack shook it. 'He's been giving us a tough time, though. Articles about how we broke our promises to everybody. Isn't that right, Mister Telford?'

'Doesn't seem the place to discuss this, Mister Murphy. But yes, that is right. And the *New York Times* article? I hope it's played a small part in shining some light in here. Promises to empty the rest of the internment camps? The Jews of Morocco and Algeria, promised they'd have their rights restored? Freed from Vichy? But now?'

'Fighting for the Jews, Jack Telford?' said Josephine. 'I'm impressed. And you, Mister Murphy, what are you going to do about it?'

'We're already working with the Jewish organisations – here in Casa. Everywhere else. And with the sultan. The camps, another problem. It just takes time. But I guess you know this, Telford – you worked with *Madame* Bénatar, yes?'

'She always appreciated the way you helped speed up the paperchase for her refugees. I'm seeing her tomorrow. Left some things with her before I headed to Brazzaville.'

It wasn't the time to push this, but here they were, two months since the landings and, for whatever reason, most of the labour camps still full of prisoners, huge numbers of Spaniards among them. Because they were Reds? Jack didn't think so. He smelled a deal between the Yanks and their new Vichy friends, who still needed the forced labour provided by the camps.

'Brazzaville – with de Gaulle?'

Baker's admiration seemed to be growing out of all proportion.

'Our Mister Telford was at Kufra, Miss Baker. Didn't you read his report?'

'I was a bit indisposed at the time. But, Jacques...?'

'I read it,' said Josephine's companion. 'I just never joined the dots.'

'Joining dots,' Murphy smiled, 'is a skill Telford seems to have in spades. At least, according to Bill Eddy. Stayed with the Resistance right through the battle for Oran.'

Jack felt all eyes turn upon him. Josephine's. Hébert's. Murphy's associate. He felt the flames claw up from his neck.

'Telford, did you say?' It was Murphy's associate. English. Plum in his mouth. 'The same Telford involved in that swimming accident at San Sebastián – what, four years ago?'

Oh, christ, thought Jack, a sudden chill in his spine replacing the flush in his cheeks.

'Indeed,' he said. 'You read about it, sir?'

'Know the family, old boy. Poor Valerie. Whole life ahead of her. Strange story.' It was as close to an interrogation as Jack had ever come across. 'Father never got over it. Simply refuses to acknowledge she's gone.' The man turned to Murphy, explained. 'Sir Aubrey. Carter-Holt. Secretary for Overseas Trade. I'm expecting him at Rabat, now we're open for business again.'

'All hands to the pumps,' said Murphy, 'if we're going to get the French to pull in one and the same direction. No offence, Miss Baker. But if you're as close to General de Gaulle as you seem to be, you might just whisper in his ear, maybe?'

Telford's turn to be impressed. Josephine Baker – close to de Gaulle? How?

'The general is his own man,' she replied. 'Well, France's man, anyway. The man for tomorrow's France. Maybe just needs your English buddies to recognise that.'

Baker raised an eyebrow towards the Englishman.

'Oh, believe me, dear lady,' he said. 'I happen to be a great admirer of the general. But forgive me, we've not been introduced.' He held out his hand, a charming gesture. She offered her fingers. He kissed them gently. 'Macmillan,' he said. 'Harold.'

'So, you like to fight for folks' rights,' said Baker, as they worked their way through the dancers, threaded between the tables. She stopped to sign a napkin for one of the coloured GIs. 'The Jews have had a bad time here.'

'I've done nothing,' said Jack. He was more concerned about Macmillan. Connection to Carter-Holt? And Sir Aubrey due in Rabat. It was all a bit – too close to home. 'Just bits,' he said. 'Bits, here and there.'

'But Kufra,' she said. 'Oran. And then this mysterious drowning at San Sebastián. Don't tell me there's no story there.'

They reached Réchard's table, took their leave, Jack explaining about the Anfa. Monique gave him a knowing look when she thought they were unobserved, whispered *bonne chance* in his ear as they exchanged farewell kisses.

'I'm really more interested in how you come to know de Gaulle,' he said, when they'd moved on and he was trying hard to forget the insinuation.

'Joséphine...' Hébert began, but she tutted at him.

'Don't look at me like that, Jacques,' she said. 'It doesn't matter now. Spying days all over, I'm afraid.'

Hébert threw up his hands in exasperation.

She stopped at the next table, signed a menu this time. Then somebody's notebook. Another. And all the time keeping up a stream of intimate greetings, expressions of concern for their welfare, the occasional cheeky innuendo.

'Hard to believe,' she said, over her shoulder, to Jack, 'but, back in the day – hell, what was it? Only twelve years ago. Thirteen. Berlin was the pleasure garden of Europe. Open for anything. The most broad-minded city in the world. Boys and girls. Girls and girls. Boys and boys.' She winked at him. 'Know what I mean, Jackie? The Germans loved me, almost as much as the French.'

More tables. More signatures.

'But then Hitler,' she said. 'All his hate for *neger* music.'

Jack remembered Auer at the Excelsior. The same phrase.

'Well,' Baker pressed on, between signings, 'when the war started – after France – I was still touring. Banned from Germany, of course. But every time I passed through a German checkpoint, in France, in Holland, just about anywhere, there were those Wehrmacht boys lining up for my autograph. Never seemed to enter their heads to worry about what I might be carrying. Or where.' Another wink. 'Intelligence, that's what de Gaulle called it.'

They'd finally reached the back of the hall, were just heading out into the foyer, when another of the GIs stopped in front of them. White, square-jawed. No mere boy, though.

'Hey, soldier,' she said. 'Want me to sign something for your sweetheart back home?'

An edge to her voice, and Jack looked into the soldier's eyes, perhaps discerned there just a hint of the venom Josephine Baker had recognised at once.

'No, lady,' spat the GI, 'I just want what you owe me.'

Jacques Hébert stepped forward, but she placed a calming hand on his chest.

'And what is it?' she said. 'What is it you think you're owed?'

'Paid top dollar to see you, girl. New York. The *Follies*. Couldn't hear a goddamned thing. Call yourself a singer?'

'Probably all those rednecks and their women, banging chairs and walking out because some sassy nigra had the nerve to sing on their stage. You one of those, soldier? A chair slammer? Because, if you are, it's you owes *me* money. I lost a whole packet of money in New York. Mind, if I'd known there was going to be twenty thousand of your Nazi friends at Madison Square, just a year after – well, I might have given New York a miss all together. Saved you *and* me some of your top dollar.'

Jack saw the GI ball his fists, his face crimson.

'You don't get to speak to me like that, bitch. Ni…'

It all happened at once.

Telford and Hébert both acted at the same time, Jack taking hold of Josephine's skeletal shoulders, moving her aside, and the Frenchman about to take a swing at the GI.

But the rest of what would inevitably have followed was choked off by the especially large fist of Lieutenant Sidney Williams, clamped around the soldier's throat, his other arm holding Hébert back.

'Sorry, Josie,' said the lieutenant. 'Thought we'd weeded out all these hayseeds. And you two!' He roared at the white-helmeted military policemen who'd so far remained motionless at the front doors, casually watching the scene with some amusement. But now, at last, the lieutenant brought them scurrying forward. 'Get this piece of shit to the stockade.'

'Sidney, it was no bother,' she said, as the prisoner was dragged away. 'Look at these two guys I got to look after me.' She beamed up at Jack, then at Hébert. 'And I told you when you asked me, this wasn't going to be easy.'

'No,' said Lieutenant Williams, 'what you told me, girl, was to go to hell.'

Jack rode in their car to the Hôtel Anfa.

'What time are you on?' he said.

'Midnight,' she replied. 'The witching hour, Jackie. Isn't that what you say? But back home, St. Louis, it was the time those rednecks came a-calling. You know they left two hundred of us dead? Children. Thousands of our homes burned.'

'And the Jim Crow laws,' said Jack.

'I was brought up with those, Jackie. Taught every day of my life how black kids like me ain't fit to lick the boots of even the poorest whites. But it wasn't like that in France. So, I think to myself, twenty years later, hell girl, things must be better at home by now. I head back to New York. I star alongside Bob Hope. But, you know, things were *worse* than when I'd left. Sure, they let me stop in a white hotel, but only if I used the rear entrance.'

Hébert put his arm around her shoulders, held her close. More than secretary or bodyguard, then.

Through the car windows, Jack could see *Les Arènes*, the bull-ring, remembered the fight there with the fascist thugs of the Falange.

'Always been the big mistake,' he said, 'imagining the Nazis are a product of Hitler's Germany, no? Other way around, I always thought. Too many millions of people around the world with bred in the bone hatred for Jews, or blacks, or – well, just about anybody who's different. They breed the Hitlers, the Mussolinis, the Francos. Never learn, either.'

'A depressing view of the world, *monsieur*,' said Hébert. 'Isn't this why we're fighting this war? For the middle ground, for tolerance? For consensus? An end to extremes? To swings from one form of insanity to another?'

'You sound like some of the *résistants* I met in Oran, Jacques,' Telford smiled.

'Jacques,' Baker boasted, 'was resistance before there *was* a resistance.'

'Joséphine!' Hébert scolded her once more.

'Unless I'm much mistaken,' she said, 'we're all in good company here.'

'Forgive me for asking,' said Jack, 'but are you two…?'

'What, married?' she replied. 'Hey, Jackie, I had three marriages already. None of them worked. But me and Jacques…'

She never finished.

They'd arrived at the land-locked ocean liner that was the Hôtel Anfa. This was how it looked to Jack. Its rounded entrance exactly like a ship's stern, and the lights on each floor were portholes along its decks. There was a welcoming committee, the hotel manager, his senior staff, bouquets of flowers. But as they made their way up the steps, Hébert pulled Jack to one side.

'*Monsieur* Telford,' he said, 'the Information Service at Brazzaville – we already had word of your loyalty to the cause. For Free France.'

'We?' said Jack. 'I take it you don't mean Miss Baker and yourself?'

Hébert smiled.

'Joséphine has been a crucial part of our network. But she's not the network itself. You follow?'

'Perfectly.'

'Then perhaps we shall have the chance to speak more soon.'

Jack felt a bit lost. Josephine escorted off to her dressing room, Jacques Hébert gone with her. And he'd been confused by Hébert. A chance to speak more? About what?

But he was also somewhat daunted by his surroundings. He could have been aboard the *SS Normandie*, the luxury wood panelling varnished so deeply he could see his face plainly in the reflection. Beeswax so strong it even cut through the cigar smoke. And he wasn't alone too long.

'Hélène,' he said, surprised to see her at the upper deck bar – and yes, at the Anfa, that's what it was called, the upper deck. 'My god, it's good to see you. I was planning to call round tomorrow, but this – let me get you a drink. And who are you with?'

Bénatar kissed him on both cheeks, tears in her motherly eyes, and his own emotions running high.

'Oh, what a *mechayah*,' she said. 'I'm supposed to be meeting somebody. But yes, a Coca-Cola?'

He laughed.

'Is that kosher?'

'Some rabbi in America has pronounced it so. Good enough for me. Maybe not for my waistline, but...'

Hélène's waistline was beyond redemption, though Jack was too polite to comment. But he ordered from the bar, a cognac for himself. She asked him about Oran, filled in some of the gaps about the work she'd done alongside another American, King, who'd helped the *résistants* in Casa.

'This is the last place I'd have expected to find you, though' he said. 'And your meeting – don't let me spoil anything.'

'I'm far too early. Excited, I suppose.'

He guessed the frock was new though it was, for Hélène, typically understated. Battleship grey, black military piping.

'That's intriguing. Hot date, Nella?' *Une aventure torride*, he'd said, realised he might have overdone it. But she laughed, slapped his arm. Then she looked around, furtively.

'Promise you won't say anything?' she whispered. He nodded enthusiastically, more pleased than he'd like to admit at simply being with his old friend again. 'But you know about the film?'

'*The* film, you mean? The one we're not going to get to see?'

'Just the point. I'm not sure how – well, I had this notion, *Monsieur* Telford.' She laughed. 'You remember the mention you gave about the committee? The article? Probably not the article at all. But, one way or the other, our work here came to the attention of Jack Warner. *That* Jack Warner, yes. I hear all sorts of stories about *Monsieur* Warner but I have to give him credit for this. He'd promised to donate the proceeds from the release of the film here in Morocco, and now, with no release here after all, a donation all the same – to the committee.'

Jack didn't know a huge amount about the Warner brothers, but he knew *this* much – that they'd been Polish *émigrés*, Jewish, and for a few years, been financing anti-fascist productions, *Confessions of a Nazi Spy* and a few others. Now, this one. Would anybody else have invested so much money in a movie about refugees? Even one starring Bogart.

'Donation?' he said. 'Enough to get excited about?'

'I'm not supposed to know.' She glanced around again. 'But it looks like…' Her voice dropped, to even less than a murmur. 'Nine thousand dollars.'

He almost spilled his drink.

'My god, Nella, that's…'

'Half a million *francs*, yes, I know. You're here alone?'

'As it happens, I came with *Mademoiselle* Baker.'

'You came here with...'

'Long story,' said Jack. There was a ripple of applause from those sitting at the tables. Piano player taking the stage. 'But yes, Josephine Baker. And her friend? Jacques Hébert?'

'Hébert,' she said. It wasn't a question. Something...

'That *is* his name, I suppose?'

'Why should you doubt it?' she replied, just a little too quickly. Then changed the subject. 'And I still have your records, of course. Sergio's sketchbook. The prints made a tidy profit, by the way. Another contribution to the fund. Maybe not half a million *francs*, but they've become quite a commodity, all the same.'

'Hang on to the records for me. The sketchbook as well. I'm still stuck at the Touring. But listen, Nella, you shared one secret with me – what about Hébert?'

He took her arm, led her away from the bar, to make room for others waiting to be served. The pianist tinkled away at *Stardust*.

'I think you might be stretching our friendship, Jack.' Her face set. This was a Hélène Bénatar he'd not encountered before. 'Have you no better things to worry about? You know how many new refugees we have here? You know what they're running from now?' He shook his head, not sure how to respond. 'A few months ago, we had some arrivals from Latvia. They brought word of a massacre near Riga.' She turned away, sipped at her Coca-Cola. 'The forest there. Twenty-five thousand. All Jews. From the Riga ghetto. Twenty-five thousand. Of course, nobody believed them. It was too monstrous. Even me – I just didn't want to hear. But then there were others. The same story. A new one, as well. From near Odessa. This time, thirty thousand, all Jews again. Five thousand of them burned alive.'

It turned his stomach just to think about it. Like Fox's news from Prague. Lidice.

'You're sure about this?'

If anybody else had been telling him these stories – anybody but Hélène...

'You know, Jack? If ever in my life I'd have wished to be wrong, it would be now. But these aren't isolated cases. Not any more. Of all the things we already knew about the Nazis, their cruelties. But this? This is something else. Tip of the iceberg maybe? Others we don't know about yet. Some policy change?'

'Policy change? No, Nella, you can't think… It's war. For christ's sake, bad enough at any time. But against the Nazis? The Japanese? You remember Nanjing. How many Chinese civilians did the Japs kill? Forty thousand? Fifty? More? There *will* be atrocities. Savages are capable of so much. But policy?'

'Have you any idea, Jack, how many the Germans slaughtered in South West Africa? That was policy. Belgians in the Congo? Policy. The Italians in Ethiopia? Policy. How many inventive ways did they find to butcher women and children? Thirty thousand of them. How any god could allow this… And the Germans even have a word for it. *Völkermeuchelnden*. Folk-murdering. Can you imagine? Having a word for the eradication of an entire people?'

'How could *anybody* – imagine that?'

He put his arm around her shoulders. Yet he hoped to garner comfort from the embrace, as much as to offer compassion. He'd often, in Spain, and since, felt as though he'd fallen down the proverbial rabbit-hole. Yet there was so much, now, things entirely beyond his ability to comprehend in this world. The endless weight of horrors, each one seemingly heavier than the last, which had formed their daily normality for year after year. He'd been thinking about his father's suicide a great deal lately. No longer visited by ghostly apparitions but plagued, instead, with reminders. Those lines from Sassoon. *I knew a simple soldier boy.* The final stanza.

> *You smug-faced crowds with kindling eye*
> *Who cheer when soldier lads march by,*
> *Sneak home and pray you'll never know*
> *The hell where youth and laughter go.*

And he'd begun to wonder whether, perhaps, it hadn't been simply personal terror which had led his father to kill himself but, rather, the pressure of a more global insanity.

'I pray,' she said. 'I pray none of us may never have to imagine such a thing. You see now, how important is this money from

Warner? They've tried to close me down so many times. But how many more might we save with this?'

He held her at arm's length, each of them conscious of the stares they attracted.

'Yes,' said Jack. 'I see. And I'm guessing that's your man.' He'd also noticed a fellow waiting at the Anfa's reception desk. Short and stocky, elegantly suited, wire-rimmed spectacles, a diminutive Glen Miller. 'But I don't think I'll stay for the show. Lost my appetite for it now. Catch up tomorrow?'

She kissed both his cheeks again.

'I'm sorry, Jack. I had no right – my burden...'

'What are friends for?' he said. 'But god, Nella...'

'Let's talk tomorrow,' she said. 'And before you go, I suppose it doesn't matter now.' She hesitated. 'The man you call Hébert...'

At reception, the wire-rimmed spectacles were being pointed in Hélène's direction. She gave the man a friendly wave, fought to compose herself once more.

'He's with the resistance? Hébert his *nom de guerre?*'

'More or less. You're resistance as well now, *Monsieur* Telford, no? Entitled to know, I suppose. He's Jacques Abtey.'

'Should that mean something?'

'He was a big wheel in the *Deuxième Bureau*. Followed de Gaulle to London. Now? So far as I now, he still reports direct to the general on counter-intelligence.'

At the reception desk he collected his hat, asked the lilac-liveried Moroccan concierge whether he might arrange a taxi back to town. He admired Josephine Baker even more now, travelling with one of de Gaulle's agents. Not just *any* agent either.

'No need for that, old boy.' Jack spun around. It was Kingsley Welch. 'Going your way myself.'

Funny, thought Jack, how you can experience such unalloyed joy at bumping into one old acquaintance and then, on the other hand...

'Thanks,' he said, 'but the taxi will be fine.'

'Oh, I insist.' Before Jack could stop him, Welch snapped instructions, in Arabic, to the bell-boy already running for the foyer to do Telford's bidding. Welch flicked a small silver coin, twenty-five *centimes*, in the lad's direction. 'Come on,' he said. 'Car's outside.'

'Just coincidence?' said Jack, shivering as he hit the cold night air and hoping to god it wouldn't be some open-topped job – the sort of thing he imagined Welch might favour. He stopped on the outside steps, lit a cigarette.

'Coincidence?' Welch looked back up at him. 'I don't know what – oh, you mean…? Great heavens, you've a high opinion of yourself, haven't you? Simply business brings me here, Telford. But I suppose I might think the same thing. *You* being here. A lesser man might think you were spying on *me*.'

'Would I have some reason for spying?' Jack scoffed, but in his heart he knew, of course, that he did. 'Not staying for the show either?'

'Hardly my scene,' Welch told him with distaste. 'Something in common, at least, Telford?' He walked across to a line of expensive parked cars. 'Never saw the attraction, myself. Here we are.'

A Mercedes 770 but, thankfully, with the top raised.

'Doing well for yourself,' said Jack. 'It's just like…'

'No, Telford. It's not *like* von Wulisch's car – it *is* von Wulisch's car. Or was. I inherited the thing after he escaped to Tangier. Rather, the *company* inherited. Services rendered, you know?'

Jack settled himself into the soft black leather aromas of the passenger seat and Welch turned the key.

'Standard oil,' said Jack. 'Big holding in IG Farben, no? How does that sit with the shareholders – helping Hitler's economy with Yankee dollars?'

'Just their gasoline business,' said Welch. The engine purred, headlights picking up the Anfa's gateposts. 'And most shareholders of my acquaintance don't care a fig for anything but their dividends. In any case, I'm not exactly on the payroll, old fellow. Private consultant, really.'

'Ever get home?'

'Home – Blighty, you mean?'

He spun the car around the bends, heading down the Anfa hill towards the racecourse.

'Isn't it – home?'

'I have a place in Surrey. Wasn't born there, though. No, born abroad.'

'Germany, by any chance?'

'Good god, whyever should you think so?'

They sped along the Avenue de l'Hippodrome.

'A guess.'

'India, as it happens. Broadened my horizons. Opened my mind, so to speak. You know, you should have come with us to the Continental. Our night in Cairo. Valerie and Brenda, what? Great heavens, put lead in my pencil, the two of them. Fancied that little dumpling of yours, though. What was her name?'

'Pamela,' said Jack. 'Her name was Pamela.'

'And did you…?'

Telford peered through the side window. In the darkness it was hard to tell but he was sure they'd turned down the Boulevard Danton.

'Oh, all night. Like rabbits.' He'd aimed for sarcasm, but it hadn't worked. 'Is this the scenic route?'

'All night, eh? Good for you, old boy. Good for you. And I just need to drop something off.'

Jack shook his head, knew he should have taken the taxi.

'Been back, to Cairo?' he said.

'More often than I should have liked. But needs must when the devil drives.'

'Trade must flow, yes? More important than ever when there's a war to be won, I suppose. But interesting you mention our little adventure there. Thought I saw you the next day. At the museum.'

'The Antiquities? Now, there's one place I've never been. You know what it's like on business trips. Get there, hotel, a few dusty meetings, travel back again. That's why our little interlude with your young ladies was so pleasurable.'

'Where are we heading, exactly? Habous?'

'One of the tobacco factories.'

Perhaps it was the speed at which Welch took some of the corners, perhaps something else entirely, but Jack had begun to feel nauseous, light-headed, as though he might faint.

'Look, I could do with some fresh air,' he said. 'Would you mind just dropping me here?'

'Don't be absurd, old boy. After bringing you so far out of your way? I'll just be five minutes and then we'll drop you off. Put you out of your misery, what?'

They swung up a steep hill, the lights of the city spreading out below them, to the left.

'It was the museum gardens, actually,' Jack explained. 'Where I saw you. Not inside the Antiquities itself.'

'No, not me,' said Welch, and in the faint glow from the dashboard, Telford saw the fellow's teeth, a rictus grin, the hawk-like beak bathed in red.

'If you say so. But these trade deals, did you ever come across Sir Aubrey Carter-Holt, by any chance?'

'Isn't he Secretary for Overseas Trade? Never had the pleasure. Though I think we're about to be graced with his presence. But you, old boy? An acquaintance of your own, Telford?'

There was something about his tone. The words forced through pursed lips. He was lying, Jack was certain. The headlights beamed across the sign for the Pasteur Institute, then the bulk of the military hospital just beyond. What was it Fox had said? *You should leave that one alone, Telford. About Welch, at least.* Maybe he'd have more success asking Josephine's companion.

'Never had the pleasure either,' said Jack. 'Nothing, really. But his name came up recently. Somebody else I bumped into. Macmillan?'

'Harold? Well, I am impressed. Certainly put yourself around, my friend, don't you? Ah, here we are.' He pulled up on a piece of waste ground, factory buildings in front of them. A fence. *Compagnie des Tabacs du Maroc.* 'As I said, need to drop something off. Why don't you get out and have a smoke while I'm away. Promise I won't be long.'

Jack didn't need to be told twice. He climbed out of the Mercedes, fished for his Gauloises, while Welch went to the boot, removed a long package, shouted another assurance he'd only be a few minutes, disappeared towards the tobacco factory's gate.

The flicker of his lighter's flame illuminated the cupped fingers shielding the end of his cigarette from Casablanca's chilly night wind.

Maybe not so clever to leave the warmth of the car's comfort after all, he thought. But he took a drag on the cigarette, anyway, watched the red glow.

He considered Welch. Was he just being stupid? The fellow was a boor, but maybe no more than that. And what was it, precisely, he suspected. Welch a German spy or something? On the basis of a single conversation he may, or may not, have overheard – possibly not even German anyhow.

Cold. Exposed to the elements. Exposed – well, just exposed. He looked around in the darkness, silent except for a dog in the distance, could discern almost nothing but the burning beacon of his Gauloise.

Then he wondered about Welch's parcel. For here – tobacco factory? Two in the morning?

He threw down the cigarette, ground it out quickly with his heel, cursed himself as it threw up a shower of sparks.

Telford dropped into a crouch at the side of the Mercedes. What had he heard? Something, nothing? He pulled down the brim of his trilby against the breeze, turned up the collar of his jacket, thanked god he'd gone for the brown, not the white – before scuttling away from the car, into the darkness, and the long walk home.

'Well?' he'd said to Réchard as he watched his friend play the roulette wheel in the Transatlantique. 'Is it true?'

It was two days later and he'd cursed himself for an idiot ever since. He'd seen no more of Welch. Just a note, left for him at the Touring.

Very rude, to wander off. Did I offend you? Then the hotel tells me they have nobody called Telford. Just somebody answering your description. Well, Mister O'Hare. A mystery.

If Jack wanted to ask that fellow Abtey about him, he'd have to wait until Josephine Baker emerged from Marrakech again, or wherever she was now. And Louis hadn't been any help either, not about Welch, but these latest rumours…

'I have no idea what you mean, *mon ami*.' Réchard set down a generous stack of chips upon the green baize. Evens.

Jack had lowered his voice. This was surely the hot tip Bill Eddy had given him, about heading to Casablanca.

'My sources tell me there's a cavalcade every morning,' he whispered. 'From the Villa Dar-es-Saada to the Hôtel Anfa.'

'Probably some son of a whore film star or other.' The roulette wheel spun, slowed, rattled towards another win for the house.

'Bogart, you mean?' Jack laughed. 'But no, this isn't the name we've heard. And no film star would have required them to turn the whole Anfa Hill into the Maginot Line. Not even a mouse could get through this amount of tanks and barbed wire without a pass signed by the Almighty.'

'Then perhaps you should keep that name to yourself, Telford. No? Though your sources appear to have had no trouble getting the information out.'

But within a few days the world and its dog seemed to know. Roosevelt and Churchill come to town, holding a conference at the Anfa. News correspondents had been excluded from the conference itself and, perhaps because of this, the world suddenly remembered Jack was in Casablanca. Wires waiting for him at the hotel. One from Sydney Elliott and *Reynold's News*. Another from Bunnelle, naturally.

And one from Arturo Barea, the contact at the BBC made for him by Father Lobo. He'd mentioned Barea to Paquita. She knew him, of course. From Valencia. Didn't really have a good word to say for the man. Not really.

'Socialist,' she'd said, as though it was a dirty word. 'One of those who betrayed Negrín.'

'No,' Jack had said. 'He was in London by then.'

'You know what I mean, comrade.'

But the messages – from Barea, from Sydney, from Bunnelle – all the same. Did he have contacts? Somebody who could secure an exclusive interview perhaps. And Louis had taken him to the Excelsior, where forty of the free world's correspondents had been clandestinely flown in from Algiers and Tunisia, along with some of the French staff officers. Something that might interest him, Réchard had said, and made the introductions. A French captain who'd been involved with those Spaniards now serving in the African Free Corps.

Yes, this captain had said, those bloody Reds were decent fighters. But just try to get them to follow a simple order without it being questioned. Impossible. Whole company of them. Putz in command – French really, and a hero of the Great War. But been a colonel, it seemed, in the International Brigades in Spain and now serving here again, helping to set up a whole battalion of mainly Spanish troops, inside the Corps. And one of the buggers – Putz's adjutant – had issued them all with little red, yellow and purple flags they'd sewed onto their uniforms. And Putz had let them.

'Did this fellow have a name?' Jack had asked, though he was certain he already knew.

'Oh yes,' the captain told him. 'Quite a name. Granell,' he'd said. 'That was it. Granell.'

Indeed. Telford remembered Amado had mentioned Putz, in Oran. He got to work on the copy straight away.

No Pasarán! Spanish Republicans in the fight for North Africa.
And a byline.

While thousands of others, ready to fight, lie languishing in Vichy's concentration camps, as North Africa correspondent, Jack Telford, *now explains.*

Well, this was the gist of it.

He'd thought about including a neat little mention of the two Spanish Republican fishermen who'd helped the American landings, and that had taken him to the harbour, where he'd found Manolo and old Uncle Emilio, mending their nets in the shadow of the valiant French battleship *Jean Bart*, bombed to hell by American planes during the naval engagement.

'Can't say we did much,' said Manolo. 'Sorted their charts a bit. Gave them a few pointers, here and there. But do us a favour, English? Leave us out of your story. The Frenchies who helped the Yanks have all ended up in those bloody Vichy camps. We'd rather not join them.'

The January sun was sinking fast into the west, bathing the sky with crimson.

'And this conference they're having.' Emilio hawked and spat on the quayside. 'Comrade Stalin not here?'

'Hands full at Stalingrad, I think,' Jack replied.

'Then there's another yarn for you,' laughed the old man. 'Good one, as well. How some of our boys who ended up in Russia are now manning the anti-aircraft guns at Stalingrad, shooting down the same German bastards that bombed them in Barcelona. *Verdad*, boy?' he said to Manolo.

Jack had heard the same story from Paquita. The friend of a friend of a friend. But she'd had another tale. About the other Spaniards fighting in Russia, the fascist volunteers of the *División Azul*, fifty thousand of them, presently at Leningrad. A down-payment, perhaps, for whatever services Hitler would render next to Franco? Perhaps here, in Morocco.

The piece was good, though. He knew it would appeal to Elliott, maybe to Barea as well. It did. Another wire, the slender slip of yellow paper, offering him accreditation as a BBC European Service correspondent – but specifically for the Spanish Section.

And a demand. Telford needed to send the copy recorded in his own voice. A touch of sarcasm. About this being a broadcasting corporation.

Recording – why hadn't he thought of that? But his more immediate problem came with a second message waiting for him at the hotel. A summons, to meet *Sidi* Muhammad. A car being sent to fetch him.

He had to wait until His Sherifian Majesty, Lord Muhammad ben Youssef, had finished the Sunrise prayers.

'My friend,' he said, 'you will take tea?'

'Gladly, Highness,' Jack replied, and they all settled upon the floor cushions. The sultan, his two sons, his twelve wise men – all of them in pure white hooded *djellabas*. And two more enormous warriors from his Black Guard.

The palace here in Casa might not be quite so impressive as Rabat, but it was a close-run thing. The Moorish gateways, the shaded courtyards, the water gardens, the orange and lemon groves, through which Jack was escorted to reach *Sidi* Muhammad's private quarters, all spoke of a culture, an artistic beauty, stretching back thirteen hundred years, unbroken.

'When I saw you in Rabat,' said the sultan, 'you mentioned a

Spanish woman, a teacher. You know it is not normal. A woman teacher. I count myself a modern man, *Monsieur* Telford, yet modernity has its limits, as the *Makhzan* constantly reminds me. Still, I believe, if our friend Gabizon was here...' He grimaced, needed a moment to compose himself, again. 'Well, you will be so kind as to furnish my secretary with her details. We shall offer her a position, see whether this modern though troubled world may cope with such innovation.'

'I'm sure you won't be disappointed, Highness.' Jack bowed, accepted a glass of mint tea. A piece of orange cake, dripping in citrus syrup. 'But I'm guessing perhaps you wished to speak with me about something else?'

'Isaac Gabizon again,' he replied. 'There are times when I miss his simple goodness greatly. And now – well, the French, the Germans, the English, they are not too difficult to understand. But the Americans, and your Mister Churchill...'

'You met him, sir?'

'Last night. Roosevelt's villa. My eldest son...' He set his arm about the boy's shoulder. 'And my two closest ministers...' A couple of the wise men nodded their heads at this acknowledgement. 'To meet the president, the president's own son – a fine young man. A soldier, did you know?'

'I didn't, Highness. The whole conference has been been somewhat shrouded in secrecy.'

'How could it not be so? They have an entire war to plan. I presented the president with a ceremonial dagger, though I am not sure he appreciated the gesture.'

Noguès had also been there, of course. And Patton. Robert Murphy, Roosevelt's eyes and ears in North Africa. And Harry Hopkins, the president's eyes and ears, they said, just about everywhere else.

'The president will want to know, I suppose,' said Jack, licking the syrup from his fingers, 'what the future holds, between America and Morocco, when this is all over. More than just a trade deal, I'd guess.'

'They offer us Moroccan engineers, scientists, trained at American universities. For now, food and machinery. Much more.

No promise of independence, yet I believed I saw, in the president's eyes...'

Above their heads, a dove fluttered, tried and failed to find a landing place among the domed ceiling's stucco stalactites of gold and cerulean blue.

'Noguès must have been furious,' said Jack. 'The beginning of the end for French Morocco?'

'Not as furious as your Churchill. The Americans have a new vision, I believe. Empire by proxy. But Churchill believes in the old and outdated image of imperialism, does he not? He became more impatient – more rude – as the evening went on. But my son...' he hugged the boy again, 'who is a great observer of such things, believes it was merely the meal's absence of both alcohol and tobacco – in deference to our beliefs, naturally – which might have incited his poor behaviour.'

Jack sipped at the sweet mint tea, the dove now strutting on the floor between the guards.

'Great heavens,' he said. 'No whisky? No cigars? I'm surprised he stayed at all.'

'He did not stay for long, of course. A dispatch rider came to fetch him. Some important business, he said. A pretense, naturally. And when he came back, yes, the smell. Tobacco. Whisky. The president, I think, is a great man. But the other one...'

'I think, without Churchill, sir, we might have sealed Britain's fate in the same way as poor France. Some cheap armistice. A deal with Hitler that would have seen us sell our soul for another piece of paper. He might not be a Roosevelt, but a mistake, Highness, to underestimate him.'

'Good advice, *Monsieur* Telford. You see, my son?' He turned to his older boy. 'We must not underestimate Mister Churchill simply because he drinks too much whisky.'

'But the Jews, sir. And the Vichy concentration camps. Is there news?'

There was a flurry among the white *djellabas*, protests from those two ministers who'd accompanied the sultan to dinner with the president. Outrage that this foreigner should dare interrogate Lord Muhammad. But the sultan waved aside their objections.

'These are matters close to my own heart,' he said. 'We have done our best for the Jews, to make sure they would not be treated as they have been in Germany. Or, indeed, in Vichy. They are my people, after all. Part of the *shlata*, the salad of races, for which I am responsible. But then I cannot be seen to be setting Jews above Muslims. It is a fine balance. So, I have agreed with General Noguès some restrictions upon the Jews which may remain. For now. But the camps? I have insisted they should be emptied. I remember the report you wrote for me, about Bou Arfa. It offends me to know, even now, that terrible place remains open.'

'I'm trying to bring this iniquity to the eyes of the world as well, Highness. It isn't much, perhaps, but...'

'No, it is a great thing. For does our Holy Qur'an not explain how Allah has taught us to write with the pen, and thus the pen helps teach mankind that which it does not know? But could it be more? Of course. Did you know your Juju General is here?'

The pen, thought Jack. Well, I hope the Qur'an is right. But when the pen in question once belonged to Communist Juan Negrín? He hoped the blessing still stood.

'De Gaulle, sir? You heard the legends then,' Jack laughed.

'Are they – mere legends? Do not say so, my friend. We are a simple people. We believe such things. But you are close to him, I think. He arrived in Casablanca just after the dinner was finished. Speak with him, *Monsieur* Telford. As Isaac would have done. Learn for me, how a French government, led by de Gaulle, would view our prospective friendship with America – would view our desire for independence.'

The Juju General, as it happened, also needed Telford, though for a different purpose entirely.

A car had been sent for him – or, rather, for *Monsieur* O'Hare. Delivered him to a nondescript villa on the seaward side of the Anfa Hill, the name of the place boarded over – for security reasons, presumably – barbed wire all along the top of the boundary wall, and American GIs patrolling the gate and surrounding area. As it happened, the entire area was an armed camp.

'Do I need to explain?' said de Gaulle, by way of a greeting, once Jack had been escorted through to the tiled terrace. There was a private swimming pool, though empty of water. 'You see? My person stands for Fighting France herself, but confined here more like a captive than a head of state. A villa not good enough for Patton but which must serve for de Gaulle.'

The general stood from his poolside table, stubbed out one cigarette and lit another, waved it towards the back of the house.

'Good to see you again, sir,' said Jack, 'all the same.'

He wondered how anybody could manage to maintain that air of ramrod rigidity, both physical and psychological, even while wearing a dressing gown, pyjamas and slippers. But de Gaulle certainly possessed the skill.

'I met Roosevelt today. Hardly the discussion for which I hoped. For pity's sake, the fellow even had his secret servicemen hidden behind the curtains. As though I might be one of his Chicago gangsters.'

Jack could remember only rare occasions when he'd seen the general so amused.

'I suppose, after Darland's assassination...'

'But is this not the point? If anybody was responsible for that little affair, the Americans, surely.'

'Sadly, they're a people who often judge the rest of the world by the standards of their own criminals. A view which eclipses all else – sometimes stops them seeing the difference between foe and friend. The wood for the trees, as we say.'

'*Bien*, the very reason we need more from you, *Monsieur* Telford. The world must know – they must see us for the forest we are. That here we stay. Free France.'

'I was rather hoping I might be allowed to rejoin General Leclerc. I'm guessing he'll now be be given the go ahead for the Fezzan?'

'It is already ours. Within two weeks, all southern Libya will be in our hands. Another two weeks, Philippe will have cut his way through to the Mediterranean, linked up with Montgomery.'

Almost on cue, the sounds of the ocean came to them, breakers on the beach just a few hundred yards away, the scent of salt and seaweed on the breeze.

'Tripoli, sir? I should be there.'

He thought about the Chad Regiment, about the distances Eze Tolabye, Abia the Bassa, Leclerc's Frenchmen and Spaniards would have travelled to reach their goal, to finally help drive the Germans and Italians into the sea.

'I arranged for the Information Service to keep you informed,' said de Gaulle, and set off around the swimming pool's perimeter. Jack followed him. 'You may take from their updates whatever you please for your writing. But if you wish to remain accredited to the press corps of Fighting France, you will stay here, focus on making sure our part has the prominence it deserves. The whole destiny of France, her future, depends on this. On this alone.'

He meant, Jack supposed, his own destiny as well.

'As you wish, General,' he said. No choice but to comply, he supposed. Not for now, at least. 'And it might help that I now seem to be accredited to the BBC. European Service. Only the Spanish section, but if I can pitch the right story...'

'The BBC? They will only broadcast whatever pleases and placates their masters. They may pretend to present balance – give equal mention to Giraud and Vichy on one hand, to de Gaulle and Fighting France on the other, but they know there are no two sides to this story. Simply the truth of Free France, and the deception of Vichy. Yet their broadcasters contine to present Giraud as though he might stand for the future. He does not. Both of us kept from the conference table as though they are thus equitably dealing with two separate embodiments of France. The truth? Churchill and Roosevelt keep Giraud out because he is irrelevant. They keep out de Gaulle because they fear the thing he represents.'

'I could not possibly comment, sir,' Jack smiled. 'Biting the hand that may feed me, you know?'

The general stopped near the shrubbery lining the outside wall, lit yet another cigarette – Gitanes, Jack noted. The general waved the packet at him.

'Impossible,' said de Gaulle. 'To find decent tobacco like this in England anymore. When we move the capital of Free France from Brazzaville to Algiers, we shall have solved this problem, at least.'

'Algiers, not Rabat? The sultan will be interested to know.'

De Gaulle literally looked down his long nose at him.

'Precisely how many masters do you serve, Telford? How many *are* the hands that feed you?'

'Not really the right question, general. More to do with the ghosts of the dead, sir – those keeping me awake at night with their demands.'

De Gaulle shivered.

'We all have our ghosts, *monsieur*. Yet *Sidi* Muhammad ben Youssef is very much alive. What is it he wants?'

'To know how you would view closer ties between Morocco and the Americans. Among other things.'

The general shrugged, looked up at the night sky, the stars now visible as the earlier fog began to clear. He inhaled deeply.

'Interesting,' he said. 'Whatever Churchill may decide, I shall never play second fiddle to Giraud. I remain free to pursue the dreams of France reborn. To win the war? Yes, of course. But that, in turn, is secondary to the renaissance of France herself. The French Empire as well. Algeria is another thing, but if the price of winning Roosevelt's support is a loosening of our ties to Morocco, a tacit recognition of Washington's ambitions there – a price worth considering, perhaps.'

'And the camps, General. In Morocco *and* Algeria. The Spanish Republicans? The Jewish resistance fighters Darlan and Giraud locked up there? Loyal friends of Free France, but now in those stinking camps.'

'All roads, it seems, lead to Algiers. We win Roosevelt to our cause – quietly, of course. Tacit understanding that Free France is the only future. Not Giraud. We signal this understanding by their recognition of Algiers as our new capital. We empty the camps, swell our ranks, gift Giraud some position to help smoothe his feathers. And then, all that remains is to liberate Paris. Shall you be there, *Monsieur* Telford, when we set Paris free once more?'

Two days later, the conference at an end, it seemed, and there was a new invitation. All those correspondents invited to Casablanca should assemble at noon in the garden of the Villa Dar-es-Saada. Jack's documentation got him inside. Not a cloud in the sky.

Churchill and the French generals de Gaulle and Giraud strolling out through the villa's rear doors to take their chairs – white dining chairs. Then Roosevelt carried out to take his own place. Camera shutters clicked. Movie cameras whirred. Barbed wire gleamed in the blazing Morocco sun. Statements and questions. Roosevelt's declaration there would be no surrender accepted from Germany, from Italy or from Japan unless it was unconditional.

To Jack it all seemed somewhat premature. A counting of chickens, perhaps. But he took notes anyway, and he watched the others until he found what he was looking for. There, a dictaphone. Portable – a Type C, the model favoured by the BBC.

'Good snapshot anyway, I suppose,' Jack had said casually to the owner when it was all over and the machine was being packed back into its case.

If there'd been an expectation of some joint statement from Giraud and de Gaulle, they must have been bitterly disappointed. But at least there'd been a shaking of hands. Not once but twice – in case any of the cameramen had missed it first time around.

'All they needed, eh?' The fellow had a Scots accent – Edinburgh, Jack thought. Early thirties, dressed in the shorts and khaki shirt of Montgomery's Eighth Army. 'Dunnett, by the way,' he said. 'Bob.'

Jack was impressed. Dunnett had quite a reputation, introduced his companion. Charlie Collingwood – ten years younger than Dunnett, Jack calculated, but a familiar name. One of the Morrow Boys, covering the war for CBS News, and boasting the very latest equipment, a Recordgraph. Collingwood demonstrated. Telford offered them dinner, later, at the Languedoc, fascinated them with his tales of Spain – the American too young to have been there, and Dunnett resentful he'd not had the sense to get out there rather than allowing himself to be trapped in the Beeb's Scotland service.

The following day, the Anfa now being all but deserted again, Jack treated them to lunch there, and afterwards he was rewarded by Dunnett allowing him to use the Type C, though only after a fair amount of tuition.

'A bit like Pandora's Box,' Dunnett had told him. 'Setting your own voice free. You'll not like the sound of it. Nobody does. It's quite a trick. And the big thing is not trying to be Alvar Lidell or Frank Phillips. Your own personality, that's what we need to hear. Keep it deep, relaxed but in command. Not flat but not up and down like a bloody songbird either. Like speaking to a friend, but with authority. And always warm up your voice beforehand. Always. Warm it up. Only get one shot at this. Oh, and before you start, for outside broadcasts, listen to what's around. Some ambient sound, very good. But nobody wants to listen if they can't hear the words for the bombs going off in the background.'

Jack recorded the piece. About Putz's Spanish battalion, and about the camps, but also a line about Fighting France, about de Gaulle. On one of the ten-inch discs, Dunnett agreeing to make arrangements for it to be dispatched safely to Barea in London, along with his own coverage.

'Impressive,' said Jack, as Dunnett carefully lifted the arm and pick-up from the black acetate.

'A bit old hat, don't you think?' Collingwood laughed.

'Reliable,' Bob snapped. 'And only thirty of these little beauties in circulation,' he said, which did nothing to assuage Telford's guilt when, the following day, Dunnett and Collingwood were flown out again, believing all their equipment safely stowed on board while, in reality, two intrepid urchins from the medina had, for a very modest amount of *bakshish*, obligingly managed to offload the Type C again.

Yes, the guilt. If it had simply been to fulfill his commitment to Barea, he probably would have settled for just sending one disc, left it there, waited to see whether a machine of his own might have been forthcoming. Though improbable. But if he was going to do as de Gaulle required, regular pieces about Free France – well, in that case the Type C was no more than a wartime procurement.

Jack would have to explain his acquisition at some stage, he supposed, replenish the case's stock of discs, but at least he had six in his possession. Enough for now.

The truck hit him four weeks later.

It hit him on the same day news arrived that de Gaulle's predictions about driving the Germans and Italians into the sea were not going to become reality without heartache along the way. In Tunisia, Rommel had launched an attack against the Americans in the Kasserine Pass, inflicting heavy losses. The offensive had eventually been halted, but at great cost.

Jack had been meeting with some of those same urchins, the ones he now called his Baker Street Irregulars. Their shadowing of Welch hadn't produced very much so far. Seemingly innocuous business meetings. But two trips on the night train to Tangier. And, more recently dinner at Bousbir with a man the lads had taken great pleasure in describing as *dhakar almaeiz*. The billy goat? They'd illustrated – a long and straggly beard, an Imperial. Chamson, Jack had decided. It had to be. The wretch now running the organisation – here in Casa, at least – that had grown from the fascist thugs of Darnand's SOL, now calling itself *La Milice*, with the blessing of Laval at Vichy, and of Noguès also, it seemed. Prided themselves on being the true resistance – the resistance to the *résistants*. It was a topsy-turvy world.

He'd seen some of them while he was waiting for the boys to appear in the market on the Place de Marrakech. A bunch of thugs. Almost uniformed, dark jackets and wide berets, pasting posters to the medina wall. Image of a red hammer and sickle daubed over by a white cross. The legend, *Contre Le Communisme*. At the bottom, *Milice Française*. One of Réchard's *gendarmes* watching them do it.

And Welch somehow connected to these fascists? Jack had wondered.

Yet, this particular day, when his Irregulars finally showed up, they'd brought him something special. From Welch's rooms at the Transatlantique. It was a passport. One of many, the boys said, hidden beneath the bed. A German passport. Welch's picture. But the name? Konrad Wagner.

'You must take it back,' Jack had told them. 'He will know – if it's missing.'

'Take it back, Lord?' said the leader of the ragamuffins. 'It has no value?'

He'd had to pay them double for their return burglary, and he just hoped to hell Welch wouldn't notice it had been disturbed.

But one of many? I bloody knew it, Jack said to himself as he stepped into the road.

To be fair, he had no idea what happened. One moment thinking about Welch, the next...

Somebody yelled. *Antabah!* He remembered the warning.

Then nothing. Not a damned thing. Until he surfaced again. The civil hospital.

Lucky, they'd told him. Broken leg, but only a minor fracture. A couple of months to heal, if he was careful. Three cracked ribs. Abrasions, his face and neck a mess. But the concussion, that's what seemed to trouble them most. His headache. His confusion. Swelling in his leg, so the doctors temporarily splinted only the calf. A few days to let it settle before a full cast. Plenty of time for him to think. About Welch. Or was it Wagner? Bizarre bloody coincidence. One minute paying the urchins to take back the damned passport, the next – hit by a truck. And why need fake passports unless...?

But, as he stared up at the ceiling fan, it struck him he was guilty of the same crime. Faked papers.

'Well,' said Louis, when he came to visit, 'as you might expect in the medina, nobody saw or heard a thing. It's a miracle you got to the hospital. If it hadn't been for our patrol – were you robbed by the way?'

Patrol? thought Jack. Probably the same wretch who'd stood by and watched those bastards from the *Milice* putting up their posters.

'Didn't have anything worth stealing, I don't think,' he said. And then there was that moment of panic again. 'Hang on, my jacket...'

Relief. Negrín's pen still in the pocket.

'Rounded up a few suspects, of course. But nothing. And Monique says you're welcome to stay with us for a while when they let you out. Until you're back on your feet.'

It was kind, but no, he thanked Louis. Though he'd be sure to let them them know if he needed anything else.

He arranged for a note to be sent to Hélène, just to let her know, but when they discharged him, at the end of the week, plaster cast to just above his knee, there she was, waiting for him.

'Nella,' he said. 'You didn't need...'

'No?' she laughed. 'You thought we'd let you languish at the Touring? On crutches?'

'I've almost got the hang of them now.'

'Face is a mess,' she said. 'Anyway, it's all arranged. Plenty of space at my place. You'll be more comfortable.'

He made all the polite protestations, but he was glad. And though she'd brought a car, a driver, her apartment was only a few blocks away in the Rue du Caporal Lugherini. A decent lift. A modest home, but a comfortable room for him with a narrow balcony overlooking a few shops. His old gramophone. His records. Listening to Brachah Zefira with Hélène.

She made arrangements for a friend to visit the Touring, a letter of authorisation so they could collect a few things for him, and any messages. The Type C dictaphone, of course. His books, so he finally settled to reading *L'Étranger* – riddled with guilt, naturally, since there was also a note from Francine, hoping she might see him again soon. A note from Paquita Gorroño also, astonished to have been offered a teaching post at the Imperial College, entirely out of the blue. It had made Jack smile.

Besides that, a letter from Sydney Elliott and a few copies of *Reynold's News*. The big surprise? A letter from his old friend and colleague Sheila Grant Duff. Congratulations on his broadcast from the conference. And a small world. She was now with the Beeb's European Service, their first editor of the Czech section. Though her real news – married, at last. To Noel Newsome, of all people.

Married to the boss, thought Jack. Married to *my* boss. Newsome, director of the whole European Service.

For the first time, these few connections caused Jack to stare down into a strange abyss. It had been such a simple ambition. Working for the BBC. His tenuous link to Barea a godsend, one which had paid dividends. Right place, right time – all that sort of stuff. But the European Service? How much did he know? Broadcasting in twenty-five different languages, maybe more. At least an hour of programming for each of those, every single day. *Dot-dot-dot-dash*. The V for Victory campaign. Everything from patriotic light music to morale-lifting messages, to persuading folks to chalk or paint gigantic V signs on walls in occupied territory, to secret codes and simple instructions for sabotage and mayhem in the jaunty tones of cookery instruction. It was enormous. Perhaps bigger than the rest of the BBC put together, now he came to think of it.

And Newsome at its head. Or was he? To whom did Newsome really answer? The Director General and the Board of Governors? Or the War Office? Well, whichever it was, Newsome had done a remarkable job. Established a service trusted without question for its veracity, a service for which folk all over the continent risked their lives daily, for the privilege of listening.

As Jack looked out over the rooftops of Casablanca, the familiar storks' nests, counted his hours by the cries of the *mu'azzins*, he began to realise just how much a part of the war machine he – and the Beeb's European Service – had become.

Meanwhile, Nella mothered him, fed him well, made sure he exercised, occasionally invited him to join the many meetings that took place in her living room. The refugee committee might have offices elsewhere, but most of her business seemed to be done right there.

'The money from Jack Warner couldn't have come at a better time, I expect,' he said to her, once all her associates had gone, one afternoon late in March. She'd brewed mint tea for them both.

'Double the work, double the cost,' she murmured, threw herself back into her easy chair, a rocker, as heavily upholstered as Nella herself, and a loud floral pattern which almost matched her frock. 'Still refugees escaping from just about everywhere. Now the camps starting to empty, at last. So, twice the numbers. The donation from the studio? Simply not enough. And the more we win – did you catch what Rabbi Toledano said? About Djerba?'

Tunisia. Still in German hands. Horrific stories of the way Jews had been treated there. And last month the rabbis in Djerba forced to collect a hundredweight of gold in just three hours from the community. Otherwise, the entire population of the *mellah* would be shot.

'We take Tunisia – and your committee gets to pick up the pieces from there.'

'It's never going to end, Jack. We all know it isn't. Yesterday we got news they finished emptying the ghetto at Kraków. The final three thousand, gone to the camp at Oświęcim. Auschwitz.'

'No resistance?'

'Of course. But those who fought back are all dead now. A year ago, there were fifteen thousand Jews in Kraków. Now...'

The bell in her hallway tinkled. Fox. And in company with Captain Raymond Dronne. Jack was pleased to see him again, had grown fond of the Frenchman during their time in Brazzaville. There were introductions, jokes – Telford prone to accidents – while Hélène made fresh tea.

'So this,' said Fox, waving his hand towards Jack's leg. 'The scorpion strikes again?'

'Oh, I've not thought about any of that nonsense in a long while,' Telford lied. 'And you two, what brings you both to Casa?'

How could it not have occurred to him? The scorpion itself. The calling card. Gabizon's shooting. The stabbing. Now this.

'Reconnaissance, my friend,' said Dronne. 'Checking the lie of the land hereabouts. Talk of the general's forces being regrouped – again. Needs a base, place to train.'

They were both weather-beaten. But Dronne looked especially like one of those desert dogs Jack had seen so often around Kufra. White patches around his eyes where his goggles had sat. His cheeks deeply tanned. Nose scarred from blistering. Beard now a sun-bleached brighter shade of ginger. He seemed to be moving with care, like a man still fragile from a medical procedure.

'And pretty new uniform.' Jack smiled. British battledress. Free French insignia at the shoulder.

'I think Monty took pity on us,' said Fox. 'After we fought our way through to the coast. Tripoli. Monty wanted to meet the general. Leclerc asked me to go with him. I'd been serving as his liaison with the Long Range Desert Group. He looked like something from *Beau Geste*. Not sure Monty knew quite what to make of him. Especially not when Leclerc put himself under Monty's command.'

'Good move though,' said Dronne. 'Montgomery arranged for the whole outfit to be re-equipped. British uniforms. Tin hats.'

'Oh, and the boots.' Fox laughed. 'Eze Tolabye and his boys have been singing about the boots ever since. Dance in them! Motley bunch, we are, all the same. The *tirailleurs*. French volunteers. The Spaniards. We've even got a whole lot of Greeks with us. Proper little league of nations. And we are now officially L Force. For Leclerc, what?'

'L Force – I like it,' said Jack. 'Felt like a fool, though. Told de Gaulle I'd like to be with Leclerc when he went back into the Fezzan. You'd already taken it. Wish I could have been there.'

'No, you don't.' Fox grimaced. 'The most miserable Christmas I ever spent. Never been so cold in my life. The only thing that cheered us up was the news Darlan had been killed. And then we were shot up very badly ourselves, just after. German planes. The Bassa, Abia – I know you liked him, but he bought it, I'm afraid.'

Yes, Jack had liked him. He remembered how Abia had first told them the legend about the Juju General, heard him singing *Der Luftballon* again, saw him laughing at the bloody horse roaming loose outside the Kufra fortress. He bit his lip, looked out the window, the light beginning to fade.

'So far away from home,' he said. 'Cameroon. Did you know him when you were there yourself?' he asked Dronne.

The captain shook his head and Hélène came back with the tea.

'Forgive me,' she said. 'But did I hear you mention Tripoli?'

'Indeed, *madame*,' said Fox. 'End of January. We drove in just behind the Fifty-First Highland Division. Right behind the Gordons. My god, what a day.'

'But the camps...'

Fox and Dronne exchanged a glance.

'There was a camp, yes,' said Dronne, taking his glass of tea from the silver tray. 'Just outside the town. But, *mon dieu*, the poor devils.'

'All Jews?'

'Three thousand. We freed them, *madame*. But I've never seen human beings treated like that. Skeletons...'

'Monty allocated all our medics to look after them,' said Fox, 'though I'm afraid many of them won't make it.'

Hélène shook her head, walked over to the cabinet, picked up the framed photograph of her late husband, Moses, carried it with her to her bedroom. Jack wondered how she bore it all, for each time there was news of atrocity anywhere in the world, it cut her personally, deeply.

'It wasn't good,' said Dronne, and Telford saw him wince, grip his ribs.

'Worse to come, I suppose,' Jack replied. 'But the reports – after Tripoli.'

'Monty moved up to the Mareth Line,' said Fox. 'Rommel's last big throw of the dice. And he hit us with everything he had.'

'I don't think Montgomery knew what to make of us either,' said Dronne. 'Stuck us right out on the left flank. A set of wells, Roman ruins, in the mountain pass at Ksar Ghilane, where he thought we wouldn't be any trouble – or get into any, either, maybe.'

'He just didn't reckon,' Fox said, 'on Rommel trying to outflank him that way. They must have had fifty tanks. But Leclerc sucked them into a trap. Not once but three times. Like bloody Leonidas at Thermopylae, old boy. And every time we thought they might break through, our bloody Hurricanes showed up to give them hell. Tank-busters. Tin-openers. At the end of the day, the biggest dogfight I ever saw. Must have been thirty fighters on each side. My god, what a show. But, between us all, our little bunch from Chad and Cameroon, from Spain and France, those Greek boys, a few Tommy sappers, our flyboys, we paid the buggers back for Kasserine.'

'That where you were wounded?' Jack asked Dronne.

'Fine now,' said the Frenchman. 'Just about. But longer than I would have liked in their damned hospital. So, technically, I think this is supposed to be convalescence.'

'And the Spanish comrades,' said Jack, 'all safe?'

'Safe, yes,' Dronne replied. 'But they certainly make me earn my pay. Fight like devils, though. All of them.'

'You'll be pleased to know there's a whole other batch,' Jack told him. 'Serving with this new African Free Corps. If the general's regrouping, he may be able to pick up some more recruits. And one in particular. A man called Granell. Amado Granell.'

She blew onto the stage at the Rialto in a cloud of billowing red, white and blue silk – parachute silk, perhaps – her hair tied up in a bun.

Below him, in the front stalls, several rows of American officers' uniforms, civilian suits, a few frocks. Enthusiastic clapping as the lights went down and she made her entrance, unannounced but to the strains of a small US army band in the pit.

Across the aisle from the Yanks, their Vichy opposite numbers, stern features, rigidly folded arms, not even polite applause. Jack could make out the heads of Louis and Monique among them.

In a small block along the central aisle itself, a few British dignitaries, still taking their places. Telford recognised that fellow Macmillan, Fox – immaculate in his number ones – showing him to his place.

Behind the Americans, a Free French contingent, yelling *Vive la Baker! Vive la Baker!* at the tops of their voices.

Jack, in the front row of the circle, with Hélène at his side, looked around at the rest of the audience when, without any introduction, and cutting through the stamping and cheering and wolf-whistling, she breezed straight into *J'ai deux amours*.

The rest of the thirteen hundred crimson velvet seats filled with GIs – white and black, with British Tommies, with the soldiers of Free France and Giraud's Army of Africa, god knows how many others standing at the back, or down the side aisles.

Her voice chimed from the chandeliers, reverberated from the gilded and fluted columns of the auditorium, trilled from the ornate ceiling. And when she hit the final high note, the crowd went wild, rose to its feet. Even Jack, though he needed some help from Nella, and from the walking stick he'd taken to using since the cast came off.

'Well,' he said, 'I suppose you can't please everybody.' And he nodded over to the far side of the circle, where a couple of fellows kept their seats. But not for long, one of them finally persuading the other that they should stand as well, though their applause was plainly begrudged, one of them with an undisguised sneer on his lips.

'They'll be Vichy supporters,' she murmured, offered Jack her best gap-toothed smile.

On the stage, Josephine was flapping her arms, the crossed eyes, the goofy grin, encouraging them all to sit again.

'You liked that, yes?' she said, first in English, then in perfect French. 'Well, they've got some great acts for you tonight, boys and girls. And thanks to all these gentlemen and ladies down here in the front stalls, the proceeds going to help the work of the French Red Cross.'

She performed a funny little dance, pointed at the banner hanging above her head, then sang *My Fate is in Your Hands*.

Jack had sat in almost the same seat the night before, to see *Star Spangled Rhythm*. My god, what a cast. And the songs. Hope and Crosby, Lake and Lamour. A fair number of tonight's audience must have also been there. But not, he imagined, those two over on the far side. Faces like thunder.

'Think they bought tickets?' he murmured.

'Who? That pair again? Way, way! Can't we just enjoy the show?'

He rubbed at his leg, pins and needles, while Josephine blew kisses to the crowd.

'Hey, you boys used this new V-Mail yet? Pretty neat. Think how much easier it's going to be, getting letters to your sweethearts back home.' All servicemen's letters, once they'd got past the censors, processed onto microfilm, enlarged again before delivery at the other end. Same process from the USA, back to the front. No more problems with bulky mail sacks. The whole system based here in Casa. 'And for your sweethearts to send you all their love. So, I'm going to dedicate this next one to all those girls thinking about you right now.'

C'est Lui, she sang. Her big number from *Zouzou*. But it was a strange choice. The man in question hardly sounded like a great catch. A bit of a cheat.

'*Il court après toutes les filles…*'

He runs after all the girls. Jack thought of Pépé le Moko, glanced along the row again, at those two fellows who seemed so out of place here. One of them, he decided, looked familiar.

Josephine Baker had run into a story about how much she'd loved her château in France. Milandes, she told them. Until the Germans had driven her out.

'Well,' she said, 'I think we had the last laugh there.'

Jack knew some of the story now. How she'd used the place to hide resistance fighters. Then how she'd used her performances, her social calendar, to spy on behalf of Abtey.

'But I'll get back there, one day,' she laughed. 'And then I'll be happy.'

Her next number, that little jazz classic, *Then I'll be Happy*.

Where the hell have I seen him before? Telford puzzled.

'Are you not enjoying the show, Jack?' said Nella.

'Mind if I smoke?' he replied, and lit one of his Gauloises when she told him to go ahead.

'Now, this next one,' said Josephine, 'I'm going to dedicate to a very brave lady, Mother Superior Marie Duval. I guess you all know the story by now.'

She repeated her words in French again. German dive bombers had hit Algiers the previous week, demolished an orphanage. And while the children had all been led to safety, fifteen nuns, including Mother Superior Duval, had died protecting them.

She sang *Sous le Ciel d'Afrique* to a huge round of applause.

'You see how easy it is – all you generals out there? Just look at this audience. Salt and pepper. Salt and pepper. And every one of us, true red, white and blue. Yeah, red, white and blue. The colours of our great alliance.'

She launched into *God Save The King*.

Shuffling in the seats, nobody except the Brits sure whether they should stand – though, at Macmillan's cue, they did. Some of the Yanks singing along, though wrong lyrics.

Telford leaned forward, gazed past Hélène to those two men on the farther end of the row. They didn't seem any happier and one of them, Jack now convinced himself, he'd definitely seen before.

The last line of the anthem, nobody certain what to do next. Stay standing? Sit down?

'I can't tell you how much this means to me,' said Josephine, and they sat. 'Here together. English and French. Under one set of colours. My own dear Americans as well. It's true, you know? My two loves. Paris, and America. Not that everything's peachy back home, right? So, here's a message for all you coloured boys out there. This race prejudice we all face. Just you wait 'til this war's over. I'll get to the States. Break it down.' *Break it down!* Somebody repeated, as if this were a revival meeting. There was a cheer, mainly from the black GIs, but from others who understood her, as well. 'This crazy segregation,' she shouted. 'All fight together. But win the war first, yes?'

Yes, ma'am. And she began the opening lines of *The Star-Spangled Banner.*

'O say can you see, by the dawn's early light,
What so proudly we hail'd at the twilight's last gleaming...'

Only the Americans joined her. But they did it with pride.

'No, no, stay on your feet. I want to dedicate that beautiful song,' she said, 'to all our boys who've been fighting these past two weeks at Enfidha, and then at Hill 609. But this next one – well, God bless you all.'

La Marseillaise.

Hardly a dry eye in the place. But, at the end, among the many cries of *Vive la France!* there were others shouting *Vive le Maréchal!* Still worshipping Pétain after everything that had happened.

And then he remembered. The market on the Place de Marrakech.

'The one nearest us,' he whispered into Hélène's ear. 'He's with the *Milice.*'

She was still clapping her hands, wiping a tear from her cheek. *Vive la France!*

She leaned forward to get a better look at the fellow.

'You're sure?'

'Yes – well, almost sure. He was watching them put up posters. Standing guard, that sort of thing. Bully boy. Strong-arm man.'

This being the case, though, he thought, strange they'd not joined in with the other Pétain and Laval supporters. And what were the thugs of the *Milice* doing here?

He glanced around the audience, trying to spot others who might not fit in, but nothing obvious. And, below, the same black lieutenant from the Liberty Club, Williams, springing up onto the stage while Baker took her bows.

'No, wait, wait,' he shouted. 'We've got another surprise for you. A little presentation to make.'

From the wings, de Gaulle, carrying a small box in his hand, and held against his medal ribbons. The place literally went wild. The military band struck up the opening notes of *La Marseillaise* yet again.

Josephine pressed a clenched fist against her teeth and, even from the circle, Jack could see her own tears. But whatever the general said to her in those next few moments was entirely lost in the roar of the audience – most of the audience, anyhow.

He presented the box to her, then stood back and saluted.

Baker opened it, held the box close to her own heart, then held up a small gold Cross of Lorraine. Plain as day, gleaming in the footlights. She tried to say something, but her face had crumpled with emotion.

And up there, in the front of the circle, Jack watched the two *milices* push themselves from their seats, make their way along the row, stop at the foot of the stairs, half-hidden behind a column, one of them furtively sheltering the other from prying eyes while the second thug reached deep inside his jacket.

Christ, thought Jack. He dragged himself upright, using the balcony rail.

'Gun!' he screamed, pointed his walking stick. 'Gun! That bastard's got a gun.'

'What the hell were you thinking?' said Réchard.

'It *looked* like he had a gun,' Jack replied.

'Oh, leave him alone,' said Josephine Baker. 'He meant well, didn't you, Jack? And, for pity's sake, sit down. Somebody find this man a chair.'

She sipped at a glass of champagne in her dressing room, sniffed at the blossoms in the bouquets surrounding her, the yellows, oranges and reds reflected in the table mirror.

Lieutenant Williams poured wine for her other guests, the theatre's owner, an accordionist, who was due to perform next, and a whole troupe of dancing girls in feathers and precious little else.

De Gaulle had been whisked away by his own bodyguards, and enough order restored in the Cinéma Théatre Rialto to allow the show's second half to go ahead. Jack could hear the strains of the band, a medley of Glenn Miller numbers.

'And they were *Milice*,' Telford protested, as Jacques Abtey fetched him a footstool from the corner.

'Sadly, there's no law against that,' said Louis.

'Well, you'd know, I suppose,' Jack told him. 'Sitting there with all your Vichy friends.'

He knew he sounded petulant, but couldn't help it. No gun, of course. Just a man with a cigarette lighter. And bored with the performance, he'd said. Outraged, naturally.

'It is my duty, *madame*,' Louis began, 'to apologise on behalf of the authorities here in Casablanca...'

He waved an accusing hand at Telford.

'Fiddlesticks,' she said. 'I might pay Jack to make a fuss at *all* my shows. Bit of drama, you know? And look at this.' She held up the gold cross. 'Cartier,' she whispered. 'How in the name of heck...?'

'What did he say to you, Josie?' Jack asked her. 'Out there on the stage?'

'He said they're going to make me a lieutenant as well. In the Free French air force. You think he means it?'

'All the same, one way or the other, Joséphine,' said Abtey. 'This changes things.'

'Changes things how?' she replied, but Abtey gave an almost imperceptible shake of his head, his eyes flickered towards Réchard, and Louis took the hint.

'Well, *madame*,' said Louis, just a little too loudly, 'it was my duty as *commandant* of Casablanca's *gendarmerie* to offer you this apology, but if you will excuse me – perhaps myself and *Monsieur* Telford...'

'I'd like *Monsieur* Telford to stay,' she said. 'But don't let us keep you, *Commandant*.'

Louis offered her a smile of sorts, saluted, made for the door.

'Look, Josie,' said Jack, 'maybe some other time, yes? I left Hélène...'

Where *had* he left her? It was all a bit of a blur: the commotion when he'd shouted the warning; Jack trying to hobble along the row, people getting in his way as they stood, trying to see what was happening; the two men, Jack's would-be assassins, grabbed by a couple of GIs, dragging them up the steps, through the crowd; and police whistles blowing, one of Réchard's *gendarmes* appearing from nowhere to help with the arrest; and, below, pandemonium, half the audience on its feet trying to see what was happening, the other half making for the exits, secret servicemen on the stage throwing a protective cordon around both de Gaulle and Josephine.

He put his weight on the walking stick, followed in Réchard's footsteps, Louis holding the door for him.

'We still need to talk, *Monsieur* Telford,' said Abtey.

'So you said,' Jack replied, reaching the door, then finding himself caught in a logjam. Some fellow with the granite features of a secret serviceman pushing his way inside, a cursory nod to the *commandant*, quick assessment of the green room's occupants.

'All clear, sir,' he called over his shoulder as, behind him, the hangdog face and heavy moustache of Britain's Minister Resident for the Mediterranean filled the doorway.

Jack retreated a few paces as Macmillan entered, three – no, four – others of a similar stamp, English upper class, at his heel.

'Forgive the intrusion, Miss Baker,' Macmillan drawled. 'Simply wanted to pay one's respects. Our troops out there delighted. Never had it so good, they say. And perhaps you might allow me to name Mister Bond, our new consul-general in Rabat.'

She offered them her most disarming smile.

'Delighted, I'm sure,' she said.

'And this gentleman...' Macmillan waved a hand towards the rotund diplomat at his side, pig-like eyes, handlebar moustache, the ends carefully waxed and curled. 'The Right Honourable Sir Aubrey Carter-Holt.'

He began to make the introductions – to Josephine, of course, and to Réchard – while Jack slid further along the wall. Pompous bastards, he thought. Right Honourable? Who else but the bloody English? He supposed he'd known it might happen, ever since he first heard Sir Aubrey was coming to North Africa. But now it was here… It all came flooding back to him, as though it had been yesterday. San Sebastián. The absurdly trivial thought that Carter had failed to inherit not only her father's politics but also any physical resemblance. Yet, what to say?

Macmillan took a final glance around the room to see whether there was anybody else he might name, and his eyes settled on Telford. So, it seemed, did Sir Aubrey's.

'Ah,' said Macmillan, 'now here's the correspondent chap…'

Jack thought he had never seen such hatred in a man.

'I know damned well who he is,' spat Sir Aubrey, and pushed his way back out of the room.

May–June 1943

Leslie Howard

'Lisbon? You want me to go to Lisbon?'

'Joséphine and myself would have gone, *Monsieur* Telford,' said Jacques Abtey. 'But with this new schedule…'

The Frenchman was perched on the corner of a cupboard Baker was using as a dressing table. Abtey wore a uniform shirt, though without insignia. And Jack thought it was more likely de Gaulle's little presentation, that Cross of Lorraine for services unspecified, had rather given their espionage game away.

'They're keeping me busy,' Josephine smiled, added a touch more lipstick, studied the effect in the mirror, turned until she could see Paquita Gorroño's reflection. 'What d'you think, *señora?*' she said. Excellent Spanish.

The makeshift green room at Temara camp's recently assembled mess hall was a far cry from the Cinéma Théatre Rialto – bare log cabin walls of freshly cut Moroccan pine. Beyond this room, filled with crates of food and drink, catering tin cans, beyond the kitchens, in the mess hall itself, the sounds of a gathering audience, the slam of folding chairs, babble of voices.

'Perfect,' said Paquita, and squeezed her husband's arm.

The performance here had been Paquita's idea, a morale booster, badly needed by the camp's occupants. The place was almost on her doorstep, buried in the forest joining the outskirts of Rabat to neighbouring Temara itself.

'There must be plenty of others who could go,' said Jack. 'And, listen, Lisbon means getting to Tangier first. Tangier, occupied by Spain just now? I have to tell you, I've *no* desire to step back on Spanish soil.'

'Doesn't Franco like your writing, Jack?' said Josie.

'I'm going outside for a smoke,' he replied, and both Paquita and Manuel followed him through the side door. 'Hell,' he said, as a blast of hot early summer evening air hit them, 'Tangier!'

At the farther end of the building, a queue was gathering, men drifting across from the rows of huts already built, others working on those still under construction. Odd mixture of men, some in threadbare civilian clothes, others in equally tattered overalls, many in the rags of uniforms, every shade of drab.

'We have comrades in Tangier,' said Paquita, and drew deeply on the Gauloise he'd given her. 'We could kill two birds with just one stone.'

'And these men?' said Jack. 'Staying here long?'

'Only for now,' Manuel replied. 'Next week they are shipped out to Libya. Sabratha, we think. Join up with the others, and then...'

The others, Jack knew, included Amado Granell, some of the rest who'd signed up with the *Corps Franc d'Afrique*, the African Free Corps. Granell and Campos *el canario*. But others already known to Amado – Bamba, Ortiz and El Gitano. Jack had interviewed them at Bizerta, two weeks before, then managed to find his old Kufra friends as well, the two *toledanos*, Alemán and El Gordo. There they all were, the Spaniards now serving with Leclerc's L Force, still part of Montgomery's 8th Army.

'And then,' said Paquita, 'if the rumours are right, they'll all be demobbed and told they can either join Giraud or Leclerc.'

'Weird, isn't it?' Jack laughed. 'Not often soldiers get the chance to vote. But if Tunis is anything to go by, I can guess where they'll end up.'

'Tunis?' said Manuel.

'You don't know the story? No, I suppose not. Two days ago. Priceless. The Allies have this victory parade, but they leave Leclerc out. On purpose. Only Giraud's men allowed to take part. Behind the Yanks and the Brits, naturally. Hell, the earache I got from Leclerc!' Jack gave a good impersonation, even down to the walking cane, but in Spanish. 'The Americans think more of Berlin collaborators than true Frenchmen.' He remembered Leclerc's words perfectly, churned them out again for the Gorroños. 'Free France undefeated. Free France never surrendered. The *Boches* have never beaten us.'

'Did he change their minds?' Paquita asked, and ground the cigarette stump into the sand and pine needles.

'Only in the way you'd expect from Leclerc. There are Giraud's men, the Army of Africa. Back of the procession. All in their old uniforms. Like something from another age. Really, they could have marched straight from the trenches of Flanders. And the crowd? Hardly any applause. They paraded past Eisenhower and Montgomery. Neither of them look very impressed. But then, from the side streets – my god, Leclerc's battle-battered Bedford trucks. All the men from Chad and Cameroon. Spaniards as well, Paquita. Singing the *Himno de Riego* at the tops of their voices. And every bloody truck painted with the names of the places they'd fought. Kufra, of course. And Murzuk. Bir Hakeim. All the rest...'

Jack couldn't finish. As choked as he'd been when he saw them.

'And the crowd went wild?' said Manuel.

Telford nodded.

'The crowd went wild,' he agreed. 'And Montgomery – the smile on his face. Come on. Back inside?'

Jack took a last look around. If Leclerc had been right, he'd soon be given responsibility for transforming L Force into the second of three French armoured divisions, now to be equipped by the Americans – the fruits of that little escapade in Tunis. And room within the division, he'd promised, for every one of those Spaniards who wanted to fight alongside him. To help him fulfil the Oath of Kufra. And to hell with whether they were Reds or not. Once formed, they'd be back here, to Temara, the site scouted for him by Dronne and Fox.

'Five minutes, *Señora* Baker.'

There was a face, a swarthy Latin face, poking around the doorway at the opposite end of the dressing-cum-store room as Jack went in again.

'Well?' said Abtey. 'Lisbon?'

'Tangier still bothers me,' Jack replied. He could have bitten his tongue – as good as a yes. 'But Paquita and Manuel might also have things for me to do there.'

'And you'll be travelling as Butch O'Hare again, no?' said Josephine. 'We've friends in Tangier as well. The sultan's brother-in-law. Remember him, Jacques? From when we were making *Tam-Tam*? They were good days.'

'I'm just not sure I'm fit enough yet for something like this,' Telford protested.

'Well enough to swim at the lido every day, though?' said Abtey.

He had the feeling Jacques didn't like him very much.

'And fit enough for Bizerta and Tunis,' Paquita reminded him.

There'd been a four-hour flight from Rabat to Bizerta, at de Gaulle's insistence, immediately after the Germans and Italians were finally driven out – a quarter of a million prisoners taken. He'd been there almost a week, then driven by truck the fifty miles to Tunis. A flight back to Rabat almost immediately after that victory parade, just time enough to wire his pieces.

'I told you in confidence,' he growled at Paquita. 'Besides, I've got things to do in Casa.'

It was true. Bilal, the leader of his Baker Street Irregulars, had disappeared. Réchard had been helpful, but in the medina? There could be a thousand explanations, a thousand things that could have happened. But it had followed so closely on the heels of their theft – albeit only a temporary one – of Welch's passport. Or, rather, Konrad Wagner's passport. And then there'd been Sir Aubrey's reaction to him. Grief? Suspicion? Or had it been something more? It troubled him. Deeply. Macmillan had been almost apologetic. Well, perhaps this was an exaggeration. Actually, the bastard had just sniffed, looked down his nose at him.

'You'll not be away long,' said Abtey. 'Casablanca will still be there when you get back.'

'But why me?'

A knock on the door, the same face again. In the background, the strains of a combo, the audience chanting.

'I have to go,' said Josie. 'Wish me luck. Come and watch when you're done here.'

'In a minute,' said Abtey, as she swept out of the room. 'And why?' Jacques said to him as soon as she was gone. 'A victim of your own success, *Monsieur* Telford. Emptying the camps? Stroke of genius. The general seems to think you might have more talents than he first gave you credit for. Personally, I'm not sure. But your credentials as an Irish correspondent – might be what we need, for this.'

Before Bizerta, the beginning of May, and the camps still not emptied, the Yanks still kowtowing to Giraud, to Noguès, to Vichy. No concessions to the Jews. No freedom for them or the Spanish Reds. There'd been all those American promises. But then there'd been his article in the *New York Times*. Scathing. And a recorded piece for Barea, his first-hand account of the camps. Djelfa and elsewhere. An affront to humanity, he'd said. Described the atrocities. Unspeakable atrocities. He'd used up another of those precious discs. Though the results almost immediate. By the time he got back to Rabat from Tunis, the camps mostly emptied. The proudest moment of his life, he thought. Extra burdens for Nella, naturally. All those Jewish refugees now released. But overall? Yes, he'd been proud.

'I'm promising nothing,' said Jack. 'But if I *do* go, what's involved?'

There, he'd done it again. As good as a commitment. But Abtey made no response, simply turned his poker face towards the Gorroños, waited until they'd taken the hint, headed out through the other door to watch the show.

'An agent travelling through Lisbon to Madrid,' said Abtey, when they'd gone. 'An important agent. Documents to be delivered to him. A briefing paper from the *Makhzan*. From the sultan. They need to be delivered personally into this man's hands.'

'How might I know him?'

In the distance, Josephine was trilling the familiar warble from *J'ai deux amours*.

'No need. You'll wait each evening in the bar at the Avenida Palace Hotel. He'll find you.'

'That's it?'

'Afterwards, you wait. See the sights. Whatever you fancy. But, each evening, you head back to the Avenida Palace. With luck, there'll be a report for us. Get it here safely – and *that's* it.'

Away in the mess hall, Josephine had raised the tempo. *Juana la Cubana.*

'This man,' said Jack. 'French?'

'English. Churchill's man. For once, we all seem to have the same purpose. Churchill, de Gaulle, the sultan – even your Spanish friends, maybe. All you need to do is deliver the documents. *Et voilà!*'

Really? Jack thought, as Abtey pushed himself off the table's edge, headed for the door.

'Wait,' said Telford, 'what rank do you hold, Jacques?'

'What?' Abtey snarled. 'Think you deserve orders in writing from some higher authority, *Monsieur* Telford?'

'Not what I meant,' Jack replied. 'You're an officer. Trained to make decisions, knowing lives may be lost as a result. The men who take your orders also know that. Know your orders may kill them. But they still obey. A contract, of sorts, between you. But me? Just a writer, Jacques. War correspondent now. It just happens I want to do more. You mentioned the camps. If I played some small part in getting those hellholes emptied – well, magnificent, but still doesn't feel quite like being in the war.'

'Kufra did?'

Jack nodded.

'Yes, Kufra did.'

'Nice speech, *monsieur*,' Abtey smiled. 'And I'm a captain. This means you'll go?'

Jack heard Josephine sing the opening lines of *Bésame Mucho.* He lit himself another cigarette, clicked his heels together. 'At your orders, Captain Abtey,' he said. 'When do I leave?'

'Tonight,' Abtey replied. 'If we can arrange the flight.'

The night train to Tangier, through Fez, was comfortable enough and a taxi driver at the station pointed him towards the Hôtel Constantine. Cheap, and he'd only need to be there long enough to catch the following morning's early flight to Lisbon – successfully organised by Abtey through the Aero-Portuguesa office.

Jack's papers – *Señor* O'Hare's papers – had been scrutinised three times at the station's exits by members of the *Guardia Civil*, and Telford had fought back the panic, the nightmare memories of how he'd been treated by their thugs in Burgos. He swore he could almost feel the cigar of *Teniente* Turbides burning through his eyeball again. Yet he was soon dismissed, sent on his way.

The Constantine stood high on one of the medina's steep streets, Jack's room looking out over the old Moorish ramparts, the coastal defences with their line of forty cannons, all captured from the various enemies that had tried to take the city during its turbulent history. But he had to close the windows against the smells from the tunny factory down past the harbour. The drive from the station had been interesting. Elegant buildings along the waterfront reminded him of Alicante, then the steep, narrow streets of the medina. A curious mixture, not just the Arabic and the European, the turban and the trilby, but the French and the Spanish. The *panaderías* along the Rue du Diable. Truly, bewitching.

Yet, in the afternoon, he headed for the sophisticated, westernised new town, the Plaza de Francia and the Boulevard Pasteur. He'd taken precious few clothes with him when he'd headed off to Bizerta, and he'd been living in them ever since. Somehow, he knew they wouldn't suffice for Lisbon. And his essentials. Hell, he hadn't changed the blade in his razor for six months. He'd finished *L'Étranger* during his travels as well, so he found a bookshop, sifted through some second-hand English editions, but finally picked up a copy of Galdós, *Fortunata y Jacinta*.

He kept the documents Abtey had given him carefully concealed in the lining of his jacket, tried to stop himself holding a hand upon them. But, with his shopping done, he settled himself on the shaded terrace of the Bar L'Hémisphère along the beachfront's Avenida de España. The menu had an interesting design, a rough map of Europe and Africa. It rather gave him an idea. He lifted the notebook and a pencil from his satchel, began to sketch a copy across two pages – well, at least the section he needed. From Spain down as far as the point where he calculated Brazzaville to be. Dakar in the west, Cairo in the east. A few adjustments as he sipped his coffee. Then, when he was satisfied, he took Negrín's pen and inked over the outline.

Not too bad, he thought. Telford's odyssey. All I need to do now is fill in...

He started with Madrid, and had just put a dot, written the word *Alicante*, when he realised the waiter was standing at his side, holding a folded piece of paper.

Car will collect you tonight. Constantine. After Maghrib. F.

He'd settled himself to wait in the hotel's small reception area, listened as the *mu'azzins* called for the evening prayers and, at eight o'clock, a limousine pulled up in the street outside. The driver wore a livery reminding Jack of an Egyptian Mameluke, ornate pointed slippers, baggy crimson trousers, a sash of imperial purple, black waistcoat over a yellow oriental blouse, and a cylindrical red hat bound with a white turban.

'*Monsieur* O'Hare?'

'Yes, where are we going?' The fellow simply extended his arm towards the entrance and, once on the street, opened the limousine's back door. 'Really,' said Jack, climbing into the vehicle's calfskin interior, 'who sent you?'

'Not far,' the driver told him, but offered no other information as he drove up through the medina's narrow alleys, out past the Tangier Kasbah, through the fortress gate until, still climbing the hill, they reached a palace overlooking the sea.

Telford was escorted past burnoose-clad retainers, scarlet tunics, at each end of the long entrance tunnel, across a first courtyard with a fountain, ornate columns, rooms and balconies on each side, then a second quadrangle, equal to the first – but with modern sculptures – to a series of gardens, terraced, running down towards the southern side of the Gibraltar Straits. From this height, he could just make out the coast of Spain, a hazy rugged line along the horizon.

'Mister Telford.' An older gentlemen in a plain tan robe, the hood thrown back, flapped towards him from a flurry of activity, two others rising from the low table, the matching divans, now bathed in the soft orange glow of a dramatic sunset. 'How good of you to come. How perfectly good. Welcome to my home.'

He held out his hand and Jack gripped it, looked over the fellow's shoulder to see Fox, smiling, wafting towards him in a billowing white *djellaba* and plain *shesh*, but worn loose and held in place by one of those black cord circlets that were rare in these parts. Very Lawrence of Arabia. With him, a younger Moroccan, absurdly handsome, Clark Gable moustache.

'Captain Fox,' Jack shook his hand also. 'But I'm sorry...' He looked to his host.

'I have the honour,' said Fox, 'of presenting His Excellency *Sidi* Abderahman Menebhi. His Excellency is a great patron of the arts. And here,' Fox bowed towards the other chap, 'His Excellency *Sidi* Ahmed Belbachir Haskouri, Chief of Staff to His Excellency the *khalifa* of Spanish Morocco, Chief of the Civil Household, Director General of...'

Belbachir held up his hands.

'Please,' he said. 'Captain Fox has a remarkable memory but, at this rate, we shall be here all night. Shall we take tea?'

'And your titles precede you, Excellency,' said Jack. They did, indeed. His reputation also. The caliph's *éminence grise*, his eyes and ears, his personal link to the sultan, *Sidi* Muhammad. More important, trusted implicitly by Hélène Bénatar. 'As well,' Telford continued, 'as a reputation of great honour.'

He had a network, Nella had told him, capable of producing Spanish Moroccan passports at the drop of a hat, and the passports issued to Jews escaping from Europe, allowing them to claim they were actually Moroccan Jews – and thus able to head to safety, South America among other destinations.

'You also have a certain reputation, Mister Telford,' said Belbachir, as they settled on the divans. Here was a man who prided himself on his use of perfect English. A servant poured fresh tea. 'Josephine, how is she?'

It caught him entirely on the hop.

'Baker?' he said.

'Who else?'

Jack looked quizzically at Fox, but there was no help forthcoming from that direction.

'I was with her yesterday,' said Jack. 'At Temara.'

'Yes, yes.' Belbachir was suddenly impatient. 'Of course. But how *was* she?'

'She was – well, sir. Very well. Performing for the Spaniards released from the last of the camps.'

'Ah, the camps,' said his older host. 'A curse upon them. An offence before God.'

'It was Miss Baker,' Fox explained to Belbachir, 'who suggested Mister Telford for this mission, Excellency.'

'An angel,' Belbachir smiled. 'Such an honour to have her in my modest abode. Tetouan, you know? I had her own personal *hammam* built for her. And a genuine berber tent – though tent is such an inadequate word in this case – erected upon the beach, as though she were the Queen of the Desert.'

'Mission?' Jack said. 'I'd assumed...'

'Don't worry. Telford,' said Fox, 'your secret's safe. But His Excellency's an important player in all this.'

'Explain?' said Jack.

'No, no,' Abderahman Menebhi interrupted. 'First, we must see my latest acquisition.'

There was a tour of the palace, more like a museum visit. It transpired that here was the son of Mehdi el Menebhi, Grand Vizier and War Minister to the old Sultan of Morocco, now living in splendid retirement in Tangier. Inherited wealth. A talented painter, it seemed. And a friend of painters. Sir John Avery. And, of all people, Churchill.

'But my greatest delight, when I was a boy,' Menebhi went on, 'was when my father introduced me to Matisse. Here, you see?'

They stopped in front of a painting. A mosque. Cobalt blue and brilliant white, pale turquoise sky. It was signed.

'Painted here?' said Jack.

'Of course,' Menebhi replied. 'But this...'

'Beautiful,' said Belbachir. 'But, as you say, Mister Telford – your mission. And Morocco, poor divided Morocco. Yet we have but one heart. One sultan. And, one day, we shall be united again. United and independent. Algeria as well, perhaps. But, meanwhile, we play the Spanish at their own game. They patronise us, Mister Telford. Because Franco still wants our phosphates. The rest of our mineral wealth. Our lands. He occupied Tangier, claiming he was preserving the neutrality of the zone – but, truly? Merely a first step in Franco's designs on all Morocco.'

Back in the gardens, lanterns had been lit, only the afterglow left to modestly lighten the western sky. There was a cool and comforting breeze blowing in from the Straits.

'You see how perfectly orientated we are, Mister Telford?' Menebhi said, with great delight. Jack assumed he meant the palace, but it could equally have been a political statement.

'And these documents Captain Abtey wants me to bring back – I gather some of them actually need to be delivered here? For the sultan's eyes.'

'If he was still with us,' said Belbachir, 'I have no doubt you would have been required to set those papers in the hands of Isaac Gabizon. But, in this cruel world, His Imperial Highness requires that it shall be my humble self who must perform this duty.'

'The rest,' Fox told him, 'myself and Abtey will make sure are delivered safely to de Gaulle.'

'The English agent?' said Jack.

'Flies back to Bristol. As Abtey might say, old boy, *et voilà*.'

Fox joined him for the ride back to town.

'Sounds easy enough, I suppose,' Jack agreed. 'But it's been my experience that those are exactly the things – and listen, I know you warned me not to push this, but Welch...'

'I don't want to hear this, Telford.'

Fox peered theatrically through the limousine's window as they passed back through the fortress gate.

'It's just – well, I remember, ages ago, he suggested I might make this very trip. To Tangier. Get to know the sultan's friends here. Did he mean Belbachir?'

'There's no damned mystery here. You know very well Kingsley Welch was heavily involved in the trade deal. Between the Yanks and Morocco. Of course, he knows Belbachir. He was part of the sultan's team, alongside Noguès.'

'Involved – yes, but on whose behalf? The Yanks? Standard Oil? Or their German business, through IG Farben? And is it pure coincidence he inherited von Wulisch's car?'

The limousine had pulled up outside the Constantine. For

a moment, Jack wondered whether he should hit Fox with the passports story. Kingsley Welch or Konrad Wagner? And the disappearance of the street urchin, Bilal, but the driver had already opened the limousine's door, waited for Jack to climb out.

'My god, Telford,' the captain laughed, 'you have a vivid imagination. Where in heaven's name do you think this is taking you. Forget about Kingsley Welch, why don't you? Just enjoy bloody Lisbon and bring back those papers we need.'

A two-hour flight, at the crack of dawn, from Tangier's airfield, at Boukhalef, eight miles southwest of the city, where the main highway to Arcila hit the coast again, having skirted the rocky peaks known simply and affectionately as The Mountain. Two hours, and a bumpy landing as the three-engined Wibault 283 delivered Jack and its nine other passengers safely to the sparkling new Lisbon Portela terminal building.

A regular bus service into the city centre, to the Praça de Figueira, across the square and its seemingly endless circuit of yellow trams, the elegantly patterned pavements, to the Francfort Hotel. His room was at the back, but a view, eastwards, rows of buildings climbing up to a wooded hilltop castle.

As soon as he'd unpacked, he decided it made sense to check how far he'd have to walk – or take a taxi – to make his assignation. The hotel receptionist laughed at him.

'*Cinco minutos, senhor,*' he said.

And five minutes, it was, even limping on his stick. Across Figueira, cutting through to the Rossio Square, and then north a hundred yards to the Avenida Palace with its superb views all the way up the Avenida itself, Lisbon's very own Champs-Élysées.

So, the rest of the day to kill. Pleasant enough, despite Lisbon's heat and the still gammy leg. Hélène had spoken often about her Lisbon contacts in the American Jewish Joint Distribution Committee, through which she also operated in Casablanca. He looked up their address, therefore. Just around the corner. Courtesy visit. Then a stroll around the Baixa's fine new shops, before jumping the tram from the Praça do Comércio out to Belém, where he found a decent fish restaurant for lunch near the Tower. In the afternoon, the Jerónimos monastery, an astonishing limestone wedding cake, housing the tombs not only of Vasco da Gama, but also Luís de Camões, Portugal's Cervantes.

He made notes, of course. Added some place names as well, over coffee and Portuguese custard tart, to the hand-drawn map of his travels. He began to also make a note of the dates. A reminder of precisely when he'd made his journeys. 280339, for example, the fateful evening they'd sailed on the *Stanbrook*. Before long, there was a whole column of numbers. Then he rode the tram back to town, in plenty of time to settle himself at the Avenida Palace, a comfortable armchair in the foyer, with his *Fortunata y Jacinta*.

Yet he'd only been there five minutes when he realised he was being scrutinised. Two men, just out of Jack's limited peripheral vision, and he was damned if he was going to turn and look at them. But now they were coming closer.

'Astonishing.' The voice was English, softly spoken. 'We had a question on the show last month. Can the *Brains Trust* explain why there are no famous Spanish authors of the nineteenth century, to compare with Dickens or Trollope? Superb. Afraid I rather waxed lyrical about Galdós. Much to Joad's annoyance, eh, Alfred?'

Alfred, his companion, looked remarkably like Churchill. Stocky, bald, smoking a cigar, handkerchief to his sweating brow.

'Pedantic,' said Alfred. He even *sounded* like Churchill. 'Did you hear it?' he asked, as Telford eased himself to his feet, mumbled that no, he hadn't. Never had the pleasure. The programme had become a BBC icon, but only since Jack had been abroad. 'Argued how, since Galdós's best work, his socialist and republican work, as Joad put it, was written *this* century, not the last...'

'It's you,' said Jack to the other man. 'Isn't it?'

He looked like Leslie Howard, but somehow not quite. And Telford couldn't quite reconcile his excitement. His awe? For pity's sake, Jack himself was on personal terms with de Gaulle. He'd been only feet away from Roosevelt and Churchill at the conference end. Virtually an intimate friend of Josephine Baker. But Leslie Howard? This was something entirely different.

'Afraid so. Would you care to join us for a drink? Any friend of Galdós is a friend of mine. With a bit of luck, we might find a quiet corner.'

They found one only after the fellow had been stopped three times for autographs. A moderately private booth. The bar was all soft lighting, ceiling fans, cool shadows and dark polished mahogany, beeswax and tobacco smoke. There seemed to be a constant ebb and flow of merrymakers at the tables and scarlet stools.

'Actually,' said Jack, setting down his trilby and the walking stick, suddenly feeling a fool for having so readily accepted the invitation, 'I'm supposed to be waiting for someone.'

'Do you have a password or something?' said Howard.

Jack thought he must have heard him wrong. It wasn't possible, surely. That the man who'd played Pimpernel Smith might actually be...

'They didn't give me one.'

'Typical,' said Alfred, and waved for the waiter.

'I was told to look for a man with an eye-patch,' said Howard. 'You've not noticed any others, I suppose? And make mine a martini, Alfred, would you?'

'Can't say I've been looking,' Jack told him, and took a packet of Luckies from his pocket, but Howard quickly pulled a cigarette case from his own jacket.

'Here, have one of these.' He offered the open case, nodded towards the Lucky Strikes. 'I may have to advertise those blasted things, but I'd never actually smoke them. Still prefer my pipe, really. And nobody mentioned the, er...'

His glance flickered towards the walking stick.

'No,' said Jack, 'a more recent acquisition. Slight altercation with a truck.'

'Jolly bad luck. But what will you have to drink?'

The waiter had arrived, and Jack happily accepted Howard's Capstan. He'd not had one of these since...

'Fox,' he said. It had been such a long time ago, when they first met. 'The password?'

Howard smiled at him, while Alfred ordered two martinis, looked to Jack.

'Fox?' said Alfred. 'It would be a good one, wouldn't it? But you've rather lost me. And your own tipple, old fellow?'

'Are you being serious?' said Jack. 'Me? You were looking for me? Oh, I'm sorry – Scotch. Just on the rocks.'

There was a list of available brands, naturally. He settled for the *Old Angus*.

'Show me your papers,' said Howard, as the waiter returned to the bar. 'Mister O'Hare,' he murmured, when he'd had a chance to turn them this way and that, in the dim light. 'This your real name? No, on second thoughts – and from whence have you travelled Mister O'Hare?'

Jack tried to measure the man against the entertaining, though two-dimensional, characters from his films. Fifty now? Perhaps older, Certainly seemed so. The hair still dark, but hints of grey at the temples and sides, threaded through the thinning waves.

'Tangier,' he said. 'And, before that, Casablanca.'

'Casablanca? Priceless. Have you seen it yet? The picture.'

'Still banned, I'm afraid. In Morocco. The clammy hand of Vichy still.'

'Yes, I'd heard. Bogey's in a real funk about it. Must be showing somewhere in Lisbon, though. You must watch it while you're in town. Franco's having it dubbed, of course. Take out all those references to Rick fighting for the Republic. Probably just in English here. Salazar doesn't seem to bother too much about those things.'

'And how long exactly, do you expect I'll be here?'

'You have something for me, I take it? The *letters of transit*? Oh, forgive me – I forgot, you've not seen the movie yet. Papers of some sort?'

The waiter brought their tray and, once he'd gone again, Jack patted the breast of his jacket.

'Next to my heart,' he said. 'But after, I just wait?'

'Isn't that what everybody does in Casablanca?' Alfred laughed.

'Great heavens,' said Howard. 'All this cloak and dagger stuff. You've not been introduced. Well, come to think of it, none of us – well, this is Alfred. Chenhalls. My manager. And my friend,' he added hastily. 'He and Bogey, my truest friends. But yes, just wait, I'm afraid. We'll try to be quick, though. Where are you staying?'

'The Constantine.'

'Then there'll be a message, instructions, at the Constantine. Soon. Been away from home a month already. British Council, you know? Lecture tour. This little jolly will be the last of it, with a bit of luck. Madrid, then back here. Arrange our flights. Home to dear old Blighty.'

'Madrid?'

'Didn't they tell you? No, I suppose they wouldn't. But I'm assuming you're carrying another bit of my script. Words of wisdom from our French friends, from the Sultan of Morocco as well. Shots across Franco's bow. More consequences if he doesn't choose his friends more carefully.'

'About as much as I was given to understand,' said Jack. 'But you're meeting Franco?'

'He's a movie fanatic, did you know? Care to come along?'

I could have killed the bastard, Jack thought. Twice.

'I already had the pleasure,' he said. Howard seemed impressed and Jack, in his vanity, was tempted to tell him. The whisky going to his head, mingling pleasurably with the *vinho verde* he'd supped with his lunch. 'But it's a very long story.'

'The *Generalísimo*,' said Alfred Chenhalls, 'has kindly arranged for us to stay at the Ritz.'

'He has a soft spot for Conchita Montenegro,' said Howard. 'Know her?' Of course, he did. The romantic interest in *The Cisco Kid*. Who could forget? 'Anyway, let's just say she's an old friend of mine. But her current boyfriend, Ricardo, he's with the Spanish Ministry of Foreign Affairs. Falange. Reasonably thick with Franco as well. Thick with Franco's perfidy. Supposedly neutral Spanish ships relaying convoy information to the U-boats. Spanish agents helping the Germans track down and kill our own people in Spain itself and here in Portugal.'

'And sending fifty thousand Spaniards to help Hitler at Leningrad wouldn't normally pass for an act of neutrality,' Jack added.

He knocked back the last of the *Old Angus*.

'Quite so,' said Howard. 'So, off we go. Tomorrow. Once we have our script, of course.'

'I'll need to unpick a few stitches from the lining. Won't take me more than a minute. Just nip to the gents.'

'Not a problem, old man,' said Chenhalls. 'But don't look now. Two fellows at the far end of the bar.'

'Don't be absurd, Alfred,' said Howard. 'Directing somebody not to look at something is the one sure way to guarantee such a thing will actually come to pass.' He made some pretense at brushing dust from his trouser leg, risked a glance. 'See what you mean,' he murmured, and took up his martini again.

Jack leaned over to use the ashtray, squinted towards the bar's extremity, near the door. There they were. One in a lightweight Styrian jacket, rigid features, cropped hair. The other in a linen suit, Hitler hairstyle and wire-rimmed glasses.

'Gestapo,' mouthed Chenhalls. 'No doubt about it. Make sure you're not followed, won't you?'

That evening he did, indeed, find a cinema, the Eden, also on the Avenida. And he sat through two consecutive showings. It was wonderful, though far from the Casablanca he knew.

The fabulous scene with *La Marseillaise*. And Rick's gambling den? It could so easily have been the Transatlantique. But Louis Renault? Hilarious. He couldn't wait until he had the chance to watch it with Réchard.

'Louis, I think this is the beginning of a beautiful friendship.'

It still made him smile the following morning when he went down for breakfast. Coffee. Freshly squeezed orange juice. Bread rolls with cheese and ham. He'd picked up a copy of *Diário de Notícias*, tried to study the headlines. A huge RAF bombing raid on Dortmund. Some local news. The ceiling fan above his table was squealing painfully and, at first, it rather masked the shrewish exclamation of surprise.

'Mister...Telford? It is you, is it not?'

He looked up from the paper to find, staring at him, the last person in the world he might have expected to bump into.

'Mrs Holden?' he said, looked around quickly in the hope nobody else would have heard her use his real name. Dorothea Holden. 'Good gracious. What are you doing here?'

He stood, out of politeness. A cursory shaking of hands. He'd last seen her at the Hotel María Cristina in San Sebastián. The fateful day when he and Carter had returned there after Santiago de Compostela. They were all supposed to be catching the same train home, but then Carter had tempted him with one last swim and, thank god, by then he'd worked out what she was all about. The rest, as they say, was history.

'As it happens...' she began. 'But your poor face. I almost didn't recognise you. So, different. Was that – the accident? We were so worried when neither of you showed up at the station. Reported you missing.'

Jack touched his fingers to the eye-patch. Yes, different, he thought. I'm certainly different.

'I heard. Good of you,' he said. 'And this? Yes, the rocks, just beyond the bay.'

'And poor girl. Such a beauty. Such intelligence. Decorated by Franco himself. I did admire her.'

Yes, thought Jack, decorated by Franco but a spy and assassin for Stalin.

'Of course, you did. Have you seen any of the others?'

'Poor Frances, of course. And Max Weston – though not in person, naturally. But his film, *Mexican Max* – have you seen it?'

Jack smiled. No, he hadn't. He was tempted, but only for a moment, to tell her he'd bumped into the young nun, Sister María Peredes, in Burgos. Though, best not to think about Burgos.

'And Professor Holden?' he said.

Her features collapsed at once into an expression of deep sorrow.

'I'm sorry to tell you that poor Alfred passed on. Oh, two years ago now.' Her voice dropped to a whisper. 'Cancer, you know.'

Her turn now to glance about her, as though the dreaded disease might somehow overhear and come for her. He was fairly sure she was wearing the same tweed twinsuit as when he'd last seen her. Hardly the right thing for Lisbon in summer. The same handbag, clutched to her midriff. The same Shirley Temple felt hat.

So, thought Jack, the old fascist bastard's dead. It was uncharitable, but he couldn't help it. Professor Alfred Holden, once a darling of the right-wing press, helped Mosley establish the British Union of Fascists. It was said that he'd written whole sections of the party's programme and ideology.

'I'm sorry for your loss,' he said. 'But look, won't you join me? Some tea, perhaps?'

He hoped to hell she'd say no, but they were starting to attract attention, and at least she might take the hint and leave him in peace. Yet, to his surprise, she murmured something about his kindness, waited for him to move around the table, help her with the other chair.

'Well, at least he didn't suffer,' she said. 'Very quick, you know? Yet, here you are. We heard the news, of course. A friend of Alfred's read one of your articles, I think. And Alfred said – oh, well never mind all that. Lisbon, just fancy. You're here chasing a scoop, I imagine. Isn't this what you newspapermen say? But not still working for your awful communist rag, I hope? Always thought you could do so much better for yourself.'

'It was *Reynold's News*,' he said, then decided there was no point trying to correct her, waved for the waitress. Dorothea ordered tea. And some scrambled eggs, as an afterthought. Oh dear, now he'd have to endure her even longer. 'And a scoop, you say? Well, I *was* following a lead, though it seems to have gone cold. But then, just when I'm wondering what I should do about that – well, fortune smiled on me, sent *you* my way. What brings you to Lisbon, Mrs Holden?'

Presumably not the Anglo-German Fellowship, he thought. Dorothea and her obnoxious husband had been active members, Nazi supporters. But their equally obnoxious society had been forced to disband when the war started, though Jack doubted whether many of its thousands of affiliates would have changed their views very much.

'Believe it or not,' she said, 'this is rather like *déjà vu*. Picking up where we left off, so to speak. Dear Alfred and I went back the following spring, you see. On the bus tour again. We'd rather enjoyed it. Apart, of course, from – well, least said, about that, I suppose. But after Covadonga... To cut a long story short, we decided to finish the rest of the journey.'

'Like getting back on the horse?' Jack offered, ordered another coffee when the waitress brought Dorothea's tea.

'Very well put, Mister Telford.' She felt the pot and smiled. 'The one good thing you can say about the Portuguese, don't you think? The only other nation in the world that understands the principles of boiling water and brewing tea.'

'I believe the Japanese, the Indians and the Chinese may also have picked up the knack.'

'Really?' She wrinkled her nose, twisted her face, at the very mention of those inferior races over the breakfast table. 'Anyway, we must have ended up on one of Swan Tours' lists. The year after, a brochure arrived. *National Spain Invites You...* Remember? Only now *El Caudillo* had added two new routes. Catalunya and Barcelona, on the one hand. Andalusia and Córdoba on the other.'

'Wait,' said Jack. 'Where are we, now? That was...'

'1940. But, by the time we'd made up our minds, there was all the silliness with France, you remember?' Yes, he remembered it very well. 'Simply impossible to travel by train anymore. But *this* route – well, ideal. Fly to Lisbon, train to Madrid, and then the bus south. We saw it all, you know. Seville and Granada. So very beautiful.'

'The War Routes,' he said, simply. But his mind was spinning. 'You're telling me...'

He remembered a conversation with Fox. He'd wondered whether the War Route tours might still be running. And yes, of course, the flights from Bristol to Lisbon remained a possibility. Precisely the way Howard and Chenhalls had got there. Three flights each way, every week. There'd been that thought, about the powerful and wealthy not letting a little thing like a war get in the way of their foreign holidays. And he'd meant to ask Paquita, but then dismissed the whole idea. Foreign holidays might be one thing, but going from blitz-blighted Britain to visit the sites of another country's wartorn miseries. It seemed preposterous. And yet...

'They're incredibly popular,' she was saying. She sniffed appreciatively at the scrambled eggs the waitress had set down before her. 'Booked up months in advance. But at least we had one last beautiful trip together, Alfred and I. And you wouldn't believe the wonders General Franco has achieved. The fellow really is a hero, Mister Telford. Brought order from the chaos, that sort of thing. You were never a great admirer though, as I recall.'

Jack bit his upper lip. He was trying not to cry, felt foolish. Too many things crowding his memory. Images. The child taken from her mother so the Republican parents could be erased from her little mind. The infants raised almost from birth to make the Nazi salute. The parents taken from their children and shot, thrown into drainage ditches, and the ditches ploughed over so there wouldn't even be a grave by which to mourn their loss. The bombing. Suicides on the quayside at Alicante. Fidel and Sergio.

'Not a great admirer, no,' he said. 'That's true.'

And I could have killed the monster, he thought. I *could*.

'Then you should sign up for this one,' she said, nibbling at the eggs. 'It doesn't seem quite so booked up as the others.'

'This one?'

'Yes, Madrid itself. We get to see Toledo. And the university, where so many of those brave soldiers died, trying to drive out the Reds. We even get to see the hotel the Russians used as their headquarters.'

'The Gaylord, it's quite something.'

'You took the tour?'

'In a manner of speaking.'

'And here I am, blathering on about things you already know. I should have thought, shouldn't I? A well-informed fellow like you, Mister Telford. But you'll never guess who we saw yesterday. Might be a story for you here, after all.'

'Perhaps,' Jack smiled. 'And who was it, exactly?'

'Why, the actor. Leslie Howard. He's Jewish, did you know?'

That look again. As though the scrambled eggs were off.

'Never gave it much thought,' said Jack. 'Are you sure?'

'Oh, certain. Dear Alfred looked it up. Father a Hungarian Jew-boy. Steiner's their real name. You could expose them perhaps. Whole filthy nest of them.'

Jack gripped the edge of the table, pushed back his chair. Dorothea Holden stood, as she'd stood so often during the week of the bus tour, for all those many things he despised about British society, riddled as it was with class bigotry. And yes, of course he'd seen it among so many of the French, but somehow...

'I think you must excuse me,' he said, through gritted teeth, unhooked the stick from the back of his seat. 'But allow me to put breakfast on my bill.'

'Oh dear,' she said. 'A walking stick. Poor man, you must have really been in the wars. But the bill? Indeed not, Mister Telford. My new husband wouldn't hear of it. The other reason for this wonderful holiday, you see. My honeymoon,' she whispered. 'Oh, my! I should have thought. Of course. There's a connection. Hubby number two knows poor Valerie's father. Yes, he's a minister of something-or-other, isn't he? And Kingsley has been involved in some overseas development work.'

'Kingsley?' said Jack. He felt himself sliding once more down the rabbit hole.

'I should have corrected you earlier, I suppose. But yes, I'm Mrs Welch now.'

'Sheila?' he said. 'Hell, this line's awful.'

He'd waited in a queue for almost an hour at the local APT office, then another fifteen minutes until they managed to make the connection.

'I know, I should have phoned earlier. But you got my letter, at least. Well, belated congratulations in person anyhow. And married life treating you well?'

It was all very banal. Hasty. This was an expensive business, after all. A courtesy enquiry about the Czech section. Her own congratulations on Jack's membership of the Beeb club. And, of course, she'd made it her business to look in on Barea, waxed lyrical about Telford's talents.

'Listen,' he said, at last, 'the other reason I'm calling...' He heard her laughing, say something about yes, she'd already worked out there must be another reason. 'Well, it's this way. I asked Sydney, ages ago, whether he could find out anything about this bloke, Kingsley Welch.' He spelled the name for her. 'Welch, not Welsh. Something to do with Standard Oil. But apart from an address in Surrey – I'll give you that in a tick – he couldn't find very much. Would you? No, it's just some research I'm doing. Thought you might – yes, the archives. And here's another lead you might follow. The Anglo-German Fellowship. Disbanded, I know. Doesn't matter. May be something. Where am I? Lisbon. Hotel Francfort. But not sure for how long. Easier if I call you back. No, don't send a wire, I'll phone. Fine, you can try to call me at the hotel, if it's easier. But make sure you ask for Mister O'Hare. No, don't you dare laugh.'

But now what? Telford thought to himself once he was back on the street. It was all just too bizarre. Dorothea Holden and Kingsley Welch? Kingsley Welch and Sir Aubrey? Jack had asked whether Welch knew him – that strange night after the Anfa, when the fellow had driven Jack out to the tobacco factory. He'd said they'd never met. Though, even then, Jack had been sure he was lying. But Dorothea had been clear enough. Sounded like they were old acquaintances. Why lie about it? And how the hell had he met *her*, of all people? Stranger still, if Welch knew Sir Aubrey, had presumably discussed Sir Aubrey with his bride-to-be, and Jack had asked him about Sir Aubrey, would he not have mentioned Jack to her, as well? She would surely have chatted with him about San Sebastián. Probably spoken his name. Yet it seemed, for all the world, like Welch must never have mentioned they were even acquainted.

He wasn't sure what to do next, either. Certainly, he didn't want to bump into the newly-weds together. And what would she have said to her husband?

'By the way, dear, you'll never guess. The fellow I mentioned to you. Remember? That thing in San Sebastián. The journalist, Telford. Small world, but I bumped into him at breakfast.'

Would it have jogged Welch's memory, so to speak?

'Oh, yes, I'd quite forgotten to mention it, but I met him. Getting old, my dear. Brain like a sieve, these days. We were together in Casablanca. Couldn't quite remember where I'd heard the name. But now you've reminded me...'

There was a café just along from the Francfort. He ordered a coffee, *uma bica*, and read the paper some more, wished he'd brought his notebooks with him. He'd spent a chunk of last night writing up his recollections of the conversations. First, with Dorothea. About the War Route tours, the details she'd given him. Would Sydney Elliott know they were still running? If not, he'd love the story. And then, with Howard, about Franco's make-believe neutrality. About the fifty thousand Falangist volunteers and Spanish regular army personnel now fighting for Hitler. About U-boats allowed to refuel at Spanish ports like Cádiz. About how Spain was helping Hitler beat the British blockade by importing goods from Argentina, allegedly for Spain's own use, but then transporting them overland to Germany – all very clandestine and almost impossible to prove.

Who knows? Telford said to himself. Maybe one day this will all make a decent article.

He'd been there perhaps forty minutes when he saw them leave the hotel, Dorothea on Welch's arm. They took a taxi, and Jack made his way back to the entrance, looking behind him to make sure they'd actually driven off. And, in this way, he collided with somebody coming the opposite way, leaving the lobby. Telford was caught off-balance, and his damned leg chose that moment to let him down.

He fell sideways, heavily, the stick knocked from his hand.

'Dammit,' he said, sat in the doorway. 'And I'm so sorry. *Desculpa.*'

But there was no reply, in English *or* Portuguese. Simply the scuffle of feet on the pavement, Jack only looking up as he reached for the walking stick, saw the man's back retreating rapidly down the street. He couldn't be certain, but there was something about the lightweight tyrolean jacket, the cropped hair, which reminded him uncannily of the fellow at the bar, one of the pair Chenhalls had been convinced were Gestapo.

'If you don't get out of my way, Telford,' Welch sneered at him, 'I'll knock your bloody block off.'

Jack was fairly sure the older man might do so, with reasonable ease. But it had taken a while to trap him, there in the hotel's restaurant toilets, and he wasn't about to waste the opportunity.

'Perhaps I should speak to your new wife about Cairo,' he said. 'What was it you said, about lead in your pencil?'

'Oh, please. You may have had a charmed life so far, but it won't last, you know. Really, you should enjoy this temporary reprieve while you can. Now, d'you mind?'

He waved a finger towards the blue and white tiled urinal, but Jack stood his ground.

'Reprieve? What the hell are you talking about?'

'Never mind, old chap. Just get out of my way.'

Jack lifted the walking stick, pressed the ferule against Welch's throat.

'It was you, wasn't it? Searched my room?'

Welch knocked the cane aside, pushed past anyway.

'If I'd searched your room, Telford,' he said, looking over his shoulder as he unfastened his fly, 'you wouldn't have known about it.'

'You're in the habit of searching rooms then, *Herr Wagner*?'

'If I ever found such a thing to be necessary, I can assure you I would do it in person, Mister *O'Hare*...' He raised a hand to silence the protest he could see forming on Jack's lips. 'Please, Telford, don't be such a bloody fool. I checked the hotel register. It wasn't exactly difficult. As I was saying, I'd have done it myself, rather than employ some clumsy street urchin to dirty his hands on my behalf. Now, if you wish to discuss any of this further...'

Jack heard the sigh of relief that accompanied the splash of Welch's water on the tiles, the slight gurgle as it trickled down the drain.

'The boy?' said Jack. 'You know what happened to him?'

'I suspect if I denied it, you'd not believe me anyway. And when was this invasion of your precious privacy supposed to have occurred?'

'I went out this morning to make a phone call,' said Jack.

'To check on me, I assume?'

'Among other things. When I got back to my room, it had been searched. Carefully. Professionally. Everything back where it belonged.'

'Then how...?'

419

Welch shook himself, turned to confront Jack once more, fastening the cavalry twill trousers.

'Because it was just *too* tidy. My notebooks perfectly aligned. Not my thing, *old boy.*'

Jack lifted the walking stick again, waved it in Welch's face.

'Last chance, Telford. I may be twice your age, but I promise you, I *shall* hurt you unless you stop this nonsense. As I was trying to say, if you want to discuss this further, you can meet me this evening. Seven. At the castle. São Jorge.'

He'd picked up the tram, the *Elétrico* Twenty-Eight, at the stop outside the Se Cathedral and jumped off again at the Portas do Dol, up in the steep streets of Alfama.

Telford studied the piece of paper, the rough map sketched for him by the hotel porter, began to climb the road towards the alleyway which would take him to the castle. If the gradient was like this all the way, it was going to be the very devil getting back down again, slow work with the walking stick. Yet he'd gone no more than a dozen yards before that stentorian voice of Welch's stopped him in his tracks.

'Mister O'Hare. Over here.'

He stood at the corner of the terrace Jack had noticed when he got off the tram. An open plaza, which seemed to hang in the air, along with the woodsmoke rising from the dwellings below, evening meals cooking, the strains of a lonely guitar, dogs barking. A railing at the far side and a couple of busy bars around the square's margins.

'You said the castle,' said Jack, glancing back up the hill.

'Seen one, seen them all. Not really worth the trouble. Just needed to make sure you weren't followed.'

Tall and straight, hawk-like, white cricket trousers, blazer and straw Panama.

'Precisely who might be following me except you, Welch?'

'You came, didn't you? Here. Beer perhaps?'

He'd led them to the nearest seats without too many other customers at the neighbouring tables. Welch removed his hat, and Jack did the same. He'd had this policy once, about never wearing hats, but now he seemed never to be without one.

'No,' said Jack. 'Nothing.'

He wasn't entirely sure why he *had* come. Curiosity, of course.

'But you won't object if I…?' Welch called the waiter, ordered a Sagres for himself. 'You're certain, old boy?'

Jack shook his head, the same sensation he'd experienced that afternoon in the waters at San Sebastián, his certainty Carter intended to kill him. He could almost smell it on Kingsley Welch, see it in his eyes. How? Would it have been poison slipped into the beer, if he'd accepted. But why?

'What did you mean – temporary reprieve?'

He lit a Gauloise, didn't trouble to offer one to Welch.

'What did you imagine I meant? Simply that, out there…' Welch gestured towards the railings, beyond which, far below, down in the middle distance, they could see the azure River Tagus, cargo ships. 'Out there, Telford, the war still rages. We are each blessed, it seems, with an interlude. A moment of respite.'

'And it it wasn't you who searched my room…'

'Supposed to be a jest, Telford? By anybody's measurement you'd have to reason that one in every twenty visitors to Lisbon, as we speak, is an agent for one side or the other. You may be travelling under false papers, old man, but you're hardly inconspicuous, are you? A person of some note. Add to this, Salazar's own PVDE men are everywhere. They'd probably search your room simply as a matter of routine. And what harm done? I can't believe you'd have left anything important for them to find. Would you?'

'A few notes for my next article, nothing more,' Jack lied. In truth, he'd not quite been able to remember how much detail of Howard's mission he'd committed to paper. The answer, when he'd retrieved the notebook, read through it again? Too much.

'And, if you'll forgive me saying so, you've some nerve, haven't you? You send that filthy little arab to search my room at the Transatlantique and here you are, accusing me of your own tricks.'

Telford clenched his fists, the words festering in his brain as the waiter brought the beer, asked if he was sure there was nothing he'd like.

'Filthy little…' Jack spat when the waiter had gone again. 'You *do* know what happened to him.'

'The truth? Can you even cope with the truth, Telford? You think he just brought my documents back and handed them over politely? No, he demanded money. Blackmail, I suppose he thought. Refused to hand it over until I paid him.'

Welch sipped at the beer's froth, wiped a hand across his lips.

'So, you killed him?' said Jack.

Kingsley Welch almost choked on his drink.

'I gave him a good thrashing and sent him on his way. The beating I gave him, he deserved it – but it was down to you, Telford. If he's gone to ground, kept out of your way, it's likely he's worked it out for himself.'

Guilt upon guilt, though he wasn't about to let Welch see it.

'Documents,' he said. 'False passports, you mean. Or was it – false? German. Spy, perhaps. Konrad Wagner. Anglo-German Fellowship. Your connection to the Holdens?'

'As it happens, yes. I *was* a member, before it disbanded. It was, at the time, good for business. Useful contacts. But the passports? You're getting out of your depth, dear boy. But without the Fellowship, I'd probably not have met Sir Aubrey.'

'Dorothea mentioned you were acquainted. But the night you gave me a lift, from the Anfa…'

A pair of storks silhouetted against the evening sky.

'The night you ran off into the dark, you mean?'

'Yes, how rude of me,' said Jack, sarcastically. 'Whatever was I thinking? But you denied any knowledge of him – Sir Aubrey.'

'I had my reasons, Telford. Don't think I owe you my life story. But he was still at the Admiralty office, at the time. Memorial service for his daughter. Never recovered the body – though you'd know that. Dorothea and the Professor were invited, of course. Apart from you, Telford, the last people to see her alive. And I tagged along with them.'

'You and Dorothea…'

'Kindred spirits, Mister Telford. It's all you need to know.'

'Interesting you mention kindred spirits. The boy – your *dirty little arab* – his name's Bilal, by the way. And he brought more than just the passport. Is that how he threatened you? Seen you meeting with Chamson, the scum from the *Milice*?'

'For pity's sake, Telford. One minute you have me mixing with German agents in Cairo, the next with *La Milice* in Casablanca. Simply figments of your imagination, I'm afraid. All the same, you should be careful.'

'Thrashing for me, as well? And these aren't figments. More like fragments. They simply don't quite fit together. Not yet.'

Jack pummelled the cigarette stump to death in the brass ashtray.

'And then what?' said Welch. 'When you think you've solved the puzzle. I'm to be traduced in one of your articles, I suppose.'

'When I write it, you can rest assured it'll not be libel you need to fear, *Herr Wagner*. Perhaps you can ponder this while you're enjoying Franco's fascist hospitality in Madrid.'

On the far side of the plaza, a man hawked and gobbed into a green and orange terracotta spittoon.

'You see? Wrong again, Telford. My duties keep me here in Lisbon. Did you not fathom? Dorothea's doing the War Route alone – well, with whoever else is on this particular tour, anyway. Hopefully, by the time she gets back, our respective missions can be completed.'

'I've no idea what you're talking about. I've no mission here. And, if you've one, I dread to think what it might be. Or from whom. No, for me, you were right. Interlude. Moment of respite.'

'It's hard to believe you can really be this disingenuous, Telford. But if we must play the game, let's just call it a lull. Yes, that might be more accurate.'

Jack left him there, decided to walk back to the hotel. But perhaps a little exploration on the way. So, after winding his way through the shadow-smeared back alleys of Alfama, he found a darkened, smoke-filled bar where a young woman was singing the mournful variety of music Jack knew to be *Fado*.

By the third dramatic lament, and his second beer, he'd come to the conclusion that, lyrical as it might be, there was a relentless monotony to the genre. He knew he was probably being unfair but at least it provided no distraction from the thoughts racing through his mind.

Respective missions? The implication they might somehow be on the same side – or, did he mean the same mission but *different* sides? Wasn't this more likely? The passports. And then the grinding sense of remorse. About his notebooks, the search of his room. Had he compromised Howard's integrity?

His leg was troubling him, and these passageways were steep, narrow. More menacing than anything he'd experienced in the medinas of North Africa. He paused outside the bar, tried to get his bearings. Downhill, that much was certain. Jack took the cigarettes from his jacket, pushed back the brim of his hat and flicked the cartridge case lighter into action. The glow illuminated the cupped palm of his hand, crimson flesh and shadow lines of deepest black.

But it lit up something else, as well. Movement in a doorway, up to his left.

'Hello?' he called. '*Olá?*'

No reply. No sound except the *Fado*'s muffled drone at his back, a stilted ripple of applause.

He waited, convinced himself it was his damned imagination playing tricks.

Jack put his weight on the stick, ventured a step forward, peering into the darkness, knowing the lighter's flame would have dulled his night vision.

Down a few steps, paused at the bottom. Still nothing. A sigh of relief.

There was a small square, bed sheets wafting gently on washing lines, a copse of clothes posts. Two old women on chairs outside their front doors, chattering in the capricious amber of a wall-mounted oil lamp set above a brick display case housing the local *Virgem Santa*.

Yet he could hear something else. Footsteps behind him. Cautious footsteps. Not bold and honest. Stealthy and furtive.

Two exits from the square, and Jack chose the one straight across.

'*Boa noite*,' he said to the women, tipped his trilby as he limped past. He was tempted to stay put, for they looked as though they could fight off the devil himself if they so chose.

He hobbled down the next stretch, reached a junction, ducked around the corner and pressed himself against a rough stone wall. Something scurried past his feet, made him jump.

But, again, he could hear nothing else, just voices, Portuguese voices, somewhere in the apartments above him.

Jack waited for what felt like an age, cursed himself for an idiot, stepped out of his hiding place.

Slam.

Something hit his chest, threw him back against the wall. Fingers around his throat, throttling him.

'*Herr* Telford.'

German? What else? But how...? And who...?

'No,' he croaked, against the grip on his windpipe. 'No. O'Hare.'

'No stupid games,' snarled his assailant. There was a second man, ripping open Telford's jacket, delving into his pockets.

There was light, from a small hand torch. It shone in his eye, then down onto his papers, his false passport, his counterfeit *Irish Press* union card. They were flung onto the ground and, in that one gesture, Jack knew he was in serious trouble.

'What the hell do you want?' he managed to say, when the pressure on his throat eased a little.

'The book, where is it now? Your codebook. We must see it again.'

The notebook? Since the searching of his room, Jack had taken the precaution of keeping it in the hotel safe whenever he wasn't using it. But codes? There was nothing even resembling a code. Unless – the dates? The column of numbers?

'Look...' he began, but the man gripped his ear, banged Telford's face against the wall, knocked the hat from his head.

'Where?'

Jack saw the bulk of the other man looming towards him, and a fist slammed into his belly, thankfully nowhere near the old knife wound, but enough to make him retch, all the same, to drop the cane, to leave him gasping for air, fire shooting through the ribs only just recovered from the truck accident.

'*Das ist genug!*' A third voice. Clipped.

The fellow with the torch spun around and, in its thin beam, there was Welch. A pistol in his hand. Jack's initial attacker still had him pinned against the wall, shouted back a stream of enraged guttural invective. And Welch answered him in kind.

For the first time, Telford had a chance to see their faces. The two thugs, naturally, identified in the hotel bar by Chenhalls as Gestapo.

'*Ich habe es dir ja gesagt! Das ist genug!*' Welch again, telling them to leave him alone, Jack assumed. And now the fellow obeyed, took a couple of steps backwards, though still pointing at Welch, arguing with him.

Telford straightened himself, painfully, rubbed at his throat.

'Do I thank you?' he said. 'Or would that be premature? Disingenuous, perhaps?'

'Get out of here, while you still can,' Welch snapped back at him.

'What? And leave you here with these two fiends? Or did I mean to say *friends*? So easy to muddle those two words, don't you think, *Herr* Wagner?'

'You should hear yourself, Telford. You can be an absurd little man, at times.'

That rather stung almost as badly as his scratched face, but Jack bent to pick up the walking stick, the trilby, and his papers.

'Well, if you're sure,' he said. He was tempted to put the cane to good use, leave these thugs with something to remember him by. But, of course, he thought better of it. 'And thanks, all the same,' he told Welch. 'Whoever the hell you are.'

A half hour's uncomfortable walk found him back at the Francfort, unlocking his room. But, this time, there had been no pretense at putting things back where they belonged. Every draw, every cupboard, every scrap of bed linen, every bag – ransacked, the contents strewn across the floor.

The message from Howard, when he picked it up at the hotel four days later, wasn't what he expected. But at least his ribs had stopped hurting so much.

Join us at once. Estoril Palace Hotel. LH.

Estoril. Fifteen miles along the coast, westwards, from Lisbon's waterfront Cais do Sodré terminus for the electrified line to Cascais.

Telford was glad to get out of town, especially after the business in Alfama. But how was he going to tell Howard, as he suspected, somebody – no, not somebody, the Gestapo, or bloody Welch, or both – had read his stupid notes, knew about this so-called mission?

He left his case at the Palácio Estoril's reception desk, knowing this place, the holiday haunt – and sometimes place of exile – for the royal families of Europe, was beyond his means. He'd have to find something more within his pocket later.

A porter directed him back out through the front doors, along the drive to the right, to the swimming pool set within those extensive gardens and overlooking the sea. And there, indeed, he discovered the actor, a twosome bathing costume, the vest pale blue and white stripes, the trunks royal blue, white belt. Jantzen, from the emblem. He was soaking up the poolside sun. No sign of Chenhalls but, on another lounger, almost joined to his own, was a real beauty. Slim, the swing-skirts of her gingham swimsuit clinging to her thighs, as she towelled her arms. On the tiles at her manicured toes, a flower-strewn bathing cap still swam in its own puddle of water, but it had left her chestnut hair perfectly siderolled.

'Mister O'Hare,' Howard beamed, 'you made it. Come and say hello to Hexy.'

She regarded him with piercing blue eyes.

'That's an unusual name,' said Jack, and stood under their parasol, though neither of them was using its shade. He took off his trilby, used his handkerchief to wipe the sweat from its headband.

'When I was a little girl,' she laughed, her accent distinctly German. 'They said I was a witch. *Hexe*, yes?'

'And easier than trying to get my tongue around *Mechthild*. Oh, I'm sorry,' Howard blushed bright red, 'I didn't mean...'

She flicked the towel at his arm.

'You bad boy,' she scolded him. Younger than Jack, late-twenties. A darned sight younger than Howard.

'Are you in the acting business as well, Miss...?'

Now the handkerchief also mopped at the perspiration on Jack's brow.

'No, no,' Howard stopped him. 'Hexy's an honest-to-goodness countess. The Countess von Podewils. But I made a terrible gaffe, didn't I, my dear? Saw Hexy so often at the beauty parlour in the Ritz, I thought she must work there. Total embarrassment. Thank heavens she's forgiven me – haven't you, Hexy? But listen, old boy, why don't you pull up a deckchair? And your face...'

There was a stack of them, folded flat. Jack grabbed one, brought it under the parasol, tried to turn it into a piece of furniture. He'd never learned the trick.

'Stupidly fell against a wall,' said Jack. 'A German name, yes? Von Podewils?'

'In Spain and in Portugal, thank goodness,' she said, and laughed at his clumsy efforts with the deckchair, 'there are no German names, or English names, or any other silly things – all nicely neutral, don't you think? All friends again, far from that awful war.'

He wished it was true. But the threat he'd faced in Lisbon was still all too fresh. And his less than satisfactory exchanges with Welch, the puzzle no nearer to solution. Well, maybe a little nearer. For though he'd seen no more of the fellow, and Dorothea gone off by train to Madrid, Jack had spoken again to Sheila. She'd come up trumps. No wonder Sydney had trouble tracking Welch down, for he had no real roots in Blighty. English father but German mother. Father a senior chemist with BASF at Ludwigshafen. Kingsley educated in Frankfurt and then in England – Westminster public school. Followed his father as a chemist, became part of IG Farben when BASF and several other outfits merged to form the company. Some record of him at IG Farben's London office – actually within the Anglo-American Oil and Standard Oil building on Bishopsgate. But for the past ten years? Still nothing.

'Strange you should say that,' Jack told her, handed the errant deckchair to a passing waiter, who instantly had the damned thing under control. 'I don't think I felt this close to the war, even when I was in the thick of the fighting.'

'And waiter,' said Howard. 'Champagne, if you please. No, wait a minute. A bottle of *espumante*. Your best Bairrada?'

The waiter beamed with pleasure.

'You are a soldier?' Hexy said to Jack, with wide-eyed

astonishment, pure play-acting. '*Herr*...O'Hare.' She hooted with laughter. 'Oh, how funny.'

'You'd better call me Jack,' he said.

'And quite a coincidence, Hexy,' said Howard. 'Mister O'Hare's a journalist. Didn't I mention? How long are you here for, old boy?'

He passed around his cigarette case. Ah, the Players again.

'I'm booked on the morning flight back to Tangier. Tuesday. So, three more days.'

Jack slipped his jacket around the back of the deckchair, settled himself into the red and green striped canvas, set down his trilby and tapped the end of the cigarette against the wooden frame before accepting the actor's lighter.

'Champion.' Howard beamed at him. 'Alfred and I are leaving tomorrow. Telegram from the studios. Time to start shooting the next one, it seems. *The Man Who Lost Himself.* Could have been made for me. Should be home in time for Sunday dinner, though. Must call Ruthie. Get her to sort out the rations. But Hexy's here a few more days, I think. Be able to keep each other company.'

Ruthie? Telford assumed it must be Howard's wife, but he couldn't be sure. And he vaguely remembered a conversation with Harmon. Something about the real love of the actor's life being – blast it, he was never any good at gossip. An actress, maybe. Suzanne something?

'Sadly,' he said, 'I'm not a good enough journalist to be able to afford this place. And who do you write for, Countess?'

'I don't think you would know it, Jack.' She spread out the towel on the foot of her sun lounger.

'Try me. You never know. Not *Der Angriff*, I hope?' He laughed, though she didn't seem to appreciate the jest. 'I understand *Herr* Goebbels has managed to increase his circulation again since we started bombing Berlin.'

'I have family in Berlin, Jack. Seems a little cruel, if you will forgive me saying so.'

'And a son, here in Lisbon,' said Howard, desperate to change the subject. 'That's right, isn't it, Hexy? The real reason she's here, yes?'

'My son, of course. My husband brought him here when we divorced. My daughter lives with me in Madrid.'

Bloody hell, Jack thought. Married *and* divorced. Doesn't look old enough for either.

'You met there, then? Madrid?' he asked, looking from one to the other for an answer.

'At one of the lectures,' said Howard. 'Hexy brought a friend along. Poet. You'd have liked him, old chap. Dionisio Ridruejo.'

'I don't think I know...' Jack began.

'But you would know his words, Jack,' she told him. 'He wrote *Cara al Sol.*'

The waiter had returned. Bottle, three glasses, ice bucket.

'Is this a joke?' said Telford. 'The anthem of the Falange?'

He'd heard it for the first time at Santiago de Compostela.

'He's very proud of it,' she said. 'Of course, they sang it for him when he came back from Russia. He was badly wounded there, you know?'

'Still in a bad way when I met him,' said Leslie Howard. 'Leningrad. Shot. Frostbite.'

'Leningrad.' Jack took a deep breath. 'With the *División Azul?*'

'Of course.' Hexy smiled at him. 'But he's out of favour with *El Caudillo* now. Dionisio can't see any reason why, once all the Reds are gone, Spain should not have elections again. Made the mistake of telling Franco so.'

'All the Reds...' Jack repeated.

'Hexy, my sweet. Maybe time for another swim? A few things I need to discuss with Mister O'Hare. Would you be a darling?'

'You men!' she said, sipped at her glass, then tucked it away, into the shadows underneath her sunbed. 'Always secrets to share.' She uncoiled those absurdly long legs from the lounger. 'But promise you won't talk about me.' Countess Mechthild von Podewils settled the swimming cap back on her head, fastened the chin strap. Then three graceful steps, like a gazelle, before she dived into the water.

'You really must stay here, old boy. Really. I wouldn't have it any other way. And apologies for...'

He waved his hand towards the pool, where Hexy was already swimming the front crawl with an elegance which would have qualified her for a part as one of Leni Riefenstahl's athletic Aryan goddesses in *Olympia*.

'Stay here?' The *espumante* was ice-cold, at least. 'I'm sorry, but isn't she...?'

'I'm afraid so, yes. Direct orders from Admiral Canaris, I should imagine. But you know what they say – keeping your friends close, that sort of thing. Besides, she's rather filling a hole at the moment.'

Jack saw upon his face an expression more melancholic than words could describe. Hurt. Pure pain, the normal *bonhomie* suddenly swept aside.

'And Franco?' he said, for want of anything more helpful.

'Couldn't have gone better.' Howard drew a last puff on his cigarette, used it to light another. 'Truly. It took a while to get to the rub but, in the end, I just had to lay it out for him. Understood how much pressure he must be under from Berlin, especially now. But used Salazar here in Portugal as an example. Not that everything in the garden's rosy with Salazar either. He might be just as big a fascist as Franco but at least understands which side his bread is buttered. Trade deals already lined up with the Allies for after this is all over. And the *Generalísimo* could have the same. But needs to show hard evidence of his commitment to true neutrality.'

The countess completed another length, waved at them from the far end of the pool.

'You got it? Some commitment?'

'In the end. There was a lot of blather about Gibraltar, of course. But I had to make it clear I was only the messenger, not the negotiator. A once in a lifetime offer. Never to be repeated. You know the strange thing? I think, despite everything, he's still actually convinced Hitler can win. Convinced, but not absolutely. Always a shade of a doubt in his eyes.'

He reached down to the ice bucket, passed the bottle to Jack.

'So, the evidence?'

'Gave me copies of the orders he's issued,' said Howard, took the bottle back and topped up his own glass. 'No more fuelling of U-boats. No more intelligence from Spanish merchantmen to the wolf packs. Claims if this is happening, it's entirely without any government backing. Protests he'll find the culprits and punish them. But he's got the message. His ships and ports will find themselves on the wrong side of the Royal Navy if there's any more of it. And the big thing? Orders for the Blue Division to start preparations for returning home.'

Jack whistled.

'Good god. How does he think that's going to sit with Hitler?'

'Oh, he'll plead economic reasons. Or unrest at home. Claim the Reds are a menace again.'

It struck Jack this could almost have been a script from one of his pictures. The actor certainly delivered his lines that way.

'But wasn't it bizarre?' said Jack. 'You meeting this Ridruejo fellow?'

'Completely. Interesting, though.'

'You've something for me, as well, I take it? Morocco?'

'Safely stashed away. More reason to stay. We'll hand them over tomorrow, before we leave. But, basically, more of the same. Personal pledges to the sultan. Tangier to become an international zone as soon as the war's over. No Spanish designs on Morocco. No designs on Morocco's mineral wealth unless by a properly negotiated trade deal. A bit more meat on the bone than that, but you should return to Rabat like the veritable conquering hero. Wouldn't surprise me if they didn't organise a triumph in your honour.'

'Change of plans! Change of plans!' cried Howard. He waved the telegram he was carrying towards Telford's breakfast table, Alfred Chenhalls at his side.

Jack had enjoyed his evening. Dinner at the hotel. His account of having seen *Casablanca* at the Eden. Notes swapped on everybody's favourite scenes, Hexy's annoyance at the absurd depiction of the Germans among the characters, the glorification of its Jews.

'But, my dear,' Howard had said, 'do you not know I'm Jewish?'

The effect could not have been so conspicuous if he'd slapped her, and she'd remained unusually silent through the rest of the meal – Howard's yarns about how he'd returned to England from Hollywood in 1940; about his friendship with Bogey, the break he'd given him during filming of *The Petrified Forest*; and about how, of all the characters he'd played, the one he despised most was Ashley Wilkes. But it all seemed somewhat rehearsed, a defensive

432

wall to fend off the chance of anything more intimate, closer to home. Entertaining though, all the same.

'Change?' said Jack.

'A wire from the embassy in Lisbon,' Chenhalls replied, in his best Churchillian voice, puffing on an early morning cigar. He was wearing a three-piece suit, despite the warmth. Howard, on the other hand, looked elegant and cool, sports shirt and cravat. 'Bloody fools are flying out a copy of *The Few*.'

It was already famous. Howard's own latest triumph. *The First of the Few*. The story of R.J. Mitchell and how he'd developed the Spitfire. Niven in the supporting role.

'Performance at the embassy cinema tomorrow night,' said Howard. 'Special showing. Just means poor Alfred will have to spend all bloody day trying to rearrange the flights. Well, if the embassy officials want us to be there, the consulate staff will just have to bump a couple of people. We need to be home Tuesday, latest.'

'So,' said Jack, 'the papers I'm supposed to be carrying back. Do I take them now, or are they safer with you until it's time to leave?'

They agreed that Howard would look after them until they knew the precise arrangements and Jack spent a pleasant enough day between the pool, a stroll on the beach with the countess – a fair amount of flirtation and her probing questions about his background, about his articles for the *Irish Press*, about whether he knew many people in the Republic with German sympathies. It was all very predictable and, despite her physical allure, a few exploratory kisses, by dinner they seemed to have become mutually bored, one with the other. She'd clearly decided she was wasting her charms, and Telford had determined there was not the slightest redeeming feature about the young woman.

The following morning, they all boarded the train back to Lisbon, Howard insisting he would accommodate everybody at the Avenida Palace again, and Jack excused himself for the afternoon. Work, he said. Articles to write. But, in the evening, there was a taxi, to take them to the embassy. Well, not the embassy itself, it seemed, but to a place called the Estrela Hall. The driver knew it, naturally.

'All sorted for tomorrow, at least,' said Chenhalls, through a cloud of cigar smoke. It was almost impossible to see through the windows. 'Flight first thing in the morning. Crack of dawn but can't be helped. Took the consulate all day to decide who they should bump.'

'Do we know who, Alfred?' said Howard. He seemed on edge, drumming his fingers against the knee of his tuxedo trousers.

'Young boy and his nanny. On their way back to Blighty from New York. Are you sure you want to do this? Tonight?'

'Of course. On our way now. But remind me then, will you? I'll write to the lad, send him something, don't you think? Feel I owe him this much, at least. And you, Mister O'Hare – what time's your own flight?'

'Just after nine. So...'

'Yes, yes. We can head off to the aerodrome together. Sort things out. Champion. And we can drop Hexy here at the station on the way. Early train back to Madrid, my dear.'

He didn't even look at her, began chewing on his lower lip. Jack wondered whether this was nerves before a performance. Because a performance, Telford supposed, was precisely what this would be. Acting for the cameras would be one thing, but Howard was also a serious stage actor. A different thing, but still acting. Like this evening's public appearance. He'd come to realise that, beneath the public persona, here was a man who was inherently modest, almost shy. Maybe a bit naïve. Must be difficult, he thought. And an event like this one, tonight? Stage fright, wasn't it? And any actor who didn't get nervous before a performance wasn't really an actor at all.

'No,' said Hexy. 'I will spend a few more days in Lisbon. You don't mind, darling, do you? If I keep my room a while longer. I still have things to do here. And perhaps some more time with Piet.'

Her son, of course. Jack had endured the whole story of her marriage, her divorce, her children. Endured it twice.

'As you wish,' said Howard. 'Stay as long as you like.'

'I say...' Chenhalls began, astounded at this absurd generosity. But Howard wasn't really listening and, by then, the driver was pointing out the embassy building. Elegant, enormous. Then the

British Cemetery, just beyond. And, around the corner, up a narrow, cobbled street, the Estrela Hall itself. Simple enough exterior, plain stucco walls painted autumnal green, perhaps to match the embassy. But a red carpet, at least, a reception committee, photographers. Howard took a deep breath, fixed a smile on his face and thanked the young diplomat who'd opened the taxi door for him.

Introductions and flash bulbs. The ambassador, Sir Ronald Campbell and his good lady wife. A senior official of President Salazar's *Estado Novo*, *Senhor* d'Almeida.

'Is he all right?' said Jack, as Chenhalls helped the countess from the car.

'Not really your business, old boy, is it?' he snapped, leaving Jack to fume at his rudeness, to pick up the tail end of their little entourage. By the time he reached the unassuming doorway, most of the dignitaries had followed their celebrated guest inside.

The procession had moved on and Jack followed them up a staircase and through the doors into a theatre with red plush seats. For about a hundred, Telford guessed.

Leslie Howard spotted him at once, waved urgently to him and Jack pushed his way through to where Howard was still in company with the ambassador and the Portuguese minister, d'Almeida. There were introductions all round, Jack seated, at the actor's insistence, between Howard himself on one side, and the Countess Mechthild von Podewils on the other.

'Can't say I'm looking forward to this,' he murmured in Jack's ear. 'Still, chin up, eh?'

'I meant to ask you, by the way,' said Telford. 'When you were in Madrid, did you meet Milanes, the consul?'

Jack remembered Milanes fondly, the consul's wife, as well. He'd spent Christmas with them in '38. With Ruby Waters, of course.

'Don't think so,' said Howard. 'The ambassador, yes. Hoare. And some military attaché. Didn't seem to want me there. Pollard.'

Yes, Jack had seen that news. He'd told Louis Réchard and Monique about it, one day at the Casablanca Lido. How Pollard, an agent of the British intelligence services, had been involved in the dirty business of Franco's initial part in Spain's military coup – and been rewarded with this plum job in Madrid as a result. Perfidious bloody Albion, as Réchard's brother had remarked at the time.

'I'm not surprised,' said Jack, as the lights were dimmed and the projector whirred into action. 'About Pollard.'

It was a masterpiece. Wonderful score. Howard's portrayal of Mitchell was moving, almost underplayed, and Jack had never seen David Niven in a better role. But about forty minutes into the film, Niven's character was recovering in hospital from a crash and a scene in which, with Howard at his bedside, a new nurse came on duty. Nurse Kennedy, as she introduced herself.

'My Dodie.' Howard nudged him.

'Excuse me?'

'My daughter, Dodie. She's good, don't you think?'

There was a spark back in his eyes, a spark that had been missing since they'd left the hotel. Yet soon it was gone, once more. Jack saw him shrink into his seat, his jaw set. Not long after, another piece of romantic interest. An actress with only a small part, though Telford vaguely recognised her from other movies. Yet the sight of her plainly distressed Howard. Jack saw his fists clenched, his head lowered. He heard him quietly sob, a single silver tear dripping onto his chest.

'Can I help?' said Jack, but Howard simply got to his feet, wiped his face, began to work his way along the row, apologising as he went.

'Call of nature, I'm afraid,' he kept repeating. 'Sorry, call of nature.'

'Should one of us go with him?' Telford asked Chenhall, but Alfred was vehement.

'Just leave him be, dammit.'

Within five minutes, Howard was back, apparently restored to his normal good nature.

The rest of the picture passed without further incident and, at its end, after a vigorous round of applause, Howard was invited to say a few words about its production.

'What was that all about?' Jack had moved to the chair alongside Chenhalls, while the actor was explaining how Mitchell – the real Mitchell – had, in fact, been a large fellow, violent temperament.

'My own performance,' he said, 'needed to be very different. But I insisted that *Mrs* Mitchell should be present throughout. So any changes I made to her late husband's character should be entirely acceptable to her.'

'The girl in those scenes,' Chenhalls whispered to Jack. 'Do I have to explain?'

'And there's an amusing little yarn we couldn't include in the film,' Howard was saying. 'It seems when the powers-that-be determined Mitchell's plane should be called a Spitfire, Mitchell himself apparently complained it was – and I quote – a *bloody silly* name.'

The audience laughed. Great story. But Jack was shaking his head.

'I'm sorry,' he said. 'I don't understand.'

'For pity's sake, that was Suzanne Clair. Violette.' Suzanne – the real love of Howard's life? Jack tried to recall. The same? But still... 'Good god, do you know nothing? Poor girl died. Last winter. Pneumonia.'

'Hell, I had no idea. And he has to sit through this time and time again?'

'So, I don't know,' said Howard, 'what poor Mitchell would make of this, but when the Yanks release the movie, that's exactly what Sam Goldwyn intends to call it. *Spitfire*, ladies and gentlemen. I give you *Spitfire*.'

Another round of applause, and the Portuguese minister stepped up to make an award, a gold medallion.

'I see death in his face,' the countess had said at breakfast. He'd not wanted to share a table with her but, in the end, it was impossible to avoid. But he made it quick, bade her farewell and at least avoided the embarrassment of the kiss she tried to force upon him.

She troubled him, and he eventually decided to broach the subject with Howard when the three men were on their way by taxi to Portela, and Jack had taken possession of the documents he must carry back to Tangier.

'I know what you said about keeping our enemies close,' he said, 'but she's only inches away from actually bragging about being a spy for Goebbels.'

'Oh, more likely for the Abwehr, I think. Yes, Alfred?'

437

'Shouldn't we have bumped her off or something?' said Jack, and it wasn't entirely in jest.

'When we sink to the level of inhumanity we despise in our enemies, that's just another way of losing, isn't it?' Howard smiled at him.

'Abwehr?' said Chenhalls. 'Almost certainly. But she doesn't know anything. Nothing crucial.'

'But the boyfriend,' said Jack. 'This poet, Ridruejo. Falange. And he may have fallen out with Franco, but sounds like he's still thick with the Falange leadership, and plenty among those still close to the *Caudillo*. If Ridruejo's picked up anything about your meeting, and he spills the beans to Hexy, Hexy reports to Berlin...'

'Good gracious,' said Howard, 'that would make a decent script. Really, old boy, I think you're making too much of all this. Poor Hexy. If she's the best the Abwehr have to offer, Hitler really *is* doomed.'

But Jack wasn't thinking about the Abwehr. He was thinking about those Gestapo thugs in Alfama. He was thinking about his notebook, the search of his room. He was still thinking about them when they'd arrived at the aerodrome, not yet seven o'clock, and many of the other passengers waiting for Howard's Flight 777 to Bristol Whitchurch.

They presented their tickets at the desk, stood on the scales with their respective suitcases – Chenhalls arguing vehemently that the bloody scales must be faulty and no, he was damned if he was going to pay the extra charge. But Jack left them to complete the immigration process. He'd have a couple of hours to kill before his own flight and, now with just his satchel and walking stick to bother about, he wandered over to the windows in the waiting area.

There was the Bristol plane, out on the concrete, the early luggage being stowed. A DC-3. It looked as though it may once have been camouflaged, but the paint had now faded to a neutral grey.

Telford had lost sight of Howard and Chenhalls. But there were twelve others around him, about to board: four men, civilians – and from their suits, he took them either for businessmen or civil servants; a youngish couple and an older man; a woman who might

438

have been Spanish or Portuguese, alone, but chatting to another lady with a young daughter – maybe ten or eleven – and a toddler, just about walking; and a Catholic priest.

One of the suited men jumped up from his seat and approached Telford.

'Excuse me,' he said, 'we heard a rumour – that Leslie Howard's travelling on this same flight. Seems like it's true. I saw you with him, just now. And I know this sounds stupid, but I was hoping – well, my wife, I know she'd love to have his autograph.'

'D'you mind if I ask?' said Jack. 'Rumour, you say?'

'I'm with the consulate,' he replied. 'MacLean. Gordon MacLean.'

My god, thought Jack. This secret mission's leaking like a sieve.

'Look. I need to buy some smokes. Why don't you come with me – see if we can find him?'

Jack wasn't entirely sure whether he should get involved. But if Howard's secret was already out and, knowing how much the actor liked to please his fans, he doubted it would do any harm. They made their way towards the shop, and there he was, Howard, deep in conversation – no, an argument – with…

Hell, it was Welch.

Telford told MacLean to stay exactly where he was, pushed himself along as fast as the walking stick would allow, but not fast enough. Welch turned, saw him, gripped Howard's shoulder and gave Jack the semblance of a salute, before backing away, heading for the exit.

'Well,' said Howard, 'this is a turn-up for the books.'

He sounded nonchalant, but there was something in his eyes. Fear.

'What did he want?' said Jack.

Howard looked about, checked they couldn't be overheard.

'Apparently the Gestapo not only know about my chat with Franco, but *Herr* Goebbels is so cross about it, he's ordered the Luftwaffe to shoot us down.'

'He told you this? Can you trust him?'

'He was there in London when I was asked to make this trip. Why shouldn't I trust him?'

'I think – never mind, you obviously can't fly.'

'That's what he told me, as well. But you see, Mister O'Hare, it's not so simple. Apparently, we only know about this because, somewhere back in Blighty, we have teams of good people breaking the German's military codes. You see the dilemma? If I suddenly change my plans...'

'Yes, I see that. Of course, I do. But you can't – and the others, over there.'

He pointed towards the seats where the passengers for Flight 777 were waiting.

'I think, Mister O'Hare, you might be taking this just a little too seriously. The Germans aren't as clever as they'd like to think. And there's a lot of sky up there. I doubt it's a serious risk.'

'Then why do you look so afraid? They're going to kill you – because you met with Franco?'

'It's probably somewhat more complex, I fear. The Germans at least seem to *think* I'm a spy. Probably reason enough. Goebbels hates me because of the films. I made fun of him, you know? In *Pimpernel Smith*. They say I'm actually number one on his personal hit list. And I *am* Jewish – well, the son of a Hungarian Jew. More than enough. On top of that, they know about the meeting. I'm not sure how. Perhaps as you said, through dear, sweet Hexy.'

Or perhaps not, thought Jack. Bloody notebook. How could I have been so stupid?

'Listen,' he said, 'I have something of a confession...'

'No, please don't. Whatever it is, it doesn't really matter, old chap, does it? Just think, though. How damned angry Hitler must be that we cost him fifty thousand soldiers. And Morocco's phosphates. Anyway, I think we'll be fine. Flights to and from neutral countries are safe enough. Slippery slope if we each started shooting down civilian flights. How would Jerry get his information and spies in and out of England without them?'

'I say!' It was Chenhalls, coming towards them, carrying boxes of nylons from the shop. 'Why so glum?' he shouted.

'Not a word,' Howard murmured. 'Alfred,' he called back. 'Need to hurry.'

There was a loudspeaker system, an announcement in

Portuguese, then in English. Flight 777. Passengers please proceed to the departure point.

'Mister Howard?' It was the consulate official, MacLean. 'Sorry to bother you, but…'

'No, *I'm* sorry,' said Jack. 'I completely forgot. Mister MacLean asked whether he might have your autograph.'

'Plenty of time during the flight,' said Chenhalls.

'No time like the present,' Howard replied. 'Do you have something you'd like me to sign, Mister MacLean?'

The man fished inside his tweed jacket, pulled out a photo of his wife, and Howard looked at it a long time before he took his pen and scrawled a message, passed it back.

'Come on,' Chenhalls insisted.

The double doors on the far side of the lounge had opened. An attendant was checking the passengers' tickets. Jack watched them begin to file through, the gentlemen standing politely aside to let that lady with the two children board first, helped by the foreign woman.

Then the rest. The priest. The young couple. The older man. Those three other businessmen.

'My wife will be so grateful, sir,' MacLean was saying. 'Really.'

He made his way towards the plane.

'Are you sure?' Jack gripped Howard's arm.

'Sure, about what?' said Chenhalls. 'And can't we get on the plane? These are awkward.'

'But good man,' Howard told Alfred. 'Enough stockings for all the girls on the set, with a bit of luck. And we'll be fine, Mister O'Hare. Trust me.'

He gave Jack a reassuring smile – or, at least, an attempt at one – and he was gone, Chenhalls balancing the boxes of nylons in his arms, at Howard's side.

The pilot and co-pilot must already be in their seats, for the engines suddenly roared into life, first one, then the other. But the other two members of the crew – the flight engineer and the attendant – were still on the apron, helping Howard and Chenhalls climb the ladder into the Dakota's belly.

Inside the airport building, somebody shouted.

A uniformed female ran out through the doors, rushed to the plane, spoke to the crew members.

Jack saw one of them poke his head inside.

Oh, please god, Telford thought. Tell me something's happened to cancel the flight.

He expected to see the passengers disembark, but there was only the priest, hurrying back towards the building.

No, not only the priest. Here came Howard, as well.

Changed his mind. Surely, he'd changed his mind.

'Father Holmes,' somebody was saying. 'The telephone, over there. But we cannot hold the flight.'

'Then you'll just have to go without me,' said the priest, and rushed off to take his call. It must have been something urgent.

'Mister O'Hare,' said Leslie Howard. He was out of breath.

'You changed your mind.'

'I'm afraid not. But don't fret – even the Germans wouldn't shoot down a civilian scheduled flight. And it occurred to me you should have these.' He took from his pocket a sheaf of papers. 'Just in case? Perhaps you might pass them to our *special* friend. Hatchet face.' He winked at Jack. 'Make sure they get back to London.'

'You mean Welch?'

'Is that his name?'

The attendant touched his arm.

'*Senhor* Howard, you must board now. No more time.'

'I never knew his real name,' said Howard.

'Good god, man,' said Jack. 'I can't decide whether you're the bravest man I've ever met, or just the most stupid. You don't have to go.'

'I'm afraid I do, old boy. Wish me luck, eh? And get those safely back to Blighty. Welch, you say?' He turned on his heel, walked quickly away, glanced back over his shoulder. 'He was only ever introduced to me as Scorpio.'

He watched it lift from the runway, twenty minutes to eight, and climb into a clear sunlit sky. But he could have wished it, rather, full of cloud. Yet they'd be safe enough, surely. Yes, he was certain of it.

442

He fretted, though, about the additional papers now in his hand. And he fretted still more about those parting words from Howard. Scorpio? This just went from bad to worse. Absurd. Absolutely bloody absurd.

Telford remembered the day he'd watched Negrín taking off, carrying with him the last hopes of Spain's Republic.

But, more than anything else, he recalled the closing scene from *The First of the Few*. Mitchell was dead, but his beloved Spitfire rose, like his spirit, into the wild blue yonder, into a brilliant new dawn.

By early evening on that same day – the first day of June, of course, he was back in Tangier. Sitting at the bar in the Hôtel Constantine.

'Is there news?' he said, as Fox came back from yet another phone call.

'Nothing. I need a drink.'

He ordered a Scotch.

'And Welch?' said Jack. 'Howard said he was there when they briefed him – but can't be right. German? Codename Scorpio? In Alfama, he might have saved my hide but, when I left him that night, he was having a cosy chat with two Gestapo agents. You still think I'm being paranoid?'

'I never accused you of paranoia, old boy. Just told you to leave all this alone.'

'I'd have been glad to, but sadly it refuses to leave *me* alone.'

'Well, our Moroccan friends are more than delighted with the documents you brought back. They want to hold a little celebration in your honour.'

Jack had been glad to be rid of them. They felt cursed, somehow. Both those for the sultan and those passed to him for dispatch to London.

'In *my* honour? Christ, Captain. It was all Howard...'

There must have been another way, surely. And he couldn't get those other passengers out of his mind. The woman with the two children. For pity's sake, it was unthinkable. They *must* be safe. They must.

He'd prayed, all through his own flight, that it was the countess, Mechthild von Podewils, who'd betrayed Howard's mission, and not Jack's carelessly available notebook. But now this all seemed so much more unlikely. Those Gestapo thugs had come back looking for still more. Codes, they'd thought, and he pulled the pad from his satchel, opened it to the map.

'Nice sketch,' said Fox, and knocked back the Scotch with one swallow. 'You've got a gift. If you're ever looking for a new vocation – but what are these? The numbers.'

'Dates, as it happens.' He took a rubber from the satchel, erased them, wished he could have wiped away his mistake so readily.

'You know,' Fox told him, 'there *are* such things as double-agents. But this Scorpio thing – the scorpion…'

'Yes, it rather implies that Welch has also been trying to kill me. So why save me from the Gestapo?'

'More things in heaven and earth, Horatio…' Fox began, but before he could finish, a young Moroccan bellboy tugged at the sleeve of his uniform shirt, passed him a telegram.

'News?' said Jack. 'Tell me they're safe.'

Fox held his gaze, bit his upper lip. He shook his head.

'Fishing boat saw them go down in flames. Off the coast of Spain. No survivors.'

July 1943 – February 1944

Sidi Muhammad ben Youssef

Howard may be dead, but he, and those other passengers from Flight 777, still haunted Telford many months later, in the dark night of his dreams.

He saw their faces, knew their names now, though this came far too late for the article he'd wired first thing the following day, back in June, to Bunnelle in London. The same article syndicated by Associated Press and which appeared, more or less intact, in the *New York Times*, just two days later.

In French North Africa, the news had been muted, overshadowed by headlines in the French language papers, special broadcasts on the now fully functioning Radio Brazzaville. A Committee of National Liberation formed, bringing together Giraud's Army of Africa and de Gaulle's Free French, the two generals serving as joint presidents. All of French Africa now united, actively at war against the Nazis. Well, that was the plan.

But Telford was determined to keep Howard in the public eye. As much of his story as he was able to tell. A condensed version of his AP copy, read out by an announcer for the Beeb's Spanish service, and the rest of the world was shocked.

Most of the world. For, in Germany, the propaganda rag published by Goebbels, *Der Angriff*, ran a slightly different headline.

Pimpernel Howard has made his last secret trip.

Jack often wondered whether the Countess Mechthild von Podewils had written the copy.

He'd told Fox all about her, of course.

'I've come across it before,' the captain had said. 'Men, women, drawn into the world of espionage. They become – I was going to

445

say reckless, but not entirely correct. Almost as though boldness becomes their shield, their armour. And for many of them, it works.'

'Howard used the old chestnut about keeping your friends close, your enemies even closer.'

'So goes the theory,' Fox had replied. 'Their problem, sometimes, after a while, is how to distinguish one from the other.'

'Welch?'

'Oh, Kingsley Welch is one of a kind.'

And so he had proved to be, though that would only become evident later. Much later.

'I can't get Howard out of my mind,' Jack had told him. 'He was so sure – they wouldn't attack.'

'Probably not. Not really. Same thing. The helm of recklessness. Go straight at the enemy. Charge of the Light Brigade. Attack as the best form of defence. It's all the same thing. Just a shame it doesn't always work.'

'Still, that first moment, when he knew he was wrong, when the game was up. You remember the Blenheim? Christ, I do. There can't be any other horror quite like it, can there? The bullets, the flames, the falling. Jesus. I live every bloody second of it, over and over.'

The strange thing?' Fox had replied. 'I don't remember a damned thing until the moment we crashed.'

'Then you're lucky. D'you think they'd have been the same – the women, the kids? Blissfully unaware until the end?'

'Yes, yes. I'm sure of it.'

It hadn't been very convincing. And there were still the faces.

Indeed, a lot of water under the bridge since June. Or, perhaps more accurately, the rabbit hole had become far deeper, infinitely wider.

'You are changed, *Monsieur* Telford,' said His Imperial Highness, *Sidi* Muhammad ben Youssef.

Jack had received an invitation to the palace at Rabat, a car sent for him at his hotel, and he had then been escorted to the stables, where the sultan had been consulting with his ostlers about the condition of the royal coach, and sheltered from the sun by an attendant bearing an enormous roundel parasol.

'Changed, Highness?'

'Yes, the walking stick.' He looked around at his twelve wise men, all in their immaculate hooded, white *djellabas*, as usual, to match *Sidi* Muhammad's own attire. 'You had an accident, they tell me.'

'A while before my trip to Lisbon, sir. I think Lisbon may have changed me rather more than the accident.'

'It was a great service, your journey to Lisbon. You deserved to be honoured for its completion.'

'Merely the courier, Highness. It was Mister Howard who made the sacrifice.'

The sultan studied him a moment and Telford was struck once more by the contrast in his features. Nothing obviously regal about him, outwardly. A benign face, blessed with a seemingly permanent five o'clock shadow of stubble – a face you would have passed in the street without a second glance. But the eyes. Now, there *was* something different. Deep shafts delving into fifteen hundred years of history.

'A tragedy, *Monsieur* Telford. Though just one among so many in this terrible conflict. Yet, tell me, do you ride? I suppose you must.'

Jack saw a pair of white Arabian purebreds being led across the yard. Beautiful, their harness, their saddles, their tasselled fly bonnets, all in bright scarlet. Beautiful, but he cringed.

'Not since I was a boy, sir. I'm not sure…'

His mother had insisted on him having lessons at some stage, but the creatures had terrified him.

'Then you will be fine. Like – riding a bicycle. Is that not what you say in England? Something you never forget?'

Thankfully, there was a mounting block, carpeted, great care taken to have the sultan comfortably in the saddle, the royal feet located with precision inside the ornate brass latticed stirrups. Jack's turn, and he handed the cane to a stable boy, climbed the steps, took the reins he was offered, and swung his leg gingerly over the red upholstery of the saddle's seat.

'Are we going far, Highness?' he said.

'To the college,' the sultan replied, and Telford breathed a sigh of relief. A few hundred yards, just the other side of the esplanade parade ground. 'I have something to show you, in lieu of the honour I should have liked to bestow upon you.'

Jack was intrigued, and it was all much easier than he might have imagined. He should have guessed, of course. For there was nothing to do but sit with a straight back, grip with his knees, and run the reins through his fingers – about all he remembered from those frightful lessons – since the horse itself was led through the palace grounds, out through the gate, across the wide open square and the tree-lined parkland beyond by his very own turbaned attendant. Thankfully, the beast had an easy gait and Jack simply wished there'd been somebody on hand with a camera. Jack Telford, in procession with the Sultan of Morroco, his personal bodyguards and most intimate advisers. Only the sultan himself, naturally, qualified for the parasol's comfort, but Jack had his trilby. Quite enough.

'You know,' said the sultan, 'I have never flown. And Allah protect me from such foolishness.'

'It seems the news speaks of nothing but crashes lately, sir. But I'm assured, statistically, it is still safer than sea travel, for example.'

News of Flight 777 had only faded from the English-language newspapers in time to be replaced by the story of Polish general and exiled prime minister Sikorski's death in a crash at Gibraltar. Just the previous week, the first week in July.

'I try to avoid sea travel also, *Monsieur* Telford. I may be a modern man, but I prefer to keep my feet firmly upon the ground.'

They dismounted – more servants appeared from the rear of the procession, bearing the mounting block, handing back the walking stick – outside the complex which could, itself have been a palace. A Moroccan version of the Oxford colleges, perhaps, the dreaming spires here replaced by amber, crenellated towers and walls of arabesque motifs, horseshoe arches of patterned tiles. Yet, inside, all was modern. If Jack had expected the simple austerity of the Islamic *madrasa*, he was soon to be surprised.

'Modern, Highness, indeed,' said Jack. 'This reminds me of my old school.'

They'd passed through a first small courtyard, surrounded by a few administrative offices and a porter's box, to a second, in which a score of young boys – *too* young, Jack considered, to be in college, most of them only seven or eight years old, but at their exercises. Parallel bars, a vaulting horse, climbing ropes and wooden gymnastic rings suspended from a solid frame. There was an instructor there, a European who looked like a circus strongman, complete with oiled, centre-parted hair and an absurdly curled, waxed moustache.

'You say so?' said the sultan. 'Your old school? Yet I fear you will never have seen such a hopeless student as that little rogue.'

He pointed to one of the lads, knee-length sports shorts and a white vest, who seemed to be stuck halfway up one of the hemp ropes. The boy heard the voice, loosed his grip and dropped into the dirt, then ran towards *Sidi* Muhammad with his arms wide open, and a grin from ear to ear. Jack recognised him now, from the time he had taken mint tea and orange cake at the palace in Casablanca.

'Father!' the lad yelled, and flung himself into the sultan's embrace.

'Abdallah, my boy. You still cannot reach the top of the rope?'

'No,' said the child, 'but this afternoon I shall succeed.'

'Then you have learned the lesson of the Prophet – peace be upon him – for how fine the man who is afflicted and shows endurance.' He turned to Jack. 'Ah, you also, *Monsieur* Telford, is it not? Enduring affliction. This is the change in you. I see it now. Come, let us move on.'

Afflicted? Jack thought. Yes, I suppose I am. But endurance? He wasn't sure. Lisbon had knocked the stuffing out of him. Guilt. The attack by those Gestapo thugs. Welch's involvement. The fellow's introduction to Howard as Scorpio. For the first time in a long while, he just wanted to run back to England, hide somewhere.

The sultan released his son, slapped his backside and dispatched him back towards the ropes, then led the way into a further wing, past a laboratory classroom to a seminar room where Paquita Gorroño was instructing a semi-circle of adolescent boys, twelve of them. Matching striped *djellabas* worn over shirts, ties and morning suits. Each lad wore a scarlet *tarboosh*. And all of them carried the same family stamp. Cousins or closer, surely. They stood as one, bowed deeply, when the sultan entered. Paquita did the same.

449

'Highness,' she said, 'I had no idea.'

'I wanted our friend, *Monsieur* Telford, to see the lesson you are now delivering to my son and heir.' One of the boys, perhaps fourteen, bowed even lower. Hassan, Jack recalled from the same meeting in Casa, the lad who had made such shrewd observations about Churchill. 'You see, *Monsieur* Telford, thanks to your recommendation, *Señora* Gorroño has become a great asset to our humble college.'

The smile of greeting Paquita had offered Jack when she saw him alongside the sultan turned quickly to a questioning curl of her lips.

'Perhaps,' she said, 'we should allow Prince Hassan to explain?'

The boy was a born politician.

'The Genesis of Morocco, the Empire of Sharif, the Kingdom of the West,' he announced, in perfect French, then spent the next ten minutes enumerating key moments, past and present, in his country's history. It was really a eulogy to Morocco's independence, the achievements of the various dynasties which had ruled his country since the Muslim invasion of the Maghreb, twelve hundred years before. He spoke dispassionately about the protection – and domination – Morocco had more recently accepted, first from the British, then from the French, after his nation had been forced into costly wars, by one European power after another. And he spoke about their new friendship with America, a country whose very name conjured the spirit of independence. 'It is that same spirit,' he said, at the end, 'which runs through the veins of our people.'

There was a murmur of approval from the sultan's entourage, clustered at the back of the room, *Sidi* Muhammad's own gently nodding head, the thoughtful expression in those profound eyes, lending their blessing to the boy's performance. He congratulated Paquita, instructed the boys to remain diligent in their studies, promised to return in due course to review their progress.

'What did you think, *Monsieur* Telford?' said the sultan, as they trooped across yet another courtyard, the roundel-bearer rejoining them to provide his master with shelter from the sun.

'You must be very proud of him, Highness. You can see it, I think, can you not? Your son ruling a free Morocco – independent Morocco?'

'I hope independence will come much sooner, my friend. The National Party is gaining ground, and you have seen the writing on the walls, I think?'

Impossible to avoid. Slogans everywhere. *Long live America. Down with France. Morocco for Moroccans.*

'But I've seen the others as well, sir. The *Milice*. Swastikas. The murdered Jews.'

There'd not been many, but enough. Unsolved crimes, that was how they were reported. But nobody had any doubts about the perpetrators. And Welch came to mind, yet again. Had Bilal and his street urchins been right, about Welch meeting with Chamson?

'They will be driven out, Mister Telford. Our friends at the Roosevelt Club have assured us. Your associate – Colonel Eddy?'

'Roosevelt Club, sir?'

They had stopped at the steps and horseshoe-shaped entrance to a further building, almost like a small fortress. It turned out to be the college library.

'My advisers,' said the sultan, as they were ushered into the cool, tiled foyer, 'have been meeting with those officials of the United States on a regular basis. Progress is slow, but it is progress. Naturally, they fear the influence of the Communists among those of our friends who seek independence. Many among the Jews, those who are bitter about the time taken to restore Jewish rights here, despite President Roosevelt's promises.'

'And Colonel Eddy?'

There was a smell, the smell of libraries everywhere. And the dusty silence of a reading room, along to their right, towards which they were now being led.

'Oh, he has his own ways of dealing with members of the *Milice*,' said the sultan, though he didn't elaborate. There was no need. 'But he will not be with us much longer, we understand. Posted elsewhere, it seems. His talents needed in Saudi Arabia, perhaps.'

'Will they help, do you think?' said Jack. 'The Americans. Are we likely to see a Declaration of Independence for Morocco?'

Inside the circular reading room, with its reference books, its wrought iron spiral staircases to the upper shelves, its study tables also arranged in the round, a scattering of students and other library users stood and bowed, were waved back into their seats by the sultan.

'Soon, perhaps,' he said. 'The National Party at least consults with the *Makhzan* about a possible manifesto. With the unions, other political groups. Even the Communist Party – another powerful link through *Señora* Gorroño. I have read their drafts and, so far, it has my blessing. And if, indeed, we are now free from the threat of Franco's ambition – well, it is why I have brought you here. See?'

In the centre of the room, a wooden lectern, its sides and slanted octagonal top gloriously hand-painted in Moorish patterns of amber, blue and brown. Sitting on the lectern's lip was a thin volume, a folder binding of carved leather, perhaps fifteen inches tall and twelve across. Beneath the lip, a brass plaque engraved in Arabic script, in the centre of which a single English word leapt out at him. *Telford*.

'Highness?' he said, uncertain about what he was seeing, but also somewhat overcome.

'Open,' said the sultan, and Jack obeyed the command, tentatively fingering the cover, lifting it, releasing the fabulous aroma of freshly tooled hide to reveal a copy of that *Life* magazine feature, for which he'd written the pieces to accompany the American photographer's pictures. It seemed like a lifetime ago. He searched on the brass plaque for any name but his own, and couldn't find one.

'I'm afraid, sir, my Arabic isn't good enough to read this, but a bit like the Lisbon trip – the credit for this article really goes to Elisofon for his photographs. With respect, don't you think?'

'There is artistry, Mister Telford, in both the image and the words. But, see? The photographer has his name here, upon the page. It is written. Yet the writer? Remains hidden, given no credit. The things you wrote have poetry but, more importantly, they revealed us to the world – revealed Morocco to the world – not as some exotic throwback to the Ottoman Empire, some quaint oriental outpost of colonialism, but as a modern nation, where tradition and technology walk hand in hand. And the plaque? It reads: *The edition of* Life *magazine, with captions from the pen of journalist Mister*

John Telford, Englishman, for whom the free peoples of Morocco shall always hold a place in their hearts.'

Jack's emotions were a mess. He was both touched and embarrassed. His ego flattered but his sense of irony and amusement tickled. His instincts brought him to the verge of tears and laughter, each at the same time.

'The free peoples of Morocco...'

'All of them, Mister Telford. You seem to have brought their stories – *our* stories – to the world and, in doing so, helped us along our respective paths, to whatever may be written next. Morocco's part in driving the Nazis from North Africa. The liberation of Jewish refugees from the concentration camps. Much more besides. You have played a part.'

'Those are kind words, Highness. But it is my job, after all. I get paid for my writing, when all's said and done. If any of it makes a difference, amounts to a hill of beans in this crazy world...'

He'd become fond of Humphrey Bogart's lines lately. Since Lisbon.

'Yet the perils you have endured in the process – your injuries.'

The sultan glanced down at his cane.

'This?' said Jack. 'I just carry it now so people will feel sorry for me. It's going in the bin tomorrow.'

'And Lisbon. The documents you brought back were vital to us. The beating you took...'

'Beating, sir? How...?'

'Why, from your friend, Mister Welch, of course.'

'He's here,' he told Paquita. 'In Rabat.'

Jack had politely declined the use of the car back into town, elected to wait for her to finish her classes, walk with her, past the Black Guard barracks and along the Avenue des Orangers.

'There must be somebody,' she said. 'Report this. Get help. My god, comrade, you're on first-name terms with de Gaulle. With Leclerc.'

'Hardly. And not the way these things work. Hell, you know that. If you'd still been at the Ministry in Valencia and some bloody journalist had come whining about a plot to kill him...'

They waited at the south side of the Bab-el-Had square, opposite the gateway into the medina – waited for the traffic to thin, then they hurried across.

'But you're not just *some bloody journalist*. And, if not your friends in the army, what about the sultan? You think he just hands out accolades like this to everybody? He may seem a mild-mannered philanthropist, Jack, but know this, you can't survive as the ruler of Morocco without having certain services at your disposal. Dark services. And you should have told me.'

He stopped her outside the gates to a Muslim cemetery on Boulevard Gouraud. There was a funeral procession making its way inside, the white-draped corpse borne on the shoulders of robed and turbaned mourners, a small crowd following on behind.

'Told you?' he said.

'How I only got the job because of you.'

'Nonsense. I did nothing but put your name on his list.'

'Listen,' she snapped, 'I'm not stupid. I don't know who or what you are really, Jack, but I learned this in Valencia. You end up on somebody's assassination list and you're not simply *some bloody journalist*. And if you're right – that, for whatever reason, there's nobody you can turn to, nobody to sort it out, you just have to do it yourself.'

'Sure,' he said. 'Why didn't I think of that? Maybe when I get back, I'll just snap my damned fingers and it'll all go away.'

'Back?'

'On the road again, I'm afraid. Sabratha. Leclerc loves me so much he wants me to spend a whole damned week making my way to the middle of nowhere.'

'Sabratha. The comrades are there?'

He nodded. A temporary base, but just west of Tripoli, almost fifteen hundred miles. All Leclerc's forces and far more besides, gathered there: those who'd battled their way across Libya; those freed from Vichy's concentration camps, Spaniards as well as many others, and volunteered to fight for the forces of Giraud and de Gaulle respectively, now hopefully more united under the French Committee for National Liberation; hundreds of volunteers from the former French National Army, or who'd escaped from German prison camps, or fought in Syria and other places.

Reorganisation taking place and Leclerc demanding his new division should have all the publicity it deserved.

'And you've new comrades here,' said Jack, 'according to the sultan. Moroccan unions – part of the independence movement?'

'Lots of new members,' she told him. 'Our own Spanish unions working with the Moroccan Confederation. It's all good.'

'Apart from that…'

They'd reached the Place de France and Jack pointed through the haze of fumes from a passing bus to the walls of the old Moorish barbican guarding the more recent archway entrance to the medina's northwest corner. Anti-communist *Milice* posters being plastered alongside an official sign reading *Défense d'afficher.* Some of the local traders gathered around, watching the thugs in berets with their buckets and paste brushes. An altercation. A wizened elder stabbing his finger up into the chest of the fellow who seemed to be acting as lookout for the bill posters.

'Christ,' said Jack, 'it's him.'

He took her arm, began to drag her through the traffic, hobbling as fast as he could manage.

'Him?' Paquita was running to keep up. 'Who?'

'Long story. Same swine. Keeping watch for them in Casa.' A truck driver blared his horn at them. 'Then he turned up at Josie's show. I thought he had a gun…'

There was almost a score to settle. Josephine still made fun of him about it, whenever the opportunity arose, and he accepted it all with a veneer of good humour, though the whole incident had made him feel a fool.

But now Jack saw the wretch push the old man away from him. The onlookers began to shout, few in number but pressing forward. The bill posters, three of them, dropped the tools of their trade. One of them pulled a cosh from his pocket. They screamed back at the kaftan-clad protestors. *Allez, bougnoules.* Towel heads, they called them. Dirty Arabs. And worse insults.

Other spectators now, a few vehicles stopping in the road, but everybody keeping a safe distance. Because the lookout *did* now have a gun in his hand, a stubby revolver he'd pulled from inside his jacket. He waved it at the traders, then pressed the muzzle into the old fellow's chest. Again and again, each time pushing the wrinkled ancient back.

He would have forced him into the road, but he must, at that moment have been aware, for the first time, of a limping European in a trilby hat, sporting an eye-patch, bearing down upon him. Or perhaps he was distracted by the rather pretty young woman, in her simple white *gandora* and headscarf, being dragged along behind him.

And maybe there was also an instant of recognition.

'You!' he said, as Telford's walking stick came down on his wrist with such fury and force, it shattered both cane and bone at the same time.

The thug's scream of pain and fury, the shock which so contorted his ugly face, was almost drowned by the piercing screech of a police whistle. He was hauled away by his associates towards the arched gateway, as the traders and the old man moved in around them, yelling, menacing but, in the end, allowing them to disappear into the medina's warren of alleyways.

Jack glanced around, bent quickly and picked up the revolver.

'What are you doing?' said Paquita.

'Souvenir,' he replied, and tucked the weapon into the waistband of his trousers, concealed by his jacket.

'*Seguro*,' she said. 'Just some bloody journalist.'

'What will you do – wait until he finally succeeds in killing you, or strike first? Kill *him*, Jack, before it's too late.'

Paquita couldn't have been more clear.

It went around and around his brain, all through the uncomfortable three-hour flight. An American supply plane on which Fox had managed to secure him a place – the first part of his journey to Sabratha, this leg from Rabat to Oran. He'd only been allowed to take one small travelling bag if, as he'd insisted, he was also going to carry the dictaphone.

There, in Oran, he renewed his acquaintance with the Carcassonnes and was welcomed like the family's saviour. The cousin,

José, who'd led the resistance in Algiers and been tossed into prison for his pains afterwards by Darlan, had finally been released back in April. So had José's father and the other *résistants*. And the family was convinced it was Jack's articles in the American newspapers, as much as the Casablanca Conference, had made the difference.

'And José's recovered?' said Jack. 'I wrote about the camps, by the way. Hell, Vichy has a lot to answer for.'

'He's in London,' Roger replied. 'Next week, I'll be joining him. We carry on the fight from there now.'

Still with a few hours to kill before the night train to Algiers, Telford hunted down the bookshop again. *La Grande Librairie de Vienne.* And there, among the English editions, just one book which caught his eye. *Republic for a Day.* He bought it, asked how the Albert Camus novel was selling. Not well, it seemed, but it was enough to make him look Francine up, take her for a glass of wine. Apologies, of course. She'd sent him that note, hoping to see him again, but he had the accident with the truck to use as an excuse.

'It didn't stop you going to Lisbon though, did it?' she snapped at him.

'How...?' he began.

'Let's just say it was a little bird.'

He'd forgotten how well-connected she was.

There was no intimacy between them. Not anymore. He mumbled something about having finished *L'Étranger*, about how much he admired the writing. And had she heard from her husband? Yes, she said. Another little bird. Albert now with the Resistance, helping to write a new underground newspaper. *Combat.*

He shared the sleeper compartment with a couple of elderly carpet manufacturers, who snored for most of the night. So, he lay awake in his upper berth, playing over more of the exchange with Paquita, toying with the revolver. It gleamed in the dim reading light, the legend *Mre. D'Armes, St. Étienne* just legible beneath the cylinder. Along the barrel, the maker's mark S.1887. It was old, but in good condition, six chunky eleven millimeter cartridges. Wooden grips. But could he use it? *Would* he use it? There'd been that time, in Burgos, the rusty old weapon he'd bought, intending to kill Franco. And look how it had turned out. Too weak. Too soft. No killer. Not really, despite – well, those times had all been very different.

But there'd been Paquita's other suggestion. About the sultan and his dark services. In truth, he'd no real idea what she meant, and his imagination simply ran rampant.

He practised opening and closing the revolver's cylinder, quietly spinning the thing, thinking about Fox, as well. *More things in heaven and earth, Horatio?* And Fox's reminder there *were* such things as double-agents. Was it a hint? Yet, still that question. If Welch was intent on killing him, for what reason? And, if so, why save him from those Gestapo thugs?

Jack tried to settle, the revolver beneath the flimsy cushion serving as his pillow. The compartment stank of garlic, French tobacco and the farts of his fellow travellers. His leg bothered him. He'd got rid of the walking stick, at least, and he smiled at the memory of its final sacrifice. More swimming, that's what he needed. He thought about the sea, but the ocean seemed suddenly full of scorpions, of astrological signs and, in this way, he eventually fell asleep.

No train onwards from Algiers to Tunis until the next morning but one, so he checked into a cheap hotel, not far from the station, just across from the busiest part of the port, and amused himself through the following day, visiting the sights, wandering the famous Casbah, imagining himself as Pépé le Moko.

But, on the fourth morning of his journey, bright and early, he presented himself to the Railway Transport Officer, showed his papers – his own, of course, not the O'Hare forgeries – along with the letters signed by Leclerc and summoning him to Sabratha.

'Sabratha?' said the British major, running a finger down his clipboard. 'This train's bound for Tunis.'

'Yes,' Jack explained. 'Tunis. Then another bloody train to Gabès. After – well, to be honest, after that I haven't got a clue, but I'll cross this bridge...'

'And these papers. No passport?'

'It's a long story.'

'But this,' the major growled. 'Emergency Certificate only, old chap. To get you back to Blighty. Signed – great heavens, four years ago?'

'Yes. Still on my way. You see, no expiry date? Can I board now?'

'Damned irregular. And what's this?' His union card, accreditation with the Associated Press. 'Union card? Some sort of Commie, are you?'

'Journalist, sir. And I've another letter here.' He fished in his pocket. 'Well, a cable, anyway. By way of a contract with the BBC European Service.'

The major harrumphed loudly.

'Why didn't you say so in the first place?'

He waved Jack along the platform, and Telford's heart sank. There was little to choose between the passenger carriages making up one half of the train, and the cattle wagons forming the other half. Derelict would have been a compliment. He'd walked all the way up to the locomotive, where the fireman and the engineer yelled banter at each other in some accent from America's mid-West. And the tender bore the painted words *General Mark Clark Special* along its side.

Well, thought Jack, as he was directed onto one of the coaches by a French guard, that's international cooperation for you. Yankee train and crew, French guards and a British transport officer.

It pulled out at nine and, for the next ten hours, it trundled at a sedate pace, belching coal smoke, soot on the windows, stopping once every fifteen or twenty minutes, hauling through the high plains and plateaux, the wheatfields, between Setif and Constantine, the fertile farmlands and river valleys towards Guelma, the wooded mountain passes around Souk Ahras and, finally, along the gorges of the Medjerda river to reach the Tunisian border and, just beyond, the station and sidings of Ghardimaou. He'd been invited by the passengers at his end of the carriage to join their syndicate. He couldn't think what else to call it, but they had a battered kettle and, at every halt, there was a roster, by which each of them in their group – Jack, the Arab children and their parents, the Algerian travelling salesman, three French legionnaires, an American nurse, a quintet of veiled Berber women who spoke no language anybody else understood – took their equal turn at running forward to the locomotive, waiting in the queue with other syndicates' agents, for their pots and pans, their teapots and tin cans, to be filled with boiling water, the makings of mint tea.

'Right, everybody out,' yelled another English officer, a captain this time, the Train Commandant. 'Out, out! *Yallah, yallah!*'

They were herded down onto the platform. Confusion. A full hour of confusion, as dusk settled and the passengers finally given to understand they'd be spending the night there, canvas awnings for their roof, stretched between a pair of warehouses and straw palliasses on the floor for their beds.

'End of the line for these bogies,' the captain explained, as Jack watched the lineside cranes already busy, lifting one of the cattle wagon bodies.

'Different gauge in Tunisia,' said Telford.

'Railway man, sir?' asked the captain.

'No,' Telford smiled. 'Just a bit of *déja vu*. Saw the same thing at Irún a few years back.'

He slept remarkably well, all things considered, and they were treated to an early breakfast, those who wanted it. Fried spam and dried eggs. Or bread and cheese. Tea with condensed milk.

By daybreak, with the carriage and truck bodies lifted onto the wider bogies, they were off again. Six hours to Bizerta. Back out of Bizerta again and two more hours to Tunis. Another hotel room.

Day six, a bone-shaking eight hours, southwards, the line around the Gulf of Hammamet to Sousse, on down the coast to Sfax and finally – finally, oh, thank god – past the signs of recent battle, burned-out tanks, trundling into Gabès. The light was fading. He rubbed at the mucky windows, initially liked the look of the place. Palm trees as far as the eye could see, a veritable oasis and, at its heart, the town. Yet the town mostly in ruins. And Gabès had hit the headlines for something else, he remembered. A couple of years earlier. An Arab mob had brutally murdered six or seven Jews, attacked and injured many more.

He found a half-demolished hotel with vacancies, right by the station, on the Boulevard Faure-Biguet, and took himself for a late-evening swim from the deserted beach.

'The old girl will get us there, sir,' said the ambulance driver, a sergeant. 'This trip's a bit of a picnic, if you don't mind me sayin'. Looked after us all the way from Tobruk to Alex, she did.'

The old Austin K2 had been parked like a charm in the square outside his hotel, a small blackboard hanging over its red cross, with the single word, Sabratha, chalked upon it.

'Still can't believe my luck,' said Jack, as they left Gabès behind them.

'Usually somebody around who needs a lift to wherever we happen to be headin' – know what I mean?'

It turned out the sergeant – seconded to this task from some unit of the Royal Army Service Corps abandoned along the coast – had made the outbound journey to pick up medical supplies which should have been delivered to Tripoli but had ended up, instead, in Tunis, and then loaded onto Jack's train.

'Six hours?' said Jack.

'Seven, more like.' Their other passenger, a young nurse from Barnstaple, Annie Wimbury, heading for Sabratha as well, a volunteer medical unit there.

Luckily, the three of them were good storytellers, though Annie had the best news – that Mussolini had apparently been voted out of power by his own Grand Council and arrested. She'd picked it up on a World Service news bulletin, part of an update on the Allied invasion of Sicily, Patton and Montgomery slowly fighting their way across the island towards Messina.

'But will they still fight alongside the Germans?' Jack asked her, but the bulletin had shed no light in this direction, it seemed, and by five they were driving along the dirt road between Sabratha's scatter of rundown adobe dwellings, its goats, its curious Libyan children. And its smell – though not the smell of the village itself. To the north, olive groves, and at the farther, northern end of the village, a small mosque. South of the mosque, Sabratha Camp, barbed wire, a sprawl of military pyramid tents, hundreds upon hundreds of them. Tents and trucks. Tanks and bren carriers. The stench of latrines for thousands of men. And the greasy stink of camp cooking. Flies everywhere, clouds of them.

A small convoy of lorries passed them as they turned in through the gates, the men in the back singing in French, all stripped to the waist and in party spirits.

'Lucky blighters,' said the sergeant. 'Off to the beach.'

'Is it far?'

'Three miles, maybe? Pile of old ruins there – Roman stuff, like. Who'd have believed it, eh? Eyeties 'ere, even all them years ago.'

They dropped Nurse Wimbury at the cluster of stretch tents flying a Red Cross flag, and Jack decided to get out there, as well. He dragged down his bag and the case containing the Dictaphone, left the sergeant unloading the medical supplies, thanked him with a packet of Luckies he'd managed to pick up, and asked a passing lieutenant for directions to Leclerc's headquarters.

'You're out of uniform, *Monsieur* Telford,' said the general, when Jack was finally admitted to his presence. Leclerc had barely looked up from the papers strewn across his table, his face set. It didn't look like he'd had the best of days.

'I didn't know I was supposed to wear one, sir.'

'New regulations. It seems we're soon to have the honour of coming under the command of the United States, both for training and operational purposes also. And their regulations are clear. Accredited correspondents shall be uniformed. No rank, no insignia – certainly no saluting. But new credentials. Green credentials, your new contract. Armbands.'

'I'm not a soldier – prefer not to be mistaken for one.'

'All the same, if you wish to remain accredited – to be fed, housed, have your transport organised...'

'If not?'

'Perhaps I phrased that badly, Telford. You signed up for this. Believe me, we're stuck with each other for the duration. And I've more to worry about than some petulant newspaperman. So, you'll damned well learn to defend yourself.'

'I came, didn't I? And you, General – your new division?'

'Division? I have one regiment of motorised infantry. One armoured regiment with no tanks. No tanks and hardly any anti-tank guns. The best part of two thousand men out there, most of them still not allocated to the units we need. Every day, a different order. Two weeks before we ship out to Temara. Two weeks to find the men and equipment we need. And for you, *Monsieur* Telford, to announce our coming – to announce the formation of the finest division in our new and united French Army. The Second Armoured Division.'

'Still room in it for all our Spanish friends?'

'Of course, but...'

The tent flap was thrust open and Massu stormed inside. Jack hadn't seen him since Brazza, Christmas. He still wore that haughty look, his nostrils pinched, but now it seemed the smell in his nose was not just unpleasant but poisonous.

'But not the *tirailleurs*,' he snarled. 'Isn't this so, General? All this way – Kufra, the Fezzan, Ksar Ghilane. And now, those bloody Americans expect us to whiten ourselves.'

'It's true?' he said later, to Eze Tolabye.

'You heard about our friend, Abia?' said the Chadian, his face gleaming in the fire's glow, a black blowfly crawling on the side of his nose, the angry buzz of insects all around them. He was spooning some sort of gruel into his mouth from a wooden bowl.

Jack had been allocated to a tent occupied by two young French medical officers, stowed his gear, followed their directions to the section of the camp occupied by the Chad Regiment.

'I heard. His spirit will be marching with Diguéal and N'Donon again, I suppose. But they will be angry at this betrayal.'

'Betrayal, English? Why is it a betrayal? And here, you must eat.'

He snapped his fingers to one of the others gathered around the fire. Jack recognised Mahamet the Hadjerai corporal, as well as Dillah and Rimdaga, those two Cameroonians who'd been with Leclerc from the start. Yet they all looked very different, every remnant of their old *tirailleur* uniforms gone, replaced now by British army battledress tunics or greatcoats, berets and forage caps. Their precious polished boots. It was Rimdaga who ladled more of the gruel from their pot, handed it to him.

'You drove them into the sea, Eze,' said Jack. 'The Italians. The Germans. And now – no longer good enough because the bloody Americans won't have black people fighting in their combat units.'

'But some of us can go home,' said Dillah. 'Is that not a good thing?'

'And the rest,' Eze grinned at him, 'still fight – but not under the Americans. Italy, my friend. We go to Italy, where the weather is warm. Even the Flying Lion has said we will be better there, better than in the cold north.'

It was pretty much what Massu had told him. Those French West Africans, the Senegalese, the equatorial Cameroonians, those from Gabon and Chad, all the men who'd chosen to fight for Free France, were being transferred to Koenig's French First Army, the Colonial Infantry Division. Yes, Sicily and, all being well, then Italy itself.

Massu had been convinced this had nothing to do with concern that black Africans should not be forced to suffer the freezing weather of northern Europe – if this, indeed, was where Leclerc's division was ultimately bound. And nor could it be lack of equipment, for who else would the general have chosen to equip first than his most hardened veterans?

'No,' Massu had raged. 'Show me. Show me just one American infantry unit with black combat troops. Fine for digging shitholes, for running supplies – but combat? Can you imagine the horror of those southern gentlemen among their bloody officers at the very thought of arming black men?'

He was right. It had made headlines when a squadron of black American fighter pilots had arrived in North Africa back in May – made headlines because it was so extraordinary. For the Americans, almost unthinkable.

'Good god,' Massu had said. 'Even their blood banks are segregated. Did you know? And their black nurses? Only used to care for prisoners-of-war.'

Telford had no idea how much of this was true, but Leclerc certainly hadn't disputed any of it. And Jack had come away with the impression the general also was furious about this *blanchiment*, as Massu had called it, this "whitening" of their ranks – just too professional to say so for Telford's benefit.

'I was hoping we'd get to serve together again,' said Jack, and swallowed some of the glutinous porridge, trying unsuccessfully, at the same time, to swat away the swarm of flies following the food towards his lips.

'Serve, English? You have no uniform. No gun.'

'I get my uniform tomorrow, it seems. But I won't be carrying a gun.' Well, he thought, perhaps the revolver, just in case...

'And you, Eze, you still have the automatic rifle, the Browning?'

'I have it. But your friend, the man who had sailed on the boat with you, who also had the same gun – you said you wanted to meet him again. Did you ever get your wish?'

'Granell? He must be here, somewhere in this camp. It's just so damned big. Have you seen the other Spaniards – Alemán, El Gordo and the others?'

'Of course. Later, I'll show you. How long are you here, English?'

'Just a few days. But listen. Maybe I can help. If I write about this, about you not being allowed to serve under the Americans – I think in some small way we might have helped liberate the camps...' He saw the puzzled expression on the faces of Eze Tolabye and his comrades.

'The camps?' said Mahamet the Hadjerai corporal.

'Never mind.' Jack knew he was wasting his time. 'It was just – I suppose this is it, then. We won't see each other again, Eze?'

'What are you talking about?' Eze smiled. 'Tomorrow is the football final. Shall you not come to watch? I think we stand a good chance of winning.'

Jack laughed, though it was only to cover his foolish sentimentality, his absurd sense of bereavement that here was a parting of the ways, the breaking of a fellowship.

'No horses on the pitch, this time?' he said.

'No horses,' Eze replied. 'And there is no need for sadness, my friend. For I think we shall meet again – before the end.'

It was the grenade that nearly killed him.

He'd received his kit from the quartermasters in the morning, then watched the men of the Chad Regiment at their drill, marching and wheeling through the heat haze of their rock-strewn parade ground. The entire camp was a frying pan.

Later, the match – an easy victory for skipper Eze Tolabye over an opposing team who called themselves the Camberley XI. The Camberley players from a tank company originally assembled in England, three years earlier, men with English fathers and French mothers, or vice versa. Young Frenchmen who'd been studying or working in Blighty when the Armistice was signed, then flocked to Carlton Gardens to join de Gaulle. But they'd seen little or no action, had been virtually exiled there at Sabratha for almost eight months.

The Spaniards had been out in force, naturally, to watch the game. Lean men, all of them, made slight by nature or by the Vichy camps, and darkened by the Saharan winds which had raked their hard labour details.

'Well, will you look at that?' El Gordo laughed. 'Proper soldier now, comrade. Spotless, but a soldier, all the same.'

And, so he was. Not a mark on his khaki shirt or those olive drab trousers, his field service shoes or the canvas puttees, his immaculate black armband with the white letter 'C' confirming his role. He felt like a total fraud, foolish.

'I see you've been introduced,' Jack said to Amado. Granell was plainly amused as well. And so were the others Telford knew by name – Campos *el canario*, Bamba, El Gitano, Ortiz and the other *toledano*, Alemán. He'd shaken hands with them all, nodded to the former International Brigade volunteers, Reiter the German and Markovich the Yugoslav. They were all together, in a crowd near the Chadians' goalpost.

There was good-natured banter, and Jack had been invited to join them later – their company's turn for a spot of rest and recreation that evening at the beach.

'Maybe a bit of fishing,' Ortiz had said when, at five o'clock, their trucks had bounced along the rutted track towards the coast, the Spaniards shouting loudly to each other, and all at the same time. It was bedlam, and Jack was struggling to follow the tangled threads of their conversations. But he'd fallen back into his own Spanish easily enough.

Telford had been doing his best to work out how all these squads fitted together, but nobody seemed to really know. The old Free French units had been formally disbanded. Fair enough, Jack supposed. An end to their dissociation from the former Vichy regiments, the goal of unifying this new French army. Yet some sort of limbo. Old battalions disbanded, new ones not officially formed, the men left under the immediate command of their sergeants or junior officers until they were assigned afresh. And though, technically, it was supposed to be an end of division, there was no way – not a cat in hell's chance – that these men who'd fought for de Gaulle and for Leclerc were ever going to give up their Free French insignia, their Cross of Lorraine badges of honour.

'Fishing?' Jack replied and passed around his smokes. He assumed they must have lines and hooks in their haversacks, but just then they'd topped a ridge and he'd seen where they were headed. 'My god,' he'd laughed. 'What's this?'

A purely rhetorical question. Ahead of them, the Mediterranean, bathed in golden sunlight, shimmering on the sea. But between these dunes and the water, ancient ruins, the columns of a Roman city, maybe, a temple, and a Roman theatre.

'They've arranged a concert or two for us,' said Campos. 'Over there. Can you believe it, *inglés*? Those bloody *macaronis* were here two thousand years ago.'

'But not anymore,' laughed Bamba. 'Now the bastards are gone for good.'

'And a whole team of archaeologists,' said Granell, 'picking over their bones. Closed off the whole damned thing. No more shows.'

The trucks pulled up close to a cluster of bivouac tents and Jack heard English voices – unhappy English voices. He rarely craved the company of his countrymen but, on this occasion, his curiosity was piqued.

'Listen,' he shouted to Granell, as the Spaniards jumped from the wagons and headed off towards the beach. 'I'll catch up with you later.'

Under the nearest of those canvas awnings, some robed Libyans and a couple of young Europeans were at work, brushing and carefully washing artefacts in wooden trays. Closest to him, the source of those angry voices. A man in his forties, a parsimonious moustache, civilian trousers, the pale shirt of an RAF officer, wings on his chest, a turban upon his head. On his shoulders, the insignia of his rank. A flight lieutenant.

'I tell you, my dear,' he snapped, 'it's Punic.' He held up the shard of red slip pottery, allowed the fading light to illuminate its edges. 'For god's sake, can't you see? Did they teach you nothing at that bloody Institute?'

She was closer to Jack's own age, slacks and a green cotton blouse, mousey hair, curled and tied back with a scarf. Elegant.

'To be precise, darling,' she said, sarcastically, 'it's *neo*-Punic. There's little distinction between the two. It's simply not accurate to brand it as Punic *per se*.'

The man turned, stared into Jack's eyes, but otherwise ignored him.

'But no damned way to do any worthwhile excavation without disturbing the temple,' the fellow explained. 'It's the only way, though. Somebody needs to give us the go-ahead to look *under* the Romans. I don't suppose that's *you*, is it?'

'Me?' said Jack, assuming this remark, at least, was aimed in his direction. 'No, I'm a war correspondent. Just came for a swim. I was curious. About the dig. You're in charge, sir?'

'I have the dubious responsibility of overseeing the allocation of grain supplies for our teams across Tripolitania. Babs here is our kingpin at Sabratha.'

'You wouldn't know it, though, would you, Mister...?'

'Telford, miss.'

'Care for a quick tour of the site, Mister Telford? I think we're finished here, Max. And, who knows, we might get some publicity at last.'

'If you say so, my sweet.'

She offered the flight lieutenant a smile, tinged with irony, and picked up a water bottle hanging from one of the tent poles.

'Come on,' she said, 'let's start with the villa. We'll walk the site clockwise.'

She led them across the open ground, past the army trucks.

'You and the flight lieutenant…?' Jack began, convinced they must be an item. Husband and wife, he thought.

'Gosh, no.'

He didn't believe her, offered her one of his Gauloises, lit them both, as they reached a jumble of fallen masonry. She showed him the mosaic floor, but thankfully without too much technical jargon.

'You were arguing like an old married couple. Working together for a while, I suppose?'

She led him to the remains of a sturdier wall. It stretched away, straight and true for some distance. Yet here there was a gap. The Byzantine wall, she explained, and this the gateway.

'Don't you know who he is?' she said. '*Mister* Agatha Christie.'

'Pardon?'

'Max Mallowan. Aggie's husband.'

They strolled along an excavated street towards the sea, columns and temples on each side. It must be like this, he imagined, at Pompeii and Herculaneum, though the gravel-throated shouting of the Spaniards, from somewhere just out of sight, rather spoiled the illusion.

'You're a family friend, then, as well?'

'You could say that. And here, the Forum.' Jack nodded his head in appreciation, while she unstoppered the water bottle, took a swig. 'Do you object to sharing, Mister Telford?' She held out the flask. The water was refreshingly cool.

There were the ruins of Roman olive presses and then she led them down through some low dunes, eastwards along the beach itself. Granell and the others were in the shallows, splashing each other like schoolboys, yelling and laughing. They spotted Jack and Babs. A few raucous and bawdy cries.

'Brothers in arms, Mister Telford?'

'Look, it's Jack. And yes, Babs, we've been through some scrapes together. They're just hoping I'll write something heroic about them.'

'Is that how you hurt your eye? In one of those scrapes.'

'This? No, an earlier misfortune. But listen, d'you mind if I ask about her stories? Miss Marple and so on. I'm a great admirer.'

A lie, of course. He massively preferred Margery Allingham. But at least Babs hadn't made any stupid comments about him looking like a pirate.

'I expect there may be something of a hiatus,' she said. 'They rather enjoy solving riddles together. And now – well, with Aggie volunteering in the hospital and Max out here. Sometimes, the three of us…'

'I suppose she needs somebody to help test the stories. And her husband – must be something of a comedown for him, living out here in a tent.'

'You *are* joking, Jack. He's been allocated his very own Italian villa. Patio overlooking the sea. Divine. Max isn't one *not* to enjoy the high life. And it *is* a wonderful villa. But yes, testing the stories.'

'Sounds fascinating.'

They finished the tour at the Roman theatre. It was in remarkably good condition, much of the semi-circular outer wall and archways intact, as well as the tiers of stone seating within, the proscenium platform beyond, and backed by the layered columns of the stage building.

'You should come to Max's villa, Jack. It could be fun. We might unravel some of life's mysteries for you.'

If only life my was so simple! Jack thought.

'Maybe after I've been for a swim,' he said and saw her bite her lip, realised his gaffe. 'Just joking,' he quickly added. 'Not tonight, obviously. But maybe before I head back to Rabat.' Yes, he decided, I would definitely be the gooseberry at that little party. 'And Babs – do I get to know your full name?'

'I think just Babs will do, Jack,' she said. 'Don't you?'

'Hey, you're just in time,' shouted El Gordo, when Jack limped down the sand towards them. His leg didn't trouble him too much now, but the circuit of Sabratha's ruins had rather taken it out of him. A swim would help.

'In time for what?' He began to unbutton his shirt, loosen the trouser belt.

'Fishing, of course,' said Amado. 'You don't think we can survive on the muck they serve at the camp, do you?' He was rooting through the contents of his haversack, took a quick look around. 'Who else brought one? Nice juicy pomegranate for bait.'

He held up the grenade and laughed.

'Bloody hell,' said Jack. 'Seriously?'

'Everybody out!' Granell yelled, waved for the Spaniards still in the waves to come ashore. Then he wandered down to the water's edge, pulled the pin. 'Down!'

He tossed the thing out, perhaps a dozen yards, crouched and folded his arms over his head. The rest did the same.

Whoosh.

Jack felt the vibration under his feet, saw the explosion of water, was amazed that, even where he was, something whistled over his head. But, by then, the Spaniards were back on their feet, some of them carrying small sticks, skewers to pierce the gills of that bounty, the dazed or dead sea bass and gilt-head bream, delivered up by the ocean.

He left his clothes and shoes, everything but his underpants, in a heap on the sand, wandered into the shallows, waves breaking around his ankles.

'Not a bad catch,' he said, and made Alemán hold up his own collection so he could admire them.

'Need more yet, though,' Amado laughed. 'And nearly time to get back.'

'Quick swim first,' Jack told him, and waded further into the sea, up to his waist, dived under the surface, felt the brine in his nostrils, the stinging freshness in his eyes, the bubbling muted rush in his ears. Stupidly, he'd forgotten about the eye patch, dislodged it. He trod water, set it straight, began an easy breast-stroke parallel to the shoreline. Almost dusk, and those Roman columns now silhouetted against the sky. Heaven, he thought, and turned towards the beach, saw his companions gathering on the sand in small groups. He'd better head back, he knew that. But one more dive first.

The water wasn't deep. He could still see the ridges on the bottom, minnows darting below him.

He surfaced, wiped the sea water from his face, out of his eye and, as his ears cleared, he just about heard the cry.

'Down!'

He saw them all drop into a crouch. There was a splash, not far away. At first, he thought it must be a fish. They'd been jumping since he arrived on the beach.

But this time there was no amusing burst of water. No, this time he felt it. The shockwave. The blast pounding into his chest. Something sliced his thigh. Something else stabbed at his left arm, near the shoulder. He spun about in the waves which no longer seemed so gentle.

There was shouting on the beach, men running. He could see Granell pointing towards him, yelling at the top of his voice at another group nearby, yelling and splashing into the water.

'Telford,' he cried. 'Are you hurt?'

There was blood, spiralling up towards the surface, a small cloud of crimson around Jack's shoulder. But the extent of it? He had no idea, though it didn't seem to impede him. He was just suddenly very cold, light-headed, yet still able to swim – swim until his feet found the bottom and he could push himself towards Amado.

'What the hell...?' he said and looked at his arm. There was more blood, lots of it, running down from his biceps. It stung like the very devil. And as the water became shallow, there was a similar dripping gash on his upper leg.

'Some bloody fool,' said Granell, gripping his right arm and studying the wounds. 'Some bloody fool! But these don't look too bad.'

Jack pulled himself free, looked along the beach to where El Gordo and Campos *el canario* remonstrated with one of the younger men. Telford didn't know his name, but the rage built within him. He pushed Amado aside, pitched himself towards the shoreline, his knees rising and falling, water splashing like fountains all around him.

As he neared the group, all eyes turned to him and the young Spaniard began to mouth an apology. But, by then, Telford had balled his fist, blinded by his own anger and fear, and smashed it into the man's face.

It hurt. The Spaniard staggered back, and Jack gripped his throat.

'Who was it?' he bawled. 'Who told you to do that?'

They both fell backwards, Telford landing on top of the youngster, now both hands around the fellow's neck. More blood ran down his wrists, mingled with the sea water dripping from them both.

'Telford!' Somebody – Granell, it must have been – gripped his shoulders, tried to pull him off. 'It was an accident.'

'Who?' Jack still demanded. 'Was it Welch? Well, was it?'

He realised he was now roaring in English. Like a maniac.

There were more hands upon his person, separating them, a blur of voices ringing in his ears until he finally felt the world collapse around him.

Josephine Baker thought it was hilarious, bit her knuckles every time she thought about it, as they waited patiently outside the RAF General Hospital at Maison Carrée.

Algiers again, just more than a week later. The tortuous bloody journey in reverse. Leclerc had at least furnished him with a Jeep, got him back to Gabès, then two days, on four different trains, before he reached Algiers just in time – or should have been – for the gala occasion at which she was performing in this new capital of Free France.

'I've got more stitches than a patchwork quilt,' Jack told her.

He was still embarrassed by it. His attack on the young soldier.

'No excuse for missing my show,' she pouted. He'd checked in at the same hotel near the station, intending to be there, for the performance, and had fallen asleep exhausted.

'It was a great show,' said Steinbeck, there on behalf of the *New York Herald Tribune*. He was easy company. An educated Yankee accent, a voice that faltered frequently. Jack liked him but was jealous as hell of his writing. 'Our girl really brought the house down. You heard, Jack?'

He'd heard. The whole point of the show was to further celebrate the new French unity, both Giraud and de Gaulle to be in attendance. But de Gaulle hadn't arrived. Giraud's presence had been politely acknowledged. And then, part way through one of her numbers, she'd been seized by a fit of emotion. De Gaulle, at last. She'd pointed him out, though he'd tried to enter discreetly.

'He's here,' she'd cried, tears of joy rolling down her cheeks, and the theatre had gone wild with excitement. Everybody. If there'd been any doubt about whether de Gaulle or Giraud was accepted as the true leader of new France, it drowned finally there, in the municipal theatre of Algiers on the Place Bresson.

'Well, I wasn't going to let you slip away again without saying hello,' Baker told him.

'I've got all day to kill,' said Jack. 'But I wasn't entirely expecting this.'

There'd been a message for him at the hotel when he'd finally surfaced. Jacques Abtey had tracked him down. Not hard to do in Algiers. A message that the sultan was in town. A state visit to neighbouring Algeria and his insistence on seeing the technological wonder of new X-ray equipment here at the hospital's burns unit. He was, after all, a modern man. And since he'd heard *Monsieur* Telford might be in town – hell, it seemed everybody knew his business – perhaps he would care to join the party, along with Miss Baker.

'And you're sure I'm supposed to be here?' said Steinbeck. 'It's not every day you get the chance to meet the Sultan of Morocco, I guess, but…'

Jack had eaten breakfast and taken himself along to the Grande Poste, its interior more like the most elaborate of Moorish palaces than a post and communications office. He'd dispatched another of his precious discs to Barea – interviews in Spanish with Amado and the others about their perceptions of the war, there at Sabratha – and wired some copy to Bunnelle, a couple of features serving to show how the slumbering giant of Free France was now gathering its strength. And then a phone call to Sydney Elliott. Nothing special. Just to keep in touch. Occasioned by the rumour Granell had picked up. That they might be heading for England? He couldn't tell Elliott, naturally. But it had suddenly occurred to him, if Leclerc's new Division was heading for Blighty…

Home? He hadn't thought of it as home for a long time. And it was still swilling around in his brain when, on his way out of the post office, he'd seen Steinbeck waiting in the queue. Well, he'd thought it *might* be Steinbeck. The man's picture had been in the paper often enough. The rugged yet amiable features, the moustache like a long chevron. Jack had read *Tortilla Flat* when it first appeared in England. Six, seven years before? Then he'd read it again, immediately afterwards. And he'd only just finished *Of Mice and Men*, a library copy, immediately before he'd set off for Spain. But he'd never managed to pick up the new one – the title which had attracted all the newspaper attention and reviews.

'Forgive me for asking...'

Steinbeck, endearing man, had been astounded that anybody should recognise him. In Algiers, of all places, for pity's sake. Mutual acquaintances, as it turned out. He'd waxed lyrical about Josie's performance. And Harmon? Yes, of course he knew Harmon. Had Jack heard she was in Sicily? Covering the air war against Rome, Milan and Turin, now the island itself was taken. Sure, she'd be there whenever they invaded the mainland. It was on the cards. Just a matter of time. And place.

'Look,' Jack had said, tentatively, 'did Josie tell you about *Sidi* Muhammad coming to town...?'

Steinbeck, it turned out, was taken with the idea of meeting the Sultan of Morocco.

'Hell, something to write home about. Folks back there have no idea. But then, I didn't have much idea myself until I started checking it out. Morocco. Algeria. My god!'

So, there they were, waiting on the hospital steps in the tenth *arrondissement* of Algiers, when the sultan's limousine pulled up in the palm-lined street below. It was quite a cavalcade, another eight cars behind. A state visit, indeed.

At the same time, Abtey came through the hospital doors.

'They're ready for us,' he said, and right behind him came the hospital's own welcoming committee: a mixture of white physicians' coats and RAF uniforms: angelic nurses in veil caps, rank insignia on their epaulettes; and an RAF photographer.

Introductions.

'Welcome, Your Highness. Group Captain Bedford, at your service.' A salute, though the absurdly tall group captain seemed uncertain where, precisely, to direct it among the group of approaching white *djellabas*. He made the mistake of settling upon the distinguished figure of Ahmed Belbachir Haskouri who, with the most gracious yet slightest of bows, the merest gesture of his hand, pointed Bedford in the right direction. At the same time, Jack spotted the almost electric spark which passed between Belbachir and Baker in the aftermath.

'Group Captain,' said *Sidi* Muhammad in his halting English. 'How very kind. And this,' he turned to Belbachir, 'is my most loyal friend, His Excellency *Sidi* Ahmed Belbachir Haskouri, Chief of Staff to the *khalifa* of Spanish Morocco. And many other honours besides. You see?'

'Yes, Your Highness. And allow me to name Flight Lieutenant Bosely, sir. Our matron – senior nurse, you know?'

She stepped forward. Young for a matron, thought Jack. He almost expected her to curtsy, but she didn't. The sharpest of salutes.

'Of course,' said the sultan. 'And let me see. Princess Mary's Royal Air Force Nursing Service, yes?'

Yes, that overwhelmed them a little. What a charmer. His boys were called forth, a few other chosen dignitaries. Then – well, no. Introductions entirely unnecessary when it came to Josephine Baker. A ripple of excitement among the hospital personnel.

Jack was named and ignored, and Josie stepped forward with an apology.

'Another journalist friend, Your Highness. I hoped you wouldn't mind. Nor you, Group Captain. But this is Steinbeck. John Steinbeck.'

Nothing seemed to register with the British party, but *Sidi* Muhammad's eyes glistened, his head turned in wonder.

'*The Grapes of Wrath*, Mister Steinbeck?' The pronunciation was imperfect, but it was impressive, all the same.

'You read it, sir?' said Steinbeck.

'I fear not,' said *Sidi* Muhammad. 'Yet we have another good friend, a collector of treasures, Abderahman Menebhi. He persuaded me to purchase a copy of the film – the movie, as you Americans call it, no? We have played it through many times, and Menebhi translates for me, where it may be necessary. He is very good at it.'

'I am deeply honoured, sir,' Steinbeck told him. '*Votre Altesse.*'

The tour began. First, the orthopaedic ward.

'You know,' Steinbeck whispered to Jack, 'it's what I love about this place. The languages. Hell, I don't think I've heard a conversation held in just one language since I got here. Bit of this, bit of that. GIs and Arabs, Arabs and Frenchies. But they all get by, just fine. It's all in the hands, don't you think?' He held out his own, palms upwards. 'Explains our writing, yes? Folk think our fingers are just the tools we use to hold a pen, or to tap on typewriter keys. But they're not, are they? There's a connection, between our brains and our hands. Expression, Jack. Expression.'

Jack looked at his own hands, the fingers which had killed Carter-Holt.

Belbachir heard them, drifted away from Josephine's side, waited for the two writers to catch up.

'Next, the burns unit, I think,' he said. 'His Imperial Highness is keen to see it. They say they have made great advances in plastic surgery here. But you, Mister Telford, no more adventures, I hope? Did you know, *Monsieur* Steinbeck, Telford here has performed great services for the people of Morocco. Perhaps for Algeria.'

'Working for the oppressed, Jack?' said Steinbeck. 'I had no idea. Another Tom Joad, maybe.'

Jack hadn't read *The Grapes of Wrath* but he recognised the name from one of those newspaper interviews. Telford demurred, while Belbachir protested.

'Oppressed?' he said to Steinbeck. 'If we are indeed oppressed, sir, it is merely through our lack of independence. French Morocco a protectorate. Spanish Morocco under Spain's control. And Algeria? Not even a protectorate. Simply territory claimed as part of France itself. Do you know there has been no traditional ruler of Algeria since the Dey of Algiers went into exile? A hundred years ago, gentlemen.'

Ahead of them, the sister for the burns unit was explaining how the ward used to be the linen store for the school, which once occupied the building.

'And independence, Your Excellency – is that a prospect?'

'In Morocco, there have been promises. From your president. You will want to plant your airbases there, we suppose. But he does not forget his promises, does he? Roosevelt? And there is a movement, here in Algeria. Ferhat Abbas. Do you know him, *Monsieur* Telford?'

Jack had heard the name. From the Carcassonnes, as it happened. But by then, they'd reached the bedside of a young man, his face terribly disfigured, yet with the left side, the cheek, the chin, displaying the blotched and pitted flesh of reconstruction, while his nose was connected to his shoulder by a thick tube of skin. Sister Hipkins explained the procedure.

'And your eye,' said the sultan. 'Can they save your eye?'

It was milky white, the lids almost non-existent.

'The Group Captain says he'll just pop it out for me, sir,' the lad smiled. 'Only need one, after all.'

'Yes,' said *Sidi* Muhammad. 'You see?' He waved Telford forward. 'This is *Monsieur* Telford. He may only have one eye, but he sees more than most men with two, I believe.'

The young airman beamed at Jack, who asked whether he'd mind giving some details, explained he was a war correspondent, would like to maybe write a feature about the hospital. Oh, and here – he introduced Steinbeck.

'He'll make you famous in the States as well, if you're lucky,' Jack told the lad.

There were photographs.

The party eventually moved on to the X-ray department, something else the sultan was keen to visit. But there wasn't enough room for everybody – not safely, anyway.

'I already got my tan,' Josephine joked. 'Maybe Jack and me, we'll wait out here.'

There were seats in the corridor.

'You've been busy, Josie,' he said. 'The papers reckon you've already done nine thousand miles. Tunisia, Libya, Egypt.'

'Palestine,' she reminded him. 'Beirut. We did a show there – a singer you won't know. Brachah Zefira. God, what a voice.'

He laughed.

'Yes, I know her. Met her once. After you, she's one of my favourites.'

She slapped him on the shoulder.

'Flatterer. Well, I auctioned that lovely cross de Gaulle gave me. Remember? Thought it should go to a good cause. We raised three hundred thousand *francs* for the Resistance. And did you know I joined ENSA? George Formby's coming out here next month. Won't that be swell?'

Jack couldn't stand the man. Whining Wigan accent. But it made him think of Max Weston, and he smiled at one of his memories. Those terrible jokes.

'Swell, yes.'

'And listen,' she murmured. 'Steinbeck. I just wanted to let you know, Jack. We're all in the same business. Get my drift? Jacques and I may be semi-retired now. But the job you did in Lisbon. Well, folk notice things. Important folk.' She winked at him. 'And Steinbeck,' she said. 'The OSS? If you needed anything doing – you know? Any little problems...'

Any little problems. How very amusing. That, somehow, he might recruit John Steinbeck to help him dispose of whatever threat Welch did, or did not, present to him.

The night train to Oran was almost empty, a soft sleeper compartment to himself. Yet he still chose one of the upper berths, lay there reading the paper he'd picked up at the station. *Liberté*. Fairly new. And here, a report from a French Committee of National Liberation meeting, held in Algiers, naturally. The speech from one of its members. Monnet? Jack didn't know him, but he liked the words, even if they might be utopian.

'There will be no peace in Europe, if the states are reconstituted on the basis of national sovereignty. The countries of Europe are too small to guarantee their peoples the necessary prosperity and social development. The European states must constitute themselves into a federation, a United States of Europe.'

Social development. Was it possible? A culture finally turning its back on racial hatreds, whether those that Baker had suffered, or those that led to the easy dismissal, the betrayal, of Eze Tolabye and other African heroes of Free France. A culture shunning the trappings of colonial domination. He didn't think so, but god, he hoped he was wrong.

He read the last few pages of his book. Hell of a story. Those borderlands where Czechoslovakia, Hungary and Western Ukraine met. Would he get there one day? Maybe. But, meanwhile, he must get hold of *The Grapes of Wrath*. See the film, if he was able.

Telford fell asleep to the sickly smell of coal smoke infused into his pillow, the rhythm of the train as it repeated some meaningless chatter along the tracks towards Oran. He was jerked awake at one of the stations along the route, the book on his chest, the dim bunk light still glimmering, and he rolled over to flick the bakelite switch.

The next time he woke, he sensed something was amiss.

The train had picked up speed.

Clickety-clack. Clickety-clack.

Tobacco smoke in the air.

Had he left a cigarette burning in the ashtray under the window? Though it wasn't French tobacco, was it? He sniffed the air. No, this was more like…

Telford rolled over, the book falling to the floor.

The glow of a cigarette in the darkness.

'Sweet dreams, Mister Telford?' It was Welch's insidious voice, of course. That wheedling, artful tone.

Somewhere in Jack's travel bag was the revolver. He'd intended to sleep with the thing under his pillow, though he'd never quite gotten around to it. Almost forgotten about it since he'd toyed with the thing on his outbound journey. And where the hell was the bag? Down there, somewhere. On one of the lower berths, with the machine. He'd not even bothered to lock the compartment door.

'I was hoping this might be another hallucination, Welch.'

He swung his legs over the edge of the bunk, saw for the first time that Welch's hand wasn't empty. The same pistol, he assumed, with which Welch had secured his release from those Gestapo thugs in Lisbon. The swine brought it up, sharply, and Jack froze, lifted his hands in a gesture of surrender, of compliance.

'Good god, are you in uniform, Telford?' Welch taunted him. 'You think it will protect you, old man?'

'You at least owe me an explanation.'

Play for time, Jack thought. Just play for time.

'Really? Like a John Buchan novel, where the villain reveals all? I have neither the time nor the inclination, Telford. Let's go for a little walk, shall we? So I can dispose of this nastiness and get on with more important matters.'

Welch backed towards the door, waved the pistol for Jack to climb down.

'A last cigarette?' said Jack and pointed towards his bag.

'Don't be a fool.'

'At least, tell me about Howard. Lisbon. At the airport. Were you bringing him the message he was going to be shot down?'

Welch laughed, slid the door open, glanced into the corridor.

'What really troubles you, Telford, I wonder? Ah, I see. You'd like to convince yourself it was Hexy von Podewils who gave the game away, who betrayed him – not your careless notebook. Come on, out!'

So, he knew Jack had written up Howard's mission, and he could only know that if his Gestapo friends had told him so, after they'd searched his room. Had Welch really been at the airfield to warn the actor, or was this a piece of playacting in itself? Had Welch, in fact, already called in the Luftwaffe attack?

'I might prefer to just be shot here. Bloody traitor.'

Jack did his best to quell his fears, to mask them with just a little of Leslie Howard's composure, his *sang-froid*. Yet he followed Welch into the corridor anyway.

'Shoot you here, Telford? But the guard would likely come wandering along to investigate. Maybe some of the innocent folk in these other compartments. And then – well, still more blood on your hands. Gabizon. Howard. You really want to add to the tally? Poor Luc Chabat, of course. My friends in the *Milice* still looking for justice, whether you were involved or not. Then, the poor chap you kicked to death in Madrid. And – oh, Miss Carter-Holt. I almost forgot.'

Welch stood aside, forced Telford out into the corridor.

'You didn't mention Major Edwin,' said Jack, stepping backwards towards the far end of the carriage. He remembered his escape from Madrid, the train from Aranjuez, his leap out into the pitch blackness rather than be captured again. The pure luck of his survival. But he was certain, now, his luck had run out.

'No, I didn't mention poor crippled Lawrence, did I? I'm sure he'd want me to pass on his regards. You see? Nothing personal. Simply owed a favour – a debt, I suppose you might say.'

Jack found himself all the way back to the connecting vestibule between this carriage and the next, the shifting plate that swayed and groaned beneath his feet.

'A debt to Major Edwin?' said Jack. 'Or Sir Aubrey?'

'Open the door, Telford. Be a good chap.'

'An accident? Fall from a train? I have to warn you I've been here before – lived to tell the tale.'

Welch raised the pistol, almost pushed it into Jack's chest.

'Oh, you'll be dead long before you hit the dirt, old boy. Now, open it.'

Jack did as he was instructed, turned the handle, pushed the door wide. The train was rattling along. Fast. The wind sucked at Telford's shirt, made his eyes water. Clouds of steam from the locomotive billowed inside. The smell of oil mixed with coal smoke.

He heard his own hypocrite's words in his brain, as he'd heard them at times in the past. *Sweet Jesus, help me.* And Father Lobo's words. '*On a battlefield, there are few atheists, my son.*'

Telford remembered the agony of his previous fall from a train.

'Please,' said Jack. 'Whatever this is about, you don't need to kill me.'

He put up his hands again, almost a supplication for mercy.

'Your stupidity betrayed Howard,' Welch sneered.

'But you knew that. Could have killed me in Lisbon.'

'I told you. A temporary reprieve. Your death there might have caused distractions.'

Telford flinched away from him, turned sideways, his back to the open door.

'Tell me, at least,' he said. 'Dorothea. Does she know – you're a German spy?'

'You think she'd care, Telford? I suspect she might admire me for it. And there you go, jumping to conclusions again. But no, the sweet girl is quite used to me being away on business. I'll make sure to give her your regards.'

'Please,' Jack said again, as Welch raised the automatic.

Telford stared into Welch's eyes, imploring, saw the sheer contempt returning his gaze.

Christ, Jack thought. He had nothing to lose. His reactions…

His cringing left hand was only inches from the gun.

Jack grabbed for the top of it, pulled it towards him and to the side, also to the left. It went off. Loud. The bullet whined off the metal doorframe. And Welch's contemptuous look now turned to confusion, perhaps disbelief.

He tried to bring his other hand across, but Jack was there before him, now with both hands gripping the pistol and twisting it in Welch's fist.

Welch was taller than him. Twice his age, but still strong. Yet he was caught off-balance. Surprised. It showed through the rage now distorting his features.

Telford pulled on the gun with every ounce of strength he could muster, swung himself around, no longer with his back to the opening.

And there was an instant.

The pistol was now in Jack's hands. Welch's hands were empty. Empty. He raised them. Palms outwards. Fingers stretched wide. His turn now to crave clemency. There was almost a smile on his face.

'Another death on your conscience, Telford? I don't think so, do you?'

Jack trembled so much he was forced to grip the gun with both hands.

'Isaac Gabizon,' he said, and raised the pistol.

'The old Jew?' Welch laughed, and the laughter was still on his lips when Telford squeezed the trigger. The gun jumped in his hand, and Welch was thrown backwards, the black maw of the night swallowing his soul.

Telford was choking, the grip around his throat tightening. His right hand was free, the fingers ripping at the sleeve, at the arm, which strangled him. But that right hand had never been the same since Spain. Weak. Lacking its full strength. He still struggled, tried to break the hold, but he could feel his will slipping away. Sinking into the dirt beneath him.

'And this,' yelled Colonel Bill Eddy to his audience, 'is the moment you'll think it's all over.' He was panting with the exertion of holding Jack down, of maintaining the grip. 'When your opponent's body goes limp. But don't be fooled. Ease the choke hold too soon and blood goes coursing straight back to the brain. Your enemy lives to fight another round.' He started screaming. Just screaming. Some sort of war cry. 'On the battlefield,' he shouted, 'you can make as much damned noise as you like. It scares the hell out of the bastard you're trying to kill, and keeps your own bloodlust burning. But hey, we don't want to kill *Señor* Telford – not today, anyhow.'

Jack felt Eddy's arm come away from his neck. He coughed, gasped for air, felt the colonel's slap on his back. He rolled over, had this upsidedown image of Granell and some of the other Spaniards, amused but bored. This was all old hat to them, of course. Amado was here to help out with the training, as much as anything else. But for the newer men, the rookies, the raw recruits, this was just another session in the gruelling programme which, hopefully, would one day save their lives.

'You see?' Amado shouted, in Spanish. He was Lieutenant Granell now, adjutant to Captain Dronne – adjutant to this recently formed Ninth Company of the *Régiment de Marche du Tchad*, the first of three companies in the regiment's Third Batallion. 'That's not the quickest way to kill fascists with your bare hands. But it's easy. Just remember...' He showed them the move one last time. 'Left arm around the throat, right hand locked over the left fist.'

'OK, Telford?' The colonel extended his hand, dragged Jack to his feet.

'Can't see it ever being any use to me, personally, Colonel, but yes, I'm fine. Glad to be of service.'

'You never know. You just never know. The krauts don't have much respect for the free press, remember?'

'I'll try. But I probably stand more chance of being able to beat them to death with my Dictaphone machine. Or a typewriter.'

'Or a pen, Mister Telford. Never underestimate the value of a pen as a weapon. I don't just mean figuratively either.'

Jack was tempted to tell him he'd already discovered this precise thing. And yes, in practice. Turbides, he thought. Telford had pushed the nib right up the *Guardia Civil* lieutenant's nostril, into his brain. Hell, Welch was right. The dead at his own door.

'Sometimes, figuratively is the best we can do,' he said. 'But this time it's not been enough to change minds – not about the removal of all Leclerc's black Africans from his ranks, Colonel.'

Jack had written some angry articles on the theme, but he'd received not a single response. Not from Bunnelle, nor from Barea, not even from Sydney Elliott.

'Let's not do this here,' said Eddy. He switched to Spanish, called to Granell. 'Thank you, Lieutenant. Carry on.'

Jack lit a cigarette as they headed for the nearest mess hut. There were almost twelve thousand men there at Temara, home now to Leclerc's Second French Armoured Division – the three battalions of the Chad March Regiment only about one third of that force. But the Chad regiment happened to include many of the former Spanish Republicans presently fighting for Free France, hundreds of them, and Dronne's Ninth Company with so many of them – the vast majority of its roughly a hundred and fifty soldiers – they'd simply become *La Nueve*.

'Coffee?' said Jack. The place might have been built to American army camp specifications but, inside, it smelled of Spanish cigars, Spanish coffee, Spanish cured ham, Spanish garlic. On the walls, photographs of La Pasionaria, of Negrín. Faded and torn Republican posters, as well. Copies of poetry, Miguel Hernández, Lorca, Machado. But other heroes also. Federica Montseny and Durruti. Evenings, here in the Spanish mess hut, could be lively, to say the least. Menacing, to Telford's ear. Old enmities still burning just beneath the new purpose.

'Not coffee,' said Eddy. 'Maybe something stronger.'

Jack ordered two cognacs. There'd had to be these concessions made as well. Red wine and cognac for the Spanish mess hut.

'And this *blanchiment*, Colonel?'

'We have two sort of generals, Mister Telford,' said Eddy. 'Us and the French, as well. The foolhardy philanthropists and the blind bigots. On our side, the former think it's unfair to give combat responsibility to poor black folks who've not got the sense to handle it. The latter are simply damned if they're going to give guns to

485

negroes. For the French? The kindly but ill-informed think equatorial Africans can't cope with the rigours of northern European winter weather. The prejudiced, the gentlemen officers of the old regimes, are just happier to see their coloureds digging latrines, fixing their vehicles, peeling potatoes, or carrying loads that would break a donkey's back. It's wrong, I know.'

'It's a betrayal, colonel.'

'But one you can't change. If you're looking for cheap beef, I'm afraid you've come to the wrong ranch.' Jack wasn't entirely certain what he meant, but he let it pass. 'I heard a story, though, *Mister* Telford. About a train journey.'

'Fox?' said Jack.

'Your friend, Réchard, as it happens.'

Jack had called Louis from Rabat, almost as soon as he'd got off the train. A month ago, now. He'd thought about it long and hard, all the way there from Oran.

'I don't care whether you believe me, Louis,' he'd said. 'He fell from the bloody train. Yes. Accident.'

Jack was lodging with the Gorroños now, whenever he wasn't at Temara, and introduced Paquita to Granell and the other Spaniards, of course. But he'd gone back to Casa for a few days, stayed with Nella Bénatar, caught up with all her news – awful news, for the most part, almost unbelievable stories, more than just rumours now, she was certain, about the fate of Europe's Jews – then been summoned to a meeting at Réchard's office. Fox had also been there, naturally. And another fellow, named Peterson. Telford had gone over the incident again and again.

'He simply said he'd been on business in Algiers. Tobacco business, I think he said. No, I'd not seen him since – well, let me see… Lisbon, of course, as I told Captain Fox, though I didn't speak to him. Oh, a few words over breakfast at our hotel.'

'Captain Fox tells me you had suspicions about Welch,' Peterson had said.

'Oh, that – just a piece of stupidity on my part. So long ago I'd forgotten all about it. No, it was tragic. The poor fellow insisted we should smoke in the corridor – instead of polluting my compartment, you know? I *think* he meant to open the window, maybe. But then the door simply flew open. All over in a flash. I made a grab for him, but...'

There'd been a search. Réchard's colleagues in Oran. But Jack hadn't been able to help much with the precise time or place of the accident. They'd bumped into each other on the platform, Jack had said, swapped compartment numbers. No, Welch had come to *his* compartment. Yes, chatted for a while. It was the damnedest thing – turned out they had more in common than Jack imagined. A mutual acquaintance. Welch's wife, of all people. Small world. And the accident? Telford had to think about it. He was fairly sure they'd only made one stop. This narrowed it down a bit. The speed of the train? Quite fast, but – yes, Jack remembered they were getting thrown about a bit. Lots of bends, which focused it still further. Almost certainly around the Oued Djer, where the line passed through the mountains. Difficult. The valley, wooded ravines. And, in the end, there'd been no sign of a body. It could be anywhere. And then there were the scavengers to consider – hyenas, vultures and the rest.

'Yes,' Jack said now, to Colonel Eddy. 'Tragic. You worked with him, of course – with Welch? Can't say I liked him very much, but tragic, all the same.'

Eddy studied him for a moment, sipped at his cognac.

'He was a valuable asset, Mister Telford,' he said at last. 'And, you know, I'm thinking you're a guy it might be easy to underestimate.'

Is this what Welch did? Jack wondered. Underestimate me? Underestimate exactly how somebody like me might react when they're in the grip of pure terror. Christ, it was the last thing I expected myself. All the flight or fight stuff.

It had all been strange, when he'd thought back on it. Like watching somebody else. He had no real recollection of grabbing the gun. Instinct? But he'd lain awake on his bunk all the rest of the way to Oran, petrified, shaking with the shock. And not exactly a new experience. He'd been through something like it after Kufra. Before that, after Alicante. Before that again – hell, too many to count. And now, here he was, planning to go off once more with Leclerc's Second French Armoured Division to god knows where. Following Eze Tolabye to Italy, maybe?

'It's far more likely people *overestimate* me, Colonel,' he said. 'And have you any idea where we might be headed?'

Eddy shrugged his shoulders.

'After Salerno and Palermo, it all looked like Italy might be easy. But now…' The Italians had surrendered, and the talk had all been about the Germans pulling out. But then German paratroopers had rescued Mussolini from prison and instead of retreating, Italy had simply become one more occupied country, the German positions strengthened, and the Allied advance ground to a halt. 'Anyway,' the colonel continued, 'your Spanish boys seem to have more idea about what's going on than the top brass. What's the scuttlebutt?'

Jack laughed.

'They're convinced it's not Italy, anyway. But they just want to get back in the fight. All this waiting.'

Training and more training. Frustration. An occasional performance to entertain them. And the preparations, of course, for the big parade in Rabat itself. Early October.

His Imperial Highness, *Sidi* Muhammad ben Youssef, Sultan of Morocco, had been invited, as guest of honour, among the dignitaries in the specially constructed *tricolore*-draped grandstand, mid-way along the Avenue de la Victoire. And Jack, in turn, had been invited to join the sultan and his two boys, to sit immediately behind them, alongside Captain Fox.

'Yet they did not consider it appropriate,' *Sidi* Muhammad whispered over his shoulder to him, 'that I should join them on the dais to receive the salute, even though my own men are part of the parade.'

No, this honour fell to the new Resident-General for Morocco, Gabriel Puaux – Vichy's Charles Noguès having finally been forced to stand down. And, of course, to de Gaulle, now undisputed president and sole leader of France's Committee for National Liberation, Giraud having resigned from his position as joint director.

'It is, sir,' said Jack, 'merely a practice run, I think, for larger – and more important parades in the future.'

The ceremonial band had already played a medley of martial music by the time the head of the column appeared away to their left, the clatter of hooves as a troop of the sultan's Black Guards trotted past. Behind them, the marching standard bearers, the battle flags, the colours of each regiment, now part of this new *Deuxième Division Blindée Française*, the Second French Armoured Division.

'All the same…' *Sidi* Muhammad began, but he was interruped by *La Marseillaise*, the command cars, and Leclerc. Everybody stood for the anthem. The first salutes. More mounted men. 'And, *Monsieur* Telford,' said the sultan, when they'd ridden past. 'Women? So many women?'

The ambulances and supply trucks of the medical battalion, including two units Telford had written about. First, the English Volunteers Group – Quakers mostly, among other conscientious objectors. And then the now already famous *Rochambelles*, the driving teams – and their ambulances – raised by the Widow Conrad in New York after she'd been forced to flee from her beloved Paris.

'Like the nurses, sir. As we saw at the RAF hospital.'

'Precisely. But these women – they shall not be sent to combat zones, surely?'

'Behind the front lines, Your Highness, but only just. They say, in the last war, more than a thousand nurses lost their lives.'

'Then may Allah protect them.'

There were lorries from the Supply and Services Sections, more command cars, the familiar figure of *Commandant* Louis Dio, leading the first of the Division's three combat command groups. He still has that look of Charles Boyer, thought Jack.

'Dio,' he said to Fox. 'You met him? No? Christ, I remember him at Kufra. There was this beautiful white horse – the Italian officer's horse. Dio took the damned thing, rode it round and round, under their walls, bullets all over the place. He's quite mad.'

And Dio still wore his white *képi*, a *shesh* about his neck.

In his wake, the First Battalion – Farret's battalion – of the Chad Regiment in their half-tracks. Not all of them, naturally, but twenty of those vehicles. Behind the M5 half-tracks, the first of the tanks. Light Stuarts, flanked by mounted *spahi* lancers – because such was their origin, like all these units, as traditional cavalry regiments. And medium Shermans – these from the former Twelfth

Regiment of *Cuirassiers* which had come over in its entirety from Vichy to join Leclerc, six months earlier.

'But this is all a far cry from Kufra,' said Fox, shouting to be heard over the rumble of the tank engines. There were clouds of smoke, the stink of oil and petrol.

'Hard to imagine, now,' Jack replied, as more armoured infantry, more tanks, roared past to the strains of fresh military rhythms. 'That ragged little band of the Leclerc Column, turned into this. Crying shame though, a disgrace – Eze and the boys not being here to see, to be part of it.'

Bringing up the rear, the third of the Division's three combat commands, this one led by *Commandant* Billotte – not someone Jack knew well, but they'd chatted a few times when he was doing interviews. But it was to Billotte's command that the Chad Regiment's Third Battalion was attached.

'There, in the command car,' said Jack, pointing to the vehicle behind the last of the tanks. 'Putz.'

'The old man?' *Sidi* Muhammad asked him. 'The officer?'

Jack laughed.

'Major Putz, sir,' he said. 'Joseph Putz. And he just *looks* old. He's every right, I suppose. Fought all the way through the last war as a young French officer. Badly wounded. Retired. Then joined the International Brigades when the Spanish Civil War started, helped recruit a lot of other Frenchmen. The siege of Bilbao, then across Spain. Wounded twice more. He was in Algeria when this one began, joined up again, of course. But his unit never reached France before the Armistice was signed. Demobilised. Worked on the railways. Met up with some of the Spaniards from the camps forced to hard labour on the Niger line and, after the Allies landed, he recruited whole gangs of them, deserters from the Foreign Legion, built them into a company for the African Free Corps.'

'Quite the hero,' said Fox.

'You wouldn't know to speak with him,' Jack told him. 'One of the most unassuming men I ever met. He's the only French officer the Spaniards will obey without *ever* questioning the orders. He had Granell with him, allowed them all to sew little Republican flags to the top of their sleeves. They still wear them. See?'

The three companies of Putz's half-tracks rolled past. Leading the first of those companies, in a new Jeep, another familiar figure.

'Dronne.' Fox smiled. 'I'd recognise that beard anywhere.'

'And Granell,' said Jack. There he was, immediately behind Dronne, his half-track neatly painted with the name *Les Cosaques*, while the rest of *La Nueve*'s vehicles carried the legends *Teruel*, *Brunete*, *Santander*, and *Guadalajara*. He could see some of the others – Campos *el canario*, himself now in charge of one of the rifle platoons. So far as Jack knew, Campos had never actually fought in Spain. In Tunisia, yes. A natural soldier, one of the best. And there, among the company, El Gordo, Ortiz, Markovich the Yugolslav.

Jack couldn't help but feel somewhat choked, seeing them, like this, in all their glory. And he was no less emotional as the last of the tanks thundered by ahead of the Division's artillery.

'You look like a new man, *Monsieur* Telford,' said the sultan, when it had all broken up and they were heading back to their cars. 'In your uniform, I mean.'

'I only wear it at the insistence of General Leclerc, sir. To be frank, I feel something of a fraud to be wearing it.'

'A fraud? You are not a soldier?'

'They've been trying to teach me to defend myself, Your Highness. I'm afraid I'm not very good at it. But I've been studying German. I think it might be more useful for wherever we're headed.'

Well, he'd survived Welch, at least. Perhaps just luck. Or perhaps Welch hadn't been such a good assassin, after all. He'd had enough chances, when all was said and done. And Reiter's German lessons weren't easy – but he was making progress.

'Mister Telford!' Fox cautioned him.

'It's fine, Captain. I'm not about to give away any state secrets. But, one way or the other, I know our days here in Morocco are numbered. Sooner, rather than later, I'd say. Wouldn't you?'

'And then?' said the sultan. 'Back to your homeland, at last?'

I certainly seem to have unfinished business there, Jack thought. He still had no idea about Welch. A favour, he'd said. For whom? Edwin? Sir Aubrey? Somebody else? Well, he'd bloody find out. Yes, the same. Sooner or later, I'll finish this. But he wasn't going to explain this to *Sidi* Muhammad.

'First, sir,' he said, instead, 'I have to gather about me all the friendships I've made here. In a way that I can keep them with me, when I have to leave.'

Telford rarely felt pride – true pride. But today?

Another month, another procession. Thursday, the eighteenth of November. Throne Day, *La Fête du Trône*, *Eid al-Arsh*, when all Morocco celebrated *Sidi* Muhammad's accession, sixteen years before. Music, dancing, endless parades, feasting, the distribution of food and clothes to the poor – almost non-stop from sunrise, apart from prayer times. It fell in this sacred month of *Dhul Qa'Dah*, immediately after the fasting days of *Yaumul Bidh*.

The previous evening, Jack had been summoned to the palace, complete with the Dictaphone machine, to record the sultan's address to the nation, which would be broadcast on all local radio stations, throughout the following day.

> *'Praise be to God,*
> *May peace and blessings be upon the Prophet, His Kith and Kin…'*

The formalities had all been scripted by the sultan's advisers, naturally, but Jack had suggested a few amendments, here and there.

> *'…Today, we proudly celebrate the sixteenth anniversary of my accession to the glorious Alaouite throne. This is an opportunity for us to ponder the state of our country and its peoples. All of its peoples. My people.'*

It was a speech about which no nationalist could complain, but above whose agitation he was easily able to rise.

'How long, sir?' Jack said to him when the recording was done. 'Before independence?'

'You know that your friend *Madame* Bénatar claims I have helped protect Morocco's Jews. And we may have taken some small measures to prevent the worst treatment Germany and Vichy intended for them. But I had the rest of my people to care for. And I still had no choice but to sign the anti-Jewish *dahirs*. Our friends in Tunisia might have taken a different stand, yet I thought it wise to maintain the façade of Vichy and hope the Americans would, indeed come. But I could have done so much more. So much more. Yet, with the help of President Roosevelt, I think we shall see independence very soon.'

'It's not simply Nella Bénatar, Your Highness. I've seen the numbers of Jews who were able to pass through Morocco to safety. With your help, sir. There must be thousands now, who owe their survival to the stance you took – a difficult stance, maybe. But now...'

'Now, *Monsieur* Telford, I no longer have Vichy snapping at my heals – simply our own National Party for Independence. They tell me they will soon declare themselves simply as the *Istiqlal* Party. But this is for another day. For now, we have tomorrow's celebrations. Tomorrow night, after the *Maghrib* prayer, there is a banquet. I need you to be there, my friend.'

There was a twinkle in his eye, something up the sleeve of his *djellaba*, perhaps, but Jack happily agreed he'd be there.

And the following day he also spent happily with his friends, enjoying the revelry. He'd missed most of the military parade, for he had an assignation, at the old Sailing Club on the Bou Regreg river, just inland from the harbour, and he was walking there, cutting through the southern corner of the medina, when he passed the same Bar Tahona de Carmen, where he'd first met Paquita, with Gabizon, all that time back.

Today, there were tables outside. It was a fine afternoon, for November, and there were two familiar faces, enjoying a beer.

'Mister Telford,' said Colonel Eddy, 'won't you join us?'

Captain Fox stood to shake Jack's hand also, admired the uniform.

Telford glanced at his watch, grimaced.

'Do you mind?' he said. 'I'm already a bit late.'

'Expected to see you with all the other newspapermen,' the colonel scolded him. 'And now you've missed out on the excitement. Good lord, there they all were, cameras flashing. Story right in their laps.'

'I'm sorry, but I don't follow...'

'Didn't you hear?' said Fox. 'Some bloody sniper. The Place de France. Right opposite the press box. Only minutes before Leclerc was due to drive past. Thank god for the *gendarmerie*.'

There was a disturbance overhead, the flapping monstrosity of a stork settling on its nest above.

'They caught him?'

'They did, old boy. Tip-off, maybe. But I was thinking about you. Mentioned him to me, didn't you? Chamson. *Milice*, of course.'

Yes, Jack had mentioned him. It was Chamson that his Baker Street Irregulars, Bilal and the rest, had seen with Kingsley Welch. The billy goat, *dhakar almaeiz*. But Fox seemed to have conveniently forgotten the connection to Welch.

'Yes, *Milice*,' said Jack. 'But what's he doing here? Casablanca's his patch.'

'Well, we'll never know now,' Eddy replied. 'The *gendarmes* finished him off. But don't let us keep you, Telford. Good to see you, though. You're at the banquet tonight?' Yes, said Jack, he'd be there. 'First class. First class. We may not get a chance to chat much, all the same. And I ship out tomorrow. Arabia, you know? They're sending me to Arabia. So, just in case, good luck to you, Mister Telford – wherever life takes you.'

He stood, offered his hand, and Jack took it.

'You've taught me a lot, Colonel. I really appreciate it.'

'Oh, I think you underestimate how much some of us have learned from *you*, young man. And I told you before, you're an easy fellow to underestimate.'

Telford had never learned to grow comfortable with compliments. They made him squirm, for the most part, so his farewell to Colonel Eddy was perhaps more terse than he'd intended. But they were, he supposed, also brothers-in-arms. The fighting at Oran last year. Yet this wasn't the thing uppermost in his mind as he rushed along Boulevard Joffre, past the Muslim cemetery and the Jewish school at the corner of the *mellah*.

Dammit, he was going to arrive all in a lather. He pulled out his handkerchief, wiped the sweat from inside his forage cap, from his brow, but thinking all the time about Chamson. A sniper? *La Milice*? To kill Leclerc? My god, he thought. Unbelieveable. Yet there was something else. Something he didn't want to let surface, because he knew, once out of the box, it would haunt him, never allow him to cage it again. An insidious, slippery creature, like a leech. It flattened itself almost to nothing, slithered through some crack in the lid of his intentions, sunk its ugly head into his imagination.

The Place de France. The press box. By rights, Jack should have been there. He *would* have been there, if it hadn't been for – And a sniper? Chamson? Chamson and Welch? Christ, what if it wasn't over, after all?

'You may just have saved my life,' he said to the young nurse.

He'd become somewhat more comfortable with the uniform shirt, with the press armband, but the army tie he wore for this occasion did nothing to help with the heat. Or perhaps the flush in his face, the sweat in his armpits, the itch behind his eye-patch, had less to do with the weather than with his companion.

'Literally, Jack?' she said.

Her own uniform, skirt and jacket, was the dress dark olive of the *Rochambelles*. He'd only ever seen her in her khaki fatigues before, and it was quite a transformation. But the face – elfin, puckish, dark curls spilling out from beneath her cap – yes, he knew, reminded him of Ruby Waters. Or maybe just coincidence.

'No, Danielle,' he laughed. 'Not literally.' Well, he hoped not. 'But if I'd had to spend five more minutes on that typewriter...'

In truth, he'd already been distracted from his work by a letter from Harmon. So many postmarks on the envelope it was a miracle it had ever found him. But she seemed to be doing well, still covering the war in Italy, the fighting at Ortona. There'd been a package from Sydney Elliott also, copies of *Reynold's News*, a couple of great features about the Battle of Kursk. Superb map of the campaign.

'Might we go, ma'am?' Danielle shouted in her native French. She and Telford were standing at the foot of the gangplank, the houseboat providing both accommodation and headquarters for the Division's *Groupe Rochambeau* ambulance unit. Their vehicles were lined up neatly along the quay. Another bit of *déjà vu*, of course. Like the *Lotus*, on the Nile. Pamela in Cairo. Houseboats seemed to be *de rigeur* in the fight to preserve the chastity of Allied servicewomen.

'You'll have her back here by ten, I trust, *Monsieur* Telford.'

Commandant Florence Conrad must have been not far short of sixty, or thereabouts. Glasses, a mop of white hair, with her cap perched on top. She spoke in French, as well, even though she was American.

'Certainly,' Jack replied, but then the door next to Widow Conrad opened and another young woman emerged. Behind her, Jacques Massu – *Colonel* Massu, now, commander of the Chad Regiment's Second Battalion. Telford knew his companion. Dani had introduced them. Widow Conrad's second-in-command, Lieutenant Suzanne Torrès. Massu's latest flame.

'Come on,' Danielle murmured, and tugged at Jack's sleeve, 'I'd rather not get lumbered with Toto.'

Toto, it transpired, was the *nom de guerre* with which Torrès had been christened by the other girls. It also transpired that she wasn't Dani's favourite person in the world. And, by the time they'd eaten in the medina, Jack had most of Toto's life story.

'But you, Dani,' said Jack. 'You climbed through the Pyrenees in rope-soled sandals so you could – what, do this? Join Widow Conrad's ambulances?'

He already knew some of her story, as well. Toulouse, the *résistants*. But her cell betrayed. And yes, she'd made it to the Spanish border, climbed up through the mountains, but detained by the *Guardia Civil* and eventually deported to Oran.

'I didn't even know they existed until I got to Algeria. Just wanted to fight. Bloody *Boches*. Lost so many friends, Jack. So many. Now I want revenge. To see the Germans bleed. And this is the closest I can get to fighting, no?'

She was fiery, Telford had to admit. Algerian father, French mother, but born and brought up in Toulouse. They watched jugglers and fire-eaters on the street, and Jack felt somebody tap him on the shoulder.

'Well, aren't you going to introduce me to your friend?'

Francine Camus had changed little, though it seemed she'd dressed for the occasion, an elegant high-necked blouse in luminous, pale gold silk. She looked stunning, he thought.

'You're a long way from Oran, Francine.'

'Arrived yesterday. Looked up Paquita Gorroño, but she wasn't very forthcoming. Knew you wouldn't be too far away from all this, though.'

'You wanted to see me?' said Jack. He was both embarrassed and flattered at the same time. Flustered.

'Jack,' Danielle almost stepped between them, 'who is this?'

'Apologies,' he said. 'Danielle Zidane, this is *Madame* Francine Camus.'

'What *is* that uniform?' said Francine. 'Nurse? And no, Jack. I brought some students. Throne Day. But since I was here…'

'Camus?' Dani replied. 'As in…?'

'Albert's in Paris,' Jack explained. 'Francine stuck in Oran.'

'And never the twain shall meet,' said Francine. 'Well, not for now, at least.'

'Not a nurse, an ambulance driver,' Danielle told her. 'With the *Groupe Rochambeau*.'

'Rochambeau.' Francine put a pensive finger to her lips. 'We sent him to help with the American Revolution, did we not? What is this – the favour returned? But you're French aren't you, *Mademoiselle* Zidane?'

'American money, French women drivers, for a French Division under American command,' said Jack. 'Simple, isn't it?'

'You don't seem pleased to see me, Jack,' Francine pouted.

'You must be missing your husband, *madame*,' said Danielle. 'War is so cruel. And your husband, in turn, will be desperately lonely without you, I imagine.'

The effect could not have been more dramatic if Danielle had slapped her face. But she composed herself quickly.

'The uniform suits you, Jack,' Francine told him. 'I just hoped – never mind, I see you've moved on in more ways than one. Good luck, *Monsieur* Telford, wherever you may be bound. And you, *mademoiselle*.'

She offered Danielle a gracious smile, though it was perhaps a little forced. Jack thought he detected a tear, but then she was gone.

'She's very beautiful, Jack.'

'But troubled,' said Jack. 'And what did you mean, about her husband?'

'I didn't want to be cruel. Albert Camus has a certain reputation. And *not* for his literature alone. Both inside the Resistance and beyond. It's obvious from his writing. And obvious to Francine. You can see it in her eyes. Poor bitch. You and she, Jack…?'

What to say? He liked Danielle a lot. Things in common. He'd been given authority to interview some of the *Rochambelles* – the nickname by which they were now known by just about everybody. And Dani was among the young women designated by the Widow Conrad to offer up their life stories.

'Yes,' he said. 'But it's been over for a while. Look – if you feel uncomfortable about this…'

'Uncomfortable? Why should I feel uncomfortable? One interview. A kind offer to show me the joys of Throne Day. Hardly makes us a couple, Jack. Hardly.'

'What about an invitation to a banquet at the sultan's palace? Might that shift us up a gear or two?'

She laughed.

'Tonight? *Commandant* Conrad expects me back by ten, remember?'

'Starts after *Maghrib* and must be finished, I guess, by *Isha*. I can arrange a car. Back on the stroke of ten, with military precision, Nurse Zidane.'

A deal, then, and Jack's suggestion that, meanwhile, they might also try to catch up with Paquita and Manuel. He had a shrewd idea they might also be at the *Tahona*, still a watering hole for Rabat's Spanish community.

Despite the holiday, Boulevard Gouraud was awash with wagons – trucks piled with second-season citrus, pyramids of potatoes, mounds of avocado, or the latest crop of volunteers in the autumn drab of Allied armies, French and American, British and Moroccan, splashes of red or blue, orange or purple, from cap and *tarboosh*, shoulder flash and regimental insignia.

At the bar, the Gorroños – as well as quite a few familiar faces from *La Nueve*, enjoying a one-day pass.

'The new company, Amado,' said Jack, after the introductions, admiring glances from Alemán and El Gordo in Danielle's direction. 'How are you getting along with Dronne?'

There was a chorus of replies from the lads, each shouting louder than his neighbour, all at the same time.

'He'll do,' said Granell. 'I think. You know the boys, *inglés*. Good soldiers, good fighters. Just useless at taking orders without a decent debate. About the how, the why, the what for. Dronne's not a toff like Leclerc, but the same principle. Maybe not Franco admirers – but no friends of the Popular Front either.'

Jack paid for drinks all round, handed over a fistful of *francs*, the wad of flimsy notes turned by the sweat that had soaked his pocket to a glutinous mush.

'And, like Franco,' said Manuel, 'they probably think the only good Spaniards are those who defend the bullfight, the hunting and the Catholic processions.'

Granell laughed, nodded his agreement.

'While those who defend basic pay,' he said, 'working conditions, medicine for our kids – all written off as Communists. And now Leclerc can't quite understand how he's ended up in command of a bunch of those same Reds.' He turned to Danielle. 'And how is your luxury yacht, comrade? This houseboat.'

She'd spent enough time tramping across Spain to understand him, replied in her own version of Spanish.

'One sink,' she said, and raised a single finger for emphasis. 'Holes in floor. Rats. This big. No comfort. But home. Watch the sea. Pleases me.'

More drinks. Cigarettes.

'If you need anything, *compañera*,' Paquita said to her. 'We don't have luxuries. But the basics? I don't suppose you'll be able to take much with you once you're posted.'

'It's the curse of all soldiers,' said Granell. 'I left Alicante with two possessions. Automatic rifle – and this.' From inside his field service jacket he pulled a carefully folded bundle. 'The last time it flew in honour was when we defended the town hall at Castellón. I wasn't going to leave it behind.'

It was a simple Spanish Republican flag, three horizontal stripes of red, yellow and purple, the legend *49 Brigada Mixta* embroidered in a semicircle across the banner.

'This, a curse?' said Paquita.

Amado laughed.

'No, *compañera*. Soldiers are like squirrels. Hoarders. We collect loot. Any old rubbish. I picked up a rug Mama's going to love. Toys for the kids. A couple of Italian watches for my favourite uncles. That is our curse. But this – Aurora will want to hang this in the kitchen. Some day, when we're able. Though when we get the order to move out, it'll all have to be left behind. The rest? I don't mind. Wherever we land next, I'll just start collecting again. We all will. This, though – somebody needs to look after this. For now, at least. Please. You'll take it?'

He set the flag in Paquita's reluctantly outstretched hands.

'Lieutenant,' she said, 'this is a great honour.'

And they sang. Their anthem. The *Himno de Riego*. And then *La Internacional*.

Arriba, parias de la tierra.

It all resulted in Jack drinking just more than was good for him. Danielle also. Almost to the point where he might have forgotten about the banquet – almost. And in the days and weeks which followed, he wondered how he would have lived it down.

He would remember that sparkle in *Sidi* Muhammad's eye, that mischief etched on those amiable features. Now explained. The reason for the sultan's insistence on him being there. The food was good. Dani was impressed. But then the announcements. Not just a banquet at all, but an award ceremony.

And Jack just one of many on the list.

An award, a *wissam* from the hands of the sultan himself. The Sharifian Order of Alaoui. Outstanding and meritorious services of a civil nature. A Knight of the Order, First Class. Suspended from an orange ribbon and gold palm wreath, a five-pointed white star on a bed of green enamelled laurel leaves and, at its centre, a red medallion with the gilt Arabic lettering of the Order.

Both Patton and General Mark Clark had received the Grand Cross version of the Order at the start of the year.

So yes, Telford was proud. Overwhelmed, but proud.

There were dead on the streets. Students, mostly. But not quite the legacy anybody had expected Leclerc's *Deuxième Division Blindée* to leave behind them.

Christmas had come and gone. *Navidad*. The New Year. *Los Reyes*.

'Mother of god,' said Paquita. 'Were you here, Jack?'

He'd met her at the *Tahona* again, partly to make sure she was still safe, partly to try to get a handle on the latest word from the medina.

'Yes,' Telford replied, as they wandered past the French tanks still parked on Boulevard Galliéni. 'I was here.'

The *Istiqlal* Party had published its Independence Manifesto early in January, and that had been followed by demonstrations, and the demonstrations had led to some violence. In the midst of this violence, a policeman killed and the party's leader, Ahmed Balfrej arrested. Then a French military tribunal sentenced some of the demonstrators to death.

'And Lord Memmeri, have you heard?' she said.

They passed through the elaborate Sunday Gateway into the Bab el Had square, with its market stalls, the mingled smells of roasting lamb and camel dung, the clack of typewriters from the local scribes drafting documents and letters for anybody who'd pay them. Life went on.

'In a bad way – but he'll survive. You know what they did to him?'

Memmeri, the sultan's private secretary, his Chief of Protocol and, in most ways, Paquita's boss – with overall responsibility for the education of the young princes. And when an angry crowd of demonstrators had gathered outside the royal palace, it was Mohammed Memmeri's task to pacify them.

'He's lucky to have survived. Hell, Jack. These are good people. But that...'

'A decent man, Paquita. I've met him a few times. You must have been with him almost every day, though.'

There'd been riots at Fez, Salé, Casablanca and other places. More policemen killed. A couple of innocent civilians as well. The medinas in each of those towns placed under military control and, in Fez, the military post attacked. Some protestors killed.

'I was terrified,' she said. 'I don't mind admitting it. But when I was going home – through the medina. There were thousands of them. I'm no stranger to demonstrations, comrade, but those crowds…'

They passed the Muslim cemetery on Gouraud. There were still mourners in there – angry, shouting mourners around the fresh graves. Jack averted his gaze, lowered his head, and Paquita pulled the edge of her headscarf just a touch further across her face.

'You think they were right to send in the army?' Telford murmured.

He'd been at Temara when the balloon went up, the Chad Regiment's Third Battalion, their half-tracks, supporting Sherman tanks sent to blockade the main gateways and thoroughfares leading into the medina.

'Perhaps they had no choice,' said Paquita. 'But the word on the street? That the demonstrations were stirred up by the *Milice*. I guess we'll never know for sure. But it all got out of hand so quickly.'

Telford had gone with them, hitched a lift with Granell and his driver. Jack had purchased a camera, just before Christmas, an old Rolleiflex, but easy to use, not too bulky.

'It's no wonder,' he said. 'The Americans made promises – I know they did. But as soon as the Independence Manifesto appeared, the bastards walked away from it. They've done the same in Italy.' Well, according to his last letter from Harmon, they had. 'Stamped all over any sort of political activity. Nothing allowed to distract from winning the war. Here,' he said. 'This is where we were.' They'd reached the Place de France, the Bab el Alou. 'They came pouring out through the gateway, hundreds of them.' He pointed across to the old Moorish bastion, the opening in the medina wall alongside. 'And somebody – Billotte maybe, though I can't be certain – gave the order to fire. Of course, the Spanish boys shrugged their shoulders. I heard a few of them muttering. About how they hadn't signed up to shoot civilians, that sort of stuff.'

'The police?'

'Bloody *gendarmes*. Didn't need to be told twice. Thirty dead – just the ones I counted.'

They wandered across to the gateway, and Jack ran a finger around one of the pockmarks left by a French bullet. He'd photographed them, and some of the bodies, then had the camera snatched from his hands by a *gendarme* sergeant, his precious film ripped from the Rolleiflex. There'd been a scuffle, naturally, and Dronne had come to his rescue.

'They're being betrayed, Jack. The independence movement. The sultan himself.'

Yes, betrayal. There seemed to be a lot of it about. Eze Tolabye and the 'whitening' of the Chad Regiment. Now this. In the dirt, around the gate, there were dark stains, the blood of those young students. They'd looked, for all the world, like they had poppies decorating their striped *djellabas*.

'He's asked to see me,' he said.

'Well, you are a Knight of the Sherifian Order, comrade. And he values your opinion. An honour as well, no?'

'It was a bad day for Amado and the boys all round, you know?' He offered to buy her a coffee and they crossed back to the opposite side of the square, sat at a terrace table of the Bar Place de France.

'Mauthausen?' she said.

He nodded. Somehow, somebody had escaped from the Nazi concentration camp. Austria. Vichy collaborators had kindly arranged for seven thousand Spanish Republicans, refugees, rounded up from all over southern France, to be handed over to the Germans. Of the seven thousand, most had now been butchered or worked to death in a stone quarry. A gas chamber, they said. To help quickly exterminate the prisoners they wanted to kill. Not just Spaniards either, but thousands upon thousands of others. And the story had spread, slowly, relentlessly, in all those corners of the world where Franco's enemies were now exiled.

Jack had interviewed Granell, some of the others. He'd seen the change in them, recorded their crippled, incredulous voices, sent the disc to Barea in London. Strange to see how their animosity towards Franco, their pledge to one day see Spain free once more, was now almost subsumed by their need for bitter revenge against Nazi Germany. After all, without Nazi Germany, Franco could never have beaten them. *No Pasarán* was a slogan they'd adopted in the full and justified expectation they could stop Franco and his Nationalists in their tracks – not that they would have to stand alone against the combined might of Franco's fascists *and* Hitler's *Luftwaffe*, as well as Mussolini's armies.

'You see?' he said, and lit a Gauloise. 'Just one more betrayal. How could they, Paquita? And why? What did Vichy gain from it?'

'They've handed over thousands of Jews, Jack. I suppose a few more unwanted Reds wouldn't have pricked their consciences very much.'

Seventy thousand Jews, according to Nella. Deported. Disappeared into the east. Like so many others. Perhaps millions. Eighteen months now since she'd first wept at the horror. The Warsaw Resistance newspaper, *Liberty Brigade*. Gas vans. Suddenly, the beast had a name. Chelmno. Though nobody wanted to believe it. And now, not one beast but many. More names than any human brain could contain. Yet still disbelief. Even the Nazis, folk said, could not, surely…

But then there was the other side of the story, the thing which kept Hélène and her teams going. The extraordinary tales of French men and women who'd helped protect the Jews remaining in occupied France – a quarter of a million? More?

'I wonder, Paquita,' he said. 'Could you do me a favour? I was thinking about it when Amado handed over his flag. But Nella's been looking after something special for me. A sketchbook. A comrade who died in Alicante. It can't be long before they ship us out, now. She'll take care of the rest of my stuff in Casa, but the sketchbook…'

She put her hand on his arm.

'Of course,' she said.

'There's this, as well.' He opened the flap on his shirt's breast pocket.

'Negrín's pen?' They'd shared jokes about it often enough. 'He's in London, Jack. You're likely to see him long before I do.'

'I wasn't thinking about returning it,' he said. 'I'd like you to have it. A gift, from one comrade to another.'

He'd never seen her cry, not until now.

'Almost time for you to leave us, my friend,' said *Sidi* Muhammad. 'Not that I know any secrets, you understand.'

It was a statement of fact, rather than a question. An entirely private audience, rather than a formal affair. A single Black Guard near the door, and the rare spectacle of the sultan himself pouring their apple tea.

'Do I have your permission to leave, Highness?'

Jack warmed his hands at the brazier on the floor between their respective cushions, almost hoped the sultan would take his question seriously, refuse his request, require him to remain.

'The Prophet – peace and the blessings of Allah be upon Him – taught us we must be in this world as though we are both strangers and travellers. And you, *Monsieur* Telford, adrift, wherever you may be, it seems to me. Yet Morocco shall always provide a refuge for you. Whenever your soul is weary, you may return. Always a place for you here.'

'Hopefully, sir, to a free and independent Morocco.'

'The Americans will honour their promises at some stage, Mister Telford. Of course, they will put their military bases here. After this war, in preparation for their next. But yes, at least we shall have an independence – of sorts. There has to be a *quid pro quo*, a balance, in all things.'

'Balance,' said Jack. 'I've been thinking about that a great deal.'

The light from a wall lamp flickered, caused the cerulean stucco stalactites to dance, as though they were fluid, mobile, tears falling to the reception room's tiled floor.

'The balance of gains and losses from your time here?'

'The scales of our lives, Highness – the good measured against the bad.'

'The fortune of reassurance you brought back to us from Lisbon, I hope, is there upon the mensurandum plate.'

Telford had to ponder this one for a moment. He chewed thoughtfully on a piece of *chebakia* before answering.

'But its mass, sir,' he said, at last, 'is more than countered by the weights on the opposite pan – the sacrifice of the actor. All I did was survive the journey.'

And even that's a lie, he thought. Or only half a truth. Howard was a hero, and betrayed by a page of scribbled notes. Or, at least, I think so. No, in this case, I'm owed no credit. None.

'Is survival itself,' said the sultan, 'not one of life's supreme achievements?'

'If you put it that way, Highness, then yes. Arriving here from Spain, in the first place. Kufra. The air crash flying from Cairo.'

He didn't even trouble to list his various other close encounters with death.

'It is written, *Monsieur* Telford, how we should lead such a life that, when we die, people may mourn us and, while we are alive, they may long for our company.'

'I count myself blessed I was able to count Isaac Gabizon among the number of my friends, sir, even for such a short span. Paquita Gorroño. *Madame* Bénatar, of course. And, if it is permitted, Highness…'

He had no idea of the protocols surrounding declarations of amity towards the Sultan of Morocco, but *Sidi* Muhammad dismissed his confusion with a flutter of his fingers.

'They are few in number, that my advisors, my guards, my own caution, would allow to gift me this simple pleasure.'

The sweep of his wing-like sleeve encompassed the inlaid table, the engraved silver teapot and matching dessert stand – and Jack himself. It was a gracious, generous gesture.

'Yet there is heaviness, sir, in the friendships. The pain of imminent separation. Perhaps a permanent parting.'

Would he ever see them again, once he'd shipped out to god knows where? He thought about Josie, so recently reported as appearing at the Cinéma Mugrabi in Tel Aviv, sharing the stage once more, as it happened, with Brachah Zefira. He also thought about Francine, his multi-layered guilt mingled with self-centered relief.

'You have already begun to distance yourself from them? If so, this is a good thing, for it is also written that the duty of every sane person is to be prepared for departures, whether within this life, or to the next one. For we do not know, any of us, when we might be served with Allah's demand upon our souls.'

'It certainly makes it easier. Though I have this sense of each of them – each of *you*, Highness – somehow also driving me away. Driving me *on*, perhaps. To different ends, maybe.'

Paquita had some vision of him following *La Nueve*'s crusade against fascism to its end – and to tell the story. Hélène? Had made him swear he would expose still more evidence of the Nazi – and Vichy – persecution of Europe's Jews, wherever that might lead.

For Jack, there was some satisfaction. His accreditations to Associated Press, to the Beeb, to Leclerc's press corps – well, he *was* Leclerc's press corps, all of it. And his medal, the Sherifian Order of Alaoui. But there was still the Pulitzer to pursue. And Welch may be dead, though it was all far from finished.

'The question, my friend,' said the sultan, 'is whether you are prepared for whatever comes next.'

April–May 1944

Raymond Dronne

As His Majesty's Troopship *Franconia* wallowed in the waves, the Bay of Biscay somewhere away to the east through the driving rain, Jack leaned on the stern rail, just along from Raymond Dronne, and recalled Fox's final words before their departure.

'Your instincts were all perfectly correct, old boy,' Fox had said. 'I'm sorry, but Welch has been playing us all for fools.'

'He's still alive,' said Jack.

He had almost been expecting it. They'd been standing on the quayside at Mers-el-Kébir, watching the first of the Chad Regiment's battalions tramping up the gangplanks, heading to their quarters for the coming couple of weeks.

'Two sightings,' said Fox, 'as it happens. The first, in Oran.' A nod of his head towards the opposite side of the bay. Oran, where Jack had landed from the Stanbrook, almost exactly five years before. 'We took it with a pinch of salt at first. But then – well, another, near his home. Just outside Guildford.'

'Dorothea,' said Jack. 'Sheltering him, I suppose.'

A crane was heaving nets of supplies up the *Franconia*'s pale grey sides, Algerian stevedores and the vessel's crew working around her own davits, fore and aft of the funnel, labouring feverishly with trolleys, back and forth, getting it all stowed below.

'The wife? Yes. You know her, Telford, don't you? My god, the tangled web in which you're wrapped. Most of the agents I know have simpler lives than you do. But she's been interrogated at length. She knows nothing. He seems to have just used her, the same as he's used the rest of us.'

'Used – how, exactly? As though I can't guess.'

They lit cigarettes.

'Short version?' Fox sucked the tobacco smoke deep into his lungs. 'Recruited by the Abwehr just before he went to London for IG Farben. He didn't need a false identity – English father, remember? Sent low level stuff back to his masters in Berlin. Nothing too significant. His codename?'

'Black Scorpion, I suppose. He always had a flair for the fanciful, yes?'

'But when the Nazi Party's own intelligence services, the SD, were formed in '31, Welch let it be known to friends that he despised Hitler, feared his rise to power. The writing, he used to tell them, was on the wall. All lies, though our boys took this as a message, turned him, as a double agent. Or so they thought.'

Now, it was the three medical units, their turn to board. The doctors, the drivers of the *Rochambelles*, the British Quakers, and the naval auxiliaries everybody had dubbed the *Marinettes*. Dani would be there among them, but in the mass of olive drab, he couldn't actually distinguish her.

'Just as the Abwehr wanted?' said Jack. 'Bloody hell, didn't anybody see it coming?'

'Seemed perfect. English father, as we've said. Blood thicker than water and all that nonsense. Good English blood. You know what we're like, Telford. English blood better than every other variety. Hell, we mock the Germans for all this Master Race nonsense, but...'

They dodged out of the way as an ambulance raced along the dockside. Not one of their ambulances, however. No, Jack had been in Casa, three days ago, seen all the vehicles, the tanks, the half-tracks, the trucks, loaded onto tank-landing ships, the flat-bottomed vessels which would carry them all the way to England. Bloody uncomfortable, but at least they couldn't be torpedoed.

'Bred in the bones of the English establishment. Yes, I know. But this?'

'The fact is, Welch was useful. Convincing. Helped set up the Anglo-German Fellowship. Brilliant. Then he could give us the names of all those Hitler supporters back home we needed to watch. But only the small fry, naturally. And all those trade delegations for Standard Oil, the stuff he fed back to us from the German Armistice Commission here. Hell, we knew every move Auer was making in Casablanca.'

Louis Réchard had made a similar comment over their final cognac together. It had, like all of Jack's partings, been emotional. But they'd shared a jest or two. The *end* of a beautiful friendship. And their mutual perplexity about whether the scriptwriters for the Bogart film had seen some reference to Casablanca's real Brigade Commandant when they'd picked the name Louis *Renault* for their own.

'The small fry because it didn't matter? We could have got the same intelligence from my boy Bilal and his mates.'

'Quite. And all the time, he was spilling his guts to Berlin. Working with the *Milice*. Christ, Telford, we were lucky. Do you know, the bastard sent them a coded message about the conference? Roosevelt and Churchill. Can you imagine? Thankfully, the German intelligence services are all so jealous of their own little machines – navy won't share with the Abwehr, Abwehr won't share with the SS, that kind of thing – by the time anybody took the message seriously, it was doubly scrambled. Bloody idiots thought Casablanca was a cipher for the White House. Can you believe it? By the time they'd realised their mistake, it was too late.'

'But it wouldn't have damaged Welch.'

'The opposite. Helped his reputation with the Abwehr no end. And they seem to have encouraged him to step up his activities a little. A bit of amateur assassination on the side. Nothing too serious, just another string to his bow.'

The Spaniards were embarking. Jack could hear them singing.

'Not Howard, though,' said Fox. 'They needed him dead a different way – so they could test out the fears about their cipher machines.'

'All makes perfect sense,' said Jack. 'Except for one thing. Where the hell do I fit into all this?'

'You want my personal opinion? You're a journalist – a good one. A nose for sniffing out the truth. Why do you think we have so many of you boys, writers in general, working undercover? You could smell what all us so-called professionals couldn't. The flaws behind the face. Behind the *double* face. And Welch, in the same way, could sense your suspicions. Being Welch, he couldn't help the amateur theatricals. The scorpion, the calling card, all that nonsense. Not high on his priorities, but you were nuisance enough for him to add you to his list of jobs.'

Nella Bénatar's analysis had been more brutal. Another tearful farewell, promises they'd each write, see each other again when this was all over. His surrogate mother. But she'd had words of advice for him. How he must go home, finish this – because, whatever Jack had done to become Welch's target, Telford could be certain this went far deeper than he could see.

'I suppose you're right,' he said to Fox. Yet he also knew, if there was truth in this at all, it was a partial truth. For what had Welch told him? That he'd simply owed somebody a favour, a debt. The rest might have been a factor as well, but Fox and Nella were correct – Telford's nose also confirmed it was only part of the story. 'And Leslie Howard?'

'Our best guess?' said Fox. 'Jerry must have had suspicions. Their codes maybe not as secure as they think. So, they use Welch to give Howard the warning. If he takes it seriously, that's another measure of confirmation they've a problem. If he laughs it off... You're sure he never told you what he'd said to Welch by way of a reply?'

A long blast on the *Franconia*'s horn. She was about to get under way. A few stragglers still climbing the gangways, and Jack needed to join them, his own dunnage already waiting for him in the cabin he'd be sharing – with Massu, as it happened.

'I'm certain,' Jack had told Fox. 'But he got on the plane, didn't he? And the ciphers – *have* they been changed?'

'Definitely classified, old chap. I'm too far down the ladder to know and, if I knew, I'd be too far *up* the ladder to share intelligence like that with a bloody reporter. Though, if they *had* been changed, maybe we wouldn't be here, having this chat – don't you think?'

Yes, he did. Something in the air, of course. Something big, like the whole world was suddenly on the move again. Invasion, naturally. But where? And when? And how? There was another thing. If this was true, about Welch, then it seemed more likely

Jack had not, after all, betrayed Howard. The Abwehr must have been well aware of the actor's mission long before Jack arrived in Lisbon and content to let it proceed, to test the integrity of their cyphers. Yet, if they doubted that integrity, had changed the codes, this endeavour on which the Allies were at last embarking would, itself, be compromised.

'I think we can read between the lines,' said Jack. 'Know when you're flying back yet?'

Fox still held his liaison post among Leclerc's staff.

'Not sure,' the captain had said, as he shook Jack's hand. 'But soon. The general's planning to be there on the dockside when you all arrive. I'll be there with him, old fellow.'

Telford was still mulling over the conversation when Dronne slapped his arm, there at the *Franconia*'s stern rail. Five days out from Mers-el-Kébir.

'Penny for your thoughts, *Monsieur* Telford?'

'I was thinking about Leslie Howard.'

'The actor – the *Boches* shot him down, no?'

'Just about here, as it happens. Or so they say. In the Bay. Somewhere north of Cedeira.'

There'd been a few poignant moments. Past Gibraltar, for example, and the Spaniards crowding along the decks as word spread that the Sierra de Cádiz was visible on the horizon. A bout of homesickness. The reminders that, while for the rest of them this war was now in its fifth year, for many soldiers of *La Nueve*, it was their eighth.

Yet good times as well. The liner might not be as grand as some of the other vessels from the Cunard fleet, but she more than compensated by way of old-fashioned elegance. Her garden lounges, covered stern decks, Tudor-styled smoking room, racquetball court and gymnasium. Entertainment, provided either by the many talents hidden among the passengers themselves, or by the lively dance band supplied courtesy of ENSA.

It all served to divert their minds from tomorrow – at least during hours of daylight. At night, no lights anywhere on the ship. And no noise. Yet plenty of opportunity for Telford to get to know Dani better, of course. And they'd fallen into a friendship, of sorts, with Massu and Lieutenant Torrès – Toto, apparently because of her diminutive size. Danielle was still less than comfortable with her, but it was all civilised enough.

The only fly in the ointment to spoil this idyll? The following day, further into the Bay of Biscay, as he walked the promenade deck with her, arm in arm, and they wondered at their convoy, spread now across calmer waters. The *Cape Town Castle*. The liberty ships visible ahead and to starboard. A couple of escort destroyers. All of them just changing course, according to their zig-zagging instructions, when one of the escorts began to veer in the opposite direction, her signal lights flashing.

Alarm bells on the *Franconia*, echoed by those of the other vessels. U-boats, everybody said. It must be U-boats. The rush for lifebelts, Telford dragging Danielle to the nearest boat station, ignoring her insistence that she should more properly muster with the rest of the *Rochambelles*.

In the end, nothing. The alarm false. And Jack left with the troubling thought that, had the ship needed to be abandoned, he would have lost his precious Dictaphone machine. Disaster!

One more thought, as well. The afterthought question for Captain Fox, when they'd shaken hands and Telford had turned back towards him.

'Meant to ask,' he yelled. 'Welch – any idea where he's gone?'

'Your guess is as good as mine, old man. In hiding somewhere. Found his way back to Berlin, maybe.'

'What language are they speaking?' Danielle asked him as the Train Commander and his team herded them onto their allocated carriages, the Crimson Lake livery of the LMS, and each coach with French flags at the windows. And so it was that there, in the once-familiar surroundings of Glasgow Central, amid the smoke and steam, the smell of rotten eggs, the babble of accents, Jack finally wrestled with the reality of being home.

'It's definitely English,' Jack told her. 'Just Glaswegian English. Don't worry, we all struggle with it.'

Danielle's own English was passable, but she'd not really understood a word since they disembarked at Greenock. The rest of the convoy had landed in the two days before the *Franconia* reached the Clyde – the liberty ships to Port Talbot, Swansea and Cardiff, the *Cape Town Castle* to Liverpool. But Leclerc, as promised, had been there, in person, to greet each element of his Division.

'The general,' she said now, as they climbed into the coach reserved for the *Rochambelles* and other medical personnel, 'he goes everywhere by train as well?'

'My friend, Captain Fox, said they'd driven from Cardiff.' Apparently, he'd stayed there long enough to get the endless processions of his vehicles on the road towards Yorkshire. 'To Liverpool,' Jack explained. 'Then flown up here. I bet he didn't get treated *this* well, though.'

All the seats in every compartment had been furnished with a gift – an American chocolate Hersheys bar and a twenty-pack of Kools.

'Long live General Patton,' the girls laughed.

They were in high spirits. Despite the efforts of *Commandant* Florence Conrad to maintain some façade of military gravitas, several of the younger ones had just discovered that their K-ration packs for the journey also included the additional reward of condoms – and one of the bustier women had the knack of blowing them up like party balloons, decorating them with lipstick. Chad faces, with the noses shaped to look like – well, just rude. And what else were good French Catholic girls going to do with bloody condoms? The slogans. *Wot, no stockings? Wot, no sex?*

'Do you mind, Dani?' said Jack. 'I think I'll go and see where the Spanish boys might be.'

'You're blushing, Jack,' she laughed. 'But don't worry.' She patted her own cardboard packs, those she'd not yet stowed in the luggage rack, and winked at him. 'I'll look after mine.'

There were four others in the compartment, including Toto Torrès, and they all smirked at Telford's discomfort. He slid the compartment door shut, their explosion of giggles following him out, and edged his way past still more boisterous women, peered through the grimy windows as they pulled out of the station for the long haul south. Twelve hours to Hull? Maybe more, depending on how busy the lines might be.

514

In the vestibule between their coach and the next, opposite the toilet, one of the men from the Friends Ambulance Unit leaned on the lowered window, blowing tobacco smoke out, allowing coal smoke to billow in. It all reminded him of that fateful train journey from Algiers. Welch. Where the hell was he? It made Jack wish he still had the revolver.

He'd handed the thing, and Welch's pistol, to Louis.

'I'll just stick to fighting with my pen now,' he'd insisted. Only he'd given the pen away. Anyway, the revolver hadn't been much use to him when he'd needed it.

He wandered into the corridor of the next carriage, three more of the Ambulance Unit boys in their British army khaki lounging outside their own compartment.

'Mister Telford?' one of them said. Jack didn't know him, but he seemed terribly young.

'Can I help you?' he replied.

'I just wanted to thank you, sir. The article you wrote about us. It's not easy sometimes, and…'

'It's my job,' Telford reminded him. 'And, whatever you do, you must *never* call me sir. Aren't you supposed to say Friend Jack or something?'

'I'm not a Quaker, Mister Telford. Methodist. Trying to be a good Christian. That's the way I was brought up.'

'Tribunal?' said Jack. The lad nodded. He would have been required to attend a hearing with the Conscientious Objectors board. 'I was brought up to be a pacifist, as it happens. The spirit's been willing enough, but sometimes life – well, it just doesn't work out the way we planned. But I'm glad you liked the article.'

Elliott had carried it. *Reynold's News*, of course. Telford had tried to reflect the experiences and conflicts of those other men – and yes, those had been Quakers – serving with the unit. The enormity of the evil represented by the Nazis and needing to be confronted, weighed against their deeply held beliefs. So, this solution, the ability to put their love of peace and healing into practice, to occasionally be able to extend this love even to the other side, and to perform that duty often in more danger on the battlefield than those who, with equal conviction, had decided to fight.

'God be with you, anyway,' said the young man as Jack muttered his thanks, excused himself, squeezed past.

He found Dronne four coaches further on, and the whole of *La Nueve* in the carriage, as well as two more beyond, boisterous songs and card games galore. He'd already passed Major Putz and another of the Third Battalion's companies, shared a few jokes.

'Well, look at you!' Telford laughed, leaned against the compartment's open doorway and stroked his own chin.

Dronne's beard. Now carefully trimmed, it formed a narrow ginger curtain only around the edge of his broad lower jawbone, a toothbrush moustache floating alone on his upper lip. He'd put on weight during their time in Temara. Positively plump again.

Granell shared the same compartment, offered Jack a jaunty salute, then shuffled his backside along the bench seat, made space for Telford to sit.

'Gave up your place with those beauties, comrade?' Amado laughed. 'Are you mad?'

Jack squeezed into the space between Granell and the soldier dozing alongside, who swore in Spanish at being disturbed.

'Still not right,' Dronne grumbled. 'Women attached to the Division.'

'My god,' Jack snapped, offered his cigarettes around the compartment, 'you fellows don't know when you're beaten, do you?'

It was an old argument, there since the *Rochambelles* and the *Marinettes* had first appeared. Fine to have women behind the lines, in the hospitals and dressing stations. But ambulances? At the front?

'The Yanks will soon change their minds,' Dronne told him, 'when the shit hits the fan. Then we'll see.'

'At Jarama, *jefe*,' Granell told him, and blew a neat smoke ring into the rest of the compartment's tobacco fug. 'Hell, those *milicianas*. You must have heard the stories, *inglés*.'

Yes, said Jack. Women warriors in the ranks of the Republic? He'd met quite a few. And the women who'd fought with the International Brigades. Formidable. As much guts as the men. More, perhaps, at places like Cerro Muriano.

'And fought to the bitter end, I suppose?' said Dronne.

Jack and Amado looked at each other. Of course not. After Guadalajara, most of the women were forced to withdraw from the Republican army. Not all, but most.

'And where will *we* be?' said Jack. 'At the end of all this?'

He leaned across Granell, wiped some of the steam from the window, pulled aside the corner of the *Tricolore* draped across the glass, and peered out at the depressing grey tenements of Glasgow's suburbs.

'Me?' Dronne replied. 'The army's been good to me – apart from a few knocks and bumps here and there. If I'm lucky enough to get through this, I'll maybe stick with it. And when I get too old for soldiering – well, there's always politics.'

'Back to Cameroon?'

'I think my colonial days are over. And I'm not sure I could look any of our old comrades in the eye again. Could you?'

Bitterness in his voice. Jack had never spoken with Dronne about the wound he took at Ksar Ghilane, but there were rumours – about how it had been a couple of the *tirailleurs* who'd saved him, pulled him to safety when the plane, one of their own, strafed them. The same *tirailleurs* who'd now been tossed aside when they'd outlived their usefulness. Yes, Dronne was bitter about the betrayal, the same as Leclerc himself.

'You Amado?' said Jack. 'You have plans? Your wife?'

Granell pinched the stub of the Gauloise between his fingers, making sure to savour every last drag as though it might be his last.

'Best not to think about all that, comrade. But here you are – back in your own country. After how long? Six years?'

'Almost.'

'And what will you do? Look up family? Friends? Did you leave a sweetheart behind?'

Family? Just his sister, of course. His mother dead now. No sweetheart, not unless you counted...

But never mind. And friends? Bloody good question. He'd truly not thought about it. Though yes, there were people he must see. Of course, there were. That other business to settle, as well. Yet how was he going to do it all?

*

517

The Feathers in Pocklington had been invaded. Flamenco guitar in the corner of the crowded lounge bar and three Frenchmen from the 501st in Huggate – the pub in Huggate having been declared out of bounds to them – were arguing ferociously about which of them was truly to blame for sinking the Sherman tank in the pond at Kilham. Poles and Irish Guardsmen from Fimber. Canadian aircrew from the local RAF base.

An enraged Mister Barker, from the dairy and the Royal Oak, tried his best to explain his problem to Captain Dronne. But he was exasperated. For some reason, Dronne – whose Spanish was excellent, and whose English improved with every day – still struggled with the local Yorkshire dialect.

'Can tha tell 'e?' Mister Barker said to Jack. 'Every bloody day in't woods.'

Of course, Jack agreed, and sipped at his beer.

'He's saying his son keeps finding live ammunition in the woods. That he's found the boy and his friends, twice now, fixing them in his workshop vice and hammering the cartridges with nails. Firing them.'

'Did it work?' said Dronne.

'Yes.'

'Were they hurt?'

'No.'

The captain shrugged.

'Tell him to lock his shed?'

Jack told Mister Barker, instead, that the captain had assured him the Spaniards would be more careful in future. Dronne had never quite forgiven his men for leaving a machine gun behind last time they'd been on manoeuvres.

It was May Day and the men of *La Nueve* had insisted on celebrating their socialism in style. They didn't quite understand the Maypole or the Morris Dancers but they joined the pageant with a will, delighted in decorating one of the half-tracks – *hastracs*, as the Spaniards pronounced the word, and normally parked with precision along the grass verge on Garths End – as a float for the Queen of the May.

They had been hugely impressed that Pocklington was so left-leaning it even had a trade union for mothers, and though Jack had tried to explain the Mothers' Union more accurately to them, it all fell on ears he suspected might be deliberately deaf.

They had, of course, been forced to clean up the *Muera Franco!* slogans daubed on the brewery walls by some of the company's younger members. Anarchists, of course. And why not? Campos had insisted. But they had been joined in the solidarity of International Workers' Day by three draymen, with the horses and wagons, all proudly sporting a small banner proclaiming their affiliation to the Transport and General Workers' Union.

The Home Guard had led the parade, music courtesy of the school band, and the procession gave Jack an excuse to wear the medal ribbon he'd been presented by *Sidi* Muhammad. The Spaniards had livened up the normal street party fare of pies, sandwiches and cakes by cooking an enormous yellow and red *paella* in the Market Place, just across from Telford's own billet at the Buck Hotel. Not quite large enough to feed Pocklington's present five thousand, but not far short.

'Flippin' eck,' the proprietor, Mrs Lumley had marvelled, 'will tha tek a gander at yonder pan?'

He'd done better than that. A photo. One of several he'd taken during the day. Pocklington's Spanish solidarity. And what better symbol than the *paellera*. It had been a joint effort, the village blacksmith helped by Ballesteros, the soldier who'd once pursued the same vocation in Priego de Córdoba. Somehow, between them, they'd even managed to procure red wine and nobody asked too many question, but seemingly from the cellars of Dalton Hall, now Leclerc's headquarters.

Yet if they'd expected the festivities to extend even so far as teatime – a concept more mystifying to the Spanish than almost anything else they'd encountered since their arrival – they had counted without the traditional English conservative approach to *fiesta*. And this was even discounting the perpetual rain.

But at least many of them had been allowed passes, the promise of more excitement in Hull, Leeds, York or Beverley. Those towns almost marked the four corners of the territory over which Leclerc's twelve thousand troops, their hundreds of vehicles, were dispersed.

And, that afternoon, Jack was bound for the fleshpots of Hull, a couple of hours from Pocklington by taxi – the Rolleiflex on his knee – in company with Dronne, Granell and a farmer from Sopelana, near Bilbao.

'It's taken until now to find them?' said Jack.

'Last week,' said Bidarte the farmer. 'I saw them for the first time in seven years. When we knew it was all over for us at Bilbao, we put them on the ship for England. Both of them.'

'How old?' Dronne asked him.

'The boy was seven, the girl only five.'

The taxi driver checked the address. Pearson Park? He asked whether it was the place where the Spanish kids lived. That was the place, Jack told him, explained how this man – Paco Bidarte – his son and daughter were there.

'What was the choice?' said Bidarte. 'Everybody knew my politics. If they'd stayed with the wife, they'd have been taken anyway. Taught to hate us. Taught to forget us. This? It seemed like the right thing. And we didn't think Franco could win. Not in the end. A year, we said. Maybe two, then we'd bring them back from England.'

Telford explained for the driver. He seemed genuinely intrigued, couldn't believe that all those kids…

'We just lost track of them,' Bidarte was telling them. 'My wife had word they'd landed in Southampton. Going north. And then…'

And then Bilbao had fallen to the fascists. Bidarte had escaped the surrender to the Italians, made his way south, fought at Madrid and Teruel. Valencia. And, after Valencia, the internment camps of Algeria.

'Your wife?' said Jack.

Bidarte shook his head, looked away.

'Last year,' he said. 'A letter finally reached me. Disappeared. You know what that means, comrade.'

Yes, Jack knew.

'But now?' Dronne asked him. 'Now you've found them?'

'We finish this,' said Bidarte. 'Then I come back for them. The Americans help us settle with Franco, and we go home. No?'

They dropped him just across from some green and pleasant park – pleasant, apart from the rain. Hazeldene it said, on the house gatepost. The youngsters were there, waiting for him, threw themselves into his arms, the boy now fourteen, the girl twelve.

'Christ,' said Dronne, as the taxi headed back down Princes Avenue, 'this bloody war.'

Jack couldn't answer, gazed out of the window, spotted a jeweller's shop, still open.

'Hey,' he said. 'You mind if we make a stop?'

He'd scoffed each time he came across stories of whirlwind wartime romance, servicemen flinging themselves into hasty marriages through some sense of their own mortality in the face of imminent action. But since they'd arrived in Pocklington, the certainty of something very big indeed just over the horizon, the fragility of their futures, had been the murmured theme of more than one lazy, bee-filled, grass-stained embrace between himself and Danielle. He hadn't actually broached the question of marriage itself, naturally, but fifteen minutes later – the taxi still waiting – saw him emerging from the shop, with his two friends, the proud but uncertain owner of an engagement ring. A small sapphire flanked by two even smaller diamonds. Telford had no idea when he might pop the question itself, but the prospect filled him with an unexpected glow.

'We shall all dance at your wedding, *inglés*,' Granell laughed, and slapped him on the back, as they walked along the small parade of shops to reach the waiting cab again.

There was a newsagent's, a sandwich board outside. *Government bans all foreign travel.*

'Maybe we're going to be stuck in Pocklington for the duration then,' Jack scoffed. 'Hard to fight if we're not allowed out of the country.'

'Foreign travel?' Dronne repeated the words. 'Who do they mean?'

Well, thought Telford, I suppose that puts an end to any more English tourists on Franco's bloody War Routes. But he also remembered a conversation he'd had with a purser on the *Franconia*, the revelation that Cunard's troopships, on their outbound voyages from Liverpool to New York, were never actually empty, as he might have expected, but still carried wealthy civilian travellers, off on their holidays in the USA. Jack and the purser had now agreed, you couldn't expect the bigwigs to give up their pleasures for a little thing like a war.

Jack started to explain, but then his eye carried to the sign above the newsagent's door. *Linares*, it said.

Impossible, he decided. But he couldn't resist.

'Wait,' he said. 'There's something…'

The bell above the door tinkled happily as he pushed his way inside. The shop was bright. Rows of entirely empty sweet jars on shelves must have been inherited from earlier occupancy. On the counter, a few copies of the day's *Express*, of the *Hull Daily Mail*, and a batch of *Sporting Greens* left over from Saturday, as well as flashes of lurid red and yellow from the *Beano* and *Dandy*. There was a smell of tobacco, stew cooking somewhere deeper within the premises.

'Mother of God,' said Lydia Linares, when she turned from her dusting and found Jack staring at her. 'José!' she yelled. 'Come, quick.'

She put her hand to her mouth, tears forming in the corner of her eyes, as she slid the comics to one side, threw open the counter's lifting hatch, and ran into Telford's arms.

This wasn't going to be a five-minute visit, and Dronne dutifully went to pay off the cabbie, while the shop filled with the extended Linares family – José himself, entirely overcome with emotion, making all the introductions afresh, marvelling at Jack's uniform, the babble of news and renewed acquaintance, a photograph taken.

It was, after all, a long way from the quayside in Casablanca and Commodore Creighton.

The Fulford Dance Hall in Beverley Road was on the opposite side of the bomb-scarred city. Even Pocklington village had a couple of bombsites from a German raid on the airfield. But here in Hull… And Glasgow, my god, what a mess. Jack felt some vague sense of shame he'd missed it all. Yet from the gay abandon of the queue outside the modest, whitewashed façade of the ballroom, apart

522

from the uniforms, you'd hardly have known there was a war at all. By seven that evening it was already in full swing. Literally. On the stage, Dunny's Dance Band belting out *Minnie's in the Money* and a batch of other jitterbug numbers.

'You told me you had nobody but your sister,' Dronne laughed. 'And there you are, half of Gibraltar thinks you're family.'

Telford had feared the worst. Sydney Elliott had never heard anything from the Linares family, despite Jack's warning they might need his help, but it seemed the document supplied by Mister Bond was sufficient, and José had wasted no time in putting their limited resources to good use, the shop here almost falling into his lap. Yes, they'd all promised, they'd keep in touch.

'Those *chicos* can certainly move,' said Amado. 'Aurora would love this. And your beautiful nurse, no?'

The floor had been monopolised by some black GIs and the local girls partnering them. Quite something. That dance, all the rage. Fast but smooth and stylish, these fellows, the young women doing their best to match their moves.

'She would have expected me to try it,' Jack replied. 'Make a fool of myself in the process.' Still, he was sorry she wasn't with him, the whole ambulance unit shipped off to York for yet more training. 'But maybe we should capture the moment, all the same.'

He slipped the camera from his shoulder, moved in for a shot, waved the Rolleiflex at one of the dancing couples.

'You mind?' he shouted, and the GI shrugged his shoulders, threw wide his arms in agreement, as though it were simply part of the dance.

'Sure, why not?' he yelled back, and his buxom blonde partner gave Jack a smile of approval.

Telford clutched the camera at his waist to steady the machine, looked down into the viewfinder and level marker. His fingers found the levers for the aperture and shutter speed, just below the lens. He fiddled with them until he was satisfied the settings were fine for the light and the movement, then he waited for the right moment and – *click*, he flicked the shutter lever, hoping he'd caught the action just right.

He waved his thanks to the dancers and was making his way

back to the bar, where Dronne and Granell swigged Coca Cola, when he spotted two white helmets near the entrance.

'What do *they* want?' said Amado. He had a natural antipathy for policemen in general, though he seemed to have set the Pocklington village bobbies in a slightly different category. But *military* policemen? Just a bit too close to the *Guardia Civil* for Granell's liking. It was fair enough, and Jack remembered his own encounters with the *gendarmerie*, the episode at the Place de France when he'd tried to take photos of the dead rioters and Dronne had come to his rescue.

'Nothing good, for sure,' Telford replied, watching the predatory heads of the MPs searching this way and that, the sneering lips mumbling, one to the other, and finally their rapacious glance settling on the dancers. A conspiratorial nudge, and they were on their way down the few red-carpeted steps towards the crowded floor, skirting the bystanders until they positioned themselves in front of the same GI Jack had recently photographed.

'You, boy! Here!'

Jack wondered why nobody ever seemed capable of writing an original script for confrontations like this. He'd have to work on that, but for now there was simply the banal routine.

The soldier, claimed the MPs, was 'out of uniform' – no tie apparently.

The GI's response, they decided, was 'sassy.'

They told him to get out and take all his n— friends with him.

When the blonde girl tried to intervene, she was met with the same sort of disdain they might have displayed towards canine excrement on their toecaps.

Amado set down his bottle on the counter and sauntered across for a closer look, and Dronne followed him. Jack knew it was all part of the routine. Steps in a different sort of dance, one that dragged him into its embrace as well.

'What you doing with this n—, girl?' drawled one of the MPs. 'You English women all stupid? Or maybe you're just a…'

A punch was thrown. The black soldier was repaid with a billy club rammed into his midriff. He bent double, retched on the dancefloor. The club came up to hit him again. And stayed there.

There was something almost comical about Raymond Dronne's appearance. A slimmer version of Oliver Hardy with the addition of a thin fringe of red beard. But he was impressively strong, fully recovered now from his wounds at Ksar Ghislane. So his grip on the MP's truncheon was solid as a vice.

The fellow half-turned, the vacuous face beneath the brim of his helmet twisted in anger even beyond the limits of its natural ugliness, his left hand slipping to the holster flap at his side.

'No,' murmured Granell, and stepped forward. '*No vale, señor.*'

He'd grabbed the man's wrist.

'What the...' yelled the MP.

'Smile,' said Jack, and pressed the shutter lever again.

The other MP, a sergeant, screamed at Amado.

'Hands off, wop. Or, by god...'

He reached for his own weapon but, by then, the wooden handle of a stiletto had magically appeared in Granell's hand. His thumb flicked the trigger tab and the blade flashed, just an inch from the military policeman's neck.

'Sergeant,' said Dronne in his best English, 'guns, they make my adjutant very nervous. And that knife, it is very sharp. There are Germans, many of them, who could tell you the same thing – if, *bien sûr*, they were still alive.'

'He's right, old boy' said Telford. 'Really, it would be better if you found some proper lawbreakers elsewhere.'

The sergeant spat on the floor, but his hand moved away from his holster.

'A limey, a frog-eater, a wop and a bunch of these...'

The sergeant glowered at the black GIs.

'Sergeant,' Jack told him, 'I don't want to teach you your business, but it's *Captain* Frog-Eater and *Lieutenant* Wop.'

'These...?' said Dronne. '*These*, they are soldiers, Sergeant. And they have done – nothing. They trouble nobody. You should leave now. *Vraiment*, you should leave.'

The sergeant didn't seem able to resist a final poke of the GI's arm, but he wasn't inclined to argue.

'You – we'll be seeing you again, boy.'

And they left, a ragged cheer from the Fulford Dance Hall's

customers. The GI thanked Dronne, offered the captain a salute.

'You need to watch out for those two,' said Jack. 'They get you in the guardhouse – what d'you call it, the stockade? But if they get you in there, they could beat the living daylights out of you. And nobody would know. Or care.'

'Living daylights?' The GI laughed. 'Is that a thing – really? But those suckers didn't take my name, did they? An' you know what they say. We all look the same to them rednecks.'

He told them he was Private Eugene King, from the Quartermaster Truck Company based there in Hull.

'You seem to have some friends here, at least,' Jack laughed. 'And yes, I've heard that saying. But I heard this, as well. People reckoning the only Americans over here with any manners are you coloured guys.'

'Hey,' said Eugene, 'you think we don't get treated like dirt by some folks in England? But I tell you, man, at least there's no lynchings in England. Most treat us with respect. And most see us as being on their side. Proper soldiers, not just donkeys for the US army.'

There'd been plenty of cases. Scuttlebutt, as Colonel Bill Eddy would have said. Even rumours of a black GI being shot in the back by MPs – somewhere in Lancashire, he thought. So many cases that the Americans had required Frank Capra to produce a film. *The Negro Soldier*, the Brown Bomber, Joe Louis in the starring role. Required viewing for all military personnel. It had been shown, just a couple of weeks earlier, at Pocklington's Oak House Cinema.

But then there'd been the letter. Mrs Foster at the Black Horse had shown it to him. From the brewery. And the brewery had been advised by the Government. The British Government had been urged by the American High Command. Please observe the requirement for racial segregation.

'What will you do?' Jack had said to Mrs Foster.

'Already done it, 'appen,' she replied, and pointed to the sign she'd placed in the window.

Black Troops Only!

The village thought it was hilarious – all but a very few.

'Well, you'll always be welcome in Pocklington,' Jack told Eugene King. 'Guaranteed a big welcome at the Black Horse.'

'Sure,' said Eugene, 'But all we want to do is fight. Really fight. You know? Hey though, I guess it's time we were going.'

Jack explained to Dronne and Amado Granell, and they agreed they should also be making a move. Another taxi. Pick up Bidarte, as they'd arranged, on the way back. They told Eugene and his friends good luck, returned to the bar, finished their drinks, availed themselves of the toilets, straightened ties and set caps on their heads before venturing out onto the street.

But as they pushed the bar on the doors, in place of the nine o'clock sunset gloom, they emerged into a dazzle of bright lights. Two trucks on Beverley Road, headlamps blazing and directed against the waste ground just in front of the dance hall.

Caught in the glare, Private Eugene King and three of his comrades, with their recently acquired girlfriends. Beyond them, silhouetted against the beams, a semicircle of military policemen. They were back, and this time they'd brought reinforcements.

'Christ,' Jack muttered.

Dronne removed his *képi* again, rubbed his head in the way he sometimes did when there was a tough decision to be made.

Amado said something in Spanish that Telford didn't quite catch.

'Told you, boy,' the MP was shouting. He slapped the billy club against his open palm, over and over. 'Told you we'd be seeing you again. Just didn't expect us this soon, I guess, did you, boy?'

Their line began to close in towards the waste ground. A couple of the girls screamed and Eugene, his friends as well, pushed them back towards the doorway.

'Get inside,' Jack shouted to them. 'Inside, now.'

'They'll just follow us,' said Eugene. 'More folks will get hurt. No, mister, this only ends one way. An' you better get out of here. Look after these fine young ladies, why don't you?'

It sounded to Jack like a good plan, but when he glanced at Amado and Dronne, he knew they were never going to walk away from this, not in a month of Sundays.

'Shit, shit, shit,' said Jack, wondered stupidly what he should do with the camera.

The line of MPs had stopped now, a dozen yards away. Telford could almost smell their sweat.

He turned to open the doors once more, to hand the girls inside, but he never got the chance. The doors burst outwards without his assistance. He was pushed aside. Almost fell. And the entire clientele of the Fulford Dance Hall poured forth, happy revellers, spreading themselves in a singing, protective ring, just beyond those black GIs.

They sang *I'm a Yankee Doodle Dandy*. It wasn't quite *La Marseillaise* in *Casablanca*, but it did the trick.

Telford rarely experienced any pride in being British. An empty concept. Accident of birth. And pride in Britain itself? There were things to be celebrated, certainly. But during his lifetime, there simply seemed to have been too many betrayals. An entire generation and more sacrificed during the previous war – for what purpose? He often thought his own father, all those countless millions more, had given their lives in that bloodbath for no better purpose than to sow the seeds for *this* one.

And though this conflict was, without doubt, different from the last, even here the betrayals of the brave simply seemed to pile one upon the next. Where had they begun? Mussolini's invasion of Ethiopia, of course, and Britain clearing the Mediterranean to allow Italy's easier transport of its armies to Abyssinia. Then Spain. The heroes of the Republic left to stand almost friendless against the forces of fascism. Czechoslovakia, naturally, thanks to Chamberlain and the general complacency of the British public. And then there was Poland. Britain and France may have declared war through their international duty to protect the Poles – but afterwards? The phoney war, until the Germans had taken Warsaw and gathered their strength again sufficiently to smash their way through France.

Yet, after that? After Dunkirk, after the Battle of Britain, after North Africa – yes, this was Britain's better side.

And tonight, at the Fulford Dance Hall on Beverley Road? Here were countrymen – and women, naturally – to make a fellow proud, as well.

He didn't really see precisely how it ended. Just the roar of truck engines, and they were gone.

Private Eugene King was at his side, fingering the armband around Telford's shirt sleeve.

'You. Newspaperman? You going to write about this?'

'Of course,' said Jack. 'But you know nobody will ever publish it.'

He offered the soldier a cigarette – he was back on the Luckies now – while Dronne and Granell went off to find a cab. It had started raining again, a thin drizzle, the smell of tar and sulphur wafting across from the local gasworks.

'Maybe one day they will,' Eugene told him.

'One day, sure. Maybe after the fighting's all done. You think you'll get your wish, Eugene – about the fighting?'

'What do I think? What I think is this. However bad this war might have been up till now, it's about to get a whole lot worse. I seen rats cornered, mister. I seen how they fight then. That's how the Germans goin' to be, when we get over there. When it starts, this army's going to need every fighting man it can get, no matter what colour we might be. An' I'll be proud to fight for my country, Mister Newspaperman. I'm proud now. So you can write that as well. Proud.' He glanced across to where the young blonde woman, her friends, hugged each other, sobbing. 'But hey, I'd better go see to the girls.'

But Jack held him back.

'And after,' he said. 'Those MPs...'

He waved his arm in the direction their trucks had disappeared.

'Sure,' said Eugene. 'America's got plenty more where they came from. Poor white trash who have to believe there's somebody further down the pile worse off than they are. All those thousands who used to be in the German-American Bund. American Nazis. Seems like human nature, don't it? We all need somebody to love – but we all need somebody to hate, as well.'

'That's a terrible condemnation.'

'Why the hell else do we fight wars? Because it's in our nature and because we like it.'

'But when the fighting's over...'

Eugene tossed away the cigarette stub.

'It ain't never over. After the Germans, after we go home, that's when the fighting *really* starts. I'm never going back to be discriminated against no more. Never! And I don't know how long it takes. Fifty years. A hundred. Maybe more. It won't stop until we make them see – those good ol' boys and everybody like them – after all this time, that a black man's life matters as much as any white.'

Telford had no idea what he might discover in London, but he was determined to bring his particular business with Welch to an end.

'You have a week, *Monsieur* Telford,' Leclerc had said to him. 'After that, I shall need you. General Patton will be here. The Division formally absorbed into his Third Army.'

They were walking together in the grounds of the Division's headquarters at Dalton Hall, fifteen miles east of Pocklington village.

'And then, sir?'

'More training, of course. And we follow our fates. An oath to fulfil, you remember?'

Jack remembered, thought about it again on the train with Dronne and the three other officers due to be honoured with the Order of Liberation from de Gaulle himself at Carlton Gardens. Telford held an invitation from Leclerc, allowing him to attend the ceremony, but he suspected there simply wouldn't be time.

And so it transpired.

He thought about a trip to Worcester, to see his sister, but when he checked out the timetables, he knew it wasn't possible. Instead, he phoned her from his hotel.

Jack thought about Ruby Waters, but the engagement ring was still in his suitcase, waiting for the right time to ask Danielle. No, not strictly true. Waiting until he had the nerve, and that moment hadn't come yet. And, somehow, he knew if he met Ruby now – anyway, he had no real idea where she might be, and the process of finding her would, he also knew, be a trap in itself.

But Sheila? Yes, his first evening, in a London very different from the city he'd left. Dinner with Sheila and her husband. Newsome was stiff, formal. Jack decided there was some jealousy there, reading more into his wife's long association with Telford than he should have done. They'd been through a lot together, but friends and colleagues, nothing more. She seemed happy enough, three months pregnant, determined that having kids wouldn't interfere with her career. And yes, Barea? Good bloke. Working at his house in Mapledurham just now, working on the third part of a book, they thought. But due back in town in a couple of days. Newsome would arrange the meeting.

The next day, breakfast and an emotional reunion with Sydney Elliott. A reunion of tears and laughter, both.

'You bastard,' said Jack. 'You told me it would be two weeks at the most.'

'Christ, Jack. Your eye – Spain. My god, I wrote your obituary. D'you know what that was like? And then you phoning me, out of the blue, from Madrid. Morocco. All this with Leclerc. We need a month to catch up. And you, in uniform...'

'But I don't have a month, Sydney. I'm supposed to be back in – oh, I don't suppose I'm allowed to say. Back with Leclerc, anyhow. And, after – well, we don't know, do we? Not officially. There's something I need to get off my chest, though. You remember the stuff you published, the stuff I sent you from Spain?'

'How we'd not lifted a finger to stop Franco handing all that mineral wealth to Hitler? Yes, it caused quite a stink. Why?'

'I'm afraid there's just a bit more to the story. And my eye? Look, I need your help, and I'm not quite sure where to start.'

But he did his best. The bewildering journey through Wonderland. Carter-Holt. Yes, she *was* a Reuters correspondent, but she was much more than that. It wasn't the most cogent of stories, but he covered all the main points. The circumstances of her death – her murder, he supposed. Yes, he was certain she'd intended to kill him, but...

His escape to Burgos. Turbides and his eye. The prison at San Pedro de Cardeña. Madrid. His suspicions about Major bloody Edwin. The papers he'd stolen and sent the story. Yes, this was how it had come about. He didn't mention Fielding, though. No, best leave that alone, for now. Then Alicante. Edwin still chasing him. How it had all ended. The *Stanbrook* and Oran – Elliott knew that part, of course. But after? Kingsley Welch and this whole sorry saga. The train from Algiers. It was all part of the same thing,

Welch long gone now, it seemed. But still loose ends. And one of those was likely to be Carter-Holt's father.

'Parliamentary Secretary for Overseas Trade – you mean *that* Sir Aubrey Carter-Holt?' said Elliott, at last. He'd sat, stupefied, through most of it. An occasional question, a demand that Jack should just go over a particular part again. 'Look, Jack, I know we joked about it. But this isn't just a two-week assignment turning into six years away. I don't know what to say. Really, I don't. Though I'm certain about this, at least. You should leave this alone now. If this Welch character's buggered off back to Germany then good riddance. For pity's sake, man, let sleeping dogs lie.'

'And how am I supposed to know there isn't another Kingsley Welch out there somewhere? Somebody else just doing a little favour for Major Edwin, or Sir Aubrey – or whoever. No, Sydney. You need to help me now.'

He thought about tracking down Dorothea in Guildford, but he knew it would be a waste of time. He'd find out nothing there to help him and it had been turgid enough having to spend breakfast with the woman in Lisbon. It might have been interesting to find out how the War Route in Madrid had gone, though, but it was hardly a priority. Still, he wondered precisely what the intelligence services might have told her about Welch's activities – if anything. Or did she still think he was away on business? Telford didn't really care, one way or the other.

Anyway, he'd decided there was another duty he should perform while he waited for Sydney Elliott to do some digging for him.

So, that afternoon, he headed for Hampstead. He'd asked at the hotel whether somebody could get him directions to the library there, and it looked as though the closest tube station was Kilburn. They were right – except, when he'd followed the directions to the corner of Westbere Road and Sarre Road, all he found was a bombsite. A couple of locals told him the place had been flattened four years earlier. Incendiaries. The librarians? Jack had asked. Transferred to the other branch, Finchley Road. A mile away, past more bomb-damaged properties.

It was a very traditional, brick-built place, on the corner of Arkwright Road. But when he asked at the counter, he drew another blank.

'Frances?' said the matronly Head Librarian. 'I'm afraid she left us, dear.'

But she gave him the address, half a mile away. Clorane Gardens.

He found her near the front gate, kneeling on a doormat and weeding a neat herbaceous border. She'd not changed much, her face still the colour and texture of milk, though smudged now by soil from the back of her glove.

Jack recalled the last time he'd seen her. Spain, of course. Heroic, as she supervised the loading of her dead husband's coffin into the hearse, on its way to the harbour and her lonely journey home.

At last she looked up from her labours, saw him watching her over the privet hedge and low wall.

'Frances,' he said. 'It's me. Jack. Jack Telford.'

When she'd recovered from the shock, fallen sobbing into his arms, scolded him for leaving it so appallingly long, stumbled through a dozen questions – about his eye, of course, and about his uniform – she made them tea, brought out some scones to a very pleasant garden room at the back of the house.

'So,' she said, as she poured the tea, 'this is your idea of coming back soon? And taking care of yourself.'

She was about Jack's own age, considerably younger than her late husband, Bertie Moorgate, had been. But the couple had shared a macabre interest in battlefield tourism, somehow reflected in her passion for the palest of gardenia face powders, for the darkest of lipsticks and nail varnish.

'You've not changed, Frances. And – comfortable? You seem to be.'

The house was very nice – it was the only way he could think to describe it – no more than twenty years old, he guessed.

'Bertie was a good provider, Jack. A *good* provider.'

He'd been the manager of the Westminster's London Foreign Branch.

'I just never pictured you weeding.'

'Did you ever picture me at all?' she said.

He had to admit to himself it had been a while. Yet, after their parting – she'd kissed him on the cheek with almost excessive tenderness – he'd missed her a great deal, surprised himself by how much he'd been attracted to her. And, somehow, it was all swimming back into focus again.

'A lot,' he told her. 'All the time I was in Spain, anyway. But then it all got a bit sticky.'

'I saw the piece in *Reynold's News* – telling the world you were still alive, after all. But I'd completely missed the earlier one. Your obituary, Jack? The funeral and so on. But thank god, my dear. I couldn't have coped, I don't think. Not you as well. And now, you've somebody in your life, I suppose?'

The engagement ring was suddenly very heavy in his pocket. Very heavy. He'd not had the heart to leave it behind, but…

'I seem to be married to the Free French army,' he said.

'Did you just avoid my question, Jack?'

'Seriously. Between General Leclerc on one side and the Associated Press on the other…'

'Your writing – yes, I'd forgotten. Is that why you write, dear man? To fill the empty spaces in your life? No, don't answer. You'll only dig the hole deeper for yourself.'

He changed the subject anyway. Told her about meeting Dorothea in Lisbon – then more or less gave her a potted and sanitised version of his own story, though in reverse.

They settled into an easy truce, swapped recollections of their time together on the War Routes bus tour, the still inexplicable way her husband had died. It all seemed like such a long time ago, a comfortable distance, a cushion upon which they could rest their reciprocal attachment, an attachment he hadn't even known he possessed.

She asked him where he was staying, and he told her, the Merchant Navy Hotel on Bedford Square.

'Jack,' she said, after a moment, 'you know there's no need. If you'd like to stay here. No strings…'

He was ashamed he even considered the possibility. But he did. And when he finally told her that, no, it wouldn't be right, it did nothing to restore any sense of moral rectitude. Nothing at all. Worse, when she kissed him goodbye – not on the cheek this time, but full on the lips, and with considerable passion – it left him with a sinking confusion. Had he just betrayed Frances Moorgate or had he betrayed Dani Zidane? Or both? And, of course, himself.

He picked up a copy of the *Evening Standard* from the news stand outside Hampstead tube station, still vexed with himself. Shouldn't have come and wondered where it had all gone wrong. He'd had the best of intentions when he settled on visiting Frances, but now, dammit…

Telford merely skimmed through the headlines on the way back into town. The Russians victorious in the Caucasus. The German stronghold at Monte Cassino finally taken. U-boats sunk in the North Atlantic. And a massive Allied bombing raid against Calais. But then an announcement caught his eye. An opening, the following day. A building called El Instituto Español. He assumed it must be something to do with Franco's embassy, here in London, but then noticed the detail. To be officially opened by Doctor Juan Negrín.

He'd forgotten. It was Paquita Gorroño who'd reminded him, when he'd handed her the pen – reminded him Jack would be likely to see Negrín before she did. London, of course. But should he go? Prince's Gate. South Kensington. Knightsbridge.

Jack made up his mind the following morning. Another breakfast meeting with Sydney. And yes, Elliott had confirmed two things. First, Major Lawrence Edwin was no longer a suspect. Ironically, killed in the Blitz, that other Great Fire of London at the very end of 1940. Well, this cut down the field, anyway. And, second, Sir Aubrey was definitely in town. Or at least not abroad, so far as he'd been able to confirm.

'But Jack,' he said, 'you can't just wander into the Foreign Office and demand to see one of its Parliamentary Secretaries. It doesn't work like that. You know it doesn't.'

'I suppose not,' said Telford. 'But I can give it a try. Besides, if it's a no-show, I can always shoot across the park and catch up with an old friend. Did I tell you about Negrín?'

Jack presented himself at the Foreign Office just before noon and his press credentials got him past the initial barriers of sandbags and red-capped military policemen. Busy receptionists told him he must write for an appointment, because surely he didn't suppose…

'But if you could simply phone Sir Aubrey's office,' he said. 'Give them my name. Telford. Jack Telford. Explain it's literally a matter of life and death. About his daughter.'

They kept him waiting almost an hour, eventually rewarded him by confirming that, yes, Sir Aubrey would see him. At three.

Jack felt his stomach lurch. He'd half-hoped it wouldn't happen, that he could convince himself he'd at least tried. With Welch out of the way, he didn't really think he was still at risk. And he supposed, even now, he had no real need to come back. Just leave Sir Aubrey wondering, maybe. But he told them he *would* be back. At three. He glanced at his watch. One way or the other, if he was quick…

The Instituto Español in Prince's Gate – at number fifty-eight – was an elegant Edwardian townhouse, not the easiest place to find, the end of a block actually on Exhibition Road, just across from Imperial College, and its entrance steps around the corner in Watt's Way but backing onto Prince's Gardens. Its interior was magnificent also. Oak panelling. Beeswax and cigar smoke. Welcome signs in Spanish. Republican posters framed on the staircase. The strains of Albéniz from a gramophone wafting down from the first floor. A young woman at the entrance lobby in very traditional Spanish dress, wide brocade skirts, white lace apron, a bright red bodice and her hair arranged into twisted buns, one at each ear, and the buns threaded by gold combs. She handed him a programme, directed him to a function room at the top of the stairs.

There were copies of a newspaper on a table by the door. *El Boletín*. And Jack was still in the act of taking one when Negrín himself broke away from some of those seated among the audience, waiting for the event to begin.

'*Señor* Telford?' he said. 'My god, I wasn't sure. And never expected…'

He pumped Jack's hand. He'd put on extra weight since Jack last saw him, still more pugilist than politician.

'Mister President…' Jack began, but Negrín raised a hand to stop him.

'Not anymore, my friend,' he said. 'But at least I'm still here. Thanks, in no small part, to you, of course.'

Telford shook his head, a modest denial.

'It's just good to see you again, sir. And this – it's very impressive.'

More visitors. And Jack found himself being introduced to the Soviet ambassador.

'Telford?' said Comrade Maisky, as though the name registered somehow, and Jack avoided the temptation of mentioning General Kotov and Madrid – for he wasn't entirely sure whether or not he remained on the NKVD's wanted list. Yet the ambassador's group soon moved on.

'I fear I'm keeping you from your duties,' said Jack.

'Not at all. Not at all. And the Institute?' Negrín's gesture embraced the whole room. 'We keep the dream and culture of the Republic alive here. Also at the Hogar Español, naturally. In the hope, Mister Telford. In the expectation. But you, in uniform. And serving with good comrades, I hear.'

Jack had to think for a moment, while yet more guests arrived.

'The broadcast?' he said.

'Barea, for all his faults, has also helped to keep the Republic alive. The Spanish Service, most of its content is excellent. And *La Nueve*? Yes, I know the name. The other Spaniards fighting with Leclerc. With Putz. Hell, there's a fighting man for you. He may be French, but we can forgive him that small sin, I suppose.' He laughed. 'And who knows, perhaps one day they'll be the core of a new army. With Hitler and Mussolini defeated, Franco will have to stand alone. And this time…'

'It's funny,' said Jack. 'I'm working for Barea, in a way. Never met him, though.'

'Then it's your lucky day. We're expecting him for the opening.' His voice dropped to a whisper. 'Though – well, you know the problem with Barea. Our Communist friends never trusted him, of course. Thought he ran with the hare and hunted with the hounds. You know Casado's here in London?'

While Negrín had been planning a last defence of the Republic in Alicante Province – hoping to hold out just long enough for this wider conflict to leave Franco standing alone, friendless – Colonel Casado and some of his Socialist Party friends were trying to negotiate their own peace with *El Caudillo*. It hadn't worked out well.

'Must make life interesting,' said Jack.

'They want me to go to Mexico, get out of London. But I won't leave Europe, not while there's hope.'

'Hope?' said a newcomer. 'There is always hope.'

Telford and Negrín turned to face him. In his early fifties, slim, receding hair, heavily oiled.

'Arturo,' said Negrín. 'We were just talking about you. And I understand you've never met. This is Telford.' Barea was delighted, and Negrín took the opportunity to leave them to their business. But as he headed towards the Soviet ambassador's party, he looked back over his shoulder. 'By the way, comrade,' he said, 'did you take good care of my pen?'

Jack could hardly believe he would have remembered but he had to admit that he'd left it in safe hands. Paquita Gorroño, he explained. Both Negrín and Barea were astonished. Each of them had known her in Valencia, each of them hungry for word of her. It made him feel – well, valued.

He spent some time with Barea. In the downstairs library. It was, he said, the third official opening and, when you'd heard one opening speech, you'd heard them all. He was an easy man to like. Affable. He'd gone into voluntary exile in Paris – ill-health, he said, though Jack suspected it was more political than anything else – at about the time Telford was arriving in Spain. But, with the civil war's end, and the influx of refugees into France, it had been made clear he was no longer welcome. Then, London. They settled into a pair of armchairs, swapped stories and yes, Barea admitted, he liked Jack's work.

'The quality of your recordings,' he said. 'Excellent. But do you mind me asking, where you managed to get hold of the Dictaphone?'

A moment Jack had been dreading for sixteen months.

'Good question,' he said, and glanced around at the well-stocked shelves. 'Almost too good to be true. Turned up on the *souk* in Casablanca.'

'That would explain it, then. Did you ever meet Bob Dunnett? He was in Casablanca.'

Barea spotted a young man, some sort of waiter in a lilac waistcoat, passing the library door, called him over and ordered coffee for them both.

'Dunnett,' said Jack. 'Dunnett? Yes, I think so. He was there for the Anfa Conference? Oh, don't tell me...'

'I'm afraid so, *señor*.'

'You think it's the same machine?'

'Almost certainly. Do you still have it?'

'In my hotel. The Merchant Navy.'

'Then I may be able to help. Let's meet again at Broadcasting House. Tomorrow. Bring the Type C back and I'll make sure we replace it with one of the new models. Riverside Portable. One of our Mighty Midgets. We've made our own adaptations, and I think you may need it.'

'Need it?'

'You're still attached to the comrades in Leclerc's Division?'

'*La Nueve*? Of course.'

The coffee arrived, still steaming in its pot.

'Then keep sending the recordings, *Señor* Telford, and we'll keep broadcasting them.'

The polished mahogany double doors closed behind him and he was left alone with Sir Aubrey Carter-Holt. There'd only been the one meeting, along with Macmillan, but he was an easy man to remember. Portly, the waxed and curled handlebar moustache, and those porker's eyes, as full of venom as they'd been on the previous occasion.

'Life and death?' he raged now, standing behind the chair at his desk, fingers gripping the top rail. 'My daughter? May God strike you down, Telford.'

'As opposed to some German spy you may have hired or otherwise procured for the purpose, Sir Aubrey?'

'What are you implying? What?'

'That was almost convincing. But I think you know what I mean. Welch.'

'Kingsley Welch is a decent fellow,' Sir Aubrey snarled. 'I told them so.'

Jack had no idea how the intelligence services might have finally caught up with Kingsley Welch, and Captain Fox either could not or would not shed any further light on the subject. But this much was certain. The same intelligence services would have followed up every lead and contact, and the connection, through those trade deals, through Standard Oil, would have given them a direct link between Welch and Sir Aubrey.

'You did?' Jack pulled up a chair, uninvited, on the opposite side of the desk, lit himself a cigarette. A Capstan – a wonderful Capstan. 'The intelligence service boys must have been impressed with your judgement of character, considering they've already confirmed Welch is an agent for the Abwehr.'

Telford still possessed the calling card, the scorpion image, and he tossed it across the table.

'Is that supposed to mean something?' said Sir Aubrey.

'Look,' Jack replied, 'you promised me five minutes, I believe. And I know what you think. You made it very plain. May God strike me down, did you say? Then let me paint you a picture, see whether it fits. Welch turned up at your daughter's memorial service. He told me so. Of course, then you just had the official version of her death. Accident. And I'm sorry, sir. You must have been devastated.'

'Condolences, Telford? From you, of all people?'

Sir Aubrey moved around his chair, sat heavily.

'I'll come to that. But you and Welch met, and your paths kept crossing. By then you were doing *this* job. Impressive office, by the way. Welch was useful. And the following year, he introduced you to somebody else. Major Lawrence Edwin. A private meeting. In which Edwin told you a different story entirely. That I'd killed Valerie. I've no idea what reason he gave. Some cock and bull story about me being a Soviet agent, I'm guessing, while poor Valerie – What, true-blue Brit? Loyal to Franco?'

'You deny it?'

The doors opened and Sir Aubrey's secretary popped her head back inside.

'Five minutes, Sir Aubrey?' she said. 'Your next appointment?'

'Never mind,' he told her. 'I'm not finished here.'

'Yes, I deny it,' said Jack, when she'd retreated once more. He stubbed out the cigarette. 'Most of it, anyway. But you may regret not leaving things there, Sir Aubrey. Or maybe you're thinking – look, let me come clean. I've no idea where Welch may be, right now. Back in Berlin with his chums, I imagine. But maybe not. Or it *could* be you're sufficiently well connected to have found somebody else.' He saw Sir Aubrey pick up a pencil, snap it between his fingers, but he said nothing. 'Oh, I imagine it wasn't a direct arrangement you had with Welch. More like King Henry and Becket, this is how I picture it. Will nobody rid me? That sort of thing? And Edwin had his own axe to grind, of course. So, Welch? Told me he owed a favour.'

'Just one more Commie hack,' murmured Sir Aubrey.

'I imagine it's what Welch's Abwehr handlers would have said. Only, you see, it wasn't me that was the Commie hack in this little story. Oh, and before we go much further, or you, Sir Aubrey, get too many ideas about finding a way to finish what Welch started, I should tell you I made two visits this morning. Early. The first to a little white-haired old lady called Nora Hames. I left with her a dossier which, by now, will be in the hands of her solicitor. I thought I owed that much to Nora, because your daughter – well, to put no finer point on it, your daughter murdered her friend. The concert pianist, Julia Britten.'

He watched Sir Aubrey jump to his feet, the chair falling behind him, and snatch up the telephone handset, pressing a button on the intercom.

'Miss Henderson,' he shouted, 'this fellow is leaving. Alert security, will you?'

Jack stood, put the cigarettes and lighter back into his uniform pocket.

'The second dossier,' he said, 'I left with a colleague of mine. Dudley Anne Harmon. She's with United Press. But, like Miss

Hames, she's under strict instructions it should only be opened in the event of anything — what should I say? Suspicious, I suppose. Anything suspicious happening to me. That set of documents should be winging its way to the States, perhaps not exactly as we speak, but you follow my drift, I think.'

'Documents?'

'Photographic evidence mainly,' Jack said, over his shoulder as he headed for the opening doors. Miss Henderson again, and a bespectacled elderly sergeant from the Corps of Commissionaires. 'A few witness statements. Couple of official papers. Anyway…'

'Wait, damn you!' Sir Aubrey shouted.

'You want me to remove this gentleman, sir?' said the sergeant.

'I just told him to wait, Albert, didn't I? And, Miss Henderson, close that bloody door, won't you?'

They backed out of the room again, flustered and confused.

'You're an unpleasant fellow, Sir Aubrey,' Jack told him, but he made no move to return to the desk. 'Welch will have a pretty tale to tell when they eventually catch him. And they will, you know. It made me wonder. Welch, working his way into the Anglo-German Fellowship, passing their names to the intelligence services, so he could convince them he was on *our* side. But only the small fry, apparently. Just the small fry. But the bigger fish, Sir Aubrey…'

He saw the fellow flush crimson.

'Documents,' he growled. 'You said documents.'

'I suppose it makes some sense to me now,' said Jack. 'What on earth would send a girl with a background like Valerie's running into the arms of the Comintern? Of course, I never counted on her father being a fan of Hitler. She never shared that with me.'

'I loved her, all the same. My own flesh and blood. And you *did* kill her, didn't you, Telford?'

'If I told you it was purely self-defence, Sir Aubrey, I think you'd be unlikely to believe me. But it *is* the truth. Still, it's interesting. You never even batted an eyelid when I mentioned the Comintern. You knew, of course. This had nothing to do with revenge, at all. You just wanted to shut me up. After all this time, you still needed to shut me up. Well, I suppose that makes sense.' Jack looked around the well-appointed office as though for the first time. 'After Overseas Trade, what next, I wonder? Something much bigger on the cards?'

'The documents,' said Sir Aubrey, and picked up his chair, sat himself down again. He seemed to have regained his composure. 'If it's money you want…'

'Oh, I was just thinking about one of the photographs.' Jack lit another Capstan, walked over to the bookcases, pretended to study some of the leather-bound volumes. 'Valerie in Vienna. Julia Britten's concert. A man called Willi Müntzenberg. And the boy, Kurt Tiebermann, who she fell in love with.'

'Just a stupid infatuation. Nothing else.'

'Still, it was Müntzenberg and young Kurt who led her into the Party, brought her to the attention of the Comintern. But then, poor Kurt killed by the Nazis. And there she was, knowing her own father admired them. My god, how she must have hated you.'

'Perhaps, at first. But she came to her senses in the end. How do you think she came to be so admired by General Franco?'

'You know, that's almost pitiful. The part Major Edwin didn't bother to tell you. The documents I mentioned. The purpose of her trip to Spain? It was to assassinate Franco himself. Comrade Stalin chose her, personally, for the job.'

Sir Aubrey's expression turned quickly from mockery and incredulity, disintegrated into open-mouthed stupefaction, and this time the colour drained from his face entirely.

'If it's not money…' he mumbled.

'Is it really so hard to understand, Sir Aubrey? No, not money. And it's no more than I told you. Insurance, of a sort. You see, I'm a fellow who fortune rarely favours. I learned that. In fact, quite the opposite. Misadventure could almost be my middle name. Often hard to tell whether the trials and tribulations of my life are deliberately engineered or simply damned bad luck. So, just in case, and to make me feel better – no more than that, if anything out of the ordinary does happen, you and I shall be going to hell in a handcart, side by side.'

He'd taken a last look at the sprawl of the Foreign Office from the farther side of the lake in St. James's Park and he smiled. Would this piece of theatre really answer? The prospect of the world discovering that Sir Aubrey Carter-Holt was, on the one hand, a secret admirer of the Nazis and, on the other, father to a Soviet agent – well, it was hardly designed to help advance the fellow's career.

And yet the newspaper photograph from Julia Britten's scrapbook had been ripped to shreds, along with the rest of its precious mementos, by the *Guardia Civil* in Burgos, six years earlier. His visit to Nora that morning had allowed him to apologise in person to her for its loss where, before, he'd only been able to write to her. But he needn't have bothered. He'd found her in a nursing home, her once-bright eyes entirely clouded over by cataracts, and her mind now lacking any memory of him. Just a snapshot of Julia Britten on her bedside cabinet.

Harmon he'd found in good spirits, though. They'd enjoyed mid-morning coffee, and she'd helped to lift him after his earlier sadness. But there was, it seemed, always somebody with a worse tale to tell. And, with Harmon, it was the yarn of her narrow escape from death, the U-boat attack, which had sunk her Norwegian freighter. All the gory details she'd not been able to tell him in her letters. Yet she'd finally returned home to the States and, since the previous autumn, she'd been here in London, chasing up routine stories.

'But hey, Telford,' she'd said, 'I didn't sign up for this. Supposed to be a war correspondent and here I am, writing stuff for the *Stars and Stripes* – folksy little pieces about how our GIs are falling over themselves to be arrested by England's first two women military police.'

'Pulitzer?' he laughed.

'You never know. But what have you heard, buddy? We shipping out, or not?'

He tried hard, in the half-hour before he had to leave her, to give a decent *résumé* of his adventures since she'd left Brazzaville. Mutual acquaintances. Poor Disher, shot to hell on board the *Walney* at Oran. Colonel Eddy. Steinbeck. And, of course, Leclerc – the formation of the Division. And yes, he was certain they'd be shipping out soon. To where? He had no idea.

'But does it really matter?' he'd said. 'Small world, after all.'

'So, you finally met Bunnelle?' Sydney Elliott had laughed, on Jack's final evening in London. They were drinking beer at the Horseshoe. 'Strange bloke, yes?'

It had been a busy day. He'd managed to track down Roger Carcassonne from Oran, and his cousin José from Algiers, now working with the French Resistance – though they couldn't discuss the details. Of course not. But it was good to see them again.

And then, Bunnelle. Lunch at the Hungaria on Lower Regent Street, before Broadcasting House and a final session with Barea.

'Bunnelle? Strange hardly does it justice,' said Jack. 'Insisted on dragging me off to Savile Row. Bespoke uniform. Said if I was going to work for AP, I needed to look the part. Stand out. I told him if we were going off to fight the Germans, standing out was the last thing I needed. But he wouldn't take no for an answer. So there I was, measured up, and the tailor insisting it'll be at Mrs Lumley's within the week.'

'Lunch good? I keep meaning to try the Hungaria, but not quite my style.'

'This your way of telling me we're eating at the Corner House again tonight?'

'Where else? And the Hungaria – like they say? Bomb-proof and boredom-proof?'

'That's what the sign claims. And yes, fair enough. Food was fabulous. Good music. Decent company. Ruthie Cowan, do you know her?'

'We've met,' said Sydney. 'Great writing. She covered the Capone trial, did she say?' She hadn't. But she had spent time in Algeria. Oran mainly, while Jack had been in Casa. 'And now?' Elliott went on. 'You think you've settled this business with Carter-Holt.'

Jack nodded, finished his beer.

'So long,' he said, 'as he doesn't call my bluff. I was always rubbish at poker.'

Early next day, he settled himself into the packed compartment on the train for Hull, along with the MSS Riverside Midget Recorder, which Barea had given him in exchange for the Dictaphone. At least it was marginally lighter, though not by much.

He'd bought himself a couple of new books, an English translation of a Russian author he didn't really know. Ostrovsky. *How the Steel Was Tempered.* And Agatha Christie's *The Moving Finger.* Seven shillings and sixpence.

The Merchant Navy Hotel had furnished him with a packed lunch, but he was already hungry, opened the greaseproof paper, munched on a cheese and tomato sandwich, offered one to the hungry-looking sailor sitting opposite him, while he skimmed through the headlines in *The Times.*

He'd been lucky while he was in London. An alert or two, though no actual air raids. And everybody said that was pretty normal these days. Intermittent attacks spread over many months, but nothing too serious, Elliott had reckoned, almost in a tone of *ennui.* The whole thing "winding down" as he described it. But Bristol hadn't been so lucky. The city had endured two full days of what was here being styled as the Baby Blitz.

Baby Blitz indeed! Bloody journalists, he thought, wondering how many poor devils had died. Why do we do this? And so, he almost missed it, the sandwich poised at his lips.

British Diplomat Found Dead

The body of diplomat Sir Aubrey Carter-Holt was discovered yesterday evening at his Belgravia home. Although investigations continue, police believe he may have taken his own life.

There were really no more details. Suicide? Jack supposed so. And he searched within himself for any sense of guilt. It wasn't there.

It began. Yet it began without them, on Tuesday, the sixth of June. And the frustration, which Telford had seen rampant at Sabratha, assuaged somewhat by the rigorous training at Temara, by their eager anticipation during the long haul that brought them to

Yorkshire, by the rumours of imminent invasion and action since their arrival – the frustration now returned with a vengeance in the form of creeping lethargy and a bitter sense of deception.

'They went without us, after all,' said Dronne, in his now fluent Spanish. It was usually Spanish when he was with the men of the Company. He stared out through the rain-washed window of Pocklington's United Services Club, leaning on his snooker cue, a forlorn Gallic warrior left behind when his tribe marched off to confront Caesar's Legions.

'Saving us for the tough part,' said Amado Granell. 'Tomorrow, maybe. Or the next day. The hard bit comes *after* the landings. Remember Oran, *inglés*?'

Jack remembered. The same with the reports from Sicily. And from Italy. My god, he thought, that mess at Anzio after it had all seemed so easy.

'Did I tell you I met Roger Carcassonne while I was in London?' Telford replied, while Granell took his shot. Amado potted a red into one of the corner pockets. It was disgusting how good they'd all become. Time on their hands, of course. And Jack no more an eye for the game than he'd ever had, even with two.

'Carcassonne?' murmured Dronne. And then, 'How the hell did they manage to land? This bloody awful weather.'

There'd been thunderstorms, breaks in the weather so sparse they'd given up all expectation of action any day soon. But, with the eight o'clock news, there'd been a broadcast, a general warning really, for those living close to the coast of enemy-occupied Europe. A few hints, mention of the Nazis' own reports, heavy bombardments at Le Havre and Calais. By nine, rumour following rumour, too many to ignore. Invasion. The short-lived excitement and the lingering sense of abandonment following in its wake.

'Carcassonne,' said Granell, watching his black go down. 'Good comrade.' He waited for Jack to collect the ball from the pocket rail, give it a wipe and set it back on its spot. 'If ever,' Amado went on, 'I was going to look for a symbol of patience personified, and patience rewarded, it would be Roger Carcassonne, I think. Don't worry, *jefe*, we'll get our turn. They can't get far without us.'

But it did little to cheer Dronne. He paced along the wall, muttered his usual curses in French when he stopped in front of the two framed prints he hated so much. A pair of battle scenes. Waterloo. Because this building had, after all, once housed the Waterloo Hotel.

'My country,' he said, reverting to Spanish again. 'And it was hours ago, the broadcast.'

Nine-thirty. It had been short and initially sweet. A second front. Normandy beaches. Bridgeheads secured. Repeated, in French. Then in Dutch. And Norwegian. In Danish and Flemish. Half an hour? But since…

Somebody shouted up the stairs in English.

'Hey, 'appen there's going to be a special broadcast. Quick. Twelve o'clock news.'

The game was abandoned, and they almost fell over each other to reach the downstairs bar. One of the locals, with a map of Europe spread over a card table, Mrs Mitchell fiddling with the tuner on the wireless. Then, John Snagge's clipped BBC voice.

'D-Day has come.'

The first official reports, he said. Northern coast of France. Normandy.

Jack translated into Spanish for those who didn't understand. A cheer went up, men embracing each other, jumping up and down, tears.

'…the Allied Expeditionary Force includes British, Canadian and United States forces.'

'No French?' yelled Dronne. 'What are we doing here?'

At the map there was a fair amount of pushing and shoving, some of the French tank drivers trying to show the Spaniards where, they thought, the landings might have taken place.

'The Allied Commander-in-Chief, General Eisenhower, has issued the following communiqué…'

'It's a message of good luck,' Jack told them. 'Basically. Oh, and a bit about how proud he is to have the forces of France under his command.'

'Are we?' said Dronne.

'A warning.' Telford was still listening to John Snagge.

'Eisenhower cautioning that a premature popular rising among the French would be unhelpful. Apparently, he said we should all be patient. Be prepared. Great battles lie ahead for us all.'

But Captain Raymond Dronne seemed less than convinced.

'Betrayed,' Jack heard him complain. 'Again.'

Telford leaned from the bed, gingerly picked up the heavy cotton bloomers with which Danielle had crowned the heap of her discarded fatigues.

'What the hell…?' he said.

'I prefer my beautiful black silk *culottes* as well, Jack.' She hugged herself, eyes closed, a sensual, weary smile on her lips. 'But when you're tearing down that six-cylinder brute of an engine on our beautiful Dodge all day, you cannot beat those trusty army-issue drawers, no?'

The strains of Harry James and his Orchestra, *I'll Get By*, drifted from Mrs Lumley's private parlour below. It had been the very devil sneaking Dani up the stairs.

'Fair play,' Jack smiled, flicked the bloomers at her, then fell back into the pillows, gazed up through the dust motes trapped within a beam of auburn evening sunlight. 'Longest day,' he said. 'Summer solstice.'

'Then we should be at Carnac. Or your Stonehenge.'

He rolled over, ran his fingernails across her belly, still not entirely certain what she saw in him. Whenever they explored each other's bodies – petting, as Scott Fitzgerald might have called it – she insisted on Jack removing the eye-patch, didn't seem distressed in the least by the mess of badly stitched socket beneath. But he tended to keep this side of his face turned from her, and now he'd buried his left cheek in the pillow.

'And what would *Père* Houchet say about that, my love. Heresy?'

She was Catholic, of course – as he knew very well from the cautious manner and method of their intimacies. Like most of the other girls, she had much better use for the K-ration condoms – English bonnets, *capotes anglaises*, as the French girls called them – supplied when they were away on training exercises. Cut up into rubber bands to secure her tobacco tins of fuses and small spares. As an extra protection for keeping sand and water out of fuel tanks and jerry-cans. For keeping damp from the distributor cap. A dozen other uses. And the medical applications? Countless. Yet she was also some strange breed of Catholic, tending more towards the pre-Christian pagan, he always thought. And superstitious? Great heavens, he didn't think he'd ever met anybody to match her on that score. It all seemed to fit perfectly with those fey features.

'The priest in my village always had a very practical approach to the old religions,' she laughed.

Jack rolled the other way, reached for the drawer of his bedside cabinet, produced the small box he'd concealed there.

'And what would he say about a proposal of marriage between two people on Midsummer's Day when they're both already naked in bed?'

He offered up the box, though she didn't take it from him.

'Married?' she said. 'You forgot about the war, Jack?'

It was so lacking in enthusiasm he was caught by surprise. Not what he'd expected. Not at all. Fifteen days since D-Day.

'Forget? How the hell could I forget? Dronne and Granell remind me every five minutes, follow every report. I see the maps in my sleep now. Carentan. The whole damned battlefront, all fifty miles of it.'

She sat up in the bed, pulled the sheets around her.

'You know it's not what I meant. So, why now? Is this like all those Spanish boys? They might be the politest men I've ever come across, but so many girls.'

'They're great ambassadors for the Republic,' said Jack, pleased to maybe change the subject, 'but Dronne's certain there'll be a whole new brood of Spanish-looking, brown-eyed kids in Pocklington after this is all over.'

'That's what I mean, Jack. They know they're going into war. Deep inside, the need to leave something behind, to live on, regardless of what might happen. And you? A ring for my finger? The same?'

He swung his legs off the bed, lit them both a cigarette. He could feel himself getting annoyed.

'I didn't just buy this,' he told her, passed the Capstan to her and put the ring box back on the table. 'It was weeks ago, the first time I headed into Hull. Remember, I told you I met the Linares family? And then the scrap at the dance hall? It was that night.'

'All this time? So, you weren't sure, either.'

'Waiting for the moment. And, for the first time, I think I'm not afraid for the future, Dani.'

The invasion was well underway in Normandy. The Eighth Army advancing steadily up through Italy. A new Russian summer offensive. Here at home, there'd been those German rocket attacks, folk killed at Bethnal Green. But, overall, everybody seemed to think a real turning point had been reached. Light at the end of a very long tunnel.

Then there was his own situation. He'd not realised how much the whole business with Welch had come to dominate his life. And Sir Aubrey? Now Jack came to think about it – and he thought about it often – he must have known all along. Not a single show of surprise. None of what Telford had told him a revelation at all. His suicide because of Valerie? No, simply the man who's sorry because he's been caught, not for whatever he's done – his dirty little involvement with Welch. And Jack's bluff about the dossiers? He doubted that would have fooled anybody. More likely Sir Aubrey knowing it was only a matter of time before the intelligence services came knocking on his door again, delved more deeply into any association he may have had with the Anglo-German Fellowship.

'You may not be, Jack – afraid for the future. But me? It terrifies me. The closer we get to being shipped out, the more I think I made a mistake.'

'You don't have to go, Danielle.'

She leaned forward, wrapped both arms around her legs, blew a perfect smoke ring.

'Of course, I have to go, like we *all* have to go. To finish this thing. But you, Jack Telford? Most of the time you don't even know who you are. And already married – to your damned typewriter. It's the only time you're whole. What sort of life would I have? You left England – six years ago? Only just returned? Is that what I can look forward to?'

'You don't love me?'

He knew it sounded pathetic, reached for his clothes, scattered along the floorboards on his own side of the bed.

'What the hell does that *mean*? It's just a word we use. But it doesn't exist, not really. You know it doesn't. We have ties. Strong emotional bonds. Shared passions, experiences, sensations. Intimacies. If we have enough of them, if we're able to set aside each other's more annoying deficiencies, we may be able to live, side by side, for a long time. But I've seen those ties broken too often. Too easily. I've seen this thing you call love vanish as quickly as it appeared, with all its stupid heartache.'

'And why should it happen to us, Dani? Hell, ties? Don't you think we've enough of those? More ahead, surely.'

'The thing we share, Jack, is this war. Ties built on spilled blood? On our hatred of the Nazis? On selling all that as news?'

'I thought they were ties built on healing the wounded. Fighting for a better world? Or giving people the truth and hope. But you're afraid of the future?'

'You might not understand this, but it feels like only yesterday. On the run from the Germans. From the collaborators who'd given us away. And even when we reached Spain, the chance we'd be sent back. The other girls talk often about being wounded. Killed, even. Though, my worst nightmare? It's being taken. That chance – even the very slightest chance – they'd find out who I am. You know what they'd do to me?'

'Yes,' he said, put his cigarette in the brass ashtray and slipped into his underpants. 'I know. But it's not going to happen, Dani. I swear it's not. After all the fuss Leclerc's made about having women in the Division at all, he'd never live it down if anything happened to one of his *Rochambelles*. Why not take the ring anyway? Decide later. Just don't say no, my sweet. Not yet. I couldn't stand it.'

'I won't say no, then,' Danielle promised him. 'But I'll not take the ring, Jack. It would, I think, be bad luck.'

'Is that the best they can do?' General George S. Patton, roaring into the East Coast wind. Somehow he was larger than life. A caricature of himself. The jodhpurs, the riding boots, the pearl-handled revolvers, and the gleaming helmet. 'Hell,' he bellowed, 'the Poles can do better than this. Even the damned Brits shoot better.'

'*Magnifique*, no?' said Dronne, at Jack's side. '*Magnifique*. Patton *and* Leclerc – no stopping us, my friend.'

Telford looked at him, saw the sparkle in his eye again. More like his old self, with action imminent and the recent knowledge that French commandos had, after all, been among the first waves ashore on D-Day.

'He doesn't seem to think much of our tank crews,' said Jack.

They were lined up along Bridlington's beach, four Shermans, their target towed back and forth across the choppy waves, three hundred yards, give or take, out to sea. The guns fired in turn. *Bang. Bang.* Smoke. The barrels recoiling into their turrets, fountains of water spouting up just about everywhere except on their mark.

'Just his way,' said Dronne. 'But Patton's panache – have you seen the way he handles a sword? And trained at the Cavalry Academy. Saumur, you know?'

Yes, Jack knew. It had been on his list of questions for the general. Yesterday, the interview Leclerc had arranged. It had been a disaster. The hothouse at Dalton Hall, looking out onto the ornate gardens. He'd even worn his new Savile Row uniform in a failed effort to impress.

'Correspondent?' Patton had said to him. 'You know what I think of reporters, Telford? That if it wasn't for your kind, and weak-kneed Congressmen, we'd have a lot less generals looking over their own shoulders rather than fixing their minds on killing krauts.'

There'd been the incidents in North Africa, Patton slapping those two GIs in hospital, calling them cowards. The press had enjoyed a field day. And then, a couple of months back, in Knutsford, he'd made some comment about it being the destiny of Britain and America to rule the world – not a single mention of their Russian allies.

'My only purpose here, General, is...

'Your articles, Mister Telford, they've not always been – what's the word? Helpful? You some sort of Commie? And what is this – bougainvillea?'

He fingered one of the bright red flowers.

'Yes, sir. Bougainvillea. But which articles are we talking about, General?'

'Well, let's see. The one about these lily-livered Quaker conchies driving our ambulances? Treating them like damned heroes?'

Jack felt almost at home here. The humidity. The tropical plants. Like Brazzaville.

'Only appeared in *Reynold's News*, didn't it?' he said. 'And anyway...'

'And your prissy little protests about Leclerc losing his blacks?'

'That one never even saw the light of day. AP didn't get any takers.'

Patton peered cautiously into the jaws of a Venus Flytrap.

'Why the hell d'you think that might have been, Telford? You seriously thought we'd let the papers print garbage like this? Good news, that's what we need – *good* news, mister.'

The news certainly hadn't been bad recently. In faraway northeast India, the three-month battle of Kohima had finally been won against the Japanese, the siege of Imphal raised. In Normandy, the German garrison at Cherbourg, cut-off and surrounded these past couple of weeks, had surrendered.

'I thought,' said Jack, 'maybe an article about some of the Commies you've got in your own ranks, General. You know? The ones who've been fixing their minds on killing krauts for nearly eight years now.'

'What the hell are we talking about here?' Patton barked. His voice echoed against the green-stained glass ceiling.

'The Spaniards, sir. In General Leclerc's Chad Regiment. You mind if I smoke, General?'

He reached into his shirt pocket for his cigarettes and lighter.

'Yes, I mind.' Jack let the pack of cigarettes sit where they were. 'Iberians, Mister Telford' Patton went on. 'Iberians. I fought alongside warriors from the lands of Hispania in the ranks of proud Carthage. Men from Gadir and Sagunto. The Battle of Zama. Great fighters.'

'These men are great fighters. They just happen to be Socialists and Communists – more than a few Anarchists among them. Since they're under your command, General, I thought maybe a quote?'

'You don't know much about the world, do you, mister? Listen, let me tell you, twelve years ago, back home, we had a different sort of army.' He sniffed at a gardenia and suddenly the hothouse was alive with the velvet jasmine-like scent. It reminded Jack of Frances Moorgate. 'Called themselves the Bonus Army,' said Patton. 'Fifty thousand of them marched on Washington, tried to start a revolution.'

Jack knew the story very well. The height of the Depression and millions out of work, many men – veterans of the war in France – clinging to the certificates they'd been issued by Congress, promising compensation for some of the pay they'd lost while fighting in the army. Their war bonus. But the certificates only redeeemable many years into the future.

'Revolution? They just wanted their money instead of the war bonus certificates, so they wouldn't starve to death, didn't they?'

'My point is, they were mostly ignorant men, uneducated, poor and unemployed. Not real revolutionaries at all but led astray by a whole bunch of bad men, real Commies, who just wanted to rule the world.'

'So far as I remember,' said Jack, 'nobody bothered to make much distinction when the army attacked them.' He really wanted to ask Patton how it had felt, as a major, back then, to lead a cavalry charge against out-of-work veterans. But he wasn't quite bold enough.

They'd come to a halt among the dwarf palms near the French doors, rain pattering against the glass.

'My point *is*, Telford, that General Franco, seeing his country also threatened by a bunch of Commies who just wanted to rule *his* world, had no choice but to destroy them. And these misguided men who now find themselves fighting on God's side, on *my* side, have been given a second chance. That's all. You want to single them out for special praise because they've had the sense to take this chance, fine by me. Just so long as you remember to put the credit where it belongs – to God Almighty and to General George S. Patton. Write that as your quote, *Mister* Telford.'

No, it hadn't gone well, and Patton had pretty much dismissed him. Delusional? Jack had wondered. Yes, certainly. There were rumours that the general had problems reading and writing but, despite this, enjoyed scribbling bits of poetry. Dark poetry, Telford imagined, full of boastful self-obsession, compensation maybe for whatever sense of inferiority his literacy problems may have inflicted upon him. But a great general? That too, without doubt, as Dronne reminded him now, on Bridlington's beach.

'He'll have us at the Rhine before we know it,' he said. 'Then into the heart of Germany itself.'

'Yes,' said Jack. 'It was the last thing he asked me before he kicked me out. Whether I speak German. I told him the lessons were going just fine. But I think it was a rhetorical question.'

As it happened, his lessons *were* going fine. Bearded Reiter had kept him at his studies, though Jack wasn't yet sure what purpose it might all serve. A bit like his weapons training. Interesting skills, though no real intention of ever using them.

'God help us all,' they heard Patton bellow from the back of his Jeep, 'if we can't shoot better than this. You expect me to present colours to units that can't even shoot.'

There was due to be a parade in just three days at Dalton Hall, some of the regiments to be presented with brand new colours, produced in their honour here in England, and the entire Division to receive their Cross of Lorraine insignia pins.

But, seemingly in response to Patton's demand for divine intervention, up came *Père* Houchet and some of the other White Fathers serving as the Division's chaplains. There were prayers, blessings and, in the aftermath, every single target blasted to pieces.

'There,' Patton shouted. 'This is more like it!'

At the general's instruction, his Jeep drove off towards the town, the three French officers who'd been watching with him now snapping to attention and saluting – the Chad Regiment's Lieutenant Colonel Vézinet; that hero of Kufra, Louis Dio, now commanding the Division's First Combat Group; and his other friend from those days in Libya, Brazzaville as well, the boyish-faced André Geoffroy, presently the captain responsible for the Third Battalion's Tenth Company.

As Telford and Dronne headed back towards their own Jeep, along the beach, Jack saw a familiar face. Another group of tanks, M10 tank destroyers, one of the crews – the TD with the name

Souffleur painted on its turret – waiting for their orders, smoking cigarettes. Among them, Pépé le Moko. He *looked* just like Pépé le Moko. Good god, the fellow could have been Jean Gabin's double. Jack caught his eye, pointed at him.

'Blame it on the Casbah,' he shouted in a poor and clownish imitation of the actor.

'Piss off, *rosbif*,' the man replied.

'He's probably had this before,' said Jack. 'Still – he looks like Gabin, no?'

'No, said Dronne. 'That *is* Gabin. He managed to tear himself away from Hollywood and Dietrich back in January, signed up with the marines' armoured regiment and – well, here he is.'

Jack looked back over his shoulder, Gabin still glaring as him.

'You believe in bad luck, Captain?'

He was still troubled by Danielle's rejection of the engagement ring.

'I'm sure Gabin will forgive you, Telford.'

Jack laughed.

'I wasn't thinking about Gabin,' he said.

Dronne's driver saluted him. He'd been adjusting the small black pennant with its skull and crossbones flying from the Jeep's aerial. It bore the same legend as the vehicle itself. *Mort Aux Cons.* Death To Fools.

'You disobeyed the order?'

'To paint over the name? I told *le patron* it couldn't possibly cause offence – except to fools. Hell, I thought he was going to have me shot. But I didn't mean *him*. Of course, I didn't. But then he just laughed, said it was fair enough – that we'd never have enough bullets to shoot all the idiots anyway. Good luck, no? So yes, I believe in it, good *and* bad.'

Something haunted about the place. The spirits of heroes, he thought, wondered how many of those who'd passed through here before him were now fallen.

Telford couldn't actually see Southampton from here, even when he was standing, but it wasn't far – though it didn't really matter. They'd been confined to this endless camp of bell tents since their arrival, a week earlier, no contact allowed with the locals, no passes. Hush-hush. Top secret. Why? He wasn't sure. This ravaged heath, stripped bare of all vegetation by successive waves of invasion forces, which had trampled the staging area over the almost two months since the first Allied forces left here for the beaches of Normandy. If the Germans didn't know they were here, it would be a minor miracle, or gross negligence.

'You know,' he said to Amado Granell, 'I don't think I'll ever get the hang of this.'

He rolled over onto his side, slid the empty magazine from the carbine. At the butts, a hundred yards away, his target rose up again above the parapet, a thick wooden pointer lifted by an unseen marker in the gallery below and stabbing twice towards the edge.

'Two outers,' said Granell, and shook his head. 'From fifteen shots. Better than last time, at least.'

The other marksmen along the firing line were being replaced by those waiting their turn to practise.

'I'm nervous as hell, apart from anything else. It just seems so big. Such a leap.'

'Then think what it must have been like,' Amado replied. 'To be the first. All those boys, *inglés*. Here, let me show you again.'

Jack stood, handed over the carbine, and Granell fitted a fresh magazine, lay down in his place, wrapped the sling around his arm.

Telford made a show of following Amado's instructions, but his mind was still fixed on the enormity of it all. And no, he couldn't imagine what it must have been like for that first wave. Excitement? Terror? Or simply awe?

He'd been living in some strange sense of veneration, himself, for a full seven days and nights. When they'd left North Africa, the Division had embarked from all those different ports, arrived in Blighty at various locations, ended up scattered right across East Yorkshire. But last week he'd witnessed the enormity, the precision, the logistical miracle of Leclerc's twelve thousand men on the move in their entirety, their hundreds of tanks and heavy artillery pieces dispatched by train to either Southampton or Southsea.

Southsea where, along with the tanks and TDs, the medical contingent, the ambulances, doctors and nurses, had been dispatched.

Since that last night they'd spent together at the Buck, he'd tried several times to repair whatever damage might have been done to his relationship with Danielle. But damaged it certainly was. Another Lady of Shalott moment in his life, the web flown wide, the spell of their romance broken. *"The mirror crack'd from side to side."* The ring, he still possessed, but he'd not seen her for more than a week, now – had no idea how long before they'd meet again. Not really.

Meanwhile, the endless convoys of half-tracks, trucks, ambulances, motorbikes and Jeeps had taken the roads south. They'd wound their way through villages and towns on a dozen different routes, sometimes cheered by children and old men waving flags but, more often, simply keeping themselves amused, by night and day, with endless streams of songs and cigarettes, of sleep and stupid stories.

'Many thanks, Lieutenant,' he said, now, as Granell got to his feet again. 'I'll try to do better next time.'

Amado held out the carbine towards him.

'There may not be a next time,' he murmured. 'Not until – well, it would be better if you kept hold of this.'

Telford felt the rush of adrenalin. The fear also. And elation in the somewhat irrational calculation that, if *he* was heading for Normandy, then so must be Dani and the *Rochambelles*, as well.

'Moving out?' he whispered, saw Granell's quick nod of confirmation. 'But I've told you before, Amado, that thing would only get in my way. Have you seen…? Never mind. You know when?'

The two dozen men of the Third Rifle Platoon's Blue Squad were brought into line by Moreno, who offered a sloppy salute to their First Sergeant – Campos, *el canario*, as it happened – and received orders to get his men cleaned up. On the boardwalk below, another squad waited to take their place, and Dronne pushed his way through the men.

'Maybe we'll find out now,' said Amado. Campos saluted Dronne's arrival even more casually in his turn, dwarfing the captain. 'Come on.' Granell slung the carbine onto his shoulder, slapped Telford on the back. 'Let's tell the *jefe* what a marksman you've become.'

There wasn't even the pretense of a salute from Granell to their company captain, and Jack knew Dronne didn't really expect one anymore. Not from his adjutant, anyway. It was all very anarchic. All very – Spanish.

'You still refusing to carry a weapon, *Señor* Telford?'

Dronne, in exchange, had given up all pretense at speaking in anything but Spanish when he was with his unit. He was fluent now – at least in those sections of vocabulary pertinent to the military, to football, to family matters, and to the aesthetic splendour of the Spaniards' profanities. He'd tried hard, as a devout Catholic, to curb their excesses when it came to those lurid and countless blasphemies, told them frequently he could readily understand why Franco and the Church wished them all to burn in hell, but he could often be heard now, in the heat of a difficult moment, calling for the most unbelievable desecrations to be perpetrated against the Host or, indeed, the Mother of God herself.

'I fear it would only be an encumbrance, Captain,' Jack told him. 'And I've already got enough to carry.'

He was right, of course. The BBC's recording machine, the size of a portable gramophone – though the word *portable*, in reference to either a gramophone *or* the Beeb's deceptively named Mighty Midget, was simply relative. His typewriter. His Rolleiflex. His Savile Row best uniform and the Jermyn Street khaki shirts Bunnelle had also insisted on providing. The rest of his kit. And, of course, his books. He was still reading the Ostrovsky. But he'd managed to pick up an Armed Services Edition of *The Grapes of Wrath*, with the yellow dust jacket common to all ASE publications and the reassurance on a red background that this was the complete book, not a digest. It was a unique edition, all the same, landscape format, maybe to help with the length. Five inches tall, seven inches wide, another mighty midget. As a bonus, an ASE copy of Steinbeck's *The Pastures of Heaven*. Finally, his own sketchpad to go with his notepads. A couple of drawing pens, bottles of ink. He still had the map from his African travels – and maybe he'd do the same in Normandy. Maybe.

'Well,' said Dronne, 'we may have just one more thing to encumber you with. Lieutenant, will you do the honours?'

Granell opened the breast pocket of his field service jacket – his combat jacket, as they liked to call them, pulled out a fold of tissue paper and, inside, one of the hand-made shoulder flashes the men of *La Nueve* had been wearing since Temara – and some of them, Amado included, for much longer. A tiny miniature of the Republican flag, red over yellow over purple.

'Comrade,' said Granell, 'the men of the Company, we'd like you to wear this.'

Jack bit at his own top lip, determined not to make a fool of himself.

'I don't think I'm entitled to this, Amado,' he said. 'But it's a great honour.'

It struck him this was even more significant than the medal he'd received from *Sidi* Muhammad and now nestling within his dunnage, wrapped in socks at the bottom of his kitbag. It choked him. Further words stuck in his throat.

'You told me once,' said Dronne, 'you were with us because you owed it to your dead. I've no idea what this means or who they might have been, my friend, but you've earned your place in this Company. One of us.'

'I was there when we took that other oath,' said Jack. 'Kufra, my god. All in it together until the *Tricolore* flies again over Strasbourg Cathedral. If I'm honest, on the day, I never gave much thought to what it meant – to how far it was from Kufra to Strasbourg.'

'German border,' Dronne replied. 'Hard to imagine. By the time we reach Strasbourg – *if* we reach Strasbourg – we'll have driven the Germans from every corner of France. A long way. A *hell* of a long way.'

I suppose I've come a long way as well, Telford decided. A strange road. And he wasn't certain it was a path entirely of his own choosing.

He could almost feel their hands upon his back, pushing him towards this next crossroads, exactly as he'd felt their pressure in the past. His father. Julia Britten. Fidel Constantino and Sergio Sifre. Gabizon. Perhaps even Carter and Welch. Among the living? Louis Réchard. Nella and Paquita. Fox – who he'd not seen since the captain was posted as direct liaison to de Gaulle's headquarters staff.

Yes, he thought. A long way. Jack Telford, war correspondent.

August 1944

Suzanne 'Toto' Torrès

It could have been Bridlington all over again. But it wasn't. This was Normandy. The stretch of coast, the seemingly endless industrial and military scrapyard, now known to the world as Utah Beach. To be precise, the low-water line just below the village of Saint-Martin-de-Varreville. Yet the same iron-grey sea. The same overcast sky. The same damp foreshore. The same illusion that this was, somehow, supposed to be summer. The same seagull screech and throb of diesel engines against the waves, the stink of oil fumes and steaming steel.

Jack snapped the photo for the third time – Leclerc marching along the landing pontoon, in his forage cap and heavy trenchcoat, the tip of his cane chiming against the rivets beneath his feet, though the limp made almost imperceptible by the sheer force of being back on French ground. Around him, his staff, his aides, and the priest, *Père* Houchet, who served as his chaplain – now in uniform, of course, like all the rest, and carrying the sacramental tools of his trade in a suitcase.

At the other pontoons, stretching away in both directions and into the distance, liberty ships, barges and landing craft, disgorging men and machines. There were tanks, temporarily abandoned below the dunes, while their crews knelt to kiss the sand. Some tears, a great deal of shouting, the rumble of half-tracks and trucks. A welcoming committee of locals waving French flags and chanting. *Vive de Gaulle!*

'That one was perfect, sir,' Jack shouted, turned the handle to wind on the Rolleiflex.

Leclerc simply nodded his response. He'd made it clear he wasn't going to do it a fourth time in any event. And it wasn't Jack's fault.

It was the blokes from US Army Pictorial Service, determined to shoot the scene to perfection. They'd been there at Southampton, filming the embarkation, just as they'd been at various points along the route south from Pocklington. These days, they seemed to be everywhere. But they did some good work, and Jack still admired the newsreel footage he'd seen, taken by the APS at Anzio. He admired their equipment – those PH-47 Speed Graphic cameras supplied to the photographers. He glanced down ruefully at the Rolleiflex. Maybe he should try to acquire an upgrade.

But, for now, he hefted the strap of the Mighty Midget to a marginally less chafed position on his shoulder and set off along the beach. He was keen to rejoin Dronne and the others who, so far as he knew, hadn't yet been allowed to land. Leclerc had insisted Telford should sail with the headquarters staff but Jack had at least been able to do an interview with him during the crossing. He'd been astonishingly unguarded.

'General Patton?' he'd said. 'He is, of course, quite mad. But I admire him, and perhaps madness is precisely the quality we need at this moment in history. Look how well it has served the German leadership until now.'

Of course, when he saw Jack's typed text, the heavy black pen of censorship redacted this to five-word simplicity.

General Patton? I admire him.

Telford found an elderly beachmaster – American naval officer's uniform, cowboy boots and raincoat – from one of the Construction Battalions, their Seabees, with the formidable task of creating order from this chaos.

'If they're where they're supposed to be,' the beachmaster drawled, a shrill whistle clamped between his teeth and directing the flow of traffic with all the dexterity of a policeman at Hyde Park Corner, 'about there. Third balloon along.'

He pointed at one of the tethered barrage balloons, those comforting prophylactics against incursion by enemy aircraft although, today, the only planes in the sky seemed to be friendly enough. And he was right. There they were, ten minutes hard slog through the sand, the rock pools, the morass of men and machinery. Dronne's Ninth Company, and Sarazac's Tenth, more than three hundred men, either crowded upon the ramp of the tank-landing ship, the black maw of the hold behind them, or packed along the bow rail, forty feet above. Impatient men, chanting.

'*A la playa! A la playa!*' To the beach. To the beach.

Yet, with most of the half-tracks finally landed – two of them had slipped off the ramp and were now abandoned in the shallows – Jack was soon surrounded by familiar and eager faces: the pinched features of Granell, of course, made somehow even thinner by the bulk of Campos alongside him; his old friends, El Gordo and Alemán; Reiter, the German, formerly with the International Brigades; the Spaniard they all called Bamba simply because his Dutch real name was unpronounceable; Fábregas the Anarchist; Constantino Pujol; and that outwardly most mild-mannered but, in truth, the hardest of them all, Fermín Blásquez, who'd served with one of the Madrid *checas*, the Dawn Brigade, which had brought so much summary torture and death to anybody suspected of being Fifth Columnists or traitors to the Republic. Even here, the lads were generally cautious about what they might say in front of Blásquez.

'Strange,' he said now, as they accepted Jack's cigarettes, 'we're further from Spain here than when we were in Casablanca. But, somehow, it's like I can smell the border.'

'Only a short hop south,' Amado laughed, 'and we'd be across the Pyrenees.'

Dronne marched up the beach, just in time to hear him.

'The war's *here* now, boys. You want revenge on the *Boches*, it needs to be here. They beat you in Spain, remember?'

'Sure,' said Fábregas. 'We remember. We remember how it took them three years to do it. And helped by the whole Italian army. By Franco and the *facciosos*. By brigade after brigade of *moros*. But here, *Capitán*? Here, the krauts kicked your French arses, on their own, in less than two months.'

'So, what would you do, *jefe Capitán*,' Fermín Blásquez laughed, 'if we just loaded up our M5s and headed for Barcelona or San Sebastián. Franco's on his own now. No Hitler or Mussolini to help him. All the *moros* sent back to Melilla and Ceuta. We'd cut through them like a knife through butter this time. Even just our hundred and fifty. We'd be in Madrid before they could spit, have the bastard hanging by his balls from a lamppost on the Gran Vía.'

And I could have killed him for you, thought Jack. There it was again. The guilt. That this was all somehow his own fault. He may have been pushed along the road, but the big driver in his life? This sense of unfinished personal business.

'To fight for the freedom of Spain,' Dronne was saying. 'Any different to fighting for the freedom of France?'

A few of the men laughed. Sardonic laughter.

'Hey,' Granell yelled at them. 'Respect, remember?'

'The only thing we need to remember, Lieutenant,' said Dronne, 'is that we're here to kill krauts.' He slapped the bonnet of the half-track behind him. It now bore the white-painted name *Teruel*. 'And if you've any venom to spit out, maybe *Señor* Telford would be happy to record your sentiments for posterity on that machine he's guarding so carefully.'

Jack was happy to oblige, and there, among the dunes of Saint-Martin-de-Varreville, he persuaded some of them to vent their frustrations on one of his precious discs. He'd send it to Barea, of course, trust him to edit the broadcast though, in practice, most of it was – to Telford's surprise – eloquently loyal to the cause of Free France.

That evening, in his tent, he also wrote a piece for Bunnelle.

In the town of Saint-Martin, in the shade of Utah Beach, there's a Spaniard who'll fight for the freedom of France. On the streets of Saint-Martin, there's a Spaniard who weeps for his own country lost, while the rest of the world slept. In the square of Saint-Martin, there's an oath they must take, with their brothers-in-arms, the Yanks and the French. And in the fields of Saint-Martin, where they sleep with their tanks, they swear they will die for the freedom of all.

It went on in the same vein, and when he'd finished, he thought about Granell's contribution to his work. Jack had asked Dronne whether, the next day, he might borrow Amado, to drive him across to the Communications HQ outside Avranches, to get his stuff dispatched from there. And when the interview was over, he'd shared another Capstan with the Valencian.

'You know,' Amado had said, 'I'd follow Dronne to hell and back. So would we all. Fábregas might have a big mouth, but he's loyal as the rest. And all that about the fight for France being the same as the fight for Spain. The boys were right, *inglés*. It's just shit.'

'Almost two hundred men,' said Harmon. 'Villagers. The Germans, men – if that's what they deserve to be called – from the Waffen SS *Das Reich* Division, shot them in the legs, then poured gasoline all over them. Burned them alive. Two hundred children, two hundred and fifty women, all shot down. All of them.'

The marquee was frantic with the chatter of typewriters, churning out the story in a score of different styles and formats. In the adjoining tent, there'd be a queue waiting for their turn at the Press Wireless Transmitter.

'Where can I work?' said Jack. There were a few empty spaces on the sixty of seventy trestle tables, but even those seemed to have folded cards, tent cards, with either somebody's name or *Reserved* scribbled on them. 'And is this the women only section?'

Seven women to be precise, those dozens of others in here, busy at their stories and sidebars, all men, a few in civvies, but the rest in the tunics, the various khaki drabs, the fatigues of the Allied forces – mostly either Yanks or British, so far as he could tell, though he'd already met a few of the Canadian and Australian reporters. A pipe smokers' convention, the air thick with the rich aromas of St. Bruno and Navy Flake, seasoned by essence of cigar.

'The top brass doesn't like us being here in the first place,' said little Ruthie Cowan – still as mouse-like as she'd been during their lunch in London with Bunnelle. 'And yes, we in our small corner. But you can use Lefèvre's place if you like.' She pointed to the vacant chair at a table just opposite, lifted her forage cap to scratch at the scalp under a tangle of blonde hair. 'He's taken Hemingway on a sightseeing tour. Can you believe it – Hemingway?'

Jack gratefully set down the precious portable recorder, his satchel and his camera case. He'd abandoned the typewriter in the Jeep.

'So, where is this place – the massacre?' said Jack, and pulled the woollen cap from his head, stuffed it in his pocket. He'd left

Granell making some minor adjustments to the Jeep's engine over at the vehicle depot, while Telford himself registered at the Communication HQ.

'Here, I'll show you.' The young Englishwoman, Babs Wace, took his arm and dragged him over to the wall map. She pointed to a spot, a long way south, halfway down the country, near Limoges. Too small to even have a name. Not yet, at least, thought Jack. 'Just about there,' said Babs. 'Oradour-sur-Glane.'

Jack lit a cigarette.

'And this was – two months ago?'

He looked to the women for an answer, saw Babs shove those absurdly large black-rimmed spectacles further up the bridge of her nose.

'There'd been rumours.' Harmon stopped typing, flicked a finger towards his Capstan. 'You got one of those to spare, Jack?' He offered her the packet. Neither of them commented on her new habit. 'But nobody wanted to believe them,' she went on. 'Like the stories we're picking up from the East. Death camps?'

'Death camps,' he said, and sat at the table, next to his kit. Jack opened his notepad, unfolded the small-scale map of France tucked inside the cover, wrote down the name. *Oradour-sur-Glane*. 'Nella Bénatar's been trying to get people to take those seriously for the past two years. What the hell's the big surprise? If Nella's right, Hitler's busy eradicating the entire Jewish race – with industrial precision. Can't even bring myself to think about what that means. But if she's even only *part* right, are we really surprised by German atrocities further down the chain of command? And what's happened to make everybody believe this story now, when apparently we were all happy to write it off as rumour yesterday?'

'Report from an American flyer,' Barbara Wace told him. 'Navigator. Shot down in the area and sheltered by the Resistance. Saw the aftermath, it seems. Only just got back to Blighty.'

Telford made a note of that as well.

'Hadn't the Resistance reported it already?'

'Of course,' said Cowan. 'But...'

'But nobody believed them? Good god, it's not as though this hasn't happened before. Châteaubriant? The massacre of all those

Senegalese prisoners-of-war? The deportations of Jews from France, the transports – What do we think happened to *them*? Thousands upon thousands.'

'Personally,' said Babs Wace, 'I thank God most decent people *don't* want to believe these things. The monstrosity of it all, Mister Telford. Yet when we *are* forced to confront it, we so quickly sink to the same level.'

'The only good German is a dead German, you mean?'

There'd been those rumours. Incidents of German prisoners shot, either in revenge for the slaughter of American troops or because, as he'd heard it said, on D-Day itself, nobody could afford to be encumbered by taking prisoners – and, for some, it had maybe set a pattern. Rumours. Alongside the instructions to the press corps. No shadow to be cast upon the integrity of the Allied cause. None. And Jack thought this was fair enough. For now, at least.

'I've been interviewing them,' said Harmon. 'Half of them aren't German at all. Boys who've been pressed into service from goodness knows where. Poles and Latvians. Czechs and Russians. Given the choice of either fighting or being shot. And women. German women, sure. But sent here to man the coastal batteries. We've got two hundred of them penned up, just the other side of Avranches while the top brass figure out what to do with them.'

'Great story,' said Jack. 'And what's all this?' He waved his hand towards them. 'Something I ought to know? United Press and AP working together now?'

'Us girls gotta stick together,' said Harmon. 'And the story? Sure is.' She smiled, gave her typewriter a friendly tap. 'It'll be winging its way home just as soon as I'm finished here tonight.'

'And you believe that, Mister Telford?' said Babs Wace. 'About good Germans and dead Germans?'

He so desperately wanted to put her in her place, took a deep breath, mostly cigarette smoke. Had she thought he'd meant the massacre – that the massacre was nothing more than a great story? But he knew if he tried to correct her, he ran the risk of simply digging the hole deeper.

'So far as I understand it, Miss Wace, the Germans are pulling troops from all over the show. To stop us, here in Normandy. As they pull out, the Resistance takes the opportunity for attacks on collaborators, the *Milice*, a German officer or two. Can't hardly blame them. But the Germans respond with reprisals. Terrible reprisals. Like at Oradour-sur-Glane. All I'm saying is – well, they're not likely to enjoy much mercy, are they? And especially not the Waffen SS.'

'Dudley says you're attached to Leclerc and the Free French,' Babs replied. 'A Spanish unit? How will they take it, d'you think – German prisoners? They've got their own scores to settle, I imagine. Guernica and so on. And, according to one of the reports, there were Spanish kids killed at Oradour. They'd been refugees, you know? Oradour took them in, apparently.'

It cut him. Oh, he knew it didn't make the atrocity any worse. But perhaps it brought it closer to home, somehow exaggerated the tragedy. Children and their families who'd been through so much, in Spain, then the exodus, the internment camps, finally finding human kindness again. Until…

'Babs,' murmured Ruthie Cowan, in her gentle American accent – cowgirl accent, he thought of it, from his fondness for westerns, 'why don't we open a bottle of the Calvados, give our friend Jack a quick nip?'

He appreciated her attempt to change the subject. There was an accusatory edge to Wace's interrogation he didn't quite understand. Or like.

'Sorry, Ruth,' he said. 'Must keep a clear head.'

'You're fine,' she shrugged. 'Busy day?'

'Driving across soon to catch up with the Division's ambulance corps. Landed yesterday afternoon and I want to get some interviews.' He patted the recording machine. 'But the Spaniards, Miss Wace – Babs? You're right, scores to settle. And, in the heat of battle – well, stuff happens.'

'A little bird tells me,' said Harmon, 'you've got more than just a professional interest in some of those ambulance women, Jack.'

'Maybe I'll take that shot of Calvados, after all,' he told her. 'For pity's sake, is nothing sacred?'

'See, Babs?' Harmon laughed. 'Told you. He's already spoken for. You'll just have to grab one of those boys who keep whistling after you.' Wace blushed, bright crimson. 'She loves it, Jack, really she does. But the only time she came close to landing a catch was when a New Jersey GI asked what part of the States she's from, and then ran a mile when he found out she's only a limey.'

The other women thought it was hilarious, while a flustered Barbara Wace made some excuse about having errands to run, picked up her forage cap and fixed it into her unruly mop of black hair.

'That's a very smart uniform, Miss Wace,' said Jack, 'if you don't mind me saying so. I don't suppose…'

'Mister Bunnelle insisted I should have it,' she replied. 'A little inappropriate, though, don't you think?' Jack didn't want to tell her he also possessed his own Savile Row tunic, thanks to Bunnelle, stowed in his dunnage. 'And he's shipping me back out tomorrow – now Ruthie's here,' Babs said to him. 'Well, good luck and happy reporting.'

She shook his hand and made for the marquee's exit.

'Errands?' said Telford, working on his notepad some more.

'She has a thing for one of the BBC's correspondents,' Harmon replied. 'Dickie Dimbleby. You know him? Shame is, he seems to be happily married, but it doesn't stop Babs following him around like some moonstruck heifer.'

'Know him?' Jack laughed. 'No. But good god, that broadcast from the beaches on D-Day itself – we listened to it in Pocklington. Set us all a high bar, don't you think? And while I'm here I should introduce myself to as many of the Beeb boys as possible, I suppose.'

Barea had given him a list. Dimbleby, Barr, Melville and the others. And Lefèvre? Jack pulled the wire from his pocket. Yes, there he was. Pierre Lefèvre. French Service. And another Frenchman, – another actor, as it happened – Jacques Brunius. They'd be looking for Leclerc, he was certain – the general now heading for Bayeux, where de Gaulle had established the latest capital of Free France. Brazzaville, Algiers, now Bayeux. Soon? Well, he thought, let's hope it's Paris again. He wiped a hand across his own pocket-book map, flattened the creases, calculated the distances, measured them against the outline he'd already started.

'What's that, Mister Telford?' said Ruthie Cowan. 'An artist now?'

'Hardly,' he laughed. 'But I managed to put together a map, of sorts. It's a bit rough, but you see?' He turned to the double pages further towards the front of his notepad, held them up. 'My odyssey through Africa, Harmon. Look, Brazzaville.' Harmon pursed her lips, gave it a nod of endorsement.

'Neat,' she said. 'And now Normandy?'

'Normandy and beyond, maybe.' He planned to do the same, keep the second page clear. If he played his cards properly, he should be able to run the Rhine down the right-hand outer edge.

'And where on that map might your sweetheart fetch up tonight, Jack?' said Harmon.

'Looks like they'll be headed for Ducey.' The place wasn't on his map either, but Granell knew how to get there. And not far from Avranches, he'd promised.

'They set up a dressing station there,' Ruthie told him. 'When we took this place.' Avranches had only been in Allied hands for less than a week.

'I read some of your pieces,' said Jack. 'Great writing.'

Cowan had been out in Normandy for a month now, but built her reputation with reports from the hospital ships. Interviews with the dying, with the wounded. Both sides.

'But when we had dinner with Bunnelle,' she said, scrutinising him closely, 'you didn't pay me no mind, I reckon. You think women correspondents shouldn't be in the war zones?'

She was right, he hadn't given her much attention. But mainly because, at the Hungaria, she'd seemed so reserved.

'My only excuse, Miss Cowan, is that those few days in London – they weren't exactly...'

His obsession with Sir Aubrey.

'Apology accepted,' she said. 'But Ducey? The krauts have already shelled it a few times. Front line, you know? Hospital or no hospital. Easy target for them. If your girl's going to be there, you'd best take care of her. Take *good* care.'

The previous night, his dreams had swept him back to Hull. One of those tea dances with pretty Ruby Waters, Jack and the rest of the boys all scrubbed up to the nines, best uniforms, close shaves – for the honour of Spain. *Their* Spain. Republican Spain. But a dream and nothing more. Ruby, so far as he knew, had never even *been* to Hull.

No, it was the similarity, he supposed, between Ruby and Danielle. Yet it raised with him, once again, the obvious troubling thought, as Granell raced them through the narrow lanes of Normandy, hedges high on either side. The *bocage*, they called it.

'Will we get there before dark?' he yelled, bracing himself, white-knuckled, against the Jeep's bouncing, swaying progress through the deep shadows cast by a sinking sun.

'Don't panic, *inglés*. Just enjoy the ride.'

His strange sense of humour. Like driving through a maze. Yet, occasionally, the hedgerows gave way to bare fields, to farmhouses, to isolated hamlets. And the open ground? More craters than the face of the moon. Dead cows, dead horses. The stink. Sickly stench. And the farms, the villages – not a single building left intact. Ruins still smoking. And, everywhere, the smell of gasoline.

'My god,' said Jack. 'My god.'

It had been bad enough, the drive across the peninsula from Saint-Martin-de-Varreville to La Haye, then south to Coutances, but here the devastation was relentless.

Yet, when they reached the apple orchard at Ducey, the light had already faded too far for anything to be visible except the dim glow from blackout lanterns hanging in the branches, the ghostly outline of ambulances parked in a neat line between the trees and the surrounding brick wall, a couple of tanks near the entrance gates, shadows cast by a small campfire and, around it, a gathering of ambulance drivers, medical staff, tank crewmen – a veritable garden party, enjoying the warm August evening. An evening alive with the buzz of insects. And singing. French singing. *Alouette.*

A cigarette glowed in the gloom as Jack climbed from the Jeep.

'Well, Mister Telford,' said Suzanne Torrès, falling into her easy French, 'home from our exile, at last.'

He already knew she was Parisienne. Nursing now, but at the start of the war she'd been with the French Red Cross, some liaison role with the top brass, wasn't it? Ended up in New York.

'How long?' he said, lifting his kit from the vehicle with Granell's help.

'A lifetime, of course. After the fiasco, to Bordeaux, then evacuated to Algiers. We flew out with Saint-Exupéry, did you know?'

He didn't, and he was suitably impressed.

'Where is he now? Any idea?'

'Not really. Flying again. Italy somewhere, I think. Lost track of him after Algiers. And with the armistice and Vichy, I headed to Spain, then Lisbon and Brazil, and finally New York. But it was funny, in New York, I came across Antoine again. Not in person, but his book. Have you read it?'

'About his crash in the desert? No, I always meant to, but then – I had my own plane crash and, afterwards...'

'Not that one,' she said, and trod on her cigarette stub, a shower of sparks from under her heel. 'He's just published a story for kids. In New York. Except, it's not just for kids. Not really. Morality tale, I suppose you'd call it. I brought a copy with me when we sailed. Lend it to you, if you like.'

Jack wasn't sure he'd enjoy it, but he thanked her anyway, out of politeness.

'And Spain, you said?' Granell asked her. 'Where in Spain were you?'

'All a bit of a blur,' she told him. 'We sailed from Oran to Alicante.'

'We know the route,' said Granell, his voice thick with sad nostalgia. 'Only in reverse, no, *inglés*?'

The *Stanbrook*. Yes, Jack remembered.

'After Alicante,' Torrès recalled, 'Madrid by train. Then Lisbon. Eventually, anyway. Neutral Spain, of course.' She smiled at Amado. 'Isn't that what they call it now? Neutral?'

'Neutral,' Granell repeated. 'If you're a Franco supporter, I suppose. Or keeping your head down. Or hiding from the Falange.'

He was thinking of Aurora, Telford imagined, back at home in Orihuela. Would he see it, or his family, ever again?

'I was hoping to catch up with Danielle,' said Jack.

'Over here, I'll show you.' They left Granell to his memories, lighting his own cigarette, while she led Jack towards the campfire where, he could now see, the women – he recognised some of the

573

Quakers as well – were cutting into a couple of huge wheels of cheese, breaking up and passing around cobs of baguette, sharing bottles of wine.

'Isn't this a bit reckless?' he said. 'The fire, considering the blackout lanterns.'

'Florence says we'll be safe enough for tonight. Girls needed cheering up a bit, after the journey. Hey, Danielle,' she shouted, over the singing – somebody was sadly butchering *Plaisir D'Amour* now, 'look what the cat's dragged in.'

Dani looked up, saw him and grinned, pushed herself from the circle of the other girls – handed the bottle she'd been holding to somebody else – then stepped carefully out of the company before flinging herself into his arms.

'Hey, steady on,' he laughed, as she led him away from the party, 'it's not been *that* long.'

'You don't know the half of it, *monsieur*,' she said. 'Three days on the bloody liberty ship, sick as a dog for most of the time, waves as high as a house. And then the job they had, getting me down the side and into the landing craft. My god, if it hadn't been for Toto...'

'Thought you didn't like her much.'

'Oh, she knows what she's doing, I'll say that much for her.'

'Whereas...?'

'Nothing really,' she said. 'Just a lot of grumbling about Florence. Whether maybe she's just too old for all this, now.'

Their *Commandant* Conrad, Widow Conrad. He thought he smelled a story, but it could wait.

'And you, Dani. Home again.'

She nestled against his chest.

'Not home, not until I get back to Toulouse. But, hell, I never pictured it this way, Jack. There's nothing left. Nothing. The fighting. When we got here last night, in the dark, down those bloody lanes. The headlights, picking up the signs. Warning signs, every few minutes. Mines. It'll take a lifetime to put it all together again.'

'But it *will*,' he said. 'Get put together again. Maybe this will be the end of it. An end to war?' He felt a fool for thinking there'd ever be an end, slapped at a mosquito on his neck. 'A finish to these little devils as well, d'you think?'

'Ate me alive last night,' she smiled. 'Slept in the ambulance. Bites everywhere, all the same.'

Jack kissed her.

'Despite the army-issue pyjamas?' he said. 'Is that possible?'

'I'm sure if you asked nicely, they'd share the secret with you.'

They spent an uncomfortably hot but reasonably interesting night in the back of the Dodge, after Danielle had slipped away to make some less-than-discreet alternative arrangements for her co-driver to sleep elsewhere, and Jack had made sure Granell could bed down with the tank crews. But he was up and about at first light, the camp already busy and, as he emerged to greet the day, there was Torrès sat against the wheel of the next vehicle, eating from her mess tin. She glowered at him.

'Nurse Zidane plainly didn't tell you about Rule Number Six,' she snarled.

In the distance, the sounds of fresh fighting. Like the firing range at Southampton, the steady *pop, pop, pop* of rifles, punctuated by the more staccato and occasional rattle of a machine gun. But muted, carried on the lazy morning air, from – how far away?

'Fraternisation?' said Jack, feeling himself colour, heat rising up his neck. 'Army rules?'

'My own,' she told him. 'And Rule Six says fraternisation's fine, just don't rub my face in it. I'll deal with her, though, just as soon as she deigns to join us. But you, *Monsieur* Telford, may put yourself back in my good books if you've got news of Jacques.'

'Massu?' Yes, of course, Massu. They'd been close, back in Yorkshire. Very close. He wondered how this stacked against the fraternisation rule – but he wasn't about to ask her. 'He landed safely enough,' Jack told her. 'Be glad to know I've seen you, I'm sure. Any message?'

She shook her head, went back to spooning the mess tin's slops.

'The cheeses,' he said, trying not to think about the gunfire, louder now, and fastening the buttons of his shirt with one hand, lifting the edge of the camouflage netting with the other. 'Where did they come from?'

'Some of the villagers,' Dani shouted from inside the ambulance, her voice muffled, coming to him in fits and starts. He

575

pictured her struggling back into her uniform, dreading whatever censure might await her from the tongue of Toto Torrès. 'Ducey,' she yelled. 'Not much left of the place. But they brought the cheese. The bread and the wine. God bless them. Tried to pay them. But they got really upset. Refused to take a single *sou*.'

'And this place?' Jack looked towards the wall behind them, fruit trees with ripening pears fastened in fans to the red brick. Above and beyond the wall, the roof of a substantial building.

'The Château des Montgommery,' said Torrès. She saw his questioning look of surprise. 'No, *monsieur*, not *that* one. *This* Montgommery was here three hundred years ago. Something of the sort, anyway.'

'But who knows?' said Jack. 'Maybe one of Monty's ancestors.'

He sat on the ambulance steps, pulled on his boots, cocked his head to pick up the drone of an aircraft. It didn't sound particularly menacing, but he could see others in the camp, the cooks from a catering tent on the opposite side of the orchard, leaving their work to peer up into the sky. *'German,'* somebody shouted. *'Spotter plane.'*

A flurry of activity, everybody making their way to cover, under the netting, against the boles of the trees, anywhere but in the open. Jack could see the crosses beneath the aircraft's wings as it spluttered over the orchard, banked to one side and made a second pass before disappearing towards the rising sun.

'Where the hell's our air cover?' said Jack, as Danielle emerged behind him. 'That bastard snooping around without a care in the world.'

'Lieutenant...' Danielle began, presenting herself for punishment, but Torrès simply shook her head, cleaned out her mess tin with a handful of grass.

'No time for that,' said Toto. 'Need to get ready. Florence has gone to get our orders. Looks like we'll be moving out again. And air cover, *Monsieur* Telford? They can't be everywhere.'

No, they couldn't, and he turned to Danielle, who was dragging a comb through her hair.

'Listen,' he said, 'I need to find Amado, get back to the Company and...'

The roar of more aircraft engines and coming fast.

'There you go,' laughed Torrès. 'Our air cover. I'm guessing that's one spotter who'll not be making it back to his *Boches* friends.'

But as they pushed back the netting for a better look, Jack felt his stomach lurch, grabbed Toto's shoulder strap and dragged her back.

'Shit,' he yelled. 'Not ours.'

They came in from the south, three Focke-Wulf fighters, the leader low, flashes from his wings, lines of tracer hanging in the air, the *hammer, hammer, hammer* of his guns, then bullets kicking up dirt in a line from the gates and up the centre of the orchard. *Splat, splat, splat.* From the other two, both higher, bombs – only…

Falling too slowly for bombs. Almost graceful. Canisters which opened as they left the plane and, from the canisters, dozens of smaller objects, each hanging from its own wings, like sycamore seeds, spiralling down towards the ground – down towards the ambulances.

'Out of here, quick,' Jack shouted, grabbed both women by their arms and hauled them out into the open, as the first of the small bombs exploded alongside the Dodge just inside the gates. It must have caught the fuel tank, for the whole vehicle went up like a torch, blew it to hell.

Then another, further up the line. Explosion after explosion. Flame and smoke. Yelling. An agonised shriek that just went on and on. The smell of burning rubber. A sound almost like hailstones, shrapnel hitting the trees. Or the clang of metal on metal as it struck the vehicles. Or the hiss of escaping air as tyres were punctured.

Somebody was screaming in Telford's ear – Danielle, he realised. He looked up to see one of the bombs spinning down directly above them. Jack pulled the women out of its path. He flung them to the grass, threw a protective arm around them. Knew it was a useless gesture.

More blasts rang in his ears, but nothing immediately near, just a thud as something hit the ground alongside them. He peaked over Dani's back to see the butterfly bomb lying where it had fallen, the device itself not much bigger than a clenched fist, its two small, curved wings still attached and spread open.

'We need to move,' he said, almost in a whisper. 'But careful. Timers. Sometimes they have timers. Or – well, just gently.'

They got to their feet. Carefully. Jack couldn't take his eyes off the damned thing. He'd not actually seen these before, but he knew about them. There'd been a raid on Grimsby while he'd been at Pocklington. Jerry had dropped thousands of these. Cluster bombs and incendiaries. The reports...

'They've gone,' said Danielle. 'Gone.'

She seemed to be right, the drone of their engines fading into the distance, leaving only the sounds of devastation here, behind them.

'Doesn't mean they won't be back,' said Toto, brushing dirt from her fatigues and looking around, assessing the damage. 'Need to get organised and – my god, what *does* she think...?'

Three of the ambulances were blazing, and a fourth seemed to have been thrown sideways. There were bodies on the ground. Others, men and women, dazed, getting to their feet. And one of the drivers – Jack didn't know her name – running with a fire extinguisher towards a burning Dodge. She'd had the presence of mind to pull a tin helmet onto her head but, apart from that, she was entirely naked except for her bra and knickers.

And, somehow, it broke the spell. A few of the other girls, coming out of whatever hiding places they'd found, were shouting to her, bawdy comments, laughing. But, at the same time, they were all galvanised into action, the endless training compelling them to their various tasks.

'I have to go, Jack,' said Danielle. 'See what we can salvage.'

She squeezed his arm, ran back towards the ambulance line, yelling to others from her own team, those who could repair a track rod end as easily as a broken leg.

'But where the hell's Florence?' Suzanne Torrès was saying, more to herself, Jack thought, than anything else.

Some of the women had gathered round her, waiting for orders, and she dispatched them, here and there, arranged their triage system. She was perfectly calm, admirable. One of the girls, it seemed, Polly, was critical, both legs shattered. Burns to be treated, a couple of men from the tank crews with particularly serious injuries.

'And get your helmets,' Torrès shouted. 'I'm guessing those damned things have got timers.'

She waved her hand towards the trees, where unexploded bombs, dozens of them, hung like ripe summer fruit.

'Can I help?' said Jack.

'The priority,' she told him, 'will be getting enough of the trucks ready so we can shift the worst cases to hospital. To Avranches. That Spanish lieutenant, he's a good mechanic, isn't he?'

'Amado? The best. Like magic. We'll get cracking.'

Jack found him, outside the gates, with one of the tank crews, ministering to a boy – he couldn't have been more than eighteen –who'd taken shrapnel to his shoulder. The lad was in agony, writhing, Granell cradling his head and crooning to him, trying to get him to sip some water from his canteen.

'So, *inglés*,' he said, looking up at Telford, 'here we are again, no?'

Without his reports – for Bunnelle on the one hand, for Barea on the other – Jack doubted he'd ever have been able to make sense of his day.

They'd headed out at the crack of dawn, from Saint-James. Yet now, here he was, in a hotel of all things, Danielle dozing in the bed beside him, Jack winding the handle on the Mighty Midget until the warning light flashed green, let him know the machine was ready to record.

Telford slipped into his best Spanish.

'Today, in Normandy, the first of our Spanish brothers-in-arms, Andrés García, gave his life for the liberation of France.'

They'd arrived at Domalain, thirty-five miles or so to the south, just before eight, but there they halted. Billotte's column, just one-third of Leclerc's Division, the rest taken other routes but presumably somewhere close, to the west of them.

Thirty-five miles. In, what? Almost four hours? Not bad, considering. And no real incidents. A few breakdowns. Bottlenecks in some of the villages. Folk blocking their way in the narrow streets. Flowers and flags. Singing. Kisses. But the column edgy, nervous. After the first flush of jubilation, a few days before, the joyous welcome to the conquering heroes, now every delay, every traffic jam, made them a sitting target.

Telford came to the end of his script, lifted the needle and slipped the disc carefully back into its sleeve, writing on the brown paper, a note to Barea.

La Nueve at Domalain, Monday 7th August. Telford.

Then he held up his closed fist, his right hand, the thumb extended.

'What's that for?' Dani murmured. 'The thumbs-up.'

He hadn't realised she was awake, laughed when he saw how it must have looked.

'Sorry,' he said. 'It's how I keep track of where we are. My portable campaign map. See? The fingers, that's Brittany. The thumb...'

'I've got it,' Dani told him. 'The peninsula. Cotentin.'

The peninsula which was, of course, now entirely occupied by the Allies.

'Correct, my sweet.'

'Your very own shorthand,' she smiled.

'Shorthand,' he laughed. 'Yes, literally. Here,' he pointed to the outer base of his thumb, the top of his wrist, 'the landing beaches.'

From those landing beaches, the Allies had pushed inland, drawn the Germans into costly fighting around Caen, and that had allowed Patton to break out of the peninsula, sweep west into Brittany – Jack's folded fingers. German units in Brittany were now cut off and being pushed back into the ports of St. Malo, Lorient and Brest. They stood no chance but how long to destroy them and regain those vital harbours?

Danielle rolled over, took his hand, tickled the underside, the lower edge of his palm, sent a tremor through his whole body.

'And here *we* are, *Monsieur* Telford.'

'Stop it,' he said. 'I've still got another piece to write. This one's about you lot.'

'The fighting *Rochambelles*,' she muttered, then rolled over, her backside and the curve of her hips tempting him.

'Something like that.'

He averted his gaze, opened his notepad. It would have to be typed up in the morning, of course, but he hoped, by then, he'd be able to find out where the Communications HQ might now be. It was all a bit confusing.

But the words flowed easily enough.

Domalain. There'd been another attack by Jerry fighters. Two half-tracks destroyed and quite a few injured. Andrés García killed. Not the same García, José, who'd been with them at Kufra, of course. Then up came the *Rochambelles*, like the proverbial cavalry.

'So, what happened?' he said. 'With *Commandant* Conrad?'

'Toto wouldn't talk about it,' Dani mumbled into the pillow. 'But, after Ducey… I don't know, it was – as though this wasn't the sort of war Florence had expected. There's a lot of gossip, among the girls. And she's still there. Of course, she is. But it's like – well, Toto's now the boss.'

Torrès had certainly got everything organised in double-quick time, that much was certain. Military precision. Dressing station for the walking wounded, ambulances to take the more critical cases – those with a large red triage letter 'C' daubed on their foreheads – back to the temporary field hospital still at Ducey. Danielle had driven one of the Dodges and Jack had gone with her, another of the girls – Yvette – in the back, ministering to the other two injured men, but mainly trying to keep El Gordo under control.

Shrapnel embedded in his back and both legs, tourniquets applied. Jack doubted the legs could be saved, but Dani had driven like the very devil, despite the lack of signposts, no real idea whether they were heading through friendly or enemy territory. El Gordo's agony must have been unbearable.

'*Moro!*' he kept screaming at Yvette. '*Moro!*' You Arab! And profanities which were much worse.

'What the hell will happen to him now?' said Jack. 'If he was one of the Yanks, it would be a ticket home – if he survives at all. But ship him back to Spain, to Toledo? Christ, they wouldn't, would they?'

It plagued him all the way to Ducey. They'd been together a long time. Since Libreville. Since Bou Arfa, he supposed, really. He told Danielle the story about the fire at the hotel there. About the prisoners' escape.

At the field hospital, an American doctor gave the Spaniard some shots, calmed him down, quietly told Jack that, yes, the left leg would certainly have to be amputated, maybe the right one. But he'd do his best.

'Comrade,' Jack had said, once the Toledan was settled in a bed, 'we have to go now, but I'll speak with Barbirrojo.' More than a few of the Spaniards used this nickname for Dronne. Redbeard. 'Make sure they look after you. Veterans' hospital, or something.'

Jack wasn't sure he'd heard, but when El Gordo finally opened his eyes and spoke, he seemed lucid enough.

'Oath,' he whispered. 'Not finished. *Facciosos*. Not finished.'

Telford squeezed the big man's hand, though it seemed shrunken now.

'Granell and the other *compañeros*,' he'd said. 'They'll finish it for you.'

Gordo turned his head, winced with the pain.

'No, English. *You* finish it. For me.'

They'd left Ducey again just after noon, Yvette driving and Danielle snuggled up against Jack.

'You sure this is the right road?' Jack had said, after they'd been driving for an hour. 'I don't recognise any of this. Shouldn't we have hit Saint-James by now?'

Yvette peered through the windscreen, gazed up at the sun.

'Still going south,' she said, cheerily, and grinding the gears badly as she shifted down for yet another bend. 'But, dammit, cramp in my bloody foot.'

Danielle had complained about it many times. The way you had to keep your throttle foot on the transmission hump.

'I told you before,' Dani told her, 'use the hand throttle, give your foot a rest.'

But Yvette wasn't listening. She stamped her foot, looked down at it.

'Watch out!' yelled Jack, saw the sharp right-hander coming up, knew they were going too fast.

Yvette hit the brake. The Dodge swerved to one side. There was a high bank, a hedgerow. And a ditch. Telford felt the ambulance leave the ground and his stomach lurched. He held Danielle tight, braced himself with his free hand against the windscreen frame, feet against the footwell. Like that damned plane crash all over again.

They landed with a sickening thump, the rending of metal, the teeth jarred in his head. He heard a bang, saw Yvette's head smack into the glass. And behind them, in the ambulance itself every damned thing must have come loose, bottles shattering, the stretchers come free from their fittings.

The whole world seemed upside down, and his ribs hurt like hell, where he'd fallen against the dash. But he'd also fallen on top of Danielle. She groaned, and he levered himself up, trying to take his weight off her. He was shaking like a leaf.

'You hurt?' he said. She rubbed at her shoulder.

'You're heavier than you look,' she murmured. 'Oh, and this...' She turned her head. Danielle, in turn, had fallen against Yvette, but against the gear lever as well. Wincing, she gripped her side.

The ditch. They were in the ditch. Or, at least, the front half, the whole vehicle tilted at a precarious angle.

'Come on,' he said. 'We need to get out.'

'Yvette...' said Danielle. The girl was out cold – or worse. Blood running down her face.

He managed to scramble out of the cab, struggled to help Danielle climb free behind him, but there was no way they'd be able to get Yvette out through the driver's door. It was wedged firmly, down in the ditch, and against the hedgerow's steep bank.

Despite his aches and pains, Telford leaned back inside, reached across the seats and, as carefully as he was able, slowly pulled her up towards him. She was a dead weight, and he was feeling a bit light-headed after the crash, but he finally eased her out and they managed to lay her on the grass. Danielle limped to the back doors, still clutching her side, climbed into the ambulance and came back with her medical kit.

'Oh, thank god,' she said, when Yvette finally came round, tearful and apologetic, but with her head bound neatly in one of Dani's bandages.

'Well,' said Jack, 'I'm no mechanic but I know we'll never get her out of the ditch without help. And aren't those bits of your

583

exhaust?' In three sections, scattered along the lane. 'But there's one stroke of luck, at least.'

He pointed down the narrow road. A church steeple, poking up above the hedge.

It was a mile, maybe a little more, but felt much further, his ribs creasing him with every step. And when Jack reached the outskirts, he was overwhelmed by what he found. First, as he hobbled down a long hill, to the right of the road stood perhaps the biggest ancient castle he'd ever seen and, to the left, a bustling American army encampment, a supply dump. Second, ahead of him, where the road climbed steeply again, following some high ramparts, the upper town almost entirely in ruins. Bombed to hell.

He begged help from the Yanks, arranged for a truck to go and rescue the ambulance, discovered they'd arrived in Fougères. And yes, the driver and his mate told him. Bombed. Twice. Just after D-Day. To stop the krauts bringing up reinforcements. Sure, said the driver, we dropped the usual leaflets first. *Urgent message to inhabitants*, that sort of thing. But some people, the driver went on, well, they just won't listen, you know? And these Frenchies...

Later, with Yvette in the care of the local medics, there was an offer to repair the Dodge. Not too much damage, after all. The exhaust mainly. Should be ready to roll next day. So, another offer. Beds for the night.

But Jack had already spotted a hotel.

It had somehow survived the devastation.

'Fougères,' he'd said, when they were stood outside with their possessions, debating whether they should take the room. 'How old, d'you think?' He'd shown her the medieval fortress down the hill, and there was still evidence of the medieval town. But mostly there was just ruin. 'My god, this must have been a place for dreamers. Once upon a time.'

'A room?' The hotel's proprietress assessed them both. She had hooded eyes, like a bird of prey. 'For two?'

Danielle switched on her most alluring French charm, made quite a play of her injuries, while Jack took note of the rectangular patterns upon the walls where paintings or photographs had once hung.

'You must be pleased,' he said. 'The *Boches* gone.'

'Always paid their bills. Paid them on time. Never quibbled over the price of butter at the market – when we *had* a market, that is.'

Destroyed in the bombing, Jack was sure.

'Still, *madame*,' said Danielle. 'Liberty for France, this has a price as well, no?'

'Yes,' said the woman, 'the price of now being under the heel of the Americans instead of the *Boches*. You want me to be honest? I preferred the *Boches*. And the *Boches* never bombed the hospital.'

They'd settled into the room, Jack checking the machine for damage before he'd begun the recording for Barea. Settled into the room, and then…

'A hell of a day,' he said, now, as he finished writing his draft for the piece he'd be sending to Bunnelle.'

'You haven't made us sound stupid, I hope,' she laughed, and the laughter made her wince again. Her side. 'Oh Lord, don't make me laugh. It hurts. But getting lost, and then the crash.'

'Gosh, no. It's about how brave you all are. Surviving air attacks. Mercy missions. That sort of thing.'

'Brave?' She wrapped herself in a sheet, went to the window. 'I told you, that night at *Madame* Lumley's. And today, when I realised we were lost, it all came back to me again. The chance we might simply have strayed over the lines. You won't ever let them take me, Jack, will you?'

'You were never in any danger, my love,' he told her, and he showed her the clenched fist, the raised thumb again. 'You see?' He pointed to the fleshy mound at the bottom of his palm. What did they call it – the Mount of the Moon? 'We're about here, somewhere. And Jerry?' He stabbed his finger into his wrist. 'Jerry's over there. Miles away.'

'And that night, in Pocklington,' she said. 'I've felt guilty ever since. Just caught me by surprise. Overwhelmed, I suppose. Wouldn't blame you if you've sold that beautiful ring by now. But, if not…'

There was a twinkle in Major Putz's eye, as though he might be about some puckish piece of mischief, rather than pitching them against the cream of the German Panzer divisions.

'Before we get down to serious business,' said the wizened old warrior, slapping the point of his stick against the blackboard of the shattered schoolroom – a blackboard with a chalked battle map. 'I see *Monsieur* Telford's joined us.'

What this about? Jack wondered. He liked Putz, and he knew the liking was mutual. The major was also popular among the *Rochambelles*, almost a father figure, and Toto Torrès saw him that way. Hell, Hemingway had even given Putz a mention by name in *For Whom The Bell Tolls*. But Telford simply pulled the jeep cap from his head, by way of a salute, fumbled in his combat jacket for his cigarettes, glanced around at the faces of the Putz Group's captains, lieutenants and tank commanders.

'Present and correct, Major,' he said.

'Then congratulations, *monsieur?*'

Word had spread, it seemed, though Jack and Danielle had shared a pact to keep the whole thing quiet. There was a brief round of applause, some raucous shouting, and that big anarchist bear, Campos, *el canario*, offering him a piece of gum.

'*Chicle, compañero?*' he growled, while Jack shouted some nonsense back to Putz about the *Rochambelles* making an honest man of him, then he turned back to Campos.

'Gum, Sergeant?'

'Better for your health than cigarettes,' said Miguel Campos.

'Here?' Jack laughed. 'Are you bloody mad? Think it matters much?'

At the board, Putz was in full flow. The Allies, of course – British, Americans, Canadians, Poles, under Montgomery and Bradley – had continued their slow push inland from the beachheads, heavy fighting south of Caen, then on towards Falaise. Now, every chance of a huge flanking movement by Patton's Third Army, including their own Division, to trap the Germans in the pocket of territory around Falaise itself. Each officer there in the briefing knew this, but the Putz Group's part in the plan? The capture of one of the towns to the northwest of their present position.

Jack was updating his notes of the road which had brought him here.

From Domalain to Sées, a hundred and twenty miles, give or take. Four thousand vehicles, almost nose to tail, in daylight and in darkness. Cossé-en-Champagne, Le Mans, then the swing north to Alençon.

Sleepy towns, sometimes waking to the thunder of their passing, cheering them on their way, while others complained at such a rude awakening. A different France, largely untouched by the war until now. Yet, during the day, it was also the France of bygone holidays, their advance celebrated like a Roman triumph. Flowers, lipstick kisses, more Calvados. Jack had written some neat pieces for AP, some good photos to go with them. The Janus face of Liberation.

There'd been attacks. German ambushes. Booby traps. Summary shootings of some captured Wehrmacht soldiers. And Jack was far beyond meaningless moral judgements.

He flicked back through his notes. Couldn't actually recall them all now, the places. Bit of a blur, though he'd scribbled about Mézières-sur-Ponthoin and La Hutte, though mainly about the action two days ago in the Forest of Écouves. That had been bad, Colonel Rémy's son, just eighteen, killed there in his tank. Jack had been with Putz's group when they'd swept across from Sées like the proverbial cavalry to save the day with a flank attack against the German 9th Panzers.

God, they'd made the bastards pay. Enemy vehicles destroyed like wooden toys.

'Joder,' Granell had said to him later, as they watched them burn. 'These are the invincible Panzers? Hell, this is going to be easier than I thought, inglés.'

Yet so many deaths. The Division's nineteen French boys they'd buried at Le Gatey alone. The fighting around Alençon, the Sablon crossroads and a dozen other battlefields.

There'd also been reunions. Back at Cossé-le-Champagne, the Division had joined up with the entire rest of Patton's Third Army, including whole sections of the French Interior Forces, maquis resistance units from the Mayenne and Orne districts – and from there on the Sarthe, Dronne's own homeground. These were tough fighters, instantly christened by the Spaniards as Los Fifi. Jack had interviewed some of them. Not just French either, but Poles in their ranks. A couple of them had poked at the red, yellow and purple flash at Jack's shoulder.

'*Republika?*' said one of them. '*Republika?*'

'Yes,' Jack had told him, pointed across to where the Chad Regiment, Putz's battalion and *La Nueve* were encamped. 'Spanish soldiers. Fight for France.'

The man thumped his own chest.

'And us. *Dąbrowszczacy*,' he said. Jack was fairly sure they'd formed the Polish International Brigade during the war in Spain, but he took them off to meet Granell and the boys – and, hell, the singing and the drinking that night! Vodka. Where in god's name had they found all the vodka?

With the incoming units, also, Fox reappeared. He travelled in with Amado, who'd skipped back to Ducey with Dronne's permission, to check on El Gordo.

'Well?' Jack had said, though he knew the answer already from Granell's tight-strung features.

'Lost the fight, *inglés*. The second leg. Good man. Very good.'

'Made me promise to finish Kufra for him,' Jack recalled. There'd been too much death to mourn El Gordo's passing deeply. 'Me, for pity's sake.'

'But you, Telford,' said Fox, offering around his cigarettes. 'They tell me your ambulance woman finally said yes. My god...'

'Christ, it's supposed to be a secret,' Jack had smiled. 'But buy you both a drink, boys?'

They found a cellar bar, busy. Mainly GIs – crazy guys from one of the Yanks' Ranger Battalions. A dozen of them, sprawled on the floor against the far wall, sharing bottles of unlabelled raw red wine. Among them, three young French women. A scarred sergeant trying to teach them to sing *Baa! Baa! Baa!* at the chorus of that daft song, *Poor Little Lambs, Who Have Lost Our Way*. Above them, filling the archway, a peeling Pernod poster, blue and white.

Cider all round, courtesy of Fox. They clinked stoneware bottles, the cider warm and hard, but fine.

'And how's *le patron*?' said Jack. 'With him at Bayeux?'

'De Gaulle? Still raging about high-handed Anglo-Saxons. Livid with Roosevelt but mainly with Churchill. About what he was – or wasn't – able to broadcast on D-Day, about what he sees as their lip service to French involvement in the campaigns so far. Just about everything.'

'No better now Leclerc's here?'

'Massively better. Leclerc and the Division. You boys.' He slapped Granell on the back. 'His hope, his dream, his vision. Reason he sent me back, I suppose. Liaison is flavour of the month again, it seems.'

'To hell with all this,' Amado snapped, punched Jack's arm. 'Tell us about the girl again.'

'Hardly seen her,' said Jack. 'But god, the gang of them. Didn't matter how bunched up the rest of us were, whenever the *Boches* attacked, there were the ambulances. The girls. Or the Quakers. When I did see Dani, it was all Toto this and Toto that. Spreading them out through the lines.'

'Widow Conrad?' said Fox.

'*Major* Conrad,' Telford corrected him. 'Florence still very much in charge, but Toto Torrès seems to have all the tactical command. But hell, there was an incident. Funny, really. Lost track of where we were. Lovely little get-together, though. Toto and Jacques Massu. Fling themselves into each other's arms. Then she notices the name painted on his Jeep. Must have been the first time she'd seen it. What's this? she says. Moido? A place? He mutters some nonsense to her. Takes her two days to find out the truth and, when she does, she tracks him down and almost scratches his eyes out.'

'Moido?' said Granell.

Fox laughed.

'The most beautiful of the Toubou women. Lived with her in Faya-Largeau. Man and wife almost.'

Jack had a vision of Dina, his liaison with her at Faya. Not the most comfortable of recollections.

'*Madre de Diós*,' smiled Amado. 'As if this bloody war wasn't bad enough already. Makes you wonder why we do it, no?'

The French girls at least seemed to have the hang of the chorus now. Not a bad set of harmonies.

'Poor Dani,' said Jack, 'made the mistake of telling one of the other girls about the ring. Went round like wildfire, and she got the summons from Toto. She has rules, you know? And Number Thirteen? Do not marry except within the Division. Seems she slapped the back of Danielle's head, asked her what the hell she thought she was doing. Englishman as well. Still not sure where I stand, but she seems to have accepted I'm at least *attached* to the Division. But listen, mind if we sit?' he said, and rubbed at his thigh.

'Hurt, old boy?'

'The leg I broke. Started to play up a bit. Nothing, really.'

His right hand was troubling him again. Stiff. Legacy of the killings in Spain. All in his head, he knew that. But, all the same. And his eye socket, ached like the very devil. To top it all, the tightness in his guts, the old knife wound. There was one table, an oak barrel, in truth, a couple of stools.

'And why do we do it?' Fox said to Granell. 'Because we bloody enjoy it, old man.'

'Is that it?' Jack replied. 'It's never going to win me the Pulitzer. I always had this idea that, because we don't have any others worth speaking about, we have to be our own predators. War. Nature's way of controlling our numbers. Know what I mean?'

He ordered three more ciders from the grumbling old owner.

'Too complex,' said Fox. 'Just think of all those Ohio farmboys.' He nodded across to the singing Rangers. 'Not a violent bone in their bodies. But six months after the Draft, here they are. Every one become a natural-born killer. It's just in us – most of us. And when it comes our way, we like it. Live and taste every moment like nothing else we'll ever experience.'

'I often think about my people,' said Granell. 'Spanish. Peaceful, friendly.'

'The more of you in one place,' Jack smiled, 'the happier you all become.'

'Exactly, *inglés*. Love peace, but as though we can only cope with so much. After that, every twenty, thirty years maybe…'

'It all goes to hell in a handcart,' said Fox. 'Some collective madness, like it has to come out. Hatred. Like lemmings over a cliff. Back in 'Fourteen. Now this. But sure, Jack old boy, in the end simply because we like it.'

It was in Telford's mind again now, the classroom at Sées. Putz had already covered the background – the Division's aim to take the town, while the Yanks would move on Argentan, further to the north and east. Between them they'd have cut off the lines of German retreat. The *Boches* would be trapped in the pocket to the west, around Falaise – trapped and destroyed.

'So, here it is, gentlemen,' said Putz. 'Tanks of the 501st, most of them, with support, under Colonel Warabiot, will push up this road, directly from Saint-Christophe-le-Jajolet and Fleuré. Our task, on the other hand, is to sweep around here, to the west, through Boucé. But then, *mes braves*, we catch the *Boches* with their pants down. Here, gentlemen.' He smacked the tip of the cane, hard, against the board. 'Écouché,' he said, nodded his head. 'Écouché.'

From Hull to hell, thought Telford, and he crouched still lower at the side of the abandoned German half-track, the vehicle itself sheltering within the shattered walls of a battle-scarred barn, one of its former occupants draped over a cart, another slumped in the corner, like camouflage-clad sacks of abandoned fodder. On the lane outside, vehicles were burning, the familiar stench of cordite, petrol and blazing rubber, pitch-black smoke. Who'd have bloody believed it?

A bullet hammered like a gong against the armour above his head, paint sparks showering his shoulders. The whine and wind of its passing brushed his whitewash-filled hair, shook him to the core. Not much more than a hundred miles to Paris and some fool had said the Germans were finally in retreat.

'I told you, *inglés*,' said Granell, 'you should have stayed with your typewriter.'

The Spaniard stood quickly, hoisted the butt of the Thompson to his shoulder and returned fire. They'd been friends for five years now, on and off, since the *Stanbrook*.

'It's not right,' said Jack, and he chose to speak the words in Valenciano – Granell's first language – rather than his everyday Spanish. 'This morning. Why the hell didn't we finish them?'

Granell hunkered down again, turned to frown at Telford, dark eyes piercing the shadow beneath the rim of the American-issue helmet.

'Shit,' he smiled. 'It's you. Always bad luck, *inglés*.'

At sunrise they'd raced into town, a squad under Sergeant Bullosa and a guide from the *maquis* – all that was left of Écouché anyhow, after the bombings back in June, which had entirely destroyed the southern part of town, around the railway and its sidings – and caught a German motorised column in the act of pulling out. Heading north.

Jack had written it all down. Every detail. The bottleneck in the narrow streets. The Germans trapped, cut down by the dozen, their vehicles left ablaze, prisoners taken. The rest would all have died as well, he was sure. Every last one of them. But a single tank, a Panther, had dug itself in, a hundred yards back down the road, at the ancient bridge over the stream – the Cance – running through this upper portion of town. The damned thing had covered the *Boche* retreat until Lozano and Rico took it out, advanced to new positions here, this farther side of the Orne. But by then the Germans had made a stand, beyond the crossroads, on the higher ground, hidden among the trees, the hedgerows, the outhouses of another farm.

'You need me, Amado,' said Jack. 'I'll make you famous one day.'

Granell snorted with laughter, as Telford straightened the piratical patch covering the violation of his left eye, and one of the other *Stanbrook* men, from Number One Section – Staff Sergeant Moreno – vaulted over the debris of the barn's doorway.

'Orders, Lieutenant?' he panted, as he flattened himself against the wall.

'Find Barbirrojo,' said Granell. 'Tell him we need this bitch of a tank shifted from that farm. And get some firepower up here – but be careful.' Moreno grinned, spat into the dust, waited for Granell to give him some covering fire before he disappeared again, back the way he'd come. 'And where's your helmet?' Amado snapped at Jack, as he crouched once more.

By late evening, stalemate, and while the firing had slackened, the Germans had dug in hard.

Jack was surprised they'd not counter-attacked because they clearly had the superior strength to do so. Here, along the northern edge of Écouché, there were only those platoons of *La Nueve*, similar numbers from the Tenth Company, a few of the tanks from the 501st and, finally, a Tank Destroyer from the Marines' Armoured Regiment – its crew all former French naval gunners, now without ships. Worse, they'd all been Vichy men, still not entirely trusted. But hell, they could shoot. Put a shell through a sixpence at almost any range.

By late evening, also, word had reached him about a section of the *Rochambelles* parked in more of the apple orchards south of town, this side of Saint-Christophe-le-Jajolet, perhaps a mile or two back.

He told Dronne he was heading that way, no idea whether Danielle might be there or not, but willing to take the chance.

'You certain, *Monsieur* Telford? Can't spare anybody to go with you, you know that. And once out of town, no guarantee you won't run into the *Boches*.'

Jack was certain, made his way back across the Cance, where one of the Shermans from the 501st had finally shifted the destroyed German tank from the bridge.

In the centre of the ruined town, with an occasional stray bullet whining from the walls, life had settled into some strange alternative reality: a nun, bent double, hustling a line of small children down the side lane to the church, another Notre-Dame; and a looter, brazen, swag sack slung over his shoulder, scrambling across the rubble from one abandoned house to another; and three old men wandering across the square from the *mairie*, towards a bar on the far side, arguing loudly, angrily, about the merits of this year's local vintage. Bizarre.

He checked his kit was still secure in the half-track *Teruel*, which had brought him the last leg to Écouché. All fine, but he left everything except his satchel, his haversack and the camera, reached the town limits, passed the burned-out hulk of their own tank, *Massaoua*, an early casualty of the morning's fighting, along with the half-track, *Don Quichotte*. He didn't want to think about the fate of the crews. Hell, the things he'd seen this day.

Beyond the town, all was relatively quiet. Too quiet. Just the rumble of distant guns to the north, the twilight sky there, like a second sunset, aglow with scarlet and amber. Argentan? Possible.

A long walk along a forest road, alive with the nerve-rattling sounds of animal life, owls, the bark of a fox, the buzz of insects.

A hand slapped his neck, or so he thought. He jumped a mile, swore, spun around, swiped away the offending attacker. Stag beetle, huge claws, now on its back on the road. His first instinct was to stamp on the damned thing but, in the end, he simply helped it flip over and away it flew.

He was still shaking when he spotted the oil lamps of the *Rochambelles* burning in the walled orchard away to his left. Always orchards. Decent protection, he supposed. And, hell, there were enough of them around.

At the nearest of the ambulances, Toto Torrès was stripped to her bra, washing herself from an enamel bowl. She turned at the sound of his footsteps.

'Isn't it Rule Six, Lieutenant?' he said. 'About never receiving male visitors dressed in less than army-issue long underwear?'

Surprisingly, she greeted him with a smile. Tiny face, but when she grinned, it was literally from ear to ear.

'I wasn't expecting to be receiving anybody, *Monsieur* Telford.' She took a towel, dried under her arms. 'Dropped in for a social call, I suppose?'

'Is she here?'

'You're in luck. Two trucks back.' She pointed but, by then, Dani had heard his voice, come running to him, settled in his arms. When she finally pulled herself free, Jack saw the silent, imploring look she directed at Torrès. 'You know how many rules this breaks?' Toto shook her head and rubbed her hair in the towel. 'Go on, see if Denise is happy to bunk down with Crapette and Zizon maybe. But if there's any fuss...'

There wasn't, and thirty minutes later they'd settled into Dani's own bunk together. Clumsy lovemaking, even with the back doors open, against the heat of the night, regardless of the mosquitoes.

Shared whisperings – Jack drawn into tales of his childhood, his mother. He held Danielle's hand.

'Ring?' he said, and she pulled a slender neck chain from inside her vest. It held both her dog tags and the ring.

'Seriously?' she smiled. 'You think I was going to get this covered in engine grease?'

They slept. The sleep of the just, Jack's best night's rest for many days. But at first light he was suddenly awake. Something wrong. The whole Dodge vibrating, as though some minor earthquake had them in its grip, At the same time, Toto's voice, deceptively forceful for her size.

'That's far enough,' he heard her shouted command.

Jack eased himself from the blankets, put his hand gently over Danielle's mouth as she began to stir.

'Quiet,' he murmured. 'Something...' He crawled to the grille between the ambulance body and the cab, peered through to the windscreen and the morning mist beyond. 'Christ,' he said. '*Boches.*'

The square hulk of a Tiger tank squatted in their path. Beyond, in the haze, stretched an entire column of vehicles, each truck, half-track and tank packed with troops.

And there was Toto, diminutive, fists balled on her hips, facing down both the Tiger and the column's commander, a major maybe.

'Don't let them take me, Jack,' Danielle begged him, gripping his arm. 'Whatever happens...'

At the back of the ambulance, a furtive movement behind the next truck. One of the doctors, an Austrian Jew, who now called himself Valéry. Jack had met him a few times, liked him, but now he was slipping quietly into the shadows and then into the forest's edge. The danger to Danielle was clear and present. The other girls as well. Several of them Jews – including Torrès.

'I have no choice, Lieutenant,' said the German officer, leather jacket, impeccable French. 'I need to search all your vehicles. And then, I'm afraid, take you all as prisoners.'

'You shall search nothing *Herr Major,*' Toto snapped back. 'Nothing. We are neutral noncombatants serving the Red Cross. This is a violation of our rights.'

'Mother of God,' Dani murmured. 'The boys at the back. They came up last night, asked to bed down here. Must warn them, get them to make themselves scarce'

'They'll have worked that out for themselves,' said Jack.

'I am *Oberst* Steiner, Lieutenant. And I have no alternative.'

There was a German soldier, a submachine gun, making his way towards the ambulance.

'I said far enough, *Herr Oberst*,' Toto yelled. 'Get that man away from there. I mean it. There *will* be consequences.'

The officer stared down at her, his face set like stone. Jack reached carefully for the trenching tool, hanging on the ambulance wall, the only thing even vaguely resembling a weapon.

'Just in case,' he whispered. 'But they won't find you, my sweet. I promise.'

He glanced back through the grille.

'Very well, Lieutenant,' snarled the German, and yelled to the soldier with the submachine gun. '*Obergefreiter*, back here!'

The soldier retreated back to the *Oberst*'s side.

'And – the body,' Danielle stammered.

'Body?'

'German,' she whispered, panic in her voice. 'The boys brought him in yesterday. Prisoner. SS, but badly wounded. Arrogant little bastard, kept telling us we'd lost the war. Some new secret weapon. We tried to give him a transfusion. But he refused. Said we were trying to poison him. Jew blood, he said. Or *neger* blood. Died soon after. They planned to bury him this morning. If they find it, the body…'

Outside, Torrès still stood her ground.

'I demand right of passage, *Herr Oberst*. And besides,' she glanced towards the German column, 'it doesn't exactly look as though you have any capacity to *take* us prisoners.'

'A search, then. Just the search.'

'Did you not hear me? No search. You have no right. And this is probably not the best place for you to squander whatever time may be left you.'

The German scratched at his chin.

'A dilemma, Lieutenant, as you say. But can I trust you? A

compromise, perhaps. You give me your parole, no? You remain here for the next two hours. After that, you're free to proceed.'

Jack saw Toto look back along her line of ambulances.

'Very well, *Herr Oberst*. But can I trust *you*?'

'Lieutenant...' he began, then shook his head, turned to the Tiger tank. 'Get moving! *Schnell*.'

The tank's engine roared into life, quickly followed by the other vehicles in the German column. Toto stood to one side, as they slowly began to pass. And it seemed to Jack that the troops turned their heads away, as though pretending the ambulances weren't really there. The German officer clicked his heels, saluted Torrès, and jumped into a passing *kubelwagen*.

By the time the last of the German trucks passed through the southern gates of the orchard, the rest of the *Rochambelles* had emerged from wherever they'd been hiding to watch them go. Jack, out on the grass, found himself stupidly still gripping the trenching tool, Danielle tucked under his arm. But Toto had clambered onto the roof of her own truck, one hand shading her eyes, watching the direction of the German retreat.

'Well done, girls,' she shouted. 'But now, let's get rolling.'

'Lieutenant?' said one of the drivers. 'Two hours?'

'Rule Thirty,' she replied. 'Know how to handle the Germans any way that doesn't result in deserving to have your head shaved. Two hours? Stuff it. We need to get to the nearest unit, report exactly where those bastards are heading. Call in an air strike.'

Jack had no idea whether the American planes would have found and destroyed *Oberst* Steiner's column, and he supposed he'd never know but, by the time he'd made his way back to Écouché, the Yankee aircraft had certainly found *La Nueve*.

Two platoons, another in reserve, had moved out to form a new line, to the north and west, towards Udon, and there the American fighters had taken them for the enemy, destroyed a half-track, the tank *Bir Hakeim*, and one of Leclerc's original Spaniards, García – who'd been with them at Kufra – shot to hell, his arms and legs. He was now in the care of a medical team. Tough devil, they'd said. He'd make it.

'And this column, *Monsieur* Telford,' Dronne pressed him. 'Never mind where it was headed, where the hell had it come from?'

'Straight down the forest road, Captain, as far as I could tell. From here.'

Dronne pushed the *képi* back on his head, scraped at his beard, studied the map spread on the table in the half-destroyed farmhouse kitchen serving as his headquarters.

'Impossible,' he muttered. 'No front line. Our units, the *Boches*, all mixed up. No idea whether the bastards are ahead of us or behind.'

'Same for them,' said Amado, leaning against the wall.

'But now an entire column's simply slipped past us in the night,' said Dronne. 'Where are the bloody Americans, the British? Supposed to be keeping them bottled up. But this...'

He thumped the table, as Reiter came in, beard even more unkempt than usual, holding a folded sheet of paper. Behind him, Miguel Campos.

'Captain,' said Campos. 'There's a boy. From Mesnil-Glaise.' A village just a mile or so away, a loop in the Orne. 'Reckons one of the *Boches* officers at the château there asked him to deliver this.'

Dronne took the letter from him and Granell came to look over his shoulder.

'Looks authentic,' he said.

'Says he's the *Oberst* responsible for the hospital at the château. Wants to evacuate his patients under a flag of truce.'

'Garrison?' said Amado.

'Wehrmacht in one wing. He has no idea how they'll respond. The other wing? SS. They'll fight, whatever happens.'

'Then it's a trap, surely,' said Jack.

'Or a prize,' said Dronne. 'Mesnil-Glaise. If we're able to take it without too much trouble, we may be able to turn the flank of our friends out there on the high ground. What d'you think, *mis cosacos*?'

His Cossacks. They loved it. The whole company. And it was appropriate. Wild warriors, fast-moving, ruthless.

'We could take a half-track each, *Patron*,' Campos shrugged his shoulders. 'Check it out. If it looks like a trap – well, we'll see.'

'Good,' Dronne smiled. 'And you, *Monsieur* Telford, how's your German coming along?'

'My German?'

'If there are as many *Boches* there as this letter implies, we can hardly expect Reiter to translate for all of them. He'll need help. You have a problem?'

Jack wasn't entirely certain. It sounded risky.

'No problem, Captain,' he replied, despite his fears. 'And it may be a good story.'

Birdsong. The forest road was otherwise quiet, peaceful. Scent of pine. It climbed the vertiginous bluff above the river, the village running along the winding bank below.

The half-tracks had ground to a halt, side by side, just in view of the château. Every village had one. Square central block with tall chimneys and Cinderella pointed towers at each corner. Jack took a photograph.

'*Hostia!*' said Campos, staring through his binoculars. 'What the hell...?'

Reiter, in the second half-track, stood behind the heavy machine gun to get a better look.

'Evacuation under way,' he said. 'Loading the wounded into trucks. Can't see...'

'Not there,' said Campos. 'The grounds.'

Jack stood also, pulled down the knitted peak of his jeep cap against the morning sun, flickering through the trees. Behind the château, the low wall and railings, a gated driveway. A convoy of lorries and ambulances each flying a white flag. Stretchers and walking wounded.

Beyond the driveway, formal gardens, and the focus of *el canario*'s surveillance, but Jack couldn't see anything significantly out of place. Just more greenery.

'Can I see, Lieutenant?'

'*Seguro.*' Campos handed over the binoculars. Jack adjusted them, gazed through the right eyepiece, found those hedgerows again.

'Good god,' he said. Not hedges at all, but row after row of German green uniforms, Wehrmacht, the soldiers all apparently unarmed, many bareheaded, sitting on the grass. *Le Déjeuner sur l'herbe*, thought Jack. Without the nude, of course – though there *was*, in the midst of the Germans, a rather splendid statue of a naked cherub. He wished he was close enough to take the snap. 'They waiting to be evacuated?'

'Not part of the deal,' said Campos. 'Just the wounded.'

'The rest?' said Jack. 'Those others'

'English,' Campos laughed at him. 'They're Germans. On the other hand...'

'How many?' asked Reiter.

'Can't tell. Maybe a hundred. Worth – Christ, could be four hundred litres. But what the hell would we do with them?'

Each half-track a rifle squad, more or less. This morning, two dozen of them in total, and that included Telford. For a hundred potential prisoners? But Jack could see the calculations being made. They'd begun taking prisoners a week ago, longer. Then realised that, while they had no value to the battalion, there was some strange process among the GIs – almost merit points for the number of prisoners they brought in. Simple, the Spaniards set up an exchange rate. Roughly twenty litres of gasoline from the Yanks for every five Germans they brought in. Three officers? A couple of sheep or a pig.

They agreed to wait, but Campos sent out his three-man scouting team to watch the road behind, and eventually the convoy pulled out through the gate towards them. As the leading truck pulled alongside, an officer sprang from the cab, an armband with a red cross, introduced himself, in French, as *Oberstartzt* – Senior Surgeon, Reiter explained – Schäfer. Yes, he'd sent the letter. Campos confirmed they were free to go, safe passage, although he couldn't guarantee what would happen further east.

'But those?' he said and pointed towards the grounds.

'They want to surrender, Lieutenant. But in the far wing, there's a Waffen SS unit. *They* will not surrender – you know this. Barricaded themselves. Good luck, *messieurs*. Oh, and I forgot. The Americans – we left them in their beds. But the SS...'

'Americans?' said Reiter. 'Wounded?'

'Wounded prisoners.' The German climbed back into his truck, sheets hanging on the side with makeshift painted red crosses.

The convoy pulled out, and they watched it wind its way down the hill.

Campos recalled his scouts and they made their plans. The whole thing sounded crazy to Jack. But the half-tracks had soon taken up their station on either side of the gates, their machine guns trained on those rows of seated Germans. Now they were closer, it was plain many of these were injured, bandaged heads, arms in slings. But they were a sorry-looking bunch. A soldier limped towards them carrying a filthy once-white rag. Reiter went to meet him, yelled back that, yes, surrender.

'And the SS?'

'He's not sure. Maybe twenty of them. The Americans in this wing. SS in that one.' Reiter pointed to the far side of the château.

'You tell the bastard,' Campos yelled. 'Tell him. These beauties stay here.' He patted the barrel of his own machine gun. 'Anything, anything that upsets my friend Pablo, and they're all dead. Does he understand?'

The soldier understood, and Campos sent a couple of his scouts to cover the rows of Germans. Jack went with them, took a few pictures. But the stink. And the scratching. All of them, lice ridden. Sunken eyes. Lost. Defeated. They reminded him of the columns he'd seen struggling into Alicante, the beaten remnants of the Republic's army. Of course, Granell had been among them, many of the other Spaniards also. A strange twist of fates.

Inside the château, it was eerily quiet. A main hall, staircase, some ancestral portraits on the walls, but mainly empty frames, the place stripped bare. There was a fireplace in the first room on the right, a dining table, perfectly clean square shapes and rectangles in the dust on the mahogany and the mantle shelf. Jack imagined the Louis Quinze clock, the ormolu candlesticks, which must once have graced the place. All gone. Looted, of course.

From one of the rooms above, coughing. Cautiously, they climbed the stairs, found a room, a hospital ward. The Americans, eight of them, a couple in a bad way.

'Leave them,' yelled Campos. 'First, we clear the other wing. *El que a hierro mata, a hierro muere.*' *El canario*'s favourite saying. Live by the sword, die by the sword. That sort of thing. But, for Campos, a simple code. No prisoners.

And clear them they did. Room by room. Floor by floor. A

few grenades, suppressing fire, until each of the SS soldiers was dead, those who were merely wounded finished with a shot from Campos's pistol.

In the following silence, birdsong once more. Birdsong, the thing Jack noticed where, once, there would have been horror – outrage perhaps – at the cold brutality of it all.

Reiter's driver was dispatched in one of the half-tracks. Ambulances needed for the Yanks. The prisoners – one hundred and twenty-nine of them, when they'd been been properly counted – started under guard for the forced march back to the Division's lines, wherever the hell that might now be.

When the ambulances arrived, it was the British Quakers, young Bill Spray – actually a Methodist, it turned out – in command of the section. In the wrong place, as it happened. Should have been over with Langlade's combat group, but welcome all the same.

Jack rode with him to Patton's new forward headquarters, relocating from Laval to the outskirts of Alençon, a field hospital and, of course, the Information and Communications Service. From there he was able to have his films developed, to dispatch copy to Bunnelle, to use the Wirephoto copier and transmitter to send his best images, and to get a censored letter off to Sydney Elliott.

He was also able to mingle with many of the other correspondents. Pierre Lefèvre again, from the Beeb's French Service. And the actor turned war correspondent, Jacques Brunius. Therapeutic. The company of colleagues, and he struck up an instant friendship with Marcel Ouimet, the French Canadian, who seemed to have been in the thick of the fighting just about everywhere.

Yet his main aim, of course, was to track Dani down. And it was Bill Spray who gave him the lead. Most of the *Rochambelles* now at Leclerc's own headquarters. Fleuré, just to the east of Écouché, a little further along the Orne.

He managed to hitch a lift with a motorcycle dispatch rider. Exhilarating, the wind in his face. Mostly open farmlands here, fields of wheat, some already reduced to stubble and bound hay bales. But elsewhere the golden harvest still in full swing, horse-drawn threshing machines, farmhands and their forks following behind to make sure every stalk and spike should be taken up by the blades. Late harvest, he guessed, after all that foul weather in June. It made a pleasant change from the French countryside to which he'd become accustomed, the blighted farms, the dead live-stock, horses and cattle, left to bloat, their legs pointing skywards. But here? The sky was blue, songbirds dipped and dived. Almost idyllic.

So, too, was Fleuré itself. Tiny, on one of the many back lanes to Argentan. An ancient church and, alongside, the *mairie*. Attached to this modest town hall, an annexe. Outside, Leclerc's command vehicles, his tank *Tailly*, as well as his personal Jeep. Across the lane, on some open ground, some of his commanders' Jeeps, half-tracks and, of course, more tanks.

All bustle, other messengers coming and going. Jack slapped his own rider on the back, thanked him profusely as he dismounted stiffly from the small pillion seat.

'Telford, old boy. *Quelle surprise.*'

Fox. It seemed he'd acquired a new uniform. British, of course. Always dapper, naturally. He ran a finger along his David Niven moustache.

'Off the beaten track, this place?' said Jack, as they lit cigarettes.

'You see? That's what makes you such a damned good journalist. Nail straight on the head. Reason they sent me back again. Balloon's gone up, I'm afraid. But fancy a stroll? Left my own wheels at the church.'

'All done in there?' said Jack as they headed back down the street.

'Doesn't trust me. English, of course. Doesn't trust any of us – apart from you, maybe, Telford. But just look at you. Getting more like a Yank every day. Woollen cap, eye patch. Quite the buccaneer.'

Jack laughed.

'A view shared, it seems, by half the Spanish boys. *Pirata*, they call me. Or *pirata inglés*. I heard the rumours about Leclerc, though. They're calling him the Scarlet Pimpernel, aren't they?'

The Allied commanders trying to work out precisely where Leclerc and his main force might be but meeting only obfuscation from Patton and his generals. The scuttlebutt reckoned there'd been agreement from Patton that, at the right moment, the Second Armoured Division might make a quick dash for Paris, almost a surpise attempt to liberate the city. But Montgomery and Bradley entirely opposed to the plan.

'Scarlet Pimpernel, indeed,' Fox laughed, as they reached the old church. 'Top brass are furious. Never know where he is. Then they pick up stories about Leclerc's men trading prisoners for extra gasoline, getting ready to take Paris for themselves.'

'Surely not,' said Jack, trying to keep his face straight.

Fox studied him a moment, raised an eyebrow but decided not to pursue the matter.

'Here's my Jeep,' he said, and received a smart salute from his driver. 'Need a lift anywhere?' Well, as it happened, Jack told him, he was trying to find the ambulance unit and Fox was happy to oblige. 'Anyway,' he went on, while they settled themselves in the vehicle, 'they're not having it. Easier to bypass the city, keep striking eastwards. Eisenhower's direct instruction. Avoid Paris. A distraction. And besides, if we took it, we'd have to manage it afterwards, feed them all.'

'And perish the thought we should do anything so stupid, yes? But if it turns out to be another Warsaw?'

Poor bloody Warsaw. Knowing the Red Army was approaching fast, on the very day Leclerc was landing at Omaha Beach, the valiant Polish Resistance had risen in armed insurrection against the German army of occupation. By then, the Russians had reached the outskirts of the city – but there they'd stopped. Despite this, for the first few days, according to reports, the Poles had begun to drive the Germans out. Street fighting as vicious as anything at Stalingrad. Afterwards, the inevitable. German counterattacks. Terrible massacres of the city's citizens, armed or otherwise. The city being destroyed, building by building. It wasn't over – but it might as well have been. And still the Russians sat on the sidelines, watched and waited.

'Thompson, pull over here, would you?' The driver swung

off the road, and they sat for a moment, gazing out over the fields, to a small wood with crows wheeling above it. 'Another Warsaw,' he said, 'is precisely what de Gaulle fears. And *le patron*, back there at the *mairie*, fears it even more. De Gaulle's due back from Washington in a couple of days. After that, we'll see.'

'But meanwhile you'll let the top brass know you've found Leclerc, I suppose?'

'Well, between you, me and the gatepost, it was just a matter of luck. Quicker than I'd thought. Don't think anybody will be expecting to hear from me for a few days. And it's damned pleasant here, don't you think? Maybe catch up with a few old acquaintances, Telford, no? There's one of those French nurses, rather took my fancy. And it would be remiss of me not to check the state of morale in the Division. Help to flesh out my report a bit.'

He asked about the Company and Jack gave him a quick account of the fighting at Écouché.

'You remember García? From Kufra?' Of course, he did. 'Shot to pieces,' said Jack. 'Though they say he'll survive.'

'Poor devil,' said Fox. 'Sometimes the dead are the lucky ones. But what about you, old chap – and that girl of yours?'

'Reason I'm here, naturally. We should find them up one of these lanes on the left.'

'Then lay on, MacDuff. Let us gird our loins and make haste to find the fair maiden. Thompson, drive on!'

They sat against the trunk of yet another apple tree in yet another orchard – not far from the farmhouse where Leclerc had his spartan personal quarters, normally no more than his campaign bed, or a simple bedroll spread on the floor. Danielle nestled against Jack's chest.

'I was wondering,' he murmured. 'Where we might live, when this is all over. England? Here?'

'After we're married?' she said.

'Yes.' He nodded his head, though that idea, being married, still seemed so alien to him.

'Then I don't care, Jack. So long as it's near the beach. For the children.'

It was like an electric shock.

'Children?'

'Yes,' she laughed. 'Like small people – tiny hands and feet. But they grow, learn how to walk and talk almost like us, my love.'

'Very funny,' he said. 'I just hadn't thought so far ahead.'

'Then you'd better start, *Monsieur* Telford. You know me, I'm a Toulouse girl. No idea about good places to be, one side of *La Manche* or the other.'

Jack knew the north coast of France pretty well, but how much of those beautiful towns – Deauville and so many others – would survive all this? How long to rebuild? It didn't bear thinking about. But the Dorset coast? Devon? Almost made him enthusiastic.

'I'll give it some thought,' he said. 'Pity I can't stay the night, though. Two heads better than one, you know?'

He tickled her.

'Bloody Toto,' she said between fits of giggles.

But Lieutenant Torrès had been plain. Even invented a new rule to cover the situation. They'd be on the move in the morning. Everything had to be shipshape. So, no romantic distractions.

'Tonight,' she'd said to her assembled crews, 'you get all the sleep you can. Tomorrow, first light, we head out. Écouché, girls. Écouché.'

The German counterattack began next morning, a Wednesday, *La Nueve*'s fourth day in Écouché.

Fox had found a room for himself in the village, at the Belleville, but Jack had gone in search of Granell, discovered him with some of the men in a ruined house, in that cluster of lanes between the Cance and the Orne. There was no roof, but the remains of the beams and floorboards put at least some sort of shelter over their heads. They'd managed to scrape spaces for their bedrolls among the rubble of the former kitchen.

'They've sent up more armour,' Jack had said to Amado. 'Anything going on?'

Tanks, tank destroyers, a couple of small artillery pieces.

'*Papi* Putz,' Granell laughed. 'Inspecting the line yesterday. Reckoned he could smell it on the wind. When the cicada sings, it's going to get hot, he said. You know? The way he does? Called up the heavy stuff. No more men, though. But, so far...'

There they slept, undisturbed by the occasional burst of gunfire somewhere in the distance. And, at dawn, one of the men settled to brewing coffee – more bartered trade goods – while Méndez took himself off to the *boulangerie* to see if there was any chance of a baguette or two. Jack went with him as far as the Cance bridge, climbed down to the stream's edge, rummaged for the razor in his haversack and shaved.

By the time he got back, there was the luxury of warm bread, the coffee, and slabs of cheese. But they never had the chance to finish their feast. One of their outlying pickets, López, scrambled through the ruins with two of the local Resistance men, *los fifi*, at his back.

'*Teniente*,' he said. 'Tanks.'

'Where?' said Granell, jumping to his feet, and the others followed suit.

'We were at the mill. The village up beyond the wood...'

'Serans?' Amado pulled a battered map from his combat jacket. 'Here?'

'Serans, yes,' said one of the Frenchmen.

'Volunteers?' Granell looked around the men with him, but the question was simply rhetorical. As if any of them wouldn't have followed Amado. They gathered their equipment, checked their weapons, while the lieutenant turned to Jack. 'Patrol, *inglés*. Want to join us?'

'You're going to look for German tanks, and then...?' Jack glanced around the faces, some of them friends now, others he didn't know, but they were all grinning at him. Telford, *el pirata inglés*. Oh hell, he thought, found himself slinging his satchel over one shoulder, his camera over the other, and settling the woollen peaked cap onto his head. 'Ready when you are,' he said.

They followed the arc of the Cance from their current position near the bridge and the main road through the village, heading east and steadily north, keeping to the farther side, the high bank like a natural trench, crowned by willows, alders and birch, the dense green of ferns. Plenty of protection. Jack knew the ground.

If they'd carried on, through the open countryside, then followed the stream's curve southwards again, in a mile they would hit the railway bridges, the line to Argentan. Yet they only needed to cover a third of that distance to a spot where the Cance divided around an island, forcing the stream's normally sluggish flow into twin torrents, mill races, the mill itself and its wooden paddle wheels sitting like a solid bastion between.

Granell signalled for one of the boys to cross, to scout the building. Nothing, the mill not in operation, just as they'd expected.

They climbed the bank, scattered themselves along the treeline – and there, clear as hell, the squeak and metallic sqeal of armour on the move not too far away. But where?

The ground climbed in front of them across open pastureland to a small wood and, rising far beyond the trees, the top of a church steeple. Serans, Jack assumed.

To their right, a fold in the fields curved away and upwards.

'Cortés,' Granell said to one of the sergeants, 'take Méndez and scout up through this gulley. See what's going on in the wood. Rest of you? Firing line, here.'

The two men set off up the slope, but they didn't get far. A stretch of open grassland and then that strange sound of curtain material being ripped apart. Burst of continuous sound, rather than a staccato of shots. The German machine gun the Spaniards had come to call the buzz-saw. What had Amado said? Twenty-five rounds every second?

Jack saw the dirt it kicked up, watched Méndez spin and fall, Cortés dragging him back into some sort of cover and, from the wood, a German half-track, running down the gulley towards them.

'Pujol,' shouted Amado. 'Help them. The rest of you, get ready.'

He checked his Thompson again, took a couple of grenades from their pouches and laid them alongside. Jack looked at them, remembered the training they'd had at Sabratha, recalled the fool who'd almost killed him there.

Pujol was in the gulley now, bent double, helped Cortés bring Méndez back to safety, just as that bloody half-track came into full view, its heavy machine gun ripping apart the branches and leaves above Telford's head, and the soldiers it carried spilling from the back, a dozen of them, spreading out in a skirmish line.

Granell took down three of them almost at once. But the machine gun, thought Jack. How…?

Away to their right, there was another thin line of trees and bushes, presumably separating one field from the next and, from there, came the means of their salvation. The crackle of flanking carbine fire, the machine gunner falling, and Lieutenant Amado Granell on his feet again, yelling to his men, like some Viking berserker, to follow him.

Telford would never understand why, but he followed, scooped up those grenades. Something told him if he stayed close to Amado, very close, no harm could befall him and the rising roll of the ground protected them from whatever else was in that woodland.

The Germans decided to fall back, or to take shelter around the half-track, one of them clambering into the vehicle, making a grab for the machine gun.

Granell turned towards Jack, snatched one of the grenades, pulled the pin as he ran forward, tossed it inside the half-track. A second blew it to hell, a blazing wreck, and by then the rest of the *Boches* were dead.

Back in the trees, Telford's old friend from Toledo, Alemán, used Cortés's medical kit – more substantial supplies for sergeants – to help Méndez. Bullet in his thigh but didn't seemed to have hit anything serious. Still, he writhed in agony while Alemán, with help from Jack, cut away the trousers, cleaned the wounds with an iodine swab, applied what was actually supposed to be the eye dressing, secured it with the three-inch gauze bandage, a large safety pin and, finally, stabbed one of the tubes of morphine tartrate into the bare flesh.

'*Inglés*, you coming or staying here?' Granell, of course.

'Where?'

'Meet up with some friends.'

Jack followed him, both of them keeping low. The rest of the boys had moved up, along the gulley, but keeping clear of the dead ground, and they were laying down fire on the wood, with its unseen enemies. Amado led the way to that farther tree line where they met up with another lieutenant, Michel Elías, a *pied noir* settler from Algeria, though a Catalan by birth. At his side, another giant of a man, Martín Bernal.

'Good job you happened along, Michel,' said Amado and they shook hands.

'Patrolling back the other way,' said Elías. 'From the railway. But all quiet. Then we heard this.'

They agreed to clear the wood, Granell's boys keeping up a suppressing fire while Elías and his men would follow the tree line north, check what was happening in the village of Serans, now ominously quiet, then double back to the trees. It took them no more than thirty minutes, two buzz-saw nests cleaned out, and the two groups resting, smoking, back near the still burning half-track.

'The village?' said Granell, and Elías shook his head.

'Nothing. They're gone.'

'What's happening,' Jack asked, getting the Rollieflex ready. 'They waiting for reinforcements? Why the caution?'

'They have no idea how many we are – or how few. And *Papi* Putz has had our own armour up and down the roads every night. They must think we've got hundreds of them. Barbirrojo's no fool either. Every day we give them shit from different positions. Keeps them confused.'

'Panzers – confused?' said Jack. He persuaded them to pose for photographs with the half-track in the background, some of the German dead. Bunnelle would like these.

Yet, as he slipped the camera back into its case, in Écouché all hell broke loose. The ground shook beneath their feet and, as they looked back along the river, explosion after explosion, tanks in action, both sides.

'Now we know why the tanks from Serans disappeared,' said Amado. 'Come on, *compañeros*. We're needed.'

He set off down to the riverbank.

'Méndez?' said Jack.

'Up to you, *inglés*,' said Granell. 'You can come if you want. Or stay with him. But he's got morphine. And you – well, you might miss a good story, no?'

Good story? Hell, for most of the day, Telford had no idea what was happening.

He remembered their march back along the treeline, the north bank of the Cance, the roaring inferno of the battle ahead more deafening with each running step they took. He remembered their brief halt at the churned terrain, west of the mill, where the Panzer division – or divisions, maybe – had crossed the Orne. He rememberd the scouts Granell sent out, returning to confirm that the whole German force was now before them, not on their flank, or to their rear. He remembered the stocktake Amado made of all their weapons and ammunition. And he remembered the lieutenant's advice to him.

'Either stay here, English. Or stick to me like glue.'

After that? Confusion. The first dwellings on the outskirts of Écouché were in view, what was left of them – those between the Orne to their right, and the Cance to their left. Jack tried to locate the ruined house in which they'd spent the previous night, but the entire district was now just flattened rubble, German tanks hull-down among whatever was left. Five of them, maybe six. *Boches* soldiers flitting from cover to cover. But into their positions, French shells screaming down from beyond the Cance bridge. As he watched, Telford saw one of the tanks picked up like a matchbox, spin into the air and explode.

Then they were in the middle of them, the closest of the Panzergrenadiers entirely unaware the enemy was to *their* rear. Bloodbath. Jack had seen most of these boys fight before. But not like this. Deadly. Ruthless. Smoke and flame, a screeching hell. Granell on the back of the tank they'd reached, pulling open the turret hatch and emptying his Thompson into the interior, then jumping down beside Telford again, dragging him to cover as one of their own incoming shells ripped up the earth just behind them.

Through the vertigo, the nausea and the mind-numbing deafness, Jack saw one of their own – he couldn't tell who it might be – simply torn apart, nothing left.

They were trapped. The remains of a house, their backs to the Cance. Come so far. Yet the bridge was still a hundred yards to their left, though even if they'd managed to fight their way through, the bridge itself was so heavily defended by the Germans, they'd never be able to cross. And they'd penetrated the enemy positions so fast, the Germans had now moved in behind *them*. As more and more of the Spaniards came in, it became clear this would be their last stand.

'Just like Oran,' said Granell. 'No, *inglés*?'

Jack was exhausted, couldn't control his shakes. But yes, he nodded his head vigorously.

'Like Oran,' he murmured, took the canteen of water Amado offered him. 'Except...'

'Except bloody nothing, *compañero*,' said Granell, then yelled to the others. '*No pasarán! No pasarán!*'

And they each took it up, the slogan which had become such a symbol of their own civil war, of the defence of Madrid. They shall not pass. Grenades. Bullets. Tank shells. An inferno of blood and death.

Except what? Telford's brain tried to register the thought. Except...

Except, in Oran, he finally realised, the cavalry had come to rescue them.

With this thought, from somewhere very close behind him, the ear-shattering *crump, crump* of artillery shells. He felt the wind of their passing, just above his head, taking his breath away. He smelled the stink of their cordite. He saw the roiling clouds of dust and flame, the punishment they rained down on the enemy. And, close by, he heard the triumphant shouts of more men from the Company as they charged in from the flanking attack made to rescue Granell's beleaguered defenders.

They might be back behind their own lines, but you'd almost not have known it. There *were* no lines anymore.

Amado had left him in the only building close at hand still with an upper floor – no roof, but an upper floor, though much of the walls destroyed. Another mill, only fifty yards west of the Cance bridge. And here their good Captain Dronne had established his forward observation and communications post. Below, two men with the radio transmitter, receiver and handset. Above, near

Jack, Fermín Pujol, a marksman, with the Springfield rifle and its telescopic sights he cradled like a coddled infant.

From here, Telford could look down, even take a few photographs of the killing grounds, that landscape between the Cance and the Orne – a landscape of blackened craters, brick and masonry mountains, burning armoured cars, occasional columns of still standing grey stone. Through this terrain, the constant echo of tanks, the squeal of their tracks as they manoeuvred from one location to another, or the bellow of their engines as they clawed their way over the mounds of debris. The stink of gasoline, smoke and oil, which filled Jack's lungs. He could taste it on his lips, his tongue. Yet, through it all, through the fog of war, he could also see the macabre and continuous dance of the men in the grip of this cauldron – men who flitted through the shadowed ruins, men who rolled from hole to hole, men who raced from cover to cover to cover, and men who were occasionally unlucky enough to be caught in the open, and inevitably paid the price.

In this way, Jack and Fermín saw the sniper's brother, Constantino, wounded and fallen. And while Fermín struggled against Telford's restraining grip, the Spaniard insisting he was going to bring his brother to safety, Jack watched in horror as a section of Panzergrenadiers occupied the same position, their officer putting two bullets through Constantino's head. With tears streaming through the grime of his face, Fermín Pujol used the Springfield to wreak revenge on the officer and most of his men. It was a better comfort than anything Telford could have offered him.

Hour after endless hour, ground gained, ground lost. Amado and one of the bazooka teams from the anti-tank squad killing two more of the enemy tanks, while a trickle of *La Nueve*'s wounded began to crawl or be carried across to this nearer side of the Cance, and here were the stretcher-bearers come to help them.

Jack decided he might be a damned sight more useful down there than skulking in the mill with his notebooks and camera. But before he left Fermín Pujol, he gripped the Catalan's trembling shoulders.

'I'm sorry, Fermín,' he said. It was entirely inadequate. Though, on this day, of all days, it stretched his eloquence to the limits.

Écouché's impressive church of Notre-Dame had stood for seven centuries. But now the solid walls of its north transept, its apse and the squat central tower were peppered with shell holes, pockmarked by bullets.

Inside, the parish priest, *Père* Berger, had turned over the entire nave to a section of the Division's medical battalion for a field hospital, doctors and nurses, as well as a couple of the chaplains from the White Fathers.

Père Berger had made quite a name for himself these past few days. Everywhere, helping to bring in the wounded, to make sure the dead were buried in hallowed ground, regardless of the whisperings from his sacristan that these were Communists, atheists. None of it mattered to *Père* Berger.

'Poor man,' said Toto Torrès, when Jack found her at the church, waiting for the nurses to finish fresh dressings, another wounded warrior about to be sent to the rear. 'His pride and joy. Thinks it's his own fault, somehow.'

A stone statue of the Sacred Heart in an alcove above the altar, Christ with his arms wide, waiting to embrace the faithful, chest bare among the carved stone robes, the heart exposed, surrounded by a sunburst motif. Yet now it lay shattered in a hundred pieces.

'I think that's called Catholic guilt,' Jack whispered.

Like everybody else, Toto's face, already grey with fatigue, was grimed with filth. Her eyes bloodshot, dark circles around them. She called to a nurse, still dressing the significant burns of her patient, asked how long before they could get him on the road to Alençon.

'Time for a smoke?' she said, once the nurse told her the boy wouldn't be ready for at least fifteen minutes.

From the porch, they slipped out through the modest double doors onto the lane and quickly round to the east side of the church, safer there, in the lee of the firestorm, where several ambulances waited to make the same journey. He felt a surge of hope, a thrill of excitement in his heart when he saw them.

'Is she…?'

'I'm sorry, *Monsieur* Telford. Danielle's at Argentan – or she was, last time I checked.'

The fighting there, just six miles away, remained at least as heavy as here, at Écouché. Day after day, the rest of Leclerc's Division tied down just to the south of the city.

'But safe? Well?'

'That's a bloody stupid question. Not a single one of the girls has had more than a couple of hours sleep over the past four or five days. I can't believe they've kept going.'

'Maybe you've inspired them, Lieutenant. And I heard a story. About a lynching?'

'Oh, I'm sure the scuttlebutt will have played it up.'

'The way I heard it,' said Jack, 'you were stopped in some village by a mob on the road, dragging two young women with shaved heads to a tree where they'd rigged up a couple of nooses.'

'More or less.'

'And you threatened to blow them to hell if they didn't release them.'

'Guilty,' said Toto, and blew a series of smoke rings into the air.

'But you don't carry weapons.'

'Fortunately, they didn't look too closely at the truck's grease gun I pointed at them.'

Jack laughed.

'Collaborators, though,' he said. 'Whores for the Germans?'

'You think there would have been anybody in that damned place who *hadn't* tried to turn a profit from the *Boches*?'

Telford remembered his road south from Pamplona, the village where a young mother's hair was being shorn from her head, simply because her husband was away, fighting for the Republic. He'd not been much help.

'Well, good for you,' he said. 'But what the hell did you do with them?'

'The girls donated headscarves, and we turned them loose on the road to Alençon. Said they had people there who'd look after them.' She threw the cigarette stub away. 'I'll tell her I've seen you,' said Toto. 'And don't worry, I'll look after her.'

Torrès headed back into the church to collect her patient. Jack helped with the stretcher, but as Toto pulled away, another truck arrived. Behind it, Dronne's Jeep, with the captain and Amado

Granell. From the truck, twenty raw recruits. Spotless uniforms and kit. Boys. No more than boys. Since the landings in June, from Normandy and Brittany, there'd been a steady number of young men wanting to volunteer, or to transfer from the Resistance to the regular army.

'Get in line,' shouted Amado. 'Now, in line.'

His orders were in Spanish. Confusion among the newcomers. The language, but also their nervous eyes, flicking towards the sounds of battle, all so horribly close. Dronne stood in the Jeep, addressed them in French.

'Let me explain something to you, *mes braves*,' he shouted, and rubbed at the bottom of his spine. His vehicle had been blown off the road on the long drive to Écouché, and he'd damaged his tailbone. 'It's true you've joined a French regiment. But this Third Battalion – well, it resembles the League of Nations: Portuguese, Brazilians, Italians, Poles, even a bunch of Germans. And French, of course. But *my* Company, our Ninth Company, two-thirds of them are Spaniards.'

An incoming shell ripped more masonry from the church tower. The replacements – and Jack – flinched, covered their heads. But both Dronne, and Amado, remained entirely impassive.

'I call them my Cossacks,' the captain went on, 'because that's what they're like. Tough. Wild. Survivors. Therefore, lesson number one. In your squads, stick to the Spanish boys – *mis cosacos*. Stick to them. Lesson number two? After this, you're not likely to hear much French spoken except, maybe, among yourselves. So, do yourselves a favour and learn Spanish. Learn it *fast*. Because, if you don't...' He looked at the astonished faces staring back at him. 'Lieutenant?'

Granell climbed out of the Jeep. He had a board, paper, a roll call, separated them into smaller sections, three or four each, told them where they'd find their respective squads, led them off up the lane.

'Is that it, Captain?' Jack asked Dronne. 'Our reinforcements?'

Dronne rubbed at his lower back again, pain etched into his face.

'*Le patron*'s just been here, with your friend, Fox. You think

I didn't ask the general the same question, *Monsieur* Telford? But the line is stretched thin, you know that. If he takes even half a company from Argentan, the *Boches* may break through there. And here? What have we got? *La Nueve* lands in Normandy with a hundred and sixty men. Now? Sick, wounded – or… Lost seven here in Écouché alone. Another dozen in the hospital.' He crossed himself. 'May God bless them. The Tenth, it's the same. But we're all there is. And, Reds or not, I couldn't ask for better. So, here we stand. Or here we all die, *mon ami*.'

Jack began his piece for Bunnelle the following morning, planned to record almost exactly the same words – though in Spanish – for Barea. Yet he soon hit a problem.

It would have been impossible to write the piece during the remains of the previous day, for the fighting had continued, still intense, far into the night. But, at last, *Teniente* Montoya – once an officer in the Republic's élite Corps of Carabineers, but now in charge of the Company's First Rifle Platoon – led a counterattack across the rivers, a flanking movement, though with heavy casualties, which finally drove the Germans back across the Orne and, once more, to the higher ground above Écouché.

Most of the men simply slept wherever they happened to be when the fighting finally abated. Yet first light showed exactly how widespread the carnage had been, as the dead – and a few wounded – were brought in, and Dronne set his already exhausted men to the task of rebuilding their defences as best they could, working as one with the men of Geoffroy's Tenth Company. The German corpses – so many of them – were dragged to the more open ground just to the east and dumped into a shallow mass grave.

It was a glorious morning, not a shot fired, though there was always the constant rumble of guns from Argentan. Relatively peaceful, all the same, and when the work finally allowed, Amado joined Jack, squatting in the sun against the wall of Dronne's observation post at the mill, for some breakfast. No coffee and fresh bread today, but their K-rations, supplemented by pieces of hard cheese and cured sausage from the pocket of Granell's combat jacket.

'How the hell long have those been there?' Jack grimaced, as the Spaniard offered to share them, flicking open his slim stiletto to cut a thin slice of the *saucisson*.

They chatted in what had become almost a personal language between them, a rare and random blend of *valenciano* and everyday Spanish, *castellano*.

'When I was a small kid, I'd kept a chunk of *chorizo* hidden in my pocket for as long as I could remember. We weren't as poor as many others, but always hungry. Every day, I'd take the tiniest bite. But kept it secret. I hadn't learned to be a Socialist back then.'

Telford took the sausage, peeled away the outer skin. Granell had always been thin-faced, but now he was almost skeletal.

'Not bad,' said Jack.

'But not *chorizo*,' Amado replied. 'And this,' he glanced about their surroundings, 'not Spain, *inglés*.' He looked over at the Jeep, parked across the street. 'You know how long it would take us to reach Spain from here? With a fair wind, we could all be at the border in just over a day.'

'But you wouldn't – would you?'

Granell turned to stare at him, biting his lip.

'*Los fifi*,' he said, 'from the *maquis*, they brought us news, about the resistance groups in the south. They reckon they have whole brigades of *guerrilleros*, thousands of my countrymen and women, everywhere from Lyón and Burdeos to *Los Pirineos*. Can you imagine? *La Nueve*, those *guerrilleros* and *guerrilleras*, a few tanks. *Hostia*, we could cut our way to Madrid, like...'

He sliced at the air with his stiletto.

'Castles in Spain?' said Jack.

'Castles...'

'Forget it, Amado. Just a saying we have. It means, wishful thinking.'

Granell laughed, nodded his head.

'But will they, *inglés*? *Los yanquis*? When this is over – help us settle with Franco?'

'They promised, didn't they?' It was the best he could find to say.

'Yes,' Amado grinned. 'They did, didn't they?'

*

The problem with the article that morning was a simple one. Jack had no idea how it should end. The beginning and the middle were easy enough.

Today, in a forgotten corner of northern France, some of the finest soldiers who ever fought under the French Tricolore make their stand against impossible odds, against the toughest divisions of Hitler's Third Reich. Yet these men are not French, they are Spanish – men whose battle against tyranny began with their fight against Franco's fascist rebels, back in 1936. These are men who seek no limelight, the forgotten warriors among the Allied ranks.

They make their stand to stop the German Panzer and Waffen SS regiments escape from the trap of nets cast around them by the encircling Americans, British, Canadians, Poles and French. If the Germans break out here, this terrible war will undoubtedly be prolonged. And if they break out, it will be over the dead bodies of every single defender. These Spaniards, fighting as part of General Leclerc's Second Armoured Division, know this stand may well be their last.

And this knowledge is shared by the townsfolk themselves.

The middle. His very personalised stories. *Madame* Dumont's certainty that, if the *Boches* took the town again, there would be reprisals, and her stoicism in the face of such a threat. Old Soulier the baker and the promise to use his ancient shotgun against the Germans, his life almost over anyway, and a chance to revenge himself for the loss of not one son, but three, back in 1940. And *Père* Berger, of course – knowing, because he'd agreed with Captain Dronne it should be so – his church would provide the last survivors of *La Nueve* with their final redoubt, their Alamo, as Harmon might have described it.

Thus it was that, with the beginning and middle of the article complete, photographs taken, it was to the church he took himself. Things still quiet, there at Écouché, though from the endless thunder from Argentan it was plain the threat was still very present.

Jack met with the priest, asked whether it might be possible to store the Riverside Portable, his Mighty Midget recording machine, there in the church.

'*D'accord,*' *Père* Berger told him, enthusiastically, showed him a cupboard in the sacristy. 'And this,' said the priest, 'if you need…'

There was an ancient typewriter, and Jack spent an hour bashing the stiff keys, transforming the half-written piece into print. But he kept his eye on the nave, still busy with wounded patients and medical staff, hoping he'd catch a glimpse of Danielle. Sadly, she never appeared, though the arrival of Toto Torrès was at least some consolation.

'Lieutenant,' he shouted. 'Do you have a minute?'

'*Monsieur* Telford,' she said, took the helmet from her head, ran fingers through her hair. 'Before you ask, Dani's not here. And you look like shit, by the way. Not eating?'

'We eat when we can. And this?' He rubbed at his chin, unshaven for days. 'But that wasn't what I wanted to talk about. Listen, if the worst comes to the worst here, before you're evacuated, might you collect some things for me?'

'Things?'

'This article. There'll be a disc with it, a recording. Try to get them to Patton's headquarters, the press tent there. Oh, and a letter for Danielle.'

'And you? Where are you planning to be?'

'It's a strange thing,' he said. 'I'm not a brave man, Lieutenant.'

'Mind if I stop you, Jack?' So far as he remembered, it was the first time she'd used his first name. 'But if this is going to be some sort of personal confession, don't you think we should drop the formalities? Call me Toto? Everybody else does.'

He laughed.

'Fair enough – Toto. But like I say, not brave. Far from it. All the same, these men, Amado and the others – hard to explain, but in some strange way, our fates… Hell, I don't even believe in any of that nonsense.'

'You know, Jack, you don't need to explain. If they stay, you think you need to stay as well? But what about Dani?'

'That's what makes it even more weird. In all my life, Toto, I've never had more to live for. I'm thirty-six. With luck, at least as many years still ahead of me. Years with Danielle. Cottage on the Dorset coast. Kids, maybe even kids. But here I am. If the *Boches* take this place, there'll be no prisoners. You know that. Oh, take no notice. I expect, whenever you're evacuated from here, I'll be riding in the ambulance alongside you.'

'Sure,' she said. 'Sure, you will.'

They came again that night. A more desperate counterattack even than the previous day's assault. Their tanks and Panzergrenadiers swept in from the east, crossed the Orne, crossed the Cance and penetrated the town itself further than any of the earlier onslaughts.

Telford volunteered to help the stretcher bearers again, almost lost his life not once but several times. More casualties. The fighting – if such a thing were possible – even more vicious, all of it house-to-house, hand-to-hand. And, everywhere, in the thick of it, Dronne spurring on his men.

It only ended when Campos, *el canario*, led his Number Three Platoon in yet another daring flank attack, the fury of which resulted in the *Boches* being routed. Hell, there were even prisoners taken, captured in the woodland above Écouché. There hadn't really been any, these past few days, neither side having the time or the capacity or the inclination to burden themselves with such an additional problem.

Yet, here they were, a bunch of wounded, perhaps a dozen other captives. Granell and Reiter were dispatched to interrogate them, and Jack joined the medics and stretchers sent to help the casualties. But even the worst injured of the Germans steadfastly refused any treatment, almost sneered at the Spaniards. More than just contempt for an inferior enemy, but for such an inferior race.

'*Spanier?*' said one of them. 'No *Amerikaner?* Not even *Franzosen? Ach du lieber Gott!* No wonder you will lose.'

More gibberish about secret weapons. German victory inevitable. Deluded, surely, if they were relying on those rocket attacks so much in the news when Telford had been in London. Or was it something else?

'Your regiments?' Amado asked them, time and again. Reiter translated. No response, simply more insolent glances. SS insignia on their collar tabs, the Death's Head emblem on the only officer's cap.

'Search him?' Reiter suggested. 'His cuffs. Looks like he's just stripped something off. Cotton threads.'

A couple of the men held the officer while Reiter went through his pockets. A few family photographs, personal letters – and a pair of matching thin black cuff titles, with the words *Das Reich* picked out in silver thread.

'*Das Reich*,' said Granell. 'Second Panzer Division. Have we seen these here before?'

They hadn't, but through the confusion of these past few days, Telford struggled to recall something important. Of course, his last encounter with Harmon, Babs Wace and the others.

'Oradour,' he said. 'Oradour-sur-Glane.'

He expected the Germans to ignore him, yet the officer had the temerity to offer him a smug smile, a shrug of the shoulders.

'Oradour?' Amado was also trying to remember.

'The two hundred men these pigs burned alive. More than two hundred women shot. And two hundred kids.'

'*Our* kids?' said Granell. 'The Spanish kids?'

Jack nodded, though he doubted whether Granell truly believed the crime any worse for the the fates of those refugee children.

They shot the wounded where they lay, dragged the rest off in groups of two or three. Jack listened to the gunshots among the trees, entirely numb to any emotion. Indeed, he almost wished he had a weapon with which he could assist in the executions.

On the sixth morning, a Saturday, this eerie silence. No gunfire. Not even the faintest rumble from Argentan. A couple of American fighters in the sky but otherwise, nothing.

It made everybody so uneasy. This ceasefire unreliable, possibly duplicitous.

But then the fighters from the *maquis*, the FFI, *los fifi*, began to bring news. From Paris, where workers on the Métro had gone on strike. They'd been supported by the *gendarmerie*, then by the police, finally by the city's postal workers. Now, a general strike.

'Paris?' said Dronne. The men of *La Nueve* were dug in again, their forward positions, the captain, Granell and Telford back in the observation post, the mill still further reduced to a state of ruin.

'Not Warsaw again,' Dronne went on. 'They cannot...'

'A hundred miles?' Amado scratched with a stick in the dirt. 'A bit more? We could be there in...'

Another broadcast coming in over the wireless transmitter. Barely audible, crackle and whistling. A broadcast in the name of something calling itself the Parisian Committee of Liberation. German columns, they said, on the Champs-Élysées yet again – though, this time, heading east. Defeated columns. *Victory is near*, claimed the announcer, *and punishment for the traitors. For now, the French Forces of the Interior in the Île de France are engaged with the Boches garrison. To the death!*

The broadcast in the name of Regional Chief, Colonel Rol.

'That name mean anything?' Jack asked.

Dronne shook his head, just as another group of his scouts came in. Nothing. Not a sign of the Germans anywhere. From across the moonscape before them, a Jeep, coming in fast. The smooth, boyish face of André Geoffroy, the captain commanding the Tenth. He jumped from the vehicle, bounded up the stairs.

'They're gone,' he laughed. 'Bloody gone. We drove all the way to La Gravelle. Met up with the boys from the Second Battalion there. The Yanks have been trying to drive out the *Boches* and the bastards are still holed up in Argentan. But the fighting's stopped and looks like they've begun to retreat. It's over, Raymond. Over.'

Dronne crossed himself.

'You're sure, André? Oh, Merciful Father...'

As if the Almighty heard his gratitude, the bells of Notre-Dame d'Écouché, miraculously still in action, began to peel. Loud, victorious, calling the faithful to give thanks for their deliverance.

An hour later, and the exhausted defenders – those who hadn't simply fallen asleep at their posts – had gathered in the church to hear *Père* Berger deliver Mass. Not the defenders alone, of course – the men of *La Nueve*, of the Tenth, and of the 501st tank crews – but also the medical teams, the resistance fighters, the townsfolk and, naturally, the ambulance crews.

Danielle threw herself into his arms. Like everybody else, she was joyful, but at the end of her tether, her eyes sunken into dark pits.

'Don't stare at me,' she begged him. 'I must look terrible...'

She began to cry, and he wrapped his arm around her, led her inside the church, found a pew upon which she could settle her weary bones.

'They've been through such a lot,' said Suzanne Torrès, coming to stand alongside them in the crowded central aisle. The place was packed. Major Putz was here. Fox as well. And so many of the Spaniards. Those atheists, Communists, Anarchists. Hard to believe. Had Écouché given them religion? But then he spotted Granell, a few pews ahead of him. Next to him, the unmistakeable bulk of Miguel Campos. Each of them had one arm behind his back and – well, their fingers crossed. What *was* this? And, as he looked around the congregation, he could see more and more of the Spaniards doing the same.

Yet, as the service began, perhaps the incense, perhaps the comforting drone in *Père* Berger's proclamation of the Word of God, Jack pulled Danielle closer to him, slipped into a pleasant sleep, which carried him through the thanksgiving, the liturgies, then the consecration of the bread and wine. He woke again during the communion, the priest's regular parishioners, some of the Frenchmen – Dronne included – waiting their turn to kneel, accepting the Body of Christ, the Blood of Christ.

When it was done, however, and the priest was about to impart his final blessing, he was interrupted. Granell, Campos and Montoya – those three most irreverent of the Spaniards – moving down the aisle towards the altar, each of them carrying a helmet stuffed to overflowing with dollar bills and French *francs*.

'*Padre*,' said Granell, when they reached the altar steps, 'it is not much, but perhaps – well, for your Sacred Heart.'

The priest fell to his knees. He wept. And wept. Muttered thanks. The benediction of God Almighty.

'Please,' he said, through his tears. 'With the blessing. I wanted to invite you all. A final prayer. For those you have lost – those we have *all* lost.'

A request they could not refuse, and they filed out behind him, to the burial ground, the fresh graves.

'So,' said Toto, 'you lived to tell your tale, Jack. I'm glad. And you don't need my delivery van after all.'

She moved on, joined some of the other *Rochambelles*.

'What did she mean?' Danielle asked.

'Just one of Toto's private jokes, maybe,' he said, and pulled her closer, as *Père* Berger offered up prayers for the dead.

'It's Jack and Toto now, is it?' she taunted him.

'You still don't like her – despite everything.'

'She's supposed to be married, isn't she? But carrying on like that with Massu.'

It seemed petty, and he was too tired to argue with her, decided to ignore it, spotted Granell, not far away.

'Fingers crossed again, Amado? For good luck?'

'Not for us, *inglés*. We use it to cancel out anything we may be doing or saying.'

Jack laughed, remembered the playground adventures of his childhood. The memories mingled somehow with the relief of his survival.

'Barley,' he said, pretty much to himself, and in English, noted the quizzical glance Amado cast in his direction. 'Protected,' he explained. 'When we were kids, playing games, if we shouted *barley*, it meant we couldn't be touched. Safe.'

'Yes,' said Granell. 'This is the same, no?'

Yet they fell into a respectful silence as the priest began to recite the names of the fallen, their makeshift crosses here, decorated with one of their identification tags – the other of the pair already collected by Amado as adjutant, for the company records – and topped by their helmets, to each of which their friends had secured the red, yellow and purple shoulder flashes, removed from their combat jackets.

Poreski. Constantino Pujol. Luis de Águila. José Reinaldo Sánchez. Manuel Sánchez. A dozen others, including those dead from the Tenth.

Heads were bowed, though very soon they were turned – by the arrival of a relief column. British troops from the Eleventh Armoured Division, as it transpired. Challenger tanks, motorised artillery, Bren carriers, armoured cars.

Relief. It felt good.

But in the evening, as they all celebrated in the town's surviving bar, Dani upon Jack's knee, just a little the worse for wear, there was a broadcast. BBC. Outside, it was raining, the first time in two weeks.

Today, Saturday, the nineteenth of August...

Telford hushed them all, convinced there might be word of the stand they'd made here. They looked to him for translation, of course. He exchanged glances with Fox. How could he tell them? The bar fell silent, waiting for his words.

'A mix-up, maybe,' Jack stammered. 'But they just reported – well, an advanced column of the victorious General Montgomery's Thirtieth Corps has, today, liberated the town of Écouché from the forces of the Third Reich.'

'Bastards,' said Toto Torrès.

Late-August 1944, Paris

Amado Granell

'All I need to know,' yelled Leclerc, 'is who gave you the bloody order?'

'It was from your headquarters, sir,' Dronne stammered. 'No name. Just said – well, your instructions, General. To turn back.'

'Where was your initiative, Captain? You should have ignored it.'

'I did, sir. Twice. But the third time...'

It had seemed odd, even to Telford. They'd been on the road for twelve hours, since seven that morning. And now, here they were. No more than eight miles from the centre of Paris, the rest of the Division far, far behind them, and Dronne's hastily gathered force within striking distance of the Hôtel de Ville – the town hall. The Hôtel de Ville their goal because, like the Préfecture and some other key locations, it was already in the hands of the Resistance, but might not remain so for too much longer. One hundred and fifty men, mostly from *La Nueve*. Twelve half-tracks. Another few for the sappers. Three tanks from the 501st.

'You had a hard time here?' Leclerc glanced around at the dead Germans, their scorched, shattered vehicles.

'The *Boches* didn't seem keen to give up the crossroads, General.'

The crossroads at Croix-de-Berny, Jack and Granell watching the exchange at Dronne's own Jeep while, around them, the local civilians began to emerge from their houses, slowly at first, and then – once it became clear there was no longer an immediate danger – the normal flowers, kisses, bottles of wine, singing. It had been bad enough earlier in the day. The delays caused by jubilant crowds. But now? Not one of them needed reminding about Leclerc's expectations.

'Well, you've had your orders, Raymond,' said the general, his temper cooling, the twitch in his cheek easing. 'Now, what the hell is this...?'

A car, hurtling down the road from the north, from Paris. It screeched to a halt just across from them, and three men climbed out. Jack didn't recognise the other two, but he certainly knew Hemingway. The fellow was in khaki shirtsleeves, a helmet set on his head. He pulled a cigarette case from his pocket. Badly overweight, sweat stains around his armpits.

'Well, gentlemen,' he cried. 'You've made it.'

'Dronne,' said Leclerc. 'Tell them.'

The captain marched towards the correspondents, held up a hand, brought Hemingway to a halt.

'We have orders,' Dronne told them. 'No correspondents without a written permit can enter the city.'

'Bit late,' Hemingway laughed. 'We've been at the Ritz since this morning. Liberated the place, you might say.'

'Orders, all the same,' said Dronne. 'I'd suggest you find accommodation elsewhere. Versailles?'

'And if we don't?' Hemingway replied, grinning at his companions. 'What will you do, Captain – shoot us?'

Leclerc took a couple of steps forward, straightened his field jacket windbreaker, tapped his cane on the cobbles.

'As it happens, *monsieur*,' he said, 'that is precisely the instruction given to all my commanders.'

Hemingway turned to the others.

'I guess it's back to the Ritz, then,' he shrugged. 'Shame, though. We'd heard there was a French column on its way. Could have given you a great write-up, General.'

'We have our own correspondents, *Monsieur* Hemingway. And now, if you don't mind...' Leclerc gestured for Moreno's platoon to block the road behind Hemingway's car. 'Head south, I would suggest.'

It seemed to Jack that Hemingway was about to argue, but he thought better of it, reached for the car's gleaming door handle, and

Telford – only a few feet away – heard him mutter just three words.

'What a jerk!'

Later, Telford realised he'd never quite fathomed the depths to which his own fate had become enmeshed with Leclerc's. There was Kufra, of course, but it was far more than this. And the insult…

Hemingway was a big man, reputation as a hell-raiser, but Jack's rage overcame whatever natural trepidation he might normally have felt about tackling such a bruiser.

'Hemingway,' he shouted, and the writer turned.

It had been one of Colonel Eddy's most basic lessons. In hand-to-hand combat, if possible, use anything but your bare fists. Unless you could land a blow which would crush your enemy's windpipe. Or both fists together, like a club. Or gouging out his eyes. Yet, if you had no choice, and it came to fisticuffs, at least to make sure it was a roundhouse punch.

Hemingway opened his mouth to speak, as Jack brought his arm through in a wide circle, fist upside down, the full force of the blow landing on the side of the man's face.

After Écouché, there'd been a brief but welcome respite. Just a few days. Still more fresh-faced French youngsters to fill gaps in the Third Battalion's ranks. Then the Division regrouping. Reassigned also. To the US First Army, though General Courtney Hicks Hodges was no Patton. Rumours. The Allied commanders still insisting Paris should not be entered, simply encircled, bypassed. Leclerc had pressed their case, threatening to make the run on the city regardless. There were those among the generals who laughed at him. Where, precisely, did he think he was going to get the fuel if the Americans refused to allow him access to their dumps. Yet little did they know.

'We may owe everything we possess to the Americans,' Leclerc had said when he came back from one of those angry meetings, 'every stitch of our clothing, every round of ammunition. But the fuel?'

All those German prisoners, the secret supplies built up by the Division.

Leclerc's insistence had finally paid off. Three days, they said, he'd spent, flying from one headquarters to another, pressing their case. The Flying Lion. The desperate pleas for help from within the city, the real threat of another Warsaw.

It was a realistic prospect, as well. Regular reports from the *maquis* confirmed how hundreds of resistance fighters had died since the Paris uprising had begun. The German commander in the city, von Choltitz, had seemingly received instruction from Hitler that Paris should be put to the torch, burned to the ground. So far, wiser voices had prevailed, including those of neutral foreign diplomats. But how long could this hold?

Finally, in exasperation, General Bradley had surrendered, almost reversed his stance entirely. Now, it was all urgency. But Leclerc still didn't trust them.

Jack had been there when the unit commanders received their orders.

'Immediate advance on Paris,' Leclerc had told them. 'But, for pity's sake, avoid the Americans at all costs. Just in case.' Paris. Around the room, many of those battle-hardened warriors wept openly. 'But we shall not enter the city looking like vagrants, gentlemen.'

Weeks of grime, mud, unavoidable neglect were washed and shaved away – as well as they were able. So, it was a somewhat refreshed Second Armoured Division which set out from Sées, filling the overcast Wednesday morning sky with even denser clouds of blue-grey exhaust fumes – it would have been the twenty-third of August – and raced a hundred miles to Rambouillet, where de Gaulle planned to establish his new headquarters.

A strange day, as they forced their way through the townsfolk they encountered. Strange, also, because they were following one of the routes of German retreat. Hard to reconcile this army with the Panzer Divisions they'd faced at Écouché. Abandoned motorised vehicles, little more than rusting heaps of junk. Dead horses and mules, overturned carts. And the debris of their passing, looted works of art, discarded equipment, filling the ditches.

That night it rained, a freezing drizzle and sleet. Demoralising. Nobody slept. But at first light, the Division's columns were on the road once more, thirty miles to Longjumeau, through countryside washed clean, now glistening emerald green. Yet, at Longjumeau it all went horribly wrong. German tanks and artillery, the Division pinned down – all except the small force Dronne had gathered around him.

His scouts believed they'd found a route clear of the *Boches*, but a dilemma.

'Well, Amado,' Dronne had said to Granell, 'here's a pretty pickle. Stay here and fight our corner, or press on to Paris?'

'Immediate advance on Paris, sir,' Amado replied. 'That was the order, no?'

And so, they'd broken free of the German traps, to Croix-de-Berny, where they caught their first glimpse of the Eiffel Tower – and where, having destroyed a small *Boches* force there, Dronne had received those peculiar orders to turn around.

'At least he didn't hit you back,' Amado shouted to him, above the roar of the Jeep's engine.

Hemingway, Telford recalled, hadn't said anything, simply rubbed at his cheek.

'I wish he had done,' said Jack. 'But he just winked at me. The bastard winked at me.'

They'd managed to get away from the crossroads around eight o'clock. It was a fine August evening, shaping up towards a glorious sunset as they followed Dronne's command vehicle. In the Jeep, alongside the captain, was a young man, little more than a lad, who'd stepped out from among the citizens of Croix-de-Berny. Georges something-or-other. Said he knew the location of all the local German outposts, and the back roads to avoid them, all the way to the Porte d'Italie.

Dronne was cautious, all the same, persuaded the lad to draw a map of his proposed route, sent one of the half-tracks ahead to take point. Ten minutes later and the rest of the column followed. But Georges was right, and they were soon twisting and turning their way through streets which seemed too narrow for the half-tracks, let alone the Shermans.

'Well, *señor* newspaperman,' said Amado. 'What did you make of it – the order to turn back?'

'It's obvious there are those among Leclerc's staff who expect the liberation of Paris to be a purely French affair. How will they

631

ever live with it if the history books record that it was all down to a bunch of Spaniards?'

Granell laughed at him.

'*Hostia*,' he said, 'why don't you tell the truth?'

Jack knew there'd be an element of reality in what he'd said. There were factions among the French officers, naturally there were. Plenty of nationalism, stored away these four years past. But he also knew he'd shied away from telling Amado what he really believed.

'The truth, my friend? How would we ever know? But this much is certain. The *maquis* is dominated by Communists. Their aim, to keep Paris Red. But now, the only one of Leclerc's officers with the initiative to be within striking distance of the city? Why, good Captain Dronne, up ahead there. In command of a remarkable company of men – though, unfortunately, half of them are Reds also. So, what will they do when they get there? Support the Gaullists at the Hôtel de Ville, or throw their considerable weight behind this Colonel Rol and his *maquisards*?'

'They still don't trust us, after all this. And you're right, *inglés*. But who, on Leclerc's staff, would have dared countermand his orders?'

'Other than one of his superiors? Is that where you're going with this?'

'I'm going nowhere except to the Hôtel de Ville, comrade. And when we get there? We'll follow Barbirrojo to hell and back. And after the captain, *el patrón*, of course. And de Gaulle? He needs to understand we're not all Communists or Anarchists – though none of that matters now. Eight years fighting the fascists. Those are the loyalties which forge us together, no? So, we'll liberate Paris in de Gaulle's name, whether he trusts us or not.'

Granell's own politics, Jack knew, remained firmly with the Republican Left, *Izquierda Republicana*, and perhaps it was this which allowed him to move so freely, as Company Adjutant, between the various other factions.

'The Hôtel de Ville it is, then,' Telford laughed.

The exhaust fumes and smoke of their passing choked them, mingled with the stench of sewers. North and east, always north and east until, a half-hour later, they arrived at the Porte d'Italie itself. The old gateway and the most recent of the city's walls no longer existed. Just another avenue, lined with apartments, lined with trees, lined with joyful citizens, alerted to their imminent arrival by the half-track Dronne had sent ahead. And there, Georges left them, a new guide arriving to help, a young Armenian, Dikran, riding a Magaty autocycle – one of those small motorbikes with pedals the French seemed to favour so much.

Like Georges, he knew precisely where the German strongpoints might be. And the worst of them, straight up the road ahead in the Place d'Italie. Dronne had to decide whether he should trust this other volunteer, but while he deliberated, they were swamped once again by more of the Thirteenth Arrondissement's townsfolk.

An old man pressed his face against Jack's shoulder.

'*Impossible!*' he sobbed. '*Impossible!*'

At Dronne's Jeep, an enormously overweight woman hurled herself onto the vehicle's bonnet. She'd had time to dig out some sort of traditional dress – a white blouse barely able to contain her buxom breasts, a black apron over long red skirts, and a black knot cap sporting a *tricolore* cockade. She'd cracked the Jeep's windscreen in the process, refused to move. Drunk as a lord. But they needed to move on, the time potentially needed to shift her more than the column could afford.

Almost nine, dark now.

'We follow Dikran,' Dronne shouted, and they were moving again, more backstreets, the woman clinging on for dear life, though shrieking with laughter.

'Can you believe this?' said Jack, and Granell glanced at him, laughed loudly.

'*Mort aux Cons*,' he said. Death to Idiots. It was the name still painted on Dronne's Jeep.

At the Pont d'Austerlitz they halted again, while Dronne's Algerian sappers checked there were no explosives planted beneath the bridge. When they were satisfied, and with one of the tanks, the engineers as well, in the lead, they crossed the Seine, turned left, heading west along the river's Right Bank towards Notre-Dame, along the Quai Hôtel de Ville.

'Thank god,' said Jack. 'At least I know where I am now.'

And, as though to welcome him back, the bells of the cathedral began to peel. Joyous. Then joined, it seemed by those of every other church in Paris.

'Been here before, *inglés*?'

'In '37. International Exhibition.'

'The Spanish Pavilion?'

'Of course. The poor bloody Republic still believing the rest of the free world would help them. But what I remember most was sitting outside the Café de Flore with a friend, talking about Durango and Guernica – and Madrid, of course. She asked me whether I thought they'd ever bomb London like that. Or Paris. And it made me think. What price would we pay, I wondered, to stop Paris being turned to rubble?'

'Well, now you know the answer, *compañero.*'

They followed Dikran's autocycle past the Rue de Lobau and the side of the Hôtel de Ville. There were lights in the building, though not many, sandbags stacked against the wall, the church bells still ringing as they turned right into the wide square, the *parvis*, in front of the town hall. More sandbags, a makeshift machine gun emplacement. Dronne spotted a flurry of activity.

'De Gaulle,' he yelled. 'De Gaulle.' Then, for good measure. '*Pour la France Libre et Saint-Denis.*'

An answering cheer from the palatial front entrance of the Hôtel de Ville, while Dronne and Granell deployed their limited force in a defensive perimeter: the three Shermans, *Montmirail*, *Champaubert* and *Romilly*; the various platoons of Bernal, Elías and Campos at each of the road junctions; and the fifteen half-tracks forming an armoured protective wall along the front of the façade's Renaissance architecture, though much of its glory masked by the evening's gathering darkness. Almost nine-thirty.

At Dronne's instruction, Amado selected an escort of a dozen men and they were led inside by an incongruous and emotional bunch of the town hall's defenders. Men in old *poilu* uniforms from the Great War. Others, a few women among them, in civilian clothes but with helmets from 1940, even one of them with a fireman's headgear. Otherwise, it was all berets, forage caps, Sten guns, pistols. But all of these *résistants* sporting *tricolore* armbands, the letters FFI, and the Cross of Lorraine.

'Upstairs,' somebody shouted. 'They're waiting for you upstairs.'

They were almost carried from the vast marbelled vestibule, up the sweeping Grand Staircase, beneath ribbed and vaulted ceilings, to the wide first floor landings and corridors, to a function room, a veritable Hall of Mirrors to rival Versailles, all hung about with crystal chandeliers.

Applause. Cheering. Cries of *Vive la France! Vive de Gaulle!* An assembly of police uniforms, of civilian suits – politicians, Jack assumed. *Maquis* officers. Journalists with cameras or recording machines.

There were introductions, and Jack soon found himself, with Granell, each of them shaking hands with Resistance leader Georges Bidault, who turned out to be one of the instigators of the uprising. He looked as though he might be in his late forties, though Telford suspected he may be older. Dapper, pale grey suit. And Bidault plainly took an instant shine to Amado.

Flashbulbs popped, the light bouncing between the mirrors, distorting the echoed images of those in the room.

Jack took notes, watched as a fellow moved forward with a recording machine and a ribbon microphone on a short boom. An interview with Dronne, then he moved on to the nearest of the soldiers at the captain's side.

'And here they are,' he said, 'our valiant French boys, the first of the Allies to arrive in the city.' He pushed the mic under the nose of that same soldier. 'So, tell me, son, where in France were you born?'

'Me?' the soldier replied. It was Dronne's driver, Pirlian, a Turkish Armenian. 'Stamboul, sir.'

The journalist moved on swiftly.

'You?' he said to another of *La Nueve*'s members.

'Frankfurt,' Reiter told him. And when the next two warriors told the man they were born in Madrid and Zamora respectively, he gave up. But by then there was firing outside on the *parvis*. Many of the civilians hit the floor, though it transpired this was simply a few young bucks celebrating, shooting their guns in the air. And there was singing. *La Marseillaise*, naturally, and the church bells

635

providing a discordant accompaniment. Yet, when that died away, a different tune. Spanish. *El Paso del Ebro*. The familiar refrain. *¡Ay Carmela, ay Carmela!*

'Well,' said Dronne, 'we've come a long way from Brazzaville, *Monsieur* Telford.'

Just twenty-four hours later, and Jack sat on the grass in the botanical gardens – the Jardin des Plantes, on the Rue Cuvier, just south of the river – his back leaning against the wheel of Danielle's ambulance. He looked up at the stars, partly obscured by scudding wisps of cloud.

'You should have seen their faces,' she laughed, from inside the vehicle, where she was brewing up some coffee. 'All those women, running up to kiss us, bring us flowers. Then realised we were women. The shock, Jack. Priceless.'

'I can imagine,' he said. 'They must have been surprised.'

A day of surprises. Yes, this was certainly true.

Danielle sang quietly to herself as she lit the small spirit stove, pottered about with the bustling sounds of domesticity, while Jack – well, Jack set aside his notepad, almost too weary to write more.

'But to see the *Tricolore* flying now from the Eiffel Tower again,' she shouted. 'From the Arc de Triomphe.'

'The price, though,' he murmured to himself.

The rest of the Division had arrived early in the morning, gone almost immediately into action. Tank battles around the Tuileries and Luxembourg gardens. Perhaps no more than the slaughter he'd witnessed elsewhere, yet somehow…

'Busy when we arrived though,' Danielle called, and he could hear the clatter of their mess tins.

The Division had lost a lot of men, and Jack remembered the Tiger tank burning in front of the Opéra. The screams from the crew members inside. He'd seen and heard worse. Of course, he had. So, what was it? Simply because this *was* at the Paris Opéra? Or in Paris itself?

'Busy?' he repeated, stupidly, as she stepped down from the back of the Dodge, handed him the coffee. He lit a cigarette for them to share. He'd never seen so many medics and stretcher bearers, and when the first of the *Rochambelles* had arrived, mid-morning, he'd not been sure whether to laugh or cry. He'd missed her like hell, but he'd never been quite so fearful for her safety as he'd been today.

'Until the Yanks turned up,' she smiled. 'Took some of the pressure off.' A little later, an entire American infantry column, as well as their own medical units. But the fighting hadn't abated. Grew more intense, if anything. And, for the first time since Oran, he saw the savagery of France's own civil war. Frenchmen fighting Frenchmen. The most brutal street fighting. *Résistants* against unbelievable numbers of the *Milice*, of the French Gestapo.

Danielle sat alongside him, rested her head against his shoulder. He lifted the mess tin, sniffed at the coffee as though it might be a fine wine, savoured the familiar bitterness of its aroma. It was a rare luxury, yet she always seemed to have a modest supply.

'And you heard the news?' she said.

'The surrender,' Telford replied. 'I was there. For some of it, at least.'

'The surrender?' she rebuked him. 'No, I was thinking about Arlette's wedding.'

There'd been many romances, naturally, but few had advanced so positively as *Rochambelle* Arlette Hautefeuille's engagement to Captain Jacques Ratard from the 501st regiment.

'They're getting married *here*?' said Jack.

'Why not? Now they've surrendered in Paris, all we need do is chase them to the Rhine and then – I suppose it will all be over.'

Telford wasn't so certain. And yes, the *Boches* had surrendered. But it hadn't been easy. The Division's assault on von Choltitz's headquarters at the Hôtel Meurice on the Rue de Rivoli had raged all through the morning until, at around two in the afternoon, he was apparently forced to surrender. Jack hadn't been there – covering the fighting elsewhere in the city, with Putz at the Luxembourg, then with Elías at the telephone exchange. Nor was he there when von Choltitz was driven to the Préfecture on the Île de la Cité for the formal capitulation to Leclerc. Yet, even then, die-hard units of the SS continued the battle. He remembered something. The black GI at the Fulford Dance Hall. Something he'd said. *'I seen rats cornered, mister. I seen how they fight then.'*

'I don't know if it will *ever* be over,' he said and, as if to underline his point, a single rifle shot, from not too far away. 'Snipers everywhere, my sweet. We must all be careful. But the SS, the fanatics, the Nazis – and god knows how many of them are still left – we'd have to kill every single one of them. All the way to Berlin and beyond.'

'You are a – a *râleur, Monsieur* Telford. At least your friend, Lieutenant Granell agrees with me, that this will all be over by Christmas.'

A curmudgeon? Yes, he supposed she was right. But there was a dark cloud he could not shake off. He recalled Granell telling him about Putz's premonition. *'When the cicadas sing, it's going to get hot.'*

'Amado?' he said. 'All Granell's concerned about just now is his new car.'

After the Préfecture, von Choltitz was driven to Leclerc's own headquarters, at the Gare Montparnasse, to sign the official surrender documents. There Telford had seen him for the first time. A sweaty, overstuffed little man, in dress uniform, driven in a luxury sedan, field grey, its swastika flags removed and replaced with *tricolores*, and a bold white Cross of Lorraine on each front wheel arch. The top was down, and two French officers sat in the car with him, one with an FFI armband, the other in the uniform of a general. Two *gendarmes* rode on the running boards, more *gendarmes* in a convoy of Jeeps and police cars. Sirens, so that, by the time they arrived at the train station, a crowd had already gathered to spit on the German, no longer Governor of Paris.

The car's driver? Granell.

The *gendarmes* forced a passage for von Choltitz and his escort through the angry citizens, while Jack – repelled in equal parts by the cloying stench of the general's cologne, on the one hand, and by the baying of the mob at his heels, on the other – had pressed his own way in the opposite direction, until he was able to run admiring fingers along the vehicle's bonnet.

'You like it, *inglés*? Horch 830. Ninety-two horsepower. A beauty.'

'Coming to see the signing, Amado?' he'd said. 'Something to tell your kids about.'

They'd left the Horch in the care of the *gendarmes*, followed the small procession into the station building, to the cluster of SNCF offices now serving as Leclerc's base.

In the Jardin des Plantes, Danielle shook him from his memories.

'Will he come to the wedding, d'you think – Amado?' she said. 'Arlette said we could invite close friends to the reception. But how am I going to buy a frock, Jack? How?'

He had to bite his tongue, irritated by her obsession with this trifle, then knowing he was being unfair.

'We'll just have to go shopping, *mon chou*. When's the big day?'

'Three days,' she said. 'Monday. The big parade tomorrow. No chance there'll be anything open. Then Sunday. Impossible.'

'Early Monday morning then,' he laughed. 'And Granell? I'll make sure he knows. But the fighting's not over, Dani. Anybody's guess what might be happening by Monday.'

The SNCF offices at Montparnasse had been crowded. But no Leclerc. And an American with a film unit from the Army Signal Corps protesting loudly about the lack of lighting. Granell in deep discussion with the Resistance officer who'd been in the car with him and von Choltitz.

'That was Tanguy,' Amado had told Jack a few minutes later, when he'd finally broken free. 'You know – Colonel Rol?'

Jack had remembered. Regional Chief of the *Maquis*. Communist. The dilemma they'd discussed. The possible concern among those close to de Gaulle. If Leclerc's Spanish Reds were the first to enter Paris, would they remain loyal, or would they throw their weight behind Colonel Rol and his Communist *maquisards*?

'He spotted the flash,' Granell had murmured, touched his fingers to the red, yellow and purple patch at his shoulder – though it was faded now, almost indistinguishable. 'Fought in Spain as well. Political Commissar with the Marty Battalion. Then for the whole Fourteenth International Brigade. And his *nombre de guerra* – Rol? The name of a friend who died there.'

'Did he try to recruit you?'

Granell had laughed.

'I told him I never had much time for political commissars. But he's a brave man, all the same. And his wife, from what I've heard. Cécile, I think. Maybe a story for you there, *inglés*.'

In the botanical gardens, Danielle took their mess tins, as Toto Torrès strolled past with *Commandant* Conrad, back with the unit now. There were greetings, and Toto reached into her canvas haversack.

'Jack,' she said. 'Glad I've seen you. I think I promised to lend you this.'

A book. A children's book by the design on the dust cover.

'Saint-Exupéry,' he said. 'Yes, I'd forgotten. He flew you out of Lisbon, didn't he? And you brought the book from New York. Worth a read?'

'You've not heard?'

There was a look of intense sadness on her face.

'Heard?' said Jack.

'A couple of weeks ago. Missing in action. But now a report his plane went down. Somewhere in the sea, near Marseille.'

Jack accepted the book, promised to read it, while Florence Conrad lightened the mood, asked if Danielle was ready for Arlette's wedding.

'Monday morning,' said Dani, when they'd moved on. 'I'll hold you to that, Jack – *whatever* may be happening. What's so funny?'

Telford hadn't realised he was smiling. He'd turned the pages of the book at random, his gaze settling on a couple of lines he decided were clever.

"It is only with the heart that one can see rightly; what is essential is invisible to the eye."

'Oh, this.' He waved the book at her. 'And I was thinking about von Choltitz signing the surrender. The event had its moments, I can tell you. The local Resistance leader, Tanguy, thought he was entitled to sign it, as well as Leclerc – but, of course, Leclerc was having none of it. But in all the confusion after it was all over, he signed it anyhow – put his own name above the general's. Then that Yank – Stevens, I think – with the film unit asked Leclerc whether they could shoot the signing all over again, though outside, in the sun, where the light was better.'

'Brave man. The general said no, of course?'

'As it happens, he agreed. And that's when he first noticed Tanguy's signature. By then the cameras were rolling, so I guess he had to bite his tongue. But it was a different story when de Gaulle turned up a while later. Oh, Fox was with him, by the way. Sends his regards. Never seen the general so angry, though.'

But there'd been nothing to be done. And Amado had saved the day. The car, of course. Despite the crowds, Granell had managed to edge the Horch closer to the station's corner, where the Rue du Départ met the Rue d'Odessa and the Boulevard du Montparnasse, through the general's security cordon. And when de Gaulle caught a glimpse of the sedan, it was love at first sight.

The world somehow looked very different to Jack the following day, as Amado Granell, and that fine Horch 830 luxury sedan took pride of place – well, almost – on de Gaulle's victory parade. Dress uniforms, the best everybody could muster, *képis* and forage caps in place of helmets.

Telford pressed the record button on the Dictaphone.

'*Below me, on the Champs-Élysées,*' Jack spoke into the mic, his best Spanish, '*the vast sea of emotion, the great waves of the Parisian populace, constrained for so long by the German occupation, now part before the tall, upright figure of General Charles de Gaulle – as though he might be some latterday Moses leading his people back to their promised land.*'

Further down the boulevard, there was an official grandstand for accredited correspondents and Jack had already met Harmon there. Ernie Pyle, as well, and Vaughan-Thomas, Downing, Don Whitehead. And Dunnett, who he'd not seen since Casablanca.

But Jack had wanted some privacy, paid the owners of an apartment with a balcony overlooking the route.

'*Around General de Gaulle,*' said Jack, '*stride the military and political heroes who have stood with Free France since June 1940.*'

Leclerc, of course, and Koenig. The politicians Bidault and Le Trouquer among many others. There were *tricolores* everywhere, singing, cheers and tears.

'*Yet, immediately behind the general and his retinue, I can see a single vehicle, the car which once conveyed the German commander of Paris, General Dietrich von Choltitz. It's now driven by a lieutenant from an armoured infantry regiment in Leclerc's Second French Armoured Division. This lieutenant, as it happens, is Spanish. He belongs to the Ninth Company of the regiment, so many Spanish soldiers in its ranks that it is known, simply, as La Nueve. This lieutenant, like all his comrades, fought all the way through Spain's civil war, defending the democratically elected Republic.'*

Jack went on to name the four half-tracks following Granell and, today, providing de Gaulle's personal escort, his guard of honour. Behind those, the rest of *La Nueve*. And behind *La Nueve*, the rest of the Division. It was quite a show.

Telford finished with a short emotional piece he knew Barea would enjoy – the Republican flags he could see, the interviews he'd done with members of the Spanish community here, among the jubilant crowds, all exiles, of course. And also with the Poles he'd met among the *résistants*, many of them formerly members of the International Brigades, but remaining in Spain when the Brigades were disbanded so they could continue the fight as part of the Republican army itself, and then become refugees in France. Still here, still fighting.

He lifted the needle from the disc, stowed everything away carefully and, slinging his equipment over his shoulder, he thanked the apartment's owners again, hastening out onto the street. Threading his way down towards the Place de la Concorde, he cut through the gardens opposite the Grand Palais and Petit Palais in the hopes that the pathways there would be less crowded.

It was a good plan, and he managed to arrive at the obelisk in time to persuade a couple of armed FFI men to help him balance on the lowest lip of the pedestal so he could take a few decent shots, the parade completing this first part of its lengthy route to Notre-Dame. Some good snaps. A half-track, parked near the Fontaine des Fleuves but so covered in pink dahlias, yellow roses, blue hydrangeas, it could easily have been mistaken for a mobile florist's stall. Smiling faces. Farmers, waiting with crates of tomatoes and apples, tribute for the conquering heroes of this Roman triumph.

Telford still had the camera in his hands when the shooting began.

*

He had no idea where the shots came from and neither, it seemed, did anybody else. But the crowds dispersed as quickly as mist on a summer morning, running in all directions, an empty space opening quite suddenly around de Gaulle and his companions. They formed an island of courage and composure as the tidal wave of fickle citizens ebbed away to whatever safety they could find.

There were those who stayed, of course. Policemen, armed members of the FFI, forming a modest protective cordon. The escorting half-tracks as well, roaring into action, a defensive square. Among them, Dronne's own half-track, *Les Cosaques*, though the captain was soon picked up by a Jeep, Fox in the back.

'Did you see where they were, *Monsieur* Telford?' Dronne shouted. But Jack had no more idea than everybody else, and the firing had stopped now.

'Could have been anywhere,' he replied.

Dronne told him to climb aboard, and Jack was grateful for the chance to set down his equipment on the floor, beneath his feet.

'Looks like we're all driving the rest of the way anyhow, old boy,' said Fox.

De Gaulle and Le Trouquer were now being hustled into a waiting black limousine, while the rest of the entourage were picked up by other cars.

It was only when he was settled in the Jeep that Jack realised how much he was shaking.

'Christ,' he said, as they hurtled onto the Quai des Tuileries. 'Bloody snipers. The bastards are everywhere. And last night I was lecturing Dani about the need to be careful. Who's supposed to be in charge of security here?'

'It's like you say,' Dronne shouted. 'Everywhere. The *Milice*. SS fanatics in civilian clothes. Just too many.'

'Well, a few less, anyhow,' said Fox, as they passed the end of the Pont Royal. There was a truck, men with FFI armbands lifting two corpses from the pavement, dumping them unceremoniously onto the back of the wagon.

They drove past the riverside majesty of the Louvre Palace, Jack wondering just how many summary executions were taking place this day in the City of Light. But he said nothing.

'You think de Gaulle will be better protected at Notre-Dame?' he asked.

'You know him as well as any of us, *monsieur*,' said Dronne. 'Insisted everything should be normal – whatever the hell *that* means.'

It didn't sound good, but they fell into an uneasy silence until, as they approached the Pont Neuf – one of Jack's favourite places in the whole of Paris – and were following de Gaulle's Peugeot along the Quai de Gesvres, Fox suddenly brightened.

'I say,' he gripped Telford's arm, 'a little bird tells me there's going to be a wedding. One of the *Rochambelles*?'

'For god's sake,' said Jack. 'Not you as well.'

'What's the matter, old man? Just the thing we need to cheer us up, yes?'

They swung over the Pont Notre-Dame, slowed for the crowds gathering on the Rue de la Cité and Jack wondered at their ability to be, so often, in the right place at the right time.

'There must be an entire network of folk in this bloody place,' Jack laughed, 'devoted to spreading the word.'

It had been in the morning papers, of course. De Gaulle's itinerary. These *new* papers, no longer needing to be printed underground. Telford had been out early to visit the closest news vendor to the botanical gardens. And there they were in all their glory. Free press, at last. *Le Parisien Libéré*, only its third edition, screaming its joyful headline, *Vive de Gaulle!* All the others. *Combat*. Yesterday evening's *Ce Soir. Défense de la France. L'Humanité*. So many others.

'Doesn't take long for word to get around,' said Fox, as they stopped by the open square in front of the cathedral, the Parvis Notre-Dame. Predictably, it was packed, a solid mass of flag-waving, singing humanity.

Ahead of them, the Peugeot was edging through a narrow avenue formed by two rows of *gendarmes*, their arms linked. But Jack could see de Gaulle leaning forward to shout in the driver's ear. The limousine came to a halt. More instructions to the policemen, the general climbing from the car.

'He's not going to walk, surely,' said Fox, casting a worried glance at the tall buildings which enclosed the square on two sides

– the river on the third side, and the magnificent façade of Notre-Dame itself, of course, on the fourth. The Hôtel-Dieu hospital to their left, its upper windows and rooftops just visible above a row of leafy trees. Behind them, back on the Rue de la Cité, the austere elegance of the Préfecture. Well, hopefully, they'd be safe from that direction, at least.

How far? A hundred yards to the cathedral's entrance? Close enough, Jack supposed. But there it was again. The sense of gathering doom. *'By the pricking of my thumbs…'*

The rest of their small convoy had pulled up outside the police headquarters and de Gaulle waited for his comrades to join him, accepted bunches of flowers, exchanged greetings with well-wishers almost hoarse with cheering. He even kissed the occasional baby proffered to him over the shoulders of the *gendarmes.*

It all *seemed* safe enough. But then, machine-gun fire. And single shots. *Crack, crack, crack.*

Like a repeat of the Place de la Concorde, folk ran.

Crack, crack.

Jack dropped into cover behind the Jeep, cursed de Gaulle for his *sang-froid,* for the general stood calmly, his long nose pointing towards the upper storey of the Hôtel-Dieu, a cigarette dangling from his lips.

Others from the crowd had thrown themselves down on the ground or hidden behind the trunks of those trees in front of the hospital, where they jostled for position among the FFI fighters who crouched there, weapons trained on nothing in particular. Their attackers were invisible, even the source of their shooting indistinguishable, the reports echoing around the *parvis,* though it seemed certain to come from above, maybe those garret windows in the hospital's sloping roof.

Crack.

Telford could see now that some of those on the ground had been shot: a man writhing in agony with a leg wound; and a woman, spreadeagled on her back, a priest in a broad-brimmed hat ministering to her, a small child weeping at her side.

The priest stood, hobbled towards de Gaulle. Jack thought he must be wounded as well, realised the fellow had a limp. He was tall, though. Almost as tall as the general himself. And as thin.

'General' the priest shouted. 'Take sanctuary. In the cathedral.'

It was good advice. But the accent? Not French, Jack guessed, this priest.

Where were the medics? Yet thank god for the soldiers who'd appeared on the scene, some of them protecting Leclerc, Koenig and the others, a few fetching their personal emergency kits, or bringing their carbines to bear in support of the *maquisards*. Nuns also, emerging from the hospital to help the injured.

Crack, crack.

More dead and wounded, too close to de Gaulle for comfort, as he was led towards the church, that priest limping alongside.

'Hurry, *mon général*,' he cried.

Something absurdly familiar.

Jack kept low, saw Fox had drawn his service revolver from its holster and followed him. They edged past the side of the Peugeot, Telford wishing de Gaulle would at least have the decency to follow the priest's advice, at least walk a little faster. But, of course, he couldn't. True nonchalance in the face of danger, or the image to uphold? The general puffed quietly on his cigarette. Jack cursed him and loved him for it at the same time.

Fifty yards.

Crack. A bullet ricocheted from the paving, no more than a yard from de Gaulle.

Screams from those too terrified to flee back towards the Rue de la Cité, cries for help from the injured. There was a smell of blocked drains, mingled with cordite carried on the breeze. More shooting.

But at least they were now almost beneath the twin towers of the west façade, the doors in the Portal of the Last Judgement open before them, tier upon tier upon tier of apostles, saints and angels gazing down at them. Surely, inside they must be safe.

The general was through the right-hand door now, others pressing behind him.

More shooting in the square.

Telford felt suddenly exposed, the proximity to safety within Notre-Dame somehow heightening his fear. So near, yet...

He remained doggedly close to Fox, still bent almost double, and a moment of further panic as he realised he'd left all his equipment unattended in the Jeep. Hell, he thought, considered for just a second whether he should go and fetch it all. He stood, looked back, but couldn't see the Jeep anyway for the confusion behind.

Yet, as he turned once more towards the entrance doors, he caught another glimpse of the priest. The merest tilt of the fellow's head when it turned in Jack's direction, the briefest of glimpses beneath the brim of the black clerical hat. Indistinct. Shadowed. Stupidity, Telford knew. But certainty, as well. That the hawk-like features he'd seen belonged to Kingsley Welch.

'For god's sake, Telford,' Fox hissed, 'this isn't funny anymore. He's either dead or in Berlin.'

Jack knew the interior, normally thought it sublime, the light, the sheer scale of its magnificence. The columns and arcades leading to the side aisles, the archways towering above the arcades and topped by the stained glass beneath the vaulted ceiling.

But today was different. The shooting. They could hear it, even there, in the nave, where a monsignor, a whole procession of clergymen, advanced from the apse and altar to berate de Gaulle – who'd apparently had the temerity to place their cardinal-archbishop, Suhard, under house arrest as a Vichy collaborator. In the pews, the invited congregation already gathered, seemingly untroubled both by this contretemps and also by whatever might be happening outside. Excited and emotional? Yes. But untroubled. For here, within the sacred walls of Notre-Dame de Paris...

'We need to tell him, all the same,' said Jack. 'Need to stop Welch.'

He was attracting attention from the nearest of the congregation, scowls and questions.

'Been here before, haven't we?' Fox whispered in Telford's ear. 'Last year, the Josephine Baker show. Remember? Screaming like a madman that some bloke had a gun. Turned out to be a cigarette lighter or something, didn't it? Now, calm down, old boy.'

At the farther end of the cathedral, choristers were taking their

647

place, a *Magnificat* to be sung in celebration of the city's liberation and the glory of God. *The Song of Mary.*

'Well, it *looked* like he had a gun,' said Telford. 'And what if it *had* been a gun? What if this *is* Welch?'

'And who, precisely,' Fox snapped, 'are we supposed to imagine might be his target? The general – or *you*? My god, pure paranoia.'

De Gaulle and his party walked slowly along the broad central aisle, towards the pews reserved for them. The general stopped to exchange greetings here and there, perhaps to reassure those still troubled by whatever might be happening beyond these protective walls.

Jack looked around, happy to at least see Dronne and a few of the others just behind them. And paranoia? Perhaps Fox was right.

'But doesn't it all seem just a little strange?' he said. 'You think they're all so bad – as snipers? Not one of them able to hit de Gaulle out there in the square? It feels like...'

It all happened so quickly.

A member of the congregation, an older man, stepped into the aisle just behind de Gaulle, and the general turned to greet him – some old friend or acquaintance, it seemed.

Crack.

Like Gabizon, thought Jack, as the man fell forward into de Gaulle's arms and Telford spun around.

'A medic,' shouted de Gaulle. 'Fast.'

One of the clergymen took the wounded man from him and the general called for calm. A little too late. Chaos. People diving for cover between the pews. Screams. A *gendarme* trying to shield de Gaulle.

Crack.

The *gendarme* died, a bullet to his head.

'Up there,' Jack cried, pointed to the organ gallery high behind them. No more than a shadow moving back from the dark latticework parapet, but he knew what it was – or, rather, *who* it was. Though not a lone gunman, Telford could see. More than one marksman up there.

The general called for calm yet again, while the monsignor made some demand that there should be no violence in this House

648

of God, but de Gaulle's immediate followers were already springing into action.

'There,' Telford shouted again, as another gunman appeared above them, a ricochet screeching from one of the stone columns, and de Gaulle led reluctantly into the shelter of an archway but urging the priest to continue – the *Magnificat* to proceed.

Somewhere, a shattering of glass.

'How do we get up there?' Jack yelled at the monsignor and his retinue. The clergyman looked desperately from Telford to de Gaulle, then to his choir, gestured for them to get on with it. At the same moment, another man stepped forward, the only one in a suit rather than clerical vestments.

'I am the organist, *monsieur*,' he said. 'I will show you. But promise me – the organ...'

They ran. Telford and the organist. Fox and others while, behind them, the voices of the choir. Plainchant.

'Magnificat anima mea Dominum.'

And, as Jack raced back towards the entrance, he heard the unmistakeable voice of de Gaulle, leading the response.

'Et exultavit spiritus meus in Deo salutari meo.'

Whatever trepidation Telford might have felt was doused in this instant. To hell and back, he thought. I'd follow that man...

A doorway to the right. Beyond the doorway, a spiral staircase, enclosed, claustrophobic, narrow, forcing them to climb in single file. Fox in the lead with his service revolver. A young French officer with an automatic pistol. The organist and Jack. Behind them, more soldiers. The clatter of boots on the fan-shaped stone steps. Shouting. Something reminding Jack of the Hassan Tower, his madcap race up its ramps, but mingled with confused images of Hugo's Quasimodo, of Esmeralda, of wicked Archdeacon Frollo.

At the top of the staircase, the French officer had pressed himself against the curve of the wall.

'Wait,' he yelled, and peered around through the open doorway, was rewarded by more shooting from beyond, a bullet whistling past his head, smashing chips from the stonework, then bouncing, whining, from wall to wall down the winding steps. A miracle it didn't hit anybody.

The officer returned fire, ran through the door, followed by Fox.

'The organ,' protested the organist. 'Pray God they do not damage it.'

'Stay here,' said Jack. 'Better to stay here.'

He ventured to the top of the stairs as well, the soldiers pressing at his back.

Telford found himself gazing out into a room with a high rib-vaulted ceiling, a room strewn with storage crates and furniture, among which he could see Fox and the French officer, their guns trained on another arched doorway in the opposite wall. From somewhere beyond, Jack could hear the muffled strains of the *Magnificat* coming to its close, and he could hardly believe the service had continued, despite this gunfight taking place above the congregation.

'Keep down,' Fox shouted to him. 'They're out there. The organ gallery.'

Jack edged into the room. The soldiers followed and, in the other doorway, a silhouette, automatic fire, echoing in that vaulted chamber, flashes of yellow light.

One of the soldiers fell, but so did the silhouette, the clatter of his gun absurdly loud as it hit the flagstones.

More shooting, though this time it seemed to come from the other side of the organ loft. Fox leapt from cover, made it safely to the opening. He fired. Once. Then again. The familiar smell of gunsmoke.

'All clear,' he called, and disappeared through the doorway.

Jack followed. What would he find out there? Welch, he was certain. Though, somehow, he felt cheated, as he stepped onto the wooden landing, saw the young French officer grinning at him from the other side of the towering pipes, the keyboards, the carved angels, the ornate trumpets and the Baroque wooden casing of the grand organ. Beams of multicoloured light shone through the rose window above and behind. On the floor between Telford and the officer, three corpses – though none of them dressed as a priest.

The French officer and Fox turned each body in turn. Two of them undoubtedly *salopards* of the *Milice* but the third still dressed

650

in his SS army tunic beneath a light raincoat.

'Well?' said Fox. 'What have you got to say, Telford?'

Jack was confused, certain he'd seen Welch. But now?

The organist was at his side.

'She is safe?' he said. 'My beautiful instrument?'

'It seems so,' Telford told him, and glanced down into the nave. The *Magnificat* had, indeed, come to a close but there the service ended. No Mass, as orginally intended and the congregation dispersing as well, though de Gaulle still surrounded by admirers.

'Our Lady be praised,' said the organist. 'The priest told me no damage had been done, but I had to see for myself.'

'Priest?' said Jack. 'What priest?'

'The one who was hiding behind the crates. He went – up there.'

He pointed back into the vaulted chamber, back to the openwork stone turret almost hidden in the corner, another staircase inside and leading up to a further door, higher in the wall.

'Where does that go?' Jack demanded.

'Up the tower, naturally,' replied the organist.

Telford ran, scrambled up the steps inside the turret, ducked through the door, found himself on another staircase, the twin of the one he'd already climbed below. More fan-shaped steps, occasionally lit by narrow open windows in the thick outer wall. The sound of feet on the stone treads higher in the tower, somebody panting for breath exactly as Jack was doing.

How many steps from the bottom? He had no idea. Two hundred maybe? More?

Above him, a door slammed, a blast of air coming down the stairs to meet him. Below, shouting. Fox, telling him to wait.

But Jack had no intention of waiting. Not now. He hauled himself up still more steps. Round and round until he began to feel dizzy. And when he finally reached the door, threw it open without really weighing the consequences, he recoiled in horror, head swimming not just from the spinning giddiness of his circular climb but also from the vertigo – of finding himself on an exposed walkway, high above the ground, with nothing for protection but a masonry balustrade and the bizarre mythical beasts, the decorative chimeras, adorning its upper rail and corners.

He pressed himself back against the reassuring limestone of the tower's upper section, keeping as far away from the balustrade as he was able. He was sure the views must be a great attraction – the Seine, its bridges, the Eiffel Tower in the distance – but Jack could barely bring himself to look. And a wind up there, not strong, but enough to unbalance him still further. It tugged at the sleeves of his uniform jacket, at his forage cap.

To his left, forty or fifty feet away, was Notre-Dame's south tower. Bridging the gulf between, only the walkway, a gallery seemingly suspended in the air. At its farther side, Kingsley Welch. The priest's robes, the clerical hat.

'Well, Telford,' he shouted, 'what are you waiting for?'

The breeze carried the words in flurries.

'For a little help from my friends, naturally,' Jack replied, his voice unsteady, head turned towards Welch, neck straining so his one eye could keep the wretch in focus while, at the same time, he might avoid staring down into the abyss.

'Your friends – will they shoot me, d'you think? Or perhaps they might be interested in a little trade. Information, perhaps?'

He had no gun. Or none that Jack could see.

'I imagine they'd prefer to see you hanged,' he called back. 'As I would.'

'I was afraid of that,' said Welch. And he turned, just then. A noise behind him. For there was the same young French officer with a couple of his men. They must have climbed the staircase in the south tower, to cut off the assassin's escape. Smart move, Jack thought, as Welch limped backwards, away from the officer and towards Telford, along the gallery. He stopped by one of the chimeras, a goat-shaped creature with a single curved horn. Welch turned towards Jack, hatred in his eyes.

'I was only curious,' said Telford, dreading the thought of Welch rushing him, hurling him from the walkway, nobody able to save him. 'About de Gaulle. You could have killed him out there, on the square.'

'Just like the train,' Welch laughed. 'Still expect me to reveal all? Well, why not? I don't suppose it matters now. Our friends in the *Milice*, old boy. Wanted him to meet his end *inside* the cathedral.

Some sort of message. How even God wanted him dead. Wouldn't protect him. That sort of nonsense.'

'De Gaulle, then – not me?'

Fox was at his side now.

'Is he armed?' said Fox.

'I don't think so,' Telford told him, and relaxed a little.

'You have a high opinion of yourself, Telford,' Welch laughed. 'And no, I had bigger fish to fry after Sir Aubrey popped his clogs. Though I suppose I owed you some retribution for the train. I must admit, I never thought for one second you'd pull the trigger.' He rubbed at his shoulder, as though the memory had caused an old wound to flare once more. 'Underestimated you, didn't I? And now, here we are again.'

'I hate to break up the reunion,' said Fox, 'but I trust you're planning to come quietly, Welch?'

'A fair trial, Captain? Are you going to promise me a fair trial – back in Blighty, perhaps?'

'I suppose that will have to be decided. But yes, our government will certainly want to see you tried for treason. As for General de Gaulle...'

'Hobson's choice, Telford, wouldn't you say? I wonder, though, old chap – Dorothea, might you find a few words? Something fitting?'

'Dorothea?' Jack began, as Welch played his final card.

It was all so quick. Welch's hand upon the chimera's horn, his foot on the limestone rail, clambering up onto the balustrade.

Despite himself, Jack pushed away from the wall, covered the dozen paces between them. No real plan. And afterwards he would convince himself he simply wanted to stop Welch cheating the hangman. But, at the time, just instinct.

Welch steadied himself, still using the chimera.

Telford grabbed for the man's heels but only succeeded in catching the hem of his robes, caused Welch to turn, stare down at him.

'You bloody fool,' said Welch and launched himself out into the void, the material slipping through Telford's fingers. He fell silently, arms crossed in front of his face, the black fabric of his soutane flapping around his legs and the *saturno* hat spinning away towards the river.

'*Attention!*' Jack yelled to those below. '*Attention!*'

He saw faces turning skywards, screams, folk running from the cathedral entrance, as Welch hit the *parvis* and Jack turned away.

'That was him,' Jack murmured, spun around to face Fox. 'Yes, that was Welch.'

'No need to rub my face in it,' said Fox. 'But what did he mean – never thought you'd pull the trigger? You told us all it was an accident. He fell from the train, you said.'

'And so he did,' Jack replied. 'Though perhaps he might have had a little help.'

The world had changed yet again. Jack stared down from the rooftop terrace of the young Parisian film star. There, across the river, just two days before, on the Île de la Cité, he had seen Welch die. Finally.

The snipers, it seemed, had all been killed or gone more permanently to ground. And Welch? They'd found a rifle hidden among the crates in that room next to the organ loft.

'But if he'd not jumped,' said Fox, 'he'd certainly have hanged. The papers we found at the Lutetia. And a couple of the Abwehr boys we caught there, happy to spill the beans in exchange for – well, it doesn't matter what for, does it? But useful intelligence.'

Harmon was at his side, in a long summer frock, yellow, small daisies. Not Harmon's style at all, made her look even taller.

'How did he get here?' she said.

'Most of their records have been burned but according to our friendly informant he'd turned up back in France, probably from Oran – the last place there was a report of a possible sighting. The Abwehr eventually transferred him here. His gammy leg – I suppose we have you and his fall from the train to thank for that one, Telford – kept him here as part of Reile's team at the Lutetia.'

'All the time you spent in my house, Jack,' she said, 'and I never did get the full story of your Black Scorpion, did I?'

'Maybe another day,' Telford told her. 'And I'm more interested in *your* story, Harmon. The Mad Butcher of Paris?'

Fox offered Jack a cigarette.

'What's this?' he said.

'I can't claim much credit,' said Harmon, wafting their cigarette smoke from her face. 'Seems like the papers here carried the story back in March. Neighbours of a man called Marcel Petiot complained about the amount of smoke coming from his chimney. Police found a furnace, a quicklime pit as well. Human remains. At least ten bodies. But then they started finding traces of other victims. No idea how many in total.'

It was good to see her again. Good to see she was still close to Fox. Just how close? He had no idea and supposed it didn't matter much. Not here, not at this moment. All peaceful now, as though it had been Arlette Hautefeuille's wedding, rather than de Gaulle's victory parade, which illuminated the City of Light afresh.

For, between the two events, more carnage. German units, Wehrmacht and SS, entrenched in the northern suburbs around the airfield at Le Bourget. The fighting had been savage, the Division supported by the FFI, heavy casualties on both sides. Jack had been in the thick of it. Photographs. But when it was over, the *maquisards* identified the SS units as being those same troops involved in a massacre of French citizens at the Jardin des Plantes just nine days earlier. The very place where the *Rochambelles* had first been encamped. The reprisals had sickened Telford.

'Jack!' shouted Danielle, peering around the corner from the farther side of the terrace. 'There you are. Come and eat.'

They'd managed to find a store with some decent dresses. A miracle, since the occupation had entirely emptied the shelves and shop windows. Only one dress Dani loved, as well. Belted, navy blue, with a wide white lace frilly collar. Not exactly Coco Chanel, but then who the hell, in those days after Liberation, would have wanted to be seen with a Chanel label? The *coutourière* herself now held by the Free French Purge Committee accused of serious collaboration with the Nazis.

'Come on,' said Jack. 'Shame to let that food go to waste.'

Fox and Harmon, however, were now deep in conversation, another correspondent, Lee Miller, apparently there on assignment for *Vogue*, reporting on the fashion houses which had survived the

German occupation and whether they were now flourishing again. Jack thought it was hilarious, wished he could have taken Miller on the desperate hunt for the dress. Yet he bit his tongue, straightened his uniform jacket, gave his apologies, and hurried to join Danielle.

On the main section of the terrace were tables ablaze with delights Paris could not have seen for the past four years. The rail networks destroyed. The city's limited food reserves stripped by the retreating *Boches*. The Allies' relief convoys a huge effort but merely scratching the surface.

Yet, somehow, this family, which had so generously hosted Arlette's reception, had managed to take their pick of culinary treats. Offerings which would have graced Maxim's, or Lucas Carton, or Lapérouse at their best. Individual helpings of *Potage Printanier*; fresh pea soup as an alternative; grilled turbot and brill; *Bouchées Montglas* stuffed patty cases; slices of beefsteak with Madeira sauce and mushrooms; champagne sorbet; *Poularde du Mans*; and *petites madeleines* with poached apricots.

Fame and fortune, Jack supposed. Because some chance encounter had put Arlette in touch with glamorous young film star, Élina Labourdette. And this apartment? It belonged to Labourdette's parents. They, in turn, had helped make the arrangements for the ceremonies earlier in the day, even furnished Arlette with her wedding dress and veil – old-fashioned but elegant – while Élina herself had helped turn the reception into this glittering affair. Film directors Jean Cocteau and Robert Bresson, actor Jean Marais, the painter Christian Bérard. A host of others, besides those invited from the Division.

'What shall we try first, *mon chou*?' Jack asked her.

But Danielle was already filling her plate.

'How long, Jack?' she said, and there was a tear running down her cheek. 'Since…'

Since clean sheets. Since a few basic luxuries. Since comfort. Yet, as Proust might have said, the vicissitudes of the guests' lives soon became indifferent to them, lost in this cornucopia of abundance.

'I don't want you getting your hopes up that our wedding will live up to this one,' he laughed.

'Soon though, my love?' Dani wiped the tear away, grinned up at him.

'Well...' he began. 'But look, Arlette and Jacques. Time to congratulate them.'

He knew he was dodging the issue, but it was truly the first time he'd seen the couple on their own. But by the time Jack and Danielle reached them, the bride and groom had been joined by two more guests, a man of about Telford's years, with swept-back wavy hair. No food, but a glass of wine, a cigarette as well, in one hand and, on his other arm, a beautiful woman, half his age, with the most prominent cheekbones Jack had ever seen.

'Dani,' Arlette beamed, 'here's somebody you must meet. This is María Casares. She's going to be *very* famous. Filming with Élina.'

The young woman laughed.

'Oh, it's a silly little thing,' she said, then dropped to a whisper. 'But it *is* Bresson.' She looked around, checking she couldn't be overheard.

'The script is brilliant,' María's companion insisted. 'Adaptation of an old Diderot story. Cocteau's given it the treatment, though. Couldn't have done it better myself.'

Modest, thought Jack, but he couldn't entirely dislike the man. Those intense eyes. Passionate.

'*Les Dames du Bois de Boulogne*,' said Arlette. 'That's what the film's called. But it could be us, no?'

Precisely where the *Rochambelles*, and much of the Division, were now camped, of course. In the Bois de Boulogne.

'Spanish, María?' said Jack and forked a piece of that fabulous turbot into his mouth.

'My accent still betrays me? But yes. From A Coruña.'

'Galicia,' said the man, sipped at his wine. 'Personally, I've never been. And Galicia is the land of others, no?'

He spoke the words as though they should have meant something to Telford. They didn't.

'Hang on.' Jack's brain was racing. 'Casares – *the* Casares?'

He recalled how Santiago Casares Quiroga had been Spain's Prime Minister until Franco's military coup.

'My father,' she smiled. Then, for the first time, she noticed

657

the patch of material at Jack's shoulder, the flash of red, yellow and purple. 'But this…' She touched a finger to the emblem.

'War correspondent,' he explained. 'Attached to Leclerc's Second Division. But specifically? I seem to have been adopted by one of his infantry companies. All Spaniards. Most of them anyway. One of them was supposed to be here with us. Otherwise engaged though, I'm afraid.'

'The fighting?' said María and lifted a hand to her lips.

'No, he wasn't at Le Bourget. He's fine. Just couldn't get away for this, sadly.'

He turned, put his arm around Danielle's shoulders, felt her tremble. They'd both been there. Scars. And they'd promised each other that, for today, just for today, they might set the horrors aside. Impossible, of course.

'And the medal?' said María's companion. 'Looks vaguely familiar.'

'Really?' Jack replied, touched the five-pointed star hanging proudly from his chest. 'Perhaps if you know North Africa…'

'The Sharifian Order of Alaoui.' The fellow smiled. 'Yes, I know North Africa.'

'Albert is part-Spanish as well,' María interrupted. 'His mother's family are Cardonas. Menorca, you know?'

'Did you fight there, *monsieur*?' said Jack, though he believed he already knew the answer.

'My one great regret. A regret we should all share, *non*? Perhaps we might have learned the lesson in time to stop the rest of this madness.'

'Lesson?'

'The obvious one, as Albert always says,' María explained. 'That being right, having justice and law and courage on your side, isn't enough to stop you being crushed. Not enough in itself. So many of us here in Paris who know the awful truth of this now.'

'Forgive me,' Jack said to the man. 'Are you Camus?'

'And you, I take it,' the fellow replied, 'are Telford.' They shook hands. 'Francine told me you bought the book.'

'You owe me a signature, I think, said Jack.'

*

658

'Well,' said Jack, 'you certainly put him in his place.'

They were heading back to the Bois de Boulogne, sharing one of those Velo taxis. A bit stupid, really. It would have cost them no more in a motor taxi, but Jack had decided this might be more romantic. A warm evening, and perhaps they'd see more of the city from the open wooden box behind the bike.

'Pompous little man,' Danielle snapped. 'His lovely wife, stuck in Oran. And him, strutting around with that trollop. Old enough to be her father. Well, just about, anyway. Has he no shame?'

'She seemed very nice,' Telford replied. He'd been glad to get away. Regardless of Albert's reputation, his obvious liaison with the young actress, he was still guilty about Francine. And yes, he'd promised to get his copy of *L'Étranger* to the author, so he could sign the wretched thing, though he had no intention of doing so in practice.

They'd just reached the Pont de L'Alma and Dani took it into her head she'd like to stop at the Trocadéro Gardens.

'Maybe we could walk the rest of the way from there,' she said.

It was still a hell of a long way, but Jack agreed, paid off the driver – or was it the right word? Cyclist maybe. Anyway, daylight robbery. Six hundred *francs*. Three quid?

'Can you imagine?' he said, turning from the Palais de Chaillot in one direction, to the Eiffel Tower in the other, back across the river. 'If von Choltitz had followed Hitler's orders, blown this all to hell?'

They climbed the stairways to reach the Esplanade.

'Jack,' she said, 'I've been thinking. Perhaps when we get married – the wedding in Toulouse?'

'Well, the city's free again, at least. Your parents safe?'

Toulouse had, indeed, been liberated. Ten days earlier. And, they said, it had been liberated principally by one of the many Spanish *guerrilla* groups operating in the south, as part of the FFI. They had apparently christened it afresh. *Tolosa Roja*, Red Toulouse, much to de Gaulle's disgust.

'I've written to them,' said Danielle. 'But heard nothing. Jack, what if…?'

They'd talked about it before. The likelihood that, if the Gestapo hadn't been able to find Dani herself, they may have hunted down her family. Likelihood? Jack thought. Almost a certainty, surely.

'You know,' he said, desperately trying to change the subject, and looking out over the gardens, 'the last time I was here, for the Exhibition, there was Picasso's painting, of course. But there was a superb sculpture as well. An obelisk. I can still picture it. Winding spiral path leading to a star at the top. A symbol that, despite the civil war, there was a goal. A dream. A hope. How there's always hope, Danielle.'

'At least I don't fear them anymore,' she said. 'The Gestapo. Both free of our demons now, Jack, my love.'

He'd not had time to think about it very much but yes, he supposed she was right. Welch dead. And even the villain's last strange request – a few words for Dorothea, something fitting. Well, he'd managed, explained he wasn't in a position to divulge state secrets but he needed to inform her that Kingsley had died for his country while involved in undercover operations. Always easiest to tell the nearest thing to the truth, whenever possible. Simply no need to mention that the country in question had been Nazi Germany. Of course, she'd undoubtedly spend the next few years waving Telford's letter in the face of the intelligence services, vainly seeking more details. But he'd done his duty. It was enough.

'You're right,' he said, and lit them a cigarette. 'No more demons.'

But the words sounded hollow, even to Jack himself.

'Then the wedding,' she laughed. 'Let's plan the wedding. In Toulouse, yes?'

'In Toulouse,' he agreed. 'But not yet, Dani. There's the oath. I took the oath in Kufra, like the rest. After Strasbourg, *mon chou*, then we plan the wedding.'

Granell stopped outside the derelict premises on the Rue du Bouloi, not far from Les Halles.

'What d'you think of it?' he said. To Jack, Amado looked some-how diminished. Always slim, slender, he now seemed famished, both physically and in spirit. He'd developed a cough, as well.

There was a sign above the boarded windows. *Le Grognard.*
The Old Soldier. The Grumbler, maybe.

'Name's appropriate,' said Jack and turned to the others. Fox
and Harmon. Danielle. And Victoria Kent y Siano.

'It's a wreck,' Victoria laughed.

She was perhaps fifty. Dark eyes, dark hair, dark-skinned,
former member of the Cortes and sent in the middle of the Civil
War to be the Republic's ambassador in Paris, helping Spanish
exiles. With the German occupation she'd taken refuge in the
Mexican Embassy and, later, the Red Cross had hidden her in an
apartment near the Bois de Boulogne. Yet now no longer a need
to hide, and there'd been a wonderful little celebration, an outdoor
feast, the reunion of a few Spanish soldiers with their wives and
children who'd also managed to find sanctuary in Paris – and a
presentation of flowers by the men of *La Nueve* to Victoria, this
representative of the Republican government in exile. She'd struck
up an immediate friendship with Granell, both of them members
of *Izquierda Republicana*, the Republican Left.

'It's obviously been a restaurant before,' said Fox. 'I suppose
that's something.'

'Yes,' Dani sneered. 'When Bonaparte was a boy, maybe.'

'I'm in no rush,' Amado told them. 'Need to raise the money
first. But what do you reckon?' he said to Victoria. 'A place for the
comrades to meet?'

'Good luck with that,' Victoria replied. 'I sometimes think
we're more divided now than we've ever been. President and the
Cortes in Mexico, Negrín in London, the rest of us here, holding
our breath, still hoping the Allies will deal with Franco when the
rest of this is done.'

'I won't hold *my* breath,' said Granell, and Danielle touched
his arm.

'Time we were *all* going home, Amado,' she said. 'And did Jack
tell you? We've decided to get married in Toulouse – when we can
get there.'

'So,' Fox laughed, 'something to celebrate, at least. Drinks on
Telford, surely?'

There was a bar he liked on the Saint-Eustache end of Rue

Coquillière and they retraced their steps, to cross Rue du Louvre, but they were halted at the junction by an excited, jeering crowd lining the street. Marching down the centre of the thoroughfare itself, a group of well-armed *maquisards* forcing, before them, the object of the onlookers' opprobrium. Six women, their heads stubbled and bleeding from some rough shearing, stripped to their underwear, each with a swastika daubed on her chest with hot tar. Other women ran forward from the pavement to spit upon them, to tear at their petticoats, to beat them with sticks.

'Look at them,' said Jack. 'Still so bloody defiant.' Had he expected them to show remorse? Guilt? Yet they had nothing in their eyes but contempt for their captors and the crowd.

It was almost impossible to avoid one of these processions, wherever he went, and he wondered which might be the least fortunate – these women, accused of sleeping with the enemy, or the collaborationist men, being shot in their droves but freed from the torments which, Jack guessed, would follow the women for the rest of their lives. 'And so many collaborators,' he said.

'What?' Fox laughed. 'You don't think we'd have had the same numbers lining up to help the Nazis if Britain had been successfully invaded or if we'd agreed an armistice with them in 1940? Folk in high places, but men and women in the street as well. We have lots of their names, old boy.'

Jack had made the same point himself, more than once.

'But just no end,' said Granell. 'Not for the rest of us, *inglés*. Only for you, my friend.'

Telford had shared his story – the true story – with Amado back in Oran. Just about the only occasion he'd told the full tale other than with Ruby Waters and Sydney Elliott. Even with Danielle, there were details he'd preferred to keep to himself.

Yet an end? Yes, Welch gone and, with him, any lasting doubts Jack might have harboured about Leslie Howard.

Good, therefore, to be free of at least one piece of guilt, though Jack didn't feel as though he'd reached the end of his particular road. As a reminder, in the distance, the sound of a marching band. *The Stars and Stripes Forever* – just one of the Yankee infantry divisions parading through the city before being dispatched off to the east, along with Leclerc's forces, through the regions of Champagne, Lorraine and Alsace to reach the Rhine. Perhaps then he'd be able to fill some of those empty spaces in his life – the ones about which Frances Moorgate had reminded him. So, Toulouse. The wedding. A cottage in Dorset, maybe.

'An end for all of us soon, Amado, no? This war can't last forever. And after Strasbourg – the oath fulfilled...'

'The oath?' said Granell. 'I wasn't at Kufra, my friend. And who knows whether I might even make it to Strasbourg. Perhaps none of us will make it.'

September – November 1944

Major Joseph Putz

They'd made good progress. One hundred and eighty miles in the four days since they'd left Paris, and many were glad to be back on the road again. Glad to be part of another combined operation with Patton's Third Army, Leclerc's Division out on the right flank of the Allies' offensive to smash through the German defences in Lorraine.

'You know what the old bastard said to me?' Amado had grumbled as they'd been driving out of the city. 'Remember him – the filthy wretch who ran the bar? Asked me what the hell were we all still doing there.'

'Conquering heroes and fresh fish both start to stink after three days,' Jack had replied. 'I think Benjamin Franklin said that.'

Outlived their welcome? Perhaps. But their short time in Paris had also been costly. The Division had lost almost a hundred dead and three times this number seriously wounded.

So, four days on the road, south and east to Chaumont, then north to Andelot where they'd run into the Germans. A furious battle, nine more soldiers of Leclerc's Division killed – but the Germans had lost a hundred men, eight hundred taken prisoner, tanks destroyed.

The same day, at Andelot, members of the Resistance had arrived. Some days earlier, they'd liberated an internment camp, forty miles to the east, a place called Vittel. Three thousand prisoners there, almost all of them women and children. But the *Boches* had come back, driven the *maquisards* away. Massu had been sent off to investigate and, by mid-afternoon, Putz and much of his Third Battalion had followed.

Jack's byline for the article he wrote that same afternoon gave the date as the twelfth of September.

A very different sort of prison camp, a very different class of internees, as correspondent, Jack Telford, *now explains.*

Internment camps were nothing new to them. Of course not. There'd been the piece Harmon had written, about the German prisoners who weren't German at all. Those pressed into their service – Ukrainians, Russians, Poles and many others – but all now detained in POW camps along with the Germans themselves, tens of thousands, while somebody tried to work out what the hell should be done with them. And then there were all those in the forced labour laagers – again, full of enslaved workers from just about every corner of Europe.

Finally, the camps for those prisoners of war recently captured by the *Boches*. Camps large and small, everywhere from Cherbourg and Brest to Le Havre, Drancy and Verdun. All throughout Italy, the reports claimed, the same. And, usually, no option except to keep the internees exactly where they were – for the time being, at least. Feed them, naturally, but otherwise Allied barbed wire must have seemed little different to that with which the Nazis had incarcerated them.

But Vittel? Yes, it was very different.

A barbed wire perimeter, like all the others. Yet, inside, luxurious hotels, leafy parklands, clay tennis courts, well-stocked library, modern hospital, food and fashion shops. For Vittel had been a spa town, a holiday resort, and ideal, the Germans had decided, to house the three thousand British and American women and their children who'd been trapped in the Occupied Zone in 1940. In addition, there were Jewish prisoners here also, Jews with foreign citizenship and some prominence abroad who might serve as hostages, potential exchanges for equally prominent Germans interned by the Allies.

'Well,' said Major Florence Conrad, now reunited with her *Rochambelles*, 'there but for the grace of God go I.'

Jack's article was a bitter-sweet affair. Heartwarming stories of Conrad's ambulance drivers entertaining the camp's kids with glove puppets they'd made themselves – entertaining them from

665

the other side of the barbed wire, however. And he even had a decent photo of the event.

Telford shamelessly recorded Leclerc's speech to the inmates, as well. About how appropriate it might be for a French general to free them – a modest gesture in return for the boundless hospitality Britain had showed towards the fledgling Free France back in 1940, for the generosity of the United States in arming his Division, for fighting to help liberate his country.

But Jack wrote about the tragedies also. The many Jews discovered, only months previously, to have forged papers, less prominence than the SS had been led to believe, and the transports arranged to take them to the east, the suicides of whole families who knew precisely what transport to the east meant in practice.

Like everywhere else, it would still be some time before the Vittel prisoners could actually be freed, returned to their homes, but there were worse places to wait. And Vittel had turned up one more story. The German commandant had evidently left in a hurry, papers in a drawer of his desk. Details of local deployments – and one, in particular, which drew Leclerc's attention. An entire Panzer Brigade at Dompaire, barely fifteen miles to the east.

By early evening, the Division's Shermans had occupied most of the high ground around the *Boches* positions, and the firefight went on all through the night. It rained, but through the darkness and the drizzle, Jack counted the blazing vehicles. In the morning, the men of the Chad Regiment went into action and Telford with them. Photographs of Putz and his men sending up flares to call in airstrikes on the German positions, American fighter planes responding with rockets and bombs, which turned the place into an inferno. French howitzers and tank destroyers completed the carnage. Hundreds of German dead, a thousand wounded or captured, dozens of their tanks left in flames.

It was a great victory – so why this foreboding? Some feeling in his bones. Like one of Putz's premonitions. But why? After all, it should have been a moment of joy. Another liberation. And yet...

'Arlette's pregnant?' said Jack, as they watched Putz, Dronne and the platoon commanders of *La Nueve* examining the ruins of an ancient bridge which had, until 1940, spanned the Moselle. Next to it, the remains of the subsequent wooden bridge destroyed by the Germans in their retreat. On the other side, the houses and church tower of Châtel, lit pink by the evening sky. It was relatively quiet, though the rumble of heavy artillery drifted to them on the breeze from further north.

'Poor girl says she has no idea how,' Danielle told him, then held up the fan belt triumphantly. 'There,' she shouted to her co-driver, Édith, who was busy emptying a rusty jerry can of gasoline into the tank. 'Got it.'

Another of Toto's rules. Never drive through deep water without first removing your fan belt. Or fitting a condom to the distributor cap.

'Maybe if somebody had given her better instruction on what those condoms are *actually* for...' said Jack. He heard Édith choke with laughter. Danielle liked her, and they'd been together – well, since not long after that crash near Fougères. Poor Yvette had never returned to active duty, her vision permanently impaired.

'Arlette's more worried about getting demobbed,' Dani smiled.

The Dodge was parked among trees at the side of the road from Nomexy, not far behind them, Jack sitting in the shade, scribbling in his notebook.

'Is there a procedure, I wonder?' he said. 'Demobbed by reason of pregnancy?'

'Don't be a fool, Jack. But listen, I don't want those two getting married before us.'

'Those two? You mean Fox and Harmon? What in heaven's name makes you think they're even involved, let alone planning to get spliced? Anyway, come and look at this. Then you can pose for a photo.'

Fox was still in Paris, liaison duties to perform at de Gaulle's offices – the offices of his Provisional Government. And Harmon? Following up the latest threads in the manhunt for the Mad Butcher of Paris.

'A photo, looking like this?' said Danielle. 'I don't think so, *Monsieur* Telford.'

She threw the fan belt inside the cab, wandered over to admire his handiwork. The latest additions and amendments to the map of France he'd begun in Normandy.

'Good job I decided to spread it over two pages,' he said. 'I wasn't sure whether to take it any further than Paris. Seemed like it might be wishful thinking, bring us bad luck. Stupid, no?'

'Superstitious, *mon chéri*? Is it possible for a heathen non-believer to be superstitious?'

He'd promised her faithfully that, despite his own agnosticism, they would be married into her faith. He still wasn't certain what this would mean? Would he have to sign something? Seek authority from the pope? Another bridge to be crossed.

'Come on,' he said. 'The photo. There should be just enough light left.'

She protested, of course. The dirty fatigues. The grease and oil on her hands. But in the end, she was persuaded. He'd already taken plenty of group photos – the *Rochambelles* waiting to embark at Southampton, or in action at Écouché – but he hadn't a single snap of Danielle on her own. A stupid omission, now corrected, though he could see she was ill at ease – and not with his camera work.

'I wish the rest of them were here,' she said, and peered down the road, through the gathering gloom.

'Won't be an attack until morning. And according to Granell, it doesn't even look like much opposition. Sounds like most of the action's up there somewhere.' He jerked his head northwards. 'Stop worrying, we'll probably have the whole kit and caboodle up with us by then.'

Tout le bataclan. But he wasn't certain. The Division was strung out along quite a front. And Leclerc was bound to send the medical units wherever he thought they'd be needed most.

He'd opted to stay with Granell's patrol. Like a good luck charm, that was how he viewed Amado, as their half-track headed south, two of the Shermans behind them, following the tree-lined river until they reached the bridge to the neighbouring village, Vaxoncourt. A simple enough plan, Putz had said. Granell would cross and approach Châtel from the east. Miguel Campos, *el canario*, would sweep round from the north and, when they were both

668

in position, Montoya's men would wade the Moselle for a frontal attack on the town itself.

Granell, Campos and Montoya, the three men who'd delivered those helmets full of money to the old priest at Écouché. What could possibly go wrong?

Jack took some photographs from the back of the half-track, the arched Vaxoncourt bridge just wide enough for the tanks, and the German outpost which surrendered without firing a shot.

They pressed on, now on the east bank, following a smaller stream, an interesting prospect opening ahead of them. A sprawl of grey ruins, no more than a mile away on rising ground. Putz had briefed them, naturally. Châtel's old curtain walls, the remains of a once-mighty fortress. Beyond the ruins, the familiar sandstone church tower Jack had admired with Danielle the previous evening.

Where was she?

Lieutenant Colonel de la Horie, now commanding the Combat Group to which Putz's battalion belonged, had ordered that, once the Châtel bridgehead was secured, there'd be an advance in force across the Moselle and, hopefully, by that time the rest of the *Rochambelles* would have come up. But they'd certainly not appeared by the time Granell's little foray had begun.

They halted at the nearest of the ruins, the first of the town's houses off to their left, running down towards the river and, to their right, a set of medieval buildings like a small monastery. Amado deployed his soldiers, and the two tanks, along the line of the old fortifications and sent up a flare, a green one. They were answered by another, rising up beyond the church – Campos also in position.

'Now?' said Jack, as he wound on the camera for his next shot.

'Now,' Amado smiled, 'poor Vicente's going to get his socks wet.'

Vicente Montoya left with the task of the frontal attack. And Danielle would cross with the Dodge shortly afterwards, he supposed – hopefully, by then, with some of the other *Rochambelles*.

'Think there'll be much opposition?'

Granell shook his head.

'Seems quiet enough,' he said – just as the firing began.

*

They'd cleared out the opposition from Châtel by ten that morning and begun to rig a crude footbridge across the river, as well as a defensive perimeter. It ran in a semicircle from the Moselle to the post office and school, to the *mairie* and the church, then to the medieval fortress – where the remains of some east-facing bastions along the old curtain walls provided strongpoints – and finally to the still habitable shell of the ancient Capuchin hospice, the cluster of medieval buildings they'd seen when they'd arrived, before meeting the riverbank again about four hundred yards along from the perimeter's beginning. The line was anchored, midway along this stretch of the river, by a modest château.

'I suppose the old monks would be pleased to see the place still serving its purpose,' Jack told Danielle, as he gazed up at the rafters of the hospice.

There were wounded here, German wounded for the most part, and just a few of their own men, including Fermín Pujol, who'd seen his brother Constantino killed at Écouché. But Fermín, at least, didn't seem too badly injured.

'As infirmaries go,' she replied, 'I've seen worse.'

She and Édith had just brought in a German officer on a stretcher. He was in a bad way, shrapnel from the mortar attack *Papi* Putz had ordered against the fortified farmhouse just outside the town. Danielle helped the medics and Châtel's doctor unload their burden, settle him on the floor with a blanket and pillow.

'Do you have to go out again?' said Jack.

'Who else?' she said. 'Until the others turn up.'

He walked with her to the ambulance parked in the lane outside. At least there was no more shooting. He waved her goodbye, yelled one of those stupid warnings to be careful, while yet more of the town's citizens arrived to help as volunteer nurses.

They'd already celebrated their liberation with a display of generosity which Jack found overwhelming. The reserves of food must have been pitiful, and yet every scrap of their precious stores had plainly been sacrificed to provide the steady flow of hot meals, stews and fresh bread to the men of *La Nueve* and the Tenth Company, to the tank and armoured car crews, to the sappers.

Telford snapped photographs, scribbled down an interview

with the parish priest and, late in the afternoon, took himself off to the château near the river now serving as their headquarters. There, he was shown by a gnarled and withered family retainer to a room on the checker-tiled upper floor where he found Granell, Campos, Montoya, Dronne, Major Putz and that bold young captain of the 501st Jack remembered from the tank battles in Paris. Branet, wasn't it? Jacques Branet. A room? It was more like a gallery running almost the length of the house, with a good view over the town. At the farther end of the gallery, an old lady – the owner, Jack supposed – embroidered a piece of linen while seated in a bath chair, and a younger woman perched on her window seat nearby, reading a book.

'Well, *Señor* Telford,' said Putz, 'can you smell it on the wind?'

The major enjoyed practising his Spanish whenever he was with the officers and men of the Company. A spaniel, Jack thought. He reminds me of a spaniel. Fifty, or thereabouts. Wide, affable mouth. Bushy eyebrows. Deep-set spaniel eyes. Long snout. His lower cheeks a little puffy. But a spaniel with the bite of a bulldog. And from the other end of the gallery, Jack thought he heard the old woman muttering something to her companion about foreigners.

'An attack, Major?' Telford replied. It was so very like Putz. Jack glanced through the windows, out across the red pantiled rooftops to the thin, high steeple of Saint-Laurent, two hundred yards away. Nothing could have looked more peaceful. That distant rumble of artillery fire from somewhere else up the line, though quiet as the grave here. Yet the major had this infallible sixth sense.

'Within the hour, unless I'm much mistaken. Well, Amado, are we ready for it?'

'Spanish, perhaps?' Jack heard the old lady's companion say, quite distinctly.

There was a small occasional table in front of the window and, on the table, a map. Granell settled a fingertip at the spot where his two tanks and his half-track had dug themselves into the ruins. Then the turn of Miguel Campos and Jacques Branet, four half-tracks there, beyond the church, the very edge of town, supported by the captain's Shermans. And, finally, Vicente Montoya, a fall-back position between the school and the town hall.

'Why are there Spaniards in my house?' The older woman paused her stitching. 'At least I could understand the *Boches*.'

'You think I should explain?' Putz asked his officers. But they decided it might be more trouble than it was worth.

'Reinforcements, Major?' said Montoya.

'The colonel will bring up support as soon as he's able,' said Putz. 'We need the sappers. New bridges, no? But, for now, we'll just hold the place – like we held Écouché. Only this feels more like home.'

'You were born in this neck of the woods, Major?' Jack asked him.

'Me? Hell, no. I was born in Brussels, of all places. But when I joined up, back in 'fourteen, my first regiment was garrisoned at Toul, just north of here. And yes, home in a different way. My family all from Alsace.'

'I'm guessing it's a long way from Alsace to Brussels, Major,' said Campos.

In the background, they could hear the companion explaining how at least they all seemed to have insignia bearing the Cross of Lorraine. Telford decided that, before he left, he'd take the trouble to speak with them.

'They didn't leave by choice, Miguel,' Putz was explaining. 'We've been fighting the *Boches* for control of Alsace and Lorraine for centuries. And after the war with Prussia, when Bismarck snatched Alsace back as part of his new German empire, my family couldn't accept it – left their homeland like so many others.'

Alsace and Lorraine, Jack knew, had been back in French hands since the end of the last war. After almost fifty years as part of the Reichsland. But he wondered how many of its citizens would now see the Allies as liberators, rather than conquerors.

'There must be plenty of German sympathisers there, I suppose,' he said, and wondered whether the old woman might be one of them.

'More than enough,' Putz replied. 'But *le patron*'s oath, to see the *Tricolore* flying over Strasbourg again – well, I must admit, it has a special meaning for me.'

'Your family from Strasbourg, then, sir?' said Donne.

672

'No, Raymond. A little further to the south. Near Colmar. But a small place. You'd never have heard of it.'

The family retainer returned, followed by a delegation, men with FFI armbands and a stocky fellow Jack had already met – the mayor, Pierre Sayer, local leader of *los fifi* as well. It turned out he was also the town's doctor, the same one Telford had encountered at the hospice.

'Forgive me, gentlemen,' the mayor blurted out. 'But we just had word from Hadigny. The Boches. Tanks. Many tanks, coming this way.'

Danielle had made the first of her runs to Nomexy, carrying Gómez, wounded in the firefight, at around six.

Since then, according to Jack's reckoning, by midnight she'd made the same journey back across the river five times, evacuating those most badly wounded. Five times, then into the thick of it once more.

The thick of it – yes, it had been thick, right enough. The first attack, early in the evening. The *Boches* had dug in at the same fortified farmhouse against which Putz had ordered the mortar attack earlier in the day. But Miguel Campos had already set a neat little trap for them, rigged explosives there, positioned his men so they could catch the Germans in a crossfire. Nothing short of murder. Two Panther tanks destroyed, the farmhouse flattened, and at least a score of Panzergrenadiers killed. The survivors fell back.

After that – well, the calm before the storm.

Almost dark before the *Boches* came for them in force. Jack had been chatting with Reiter and one of the machine gun crews hidden among the debris of the flattened farmhouse. They'd appeared out of the gloom, in serried ghostly ranks, across the open field beyond.

Jack almost wanted to shout, to warn them. What the hell were they thinking?

The machine gun opened up, only a yard from him. He covered his ears, ducked his head, but looked up again in time to see them fall. They fell in neat rows, like lines of skittles.

Another machine gun, from a half-track hidden in a clump of trees away to Telford's left. But then the screech of incoming artillery fire and the half-track exploded in a ball of molten iridescence, the gunner hurled into the air and thrown almost to where Jack lay. It was the sergeant, Díez, though hardly recognisable for the scorched and blackened flesh of his face. He was moaning pitifully.

'Benítez,' he murmured, as Jack reached into his own haversack, dragged out the medical kit, wondered what the hell he was supposed to do for facial burns like these. 'Benítez?' the sergeant said again.

Telford glanced over to the burning wreckage. There'd be no other survivors, but he couldn't bring himself to tell Díez so.

In the light from the blaze, he found one of the tubes of morphine tartrate, scissors to slice open the sergeant's trouser leg, stabbed the needle into his thigh.

'*Ayuda*,' Jack yelled. '*Médico.*'

'Wasting your breath, comrade,' Reiter told him. 'Think you can get him to the dressing station on your own?'

Across the field, there were tanks, and now Campos was at their side.

'Pulling back from here,' he said. 'Join up with Montoya.' Miguel looked down at Sergeant Díez. 'José – will he make it?'

'I'll get him to the hospice,' said Jack. 'After that...'

Telford half-carried, half-dragged the sergeant across the broken ground to the narrow lane running between the first of the houses, the sounds of fury behind him, the remaining three half-tracks from Campos's section breaking from their cover and rumbling back into the centre of town.

Jack stumbled past the church, stopped to draw breath as he skirted the tumbled, moss-scarred stones of the old fortress, sheltering behind the shoulder-high remains of a round tower. Inside the ruins, Granell's men in action. Flashes of rifle and carbine fire in the blackness. More machine guns. The dull *crump* of grenades.

Díez was still groaning and Telford bore him the final two hundred yards to the carbolic miasma of the dressing station, left the sergeant in the care of the mayor, Doctor Sayer.

'This man needs more care than I can give him,' Sayer told Jack. 'The ambulance, perhaps? Get him to Nomexy.'

Yes, Jack agreed, he'd find the ambulance. But when he'd asked some of the volunteers, they thought Danielle was already making yet another run across the river. And there was no sign of any more ambulance crews. Nancy itself, to the north, had been liberated, some of the *maquisards* told him, but still heavy fighting around the outskirts. Patton's Third Army. Many casualties, they said. Perhaps some of Leclerc's ambulances had been needed there, as well.

Telford had no choice but to steady his nerves, wait it out, decided to head for the château, find out from Putz how the battle might be going – because, sure as hell, there was certainly no way to tell, out in the chaos of it all, the darkness, the smoke, the noise.

'Telford, have you seen Reiter?'

The major had joined Montoya's section, the upper storey of a large house in the defensive line they'd established between the château and the church, machine gun nests in some of the buildings, Branet's Shermans hidden wherever they could use their greater speed, their mobility, to counter the superior armour and firepower of the German Panthers and Tigers.

'I heard Campos telling him to fall back – to here,' Jack replied. 'But that was a while ago.'

'No Campos either,' said Branet.

'Dammit.' Putz turned to the radio operator at his side. 'Are you sure you can't make sense of it, Corporal?'

The radio set crackled, whistled, emitted odd words. German?

The corporal turned the squelch button, cut out the worst of the interference, adjusted the frequency tuning knob carefully. Better.

'But I don't speak German,' he said.

'Then where…?' Putz began.

'My German's a bit basic, Major,' said Jack, 'but I'll give it a go.'

And thus they managed to intercept the messages between several of Manteuffel's Panzer units.

'Hungry for revenge, I suppose,' said Putz. 'The same brigades we mauled at Dompaire – what's left of them, anyhow. Any idea

675

what they're planning, *Monsieur* Telford?'

'A lot of it was just gibberish,' Jack replied. 'But I picked up the words *Fraize* and *Nancy* a few times. And it seems they mean to take the town at any cost.'

'You have the map, Captain?' Putz asked Branet. 'Here,' he said, when he'd had chance to examine the thing. 'They're planning to swing round through this woodland, the Bois de Fraize, then come in on the Nancy road. Hit our left flank, *messieurs*. Don't you think? They've already tested our centre and right, found it a bit too hot. So now...'

He prodded the map once more.

'Then we'll be waiting for them, Major,' said Branet.

It lasted two hours. The destruction of those German units.

There'd been enough time for Putz to organise his defence, to take a calculated gamble – bringing half of Amado's section from their right flank, from their strongpoints among the fortress ruins, to the more exposed positions in the trees separating the riverbank from the lane to Nancy.

'Have you seen her?' Jack had asked Granell, as the lieutenant organised his men, Cortés and a bazooka team, machine guns.

'The ambulance? *Inglés*, she's doing her job.' He'd become more irritable, Jack had noticed. Almost peevish. The cough worse, the circles under his eyes even darker – though Jack couldn't actually *see* his eyes now, in the night's gloom and under the rim of Amado's helmet. 'And we need to get on with ours,' said the Spaniard. 'But you? Either pick up a rifle, pick up your pen or help pick up the wounded – we'll have some, soon enough. All the same, we've been in worse scraps than this one. Why all the panic? Danielle can look after herself.'

'But the more fights, the more we tempt providence, don't we? The more we shorten the odds. Look how many we were when we left England – how many of those we've lost. And it's not been much more than a month.'

'For you, maybe. For the rest of us – and that includes your woman. How long was she fighting with the Resistance at Tolosa? But even you, *inglés*. Oran? Before – in Spain?'

'Me?' said Jack. 'I suppose I never had anything I feared losing so much before. And it's too dark to write, so I suppose it had better be picking up the wounded again.'

It was prophetic, for in those following two hours there were wounded aplenty. But there was help, at least. A couple of tank destroyers, a mortar squad and more half-tracks come up from Nomexy. And yes, two more ambulances, as well as a half-track carrying some of the Quaker stretcher-bearers.

They were needed, as the lane from Nancy, the open ground between the road and the forest turned into a bloodbath. Some Doré illustration for *Paradise Lost*. The strewn dead and the writhing, mutilated damned, in shadow and light – the light from a hellish halo, more burning wrecks, dancing flames across the black background.

Jack had been twice to the hospice, helping to take away their own wounded – Cortés the bazooka man, among others. But he watched now, open-mouthed, as the *Boches* attempted their final madness. Yet more Panthers sent forward, towing chains attached to those of their tanks immobilised but not entirely beyond repair. And, as they tried to drag them away, those Panthers died in their turn. Mortar fire. The tank destroyers. Branet's Shermans now on the advance with no opposition.

Two hours, thought Jack. But looks like we'll live to fight another day, after all.

It was after three in the morning when he finally saw her, at the hospice, heading back in the darkness with Édith along the Hadigny road where, she said, they had more wounded, crewmen from one of the tank destroyers, sent up to support them. And Reiter was missing, she told him.

'But where the hell are the others?' he said to her. 'Where?'

Naturally, she had no idea. It was just a simple fact. Their old Dodge was still one of the few ambulances east of the Moselle. Just those two others which had crossed the river earlier.

'Don't worry,' she told him. 'We'll be fine.' And she reached inside her fatigues, the shirt beneath, pulled out the neck chain with her identity tags and the engagement ring. 'See? My rabbit's foot.'

'Trust bloody Reiter,' he said.

The German's flanking movement might have failed completely, but there was still gunfire out there, flashes of intermittent lightning against the night sky, but distorted by the rain which had now also started to lash them.

'They want us to pull out?' Putz yelled. Bulldog Putz, thought Jack, not the spaniel. The major lifted the *képi* from his head, scratched at his thinning hair, spoke in Spanish to Granell. 'And these good people of Châtel?' he said. 'We leave them to the mercy of the *Boches*?'

Twelve long hours after they'd received word of the German advance. They were back in the same gallery room, the same small château, which had now become part of their last line of defence. The same – only now most of the glass was gone from the windows and the bookcases, the display cabinets, the fine paintings, which had once graced the interior wall, were ripped to ruination.

'Can't we evacuate them?' Jack asked, knowing it was a stupid question. The latest intelligence. The *Boches* massing for yet another massive assault, and the rest of the Division still too scattered to mount a relief.

'The *jefe*,' Amado reminded him, 'insists we should do it quietly, use whatever hour or so of darkness still left to get the boys back across the river without too much fuss.'

He meant, of course, without the Germans trying to stop them. The *Boches* had become cautious, this latter part of the night, learned just how vicious the bulldog's fangs could be. But still a threat if they coordinated their attack properly.

'Not just the boys, though,' said Jack. 'The ambulances. And maybe get some of the people out that way. The kids? And our friend the mayor. If they find out how he's helped us...'

'But retreat?' said Putz. 'We've *never* retreated. Not once. Even at Écouché.'

'We could just ignore it, sir?' Branet suggested. '*Le patron* will just have to come and relieve us.'

Putz glowered at him.

'Never retreated, Captain. And never disobeyed his orders. You understand? Now, are the wounded all evacuated?'

Jack confirmed the names he already knew.

'Lieutenant Montoya, Major. Bellver, Izquierdo and Gómez.'

'What about Fermín?' said Amado.

'Pujol?' Jack replied. 'And Détenger. Both still here. Refused to be evacuated. Díez died in the hospice. And Cortés – *Gitano* – still there. Too bad to be moved, according to the doctor.'

Granell shook his head.

'Poor devil,' he said. 'Did you see how many of their cans he lit up? But he'll make it, if anybody can.'

'And Reiter,' said Miguel Campos. 'Still missing. Bloody German idiot.'

'Well, gentlemen,' Putz smiled, 'looks like there's a first time for everything, even a retreat. And Telford, you seem to have better links to the *Rochambelles* than the rest of us.' The others laughed. 'Why not see whether it might be possible for them to take the mayor and his family with us? Maybe a few more as well? But remember, it's all got to be done quietly.'

When they'd halted in Nomexy, just two nights earlier, the place had been full of French flags. But now, as Putz's group straggled back into town, at first light, the flags were all gone.

'They've heard we're retreating,' said Granell. 'Think the *Boches* will be on our heels.'

Jack barely heard him, stared back from the half-track for any sight of Danielle's Dodge. There was an ambulance, further to the rear, still the other side of the canal, but he couldn't make out whether it was Dani or not.

It was all confusion simply because other units of the Division were still arriving from the opposite direction. But many of them came together around the church, almost the twin of the one in Châtel. At the rear of the church, a cluster of buildings and these had been turned into a temporary hospital. Danielle would have been bringing her injured here. Granell dropped him as close as he could get and went off to find Dronne.

'You've lost her again, Mister Telford?'

Bill Spray, the same Methodist with the Quakers who'd once pointed him towards the *Rochambelles* when they'd been quartered at Fleuré.

'Seems that way,' said Jack. 'Danielle – she would have been here during the night. Is she back?'

'I'm sorry,' said Spray. 'Not seen her since – I don't know, it's a few hours now. But perhaps…'

Spray pointed to an ambulance just turning along the side of the church. Telford recognised the driver, little Jacqueline Fournier, known by just about everybody as Jacotte. She jumped from the cab, ran to the back and opened the doors – helped three women and several small children to climb down.

'Jacotte,' said Telford, when he'd reached them. 'So, we managed to get some of them out.'

'*Madame* Sayer,' she said. 'And her kids.'

The woman held her head high, an arm around the boy and girl at her side.

'The mayor?' said Telford, and Jacotte shook her head.

'Refused to come. Duty to stay, he told us.'

'And Danielle?'

'Isn't she here?'

'She was supposed to be heading off to pick up the last of the wounded. Reiter, maybe.'

'That can't be, *Monsieur* Telford. Reiter's here. I've seen him.'

Like a knife in his guts. He walked to the corner of the church, looked back up the road towards the canal. Just the stragglers coming in, the last of the half-tracks, which had formed their small rearguard.

He fretted. Where the hell is she? Where?

But maybe Jacotte was wrong and Dani was already here as well. If Reiter was back…

He asked where the various platoons of Dronne's Company might be and was directed to the old watermill, where he found Reiter easily enough, a bandage around his head, blood in the unruly beard.

'Johann,' said Jack. 'Badly hurt?'

'Scratch,' said Reiter. 'But bled like a pig. Fine now.'

'But did Dani bring you in?'

She hadn't, and he'd not even seen her.

'She'll be here somewhere, though,' Reiter told him. 'Don't

look so worried. You know the score. If she's not here, she'll turn up. Like a bad penny, your girl. Or maybe hiding up somewhere.'

'Hiding up?' said Jack. 'You mean, back there?'

It was Sunday, of course. Mass at the church, and Jack showed his face, just on the stupid offchance she'd be there – perhaps hadn't even thought he'd be worried about her. Or maybe just got together with the other girls and…

Then, later, he walked the mile back towards the ruined bridges over the Moselle but kept himself in cover because he could see the Germans already occupying the town again. A couple of tanks. Machine gun posts and sandbags. Not much sign of life otherwise.

He waited there, with no idea why he did so. If she *was* the other side of the river, she certainly wouldn't try to break through the *Boches* lines here. But maybe further south, at Vaxoncourt, the bridge Granell had used.

He spent much of the afternoon walking that way, reached the bridge, found the Germans there also, then retraced his steps to Nomexy, cursing himself for a fool, certain she'd have appeared by now and probably worried sick about *him*.

Yet she wasn't there. And now there was no doubt about it. Because the rest of the *Rochambelles* had arrived. And Toto had arranged search parties, scoured the area.

It was definite. Danielle was missing.

He slept little, and when he *did* sleep it was troubled, full of nightmarish visions.

But he was thankful, at least, the night was so short.

Leclerc had insisted that Châtel should be taken afresh and, this time, with plans for a permanent foothold, another three-pronged attack to begin at first light, five in the morning.

Three mixed columns, including Putz's platoons wading waste-deep across the Moselle – and caught the *Boches* napping yet again.

Telford had been straining at the leash since three, but Dronne had forbidden him from joining the assault until they'd won their battle. A liability, he'd said. He'd be distracted. Yet the captain swore, as soon as the place was secured, they'd pull out all the stops.

'It's family, *Monsieur* Telford,' Putz told him. 'And never fear, we'll find her safe and well somewhere. I can feel it in my bones.'

It was the most reassuring thing anybody had said to him. Putz was never wrong, after all, and Jack watched with growing anticipation as the second fight for Châtel unfolded. Almost as easy as the first time. A few hours, the town taken and the sappers there, unloading and erecting the parts for a pontoon bridge. By late morning the armoured cars of the First Moroccan *Spahi* Regiment were pouring across, light tanks as well. Pursuit. This time, the *Boches* would be given no chance to return.

Jack was over immediately afterwards, in time to find the town's citizens emerging from their cellars or wherever else they'd been hiding.

Major Putz arranged for a loud hailer to be brought up, spoke in the town square from his command car. But there was no positive news. Only the grim information that, during the previous afternoon, members of the *Milice* had arrived, part of an SS unit, and taken away the mayor, Doctor Sayer, and four other members of the FFI.

Madame Sayer and her children were there to hear the report.

'Where?' she said. 'Where did they take them?'

There was a reluctance to tell her but, finally, somebody confessed that, soon after they were taken, there'd been shooting, out on the forest road, the Bois de Fraize.

Putz instructed Amado to take a party and investigate, and Jack begged leave to join him.

'Perhaps, Major,' he said, 'afterwards, you'd permit us to check along the Hadigny road as well. It's where she said she was heading, last time I saw her.'

Putz agreed, but with the obvious warning. Hadigny itself was still in the hands of the *Boches*. Not for long, naturally, but just now…

They found the bodies easily enough. Five of them, including Pierre Sayer, where they fell, on a carpet of pine needles, just off one of the forest roads. They'd been beaten, then shot.

Granell had taken two half-tracks and a Jeep, a sombre cortège as it made the return journey to Châtel, where it was met by an equally solumn procession of mourners, led by the mayor's wife. Thankfully, Amado'd had the presence of mind to take some blankets, a couple of French *tricolores* with them, and these he had draped respectfully over the bodies.

But within half an hour, the fallen and their widows left in the care of the parish priest, Granell and Jack were on the road once more, heading in the Jeep for the road to Hadigny. From the outskirts of town, there was open farmland, the wrecks of German tanks, Hanomags, trucks and light artillery pieces. Their dead as well, of course.

Beyond the farmland, less than a mile from Châtel, there was more dense woodland to their left, more thinly wooded areas to the right. A couple of gentle bends, a long straight stretch and, some way ahead, they could see the ambulance, run off road among some trees and scrubland.

'Accident?' Jack shouted as Granell pressed the accelerator and sped forward. 'Please god...'

Yet he knew the two women had been missing for over thirty-six hours, plenty of time for them to get back to town, even if they'd been injured. One of them, at least, surely.

Telford leapt from the Jeep even before Amado had brought the vehicle to a halt, scared a couple of crows from the open front door, sent them flapping and cawing back into the oak which, he could see now, the Dodge had hit. From the damage to the front, it must have been a collision at speed, the bonnet bent almost double.

The driver's door was open and, sprawled across the seat, head hanging out of the truck but her feet still in the foot well, was Édith. Her scalp was matted with blood and there was a terrible gash on her forehead. Her neck, where it showed through her hair, was mottled red and purple, and the face livid, blue about the nose and lips. Yet her eyes were missing.

'Bloody filthy crows,' said Granell, but he was examining the wide spider's web on the passenger side of the cracked windscreen, a pool of dried ebon at the web's centre, streaks of deep carmine and lighter blush stretching like fingers along the threads.

'Somebody's tried to drag her out,' Jack murmured, but he

stared all around, seeking any sign of Danielle. Where the hell was she? 'Searched her.'

Édith's pockets were open, and emptied, her sad possessions scattered on the cab's floor or in the grass. A personal diary. Stubby pencil. Lipstick. The small striped box from her K-ration breakfast pack, the contents strewn across the road – a tin of chopped meat, biscuits and a fruit bar.

'Look here, *inglés*. Run off the road.'

The front wheel arch was crushed, paint stripped from the driver's door, the side of the bonnet. Streaks of black paint overlaying the army green. Tyre marks on the road itself.

'Danielle!' Telford yelled at the trees. 'Dani!'

No response. Naturally there was no response. What was he thinking? That she was hiding in the woods, just waiting for him to fetch her?

But if Amado was right, and the girls had been forced to crash, who'd done this? The *Boches*? He didn't believe so. And he couldn't help thinking of those murders – the mayor and those other *résistants*. So, the *Milice* then. Or worse. If so, what did they want with her? More to the point, where would she have been taken?

'Where?' said Amado, as if he'd read his thoughts.

'If she's been taken, they've got at least thirty hours head start.'

'Want to look, my friend?'

He nodded his head towards the Jeep.

'A minute,' said Jack. 'Let me check the back.' It was a mistake. For as he threw open the rear doors of the ambulance he was hit by nothing but the recollection of all those times they'd spent in there together. He slammed the doors shut again. 'What if she's in the forest?' he said and looked towards the trees again. If she *was* in there, he didn't really want to think about it.

'I'm no tracker but see for yourself. No sign of a struggle, or the undergrowth disturbed.'

They drove on, but not far. There was a path into the woods, though it didn't look as though anybody had been there recently.

'Go a bit further?' Telford suggested. He was desperate now, all his hopes of finding Danielle safe and unharmed dashed. 'See how the land lies,' he said, 'then look after Édith, at least. If we're going to find Dani, we'll need more men, no?'

Amado agreed and, as they climbed back into the Jeep, Granell said something Jack didn't catch. If he was honest, he was struggling with his Spanish, his thoughts too scrambled to focus properly. Confusion. Terrible images which he had to keep sweeping away. He was hardly aware of the further mile they covered towards Hadigny, but he couldn't fail to notice when, with the village in sight below them and a cluster of farm outbuildings just ahead, a burst of machine gun fire sent Granell spinning the steering wheel and bouncing over the fields and uphill again.

'*Joder*,' he shouted. 'No cover.'

Open country. Behind them, from the farm, one of those German six-wheeled armoured cars. Jack couldn't hear its weapon for the roar of the Jeep's engine, but he could see the clods of earth it kicked up as Amado swung one way, then the other. How far back to the forest? At least a mile, and Telford clung on for dear life.

He glanced back.

'They're closer,' he yelled in English. 'Bloody closer.'

He couldn't actually be certain, but he wished Granell would get them back on the road again. Jack felt as though his teeth were being shaken from his jaw but, yet again, Amado seemed to know exactly what he was thinking.

'Listen, *inglés*, they can outrun us…on the road…or on the tracks…through the forest.'

'Then…' Jack began, as the machine gun's bullets pranged against the Jeep's side. 'Christ.' He pushed himself further down in the seat. And, against all the odds, there was the long green wall of the woodland's edge within striking distance. A lane – not the Hadigny road but a forest track, further north, Telford calculated. 'I thought you said…'

It became clear Granell had no intention of following the track very far and, as soon as he was able, he jumped the Jeep up a low bank and between the trees themselves. The armoured car followed but not very far. A final few shots, and they were free.

Two hours later, Toto Torrès supervised their efforts to tow Danielle's Dodge back to Châtel.

Jack and Granell had recovered Édith's body. For Jack it was all so horribly familiar. Déjà vu. His recollections of pulling Yvette free from that other crash near Fougères. Yet they'd carefully taken Édith to town, sheltered under a tarpaulin and a blanket from the ambulance.

'Yes, family,' Putz had repeated, gripped Telford's arm, an embrace of great intimacy which made Jack choke back his tears, and not for the first time. He felt lost, useless. But the major had insisted that, when they went to recover the vehicle, at least two of the half-tracks should go with them – head further along the Hadigny road to make sure they weren't interrupted.

In practice, however, it seemed half the battalion turned out as volunteers to help in a search of the entire forest. In case.

Jack knew it was useless, naturally, but he appreciated the gesture.

'I'm sure she must be safe, Jack,' said Toto when they were finally ready to move the Dodge.

'I don't know what to think,' he told her, as the towing truck took up the strain on the ropes. It required no small effort to pull it from the tree, parts of the vehicle's front end embedded in the trunk. Yet, finally, it broke free and was heaved onto the road.

Granell had parked up ahead and Jack told Torrès he'd travel back to town with his friend. He would have preferred to be alone, to walk, but he thought there was little chance of him being allowed to do so. Anyway, it was raining again.

He pulled the woollen cap from his combat jacket, waved Toto a regretful farewell, headed for the Jeep. But, as he passed the patch of ground where Dani's ambulance had rested until these past few minutes, something caught his eye. A glimmer of light, almost invisible in the grass and fresh-scented nettles.

Telford reached down, wrapped his finger around a length of thin chain. He knew what he'd found, of course. And there, attached to the chain, Danielle's identity tags. Next to the tags, the ring. No doubt now. She'd been taken, but had enough time, enough presence of mind, to get rid of the only thing which could betray her real name – and also, perhaps, to leave a message, a farewell message, for Jack himself.

Telford's life had changed yet again, fallen into a new pattern.

Putz's battalion, as well. The whole Division organised afresh, the Combat Command Groups all broken up into smaller, more mobile mixed units. For Jack, it was all a bit of a mystery. But Dronne and the platoons of *La Nueve*, in action again through the rest of September and into early October: Granell's defence of Vaxoncourt; the firefights to protect their sappers as more and more pontoon bridges were thrown across the Moselle; the capture of Hadigny and a dozen other local villages; the Germans finally driven out of Épinal; the fighting at Rovilles-aux-Chênes, where fresh-faced André Geoffroy had died, a friend and comrade since Kufra; the advance towards Mortagne, the northern foothills of the Vosges, twenty miles – an advance completed faster than the *Boches* could retreat; the crossing of the Meurthe and their defence of Xaffévillers; and their counterattack towards Ménarmont, where that closest friend and comrade of Miguel Campos, fellow Anarchist Fábregas, was cut down in a hail of machine gun fire.

'He'll never be the same again,' said Raymond Dronne, as he stared out at the rain which now seemed set in for the month. It came down in bucketsful. 'Campos, I mean. Not quite with us anymore.'

The death of his friend had shaken Miguel to the core and, somewhere within Jack's own emotions, sympathy stirred. Yet he had other things on his mind today.

'The major says we won't be moving on anytime soon,' he said. They were just about out of fuel, food supplies and spare parts low. The awful weather. 'And all this with the prisoners...'

This was the pattern. Every village, every town, every roadside surrender, and Telford had insisted on interrogating the Jerries they'd taken. He'd managed to get his last film developed – with the help of Doctor Sayer's widow back in Châtel, as it happened, for the mayor had been a keen amateur photographer, a makeshift darkroom in the cellar of their house. So, he had the snap of Danielle. A good likeness, though the original was now becoming somewhat dog-eared. He'd eventually had to restrict himself to simply questioning the officers, showing them the photo. Just too many prisoners of war, but their response was always the same. Why would they have taken an ambulance driver? Why?

'Amado tells me you want to visit some of the camps,' said Dronne.

'Not much for me to do here, Captain. But can you spare him?'

'Have you forgotten? Still a job to be done. The general will expect you to do your duty, *Monsieur* Telford.'

To hell with my duty, Jack thought.

'Two weeks,' he said. 'No more. I'll be back here, and at my typewriter, long before we move on Strasbourg.'

'I suppose it might be good for Granell anyway. Two weeks, then. And make sure he takes care of the Jeep.'

There was the other thing. Granell. No more himself than Campos. But he'd already made one excursion with Telford, while they'd still been at Châtel. Jack had heard how the Yanks' Seventy-Ninth Infantry Division, just north of them at Charmes, had made a huge catch – German prisoners galore. So, they'd driven up that way, to the temporary camp constructed to hold them all. No good, naturally, but Telford had noticed the change in Amado, the lightening of his mood, just in one day.

The camps which he wanted to visit now, however – these were a different kettle of fish. And here some of the German officers, or local contacts among the *maquisards*, had been hugely helpful. At least he now had a list.

It was a hundred miles north, but two days' tortuous drive, through Metz and Thionville, to reach Villerupt and the remains of the Germans' prison camp at Thil-Longwy. A hell of a long way, no logical reason why Danielle might have ended up there, but no stone would be left unturned.

At Thionville, they met members of the FFI, the new mayor, with yet another lead. For the retreat by the *Boches* had left many more refugees on the roads and, yes, some of those were also former captives, slave labourers and the like. As a result, work had begun on a Displaced Persons Camp, another of the many already scattered across France. This, the mayor proudly announced, would be DPC Number Eight. Already some inmates, but Danielle not among them.

And nor was she at Thil-Longwy, just to the north. Their *maquisard* guides shook their heads as Jack and Amado wandered between the rows of wooden huts, rising up this fold in the countryside towards some wooded hills. No, they said, here there had been only slaves, forced to work the Tiercelet mine, to dig out the iron ore until the previous month when, with the Americans about to arrive, the remaining prisoners were packed like sardines into wagons where most of them died of suffocation.

Beyond the barbed wire fences, more huts – for the guards – and, almost built into the foot of those woodland slopes, a brick construction. There, the *maquisards* told them, they'd found the ovens, the burned remains of the men and women who'd died in the wagons, more than a thousand of them.

'No survivors?' said Jack.

'Yes,' said the guide. 'A final transport, just before the Americans got here. Sent across the border into Germany. Rebstock, near Dernau. That's where they've sent anybody they took during the retreat. Anybody from this part of Lorraine, anyhow.'

It wasn't likely, but he added the name Rebstock to his notebook.

'And this one,' said Jack, pointing at the page. 'Les Mazures. Near Sedan?'

'Closed,' the *maquisard* replied. 'Early in the year as well. Transit camp. But only for Jews, we think. On their way to the east. Nothing there for you, comrade. But we lost some good people at Sedan, and not by the Boches.'

'*Milice?*'

'No, *Francistes*.' The other principal body of French fascists, devotees of arch anti-semite, Marcel Bucard, and many of them also members of the *Carlingue*, the French Gestapo. 'Bloody butchers. Run like the dogs they are, of course. But we'll find them. One day, we'll find them. And then, by god...'

There was another name on Jack's list. Fort-Barraux. But it was a long way south, near Grenoble. And his notes were sparse. A prison camp for French Jews, Communists and others, before they were also sent east. The *maquisards* at Châtel had used their contacts, told him the place had been abandoned back in June, just before the local Vercors Resistance launched their premature attempt to liberate the area – and were put down by the *Boches* with the loss of six hundred freedom fighters. Only weeks later, the US Seventh Army had arrived with de Lattre's First French Army. Many of his men were Moroccans, Algerians and *tirailleurs* from Equatorial Africa – Jack wondered whether Eze Tolabye might be among them – and more units of the FFI.

'So, where next?' said Granell. The Jeep had a canvas cover but it was pretty useless, the rain sweeping in around the sides of the windscreen and soaking them.

'Last one on the list,' Jack replied. 'Two, to be precise. One at Schirmeck, the other at Natzwiller.'

'Behind enemy lines?'

'Well,' said Telford, 'maybe just for now.'

They rejoined the Division in time to hear the news. The very end of October, a month of monotonous drizzle.

'We should have been *there*, not here,' Miguel Campos snarled, and spooned some of the stew into his mouth.

Xaffévillers had little to offer, though most of the battalion had managed to find relatively dry accommodation in the barns, which seemed to outnumber the village houses. In this particular barn, Miguel's much depleted Number Three Section had made its home, nestling in the straw, a fire pit dug deep into the packed earth floor, the area around it completely cleared. Warmth and freshly cooked stew, not quite *cocido*, grumbling about the lack of *garbanzos*.

'And look where it got us,' Amado replied. Dronne had sent him, knowing there was unrest, but Granell's normal diplomacy seemed to have deserted him tonight. 'Like Grenoble all over again. They jumped the bloody gun, Miguel. Reconquest of Spain, my arse. Why the hell didn't they wait?'

Through the heart of the Pyrenees, the Aran Valley, thousands of *guerrilleros*, having liberated so many of those southern French cities like Toulouse, had taken the weapons supplied to them as part of the Resistance and driven a Republican wedge – forty or fifty miles, they said – into northern Spain, towards Lleida. Eleven brigades.

'Wait?' said Campos. 'Was it too much to hope for? That

having given so much to help the bloody French – the so-called *Allies* – de Gaulle, Churchill or Roosevelt might have spared them just *this* much help to crush Franco. And now, when they needed it, not some pie in the sky promises about tomorrow, or the next day.'

Jack lit a cigarette, more concerned with where his search for Dani might take him next. He toyed with her dog tags, with the ring. Reiter lay next to him, weak from some fever he'd picked up, wrapped in blankets, barely able to walk.

'No luck?' whispered the German.

Telford shook his head.

'But tomorrow or the next day,' Granell was saying, 'we'll have finished the job here. Have you forgotten, Miguel? Hitler's our enemy as well. And when it was done, we'd all have been free to go south – make a proper fist of taking Spain back. But the Communist Party again, my friend – what were they thinking? They could *force* the Allies to help them?'

Campos threw back his head, laughed – a sardonic laugh, spraying those near him with bits of chickpea and cured sausage.

'Why not? Well, why not? And when Hitler's beaten, you seriously think there'll be enough of us left? No, Amado, we'll all be dead – like Fábregas. All dead. No, this was the time. Communist Party? Yes, but I'd have been there with them.'

A couple of the other Anarchists in the section agreed with him.

'Where next?' Reiter murmured, tried to reach for his water bottle.

'No idea,' said Jack, and helped him take a drink. He was having trouble thinking straight. Guilt simply at not being able to find her. And this strange thing. About loss. About grief. The thing it did to time. Every second now an hour. Stupid confusion. His recollection of the way Frances Moorgate had kissed him. It kept coming back to him. The way he'd savoured it. A betrayal. And now he was paying the price.

'And you'd have died there,' Granell shouted back to Miguel and his supporters. 'How many were they? Six thousand? Seven? And Franco threw six or seven times that number against them. It was only going to end one way.'

691

'It was the *moros* again,' said Miguel. 'Always the *moros*.' According to the reports, perhaps forty thousand Moroccans from Franco's Army of Africa. 'So, what about all those promises, *inglés*?' Campos turned to Jack. 'That your precious sultan, your friends in Rabat and Casablanca, could stoke up trouble in Ceuta and Melilla if Franco ever tried to use them against the Allies?'

Reiter reached up and touched Telford's elbow. Jack had only half-heard the question, still sunk in his own thoughts, surprised himself when he was able to put together a cogent answer.

'I suppose it's Amado's point, Miguel,' he said, and threw the stump of his Lucky into the fire pit, sent up more sparks than he'd intended. 'If the Party had bothered to keep everybody in the picture, instead of going off half-cocked, maybe – just maybe – the comrades in Rabat and Casablanca could have done just that. Then, without the *moros*, the people themselves might have risen up.'

It hadn't happened. And little more than a week after their offensive began, the survivors of the failed invasion were pouring back over the mountains, back into France.

'But they didn't,' said Granell. 'They didn't rise up. Too late now, comrades. And tomorrow we've got our own battle to fight.'

'Again,' Campos snarled. 'They've shit on us again.'

Baccarat. The town was called Baccarat. Jack had played the card game just once, a casino in Paris on his first trip there. But he had no idea whether there was a connection between the name of the game and the town.

He'd not been there, staying to take care of Reiter. But it had been hailed as a great victory – though Campos had been wounded in the process. Not fatal but enough to force Miguel out of action when, on the following day, the first of November, *La Nueve* took Vacqueville as well.

By then, Jack was no longer able to keep himself from the fray. Indeed, he needed it, thought he was going mad.

Yet another three-pronged attack, Telford and his camera riding with one of the tank destroyers, its crew of French marines. Dronne had planned it to perfection. Granell's assault through the centre, supported on both flanks by two sections of Shermans, mortars and artillery. There were photographs, the burning Panther taken out from an upstairs window by a bazooka team. The Hanomag half-track taken, single-handed, by Sergeant Gualda. The dead – Perea and Carreño. The captured Germans forced by Dronne to clear debris from the streets to allow the tanks a clear run. And the smoking, flaming pandemonium caused by the Yanks' air strike, which finally put an end to the opposition.

'Well, *Monsieur* Telford,' said Leclerc, when he came to inspect the scene of this latest victory, 'does this mean you're back in the saddle?'

His command car was parked outside the town hall building. It was badly damaged, though not so severely as the Church of Saint-Rémy across the road, just a smouldering ruin. Jack asked whether he might take a photograph and Leclerc struck a pose, leaning on his cane, gazing out over the river, towards the glass factories.

'Doesn't mean I've given up, sir,' Telford told him, when he'd taken the snap. 'I'll find her, I swear I will.'

'Prepared for the worst, but hoping for the best, my friend. Your Disraeli, I think.'

'Though not your own philosophy, General. *Hoping* for the best? Planning for it, surely. But my thanks, all the same.'

'Thanks?'

'Yes, sir. Your visit, apart from anything else.' The general had made a social call, back in Châtel, as soon as he'd heard about Danielle's disappearance. 'It meant a lot. But naming me your friend? I can think of no greater honour. And a journalist, of all things.'

Leclerc walked onto the bridge, Jack at his side, while two trucks roared past, each filled with more green recruits.

'Well, *Monsieur* Telford, there are journalists – and there are journalists. I'm pleased to say you fall into the latter category.' The Flying Lion smiled. 'And you see? Replacements coming in. Fuel and supplies, as well.'

At the far side of the river stood an abandoned warehouse, also partly demolished, some of the men from Putz's Tenth Company guarding prisoners there, Wehrmacht and SS. Jack photographed them as well, saw their arrogance yet again, still boasting how victory for the Third Reich was now inevitable.

'Your new rockets?' said Jack and laughed. 'What do you call them? *Vergeltungswaffe Zwei*? Retribution Rocket Two, General,' he explained to Leclerc, then turned back to one of the SS officers. 'The ones you sent against Paris hit nothing at all, did they? Against Antwerp, the same. And those couple you fired towards London – more damp sqibs.'

'Then why,' said the German, 'has your Churchill not allowed any mention of them?'

It was a fair point. Telford only knew about the attacks from the Resistance. And he suspected that, if the damned things were being kept quiet, they must actually pose a real threat.

'Never mind, *Monsieur* Telford.' Leclerc pulled him away, gazed around at the signs of destruction all about them. 'The battle for Lorraine is over. Next, the battle for Alsace. The liberation of Strasbourg, our oath fulfilled. You were there, *monsieur*. There, with me. And after Strasbourg, across the Rhine. Finish this thing.'

'I don't believe it,' Dronne laughed. 'A pass. Fifteen days.'

They were ankle-deep in freezing rainwater, trying to salvage their kit, planning a move to a more habitable ruin after their first few days rest in Azerailles. Rest? Most of the time had been spent repairing the vehicles, recovering from the fight for Hablainville; cleaning a whole month's worth of mud from their systems; training those raw recruits; picking up the duties of the many who'd fallen sick with the perpetual damp and cold; or providing temporary shelter for the sixty or seventy families left homeless when the town had been destroyed.

To Jack, it had seemed interminable. Almost two months since Danielle had gone missing – he tried to avoid the word *taken*, for it conjured up too many evil thoughts – and his brain hurt with the effort of trying to invent new ways to track her down.

'Some people have all the luck,' said Granell, and while he might normally have made the comment in jest, today there was an edge to his voice, some bitterness.

'Well, indeed,' Dronne replied. 'This leaves you in command of the Company, Lieutenant. And may God have mercy on your soul.'

The dispatch rider had brought the permit only minutes earlier, and brought news, also, of Putz's promotion. Lieutenant Colonel now.

'How long?' said Jack. 'Since you saw them?'

'The last time?' Dronne replied. 'If I'm honest, I don't remember. It would have been about – this time, five years ago? Yes, five years. My little girl, Colette, she was just two.'

A long time. Imagine…

'Well, good luck with the journey,' Telford told him. 'Couple of days – to get home?'

'At least. Nancy to Paris. Paris to Le Mans. Then a short hop down to Écommoy. Just need to get to Nancy first. Hey, has Moreno's platoon headed off yet?'

Granell looked at his watch, while Jack wondered about Nancy. The city had been liberated while they'd been at Châtel and Nomexy, of course. No reason why Danielle might have fetched up there. Yet he kept imagining her, lost and dazed, perhaps her memory gone. It was the least painful of his possibilities, his fantasies. And Nancy was a stone which remained unturned.

'Any minute now,' said Granell. 'Due to leave at ten. Just make sure you come back, yes?'

The forty men remaining in Moreno's section had been given leave as well, by their Combat Group Commander, Lieutenant Colonel de la Horie. Twenty-four hours and – to Dronne's good fortune – in Nancy itself. They found their trucks and Jeeps in the square, where the town hall had once stood.

'Well,' said Jack, as they waved farewell to the small convoy, 'some of them must have found a dry corner in this godforsaken place. But I wouldn't have minded a trip to Nancy myself.'

He had his chance within the hour.

Papi Putz in his Jeep arriving outside one of the only buildings in the village still with a roof, the old post office, now serving as the Company's command post. Just about dry enough for Jack to stow his own equipment there.

'*Teniente*,' said Putz, as he ducked under the fallen door lintel, 'the bloody radio.'

'Hasn't worked since we arrived, sir,' Granell told him. Two of his men were working on the thing, even then. But, like everything else they possessed, it had suffered badly these past few weeks.

Putz shook the rain from his poncho.

'This army,' he growled. 'How the hell do they expect us...? Anyway, never mind all that – Moreno's section, they're still here?'

'Left an hour ago – Colonel.'

Again, an edge to Granell's words. Telford heard the inflection, saw the frown on Putz's face, though he wasn't certain whether this might simply have been a response to the news about Moreno.

'Yes, congratulations, sir,' said Jack.

'*Lieutenant* Colonel,' Putz corrected Amado. 'But I don't expect the pay rise any time soon. And you, Granell. Better get after them.'

'To Nancy?'

'Of course to Nancy. Gather up as many of them as you're able. We've orders to move out. The Yanks need our help, it seems. Take some of the pressure off them.'

Leclerc had been slightly optimistic, the battle for Lorraine not quite over, two infantry divisions of Haislip's Fifteenth Army Corps – to which the French Division was attached and formed Haislip's right flank – were bogged down thirty miles to the north and east, around Sarrebourg.

'Again?' said Granell.

'Yes, *Teniente*,' Putz replied. 'Again. De la Horie says we're going to hit the *Boches* positions at Badonviller. And the *jefe* thinks it's a good plan. Opens up his road to Strasbourg. But, for now, get those men back from Nancy. We move out tonight.'

Jack clutched his satchel and Rolleiflex, while Amado drove Dronne's Jeep like a maniac, all the way to Nancy.

'Just how the hell am I supposed to find them?' Granell complained, over and over again. Or he grumbled about them supposedly being in reserve. Hadn't they done enough already? And if he couldn't find them? A third of the Company on leave, raising hell. At best they'd be pissed as rats. So many of the half-tracks out of action as well. In god's name, what were they going to use to get them there – to this Badonviller.

But Telford was more concerned about his search for Danielle.

So, in Nancy — yet another city of accusing masonry fingers pointing to the grey heavens, of cupped craters filled with celestial tears — he began at the Hôtel de Ville, and from the Place Stanislas they referred him to a small office on the Rue Henri-Poincaré.

It was an office belonging to the Ministry of Prisoners, Refugees and Deportees. Telford didn't know such a Ministry existed but a clerk – a young woman in a pretty green frock – informed him, with some pride, that General de Gaulle had established the department a whole twelve months earlier, then still in London, but now with its main operation in Paris.

'We have more than our fair share,' said the clerk, and set her cigarette down in a half-filled ashtray. '*Nancéiens* and *nancéiennes* still in German camps, *monsieur*. Refugees arriving here on their way to god knows where and can't get any further. And then – the missing...'

The fighting to liberate Nancy had lasted ten days and, during this time, families divided, children lost.

'We have a dozen children's homes in the city alone. Two hundred kids. You'd think, by now...'

Jack hadn't written anything since Châtel, but as he showed Danielle's photo to the clerk, as she shook her head and apologised, it struck him this was a story for Bunnelle. No, that wasn't quite right. Here was a story, he realised, which Dani would have expected him to write.

'The homes,' he said. 'Is there one near here?'

She wished him good luck, directed him to an old convent just across from the Promenade de la Pépinière, where he scribbled down names, delved into a dozen other tragedies of separation, photographed tiny faces. Then he took himself off to a bar opposite the station, where Granell had found the Company's trucks. Telford spent an hour writing his copy, keeping his eye on the vehicles at the same time. When it was done, he wrote the words *For Danielle* at the end.

With his second cognac and coffee, his umpteenth cigarette, he wrote a letter – to Sydney Elliott, telling his own story, trying to set down on paper, in ink, just a few of those tangled emotions he felt.

'Any good?' said Granell, when they were driving south once more. 'Clues?'

Amado seemed more himself. He'd somehow managed to track down all but two of Moreno's section.

'No,' Jack replied. 'But I came across a story.'

He told Granell.

'At least here the poor mites won't be dragged off for re-education,' said Amado. Those stories from Spain, from Beto and others, about the thousands upon thousands of children, forcibly separated from their parents and taught by the nuns to be good little Nazis, to give the fascist salute on demand. 'And you, *inglés*. You seem – more like your old self.'

'The writing,' said Jack. 'Somebody told me, just a few months ago. How I write to fill the gaps in my life. Never been truer than now.'

If they'd been through seven kinds of hells at Écouché, at Châtel, at a dozen other places, they'd never experienced anything quite like Badonviller over the following two days.

Branet's tanks ambushed time and time again by German Eighty-Eights hidden in the most deviously camouflaged emplacements. The losses they'd suffered in the process of destroying those killer guns. The house-to-house slaughter as Granell's woefully inadequate numbers prised fanatical *Boches* defenders from every last bloody building.

In the afternoon of the first full day – Jack's notebook showed it to be a Friday, the seventeenth of November – Telford was with Granell again, his lucky talisman, in the middle of town. They'd come this far, but the survivors had dug in now, only capable of defence, of holding on, stretched in a thin line of pale khaki, olive drab and filth, from the train station on their far left to the remnant of the *mairie*, just here, to the right.

'You still taking pictures, *inglés*?'

'Out of film,' Telford replied, held up the camera to show how redundant it had become. They were lying on their backs behind a pile of rubble which had once been the crossroads, the heart of Badonviller. 'Shame too,' said Jack. 'Might have won a prize with that one.'

Just above their heads was the water fountain. Before today

698

it must have graced the crossroads itself, though it had now been uprooted, tossed on top of this mound.

'Very artistic, said Granell without opening his eyes. He looked like he could have slept for a week. 'But *hostia*, my friend. I wish you'd wear your bloody helmet.'

Jack had come close a few times, so many near misses he'd become convinced Welch must be out there somewhere.

'I'm starting to take this personally,' he said, as yet another sniper's bullet smacked the fountain's trough, no more than a foot away. He slid further down among the debris.

He wondered at his ability to get used to it all. The burning, the stink, the blood, the incessant mechanical grind of tracked vehicles. And the danger. Of course. Though, since Dani, since Châtel, he was hardly conscious of the risk.

'Where is that bastard?' Amado yelled.

The sniper. Jack rolled onto his side, looked past Granell's knees to the street corner. The remains of a shop and, next to it, a house with stone steps leading up to a small terrace and the gap where the front door had been. Sheltering behind the steps, Sergeant Mateo. He had a small mirror, stuck with *chicle* to a pencil, used it to look up the street ahead of them.

'The church,' he called back. 'Can't be anywhere else.'

The last time Jack had looked, there wasn't much left of the church. The clock tower, rising from the square bulk of the building, had mostly been shot to smithereens but, remarkably, its lead-lined dome remained in place – more or less. Equally remarkable? The dome looked, for all the world, like a Yankee helmet, now worn at a jaunty angle, but still in place.

'Left my tin hat in the half-track,' said Telford. He lifted the peak of his jeep cap, brushed some of the filth from the top of his head. He had to admit the knitted green wool wasn't much protection.

From their right, down the road, the sound of an engine. Jack turned onto his back, saw a cloud of terracotta dust coming towards them.

'Amado...' he began.

'Ours,' Granell told him, without stirring himself. 'M8.' The armoured car stopped just short of the junction, and Lieutenant

Colonel de la Horie jumped down from the side of the gun turret. 'Might be useful, as well,' said Amado. 'Covering fire!' he yelled.

The men around them emptied their carbines in the general direction of the church, the houses lining the street between, while Granell grabbed the shoulder strap on Jack's combat jacket, dragged him along as he sprinted, bent double, across the fifteen yards of open ground.

'Well, Lieutenant,' said de la Horie. He spoke in French. Natural enough, Jack supposed. 'Can't stay here all day. And where's Major Putz?'

'Lieutenant *Colonel* Putz, sir,' Amado replied. His French wasn't bad, as it happened. Jack sometimes thought his native *valenciano* was more akin to French than to Spanish.

'Yes, yes. I'd forgotten. But where the hell is he?'

'Holding the other end of the line, last time I saw him.'

It was easy enough to hear the fighting, half a mile away. Artillery. Tanks. But Granell's response still sounded insolent.

'The train station,' said Jack. 'It's pretty key, sir.'

He thought it might be helpful, but de la Horie simply looked at him with contempt. He was a few years older than Jack but, like poor André Geoffroy, he seemed younger. His scarf was tucked into the neck of his combat jacket, and Telford saw his forage cap bore the five silver and gold bars of his rank in the French fashion. As it happened, Jack liked him. He had guts. And he had a job to do. A whole Task Force to command, and Leclerc wasn't a general to suffer fools gladly. If de la Horie had *le patron*'s confidence, it was good enough for Jack.

'He's supposed to be a battalion commander, Lieutenant. Not a bloody sergeant. Not a bloody junior officer.'

'It's probably something to do,' said Granell, 'with most of our bloody sergeants, most of our bloody lieutenants, being dead or out of action. You understand, sir?'

'You're damned impertinent, Granell. But I'm giving you an order. You have to press this attack.'

Amado glanced back towards his defensive line.

'Look at them,' he said, and now simply sounded more weary than defiant. 'Just this section. Five dead. Twice that number wounded. And those three?' He pointed to a trio of his men, sheltering behind the remains of a half-track. 'Their first fight. They've done fine. Just fine. But if I was thinking of sending them out there again, I might as well just shoot them myself and be done with it. They won't make it, sir.'

'Are you telling me they'd disobey your orders, Lieutenant?'

'No, sir.' Granell snapped to attention, saluted smartly. 'I'm telling you that if you order another attack, I will gladly jump in my Jeep and fight those bastards on my own. But I won't be passing on your order to any of the men under my command. *Sir.*'

'*Monsieur* Telford,' said the Lieutenant Colonel, 'I would appreciate a moment with Lieutenant Granell.'

'Of course,' Jack replied, and wandered over to the armoured car.

Back at the crossroads, the firing had intensified again. And whatever passed between Amado and de la Horie, it didn't take them long.

'Sergeant,' the Lieutenant Colonel shouted to the M8's commander, as he came back to the vehicle, Granell immediately behind him. 'You're staying here. Give these men some support, won't you?'

'You, sir?' said the sergeant.

'Don't worry, I'll find my own way back.' He turned to Granell. 'Well, good luck, Lieutenant. And well done. Did I forget to say it?'

Amado refused to say any more about the exchange, but the M8's cannon made short work of the opposition in the church – though its armour was too thin for it to be any use against the Panthers which came up later in the day. Yet, by then, reinforcements had arrived, men from Putz's Tenth and Eleventh Companies, a couple of Shermans, and one of the tank destroyers. Those were the units brought up to press the attack, to drive the *Boches* to the very outskirts of town, though no further.

That night, what was left of *La Nueve* slept in comparative comfort. In the old earthenware factory, among crates of stoneware jars, plates, bowls and jugs.

'Are you not going to tell us?' Jack said to Granell.

The men shared a pot of potatoes brought to them by an old man and his wife.

'Nothing to tell,' said Amado. 'Didn't you see, *inglés*? We were left in reserve. Others sent up to take our place.'

Jack didn't believe him, but there seemed no more to say on the matter. He slept better than he'd done for the past two months, even the noise of shelling, which went on through most of the hours of darkness, failing to keep him awake.

Next day, the fighting resumed in earnest, though with *La Nueve* holding their defensive line, still pretty much in reserve. So Amado wasn't invited to the briefing between de la Horie and his officers later in the morning. In Granell's sector it was noisy but the shells falling away from their positions, and there were no more dead or wounded. But when *Papi* Putz came to visit, it was plain there was something wrong.

'Did you hear?' he said.

'Hear what, sir?' Granell replied.

'De la Horie. Dead. Brémentil. He was briefing us. A bloody mortar shell came through the window. Shrapnel. Killed him outright. Mazieras as well. And Branet wounded.'

Mazieras, commander of the battalion's Eleventh Company. Mazieras, who'd brought up his men only the night before to relieve them.

'We've lost so many good comrades here,' said Amado. 'So many.'

Jack had listed their names. He would write about this battle, he'd decided. For Barea. For the dead. Bullosa and Duros. For Martínez and the Frenchman, Roger Botcazon. For López and Duchastel.

During the early part of the day, an ambulance had driven past their line. It looked for all the world like Danielle's old Dodge. And his heart had begun to pound, until he saw it was Toto Torrès waving to him from the driver's seat. He was able to blow her a kiss, at least, and she put her head through the open window, gave him her warmest smile.

'And women,' he said now. 'Mustn't forget the women.'

'Of course,' said Putz. 'Not the women either. And you, Amado. I understand you'll be leaving us.'

Jack turned in surprise, initially pleased for his friend.

'You've got leave,' he said.

'No,' said Granell. 'Leaving the Company.'

'Leaving…?'

'It was a surprise to me, as well, *Monsieur* Telford. But one of the last things de la Horie told us. My god, Amado, that man had some respect for you.'

Granell nodded.

'Yes, sir, I know. And he'll be a great loss to the Division. The *jefe* will need men like him if he's going to take Strasbourg.'

'But not men like you, Amado?' Jack said to him later. Somehow, the citizens of Badonviller had got the church bell to ring. The fighting was over and, as the parish priest had told him, all they needed now was the return of those from the town who'd been taken as prisoners, deported to the east, or sent to the forced labour camps.

'What do you mean?' Granell shouted over the noise of the bells.

'You told Putz. How Leclerc would need men like de la Horie for Strasbourg. But not men like you? You won't be there?'

'I told you, *inglés*. I never took the oath. I'm forty-five but I feel twice that. I'm finished. Lately – it's hard to explain, but I've not missed a single day's fighting in – what is it now? Nearly four months. And before that, Oran. Before that again. Madrid and Teruel. All those other battles between. Of the officers, the Spanish officers, I'm the only one left. Besides, I have things to do in Paris now. I've been asked to help. Seems I'm famous.'

'Photo in the newspapers,' Telford laughed. 'What d'you expect? And help – with what precisely?'

Granell refused to be drawn.

'Perhaps when we meet again,' he said. 'I'll have a clearer picture.'

'When do you leave?'

'Four days. I have four days to reorganise the Company – what's left of it – then I'm off to Paris. Training some of these bloody recruits. And then de Castellane takes over until Barbirrojo gets back.'

'I don't know what to say, my friend,' Jack told him.

'I guess you'll find a few words eventually, comrade. You usually do. And I think this will only be *hasta luego*, not *adiós*.'

Telford wasn't so sure, but by the time Granell left them, he'd used one more of his precious discs, wrapped it carefully, addressed it to Barea and made Amado promise faithfully he'd see it posted as soon as he reached Paris.

Jack had practised the Spanish over and over before he made the recording. It had to be perfect, this one.

'*The mountains, valleys and forests of Lorraine in the far northeast of France are now free.*

'*Perhaps it may seem wrong to highlight one group of the region's liberators above any other – or, indeed, one man over the tens of thousands, those comrades in arms, who have fought through this campaign.*

'*From valiant Verdun and the mighty Meuse to the Vosges Mountains, a final struggle now known as the Battle of Badonviller – many lives lost, much blood spilled. In the case of Badonviller, Spanish blood.*

'*The blood of men unable to write final letters to sweethearts, wives and lovers, lest it exposed their families, still in Madrid, Zaragoza or Cartagena, to reprisal from Franco's death squads. Men unable to even fight under their own names for this same reason. Men whose only brothers are those here beside them, holding them close as they lay down their lives. Men whose possessions are few, whose bellies are taut. Men who sing in the rhythms of Córdoba and Cádiz. Men who long for the strong tobacco of Tenerife.*

'*One of those men, a lieutenant of my acquaintance, has already fought for freedom and democracy in Spain itself. Three years. And now here, in France, against the same foe.*

'*He remembers their names, each and every one, who served under his command and fell into darkness, into endless night – at Guadalajara, at Belchite, at Brunete, at Teruel and along the Ebro. He remembers, as well, the names of those who have perished at Écouché, at Châtel-sur-Moselle, and at Badonviller.*

'*It is possible some of them may have been less than heroes, were fearful, or faint of heart. Yet, if so, I never saw sign of such human frailties, nothing but the cause which brought them here, all together, in this common hardship.*

'*Lorraine in the far northeast of France is now free, though a chill wind blows through its mountains, valleys and forests, a wind blowing south towards the Pyrenees, a wind which will one day also sweep away the despotism of General Franco, bring freedom and democracy home to Spain itself.'*

Strasbourg. And yes, Leclerc needed men like Amado Granell and Jean Fanneau de la Horie, though neither of them was present, of course. De la Horie dead and Amado making the journey back to Paris. But there were others. Men like Lieutenant Colonel Joseph Putz and Captain Raymond Dronne.

'How many times must we win Alsace back from the *Boches*?' Putz yelled now, above the engine roar of his Dodge command car.

'They've still not woken up to us being here,' Telford replied from the heavy vehicle's rear seats. He was being thrown about, trying to protect the camera and the recording machine. It was cold, and he'd thrown on as many spare items of clothing under his combat jacket as he'd been able, the jeep cap pulled down over his ears, fingerless grey woollen gloves on his frozen hands.

To reach Strasbourg, they'd faced the problem of crossing the Vosges Mountains with the Germans holding all the passes – or, at least, all those it was possible to cross in this already bitter winter. So the Division had, at the Flying Lion's instruction, used the impossible ones instead, negotiated them like Hannibal over the Alps, driven down into Alsace itself.

It was the victory won by de la Horie's Task Force, of course, and by *La Nueve* – before the lieutenant colonel's death – which had opened the way to Strasbourg itself. It would always be his epitaph.

Yet there'd been skirmishes, then Reiter and Telford employing their language skills to phone the enemy's headquarters in the city. Innocent enquiries after *Hauptmann* such-and-such, or *Oberstleutnant* what's-his-name – real names carefully gleaned from interrogation of recent prisoners. Subterfuge, but the unsuspecting *Boches* operators had been hugely helpful in divulging the intelligence Leclerc needed – at least the major dispositions of their troops.

'They didn't think we could so easily cross the Vosges, *Monsieur* Telford, no?'

'Fair enough, sir. Four years ago, none of us thought they could get past the Maginot Line.'

Putz laughed, pulled up the fur collar of his coat, his breath condensing into misty clouds.

The past two days, this madcap race across the plain of Alsace, led by Massu's Combat Command Group. They'd taken Saverne and, yesterday, Putz's battalion had liberated Marmoutier, spent the night at Birkenwald. This morning – a Thursday, Jack's notebook had recorded, the twenty-third of November – the various Combat Groups and Task Forces between which the Chad Regiment was now divided, with full support from the Division's tank busters, from its Shermans, from its *Spahi* armoured scout cars, from its medical units, was charging in five columns towards their objective. And now, there was Strasbourg itself, the spire of the cathedral clear for all to see, to the southeast.

As usual, Putz was out on the right flank, sweeping around to hit the western suburbs. But first there was another objective. The fortress known to the Germans as Fort Fürst Bismarck, just one of eleven such fortifications encircling the city on this side of the Rhine. Formidable, all of them. Built by the Germans after 1870.

It certainly seemed ominous when they reached the outskirts of Wolfisheim – machine gun nests and Eighty-Eights to be cleared. Yet this delayed them no more than half an hour, *La Nueve* taking the whole thing in its stride, squads riding into battle on the Shermans.

Putz had watched them through his binoculars from the upper floor of a farmhouse, only a hundred yards from the crossroads. The farmer and his wife had been astonished. Overjoyed but astonished. Where had they come from? And the *Boches*, where had they all gone? At the time, Putz hadn't quite understood the question, but persuaded the gnarled couple to take shelter in their cellar anyhow. Things, he said, were likely to get nasty.

'I wasn't sure about them,' he said, when the Company's prisoners, scores of them, were being led along the lane. 'All those new recruits. New officers. But a good job, *Monsieur* Telford. A good job, indeed.'

Seventy new recruits, many of them for *La Nueve*. All Frenchmen, of course. Moreno now serving as adjutant, but Captain de Castellane a different kettle of fish from Dronne. Efficient and brave, certainly, but refused to allow any of that Spanish nonsense, he said. A French unit, and they'd just have to bloody learn to take orders in French, wouldn't they?

'Still enough of the old hands left to look after the new boys,' said Jack. 'And as you say, sir. A good job. Caught them on the hop again.'

Putz laughed once more. 'The *Boches*,' he said, 'had enough imagination to invent *Blitzkreig*, but not enough to consider we might ever use it against *them*. Let's just hope our luck holds with the fort.'

Yet, when they reached the place – its solid earthworks, bastions, deep protective ditches – they found the drawbridge lowered, no signs of life. A trap, certainly.

But no, simply abandoned. Uncanny. A mystery. Though at least it gave Putz a solution to one problem, their prisoners soon shifted to a yard at the fort's heart. Fort Kléber again, as Captain de Castellane had instructed some of the boys to paint on the gates, restoring the name Fort Fürst Bismarck had been christened when the region was taken back from the Germans in 1918.

'And now, sir?' said Jack.

'Now? Reminds you of Paris, doesn't it? Now, *Monsieur* Telford, we seize the day. *Carpe Diem*.'

They rushed on, headlong into the city, three miles, crossed a canal bridge, amazed to find it intact, passed the main station away to the left.

'Not like Paris at all,' said Jack. Because, in Paris, there'd been warning of their coming. All those flowers. Kisses. Impenetrable crowds on the streets. Here? Open-mouthed astonishment. And not a single shot to spoil the morning.

On they sped. Another bridge, a wider tree-lined river, with glimspes of the cathedral's spire through narrow streets of half-timbered Alsatian houses, steeply pitched, clay tiled roofs. But close. The city's centre. And still Putz pressed on. A hospital, the university buildings, a citadel and ancient fortifications, one more bridge, a couple of dockyard basins – warehouses, barges and small ships.

Then, the Rhine. Three hundred yards wide, Jack supposed. The other side, Germany.

Putz's ultimate objective, as Leclerc had instructed all his commanders. The Kehl Bridges, he'd said. Take them and cross. The Division to be the first Allied unit beyond the Rhine, into Germany.

But Putz had been beaten to the punch. At the riverside, a huddle of officers around Colonel Rouvillois, whose Combat Command Group had arrived ahead of them. There was jaunty jeering, as well, from some of the soldiers resting at the edge of the road, other men from their own Chad Regiment, though these boys from the First Battalion. What kept you, lads? they yelled.

Yet the rivalry wasn't the worst of it. Because Rouvillois had also failed. The Germans may have been asleep earlier, but they'd woken in time to blow the bridges. Two great girder structures, one for road traffic, the other for the railway. Each collapsed at its central point into the river's depths.

The Flying Lion's advance into Germany would have to wait.

'If they'd not been in such a hurry to get here,' said Jack, 'perhaps somebody might have remembered to bring the flag.'

The oath. How long had it been since Kufra? Three years and eight months. Their purpose for all that time. The pledge to fight until the flag flew above Strasbourg Cathedral once more. So where was Leclerc? Where was the flag?

'He'll be here,' Putz replied, seated on the bonnet of his command car. Their half-tracks, their tanks, their tank destroyers, their armoured cars and ambulances were now trapped, surrounded in a sea of citizens, tens of thousands, packed into the square facing the glorious West Front of the cathedral and the even wider *parvis* on its southern side.

The battalion had driven back into the centre. Still no opposition. It should have been the easiest place in the world to defend. Fortresses around the outskirts, the river, or canal, completely encircling the city's centre like an enormous moat. Only the German garrison still held out at their headquarters, one of those forts, three miles north of the city, sections of the Division already laying siege to their position – and Leclerc presumably there as well.

But around Notre-Dame de Strasbourg, crowds continued to grow. The same crowds still unable to believe they'd been liberated, pinching themselves. A dream surely. They had indeed looked like sleepwalkers as the half-tracks had driven past. An ordinary day at the school, the office, the factory, the shop – or so it had started. No more. Now it was time to celebrate, in a no-nonsense Alsatian sort of way, naturally.

The Oath of Kufra had become something of a legend. And when a legend is about to become fact, history rather than myth, fairytales come to life, it will attract multitudes. And, within this particular throng, folk were growing impatient. They were still singing, of course. *La Marseillaise*. And why not? Had Rouget de Lisle not composed it here? And another song Jack hadn't heard before. It sounded like some of the crowd sang in German, others the same tune but in French, but both groups waving red and white flags.

'Well,' said Telford, 'if we had some blue cloth, I suppose we could make one of our own. And what *is* the song, sir?'

'The Alsatians' own anthem. Sadly, it was written in German when Alsace was – well, you know the story, *Monsieur* Telford.'

Toto Torrès had parked a couple of her ambulances close to the Lieutenant Colonel. As usual, Telford couldn't help himself – searched the familiar vehicles, just in case…

'But the French version,' Toto was shouting, 'stands up well, don't you think? *Hymn to the Alsatian Flag*.'

'Forgive me, sir,' said a man pressed up against Putz's vehicle. 'I couldn't help but hear. And – well, if you'll allow me.' It turned out he was a pork butcher, *Monsieur* Lorentz, but his wife quite a hand with needle and thread. 'Just so happens,' Lorentz told them, 'the tablecloth in my shop is just the right shade of blue. More or less, anyway. If we borrow somebody's Red and White…'

Torrès volunteered a couple of her girls to assist, and Lorentz led them off to his shop. Not far, he said. Place Saint-Étienne.

'What now?' said Jack. He lit himself a cigarette. 'If they don't get back with the bloody flag soon, there's likely to be a riot.'

It was cold, a light drizzle falling. Yet they were saved by a procession of men in heavy winter coats, carrying musical instruments. A brass band. They arranged themselves around the corner of the cathedral and were soon playing a medley of dance tunes, to the delight of the crowd. Within minutes, the whole square was alive with spinning, dancing couples, fluttering scarves and swirling coat tails.

A young officer in the uniform of the *Spahi* Regiment approached Putz's command car. He wore his driver's helmet but around his waist a wide red sash.

'We heard, sir,' he said. 'About the flag. When it arrives, if you need somebody to climb up...'

He glanced up at the spire, and Jack followed his gaze. He hadn't thought about it before.

'I don't imagine General Leclerc intended – not literally *above* the cathedral. Surely...' Telford felt dizzy just looking up so high. To the top of the spire? Christ, it must be five hundred feet.

'I'm a climber, sir. Asked my lieutenant. It would be such an honour. I wasn't there at Kufra, of course. But the oath...'

'What's your name, soldier?' said Putz.

'Lebrun, sir.' He came to attention, saluted.

'Well, Lebrun, it looks like you'll have your wish.'

Pushing their way through the dancers came Toto's girls, and *Monsieur* Lorentz, proudly bearing the *Tricolore* between them.

'But it's not possible,' Telford protested. 'Look at the damned thing. You can't climb up there.'

'I'm told, *monsieur*,' said Lebrun, 'there'll be a steeple ladder somewhere. So long as there's somebody to steady it – I've done worse.'

'Just a shame *le patron*'s not here,' said Putz. 'But I suppose, so long as the oath's fulfilled. He'll expect a record, though, don't you think, *Monsieur* Telford?'

'Of course, sir,' said Jack. But then, a pricking of his thumbs... He could almost feel Danielle, peering over his shoulder. *Careful, Jack.*

'And, of course, a photograph from down here – it wouldn't show very much, would it?'

'It's a wonder what they can do now,' Telford replied, feeling one more trap closing about him, still hoping to avoid being snared. 'When they develop film. Enhancement. Enlargement. All the rest.'

'But not so good as a snap from shorter distance, my friend. Yes, the more I think about it, the more certain I am. We'll need you up there, with Lebrun.'

'These photographs,' said Leclerc, early next morning, 'astonishing. I wish I could have been there, *Monsieur* Telford. And a pity, we can't see the flag from here.'

The doors to the balcony of the Hôtel de Ville, the Hanauer Hof, opened onto the Place Brulée, with its cropped and bare winter trees, looking north, rather than towards the cathedral. The room was far less exotic than the rest of the city hall's opulence, but it suited Leclerc. A hive of activity. Telephones, typewriters, heavily padded dispatch riders coming and going.

'It was good to get them developed so quickly, sir. And worth the climb.'

Telford was astonished he'd even been able to hold the Rolleiflex. Lebrun had gone up those hundreds of steps inside the tower like a mountain goat, the flag in a haversack at his side. Jack laboured behind him, happiest in the darker stretches, where the windows were small, closing his eye as best he could when he reached those sections where the freezing wind whistled through absurdly exposed spaces. The higher he climbed, the more this place was built like a latticework, the openings – when he had no choice but to open the eye – looking down onto the flying buttresses below.

He'd wondered why the hell he'd not simply refused, but the idea of being shamed before Putz had been too much, like not letting his father see him cry when he'd fallen off his first big boy's bike. Though, when he'd eventually emerged, on his hands and knees, onto the wide platform at the top of the tower itself, he'd collapsed in a relieved heap on the solid stone of the roof. Flat and safe.

'Just look at these,' Lebrun had said, and Jack saw he was admiring sculptures in the sandstone recesses of the wall behind them. 'You'd have no idea they were even here – not from the ground.'

'No,' Jack had said. 'You wouldn't.'

'And a shame they never built the other one, no?'

Jack hadn't been sure what he'd meant, but as he got his breath back, relaxed just a little, he saw that, on the farther side of the

711

platform was a flat-roofed structure. It must have been a fair size, and he slowly realised something which hadn't been apparent to him from below. This cathedral was obviously intended to have been built with *two* spires, not one.

And here was his nightmare. He looked again at Lebrun's sculptures, saw them in more detail this time, but then followed the wall into which they were built, followed it up – and up. They weren't at the top at all. A second tower, obvious from the ground, though it all looked so very different from here. Open at its core, octagonal.

'Well,' said Lebrun, 'shall we get this done? They'll be waiting, down below.'

'Is this it – the spire?'

'Lord, no, *monsieur*. The spire's above this one. Next level.'

The worst still to come. The steps up the corner of this tower inside a tracery of entirely uprotected apertures – or so Telford felt. He groped his way higher and higher, emerged through another door, a balcony with a balustrade. And here was the spire – the start of it, anyway.

'Not far now,' said Lebrun, found yet another staircase, mercifully this time more enclosed, until they reached the pinnacle gallery.

Here, there'd been nothing. Another balustrade, yes. But for all the comfort it provided it might as well not have existed. Telford had tried not to look, because everywhere about him was the void, the wind whistling and whipping about the slender final pieces of masonry, too fragile up there, he'd thought, not to be blown away.

'Here it is, safe and sound,' Lebrun had laughed, and heaved an even more slender ladder from its frame on the inner side of the balustrade. 'Can you just steady the foot for me?'

'What?' Jack had yelled. 'No, Lebrun, this is high enough. For god's sake, just fasten it to the rail.'

But Lebrun had already hoisted the ladder skywards. There were hooks at the top to secure it in place and Telford saw, above the final stones, a weathervane, and lightning conductor.

'No, don't do that,' he'd yelled into the wind as Lebrun began to climb.

But the young daredevil had managed the task and, somehow, Jack had steadied the camera long enough, bracing himself against the balustrade, to take not one decent snap but three – the final one with Lebrun holding the weathervane. Just one hand, one foot on the ladder, his other arm and leg stretched out, the homemade flag of France – its blue, white and red transmuted to shades of grey – snapping in the breeze above his head. Until it flew so proudly up there Telford had no idea Toto and the butcher's team had managed to also stitch a black Cross of Lorraine on the central white panel. Against all the odds, he'd captured that, as well. And no need to tell anybody how many spoiled negatives, shaky exposures, indistinct images he'd been obliged to destroy.

'Astonishing,' said Leclerc again, as he examined the pictures for the fifth time. 'You deserve a Pulitzer for this, *Monsieur* Telford.'

'And perhaps a medal for young Lebrun, sir.'

'All the same, I'd like you to be around later. The parade. My Order of the Day. One of your articles, to put the eyes of the world on us again.'

He was angry, Jack knew, the tic in his cheek. The Division hadn't even been first to reach the Rhine, let alone cross into Germany. No, this honour had fallen to General Jean de Lattre's First French Army. No love lost between the two men, of course. De Lattre may have finally defected to de Gaulle, but all that time as part of Vichy's Armistice Army... Rumours, as well – how de Gaulle intended to put the Division under General de Lattre's overall command.

'I'll do my best, sir. But perhaps if I could see the Order beforehand?'

'There, on the desk.'

Jack read it. *Order of the Day, Number Seventy-Three.*

Officers, NCOs and soldiers of the Second Armoured Division. In five days you have crossed the Vosges despite the enemy's defences and liberated Strasbourg.

The Oath of Kufra is fulfilled!

Telford realised there was a tear running down his cheek, wiped it away.

'An emotional moment for us all, yes?' said Leclerc. 'And you were there. At Kufra. You've been with us all this time. If anybody deserves a medal, *monsieur*, perhaps it is you.'

Kufra. It was always going to be Kufra. The first time, the one he would always remember, like his first lovemaking. The gut-wrenching fear of knowing that, there, those Italian planes, those enemy soldiers, the incoming fire – all directed at him. Personally. Not as part of some anonymous bombsight unpredictably. Nor the accidental hazards Telford had encountered in Spain. At him. And then the shocked realisation he'd survived. The bullets had passed him by, left him unscathed. At least, physically unscathed. The shakes, and the irrepressible joy of still being alive. But the thought, also, that next time…

'I'd gladly exchange the medal for a chance to see Paris again, General. You know the most remarkable thing about Lebrun, sir? He only told me when we were on our way down again, but the thing which most bothered him was the prospect of German snipers.'

'He took a calculated risk. We soldiers do it all the time.'

'Yes, you're right. He'd worked out the wind speed, the distance to the nearest building, calculated it would take the very finest of snipers to take the shot. But, of course, he said, there was always the chance…'

An orderly brought them coffee. Hot and strong.

'That the finest of snipers might just *be* there.' Leclerc smiled. 'And here's the advantage of being a general. The piece of the calculation Lebrun couldn't have made. That the Boches had all gone. Every last one of them. At least, all but those fools holding out at Fort Ney. But we'll winkle them out of their shell tomorrow, at the latest. For the rest – I'm ashamed for them.'

Late yesterday evening, Jack had taken more snaps, of the ammunition caches found all over the city.

'They were ordered to fight to the last round,' said Leclerc. 'So, they threw their ammunition away, then surrendered. Claimed they'd done as they'd been instructed. The last round.' He snorted with derision.

Nine thousand prisoners in less than a day. Even the SS hadn't bothered to stand and fight, simply looted the city and headed for home. They'd taken with them the civilian mayor, his deputy, the Chief Magistrate — each of them a collaborator, a traitor to Strasbourg, to Alsace and to France.

'A great victory, sir. And I'm happy to file more stories. Heaven knows, there's enough here to write about. But, then, General, I'd like to be relieved of my duties.'

'Too many ghosts?'

'Too many.'

'The worst betrayal, *Monsieur* Telford, would be if we allowed them to be forgotten.'

'I've no intention of letting it happen, sir. Not if I can help it. I'm not sure how many lives I have left, if you get my drift. Somehow I've managed to survive quite a few battles. But who knows what tomorrow might bring? *La Nueve*'s been my home for a long time, as well, though the outfit's not the same anymore, either. Dronne will be back in a few days, and I'd like to see him again. After that...'

'You're an accredited correspondent, Telford. Not enlisted. Of course, you're free to go as you please. But you'll be missed. You know you'll be missed.'

General Philippe François Marie Leclerc de Hautecloque reached across the desk, his hand extended for Jack to shake – and Telford knew this would rank among the proudest moments of his life.

He left the Hôtel de Ville through the courtyard, still a little shaken by the warmth of Leclerc's farewell, found Reiter waiting there for him.

'Telford,' said the bearded German. 'Got something to show you.'

The yard was full of army vehicles but, at the far side, there were also garages. Reiter led him there, stopped in front of a black sedan, a Citroën.

'Nice motor,' said Jack.

'No, *kamerad*, you're not looking.'

He showed Jack the nearside wheel arch. It was badly damaged. The side of the bonnet as well, and the running board.

'I'm still not sure...' Jack began.

'Châtel,' said Reiter. 'The damage to the ambulance.' He pointed to the missing paint, primer beneath, but rubbed into the scratches, traces of olive green. 'You see?'

'All the way here – from Châtel? Hell, Juanito, how many Citroëns on the road between here and there with a bit of crash damage?'

'I just thought...'

'No,' said Jack. 'Good you found it. Thanks for looking. But it's not likely – wait, just a minute...' He reached into the pocket of his combat jacket, took out his notebook, skimmed through the pages. 'Dammit, I almost forgot.' There'd been those last two camps on his list. Behind enemy lines – until now, at least. 'D'you know these places? Schirmeck, and the other one is... Natzwiller?'

Reiter didn't know, but he promised to make enquiries and, an hour later, they were on their way out of town again – in the borrowed Citroën, naturally. Under banners hung across the streets. *Merci pour la délivrance. Tricolores* everywhere bearing the Cross of Lorraine. Then west into flat, open farmland until they reached the foothills of this southern section of the Vosges Mountains, snow-covered wooded valleys and steadily rising ground.

They chatted, Jack finally – after all the time he'd known the man – hearing the story of how Reiter had joined the International Brigades: his father, a prominent German general of the old school, an outspoken critic of Hitler, having been shot by the Nazis in '34; and the beginning of Reiter's personal commitment to fight fascism to the bitter end. The rest of his family? Disappeared, it seemed, while Reiter had been in Spain.

'Then perhaps we both have the same quest,' said Telford, as they turned off the main road through the Bruche Valley into the village of La Broque – Vorbruck, as the sign in German still named it.

They found the station easily enough, and the small town hall where, after a few attempts, they came across a member of the FFI willing to show them the Schirmeck camp.

'To be honest,' said the young woman, Erika, 'you can't really miss it. And French or German?'

She meant, of course, which language would they prefer to use, but they settled on French. She wore an old helmet, a brown winter coat with the usual armband, and a long green scarf wrapped round and round her neck.

'When they first built the place,' she explained, 'the barbed wire was right under my window. And the prisoners – well, they were mostly folk from the region who'd not cooperated with the *Boches*. They called it an education camp. Teaching them how to be better Nazis.'

Erika showed them the house, and she was right, the camp almost an extension of the village.

'And prisoners here recently?' said Jack.

'The *Boches*, you mean? The Americans used it for a few days after they came through. We still can't believe it – being liberated, I mean. Only a week. Still only a week.'

She led them through the gate. It was remarkably similar to the camp he'd visited at Thil-Longway. Presumably, he thought, the German mind would have a uniform plan for concentration camps, wherever they might be.

'No, Erika,' he said. 'Before the Americans. Were the *Boches* still using it?'

'Don't you know, *monsieur*? I thought perhaps it was the reason you've come. Since September, they used the camp as the base for their operations against the *Maquis*. Against British agents in the area. Reprisals against anybody they suspected of helping them. All the way from here and along the Rabodeau Valley to Moyenmoutier. The third time, only three weeks ago. So far as we can tell, they took eight thousand of us – for forced labour. Processed them here, then transports. Somewhere into the east. *Waldfest*, the Boches called it.'

Forest festival, thought Jack. Sick bastards. He took notes, the names Erika knew, of the Wehrmacht, Gestapo, SS and *Milice* or *Francistes* commanders responsible for the operation, here at Schirmeck. Maybe useful, he thought.

'Did you hear of any more?' Reiter asked. 'Prisoners taken in other places – maybe Lorraine?'

They walked through slushed snow between the rows of identically drab, grey wooden huts.

'There were rumours,' said Erika. 'Prisoners they already had in Strasbourg. But we never picked up details.'

'There's another camp, as well,' Jack told her.

'You mean Natzwiller?' She shivered. 'Nobody there since August. Nobody but ghosts, anyway. I was in the place a few days ago, with the Americans. Oh, *monsieur*, we'd heard stories, but...'

There'd been a quarry. Prisoners worked to death. And the rumours? Medical experiments, somehow involving the university in Strasbourg. And when she'd been there with the Americans, a gas chamber discovered – a gas chamber for more experiments, the efficacy of mustard gas and typhus as a means of extermination. There'd been meticulous records, it seemed. And among them the Yanks had found details of three Special Operations Executive agents executed there.

Erika spoke their remembered names with reverance: a Frenchwoman, Denise Borrell; and two English girls, Diana Rowden and Vera Leigh.

'Of course,' she said, 'I knew the place from before the war. So different then. You know? A ski resort. It was beautiful. It was really beautiful.'

It seemed the Division had taken over the entire L'Aubette building on Place Kléber for its celebrations – the last of the *Boches* now surrendered – and Lebrun had insisted Jack should join him and his comrades from the *Spahi* Regiment for dinner in the ground floor café-brasserie. It was all very modern, cubist paintings on the walls, vivid oranges and blues – colours clashing somewhat with the soldiers' khaki, the scarlet of their sashes and berets.

'Nerves of steel, this man,' yelled Lebrun, and waved the copy of the photo Jack had brought along.

'Take no notice,' Telford shouted back. 'I was shitting myself all the way up. And don't even ask how I got down again.'

The long table was filled with food, but mostly simple stews, sausage and evil-smelling Munster cheese, fresh bread – and wine. Good Alsatian wines, Rieslings mostly, a few rare bottles of red, plenty of Schnapps.

'I hope you saved us some of that wine,' called Toto Torrès from the doorway, and the table fell silent. Astonishment as Toto led a small procession of her girls, eight of them, into the room, waiters clearing tables for them, taking their heavy trenchcoats. Jacotte, Rosette, Madeleine, a couple of the others Jack knew by name.

When was the last time anybody had seen them without their fatigues? Back at Dalton Hall for the parade, Jack guessed, though he was thinking more of his first date with Danielle, in Rabat, when he'd picked her up at the houseboat then serving as quarters for the newly arrived *Rochambelles*. But here they were, dress uniforms again, skirts and tunics, shirts and ties.

The silence didn't last long, erupted into laughter, some banter as well, naturally.

'So, how are things with you, Jack?' said Torrès, a while later, after she'd squeezed herself onto the bench alongside him.

'Feeling luckier than I've done for a while,' he smiled. 'Managed to survive that bloody spire. And Jacques?'

One of the soldiers passed a Schnapps bottle along and they both filled their shot glasses.

'Rule thirty-six,' she laughed. 'Only drink Schnapps after eight in the morning. And Massu? Preening himself for being the first into Strasbourg.'

'He's a lucky man.' Jack swallowed the liquor.

'Jealous, Jack?' She offered him her most wicked smile.

'Are you flirting with me, *mademoiselle*?'

She laughed again.

'Flirting? No, I can safely leave the flirting to these boys.' He remembered Danielle telling him she had another rule. Something about warning an officer whenever more than two of the Red Berets – the *Spahis* – arrived unannounced. 'And I meant jealous of his luck. You still feeling life's let you down? You shouldn't, you know.'

'Let's get pissed, Toto.' He poured them two more shots. 'And what am I supposed to do – count my blessings?'

He thought about his meeting with Sir Aubrey. Misadventure his middle name.

'For the time you had with her? Of course. And have you given up now – the search?'

He dug in his pocket, pulled out the chain, the dog tags, the ring.

'I still have no idea what to do with her tags,' he said. 'And given up? I keep thinking it's exactly what I should do, but then there's always something. Yesterday, I went with Reiter to an old internment camp. At La Broque. A young *maquisarde*. Erika. Told me there'd been prisoners there recently. From here, in Strasbourg – maybe brought from further west. Probably nothing, but...'

Torrès took his hand.

'The dog tags?' she said. 'I'd keep them if I were you. Or speak to Florence when you get back to Paris.'

'How the hell did you know...?'

'There are no secrets for very long in this Division, Jack. You should know that.'

'But I only told Leclerc.'

'And *le patron* told Jacques, and...' She laughed again. 'So, what next? If there were prisoners at this camp, they'll all be a long way over the Rhine by now. Think you can follow up this lead from Paris?'

'Maybe. Though there's something else. In Nancy, there was a convent, a home for kids. All separated from their families, some of them forever. I wrote a piece. Not heard anything yet. But this is bigger than just Danielle, Toto, isn't it? And I've got this feeling it's what she'd want me to do. Search? Yes, I guess I'll never quite give up the search, but more stories to track down out there, as well.'

She leaned over, kissed his cheek, just as Jacotte came over to their table.

'Hey, what's this?' Jacotte smirked. 'Isn't there a rule? About kissing newspapermen? But listen, you two, we're going downstairs. Fancy a dance?'

It was a nice offer, but Jack thought he might take a rain check.

'I'm afraid not, *Monsieur* Telford,' said Toto, and dragged him to his feet. 'You're not getting away with that one.'

'Really,' said Jack, and threw down a fistful of *francs*, enough to more than cover his share, he hoped. 'Toto, I'm not in the mood.'

'Believe me,' she growled. 'Danielle would have wanted you to do this. Don't you dare spoil things.'

He had no idea what she meant, but she sounded serious, and

he allowed himself to be hauled out of the Café-Brasserie L'Aubette and down the stairs to the basement, following Jacotte and the girls, past the signs for the toilets, the telephone booths and the *Cabaret-Danse*. He turned, saw Lebrun and some of the others from his unit following them down the steps.

The music which met his ears from the dancehall was familiar, something he'd heard in Madrid. The tango, *Por una cabeza*. Yet he knew something was wrong, long before he went through the doors. That old sixth sense again. And Toto hanging on to his arm like grim death.

'Toto…' he had time to say, as the doors opened. A moment of dangerous silence.

He looked up to see a banner strung from the chandeliers.

It read, *Hasta Pronto y Buena Suerte*. So Long and Good Luck.

'Oh, christ,' he said, as the singing began. The tune. *For he's a jolly good fellow*. But the words?

> *Telford se fue a la guerra,*
> *Telford se fue a la guerra,*
> *Telford se fue a la guerra,*
> *No sé cuando vendrá.*

Telford went off to the war. I don't know when he's coming back.

The whole Company must have been there – what was left of *La Nueve*. The small and perpetually unhappy features of Ramón Gualda. He waved at the Catalan brothers, Juan and Paco Castells. Broad grins from Faustino Solana and Pablo Moraga.

Another verse, another chorus, and Toto released his arm at last.

> *Es un chico excelente,*
> *Es un chico excelente,*
> *Es un chico excelente,*
> *Y siempre lo será.*
> *Y siempre lo será,*
> *Y siempre lo será,*
> *Es un chico excelente,*
> *Y siempre lo será.*

For he's a jolly good fellow. And so he'll always be.

'You should have warned me,' he said, felt tears welling again. Shit, he hated all this emotion stuff. And there was cheering now, men coming forward to slap his back, to shake his hand.

'You wouldn't have come down, *monsieur*,' Torrès laughed.

Dronne came to shake his hand as well.

'Captain,' said Jack, 'you're still supposed to be on leave.'

'Only a day early, and if I'd left it until tomorrow – you'd have been gone, no?'

Dronne embraced him, kissed him on both cheeks, and Jack saw two more comrades behind him. Federico Moreno. At his side, Miguel Campos, *el canario*.

'Miguel,' Telford shouted, stepped forward with his arms wide, though Campos moved backwards, and quickly, put up his hands to protect himself.

'Careful, comrade,' he said. 'I may look like I'm all in one piece but this bloody shrapnel...'

The tank shell, which had hit the building in which he'd taken cover at Vacqueville.

'You should still be in the hospital,' said Jack. 'And I don't deserve...'

'Don't flatter yourself, *inglés*,' Campos growled. 'Somebody told me there was free wine. And d'you have a smoke?'

Telford laughed, handed him his Luckies, spotted Reiter leading another round of singing.

'You'll find things have changed a bit,' Jack told Dronne.

'More Frenchmen than Spaniards in the Company now, they tell me.'

'Hell, I've even heard the new boys calling it *La Neuvième* instead of *La Nueve*. Bloody heresy, isn't it?'

'Times change,' said Dronne. 'Even in a war. They say the Division's going to be put under de Lattre's overall command. You heard anything?'

'Seems that way. Last time I saw the *patron*, it was plain he thought he'd been betrayed.'

'There's a lot of it about these days,' said Campos.

*

722

It had been a good night, but tomorrow he'd be on the train.

Telford said his final goodbyes, apologised for leaving the party early, but it had all been somewhat overwhelming. He felt like a deserter, hadn't understood how much he'd become rooted in their company. And the presence of Toto, the other *Rochambelles* – just too painful.

There'd been a parting gift, as well. He turned it over in his hands while he waited at the cloakroom for his trenchcoat.

Outside, it was raining again. Thankfully, he only had to walk across the square. To La Maison Rouge. One of the girls, Madeleine, had told him it was Strasbourg's finest hotel and, from the price of his room, he could believe it.

'Mind if I join you?'

Putz was also sheltering from the rain under the L'Aubette's canopy.

'Colonel…'

'My name's Joseph, *Monsieur* Telford. Perhaps for tonight we can just dispense with the formalities. Where are you headed?'

'Just there.' He pointed to the façade of the hotel, ghostly through the downpour. 'You?'

'Other way, as it happens.'

'You should have come to the party,' said Jack.

'Not my thing,' said Putz. 'And the men needed some fun before we head back into action again. Without *Papi* Putz breathing down their necks.'

'Soon?'

'Soon. And we'll never have it as easy as Strasbourg again. Never. Going to be a bitch from here on in. But I understand they were planning to make a presentation?'

Jack delved in the trenchcoat pocket, pulled out the tissue-wrapped gift, passed it to Putz.

'Cigarette lighter. Always useful,' said the man Jack had come to see as a father figure. Hell, the whole Company saw him that way. Putz pulled a pair of spectacles, wire-rimmed, from inside his own coat, examined the lighter in the glow from an overhead lamp. 'Hallmark,' he smiled. 'Crown and sun. German, of course, as I'm sure you worked out. And the inscription?'

They'd had it engraved.

Telford, periodista. La Nueve. Nunca olvidar.

Telford, journalist. The Ninth. Never forget.

'And I won't,' said Jack. 'Forget.'

He bit his lip. Damned emotion again. One oath fulfilled, another sworn.

'You know,' said Putz, 'we're likely to be transferred into the First? De Lattre demanded to see me, asked me how I accounted for my successes. Successes – the man's a bloody fool. But I told him. Whatever the battalion's achieved, the battles we've won, often just a matter of luck. Sometimes a measure of good judgement. But always? Always it's the heroism of those soldiers, the ones who earn our medals for us. Isn't this the worst betrayal, Telford? That we go home with chests full of medals, and they go home – if they're lucky enough to go home at all – shot to hell, or blind, or missing their arms, their legs. You'll keep writing about them, won't you?' He passed back the lighter. 'Every time you light a cigarette, you'll remember.'

'I will, sir.'

He was right, of course. Always two sorts of heroes in our lives, those we put on pedestals, admire from afar. But the real heroes? No statues for them. Those ordinary but quintessential folk, like Gabizon, Eze Tolabye, Reiter – and Danielle Zidane. *Los imprescindibles*, as the Spanish would call them.

'And safe travels,' said Putz.

They shook hands, and Putz walked off, to make his way back to his own quarters, Jack heading for the hotel. But then Telford remembered...

'Sir,' he yelled, and Putz stopped, turned back. 'I forgot to ask. How the hell did they afford the lighter?'

'Afford?' Putz shouted back. 'You should know them better by now, Telford. You have Granell to thank for this one. He spotted it on the desk of that German commander in Paris. Von Choltitz, remember?'

Late May 1945

Epilogue

Jack had been back in Paris since December. Lost in an endless quicksand of futile enquiries.

'You checked them all?' said Josephine Baker. This was *La Baker* at her ease, a simple grey blouse, striped slacks, sunglasses. She poured his tea from the oriental silver pot he suspected had come from Fortnum and Mason.

Telford leaned on the stone balustrade, the shaded terrace looking out over her lake. Lily pads, green reflections of weeping willows, splashes of yellow from the Asiatic blossoms. Not quite Givenchy but pretty.

'All of them,' he replied. 'Lost count.'

And so he had. The offices of the British Red Cross, the American Red Cross, the Swiss Red Cross. The Relief and Rehabilitation Administration Centre. The dozens of Refugee and Displaced Persons organisations with which Nella Bénatar had put him in contact. Committees and individuals. False leads which had taken him to other camps in Metz and beyond, to some of those places, the names of which he'd rather forget. But how was this possible? The images. The horror everywhere.

The Soviets had liberated Majdanek the previous summer, then Auschwitz this January past. Stutthof, Ravensbrück and Sachsenhausen over recent weeks, while the Americans had reached Dachau and Mauthausen, the British army at Bergen-Belsen. As if that wasn't enough, there were new tales. The death marches. He'd only been to the closest of them, to Haslach, across the Rhine in the Black Forest – just one of the secondary camps to which prisoners from Natzwiller had been relocated.

'Looks like you need some rest, Jackie.' She passed the cup to him, and he knew how he must appear. Those four months fighting their way across France had kept him lean and leathery, but now the face staring back at him each morning from the shaving mirror was painfully pinched, gaunt.

'Rest?' he said. 'You remember Paquita – Gorroño? She expected me to follow Granell and the others to the end, tell the story of how they finally won their fight against fascism. And Nella Bénatar. Wanted me to dig out more evidence of persecution against Europe's Jews. Christ, Josie, how much more evidence can we take?'

'Carrying the weight of the whole world on your shoulders, Jack? That can't be.'

A plane roared over, and Jack instinctively ducked his head, slopped some of the tea down his cricket flannels.

'Dammit,' he said. Looked up in time to see the distinctive shape of a P-38 disappearing eastwards.

'So bad?' said Josie, took a serviette from the tray and offered it to him.

'Can't remember the last time I had a decent night's sleep,' he said. 'Makes me jumpy.'

'Apartment not comfortable?'

She'd kindly allowed him to use one of her properties, in Montparnasse.

'Perfectly comfortable,' he smiled, sipped at the bone china cup. 'But you're still planning to sell?'

'Well, I can't stay here, that's for sure.'

She shivered, looked back towards the Gothic majesty of the villa. It's what she called it – a villa, though Jack had seen more modest châteaux. It was a beautiful property, set in the leafy meander of the Seine, one of the finest houses in a whole district of fine houses at Le Vésinet, barely a dozen miles north and west of the city.

'Ghosts?' he said.

'The filthy *Boches*,' she told him. 'They left the place tidy enough, but every time I touch anything, it's like I can smell them, hear them. Besides, I want to go back to Les Milandes – and there's no way I can afford to buy a castle *and* keep Le Beau Chêne.'

She'd spoken often of Les Milandes, the property she'd rented for so many years before the war in the Dordogne.

'It's been good to have somewhere to stay, Josie, but time I was moving on now.'

'Hey, you stay as long as you like. I don't need to sell the apartment as well – not just yet, anyway.'

A young woman emerged from the *portes-fenêtres* onto the terrace, asked whether she should take the tray, and when Jack confirmed he'd had enough tea, Baker suggested they might take a turn around the gardens.

'All the same…' Telford said, and picked up his Panama hat. Josephine took his arm and they headed down the broad steps towards the lawn.

He was surprised she'd not had to put the apartment on the market already. She'd pawned most of her jewellery, after all. To help feed those Parisians still at risk of starvation. A cruel winter in more ways than one. The Allies bringing in convoys of food. The surrounding districts helping as much as they were able. But the distribution systems were often flawed, too many reliant on black marketeers, and the poorest, the oldest, without the means to feed themselves – until Josephine and others like her had stepped in.

'All the same?' said Josephine. 'You've had a better offer maybe?'

'Nothing else for me to do here. And I have a friend, with good connections. I've asked her to use her influence. Maybe a transfer to the German section of the European Service. Maybe more clues further east.'

And there it was again – his certainty, on the one hand, that he could never find Danielle and, on the other, his total inability to stop searching.

'Not at home with the Spaniards anymore?'

'Granell's still around. Over there somewhere, as it happens.' He pointed beyond the lake and her orchards, the river. Beyond the Seine, the forest of Saint-Germain-en-Laye. 'No more recruits to train, of course. But not demobbed yet. And then there's the whole Spanish community in the city itself. But can't face them. All those promises, Josie.'

The pledge – more than simply implied – that, with Hitler and Mussolini defeated, Franco would be next. Well, Hitler was dead in his bunker now. And Mussolini? Shot, along with his mistress and other leading fascists, their bodies taken to the Piazzale Loreto in Milan, hung by their heels with meat hooks from some sort of scaffolding. But the promises – they'd come to nothing.

'Nobody told their story better than you, Jack. Just nobody wanted to listen.'

They paused at the lakeside, the hum of insects, and fish jumping here and there.

'I wasn't there for the end of the story,' he said. 'Feel like I betrayed them.'

Dronne had kept him in touch with some of it. The strange tale about Miguel Campos, *el canario*, how he'd gone out on a perfectly routine patrol, alone, just before Christmas, and had never been seen since. Disappeared, just as Danielle had done.

And then there'd been the news coverage of the fighting at Grussenheim, at the end of January. The Americans had been dying in their tens of thousands, further to the north around Bastogne and through the dark forests, the snow-covered hills of the Ardennes, during Hitler's final throw of the dice, the German offensive the whole world now knew as the Battle of the Bulge.

But the world seemed to have forgotten how, through that same wicked winter, over the same sort of terrain, and against equally determined *Boches* Panzer divisions, other Americans, the French First Army and Leclerc's forces were engaged in a life and death struggle to reach the Rhine. At Grussenheim, *Papi* Putz and several of his officers killed by a shell. It had moved Jack beyond words. The irony. Putz had been almost at the threshold of the district from which his family had moved, seventy years earlier. Almost home, Telford had thought, after all this time. He'd felt the loss more keenly than the deaths of his parents.

'There you go again,' she said, and thumped his arm. 'You can be annoying, Jackie. You know?' She dragged him back onto the path, towards the walled garden. 'You think de Gaulle scatters medals around like confetti? And to somebody who's betrayed his best fighting men?'

A fox broke cover from the shrubbery along the brick wall, a flash of reddish orange against the deeper red of the flowering quince.

'I didn't say I'd betrayed *them*,' Jack protested. 'Well, not directly, anyhow. A betrayal not to be there, with them. Confetti? Sure, it felt a bit that way. But you, Josie, at the première – in uniform, dripping with medals.'

Back in March, Telford required at an award ceremony in Paris. De Gaulle had pinned a *Croix de Guerre* to his chest. But to Josephine? Medals were old hat, of course. Not only the *Croix de Guerre* and the *Rosette de la Résistance*, but also a *Chevalier* of the *Légion d'Honneur*. She wore them all, along with her lieutenant's French air force tunic, at the Théâtre des Champs-Élysées, for the first showing of *Une Fausse Alerte*, the film she'd made back in 1940.

'If you've got it, flaunt it. Ain't that what they say?' She smiled, crouched down, examined the strawberries just beginning to ripen. 'Not quite ready. But these gooseberries – hey, did you know we can't grow these back home? Some stuff about them spreading disease. Hell, I don't know.' Jack didn't know either. 'And is it right – you guys think babies are born under gooseberry bushes?'

'Aren't they?' he said. He was pleased to see he'd made her laugh. He loved her laugh. But the joke made him think about Arlette Hautefeuille. Pregnant without knowing how. And Jack had joked with Danielle about gooseberry bushes as well.

'I want kids, Jack.'

'So did Danielle. Is Jo going to oblige?'

The new love of her life, Jo Bouillon, the band leader.

'Jo?' She laughed again. 'Hell no. I mean some of the street kids. The orphans. The ones who've lost their parents. But it should have worked out different for you, Jackie.'

She stood, hugged him tightly.

'I know it sounds awful,' he said, 'but if I knew for certain...'

'Knew she was really gone?' said Josie. 'Not awful at all. But time heals, you know?'

'Never fast enough. Never.'

'I guess not. But say, you never told me what happened in Toulouse.'

729

'You really want to know?' he said. 'Not quite the way I expected.'

Back in late February. Snow. And he'd received a note from Florence Conrad, herself still in Paris, yet another reorganisation of the *Rochambelles*.

Telford made his way to Conrad's office at the Val-de-Grâce hospital on the Boulevard de Port-Royal.

'A letter, Mister Telford,' she said. 'We've had a letter.'

'How are the girls, Major?' he replied. 'Toto and the others.'

'Can you imagine what they've been through? Grussenheim. All those weeks in the ice and cold. My goodness, it would have killed me.'

She looked far more than her sixty years, but her uniform was still elegantly pressed.

'Arlette?'

'Baby's due at the end of April. She's living with Ratard's mother and grandmother in Brittany. Seems just fine and dandy.'

He nodded. 'Good,' he said. 'We were pleased for her. Me and Danielle. But I'm sorry, you mentioned a letter?'

'Well, this is the point. It's from Toulouse. Danielle's parents.'

'She wrote to them,' he said. 'When we were here in August. But she didn't think – well, to be honest, it was me. I was sure they couldn't have survived. Parents of a fugitive *résistante*?'

'Here it is, all the same.' Conrad pushed the letter across the desktop. 'You see? It's been all over the shop. Isn't that what you say?'

Jack smiled.

'We'll make an Englishwoman of you yet, Major.' He picked up the square brown envelope, saw the number of different addresses, a reminder of how many times Conrad's office had been moved. Pillar to post, he thought. Yet there, on the back, a return address. Rue Saint-Germier. Still in Toulouse. The letter itself? Brief, just a few lines. Almost terse. Confirmation they were still alive, though now at this new location. And because they'd moved, Danielle's letters to *them* – there'd also been previous letters, it was clear – had taken many months to find them. They were pleased to hear she was safe. Jack turned the page, looking in vain for more.

'Short and sweet,' said Conrad. 'Will you write back?'

'I'd prefer to go and see them. Hard enough for me to think clearly about what's happened. Still don't know. Putting that in a letter? Besides, this has made me think.' He put his hand into the pocket of his trenchcoat, pulled out the chain, the identity tags, the engagement ring. 'I meant to get in touch with you anyway. The dog tags – aren't you supposed to have it, Major?'

Florence Conrad reached across, took the chain from him.

'Technically?' she said. 'Danielle's missing in action. When our soldiers are missing in action, by definition we don't normally recover their tags. If, on the other hand, I accept Dani's tags – well...'

She passed back the chain.

'I understand the conundrum,' said Jack. 'And if I gave you just this one...' He played with the thin discs. 'If I did, it would be like accepting...'

'Yes, Mister Telford. Accepting she's gone.'

'On the other hand,' he weighed the chain, tags and ring in his hand, 'if I kept hold of them...'

He'd delayed the journey until early in March, until the snows began to melt. But when he finally set out for Toulouse it all felt eerily akin to that other trip, almost seven years earlier – the one with which this had all started, his assignment to report on Franco's battlefield tours, his War Routes of the North. The same glass-domed baroque cavern of the Gare d'Orsay. The same 2-D-2 'Pig Nose' electric locomotives to cope with the steep gradients. But this wasn't the Sud-Express, and there were no luxurious pullman carriages.

The Toulouse train – its final destination at the Spanish border, Port-Bou, where onward passengers could change for Barcelona – was busy, but he was finally settled in his seat, his overnight bag stowed in the luggage rack. He chatted with the other passengers, he dozed, he worked his way through the newspapers, and he read some more of *The Little Prince*.

When he'd made his other journey, on the Sud-Express, he'd been carrying a copy of the *Beano*. Eggo the Ostrich. And now, he thought, I've graduated to *The Little Prince*. Progress, he supposed. Back then, reporter for *Reynold's News*. Nothing wrong there – a very respected publication though, yes, only a Sunday paper. Now? War correspondent. Associated Press. The Beeb's European Service. Accredited to de Gaulle's press team – or had been until he'd abandoned the Division.

The day dragged a bit. An early start. But by late afternoon they'd pulled into the stone palace of the Matabiau station, and he'd checked into the Hôtel Régina, just opposite. More than his pocket could afford now – he'd not made much money these past few months – but it was an easy option, and they had rooms. He ate at the hotel's brasserie, where one of the waiters gave him directions for the following morning, as well as a hand-drawn map.

Jack kept it safe within his notebook and, after breakfast, set out to find the Zidanes. He'd written to them, warned them of his visit – another reason for delaying the trip – and just hoped his letter had reached them, hoped they'd actually be there. He'd kept it short: a friend, he'd said, who'd worked with Danielle; his sad duty to inform them she was missing in action; and he'd appreciate the chance to meet with them.

Across the Pont Riquet, over the canal, then following the map to reach the Faubourg Arnaud-Bernard, to the Boulevard d'Arcole, where an old lady directed him to the Rue Saint-Germier. Their apartment was on the third floor of a building which had seen better days.

The Zidanes weren't what he'd expected. Older. Much older. They could have easily been Danielle's grandparents. And while the apartment block itself may have been seedy, their clothes, their furniture, spoke of a more affluent past. They stood stiffly in the doorway when he knocked. Aloof. He'd wondered for a moment whether they intended to invite him inside but in the end *Monsieur* Zidane stood aside, though made a point of pulling a watch from the pocket of his waistcoat, studied the time.

A short visit then, thought Jack, but still he handed over the paper-wrapped package he'd carried so carefully from the *pâtisserie* on the boulevard. A couple of *éclairs*, for which he'd been required to present his ration card – the card acquired for him with so much difficulty by Josephine when he'd returned from the front. Not a French citizen, though the Ministry had eventually accepted his papers, his credentials signed by General de Gaulle himself.

'A small token, *madame*,' he said, earned almost the shadow of a smile. She brushed imaginary crumbs from the front of her pinafore, gestured towards an antique polished table with gold ormulu edgings, far too big for the room. They sat, and he imagined he might have been offered coffee, yet there was no hospitality to be found there.

'Missing, *monsieur*?' said Danielle's father, looking down his long nose, spectacles perched on the end. 'You mentioned she's missing.'

It was all very cold. Formal. Some way of dealing with their grief? Jack explained his role as a correspondent, how he'd spent time with the *Rochambelles*. He knew Danielle had written to them, he said, about the ambulance unit.

'Yes,' said *Madame* Zidane. Nothing more.

He explained about Châtel, kept the details sparse.

'You sound, *monsieur*,' said the father, 'as though there may have been something more between you. Merely a friend? A long way from Paris to Toulouse, when a friend could simply have told us this much in a letter.'

Telford tapped his fingers on the tabletop, unsure whether he should explain but he finally reached inside his satchel, pulled out another small package, unwrapped the chain, the identity tags, the ring. He held up the ring, hoped it might need no further words.

'I was very privileged,' he said. 'I proposed marriage to your daughter, and she accepted.'

He looked at them, expected some response. Nothing.

'Missing,' said *Monsieur* Zidane again. 'Yet you have her identity tags.'

Jack explained the way in which it had been found.

'Then is our daughter – dead, *monsieur*?' said the mother. It was all very matter of fact.

'I think…' Jack began, felt tears welling into his eyes. Of course she was bloody dead. How could she not be? But he couldn't quite give up that one chance in a million. 'Anyway, I thought you should have these.' He set them down on the table, but neither parent deigned to touch them. 'She was always afraid,' he said. 'For you. The Gestapo...'

'How do you think we come to live in this hovel?' murmured *Monsieur* Zidane. 'In this part of town. Full of damned foreigners.'

'Foreigners?' said Jack.

'The place crawling with those Spanish beggars. You think the Gestapo didn't interrogate us, after... The hoops we had to jump through, *monsieur*, to prove our loyalty to Vichy. To...'

His wife put her hand upon his arm.

'*Monsieur* Telford doesn't want to hear all this, my dear,' she said. 'But yes, we lost our beautiful home. Forced to move here. And then – *Tolosa Roja*, have you heard the term? After the *Boches*, the Communists. Spaniards again. Vernant and his *maquisards*. But Communists, *monsieur*. And Spaniards. No better than gypsies, are they?'

'Our daughter put us through all that,' said the father. 'What did she think she was playing at?'

'She was a brave young woman,' Jack replied. 'Working towards the liberation of her country. Doesn't it count for anything? You're her parents, for pity's sake. Did you not love her?'

'Did *you*, monsieur?' *Madame* Zidane snapped at him. 'Proposed marriage, but didn't marry her?'

He thought about how much she'd wanted to marry when they were in Paris. But there'd been Strasbourg to reach, the oath to fulfil. And he was too choked to say any more.

Telford stood, nodded his head by way of farewell, left the ring and the dog tags there on the gleaming mahogany. No, not quite what he'd expected.

There'd been one more call to make in Toulouse. Amado had asked him to do it, and yet another reason for the delay in travelling.

But he'd been early, the brevity of that meeting with the Zidanes. And he didn't know Toulouse, but after he'd crossed the Boulevard d'Arcole again, heading south now and still following the hotel waiter's directions, after no more than five hundred yards he came out of the narrower streets into the Place Saint-Sernin, a great oval space with the basilica towering in front of him. On the far side of the basilica, the road he was seeking, Rue du Taur, and along the street, a church with a brick façade, almost Moorish, and a welcoming open door.

Time to kill. Time to settle himself in one of the pews. Time to chew over the morning's strange encounter. Time to reconcile himself with the crippling thought – if only, in Paris.

He couldn't help thinking about Arlette, safe with her husband's people in Brittany. What if…?

Above him, in a recess, a Virgin and Child. Unusual, black faces. Something about the serenity of the place. He didn't consider himself to be a spiritual man, not by a long chalk, but here he relived each of the times he'd spent with Danielle and, at the end, he wept openly, as he'd not wept since her disappearance. He wept for a long while.

Later, when he'd steadied himself again, he left the church, washed his face at a street fountain, walked back up Rue du Taur until he found the office, signs outside. *Partido Socialista Obrero Español* and *Unión General de Trabajadores*. Exiled organisations. The Spanish Labour Party and their General Workers' Union.

At the reception desk, he confirmed his appointment with the General Secretary. The fellow checked a diary.

'Here it is,' he said, stabbed at the page with fingers gripping a cigar. 'But *Señor* Llopis isn't here yet. On his way, I imagine. Coffee?'

Llopis, Granell had told him, lived in Albi. Forty-five miles away, but Llopis came every day of the week to the office in Toulouse. Since he was General Secretary for both PSOE *and* UGT in exile, a convenient arrangement.

Telford thanked the man. Yes, he'd said, coffee would be fine, and he took a chair in the wood-panelled reception area, expected to see Llopis enter, but there must have been a rear entrance. The intercom buzzed on the reception desk and Jack was directed into an office along a narrow corridor.

'*Señor* Telford.' Llopis was perhaps fifty, bushy eyebrows, bow tie, tweed jacket with leather patches at the elbows, a quizzical twist to the corner of his mouth. 'Amado has told me a great deal about you. Please, sit.'

Llopis came from behind his desk, joined Telford, sat next to him in one of a pair of matching green leather armchairs. On the walls, posters – union and PSOE posters, propaganda posters from the Civil War. ¡No Pasarán! They exchanged some pleasantries until the coffee arrived and Jack decided he must get down to business. He'd spent enough time with Spaniards over the past years to know that, left to his own devices, Llopis would have been happy to chat for much longer.

'Apologies, señor,' said Jack, and sipped at his tiny coffee cup. 'Granell asked me to interview you but I wasn't able to bring a recording machine. If it's all right with you, maybe we could do it the old-fashioned way?'

The introduction was almost unnecessary. If Barea decided to use the piece – and Jack could think of no reason he wouldn't – there'd be nobody listening to the broadcast who wouldn't know Rodolfo Llopis.

Llopis shrugged, reached for a wooden box from his desk, while Telford pulled his notebook and a pencil from his satchel.

'Sure,' he said. 'Interview – it's fine. And Amado tells me you were on the *Stanbrook*. In that case, we have a connection. You remember the French authorities impounded the vessel – refused to release the ship, allow the rest of its passengers to land, as surety for the cost of running their damned internment camp?'

He opened the box, offered Jack one of the cheroots. Telford selected one, took the fancy gold lighter from his pocket.

'I remember it very well, sir. Quarter of a million *francs*. And neither the British government nor the *Stanbrook*'s owners willing to stump up the money. Negrín's Refugee Committee paid it in the end, yes?'

'The Refugee Committee, of course. But the negotiations were my responsibility. Through our PSOE office in Oran.'

He waved his own cheroot towards the wall near the door, a wall lined above the wainscoting and chair rail with framed photographs and there, sure enough, one of the *Stanbrook* in the harbour at Oran, decks still crammed with her refugee passengers. Did it fill Telford with nostalgia? No, simply anger, burning as brightly as it had done at the time.

'You paid all that money, *señor*,' he said, 'but it brought the poor bastards no comfort. Not a crumb. No, it was left to all the local committees, the volunteers, trying to bring them food, clothes, blankets, medicines, every day.'

'Including our PSOE activists, *Señor* Telford. Our *militantes*.'

Jack nodded his head. He'd been a volunteer with one of the other groups, though it gave him no pleasure to remember.

'You know she was torpedoed eight months later?' he said, and took his seat once more, flicked the end of his cheroot into the desk's ashtray. He had a vision of Commodore Creighton, imparting the news, on that other dockside in Casablanca.

'Survivors?'

'None,' Jack told him.

Llopis grimaced.

'I managed to beat them down somewhat,' he said, as though this might be some consolation. 'On the price. In the end. But not much. Still, the advantages of being a Mason – I assume Amado will have told you.'

'I had no idea, sir. Neither the negotiations. Nor...'

'We have our own Lodge here. A Spanish Lodge, in Toulouse,' Llopis boasted. He plainly expected some enthusiasm, but when Telford simply showed appreciation for the cheroot, the Spaniard went on. 'The Allies,' he said, 'have made promises, *señor*. About Spain. But none of us need more bloodshed, yes? The solution is easy enough. The Americans, the British, the French – easy enough for them to apply economic pressure, just sufficient to make Franco want to negotiate.'

'Negotiate, sir?' Jack drained the last of the coffee.

'Simple enough. Last year, we formed an alliance. The *Alianza Nacional de Fuerzas Democráticas*. Liberals, Socialists, the Republican Left, the unions – most of them, anyway.'

'Negrín? The Communists?'

'Not yet. Though we're still hopeful. But our manifesto is clear. Based precisely on the Atlantic Charter.'

He certainly didn't *sound* hopeful – about the Communists. But the Charter? It had been signed by Roosevelt and Churchill back in 1941. Optimistic, though a blueprint, rules, for how the free world should be regulated after the war was won. And neither Roosevelt nor Churchill had any doubt it would, in the end, be won.

'Common principles,' said Jack, blew a cloud of smoke into the air. 'Freedom of labour, economic and welfare standards. All peoples to choose their own form of government. So, no more dictators? But I still don't understand – the negotiations.'

'There's an obvious sticking point. But this is not for publication, *Señor* Telford. Is this clear? Off the record?' Jack closed his notebook. 'Even if Franco can be brought to the table,' Llopis went on, 'even if he can be forced to agree some phased return to democracy, he – the Church – will never accept any proposals which don't include the monarchy.'

'And you have somebody who can negotiate with Don Juan?'

Juan de Borbón, heir apparent to the Spanish throne but still in exile.

'We expect him not only to support our own manifesto, but to present one of his own. A demand he should replace Franco as head of state.'

'Your negotiator, sir?'

'Who else? Granell, naturally.'

'My life,' he said to Fox, 'seems to be an endless round of vertiginous adventures.'

The very end of May, and they were sitting in the front row of the highest balcony at the Salle Richlieu, the main theatre for the Comédie Française. A special performance tonight.

He'd dutifully marvelled at the foyer's marble busts, its columns, and Molière's armchair – the one in which the playwright had apparently eaten out his heart so memorably as part of his performance of *Le Malade Imaginaire*, his last play. Telford had shared Fox's enthusiasm for the gleaming chandeliers above the Grand Staircase, and the corridors adorned with portraits of its most famous actors. But he'd balked entirely when they'd been shown to their seats in the front row of this dizzy tier above the stage.

'Wonderful view though, old boy.'

Jack followed his glance to the box around to their right, where General de Gaulle, Chairman for the Provisional Government of the French Republic – effectively now President of France – sat alongside his modestly attired wife. Jack recognised her from the papers. Next to *Madame* de Gaulle, the slim and elegant features of Leclerc's wife, Thérèse, the general himself at her side. At least, Jack assumed this must be Thérèse, though he'd never seen a picture.

'They seem to be friends again,' said Jack. 'Or is this just for show, d'you think?'

Leclerc had retaken sole command of the Division towards the end of April, in time to rush them towards Berchtesgaden in the Bavarian Alps, the town in which Hitler had taken his holidays and where, it had been feared, the Nazis might make a last stand. As it happened, the Yanks had got there first – though they'd not reached Hitler's personal hideaway, at the Eagle's Nest, perched atop its rocky outcrop above Obersalzberg. And that was where the batallion had successfully fought the last battle of the war, though they'd lost yet more men in the process.

'Touch and go for a while, I think,' Fox replied, 'while de Lattre had command. But those two have been through too much together to allow a minor spat to come between them. Don't you think? And you still mean to go through with this? He probably won't see you, Telford.'

'I owe it to too many people not to try. And it was good of you to bring me. Hopefully it won't queer your pitch?'

'Me? Heavens, no. My time here's just about finished anyway. I'm not sure what Berlin will bring, but it's where the brass think I'm needed, so off I go. I suppose there's this consolation – if de Gaulle has us shot for treason, we'll have enjoyed a good show beforehand.'

He was right. A good show indeed. And poignant, especially for Jack. The actress Béatrice Bretty starring in Courteline's comedy, *Les Boulingrin*. Amusing enough. Yet the thing which had brought de Gaulle and a cohort of France's other leading politicians here? Bretty's first performance in almost five years. Effectively banned from the stage by Vichy for her relationship with Georges Mandel.

'Remember when he arrived in Casablanca?' whispered Jack as blonde *Madame* Bretty – Junoesque, as somebody had described her

– made her first entrance, every member of the audience getting to their feet, an ovation lasting a full five minutes. Not for her alone, but for Mandel also. Mainly for Mandel, perhaps.

'I remember it well,' Fox replied. 'The *Massilia*.'

A day of great activity in Casa's dockyards. Comings and goings. Two dozen members of the French government – those who refused to accept the idea of armistice and betrayal – confined to the *Massilia* and eventually arrested.

Jack had liked Réchard, but there'd been moments...

'Arrest him?' Jack had said. 'You can't, surely?'

'You think I'd have a choice?' Louis had replied. 'And anyway, he's a Jew.'

Chilling. And Mandel had remained in prison for four years. But then, in the previous July, with the Allies almost in Paris, the *Milice* had hauled Mandel from his cell, taken him to the Forest of Fontainebleau and shot him, dumped his body there. But they'd overlooked his notebook, recovered when members of the Resistance eventually discovered the crime, and his moving last words had been published in *L'Ordre*, as well as some of the world's press.

At the play's end, another standing ovation, during which Telford and Fox made their escape, walked quickly along the corridor to the upper private boxes. Yet, when Jack saw the bodyguards, the *Sûreté* men with their submachine guns...

'Perhaps this was a mistake,' he said. 'I could always...'

'*Capitaine* Fox,' beamed de Gaulle as he came out onto the plush red carpet. His wife was on his arm. 'We thought you'd been posted to Berlin.'

'Next week, sir.'

'And *Monsieur* Telford. Out of uniform, I see.'

'I have been for some time, General,' said Jack. 'Quite some time, in fact.'

Hadn't anybody noticed?

'Although Telford has continued to serve us,' said Leclerc. 'Some very good pieces. Almost as though you were there, *monsieur*. Dronne, I presume?'

There were introductions. *Madame* de Gaulle, Yvonne. And yes, of course, Thérèse. Then that awkward moment.

740

'Well, gentlemen,' said de Gaulle, 'wonderful to see you both again, but now...'

'Actually, General,' said Jack, 'I wondered whether you might spare just a few moments.'

'My regrets, *Monsieur* Telford. But another engagement, you understand? Though if you care to contact...'

'Sir,' said Leclerc, 'I'm sure they'll hold the table. And for *Monsieur* Telford, perhaps...'

De Gaulle was less than pleased, his jaw set, but he asked the ladies whether they'd mind. Just a few minutes, he said, as an orderly led them off to the cloakrooms.

The door to the box was opened again. Below, the audience was finally dispersing, though still the clamour, enthusiastic conversations carrying up to the ornate theatrical ceilings.

'I have to say, *monsieur*,' said de Gaulle, when they were seated, somewhat uncomfortably – the arrangements not lending themselves to such a meeting, 'I rather resent being bearded in this way. If it weren't for our past relationships...'

He stressed the word *past*, Jack thought.

'Truly, General, I apologise,' he said. 'But I'm still on contract to the Associated Press, and they tell me their American readers are curious about a couple of stories. They're being reported rather unfavourably by some of UP's correspondents and I wondered whether you'd like me to counter them.'

It was only half true.

'Stories?' said de Gaulle, and pulled at the buttons of his uniform tunic, reached for his cigarette case.

'Yes, sir.' Jack wished he'd brought his notebook though, somehow, it wouldn't have fitted anywhere within the tuxedo Fox had insisted he should hire for the occasion. 'Like Thiaroye.'

'Poor devils,' de Gaulle replied. 'I arranged for them to be shipped home as soon as they were liberated. But rebellion is rebellion, *Monsieur* Telford, regardless of the justification.'

'They simply wanted the pay to which they were entitled, did they not?' said Jack.

December, and many of the Senegalese *tirailleurs*, hundreds of them, held in Nazi concentration camps since the fall of France, had been shipped home to Dakar for demobilisation. Protests about their pay, about a failure to honour previous commitments they might become equal citizens of France. French soldiers, other *tirailleurs*, fired on them. Armoured cars, machine guns. The official reports said thirty-five dead. Others claimed it was closer to three hundred.

'It's still under investigation, Telford,' said Leclerc. 'The General's not really been involved.'

Jack had wondered whether, somehow, Eze Tolabye might have been caught up in the massacre.

'Some of the American papers are calling it a betrayal, sir,' he said.

'I don't think we need to take lessons from the Americans,' de Gaulle snapped, 'on the treatment of our black people. Now, if we're done here...'

He rose to his feet, straightened the impeccable creases in those long trouser legs, cigarette still dangling from the corner of his mouth.

'Actually, General,' said Jack, 'I wanted to ask about Sétif, as well.'

Far more recent. Beginning of this month. Oran, and nationalist protestors clamouring for Algerian independence. French soldiers had opened fire. And after Sétif, a whole catalogue of other atrocities. Even official sources put the death toll at a thousand. But Radio Cairo claimed it might be as high as forty-five thousand over the intervening weeks.

'Violent crowds,' said de Gaulle. 'Outright revolt. Duval was quite correct.'

'But Radio Cairo is claiming General Duval took his orders directly from you, sir.'

De Gaulle didn't answer, simply climbed the steps towards the door, which was opened by one of his bodyguards.

'Telford,' Leclerc snapped, as he began to follow de Gaulle. 'What's happened to you?'

The Flying Lion glowered at Fox in equal measure and Telford knew he'd just killed all the goodwill built up with his hero since Kufra.

'I wanted to ask him about Spain, as well,' Jack shouted after Leclerc's retreating back. 'Another betrayal?'

'And I'd been hoping to find out more about Karlstein from Leclerc,' said Jack.

Fox had taken him off to the Café de Flore, on the corner of Saint-Germain and Saint-Benoit. Jack liked the place, but he'd last been there in July, eight years earlier, with Canadian art critic, Angela Alexander. He'd told Granell about it. Covering the Exhibition, talking about Guernica. It was noisy. A furious argument going on behind them, on the terrace, coincidentally about the respective merits or otherwise of Picasso's paintings.

'Did you get a chance to follow it up?' said Fox. 'About Karlstein?'

Jack set down his empty cognac glass.

'Not really. But it was interesting information from Dronne.'

The same day as the German surrender. The Company had been overjoyed, fresh from its victory at Inzell three days previously, and they'd received the capitulation of a Waffen-SS unit. Charlemagne Brigade. Frenchmen, though they didn't deserve the name. Fascists. Some of them had been serving Hitler since the Armistice. Others, more recent recruits, according to Dronne – members of the *Milice* who'd fled to Germany as the Allies moved east towards the Rhine.

'And Châtel, old boy – he was certain some of them were from Châtel?'

Fox ordered two more cognacs. If he was honest, Jack thought he'd probably had too much already, but he'd certainly needed a couple to help him get over that encounter at the theatre. What *had* he been thinking?

'Certain. Reiter had been working on them, trying to find out whether they were responsible for Doctor Sayer. And maybe – maybe for Dani's disappearance as well. Only the slightest possibility, but the car in Strasbourg. They might have thought she was a catch. Potential hostage. Or a means of buying their way across the Rhine. American ambulance driver, not realised she was French.'

Then taken her to Strasbourg, he thought. And the Gestapo there, with their usual efficiency might have nailed her as the escaped *maquisarde*, still on their wanted lists. It had always been her fear.

'Bit of a stretch, if you don't mind me saying so, Telford.'

'But I can't come up with another one. And, even so, if they *did* take her – well, it's all the same, isn't it? A transport off to the east. Hell, I can't bear to think about it.'

Jack took off his trilby, used his handkerchief to wipe sweat from the hat band.

'And now, the evidence is gone,' said Fox, accepted his next cognac from the waiter's tray, offered Jack a Capstan.

Gone indeed. Leclerc had apparently ordered their summary execution, every last one of them, even though the war was technically over. But Jack didn't blame him. Not really. Though apparently it had caused a bit of a stink within the Allied High Command.

'Shame I didn't get a chance to ask about Spain, though. Christ, all those promises they made. The number of times we had to argue with the boys, assure them the promises would be kept.'

'You need to remember we've had Yalta since then. Did you forget? Only three months ago, Telford. Dear me. It's all Berlin now, old boy. Not Madrid. There we are, Germany carved up into four zones – and poor Berlin, a hundred miles inside the Soviet Zone, carved up four ways as well.'

Along the Boulevard Saint-Germain, a convoy of American trucks, exhaust fumes wafting into the terrace. It was late, but the road still heavy with traffic, blaring horns and, behind them, that incessant squabble. Bloody Picasso.

'But you've read the manifesto,' said Jack. The manifesto produced by Llopis, by the *Alianza Nacional de Fuerzas Democráticas*. 'Precisely the same principles as the Atlantic Charter. Churchill and Roosevelt, for pity's sake. Self-government. Democracy. No more bloody dictators.'

'Beautiful idea, old boy – but with the Soviets now in Berlin? The Commies at the gate. Yesterday's friend, tomorrow's foe. Franco's persuaded Churchill and de Gaulle this is just another ploy – Commies ready to take over Spain yet again. Salazar in Portugal telling them the same. So, principles of the Atlantic Charter? Of course. But not right now, thankyou very much.'

Jack had no sooner been back from Toulouse, his interview with Llopis, when Juan de Borbón had published his own manifesto. Demanded he should replace Franco as head of state forthwith –

claiming a restored but constitutional monarchy was the only way to prevent future excesses of a republic on the one hand, and a dictatorship on the other.

Since then, it had all gone rather quiet. Nobody talked about the Spanish anymore. *La Nueve* had slipped from the headlines. Barea hadn't even responded when Jack sent the copy of his interview, certainly hadn't broadcast the content.

'All things considered,' said Jack, 'it doesn't feel like I've achieved very much. Like *we've* achieved very much.'

What had been Paquita's dream? 'Defeat for Germany and Italy,' she'd said. 'Defeat for Franco. Independence for Morocco. Spain a Republic once more.'

'We won the bloody war, didn't we?' said Fox. 'And at a personal level, if you had to set your gains and losses on a balance, how would that look?'

'I'm not really in a mood for games.'

Telford looked around at the men arguing about Picasso, glowered at them. It sounded like they might even come to blows. Beards and brown bowler hats, as though they'd stepped out of a painting by Lautrec.

'No game,' said Fox. 'Come on, humour me. It may be the last chance you'll get. So, regrets? What would you put on the regrets side of the scales, old fellow?'

'Danielle, of course.'

He reached in his pocket for the dog tags and ring, remembered he'd left them with the Zidanes, regretted he'd done so.

'That all?' Fox pressed him.

'I could have killed Franco. Cocked it up.'

They lit fresh cigarettes, Fox's Capstans again.

'No more?'

Jack thought about Ruby Waters. Yes, he'd lost Ruby as well. But it would take too long to explain.

'Nothing I can think of right now.'

'Pleasures, then. Do I mean pleasures? Opposite of regret. Satisfactions, I suppose.'

He called for the waiter, ordered coffees, asked for the bill.

'I no longer seem to be hunted. Still alive, survived the war. A few friends – I hope. The piece I wrote for the *New York Times* – the one that helped finally empty the camps. Sunday journalist to war correspondent. Not a bad move. Dani, of course. Other side of the coin. Better to have loved and lost, isn't this what the bloody fools say? But all this endless pain. Is it – better, I mean? I suppose I understand. In a way, she brought me…'

He couldn't finish.

'And you saved de Gaulle's life?'

Yes, he had. And been rewarded with a *Croix de Guerre*. A medal. He wasn't sure where to place the medals, this one and the Sherifian Order of Alaoui – which side of the scales.

'Sometimes,' he said, 'our lives just take a turn. Free France, Leclerc and de Gaulle gave a purpose to my life that wasn't there before. Gave me – a home, I suppose. For a while.'

'Didn't you tell me you saved Negrín's life as well – in Alicante?'

'More of a joint effort,' said Telford. As it happened, he now had Negrín's pen in his possession once more. Sergio Sifre's sketchbook as well. Paquita had returned them, a letter saying she felt bad about keeping them. They'd arrived at the apartment, on his birthday, as it happened. April. The twenty-fifth. A month ago. Nice gesture, though it had made him maudlin all over again, the realisation he and Danielle had never shared a birthday, nor a Christmas. Not one. And never would.

'Pulitzer?'

Jack laughed. After all this time. The letter back in mid-April. The Correspondence Award for his work during the previous year. Distinguished war correspondence. Invitation to the luncheon awards ceremony.

'It was certainly an honour. And, for a while…'

'I still don't understand. You turned it down?'

The coffees arrived and Jack insisted on settling the bill. There was the usual wrangle, but Telford won in the end, pulled out enough twenty *franc* notes to leave a decent tip as well. In the process, he also accidentally pulled out his crumpled photo of Danielle, tucked it away again, knowing he was in danger of making a public spectacle of himself.

'Can't say I wasn't tempted,' he said. 'But, in the end? I

remembered what Putz said to me. All those who helped me earn the damned thing are either dead or gone. Or betrayed. Accepting the Pulitzer would have been like betraying them as well. Anyway, I'm sure another one will come along.'

'Betrayals,' said Fox. 'Seen our fair share, yes? But trying to confront de Gaulle with them – can't lay it all at his door, can we? And all that about the United Press. Was it true? Harmon tell you?'

'A white lie, maybe. And Harmon – you two…?'

'Just good friends, old boy. But the betrayals? War, after all. Dirty things happen in war, Telford. But this one was justified, at least. Perhaps the only war there's ever been which has some proper rationale. Redemption.'

'Never justified,' Telford replied. 'Not one of them. They never are. We caused this one as sure as eggs are eggs. Could have stopped it in its tracks, but we let them all bleed – Abyssinia, Spain, Czechoslovakia. Even Poland. And now? Here you are – off to Berlin. Soviets this time. Christ, haven't we had enough?'

Inside, somebody had switched on the gramophone. Damia. *On Danse a la Villette.*

'I'm just a simple soldier, old fellow. Do as I'm told. Leave all that self-flagellation stuff to you poor bloody writers. And God help you!'

'You know, Captain, there were times when I thought…'

'You didn't trust me either? Then I must have been doing my job, old boy. But time I took a taxi. Can I offer you a ride?'

'Thanks, but I think I'd like to walk.'

They left the table, shouted goodnight to the waiter, stepped out onto the pavement. A strange evening. Cloudless sky above, a Van Gogh star-filled night but, at street level, a low rolling mist. He recalled the closing scene again. From *Casablanca*. Hardly a beautiful friendship, this one, but all the same…

'I suppose I shall miss you, Telford. Life's likely to be dull without you. But always room for a bloody good war correspondent in Berlin if you get bored.'

They shook hands and Jack dodged the boulevard's traffic, the blaring horns, somewhat unsteady after the cognacs, headed down the Rue de Rennes towards Montparnasse and Josie's borrowed apartment. What was it she'd said? A man who's never lost anything can't understand the value of the blessings he still possesses. Wasn't that it?

Telford thought about his train journey to Toulouse. He'd read *The Little Prince* on the way south – then read it again on the return trip back to Paris. There were some memorable lines – for what was supposed to be a fairytale. But one short piece had stuck with him, almost haunted him.

"A rock pile ceases to be a rock pile the moment a single man contemplates it, bearing within him the image of a cathedral."

That just about sums it up, he decided. It's what I do. See my life as a jumble of fallen stones, obstacles, rather than the thing I could build from them. Perhaps, he thought, this time something beautiful – something beautiful after all.

The End

Historical Notes and Acknowledgements

As I said at the beginning, this *is* a novel, a work of fiction. But it's shaped by actual historical events, and the real-life characters who participated in them. Even before I finished writing *Until the Curtain Falls*, I'd developed a fascination for the fates of those Spaniards who'd fought against Franco, Hitler and Mussolini throughout their civil war and became exiled from their own lands. It wasn't long before I came across references to *La Nueve*, the company of former Republican soldiers who went on to fight for the Free French and were, literally, the first Allied troops to enter Paris when the city was liberated in August 1944.

La Nueve's remarkable war – and that of the Chad Armoured Infantry Regiment's Third Battalion to which it belonged, or indeed the whole of Leclerc's Second French Armoured Division – did not end, of course, at Paris. *La Nueve* went on to fight its final battle at Inzell on 3 and 4 May 1945 and arrived at Berchtesgaden on the following day. By then, the battalion's Twelfth Company had advanced all the way to the Berghof, Hitler's Eagle's Nest, and taken it. There's a legend that, of the 146 Spanish Republicans who formed the original core of *La Nueve*, only 16 survived the war – though this must be entirely incorrect. We have details and names of all those who were killed and they number less than forty. There were certainly many wounded and, as Robert S. Coale – one of the world's most eminent experts on the subject – reminds me, some of them unlucky enough to be wounded twice. But most of those survived and were discharged from service.

I owe a debt of gratitude to Evelyn Mesquida for her 2015 book *La Nueve, 24 August 1944: The Spanish Republicans who liberated Paris*, since it gave me a starting point for my research. And I took a second step along the road by reading the book written by

La Nueve's captain, Raymond Dronne, *A Spanish Company in the Battle for France and Germany (1944-45)*.

For lighter reading, there's Paco Roca's superb graphic novel – with an epilogue by Bob Coale – entitled *Los Surcos Del Azar*, in English edition as *Twists of Fate*, and the French version simply *La Nueve*.

But the volume which provided the best Spanish overview, and again thanks to Bob Coale, was *Republicanos Españoles en la Segunda Guerra Mundial (Spanish Republicans in World War II)* by Eduardo Pons Prades. It may be somewhat outdated now, yet this was a text that helped me, in Bob's own words, to "keep the fictional story within the limits of historical veracity" – which should, of course, be the very minimum requirement for every historical fiction writer.

Similarly, for Leclerc's Second Armoured Division as a whole, there's William M. Moore's biography of the general, *Free France's Lion*, and *Free French Africa in World War Two* by Eric Jennings. But there's also the French website *voiedela2edb.fr* organised by the Maréchal Leclerc de Hautclocque Foundation.

For those who want to physically follow *La Nueve* and the Division, there's a wonderful Michelin guide, which defines their route from the beaches of Normandy to Strasbourg, with a commemorative marker post in all the towns and villages along the way. It's free to study online or can be picked up at any of the tourist offices in the towns on the route.

Then, among a mass of other sources, there's the wonderful website authored by Gaston Eve whose Anglo-French father, of the same name, left such detailed diary entries and recollections of his time with Leclerc's Free French armoured units, from the time he volunteered to join de Gaulle in London, his passage to Pointe Noire and Brazzaville, his experiences in North Africa, his brief return to England before being shipped to Normandy, and all the way to the Obersalzburg: *gastoneve.org.uk*.

And I mustn't omit the two books that provided so many of the "human" stories for the Normandy and Paris sections: *Women of Valour, The Rochambelles on the WWII Front* by Ellen Hampton and *Quand J'Étais Rochambelle*, the remarkable first-hand account written by Suzanne Massu, formerly Suzanne 'Toto' Torrès.

For the story of *La Nueve* in England, I can't recommend anything more entertaining than the YouTube video of a presentation given by the Pocklington and District Local History Group, entitled *La Nueve in Pocklington and the Liberation of Paris*.

To understand the Normandy campaign overall, I most regularly – among many others – returned to Antony Beevor's *D-Day: The Battle for Normandy* and his *Paris: After the Liberation, 1944-1949*, written in conjunction with Artemis Cooper.

But this quickly became a story about much more than *La Nueve* alone. In part, it became a snapshot of Spain itself between 1939 and 1944 since, too often, I'd heard this period simply "written off" by folk claiming that, because Spain was officially neutral during the Second World War, she played no part in the conflict – which is plainly nonsense.

And since the fates of those Spanish Republicans at the heart of the novel – who went into exile in North Africa in 1939 – are so closely tied to the rich and colourful story of North Africa itself in those years, the novel also quickly became a partial account of Morocco's role in the war, and far more than just the military campaigns with which we might be more familiar. Some of this story, I found in Meredith Hindley's *Destination Casablanca: Exile, Espionage, and the Battle for North Africa in World War II*. And more I discovered in *Españoles en Marruecos, 1900-2007*, by Oumama Aouad and Fatiha Benlabbah, as well as Paul Feron Lorenzo's *Investigación sobre el exilio y la emigración de los españoles en Marruecos*.

So, what about the fates of the real characters in the story and, first, those who, as Jack's heroes and heroines, give us the titles for the novel's sections?

Brachah Zefira continued to perform in Palestine until 1947, then toured successfully through Europe and the USA until 1950 but her popularity waned over the next 20 years. She gave her farewell concert in Tel Aviv during the mid-1970s and died in 1990 at the age of 80.

T.E. Lawrence – Lawrence of Arabia – had died in 1935, at the age of 47, following a motorcycle accident, just after leaving military service. He therefore can't appear directly in the story but features as an influence on the more "romantic" side of Jack's life.

Paquita Gorroño (Francisca López Cuadrada) *may* have taught at the Imperial College in Rabat, though her official role was as secretary to the college director. She later worked as personal secretary and interpreter to King Hassan II of Morocco, but none of that detracted from her work with the Spanish unions in the region, among whom she was universally known as *La Pasionaria Rabat*. She died in Rabat at the age of 103, as recently as 2017. It's said she had in her possession, at the time of her death, a torn and tattered Spanish Republican flag, though nobody could say precisely where it came from.

Archibald Dickson, the heroic Cardiff skipper who had helped so many Republican soldiers to escape from Alicante on board the *SS Stanbrook* (who also does not feature directly in the story), did indeed meet his end, along with his entire crew, when they were torpedoed in the North Sea during November 1939.

Hélène (Nella) Cazès Bénatar had been Morocco's first female lawyer. After the war, she continued to help hundreds of displaced Jewish refugees and support their relocation to Israel. She toured the USA in the mid–1950s to raise funds for her charity work. She died in 1979, aged 80.

Philippe de Hautcloque, *nom de guerre* Philippe Leclerc, continued his exceptional military career after the end of the war in Europe, taking command of the French Far East Expeditionary Corps and representing France at the Japanese surrender later in 1945. Great things were expected of Leclerc as France emerged from the conflict, but he was tragically killed in an air crash in 1947. His body was returned to France, where it was taken to Paris along the route followed by his now famous Second Armoured Division in August 1944. His enormous state funeral service took place at Notre-Dame Cathedral, where Charles de Gaulle wept openly, as did all those others in attendance who had served with him. His body was then laid to rest in the crypt of *Les Invalides*, near the tomb of Napoleon Bonaparte and other heroes of France.

Dudley Anne Harmon covered the Nuremberg trials for the United Press and reported from the United Nations European headquarters in Geneva from 1948 to 1952. Harmon also served as a member of the United Press staff covering the U.N. General

Assemblies in 1948 and 1950. Returning to the USA in 1952, Harmon worked as Acting Publicity Director for the League of Women Voters in Washington, D.C., as a consultant to the Ford Foundation in New York City, and as Acting Publicity Director for Sarah Lawrence College. She returned to Smith College (from which she'd earlier graduated) in 1955 to assume the position of News Director. In 1962, Harmon was named Manager of Information Services for CBS News, Washington Bureau, the post she held until she died on 14 September 1966.

Colonel Bill Eddy served from 1943 until 1945 as US Minister to Saudi Arabia. He was instrumental in the creation of the CIA. Later he worked as a consultant for the Arabian American Oil Company and he spent his final days in Beirut, where he died in 1962, at the age of 66.

Josephine Baker received the Croix de Guerre and the Legion of Honour, along with other recognitions of her wartime service. After the war she returned to the Folies Bergères and then toured the USA to huge acclaim – until an incident at the Stork Club, over racial segregation, led her into a series of public relations disasters and the cancellation of her work permit. She worked ferociously for the Civil Rights movement and, during this time, she began to adopt children, her "rainbow tribe." She continued to perform periodically but returned to the stage more fully in 1968 and, following landmark performances at the *Bobino* in Paris, she died peacefully in 1975. Her story is a remarkable one.

Leslie Howard needs almost no additional explanation. One of the great movie idols of the 1930s and early 1940s. A huge amount of mystery and controversy still surrounds his death on that fateful flight on 1 June 1943 and I simply chose the version of events which best fitted the story and, for me, was the most plausible in all the circumstances. It's also the version fitting most neatly with the confessions made by the real-life Countess Mechthild "Hexy" von Podewils to the Spanish newspaper *El Mundo* in 2009, just before she died.

Sidi Muhammad ben Youssef, Sultan of Morocco, continued to argue ever more vociferously for Moroccan independence – to such an extent that the French authorities sent him into exile in 1953 and replaced him with a puppet monarch. Violence ensued and *Sidi* Muhammad was brought back to Morocco, restored as sultan. He then successfully negotiated independence with France and Spain and was crowned as King Muhammad V of a free Morocco in 1957. He died in 1961 and was succeeded by King Hassan II, his eldest son, who also appears in the novel. And there was, I must confess, no such position as the "Sultan's Jew" in the court of Muhammed ben Youssef, though this had been a position of some repute and respect during the previous century. Here it was simply a fictional device to allow an equally fictional Gabizon the status I thought he deserved.

Raymond Dronne resumed his leadership of *La Nueve* from 27 November 1944. He campaigned all the way into Germany and as far as the Eagle's Nest at Berchtesgaden – though he'd been promoted to the rank of major in March 1945 and, at that point, gave up command of *La Nueve*. Later, he commanded an armoured infantry battalion in Indochina, leaving the army in 1947 with the rank of colonel and received the Legion of Honour. He became Mayor of Écommoy in his native Sarthe district, and later a Senator, then Deputy for the region. He also served as President of France's National Defence Committee. He died in 1991. I cheated a bit with Raymond Dronne – apart from all those fictional engagements with Jack Telford, naturally – in so far as he was actually made a Companion of the Order of Liberation in December 1944, rather than June, as I've suggested here.

Suzanne 'Toto' Torrès, after the war, remained at Leclerc's side and commanded the army's ambulance services in Indochina. In 1948, after divorcing her husband, she finally married Jacques Massu that same year. In 1957, with Massu commanding forces in the Algerian war, she organised a charity to support Muslim street children. She published her memoir, *Quand J'Étais Rochambelle*, in 1969, and she continued her charitable work until she died, of cancer, in November 1977.

Amado Granell was the son of a timber importer from Burriana, Valencia. He married Aurora, the couple operating a motorcycle shop in Orihuela, south of Alicante, until the outbreak of the Spanish Civil War in 1936. He served with distinction for the Republic and escaped from Alicante on the *Stanbrook*. After the war, Granell received the Legion of Honour from Leclerc but rejected an offer of promotion within the French army. He was certainly part of the comings and goings through which Llopis and the ANFD (*Alianza Nacional de Fuerzas Democráticas*) hoped to negotiate a return to democracy. But by 1950 he'd opened a restaurant, Los Amigos, on the Rue du Bouloi, Paris, which became a meeting point for Spanish Republicans. He later returned to Spain, and finally to Alicante. He died in a traffic accident on 12 May 1972 while heading to the French consulate in Valencia about the payment of a grant for his service as a French army officer.

Major (later Lieutenant Colonel) Joseph Putz, that valiant old warrior, veteran of the Great War and the Spanish Civil War as well, tragically met his end fighting at Grussenheim in January 1945.

Then, there are all the real-life characters who have "speaking" parts in the novel, and though there is no space here for their later stories, they are each easily researched online or through library services. But they include: Leonard Hurst, Consul General at Rabat; William Bond, Consul General at Casablanca; the astonishing Commodore Creighton; Leclerc's various named officers – Dio, Massu, de Guillebon, Rennepont, etc; Francine Faure Camus; Roger Carcassonne and his family; Lieutenant Sidney Williams; Robert Murphy; General Edward Spears; Jacques Abtey; Harold Macmillan; General Charles de Gaulle; Gordon MacLean and the other ill-fated passengers on Flight 777; their excellencies *Sidi* Abderahman Menebhi and *Sidi* Ahmed Belbachir Haskouri; at the Sabratha dig site, Agatha Christie's husband, Max Mallowan, and archaeologist (later to become Mallowan's second wife) Barbara Parker; John Steinbeck; at the RAF hospital in Algiers, Group Captain Bedford and matron Flight Lieutenant Bosely; Félix Éboué and André Parant; in Pocklington, Mister Barker, Mrs Lumley and Mrs Foster; General George S. Patton; Bill Spray, the Methodist among the Quaker stretcher-bearers; *Père* Berger at Écouché; in Paris, Ernest Hemingway, María Casares and Albert Camus; the other real-life *Rochambelles* Florence Conrad (who, in 1946, married Colonel Paul Lannusse, another of Leclerc's officers),

Arlette Hautefeuille and Jacqueline 'Jacotte' Fournier; and Rodolfo Llopis, the elected Deputy for Alicante in 1931, 1933 and 1936.

It's maybe worth noting that I never intended to have this number of real people in the story, but I'd already mapped an outline of Jack's travels, the timescales for his stay in, say, Casablanca, or Oran, or Brazzaville, or Paris. But as I researched each of these locations, during the time Jack would have been there, and moving in the circles I'd written for him, I realised he couldn't possibly have been there without bumping into many of these real-life individuals. It gave a whole new meaning to the requirement about "keeping the fictional story within the limits of historical veracity." But sincere apologies, once again, if any of their families think I've portrayed them unreasonably.

I'd said that I wanted this to be a story, not only of *La Nueve*, but also of those other Spanish Republicans who continued their fight against fascism all the way through the Second World War – though this, as it turned out, was impossible. From the very start of the conflict in 1939, Spanish Republicans, exiled in France, Morocco and Algeria, joined the ranks of the French Foreign Legion and fought with distinction in the ill-fated Norway Campaign and then in the 1940 battle for France itself. After the armistice, and unable to support the Vichy government, thousands of them deserted the Legion and transferred their loyalties to the forces of Free France and General Charles de Gaulle. Many more, of course, ended up in labour battalions and were badly treated.

Again, the Spaniards made quite a name for themselves in the fighting which eventually drove the Germans out of North Africa and the Middle East. By then, thousands of others, who'd taken refuge in Soviet Russia, were helping to defend cities like Stalingrad. It's estimated that several thousand Spanish Republicans fought either as part of the Red Army or within specifically Spanish *guerrilla* units. Elsewhere, perhaps three thousand more Spaniards formed nine distinct guerrilla divisions within the French Resistance all across southern France.

So, back to *La Nueve*. There are a few fictional characters within their ranks in this story – like the men from Bou Arfa, or El Gordo and the character with the nickname Alemán – but most of those named actually served and fought within that astonishing Company of the Chad Armoured Infantry Regiment. They include Amado Granell and Miguel Campos, as well as Manuel Sánchez, Luis de Águila, José Reinaldo Sánchez, Michel Elías, Martín Bernal, Andrés García, José García, Constantino Pujol, Fermín Pujol, Johann 'Juanito' Reiter, Antonio 'Bamba' van Baunberghen, Manuel Bullosa, Luis 'Gitano' Cortés, 'Cariño' López, David 'Fábregas' Ramón-Estartit, Manuel 'Lozano' Pinto Queiroz, Victor 'Rico' Baro, Pablo Moraga, Ramón Gualda, Juan and Paco Castells, Faustino Solana, Federico Moreno, José Mateo, Francisco Perea, Felipe Martínez and Rafael Gómez Nieto, among others.

Strangely, the last surviving member of *La Nueve*, Rafael Gómez Nieto, died in a Strasbourg nursing home on March 31, 2020, at the age of 99. He was a victim of Covid.

And Cécile Rol-Tanguy – valiant Resistance fighter and wife of Colonel Rol-Tanguy – also died while I was writing the book.

Naturally, there are bits of the story I've condensed for the sake of the narrative, or incidents I composited and abbreviated for the same reason. But most of the incidents and events in the novel are true enough. There were certainly a few places where I took some 'artistic licence' and tweaked the truth, so I owe a huge debt to Bob Coale who, as I mentioned earlier, has been indispensable in reminding me of those transgressions and, often, with great patience, suggesting corrections.

The camp at Bou Arfa, for example, was probably not open as early as I've told the story here, and there was almost certainly no open resistance, nor quite the level of cruelty. Not at first. All that came later. It's also unlikely there would have been "internationals" in the camps at that time. Foreign nationals arrived later as well, having been released from the Legion after the 1940 fall of France.

There *was* such an article about Sidi Muhammad in *Life* magazine, but this was 26 April 1943, and Jack didn't write the captions – though Eliot Elisofon *did* take the pictures.

In my reference to the *Stanbrook* and its skipper, I've said that Captain Archibald Dickson helped "almost two thousand" to escape from Alicante. There are accounts putting this figure as high as *three* thousand but in Dickson's own account, sent to the *Daily Dispatch* from Oran immediately after the *Stanbrook* arrived there, he says that he initially thought there were 2,000 refugees on board but "later I determined there were 1,835 in total."

Then, in relation to Miguel Campos, it's unlikely he was actually detained in the camp at Djelfa and, if he took part in the battle for Oran at all, it's even more unlikely he would have been with Amado Granell. In reality, these two men were poles apart politically, Campos the Anarchist and Granell the centrist Socialist – though I brought them together frequently for the sake of the narrative.

The scene in which I have the French captain, Raymond Dronne, with Jack, in Hélène Bénatar's apartment also could not have happened since, at the time, poor Dronne was still in hospital in Cairo, recovering from the wounds he'd suffered at Ksar Ghilane. He was still in hospital, as well, during the parade in Bizerta.

Amado Granell didn't arrive at Pocklington until June 1944, having only recently been transferred to *La Nueve*. Indeed, it's certain that *La Nueve* itself would not have arrived at Pocklington in time for May Day. And nor would they have factually been allowed to wear Spanish Republican colours on their uniforms.

During *La Nueve*'s frantic drive into Paris, there was indeed an altercation with journalists, though it's unlikely Hemingway was among them. And, during General de Gaulle's triumphant procession from the Arc de Triomphe to Notre-Dame, there were certainly sniper attacks as I've detailed, though they didn't *quite* conclude with Jack's dramatic involvement.

And the battles? I studied each of them endlessly but then realised that, first, these are only witnessed from Jack's point of view; second, they needed to appeal to a wider audience for whom the precise military details might be tiresome; and, third, they needed to fit the dramatic narrative. So, for example – another of Bob Coale's reminders – there was no tank battle in the streets of Écouché; no actual fighting in the taking of the Mesnil-Glaise château; no penetration into Écouché during the German counterattack; Putz was not actually at Châtel-sur-Moselle; and I significantly played down the parts played there by Campos, Moreno, Reiter and Dronne.

A word about the ambulance teams, as well. The *Rochambelles* were attached specifically to that section of the Division to which Putz's battalion of the Chad Regiment initially belonged. But I also wanted, for various reasons, to give mention to the medical units which, in practice, served other groups in the Division – and especially the Quakers of the Friends' Ambulance Unit. Those volunteers, Quakers *and* Methodists, therefore crop up from time to time in the wrong places. Apologies.

Telford, of course, didn't win the Pulitzer Prize for Correspondence in 1945. This honour fell to newspaperman Hal Boyle, also contracted to the Associated Press. A collection of his writings appear in his book, *Help, help! Another day!* And I've tried – probably without success – to shape Jack's own journalism around Boyle's work.

Finally, the performance by Béatrice Bretty at the Comédie Française to help commemorate the sacrifice of Georges Mandel actually took place on 24 February 1945, not the end of May that year, as I've detailed it in the story.

So far as resources go, there's a more complete list on my website but, apart from those I've already mentioned, I'm grateful to a couple of complete strangers.

First to Mohamed Dekkak, Moroccan-born businessman, investor and philanthropist, whose blog about Morocco, about Casablanca, its history and architecture, helped me learn more on the subject than anything else I've read.

Second, I want to pay particular credit to the author Patrice Nganang, whose stunning novels tell the story of Cameroon during the Second World War exclusively from the viewpoint of the black Africans who fought and died for France – *Mount Pleasant* and *When The Plums Are Ripe*.

And, while I'm thinking about Patrice, I should note that Chad became fully independent in 1960; French Cameroun, Gabon and the Republic of the Congo in the same year; Algeria in 1962 after an eight-year vicious struggle with France; and Spain only fully gained its freedom from dictatorship after Franco's death in 1975 and the adoption of the Spanish Constitution of 1978 – a constitutional monarchy, with King Juan Carlos on the throne, the son of Juan de Borbón.

As usual, my deepest thanks to the regular crew – Helen Hart and her publishing team at SilverWood Books; cover designer Cathy Helms at Avalon Graphics in North Carolina; Julie Whitmer at Julie Whitmer Custom Map Design in Ontario, Canada, for Jack's maps; editor Nicky Galliers, who this time was faced with a daunting task, simply because of the novel's size and scope, but whose comments, corrections and encouragements were invaluable – particularly in relation to Fougères, a location which she helpfully knew very well; my ideal beta reader Ann McCall; friend and fellow-author Elizabeth Buchan for her endorsement; and all those others who took the trouble to read advance review copies or a million other things to help me finish this.

If you've travelled with me this far, you must at least have some stamina. This was truly a labour of love, which grew like topsy. But I hope you've enjoyed the story and, if you want to keep in touch, I send out regular monthly newsletters, as well as always being happy to chat and answer questions. My website is: davidebsworth.com. You can also sign up for the newsletter there. I'm on Facebook – my personal page, dave.mccall.3 plus my David Ebsworth author page, @EbsworthDavid – and occasionally Twitter: @EbsworthDavid. And if you liked the books, a short review is always welcome.

Thanks again for taking the time to read all this and best wishes.

David Ebsworth
April 2021